Du Rose Legacy

THE HANA DU ROSE MYSTERIES

K T BOWES

Would you like to be part of it?

I'm a believer in 'try before you buy.' There's nothing worse than forking out your hard-earned cash on a doozy and regretting it.

I don't want stinky reviews. I want you to love my work and feel like you got value for money.

If you'd like to join my mailing list, you can grab 4 free eBooks which will be delivered right to your inbox.

You can do that at ktbowes.com

Acknowledgement

For Maureen, who would rather have been Naomi.

The story so far ...

Hana Du Rose is forty-five, newly married and unexpectedly pregnant to her English teacher husband, Logan. As she deals with the problems in her married life, she is forced to contend with the constant threat of a conman who preys on widows for their wealth. An old lady's last will and testament, with the potential to overthrow the crook's claim on her estate, has somehow ended up in Hana's possession and makes her the subject of his interest. Hana and Logan become deeply embroiled in the mystery, forced to go to extraordinary lengths to live their lives in safety. But Hana's rebellious spirit constantly puts her in danger.

Her own adult children are struggling to accept her secret marriage to Logan, amidst serious problems of their own and Hana tries desperately to fit in with the fickle, feud-ridden Du Rose *whanau*. Logan's mysterious past and secret life hinder his future with Hana and he finds himself the subject of a criminal investigation. An event at the secondary school they both work at means that things come to a dangerous head as the doors are thrown open to the public and Hana becomes immediately vulnerable.

Chapter 1

Logan felt for a pulse on his friend's blood soaked neck and found nothing. His grip slipped in the red slick and he forced his index and middle fingers into the space beneath the left side of Boris' broken jaw. Closing his eyes, he waited. The weak, irregular beats forced a sigh of relief from his pursed lips. "Let's hope you're lucky, mate," Logan breathed. He reached for the phone in his pocket and dialled triple one for emergency, explaining his location to the efficient operator. "Yeah, it's bad," he said, casting an experienced eye over Boris' twisted body. "Multiple breaks and blood loss."

While the dispatcher chattered in his ear, Logan felt around Boris' limbs, finding a broken arm and perhaps dislocated knee. He snatched a cloth from a sideboard and balled it up, slipping it beneath Boris' head and wincing at the groaned response. "He's moaning, but not conscious," Logan relayed. The bloodied phone clattered to the floor as he leaned over the injured man's mouth. Guttural breathing rewarded him. "Come on, man. Help is on its way. They won't be long. What the hell did you get involved in?"

"Don't move him," the ambulance operator stated when Logan picked up the phone again. "Stay with him, monitor his vital signs and talk to him."

Logan hung up before the man could tell him to stay on the line and dialled Bodie's number. The young police officer let out a string of swearwords. "What the hell are you doing? I told you to leave this alone. You know what will happen now, don't you? Geez!" Logan heard the rage in his voice. Then Bodie's voice changed. "Did you get blood on you?" Logan looked down at his soaked fingers, the dripping phone and his bloodied shirt. He didn't reply. Bodie snorted. "Then you're an idiot and you get whatever you deserve. I spoke to Detective Sergeant Odering and he left half an hour ago to speak to Boris. If you'd stayed at work, you'd have an alibi!"

Logan ground his teeth at the hint of victory in his stepson's tone. "Way to go, Du Rose," he mouthed at his own stupidity. Boris stirred and he dropped to his knees, rocking the man's shoulder. "Boris, wake up, mate. Who did this? Did you know them?"

Bodie snorted. "Too late Du Rose. You put yourself in the frame and you can stay there for all I care. I'll take care of my mum and your kid." The call ended and Logan felt a flicker of fear. Sirens split the gentle, rural atmosphere and he checked Boris' weak pulse again. The sound of tyres on gravel heralded more than one vehicle.

The ambulance men arrived, kneeling next to Boris and firing questions at Logan. He answered with stiffness, knowing whatever he said would incriminate him.

"No, I found him like this about ten minutes ago."

"No, he groaned but didn't regain consciousness."

"No, I don't know what happened."

"Yes, the faint pulse was there when I arrived. No, I didn't resuscitate him. His breathing stayed slow and shallow. Yes, it sounded like that." Logan regurgitated the information he gave the operator, keeping his story straight.

The second vehicle disgorged two cops who entered hot on the heels of the medics. "Just procedure," the older cop said, halting Logan with his outstretched palm. He peered over the head of the ambulance crew.

His younger colleague jumped to the obvious conclusion and took a firm grip of Logan's shirtsleeve. "Come on, sir, up you get!" he told him, hauling on the material until the seam split. Logan gritted his teeth and tried to put his hands down to stabilise himself, the cop's tug on his shirt overbalancing him. The light from the doorway highlighted the man's ginger hair like a halo.

"Wait!" he snapped. "My legs have gone to sleep." The cop's blue irises became glassy and Logan saw the moment when the man decided his guilt. He staggered as he rose, taking a moment to give his blood time to refill his legs. Bending to rub at his numb calves, he sensed the atmosphere change.

"Hands behind your back," the young cop demanded, slipping handcuffs from his belt.

"Sod off!" Logan bit. "Is it a crime to call for assistance when you find a mate collapsed now?"

The young cop drew his baton and Logan ground his teeth. "Hands behind your back," the man asserted and Logan raised an eyebrow.

"You really wanna do this?"

Racism oozed from the ginger-haired cop and Logan's heart sank into his stomach as a familiar disappointment returned. More than just anticipation laced the cop's freckled face. His eyes blazed with excitement and his nostrils pulled upwards in a sneer. "Come on, dude," he hissed at Logan. "You lot are all the same."

Logan's gaze slid to the older man, seeing him distracted in conversation with the paramedics. He looked back at the ginger cop, assessing him and shaking his head. "I won't give you the satisfaction, mate," he said, loud enough for the other man to hear. "I'm sorry you don't like my kind."

The older man glanced across and his face fell. His lips parted in a gape of realisation as though it wasn't the first time. He stepped in Boris' blood as he hurried towards them. "What's going on?" he snapped, his eyes wide. Logan turned around and presented his hands behind his back.

"Your colleague thinks I need handcuffs," he said, forcing his voice into a reasonable tone. "He'd like to use all his new toys." A mirrored dresser opposite showed the young cop babbling like a fool with no sound emerging from his lips. He folded his nightstick at speed and shoved it back onto his belt.

"This dude lurched at me," he managed, avoiding the older man's eye. "He's dangerous."

"My legs went to sleep." Logan turned around but kept his hands behind his back. "How's Boris?"

"Not good, son." The older man glanced backwards and looked at Logan in sympathy. "You called us?"

"Yeah." Logan sighed and when the older man turned aside to speak into his radio, slid his gaze back to the young cop. Little over twenty, he looked inexperienced and still thrilled with his own sense of power. The latent racism handed down by his white parents lay just beneath his veneer of professionalism. Logan shook his head, hoping the police service recognised it before it got out of hand. The cop's skin, pale and freckled, flushed with excitement and his carrot orange hair stood out from his head like the fluff of a soft toy. Logan recalled a hundred boys just like him, the butt of schoolyard jokes and bullying. It seemed a slender line sometimes between victim and aggressor. History proved often how oppressed became oppressor in a crooked twist of circumstance.

The paramedics pulled Boris' distorted limbs into some semblance of normality and he groaned again. The older cop turned around to observe them sliding a splint under his leg. An image of Hana's trusting face floated past Logan's inner vision and he put a hand up to rub his eyes. She would freak out and accept Bodie's consolation. At his sudden movement, the young man twitched and Logan experienced a spark of temper. "How much longer do I need to put up with this joker?" he snapped.

Aged around fifty, the older cop raised an eyebrow. "Exactly what I keep asking," he muttered under his breath. Tugging on Logan's sleeve, he moved them aside as the paramedics shuffled Boris onto a stretcher. He let go and drew a notebook and pen from his pocket. Flipping open the book, he jabbed a finger at the young man. "Now you've drawn your nightstick, you need to record it in your pocket book." He kept the timbre of his voice slow as though speaking to someone with limited understanding of English. Logan kept his face straight and stared at a dent in the skirting board. The ginger fluff rustled as the kid reached for his book.

The older man turned to Logan with a casual smile. "I'm sure you understand, sir, as the first person on the scene we'll need to ask you some questions. I'll do that now, but we will revisit this at a later date. Do you understand?"

"Yeah, sure." Logan exhaled and moved his head to get a better view of Boris. The unconscious man made tiny grunts as the paramedics collected their gear and the stretcher wheels squeaked on the wooden floor. "Excuse me," Logan said, reaching out a hand towards the nearest paramedic. The young cop went into another paroxysm of excitement, redrawing his baton again.

"Bloody hell!" The older policeman exclaimed. He looked away, rolling his eyes at the younger cop and shaking his head.

"Hey, how is Boris?" Logan asked, his tone urgent. "Will he be okay?"

The man barely broke his stride. "Too soon to say, mate."

Logan bit his lip, seeing his disastrous day progressing down the gurgler faster than anticipated. He reran the morning's conversations, unable to count the threats he made against Boris' wellbeing. He groaned and put his head back, closing his eyes against inevitability.

Both cops rustled the pages of their notebooks, one logging his baton frenzies and the other waiting for Logan's attention.

Logan turned towards the friendlier of the two and made a valiant effort to stay on track. The questions began, going in the direction he expected. "I told the despatcher his name, age and all that." Logan cringed as the ambulance siren screeched into the sunlit garden and birds scattered into the sky. The cop made him repeat it all so he could scratch it into his book with a capitalised script. "When did you last see Boris Lomax?"

"Earlier this morning."

"Where?"

"At work."

"Where is that?"

On it went until Logan grew bored. He answered with feigned interest until the man asked if he knew how the injuries to Boris occurred. His eyes narrowed at a memory. "As I pulled into the driveway, I almost hit another vehicle coming out. Dark coloured saloon with tinted windows." He closed his eyes. "I saw two faces in the front but I couldn't see in the back seats."

"Registration number? Identities?"

Logan shook his head. "Too fast." He eyed the younger cop sideways. "Boris got into debt to Ted Larne. When I saw him this morning he showed signs of injury. He limped and looked uncomfortable as though he might have broken ribs."

"Who's Ted Larne?" The young cop knitted his orange brows and sneered at Logan. "Are you trying to pass this off on someone else?"

The older man slapped his colleague on the back. "No, son. You'll meet Mr Larne's thugs one day. Then you'll need your night stick." He held out his hand to Logan, palm upwards. "Phone please, Mr Du Rose."

"What?" Logan looked from one to the other. Realisation dawned and his shoulders slumped. "You're kidding? I'm here, so I must be your suspect? Sterling work guys as always." Logan pursed his lips and remembered his ill-timed call to Bodie. Hana's image turned the thought of karma into a regret. He drew the stained device from his jacket pocket and dropped it into the bag the young cop held open in front of him. "I'm wasting my time here," he said. "I want to talk to Detective Sergeant Odering and I'm saying nothing until he gets here."

The cop wrote that down and shut his notebook with a snap. He nodded towards the ginger cop. "Call it in. Get Odering here." He pulled Logan's arm and led him towards the door. "Until then, you can sit in the car, Mr Du Rose."

The slender detective arrived fast. Logan fought frustration as he tapped his boot heel on the gravel with poorly disguised impatience. Ginger cop stood over him, his fingers itching to pull his baton free of its clip. The other man cordoned the house off with police tape.

"Victim's reached the hospital," ginger-cop gushed with excitement as he listened to chatter on the radio. His colleague approached wielding a roll of marker tape. "Shall I take the suspect in now?"

Logan let out a snort and shook his head, experiencing another wave of exhaustion. He sat in the back of the police car, his bum on the seat and his feet on the gravel drive. "How is he?" he asked, ignoring the bouncing idiot at his side.

"Too early to tell, sir," the older man replied with respect. "Detective Sergeant Odering is here now."

"Typical Māori lazy arses," the young cop hissed beneath his breath. "You think you're owed because that's how you're raised."

"Hey, enough of that crap!" the older man rebuked him. His blue eyes narrowed into slits. "I'm not having this. You go on report the minute we get back to the station." He curled his top lip back in a snarl. "You can make a complaint, if you want." He directed his last comment to Logan and he shrugged in response.

"What's the point?" He massaged his scarred knuckles and worked hard to control his temper, watching Odering descend from the car. He wrinkled his nose as the detective spoke to a colleague directing operations with a practiced air. They whispered with their heads bowed together as though in prayer. Then Odering nodded and turned towards Logan. His shiny shoes crunched across the gravel and Logan watched his progress, noting the heaviness in his step.

When Logan tried to stand to greet him, the older cop pushed him back to a sitting position. The Detective Sergeant stood with his hands on his slender hips and looked at Logan. "What a bloody mess, Mr Du Rose."

He nodded. "Yep." Gritting his teeth, he stared at a point in the distance, watching a white cloud scud overhead. The detective's superiority galled him and he cursed his diminished circumstances.

Odering bent to his haunches, one neatly pressed trouser leg resting in the gravel. "I know you didn't do this, Logan," he whispered. "It's not your style. But you must go to the station and ride this thing out through due process. I suggest you comply with everything asked of you for the time being."

Logan saw the detective's infuriating upward lift of mouth and eyebrow. "You're enjoying this," he hissed. His grey eyes flashed in the sunlight, speaking threat and revenge. Odering grinned. "Mr Du Rose can go to the station now, please. Do the usual checks and hold him until I get there." He stood. Through the corner of his eye, he spotted the ginger cop drawing his handcuffs. Logan endured a poignant moment of hesitation aimed at unsettling him further. "There won't be any need for that thank you. I don't think Mr Du Rose has any intention of running." He looked hard at Logan. "He has more reason than most for needing to sort this out."

At the police station, Logan donned a white, hooded jumpsuit with integral booties and watched them take his clothing as evidence. The charge sergeant took his gold St Christopher and dropped it into a plastic bag along with his watch and wedding ring. Logan's brows knitted at the sight of his bare finger, accustomed to the mark of marriage even after such a short interlude. "Sorry, Hana," he whispered to himself, waiting for fingerprints and photographs.

Each facet of the procedure reinforced his status as an animal at a cattle market, a criminal without relevance. After sitting for an indeterminate amount of time in a bare cell in the bowels of Hamilton central police station, the cop on duty allowed Logan a single phone call. He couldn't bring himself to alarm Hana and without his phone, other helpful numbers escaped him.

"What?" Pete screeched amidst the throng of sweaty males. "I can't hear ya." He turned aside and lost his place in the tuck shop queue. "What?" A swarm of boys filled his place, surging forward like water as Pete wedged a pudgy finger into his ear to drown out their chatter. "Logan?" he yelled and then the colour drained from his face. "Oh, bollocks!"

Chapter 2

“That’s the bloody last time I lend Du Rose my stuff,” Gwynne complained when Pete broke the news about his impounded car. “I should have gone with him.” He thumped his palm against the post room door.

“What? To beat Boris up?” Pete’s eyes bugged like a frog’s. He snorted and a bogey dived from his hairy nose onto Gwynne’s shoe. They both stared at it for a moment. “Hey, bro?” Pete postured and tapped Gwynne on the shoulder. “What if the cops find the drugs under your front seat when they search your car?” He snorted again, thrilled with his own humour.

The older man fixed him with a penetrating stare that went on far too long for Pete. Moving close and invading his personal space with deliberate threat, Gwynne’s face creased into a grin that didn’t reach his eyes. “I’d worry about the gun in the glove box,” he hissed. “And keep your bodily fluids to yourself.” He turned on his heel and stalked away.

“He’s got a gun,” Pete squeaked, pointing at Gwynne’s retreating back. “In his car.” He glanced at the Scottish hockey coach who walked in to grab his mail. The man shook his head.

“He’s joking Pete. Can ya still not tell?”

“Oh.” Pete swallowed and edged away. “Are you sure?”

"Yep." The coach dismissed him by turning his back.

Pete pulled his collar away from his throat, feeling rattled. He hopped from foot to foot, reluctant to break the news of Logan's predicament to his wife, Hana. His perpetual state of cowardice sent him in search of the school principal, hoping he'd do the dirty deed instead.

"Mr Blair is delayed at his meeting and won't be back for at least fifteen minutes," the principal's-personal assistant informed him.

"That's okay. I'll wait here." Pete made a beeline for a stack of women's magazines on a credenza and clapped his hands. The secretary grimaced.

"Snip anything out this time and I'll kill you," she snarled, menace dripping from her sentence.

"I don't have my scissors," Pete said with regret. His bottom lip protruded at the sight of Rachel Hunter on the front cover. "Damn. I don't have that one," he muttered, making snipping motions with his stumpy fingers. Denied his favourite pin up, he got busy fingering ornaments and trophies and knocking over a bowl of peppermints.

When Pete upset the bowl a second time, he dropped to his knees and collected the mints using the tiddlywink method. The secretary stood up and screamed, "Out! Out!"

"I'm nearly finished!" he grumbled. "Keep yer hair on." He blanched as she produced a cricket bat signed by the Black Caps. "You wouldn't!" he gasped as she wielded the priceless object.

"Watch me!" she hissed and chased him into reception, slamming the door in his face. Pete glared at the receptionist before noticing another stack of magazines.

"Yay!" he exclaimed. He skipped across to the mountain of bikini bodies and started tearing out the blondes.

Angus Blair glided through the double doors, backside first. "It's raining," he announced to a group of boys who waited for him to get out of the way. His arms performed a flapping action with his soaked umbrella, shaking off the droplets. His face scowled with dismay at the sight of a giggling Pete attacking a guest magazine with his teeth.

"Peter North! Go to class!" he bellowed. He strode into his office with a cursory nod at his assistant. He misunderstood her squeak of rage as a greeting, until he turned to hang his coat on its hook and came nose to nose with Pete.

"Hi, Angus." Pete smiled and withdrew his finger from his left nostril with a pop.

"Go away, North," the principal replied, pointing towards the door. "I'm busy."

Pete nodded in sympathy, his bulbous eyes wide. "Me too," he said. "Sucks, doesn't it?"

As Angus filled his lungs with the intention of blasting the silly little man, Pete dropped his bombshell. "The cops arrested Logan."

He explained the situation and left Angus to break the news to Hana. It wasn't the plan but he missed lunch and if he hurried, there might be a pie left.

Angus sent for Hana and her face remained impassive as he repeated Pete's tale. "Logan is suspected of assaulting Boris." He narrowed his brow. "I rang the hospital. Boris is unconscious." The tremor in his Scots lilt betrayed his private anxiety and irritation. He shook his sandy head. "Logan Du Rose has always behaved as a law unto himself! I'm sorry my dear, but he's a loose cannon."

Hana sat in front of him, her stillness accompanied by an unnerving silence. When she spoke, Angus raised a red eyebrow. "Logan wouldn't hurt Boris."

Angus sighed. "Your husband has exacting standards, Hana. He shows little tolerance for those who don't meet them."

"I think I know my husband," Hana replied, her tone sharp. "He wouldn't hurt Boris."

Angus rolled his eyes and left his gaze peering at the ceiling. "I'm inclined to agree with you, Hana. But the mess remains, I'm afraid."

Hana leaned forward in her seat and hugged her knees with her good arm. The other hung from the sling around her neck, the cast clunky and awkward on her slender frame. "Do you know what happened?" she asked. Shifting in her seat, she ran her palm across her swollen abdomen and the principal's eyes widened in realisation.

Leaning back in his seat, he steepled his fingers and tried to fit the pieces together for her. "Boris admitted to me this morning that he developed an online gambling addiction. He got into financial difficulties and made a foolish loan from a drinking acquaintance. When he couldn't pay up on time, the debt became the property of a small time money lender called Ted Larne. He received threats and they roughed him up a couple of times. He wasn't sure how or when his job at the school became part of the mess, but he received a visit from Larne some months ago. They demanded your address."

"Mine?" Hana screwed up her face and shook her head. As the puzzle took shape in her mind, the colour drained from her cheeks. "Oh, no."

Angus waggled his eyebrows and leaned on his elbows. "Quite. He ignored them at first and kept them at bay with little payments. He took a beating a week ago and gave your Achilles Rise address."

"They already knew that." Hana shook her head and squeezed the bridge of her nose between finger and thumb. "Laval's men knew I moved."

Angus pushed his glasses up his nose. "Who knows how these people work?" he sighed. "I certainly don't. I think we can safely link what happened to you last week to whatever information Boris gave them."

"It doesn't make sense. The blonde man works for Laval and he turned up there too. Yet that wasn't new information. He attacked me there before and staked out my house. I'm understanding none of this." Hana closed her eyes and rocked in her seat. "Perhaps Logan's right. I should go to his parents' hotel until this is all over."

"Only you can decide that, Hana." Angus rose to his feet and walked around his desk. He rested his backside on the corner and patted her shoulder. "I can give you a leave of absence if you wish."

"I don't know what to do." Hana shook her head and stared through the tiny slit of a window, desperate for a touch from the watery sunshine she saw outside. "I don't understand why my husband is in jail."

Angus inhaled. "Something happened this morning and Logan chanced across an indirect exchange between Boris and Larne. What Boris said to Logan suggests he'd done something foolish and regretted it. Logan didn't know what he meant at the time, but obviously we all do now." He spread his arms wide in defeat. "We don't know if Boris told them your new address or not. I'm guessing Logan went to find out."

Hana sighed and closed her eyes. "Logan came to my office and made me promise not to leave the building. He came back later and found Boris." She clapped a hand to her mouth. "I'm so stupid. I almost gave Boris our address." Her green eyes filled with tears. "Logan stopped me writing it down for him."

"Ah." Angus' shoulders sagged in relief. "Then he doesn't know where you live."

"He almost did." Hana looked tiny sitting in the big armchair, her slender frame taking up little of the space. She ran a hand over her cast. "I still don't understand what happened to Logan. Last time I saw him he walked away with Boris."

Angus swallowed. "Ah, yes. I'm afraid I mishandled the situation and sent Logan away to avoid a punch up in my office. It seems it only delayed the inevitable."

Hana exhaled amidst an exasperated tut. "Logan's not stupid. He and Boris used to spar in the gym before he broke his arm. He always said they were a good match. Logan's arm is still knackered anyway. He goes to physiotherapy twice a week."

"It's still weak?" Angus looked hopeful as he scratched his nose. "That might help his case."

"Logan didn't hit Boris." Hana gritted her teeth. "Something else happened." Her fingers picked at a frayed edge of her cast and she held the principal's gaze. "How do I get Logan out?"

Angus quirked an eyebrow skywards. "Why, Hana my dear. You're sounding like a mafia princess." His lips parted in a smile.

Hana jerked her head back. "Where did that come from, Angus? What a weird thing to say." She sighed, a sound like an irritated snort. "Where did all this happen?"

"My rental in Gordonton. The police have cordoned it off." He settled back in his seat. "I feel more like retiring by the hour," he grumbled. Hana stood and walked across to the window. Flanked by taller buildings, it enjoyed an impeded view of the rugby fields. She watched a sports class cavort around on the grass. A thin, dark-skinned boy captured the rugby ball and ran for his life as though the hounds of hell chased him. He reminded her of Bodie with his long-legged gait. She touched her fingers to the glass and felt the chill from outside.

"Did you know a mother can recognise her child by their scent?" she asked. Memories of Bodie's school days flooded back and she sighed. "He was so naughty here, wasn't he?"

"Bodie?" Angus gave an upward jerk of his head. "Yes. He and Marcus led us all on a merry dance. But they turned out okay, didn't they?"

"I guess." Hana wandered back to her seat and settled into it. "I hope Bo didn't arrest Logan. There will be no coming back from something like that."

"Sure won't." Angus widened his blue eyes and gave a slow shake of his head. "What does he want from you, this man, Laval?"

"A box." Hana licked her lips. "We think a boy put a metal box beneath my car. Perhaps the boy who attacked me in the chapel car park. We don't know when. It fell off in my garage and I didn't realise. To shorten the story, we found it again and Logan located the contents. The police detective has it now, but Laval doesn't know that."

"What did the box contain?" Angus lifted his eyebrows in a show of open curiosity.

Hana shrugged. "Property deeds, a will and an engineer's report. It makes no sense but this man wants it. The cops believe he killed an old lady over it."

"So, why can't they arrest him?" Angus knitted his brow and spread his hands in question.

"He hides himself well. A blonde man does his dirty work and so far, he's evaded the cops too. The police can't charge him with murder when they never found the woman's body. It's stalemate and I'll stay in the middle of it until something dreadful happens."

"I think it already has." Angus patted her shoulder again. "Oh, Hana. Go to Logan's parents' place. Stay safe."

Hana shook her head and stood. "I need to get Logan out of jail. And Sheila wants me to work on the expo." She walked to the door and placed her hand on the handle.

"Hana!" Angus' tone sounded sharp and authoritarian and she braced herself for his rebuke. "Family first, my friend! Go home."

"And do what, Angus?" Hana turned the handle. "Worry? Sit by the telephone and wait?" The huge sigh seemed to come from her boots. "Besides, Logan hid the car this morning and I don't know where." She left the room, her steps sounding heavy on the parquet floor of the reception area.

Angus waited for the click of the doors leading upstairs and then heard silence. He slumped in his throne and drummed his fingers on the old desk, deep in thought. Generations of principals lined the walls around him and yet none remained to provide advice. Austere expressions faced him with no clue how to proceed. Angus stared at his predecessor's portrait. "Your quiet wisdom might prove useful about now, my friend," he muttered. When the tight-lipped man in the painting remained silent, Angus shrugged. "Bugger you then. I'll sort it myself."

He made a phone call. "Ah, Mr Singh Johal," he breathed, hearing Bodie's sharp inhale across the connection. "Angus

Blair here. I'm sure you're aware of our mutual friend's predicament."

Bodie snorted. "Yeah. Logan's in the cells downstairs and he's not my friend. And his circumstances are not a predicament, but a result of his own stupidity."

"That may be so." Angus snatched his glasses from the bridge of his nose and peered at the greasy smudges on the left lens. "I'm sure you're capable of lessening his burden."

"I don't want to." Angus imagined the young policeman's eyes narrowing beneath a single dark line of brows. "Logan Du Rose is bad news for my mother. I want him out of her life."

"Oh, that won't happen." Angus sighed. "I've known Logan many years and doubt he entertains any plans of abandoning Hana. Not now."

"The baby." Bodie spoke through gritted teeth and Angus grinned. No matter how old they got, boys always fell for the same ruse.

"Thank you for confirming that. I suspected as much," he said, listening to Bodie's silent agony at the other end of the call as he realised he'd blurted something private. "Hana needs to leave but has no ride home. Logan hid her vehicle before work and has all her keys. Are you able to help?"

Bodie huffed out a breath. "I suppose so. I'll finish my shift and pick her up."

"How is Boris?" Angus asked. "I wish to see him."

"He just got out of surgery. They plated one of his arms and wired his jaw. He's a mess. They have him sedated now while everything settles. He'll stay in intensive care with a police guard for at least a few days."

Angus hesitated. "A guard? That's interesting. Why does he need a guard if your colleagues arrested Logan at the scene and incarcerated him? What do they think he might achieve from the cells beneath your station?"

"I don't know." Bodie conceded without grace. "Maybe he had an accomplice. Or maybe he's well connected."

Angus smiled, recognising a fishing exercise as one who felt himself an expert. He hadn't spent forty years teaching boys to miss obvious ploys. "I need to speak to our board of trustees," he mused, changing the subject. "An emergency meeting is in order, but what will I tell them?"

"That's your decision." Bodie sounded sulky. "They'll fire his ass and then maybe he'll leave town."

Angus sighed. "It's funny, you know. I was only thinking yesterday of that incident with the marijuana in the gully. It's amazing how the account of it never made it into your student records. I might have a wee poke around in the archives and see if I can locate it. It doesn't sit well with me knowing a student doesn't have a complete file, especially with you enforcing legal rules for a living." He paused, hearing Bodie swallow.

"Blackmail is a criminal offence."

"It certainly is." Angus struggled to keep the smirk from his voice. He lifted the phone away from his mouth and stifled a snigger. "I wouldn't condone it on any grounds. Sometimes secrets are like flatulence, don't you think?"

"How so?" Bodie ground his teeth and his voice sounded tight.

"Well, better out than in."

"What do you want?"

"Oh, how kind. We do so love it when our Old Boys stay in touch."

Bodie inhaled and his answer emerged as breathy and laced with temper. "Fine! I'll give you regular updates."

"And pick up poor Hana." Angus flared his nostrils and blinked to disperse the tears of mirth. "Speak soon then." He hung up the phone and clapped a hand over his mouth, allowing himself a muted chuckle. He winked at the photograph of his stern predecessor and placed a finger over his lips. "Don't judge, dear sir. I'm sure you did it too. We told them often enough to live as though in front of witnesses. It's not our fault they weren't more careful."

At the other end of the site, Pete dealt with Logan's other request. He liked this one even less, but could think of no suitable candidate to palm it off onto. He took deep breaths like a pervert and dialled the number scrawled on the back of his hand in vivid, waiting for someone to pick up. A woman's voice answered. "Hello, you've reached the chambers of Eliza Du Rose. How may I help you?"

Pete felt the pressure of dollar signs racking up with every passing second. "Hi. Put Liza on."

"What?" The slick voice slipped from obliging to hostile. "Who is this?"

"It's Peter North. She knows who I am."

"Give me your phone number." Pete rattled it off, his eyes crossing at the close up view of a bogey on his index finger. "She'll call you back."

"No, she won't." Pete sighed. "She hates me. But Logan needs her. I have to talk to her myself." He rubbed at the black pen mark on his hand where he wrote Liza's number during Logan's frantic call. It remained solid like a bold tattoo. Pete reached out his tongue and licked it. It tasted foul and he rubbed it into a dirty bruise up his thumb and the bones in his wrist. The line went dead and he paused in his licking, sighing with relief as music sounded through the device. "Bitch put me on hold," he whined and licked his hand some more. A whiff of meat pie called to him as staff closed up the tuck shop for the day. He sped across, holding the phone to his ear. "You got any steak and cheese left?" he demanded through the open hatch.

"Maybe one," the girl behind the counter answered. She walked to the oven and peered inside. Hauling the contents out using tongs, she shoved it into a paper bag. "Only this one left," she said, sounding like she didn't care. "That's two dollars fifty."

"I'll pay you tomorrow." Pete snatched up his prize and back-stepped out of range.

"You're not allowed a tab!" the girl called with indignation. Pete turned his back on her, strolling to a bench out of sight and slumping onto it. He held the phone one handed and bit into the pie using the other.

"It's apple!" he wailed, the sound echoing off the surrounding buildings. "Henrietta's cursed me!"

A woman's voice spoke into his ear and he almost dropped the phone in fright, spitting warm apple onto the flag stones in disgust. "What?" he shouted into the handset. "Just what?"

"You rang me, dickhead." Liza's voice slipped across the distance between them, controlled and lethal.

Pete let out a squeak of fear. "I didn't want to. Logan made me."

"Let's have it?" she sighed. "If he's got you doing his bidding, it must be bad."

Pete threw the offending pie in the trash and clutched his groin. The sound of Liza's acid tones went straight to his bladder on its way to his bowels. He stammered the details to her, picturing her haughty nose wrinkled upwards in distaste. She intrigued and terrified him. Visiting Logan's home in the holidays as a boy when his parents didn't want him, Pete developed a monster crush on Liza Du Rose. He sought her out despite knowing the consequences, retiring from her company with his self-confidence in pieces. Yet he repeated the pattern many times on a loop of destruction, always with the same result. A thread of utter thrill ran within the overwhelming sense of terror, enticing him back like a brown moth to a naked flame. "He mentioned none of this last time we spoke." Liza let the anger creep into her tone. "Who's this Laval?"

"He got me bashed," Pete said, craving sympathy. "On the head."

Liza snorted. "Did it knock any sense in?"

"They broke Hana's arm."

"The English wife?" Liza spat the words and Pete nodded, forgetting she couldn't see him. She inhaled.

"Has anyone set bail?"

"I don't think so. They let him have one phone call, but he couldn't tell me details. Someone in the background told him to shut up."

Liza inhaled. "And he wasted his single phone call on you? That's an act of faith. Where is the wife now?"

"At work." Pete swallowed. "Are you coming down?"

Liza tutted. "Yes. That woman's made my brother soft. What was he thinking?"

"He's trying to keep her safe." Pete pouted and imagined seeing Liza again. All thoughts of Henrietta faded. "You can stay at my place, if you like." He narrowed his eyes. "Can you find out if the police cordon is off though? Otherwise we'll need to get a hotel."

"In your dreams," Liza snorted. "I'll stay at my brother's house. Give me the address and hurry up."

Chapter 3

Hana used the mindless administration and Sheila's constant demands to drown out the panicked, screaming voice in her brain. She left her phone number with the secretaries of numerous lawyers, warned they might prove too busy to help. Staving off the sense of powerlessness through futile activity, she knew she wasted her time but did it, anyway. Traipsing around the school site, she counted power sockets for the expo, jotting their location on the floor plan. When she arrived back at the office, Sheila changed her mind about one of the presenters. "I don't want them in there." She flicked a manicured nail at the map. "I want them in Q block. They need a data projector. Did you see one there?"

"No." Hana sighed and turned to leave again. Her footsteps dragged on the carpet. "I'll check."

Sheila's brows knitted into a thin, pencilled line. "Is something wrong, Hana? If you're tired, I can send Pete."

Hana shook her head and produced a less than convincing smile. "I'll go. I need the exercise."

Time passed in a strange blur, the hands of the clock speeding up as she retraced her steps. Everything reminded her of Logan. She trailed her fingers across the cupboard door on the split-level staircase, remembering how his kisses took her breath away in the darkness a lifetime ago. The steps to the gym forced her to recall the muscle definition on his naked back and the thought raised a blush to her cheeks. "What now?" she sighed. "Am I destined to raise my children alone again?" Only the occasional raised voice or scrape of a chair answered her.

Bodie waited for her in the common room. He watched her climb the back stairs as though every step drained valuable energy. His jawbone showed through his cheek as he ground his teeth. "Hi, Mum," he said.

Hana stopped half way up the stairs and gripped the bannister rail in white knuckled fingers. "Hi, Bo." She swallowed and drew on her dwindling strength to stop herself crying. "I guess you've heard what happened?" Disaster waited above her head, poised like a cloud burst.

Bodie nodded and waited for her to reach the top step. "Yeah, Mum. I heard." He opened his arms and Hana allowed him to enfold her. She waited for his inevitable victory speech and tensed.

"I won't say it." He read her mind and patted her back. "I'm here to give you a ride. Angus asked me."

"Thanks." Hana smile looked forced and tightened the muscles in her jaw. She gathered her belongings from the office and left the amended floor plan on Sheila's desk. Bodie led her down the back stairs, the silence between them creating an air of awkward foreboding.

Outside Amy's house, Hana flew into a rage, the misery of her situation mounting into a storm of emotion. "I want to see Logan!" She locked the passenger door with her elbow and stamped her foot. "Take me to the police station right now!"

"No." Bodie shook his head. "You can't see him, Mum. Nobody can. Odering will question him and Amy promised to ring me if there's anything to know. She's the desk sergeant tonight. She'll know before anyone else because she'll be the one charging him!"

Hana ground her teeth as he got out and slammed his door. She watched him step beneath the porch and fit his key into the lock. The temperature dropped and she followed him in with great reluctance. "You look very at home here," she grumbled, throwing her handbag onto the kitchen table and slumping into a chair. "Are you a couple?"

Bodie inhaled through his nostrils and let the breath go before turning. "No. I'm doing my share with Jas at the moment. That's all."

"Well good for you!" Hana closed her eyes, ashamed of her behaviour. The sound of a car door slamming preceded small feet running up the concrete driveway. Bodie's son barrelled through the doorway, clattering against the wall as he made a beeline for his father. He waved over his shoulder at Hana.

"Hi Hanny, lovely to see you sitting there in my kitchen." He turned his attention to Bodie. "Dad! I maked you this." He waved a lumpy dough ball at Bodie's stomach, growling as a blob detached itself and landed on the floor.

"What is it?" Bodie asked, narrowing his eyes in confusion. He poked it and left a depression in the ball. Jas jerked back, taking offence at his father's inexperienced questioning.

"It's goo!" he complained, bending to pick up the lump and add it to the mess. "You're not having it now for being rude."

A delicate little girl nosed her way through the open door and Bodie gave her a nervous smile. "Hi," he said. "Who are you?"

Hana bit her lip at her son's complete lack of diplomacy. She smiled at the girl and gave a tiny wave. The child returned her greeting as though complicit in some intrigue Bodie wasn't invited to take part in.

"Hello." A blonde woman stepped into the room and the small kitchen became full. Hana pressed herself into the back of the seat and fought a sudden wave of fatigue. Her awful circumstances didn't foster a desire to be sociable. The awkwardness sizzling in the atmosphere drove her to act.

"Hi." Hana stood and held out her left hand. "I'm Hana. Nice to meet you."

The woman looked relieved. She took it and gave a gentle shake, acknowledging Hana's broken right arm with a nod of understanding. "Sharon. Likewise. Amy and I share the kids. We often work opposite shifts, so we sort it out at the start of the month."

"That's awesome." Hana cast her mind back to a conversation with Amy and pointed to the children. "Jacinder, right?"

"Yes." Sharon nodded with too much enthusiasm and observed Bodie through the corner of her eyes. She checked him out and her cheeks pinked when she noticed Hana looking. "I'll take mine home," she said, gnawing on her lower lip as Bodie remained silent. "Amy said to bring Jas home today, so I didn't feed him."

"That's fine." Hana gave her a beautiful smile and the woman relaxed.

"See you again, Hana," she said and grappled for the hood of her daughter's coat. She missed.

Jas seized the child's hand and led her into the hall. "Poppa Logan cleaned my room," he said, the hitch of excitement in his voice as he marched towards his bedroom. "And he got me new sheets with soldiers on it. Come and see."

"We need to go," Sharon gushed, catching the hood and almost garrotting Jacinder. "Jas wants to spend time with his daddy."

"No I don't," Jas argued. "Jacinder can have him if she wants. I've got Poppa Logan now."

Hana winced at the look of thunder in Bodie's eyes. His upper lip twitched and he walked into the hallway. "So, you don't want the burger I got you?" he asked.

Hana heard a long pause and saw her son's spine tense. Then pattering feet grew nearer and Jacinder left with a flustered Sharon. Jas followed Bodie into the kitchen and peered at the squashed offering in the paper packet. He wrinkled his nose. "Did you sit on it?"

"No!" Bodie's head jerked backwards as though slapped and Hana saw a man so far out of his depth, he drowned each time he opened his mouth.

"I'll microwave it." She picked up the greasy mess and found a plate, pushing it into the microwave and struggling with the settings. "It's nice of Daddy to get you something, isn't it?" She turned to see Jas nod with reluctance.

She sat with him while he ate, avoiding conversation with her son. Bodie leaned his bum against the counter and folded his arms, watching how Hana interacted with Jas. She ached to soothe away the lost look in his eyes, wondering how it must feel to come into his son's life so late.

"Wanna come play, Hanny? You do good games," Jas asked, his brown eyes wide and hopeful. He wiped his greasy mouth on his sleeve and hopped down from the table.

Hana tugged on his arm. "Get back up and ask to get down," she said, her tone discouraging argument.

"Why?" he asked, although he complied.

"It's manners." Hana waited while he repeated the sentence and then looked to her son for authority. "Is that okay, Daddy?"

"Yes." Bodie swallowed and nodded.

"Seems a bit of a waste of time to me." Jas shrugged and slouched to his bedroom as the tense atmosphere descended over the kitchen in his wake. "Up down, up down," he chuntered like an old man.

Bodie sighed and ran a hand over his face. "Thanks," he conceded. "He won't listen to me."

"Don't give up." Hana threw the burger wrapper in the dustbin and flicked the kettle on to boil. "The best things take time." She sighed and her mind returned to Logan. Her husband exhibited unending patience, his experience with horses lengthening a quality into a formidable skill.

"Are you thinking about Logan?" Bodie's voice broke the silence.

Hana jumped. "Yeah. I hope he's okay."

Bodie ground his teeth. "He dropped me in the mess with him. Did you know that?"

"I don't know anything." Hana stared at crumbs on the table and pursed her lips. "He wouldn't do it on purpose."

"Whatever." Bodie rolled his eyes. "He rang me from the scene to ask what he should do."

Hana's lips parted. "He rang you for help?" She gritted her teeth to stop herself releasing any comment about the state of desperation which might drive Logan to make that call. "What did he say?"

"That he found Boris messed up. He called the paramedics."

Hana nodded and gave a slow exhale. "I never doubted him."

"Well, you should." Bodie pulled out a chair and sat down. "They took his phone as evidence and traced the call to me. I spent an hour in the inspector's room under threat of disciplinary."

Hana shook her head. "He wouldn't do it intentionally, Bo. I know you don't want to believe me, but it's true. He's a good man."

Bodie pressed the flat of his hand against the table and shrugged. "I'm so worried about you, Mum. Why won't you listen?"

"Because you don't say anything with any substance. It's all speculation and your off kilter gut feeling." She stood to make herself tea, waving a mug in his direction and sighing at his refusal. "You give me nothing concrete, Bodie but you seem desperate to hate him."

Hana took her tea to Jas' room and played with him. She read a story about an angry hedgehog and they fell asleep on the bed together, curled up into a comfortable ball of cast, arms and legs.

Amy arrived home after six o'clock and Bodie woke Hana with a gentle shake of the shoulder. She woke feeling groggy, with a toy soldier stuck in her fringe. Amy tutted at the sight of her sleeping son. "He won't sleep tonight now," she grumbled, pulling the elastic tie from her hair. It cascaded to her shoulders in a ruffled, attractive bob.

"Sorry." Hana yawned and peeled Jas' slender arm from around her waist. "In his defence I think I nodded off first."

"It's okay." Amy's gaze slid sideways towards Bodie and he ignored her. She leaned over Jas and stroked his hair. "Come on dude. Let's get you washed and ready for bed."

Jas leaned across and planted a wet kiss on Hana's cheek. "Night, Hanny," he said and yawned.

"Night baby," she replied and gave him a little wave.

"I should get you home," Bodie said. "Want me to stay with you?"

"That would be nice." Hana felt a wave of gratitude at his olive branch. "I'd like to speak to Amy before we leave, in case she saw Logan."

Bodie tensed but allowed her to straighten the bed covers and tidy up while she waited for Amy's return. Jas pounded into the room first, wrapping his arms around her thighs. "I love you so so so much, Hanny," he purred, kissing the front of her shirt.

"I love you too." She smoothed his curls flat with her palm and patted his bare bottom. "Get your jamas on, gorgeous. I need to speak to Mummy."

"About me?" Jas used his trousers like a sail and ran naked around the room.

Hana laughed. "Maybe. And maybe not."

"I love riddles." Jas pushed a bare foot into one trouser leg and hopped around.

Hana shot a sideways look at Bodie and walked into the hallway. She stopped him with an outstretched hand as he tried to follow. "Spend time with your son," she instructed. "I'll talk to Amy."

Bodie frowned and stared at the maniac bouncing on the bed in camouflage pyjamas.

"I can't tell you anything," Amy groaned in the kitchen. "It's against the rules."

"Can't you tell me if he's okay?" Hana pleaded. "He must feel terrified."

"He's fine." Amy sighed and poked in the fridge for leftovers. She dropped a crinkled carrot into the dustbin and leaned in, pulling out the burger wrapper. "Please tell me Bodie didn't feed Jas this crap for his dinner."

Hana swallowed. "What can I do to help Logan? I feel powerless."

"He's got a lawyer." Amy dropped the wrapper into the bin and stood. She narrowed her eyes. "I knew her. She was at your wedding reception."

"Mine?" Hana knitted her brow. "I can't think who that is."

"Eliza Du Rose." Bodie leaned against the doorframe and Hana heard Jas pulling toys out onto the bedroom floor. "His sister. Odering behaved like a man with a bee up his ass when he saw her arrive."

Hana's face changed at the mention of the woman who confiscated her phone and stopped her calling for help when Tama attacked Logan. "What did she do?"

Amy's shoulders slumped. "Pushed everyone around. The evidence against Logan is circumstantial."

Bodie snorted. "Apart from his threats against the victim."

"He didn't mean them." Hana sank into a kitchen chair. "He just learned that our mutual friend sold my safety to the highest bidder. I'd rather like to bash Boris myself." She rubbed her eyes and the paleness of her complexion betrayed extreme tiredness.

Bodie straightened upright and nodded to Amy. "I'll take her home. I'm sure you'll get the pleasure of giving her mafia husband breakfast in the morning. I'd like to forget him for tonight."

"Don't be such an ass!" Amy rebuked him.

"Mafia husband?" Hana scraped her chair back with her legs. "Why do you say such mean things?"

"Ass!" Jas squeaked, flying one of his dolls around the table. The doll's cape flew out behind its shoulders and he distracted Amy as she tried to stop him falling over chair legs and the dustbin. She grabbed him by the forearm and hauled him up onto her hip.

"Stop repeating grown-up language. Say night to Hanny," she said, dipping him forward so Hana could kiss his lips. He blew a raspberry and giggled.

Hana climbed into Bodie's car in silence. He started the engine and turned towards her. "Do you want to see if your vehicle is okay?" he asked.

She nodded and made suggestions about where Logan might have hidden it. They located it in a side street in Fairview Downs, a short walk from the school. It nestled between a truck with a wheel missing and a decent saloon. Bodie nodded towards it. "Looks safe enough for tonight. Without the keys it will have to stay there."

Hana pressed a hand over her stomach and fought to maintain her composure. Logan's efforts to keep her safe spoke of devotion and his awful predicament unpicked her from the inside. "He'll be home tomorrow," she insisted. "He can pick it up."

"Don't count on it," Bodie breathed. He turned his car around and headed towards Ngaruawahia.

Pulling onto the bottom of Hana's driveway, he didn't expect to almost rear-end the sleek red Mercedes blocking the gate. "Oh, no!" Hana hissed and hid her face in her left hand.

"Who is it?" Bodie demanded, undoing his seat belt.

"The last person in the world I want to see," she groaned.

Liza's long legs preceded her haughty face from the driver's door and she strode towards Bodie's window. "Open the gate," she demanded. "I've had a long day and what's-her-name isn't replying."

Bodie's lips parted in surprise and he opened his window to run a critical eye over the spectacular woman in front of him. "Mum's here," he managed with a stutter and Liza made an irritated sound with her lips.

"Open the damn gate then!" she rebuked him. "It's freezing out here." Her gaze slid over Hana's cast and up to her face, but she made no comment. Her expensive heels clicked in the gravel as she walked back to her sports car.

Hana exhaled and looked at Bodie. "Are you still staying the night?" she asked, hope in her voice.

He shook his head. "No thanks. It's not appropriate under the circumstances. It's bad enough your husband phoned me after finding Boris, but if I spend the night in the same house as his lawyer they'll fire my ass for sure."

Hana swallowed. Liza's car ground up the driveway, navigating the turns with car. The exhaust pipe hung about five centimetres from the concrete and Bodie hissed as she almost lost it at the top of the rise. Liza blocked the ramp to the garage, so Bodie dumped his car in front of the porch steps. Hana struggled to extract herself one-handed and emerged in time to see Liza dump her briefcase and an overnight bag in his arms. "Don't put them on the floor," she threatened and Hana saw her son's back straighten in irritation. She almost laughed as he turned towards her with a mystified look on his face.

Liza clumped to the top of the porch steps and tried the door handle. She snorted like an angry bull. "Open the door then!"

Hana shrugged. "Logan has the key."

"I've got mine." Bodie struggled to support both bags in one hand while he fumbled in his pocket. Hana clutched her handbag and kept her left hand under her cast, not wishing to end up as a bag carrier either. She stood on the drive and observed Liza's long legs and the expensive cut of her power suit. The youngest judge on the circuit cut a dashing figure, even in the darkness.

Bodie unlocked the door and deactivated the burglar alarm, shoving the briefcase under his arm. He eyed the floor and bent as though wishing to drop Liza's bags. "Don't you dare!" she warned and he stood up straight and glared at Hana.

"Put them in the room you used," she said with a sigh. Bodie clumped towards the open bedroom door and Hana smirked as he ditched the bags on the bed without care.

"He can't stay here." Liza pointed a manicured fingernail in Bodie's direction as he walked towards her. "If he's involved with incriminating my brother, he can't hear anything I have to say."

Bodie held his hands up in front of his face. "Don't worry, I'm leaving." He raised an eyebrow and shot a cautious look at Hana. "I hope you realise this is your life now, Mum." He shrugged and stepped onto the porch. "Don't say I didn't warn you."

"What's he talking about?" Liza sneered as the front door closed.

Hana sighed and set her handbag on the floor. She fumbled the zippers of her boots one-handed. "He thinks Logan is a mafia boss and that I'll spend the rest of our marriage prison visiting."

Liza laughed, a musical, tinkling sound. "This is Logan's first arrest and purely circumstantial." Her face softened. "My baby brother's an idiot, not a criminal."

Hana nodded. "I know." She stood up straight and inclined her head towards the kitchen. "Have you eaten?"

Liza nodded. "I dined with a local parliamentary minister after I finished with Logan." The snooty air returned. "I'll get changed and then we'll talk."

"Okay." Hana pointed towards the allocated bedroom and Liza's nose wrinkled.

"It isn't what I expected of my brother," she said, the words snide on her tongue.

Hana shrugged. "That's because it's mine," she replied and turned her back on her sister-in-law.

The kitchen smelled of Logan's aftershave and Hana closed her eyes. She felt defeated and Liza's presence in the house gave her no space to unleash her negative emotions. Flicking the kettle to boil, Hana pulled mugs from the cupboard and set out milk and sugar.

Liza appeared in the doorway, her clothing expensive but casual. She'd released her long, dark hair from its severe bun and it cascaded around her shoulders in ringlets. Inclining her head towards the teapot Hana laid on the table, she asked, "Don't you have anything stronger?"

"Not really. We don't drink anymore." Hana pulled open a cupboard door and found a dusty bottle of cooking sherry. She plonked it on the table and watched Liza struggle with the rusty lid.

"Help yourself." Hana pushed a mug towards her and watched Liza pour black tea and add a glug of sherry to the dark mixture.

"That's better." Liza closed her eyes and a smile lit her tight lips, curving them upwards in a beatific expression. Hana watched in surprise as she lost the hard look and mirrored Miriam's fragile beauty. "I'll get him out," she said with confidence, savouring her drink.

Hana nodded and replied with a nod. She poured tea for herself and sat opposite. Her stomach rumbled but the thought of eating induced nausea and she ignored it. "How's Logan?" she asked. "I know he didn't do it."

Liza inhaled. "The victim regained consciousness as I left the station," she said. "The detective went up to the hospital to speak to him. My brother has no previous record of violence, so their only evidence is circumstantial and the fact he ran his stupid mouth off before following the man."

Hana nodded. "With good reason. Boris betrayed us."

Liza looked at Hana over her mug, "My brother can take care of himself, but hitting someone from behind isn't his style. If he had questions for the man, why hit him with a sharp object over the back of the head and then call an ambulance? Logan isn't the type for regrets."

Hana sighed. "Logan's left arm is still weak from the break. He's having physio and chopping wood to regain its strength."

Liza tilted her head and frowned. "But an angry man can do extraordinary things. It's not a reasonable defence, although it can be argued to influence a jury."

"A jury?" Hana swallowed. "It won't go that far. Will it?" Her eyes glazed over in horror and Bodie's threat returned to taunt her.

"No." Liza sniffed. "The doctors found splinters in the wound. Someone hit him with a sharp, wooden object. They haven't found it yet."

Hana closed her eyes and imagined the villa's hallway. "I don't remember seeing anything like that. But there's a garage." She bit her lip. "Logan might have touched any number of things in there. He still keeps a car on the property."

"Just let them find what they find," Liza said, taking another sip of her laced tea. "We'll deal with it then."

Hana let out an audible sigh but Liza, used to other people's misery in her line of work, finished her drink without further comment. She scraped her chair back from the table and stood. Pausing in the doorway, she said, "If anything changes, they'll call me and I'll go. They can only keep him for twenty-four hours while they get their evidence together. They can apply to a judge for an extension but I've already spoken to their list of possible signatories. They've promised to make themselves unavailable. Nothing will happen tonight. I can't imagine they'll wake him up for questioning when they have all of tomorrow morning."

"Unless Boris dies." Hana lowered her gaze and tried not to allow the possibility to permeate her fears too far. She opened her mouth to thank Liza for her efforts, but the other woman's parting shot left her speechless.

"You're the problem. You've made him careless and that's on you."

Hana sat at the kitchen table long after Liza closed her bedroom door. Logan's family seemed determined to blame her for everything that went wrong. She sighed and pulled herself to the pantry to pour kibbles into Tiger's bowl as he wrapped himself around her feet. "Don't go climbing into bed with her by mistake," Hana warned him as he crunched on biscuits. "Although she probably sleeps upright in a coffin."

Feeling jaded and fretful, Hana shuffled off to bed. Sleep wouldn't come. The shirt of Logan's she pulled on smelled of him and underlined his absence while the moreporks sounded louder in the bush as though on purpose. The baby danced a jig in her womb and at midnight, Hana admitted defeat and got up again. She wandered to the kitchen without turning lights on and closed the door behind her. Flicking the spotlight on over the hob filled the room with a calming glow and she started to relax. The boiling of the kettle sounded deafening in the silence and Hana made tea for herself. It didn't take long to ferret out the chocolate biscuits Logan hid in the cupboard under the sink and she smiled to herself at his rubbish hiding place. "I told you I didn't want to find them, Du Rose," she sighed. "You're slipping." Liza's accusation came back to torture her and Hana put them back without taking one. A note fluttered to the floor as she shoved the biscuits behind a can of furniture polish and she pulled it out.

"You're not fat," Logan's slanted handwriting proclaimed. "You're beautiful and I love you just the way you are. Eat them all."

"Oh, Logan!" Hana sank into a kitchen chair and pressed the paper to her forehead. "How do we put this right?" The baby jabbed her with a sharp kick as though to remind her of its presence. She rubbed her left hand over her growing bump, grateful for the solidarity.

Hana drank her tea and stared at the pile of mail in the centre of the table where she left it. A flesh creeping itch worried her beneath her cast and she twitched, trying to shake it free. Distracting herself, she reached for the envelopes, noticing holes in the electricity bill where a slug made free with the post box. She flicked it aside with her fingernail, deciding Logan would deal with it when he got home. When. Not if.

"Not again!" she groaned, staring at the address label of the one underneath. "How many more times?" Her brow knitted in irritation at the idea that a company named, 'CircleLine Holdings Ltd' might be using her address. She'd sent four letters back to the sender, marked as 'unknown at this address' in the past month.

"I should search for them on the internet," she told the cat as he lapped up water from his bowl and purred. "You'd think the black vivid and capital letters I wrote it in last time might give them a clue that they're writing to the wrong address."

Tiger yawned. It didn't affect his wellbeing and he didn't much care what arrived or left in the post. As long as it wasn't him.

Hana fingered the envelope one-handed and contemplated opening it. She rejected the idea, knowing she couldn't do a proper job of disguising her nosiness with only one hand. "I think it's illegal to open someone else's post too," she said to the cat. "And we're in enough trouble for one day."

The kitchen door creaked open and Hana jumped in guilt. She slid the offending envelope beneath the chewed power bill. Liza stepped into the room, her clothes still immaculate as though she hadn't slept. She eyed Hana's cup of tea and sighed. "I'll get you one," Hana said, jumping to her feet.

"Thanks." Liza scraped out a chair and sank into it. She watched Hana's quick but clumsy movements, her gaze taking in the man's shirt and bare legs. When Hana turned, she gasped and swore.

"What?" Hana panicked and looked down at herself, imagining the slug transferring itself from the envelope to her. She swirled on the spot, inspecting herself for unwelcome creatures.

"You're pregnant!" Liza spat. "You kept that quiet."

Blood rushed to Hana's porcelain cheeks and she remained silent, making tea with a shaking hand. It bought her time to think as she waited for the kettle to re-boil and picked at a loose strand on the end of her plaster cast. No sparky answer presented itself to her exhausted brain. She put Liza's tea on the table and stepped back. "I'm going to bed," she said with a tight smile and headed for the door.

"When is it due?" Liza demanded, turning in her seat.

"January." Hana gripped the doorhandle in her fingers.

"So that's why he married you."

Hana bridled with natural indignation. "No!" she spat. "Just a little wedding gift and none of your business."

Liza snorted. "That's what you think."

Hana gritted her teeth and snorted through her nose. "In case you hadn't noticed, Logan is a grown man and makes his own choices. We don't need your permission to have children." She stumbled from the room and slammed the door behind her. "Bitch!" she hissed into the empty hallway.

Sleep arrived with surprising ease after Hana's spat with her sister-in-law and the alarm clock woke her from a deep slumber. After a messy one-handed wash, she found Liza at the kitchen table eating toast over an expensive laptop. She swallowed her pride. "Please can you give me a ride into town?"

"I'm leaving now." Liza shoved the last piece of toast between her glossy lips and snapped the laptop lid closed. Hana groaned and abandoned any thoughts of breakfast.

Liza's lips quirked upwards in amusement as Hana slammed the front door behind her. She hopped down the porch steps wearing one boot, trailing the other along with her handbag in her left hand. Dropping into the low-slung car with her possessions and hamstrung arm proved awkward. Liza made no attempt to help. Hana fumbled her seat belt into its fastening and sat back with a sigh. Liza glanced sideways at her stomach. The tight cream jumper revealed either a budding baby bump or a serious case of pie eating and Hana wasn't sure which she preferred. Liza inhaled and started the engine.

Exchanging only directions on the way through Hamilton, Hana found herself spat out in the front car park of the school, still wearing only one boot. Liza left with a squeal of tyres and a flick of her luxurious hair. Exposed in her revealing jumper, Hana's confidence left and she felt naked. Her body betrayed her by indicating to the school population that she'd enjoyed great sex on enough occasions to get pregnant. Her hurried marriage seemed only five minutes ago and Hana's lips tightened into a smirk at the memory of her energetic husband. In his absence, the child brought her comfort.

She walked towards the front steps, her heart yammering in her chest. The boys who held the door open for her seemed not to notice, issuing a polite greeting before bounding down the steps. The staffroom proved a different matter.

Fingers pointed and the general hubbub silenced as Hana stalked through to fetch the post. Hushed conversations took place behind hands and she sensed the prickling sensation of a painful blush sinking into the roots of her hair. Angus accosted her below the guidance counsellors' post box as Hana reached up for a stack of envelopes. He jerked his head towards her protruding belly. "Very clever," he said with approval. "Are we trying to detract from your husband's current predicament?" He used the term we in the royal sense, already distancing himself from the aftermath of Logan's arrest.

"Not on purpose." Hana shrugged and stared through the glass partition into the staffroom. Sheila waved, enjoying her few moments of fame at having known about the baby for a while. Keeping silent almost killed her.

Angus leaned back against a bank of pigeonholes. "So, when everyone wants to congratulate Logan and can't find him, what will you say then?"

"I don't know." Worry returned, a wave crashing over her head like an icy bath. "I know nothing." Hana ran a hand over her face. "I'm living from hour to hour and thought work might help."

Angus placed a hand on her shoulder. "Yes, keep busy. News will come. Our Logan's not a fool."

Hana snorted. "If you listen to his sister, then it's clear I've made him into one."

"A fool for love?" Angus removed his hand and tapped his chin. "I like that. It's so contrary to my understanding of Logan Du Rose that it entertains me." He inhaled through his nose and smiled. "I've told the board of trustees nothing as yet. I'm hoping I don't need to."

"They'll suspend him." Hana's shoulders sank. "Then they'll fire him."

"Maybe not." Angus winked and sauntered away, his hands linked behind his back in a casual stance.

Hana got on with her work, jumping at every sudden noise. The sound of the bell seemed louder than usual and she spilt a cup of herbal tea over a student's psychological assessment. "Bloody hell!" she groaned as the pink liquid spread like a rash.

"Any news yet?" Pete stage-whispered in her ear. He sprayed the side of her face with foul smelling spit.

Hana shook her head. "No. Please tell no one where he is."

"Gwynne knows," Pete hissed. He rolled his eyes. "I needed to break the news to him about his car. The cops impounded it as evidence." He shivered and leaned closer. "That guy is one crazy assed dude, but he won't tell anyone."

Hana sighed and nodded. Her arm itched beneath the cast and the joint ached. "Logan will take me to the hotel when he gets out. I'm not safe in Hamilton, thanks to Boris."

Pete nodded in sympathy. "Yeah. Sorry, Hana."

Sheila regaled everyone with excitement over the expo, unaware of her assistant's agony. "I can't believe it. This year, we're so organised." She beamed. "Everything is ready and we're a fortnight out from the event still. I'm amazing, don't you think?"

Pete's gaze slid from Sheila to Hana and back again. He opened his mouth and closed it. Hana swallowed; glad she'd finished her tasks early. If the worst happened, Sheila could manage without her.

As Pete shot off to the tuck shop at the sound of the interval bell, Hana lifted the handset of her office phone. Sheila emerged from her office and shook her head. "He's addicted to those pies," she groaned. "I won't touch them. I dated a butcher once and he said they're full of ear holes, eye holes and ass holes."

Hana swallowed down the acid which leapt into her throat and allowed herself an involuntary shiver. Then she wrinkled her nose. "So, they're full of nothing then?"

Sheila cocked her head and her face creased into a smile. "Oh. I never thought about it like that. Yes, all holes. Brilliant."

She drifted from the room and Hana heard her berating boys in the corridor for leaving orange peel on the floor. Taking a deep breath, she picked up the phone and dialled the hospital's number.

"Are you a family member?" the receptionist asked. Hana heard a trolley moving past in the background. She considered impersonating a fake German sister and then pushed the ridiculous thought away.

"No. Colleague. And friend," she replied.

"I can't give you any details," the woman said. "He's comfortable."

"Comfortable? Thank you."

"Can I say who's calling?" The question proved slick enough to force Hana into a stutter.

"Sheila," she rasped through a dry throat. "Jennings." Then she hung up.

Her forehead hit the table with a bump. Her idiocy rose up to bite her at her near mistake. Giving her name when Logan sat in a jail cell smacked of a death wish, but giving Sheila's reeked of dishonesty. With a sigh of regret, Hana continued with her work, guilt driving her past home time.

"See you tomorrow, Hana." Sheila smiled as she grabbed her car keys and handbag. She jerked her head towards Hana's stomach. "You look amazing. Don't listen to the gossips."

"What gossips?" Hana's muscles tensed in dread and she watched as Sheila bit her lip.

"Nothing. Don't worry about it. I'll see you tomorrow."

Hana pushed her keyboard away with her left hand and groaned. She listened to Sheila speak to someone in the corridor outside and stared at her silent phone. Nobody called to offer her a ride home and she contemplated her dilemma. The buses didn't run as far as Hakarimata Road and a taxi would burn holes in Logan's credit card. Tiredness turned her limbs to concrete and she lay her face on the desk and closed her eyes. "I'll sleep here," she sighed. "Nobody will care."

"I'll care."

Hana sat up so fast she jarred her arm. The chair swivelled around to face the door. "Logan," she breathed. Relief wrenched a sob from her throat and she pressed her fingers against her lips to prevent its escape.

Logan leaned against the doorframe with his hands jammed in his pockets. A nerve twitched below his left eye and exhaustion hung around him like a shroud. "You didn't think I'd leave you here, did ya?" He smiled through a dark shadow of beard growth. Yesterday's clothes looked rumpled and dirty.

Hana sniffed and stood, crossing the distance between them with quick footsteps. "Thank God!" she breathed into his chest.

"I smell sweaty," he apologised, cradling her head and pushing his fingers into the back of her hair. "They didn't let me shower."

"I don't care." She threaded her left arm between his jacket and shirt and held on, breathing in his familiar scent. "I'm so glad you're here."

Logan winced and wrinkled his nose. His sigh covered the news he'd need to deliver later. The sound of the vacuum cleaner broke the moment and Logan stirred. "Let's get out of here," he said, kissing the top of her head. Hana lifted her face and pursed her lips and he shook his head. "I didn't clean my teeth, babe. I found a mint in the car and ate that." He ran his tongue over the front of his teeth and rued his compulsive tendencies. "I need to get clean."

Hana nodded and snatched up her phone. She yanked her handbag from the bottom drawer and almost forgot her jacket. "Is the car okay?" she asked. "Bodie drove me round to check on it last night."

Logan nodded and his smile looked tight. "Yeah. It's fine. I parked out front." His gaze roved over her attire, the tight cream jumper hugging her rounded belly. A light flicked on behind his eyes, pushing away the threatening darkness. He smiled and the action seemed more genuine. "I love you, Hana. Don't forget that."

"I won't." She killed her computer and followed him from the office.

They passed through the empty reception and almost reached freedom before Angus called Hana's name from his office doorway. Logan kept walking, head down and thoughts miles away. He landed on the front steps before realising she'd let go of his hand. "Yes, Angus?" Hana asked.

The principal raised his eyebrows in question and jerked his head towards Logan. "Is there any need for an emergency board meeting?" he asked.

Hana glanced through the glass doorway at her husband's distracted expression, suspecting he held something back. But for Angus, she manufactured her brightest smile and shook her head. "No. Everything's fine now."

She bolted through the doors and grasped Logan's hand, urging him to walk fast. "What's wrong?" he demanded.

"Angus, asking questions. Keep walking and don't look back."

Logan sighed. "I'll need to speak to him sometime," he said.

"Not tonight." Hana shoved him towards the car and took the keys from his hand. "You look knackered. I'll drive."

Logan didn't question her, sliding into the passenger seat and sighing with relief as the engine started. They reached the expressway before he glanced across and remembered her cast. "Bloody hell, Hana! You can't drive like that."

"You did." She stuck her nose in the air and refused to pull over. They reached home with more luck than judgement. Hana steered the vehicle and let the automatic gear changer do its work, but she didn't indicate once. Logan grumbled for half the journey and then fell asleep.

He woke as the gate clanged shut behind them and the Honda strained at the hill. Hana slowed as they reached the house. "I didn't leave any lights on!" Her voice sounded strained as she stared up at the welcoming porch light and the sound of music coming from inside.

"I'll check it out." Logan heaved himself up the porch steps and tried the doorhandle. It gave way. He disappeared inside and returned to beckon her in. "It's Maihi," he said with a yawn. "She's made dinner."

Hana's shoulders slumped with relief and she kicked off her boots. Maihi met her at the kitchen door. "Hey tamariki," she said with a smile. "I've brought you a wee thank you for letting us use your paddocks for grazing. I've done a roast for youse."

Hana swallowed and her voice sounded croaky. "Gosh Maihi, you're amazing!" she breathed.

Maihi patted her cheek and planted a kiss on her forehead. "Want me to help you dish up?"

"Aren't you staying?" Hana asked, glancing back at Logan.

He avoided contact with the old woman and waved a hand in their general direction. "I need a shower," he said. "Thanks Maihi."

They listened to the bathroom door shut and water ran through the pipes within seconds. Hana sighed and sank into a kitchen chair. "He doesn't mean to be rude," she said, scrubbing at her eyes with her hand. "He's had a terrible few days."

Maihi tapped the side of her nose. "Maihi already knows what's goin' on, girly. I have my spies."

Hana exhaled and nodded. "When did you find out?" She narrowed her eyes. "How did you find out?"

Maihi pulled out a chair and sat next to her. "My cousin rang me this morning. She cleans at the police station. A detective spoke to a colleague on the phone and she heard him mention Logan's name. She took a while emptying the dustbin and listened to all the details."

Hana nodded. "He didn't do it. Logan didn't bash Boris."

"I know, I know." Maihi patted her fingers. "He'd bury the body and not ring an ambulance."

Hana gasped. "Maihi! He wouldn't."

The old woman smirked. "What's happening now then?"

"I don't know." Hana shrugged to emphasise her hopelessness. She listened to the shower pound against the bathroom tiles. "He fell asleep on the way home. I don't know if they let him go or if they want him back."

"Perhaps he broke out." Maihi waggled her eyebrows and widened her eyes. She crinkled her weathered face into a smile. "We look after our own," she said with sincerity and kissed Hana on the cheek. "Don't you fret about nothing. Now, old Maihi needs to go home and leave youse two lovebirds to sort out yer problems in peace." She hugged Hana, grabbed her coat and boots from the hallway and left.

Her words gave Hana a feeling of profound safety and she basked in its warm glow. The roast beef sent delicious smells into the kitchen, reminding her she hadn't eaten.

"Hey." Logan stroked her hair as he passed, heading for the oven and peering through the glass door. "This looks amazing." His pyjama bottoms hung low on his hips and his back muscles rippled as he bent.

"Are you hungry?" Hana asked, pushing herself upright.

Logan nodded and turning, held out his arms to her. His downy chest hair smelled of lavender shower gel and Hana closed her eyes and drank in his nearness. Water laced with hair conditioner dripped onto the top of her head as she nestled close. "I missed you so much," she breathed.

"I know, babe. We need to talk," Logan replied.

Chapter 4

Hana sat at the kitchen table and squirmed with discomfort at the itch beneath her cast. Using her left hand, she pushed Maihi's perfect beef and vegetables around the plate. Logan grabbed himself a second portion and sat next to her, running a hand across her shoulder. "I think we should move in with Maihi," he suggested, scooping potato into his mouth. "Or dig a tunnel to her kitchen and use it at meal times." Hana's chin wobbled and he knitted his brow and laid his cutlery across his plate. "Joke," he whispered. "Everything will be okay, babe."

"You don't know that." Hana used her sleeve to wipe her damp eyes and gave an unladylike sniff. "You're guessing."

She stood and took her plate to the dishwasher, dropping the knife on the floorboards half way across. Retrieving it distracted her and lessened the impact of Logan's watchful gaze. A teaspoon plunged onto the floor of the machine and she leaned in, trying to pick it up without removing the trays. She failed and almost fell in trying to grab it. Strong fingers closed around her waist. "Geez, Hana! Be careful!" Logan hauled her upright and she made a desperate grab, snatching the handle at the last moment. Exasperated, she threw it into the cutlery tray head first.

"I'm fine, Logan, really." She shrugged herself free and backed towards the counter.

Logan made a pot of tea, got the cups and spoons together and nudged Hana towards the table. "Liza's amazing," he commented. His lips curved upwards in a grin. "Odering is terrified of her. She told him his evidence is circumstantial. The blood on my jacket and hands came from trying to help Boris and I could account for how I got it."

"Liza said Boris regained consciousness as she left last night. He could tell them you didn't hurt him."

Logan sighed into his mug and looked sideways at Hana. "Thanks." He reached for her hand as her face creased in confusion. "You haven't once doubted me. You know I didn't do it and I'm grateful for your faith in me." He shook his head with sadness in his grey eyes. "Boris refused to clear me or implicate anyone else. He's keeping quiet."

"Can't he remember?" Hana stirred milk into her tea and watched her husband shrug. The slight action filled her heart with foreboding.

"I think Boris remembers perfectly well what kind of trouble he's in." His tone sounded jaded.

Hana pressed her fingers to her lips. "No, he wouldn't do that to you. You're friends."

Logan shook his head. "Not anymore, Hana. Odering charged me with wounding with intent and I'm on police bail. Boris could clear me with a single word, but won't. Liza says they will drop the charges but until then I must check in with the cops at the station every day."

Hana's face paled. "So Angus will suspend you then?"

Logan nodded in misery. "He won't have a choice. My teaching career's over, you know that?"

Maihi's lovely roast turned to ash in Hana's stomach as sickness and fear fought for dominance. "Odering must know you didn't do it, Logan," she pleaded, her eyes growing glossy with tears.

"Yeah, he does. But I'm a handy body at the moment. He's not playing by the rules and will use me to catch Laval."

"He thinks the blonde man bashed Boris?" Hana rubbed her eyes and pushed her mug away.

"I dunno." Logan sighed. "He knows I didn't, but he wants them to get cocky and make a mistake. He's desperate and his career is riding on it."

"So, you're a sacrifice?" Hana's eyes widened as she processed the appalling truth.

"Yep." Logan stood and pushed his chair in, offering his hand. "Come on. I'm beat. How about an early night?"

She nodded and accepted his outstretched fingers, hauling herself upright and allowing him to pull her into his chest. "I'm so sorry," she whispered. "All this started before we met. It's my problem and now it's ruined your life too."

Logan tutted and kissed the top of her head. "It's not that simple," he sighed. His lips curved upwards in a tired smile and his eyes crinkled at the corners. "Anyway, your problems are mine. Remember?"

The house felt safe and cosy, but outside the oppressive darkness contained a sense of threat. Hana slept in a series of fitful dozes, her dreams filled with jail cells and the clang of metal doors. Logan shifted around in his sleep, his mind still running scenarios and solutions on a futile loop. When he woke in the early hours, he lay and listened to Hana's steady breathing and placed a gentle hand over her stomach. His child kicked him and he allowed a smile to play across his lips. The tiny form bore the weight of his hopes and dreams for the future and it pained him. Closing his eyes, he prayed to Hana's God for justice, vindication and peace. When the alarm disturbed him at six o'clock, he sensed the shift which told him somebody heard.

Hana sat up and rubbed her eyes, her hair standing out from her head like a halo. She yawned and stretched. "Did you get any sleep? I don't think I did."

"Yeah, you got a few hours." Logan turned onto his back and rested his head on his arms.

Hana wrinkled her nose. "That means you didn't."

"I'm okay." Logan smiled and jerked his head towards the door. "You grab the first shower and I'll boil the kettle for tea."

A blip in the power gave Hana a douse of cold water half way through her shower and she screamed in shock and irritation. The morning went downhill from there. She poked mascara into her right eye and tore a hole in her tights, the blonde man's influence stretching over her life further through her broken arm.

"I'll drive," Logan said with a tight smile, snatching up the car keys. "I'd like to get there alive." He frowned and pursed his lips as the awkward meeting with Angus loomed before him.

"It might not go the way you think," Hana soothed, reaching out to stroke his sleeve. "Angus isn't stupid." Hana followed him to the front door, carrying the envelope she'd found in the post box. Her left handed writing looked childish and she flapped it in front of her.

"What's that?" Logan asked, holding out his hand.

"Someone keeps writing to CircleLine Holdings Ltd." Hana placed the envelope into his palm and bent to grab her handbag.

Logan's eyebrows narrowed as he peered at her scrawl. "Not known at this address," he repeated. "How many have you sent back?"

"That's number four." Hana yanked a pair of gloves from her bag and stared at the right one. Shaking her head, she stuffed her left hand in and put the other one back. "Five. No, four. I don't know. They started last month. They're annoying me because it's hard to write now."

"I'll deal with it." Logan pushed it into his jacket pocket and gave her a tight smile. "Give them to me from now on."

"We shouldn't get any more," Hana protested. "I need to find out where they're based and ring them."

"I said I'll deal with it."

Hana blanched at Logan's tone and dropped the matter.

Logan put the car into gear and drove down the slope, avoiding conversation throughout the journey. Hana fidgeted, sensing his unease and unable to help. "Would you like me to come to your meeting with Angus?" she asked.

Logan shook his head. "No, thanks."

"I don't mind." Her gloved fingers danced in agitation across her knees.

"I'm good. Thanks."

Hana's lips parted in surprise as Logan drove straight to work. He didn't deviate their journey in case Laval's men sought them, but used the expressway and entered through the front gates. She bit her lip and said nothing, suspecting he desired to hasten a confrontation with the blonde man. A student teacher fought him for Hana's parking space and he claimed it at the last second. She slammed her door and stormed towards them, leaving her engine idling. Staff cars piled up behind her steaming exhaust. "I've parked there all term!" she raged. "That's my space."

Logan ground his teeth and Hana held her breath. "Don't, Logan," she begged. "Don't make it worse." She managed to exit the car before him and headed the young woman away from the driver's door.

"It's my space," she asserted. "I've parked here for the last fifteen years." She held her hand up as the girl opened her mouth again. "Find somewhere else."

"But I like that space." The girl pouted and blonde hair whirled around her head in the breeze.

"So do I." Hana turned and met Logan at the driver's door, herding him towards the chapel. The honk of a horn sent the girl running back to her vehicle.

"What did you think I'd do?" Logan hissed under his breath. "Bash her too?"

"Logan!" Hana stopped dead and her face drooped in misery. "Stop!"

"Sorry." He shook his head and blinked a few times. "I'm wound up, Hana."

"I know." She reached for his arm and walked next to him, her handbag swinging between them. "And no, I didn't think you'd bash her. Your glare would melt her first."

Logan snorted and stepped back to hold the front door open. Two boys emerged at speed, treating Logan as a doorman. They pushed past Hana and almost knocked her flying backwards down the stairs. Hands in their pockets and heavy rucksacks on their backs, they kept walking without concern. Logan lurched, hauling them back by their bag handles. "What the hell do you think you're doing?!" he snapped.

Hana steadied herself against the wall as Logan turned the boys to face her. Colour drained from their complexions and they stammered apologies like fools. "Get back in there!" He shoved them towards the doorway and then let go as they stumbled up the step, falling over each other. He indicated Hana with a jerk of his head, grey eyes glowering as though on fire.

"Sorry," they chorused in unison, seeing her tiny baby bump and widening their eyes. Logan backed them up and then turned holding his hand out for Hana

"Here you go," he said, his brow creased in anger. Hana saw him grapple with his emotions as she stepped through the doorway and watched him meet the gaze of the nearest terrified boy. "That was wrong on too many levels to count," he said, his tone acidic. "That's not how you should behave. Ever!" His jaw flexed and released as the boys apologised again. "Get to registration." Logan stood rigid as they bolted for the door. He pulled Hana clear of the opening and she felt his fingers trembling against hers.

"I'm fine," Hana whispered. "The baby's fine."

"Yeah, but how many more near misses can we dodge?" he demanded, his voice icy. He sighed. "I can't leave town, Hana. But you can. I need you to go to the hotel. I'll get one of the guys to drive down and fetch you."

"No." She exhaled and her breath caught in her chest as Logan let go of her hand. With a rigid back, he strode towards

Angus' office. The principal leaned in his doorway stifling a smirk. Hana read his lips as she saw him lean in towards her husband. "That's my boy," he muttered under his breath. "Twenty seven years and I still can't help but like you, Logan Du Rose."

"Whatever!" she heard Logan reply as they disappeared into the office and the door closed behind them.

Angus slid into his chair and watched the sky brighten through the slender window. Logan remained standing, his jaw working as he fidgeted. "Sit." Angus pointed to the chair opposite and Logan shook his head.

"No need. I quit."

Angus snorted. "And I refuse to accept your resignation." He leaned back in his chair and shivered. The fireplace burned with a fierceness which mirrored his assistant's lighting of it. He imagined her cursing as she lit the newspaper. "Bloody room," Angus shivered. "Worse designed room in the whole site and it's mine."

"I'm sure you're used to it." Logan took a step forward and held out his hand to Angus. "Thanks for everything."

Angus stared down at the calloused palm and the myriad scars. He shook his head. "Take a leave of absence. Go somewhere safe with Hana. Think of your child and come back when you can."

Logan sighed and his shoulders slumped. "I can't, Angus. Odering charged me."

"You're the best thing to happen to my English department in years. It's never run with such ease and I don't intend to let you walk away like this." Angus steepled his fingers and rested his chin on top.

"You need me to resign. The board will insist."

"Why? You're assuming the board are aware of your misfortune."

"You didn't tell them?" Logan's brow narrowed into a dark line and confusion played in his grey irises.

"I didn't need to." Angus watched his flounder, enjoying the upper hand. He indicated the chair opposite again. "Sit, Du Rose. Don't make me break out the cane."

Logan snorted and moved towards the chair. "Yeah, my ass still hurts from the last time."

Angus waved a hand in dismissal. "Don't be ridiculous, man. You were fourteen." He leaned forward in his seat. "I took the liberty of visiting poor Boris last night. His relatives are overseas and as his sponsor, the police permitted me access. Senior Sergeant Singh Johal has provided me with regular updates since yesterday although he's somewhat angry with you."

"Me?" Logan's head jerked back in surprise. Realisation made him wince. "Ah, yeah. I rang him when I found Boris and then they confiscated my phone as evidence."

Angus raised an eyebrow and continued, "Boris regained his memory for long enough to assure me you weren't his attacker. On that basis I will not require your resignation." His Scots accent rapped out the words like a staccato beat.

Logan shrugged. "They still charged me, Angus. Boris won't clear me to the cops. It's his word against mine."

"And mine against his." Angus smiled. "We'll wait for a few days to see if our young man comes to his senses. If not, I shall intervene."

"It won't help." Logan shifted in his chair, pent up frustration making his movements jerky. "He needs to tell them, not you."

Angus stood, indicating the meeting at an end. "Teach your Year 12 and 13 classes for the next few days, Mr Du Rose. I'll give you cover for the rest. I suggest you use the time to sort out your issues. As soon as the expo is over, take Hana to your hotel and keep her there."

Logan winced and bit his lip. "My parents' hotel," he said, his eyes flashing.

"If you say so." Angus raised both bushy red eyebrows and jerked his head towards the door. "Boris will tell the truth about who attacked him, Logan. Patience is a virtue."

Logan cocked his head and eyed the principal sideways. Something about Angus' confidence irked him. "You recorded him, didn't you?" he said, his eyes narrowing. "Like you did when Pete confessed to smuggling those girls back to his dormitory."

Angus snorted and his body rocked with mirth. "Let's hope our mutual friend fares better with the lovely Henrietta," he chortled. "All promise and no delivery, that boy." He reached for his cooling mug of coffee and took a sip.

"Really?" Logan stood and his eyes brightened. "He said they had a threesome."

Angus sprayed brown liquid far and wide. Logan dodged backwards as droplets fired across the desk. Laying the mug down, Angus reached for a handkerchief in his top pocket and wheezed into it for a moment. He flapped his hand in dismissal.

"What did they do?" Logan's lips twitched upwards. "You have to tell me now."

"They ate toffees and looked at his car magazines," Angus rasped, mopping his mouth.

Logan paused on his way to the door. "But he said you recorded his confession."

"I did."

"And you kept him on detention for a term." Logan's eyes narrowed. "Why?"

"He begged me to." Angus' eyes streamed with the effort of concealing his laughter. He pointed at the door and shook his finger. "Out, Du Rose. Out."

"Lying little bugger!" Logan breathed, backing out into the assistant's domain. She glared at him and tutted at his language, herding him through the door and closing it behind him.

In his office, Angus lay back in his chair feeling every bit as old as his years. He toyed with the idea of retirement. Logan's offer of resignation tickled him. "I didn't mark you as a quitter, Du Rose," he sighed. He grinned at the memory of Logan's veiled surprise as he instructed him to hide his wife at his hotel. "It's amazing what land agents can find out nowadays, Du Rose," he sighed, patting his stomach and wishing he hadn't imbibed in that last packet of biscuits. He thought back to his Auckland north shore grammar days and the silent teenager with the grey eyes who perplexed him even back then. Close knit and secretive, the Du Rose boys reeked of emotional neglect and the elder deferred to the younger.

Logan winged his classes with considerable skill and years of practice. "I'm sorry," he apologised. "I haven't marked your Year 13 internal exams but I'll deliver tomorrow." It seemed inappropriate to add marking wasn't permitted in a police cell, owing to the stabbing risk with ball point pens and the choking hazard of paper.

At interval, he jogged to Hana's office to tell her the result of his meeting with Angus. She cried with relief, giant tears rolling off her chin. "I assumed the worst," she sniffed. "And I knew the cops had your phone so you couldn't text me."

"Sorry." Logan smoothed the streaks from beneath her eyes and kissed her forehead.

"I don't want to go to your parents' place," she sniffed, wiping her nose on her sleeve.

"Why?" Logan held her at arm's length and knitted his brow. "Don't you like them?"

Hana squirmed free of his embrace. "I don't know them. It's not fair to leave me there by myself."

Logan sighed. "Look, I'll teach this next class and then head home. I'll come back for you at the end of school."

"Okay." Hana forced a smile onto her lips. "I'm glad Angus backed you."

"Me too." Logan winked at her and walked towards the door. Pete barged through, stopping dead at the sight of him.

"What happened?" he hissed. "What did Angus say?"

Logan smiled, the expression smug and self-satisfied. "He said lots." He chewed his bottom lip and amusement lit his eyes from within. The bell rang and he glanced into the common room as boys filed in. "But it will keep."

Pete watched him stride through the throng of male bodies and disappear across the bridge. He held his arms out sideways and shrugged. "What happened?" he demanded.

Logan taught his next class and then drove to Amy's. Bodie answered his knock and his lips curled back in a snarl. "You bastard!" he growled, stamping back to the kitchen and leaving the front door open. Logan followed.

"I didn't mean to drop you in it," he said, his tone sombre.

"Well, you bloody did!" Bodie snapped. He eyed Logan's smart clothes and his brows knitted. "Why are you here? Did the board fire you?"

"No." Logan pulled out a chair and sank into it. "He saw Boris and got the truth."

"Boris said who attacked him?" Bodie stood up straighter, excitement making his eyes sparkle.

Logan winced. "No, but he admitted it wasn't me." He rolled his eyes. "Angus is a wily old dude. I think he recorded him saying it."

Bodie shrugged and resumed his stance, leaning against the counter with his arms folded. "It's not admissible. Means nothing."

"Why don't you like me, Bodie?" Logan asked the question and watched him struggle to answer. He recognised the moment when he chose to lie.

"I don't dislike you." A vein twitched in Bodie's left eyebrow and Logan memorised the tell for future reference.

"Then we're good?" Logan leaned back in his chair and Bodie shrugged. Backing himself into a corner left him no choice.

"I guess so."

Jas appeared from beneath the kitchen table. He popped up and plonked himself and his Action Man bungee jumper on Logan's knee. "Hi Poppa," he said, grinning and exposing his baby teeth. "Daddy doesn't accept sorries. Mummy said. She says allergies to him all the time and he never takes them. He's a right ass."

Logan clamped his teeth over his bottom lip and tried not to laugh as the child echoed his own sentiments. "Is that right?" he said, keeping his voice level.

"Yep. Mum said." He wrapped a scarf around his doll's head and arranged it so his eyes showed. Logan resisted the urge to check out Bodie's expression. Jas glanced up at his father. "Youse meant to make drinks for peoples when they visit," he rebuked his father.

"Would you like a drink, Logan?" Bodie asked, enunciating every word.

Logan nodded and muttered his thanks. Bodie covered his confusion by reaching into a cupboard for two glasses and retrieving a bottle of cold water from the fridge. He plonked it onto the table and sat down opposite Logan. Jas let out a huff of exasperation before hopping off Logan's knee. His little bare feet made a pit-pat sound on the floor tiles as he headed to the cupboard. He opened the door and stuck almost his whole body in, emerging with a plastic glass in his hand. Tottering back to the table with exaggerated movements, he thumped it on the table. With one hand on Logan's knee, he stood on tippy toes to push it towards the other two glasses with a clink of plastic on glass.

"You look like Hanny," Logan said, failing to hide his amusement. Jas cocked his head on one side and tilted his right eyebrow.

"Dunno what you mean," he said. "Can I tell you about kindy this morning?"

"Yep." Logan lifted him back into his lap while Bodie poured water in the glasses. "What happened?"

"Well," Jas began. He settled himself for a saga and laid Action Man on his chest. "Two naughty boys argued over a bucket in the sandpit. One had a plastic hammer and the other poked his thing. His ass. What's it called, Daddy? Ass?"

Bodie swallowed and his eyes widened in horror. Logan provided the word. "Assailant?"

"Yeah, fanks Poppa Logan," Jas smiled up at him. "He poked his assailant in the eye with a headless Barbie doll. He uncovered it out the sandpit. I fink he hid it there. There was lots of screaming and crying. I wanted to arrest both of them for assault with a dead weapon." He rolled his eyes in exasperation and gave a noisy exhale. "Mrs Wright didn't let me. She shouted at me, 'Sit on bottom!' so I did sit on my bottom. But she scared me so I sat in Jacinder's lunch and she cried and cried for ages."

Bodie closed his eyes as though picturing the scene. "How did you sit in her lunch?"

"Daddy! You don't listen. I was standing on the table when Mrs Wright shouted, 'Jaspal! Sit on bottom!' so I sat on Jacinder's lunch."

Logan opened his mouth to enquire why Jas found it necessary to stand on the lunch table. Then he closed it again without asking. Jas gave him a beatific smile. "Wanna join my army?" he said in a sweet voice.

"I need to talk to your dad." Jas' face crumpled into his characteristic meltdown expression and Logan shook his head. "Don't go there, mate," he warned.

Jas shrugged. "Okay," he said with affable cuteness, as though the dark storm of temper never crossed his childish features. "Don't leave without hugging me bye." He unhooked Action Man's belt from his bungee rope and reaffixed it to the back of the doll's shirt collar. Then he dragged him along the hallway, making grunting sounds and muttering, "Come on prisoner, let's see what the cops can find out from you under torture."

Logan grinned. "Been listening to Mummy and Daddy talk about work again, has he?"

Bodie's face creased into a sarcastic smile and he produced a fake laugh. "Yeah, whatever!"

Logan relented. "Look I already apologised, Bodie. Calling you wasn't my finest moment and I regret it. It wasn't intentional but I am sorry for the trouble it caused for you."

Bodie's body language softened and he nodded. "Okay. Let's leave it now. What do you remember about arriving at the Gordonton house?"

"Not much. I told Odering everything I saw. Boris lay on the hall floor on his back and I could see he'd broken bones. I felt for a pulse, called for an ambulance and then rang you, for which I am sorry."

Bodie rested his elbows on the table. "If Boris told Angus you didn't attack him, why wouldn't he tell us?"

"Scared." Logan shrugged. "Or paid to set me up, so it leaves Hana vulnerable?"

Bodie nodded. "Either would certainly fit."

Logan sighed. "I saw a black saloon as I turned onto the driveway. The bushes obscured it until I made the turn and then I almost clipped it. My wheels slewed across the track and back again. You must still be able to see the mess I made."

"Did you see the blonde guy in the car?"

Logan shook his head, the exaggerated movement expressing his irritation. "Tinted windows. And I didn't look. I struggled to turn the wheel and slow down and they'd gone by the time I looked in the rear view mirror."

"What make was the car?"

"I dunno. Black, sleek, a five door saloon. I didn't take enough notice."

"Who did you think might be in the car?"

"What?" Logan halted and stared at Bodie in confusion.

The cop poured himself more water and sipped, looking at Logan over the rim of the glass. "It's a private driveway leading to a rental property. The only people using that track live there. Did you know the car?"

Logan stopped as though the wind disappeared from his sails. He closed his eyes and fought for a buried memory. "Geez, you're right. Nobody asked me that."

"So, who did you think it was?"

"The rental agent. He drives a car the same as that."

"How do you know?"

Logan huffed out a breath. "He called by twice while I lived there. The first time was to give the plumber access to fix a leak and the second was a routine inspection. He asked Pete to tidy his room." Logan blinked in rapid succession. "He parked the car in front of the garage so I left my bike outside. I forgot about it and it rained."

"So what sort of car is it?"

"Black Nissan Skyline, 1990s manufacture." Logan ground his teeth and struggled to remember. "They've modified it though."

"How?"

Logan remained silent and focussed on a patch of blank wall as though running the scene back through his mind. "Aerofoil," he said after a long while. "It looked odd. The agent's doesn't look like a boy racer car but this did."

Bodie's lips parted into a satisfied smile. "That's because it is." He slapped his palm on the table. "Nicked a few nights ago from outside a kid's student flat. Find the car, find Laval."

Logan cocked his head on one side and eyed Bodie with renewed respect. "Dude, you're good at this. Why aren't you a detective?"

Bodie picked up a toy soldier from the table and turned it over in his fingers. "Never got the opportunity," he replied. With a swift movement he lobbed the little man at Logan, watching as his step father caught it in his hand. Logan winced and laid it on the table, moving his right hand up to rub the space above the elbow.

"What did you do that for?" he grumbled.

"Proof." Bodie rocked back in his seat. "You're left handed and your arm is still weak. You favoured it even though you might not make the catch. Whoever hit Boris over the back of the head did it with force. From behind. Odering is looking for a right handed assailant hitting from a particular angle and that's not you."

Logan snorted. "No shit, Sherlock." He closed his eyes but not before Bodie saw the force of temper glittering in the grey irises. "Yet here I am, signing into the police station every day with conditions set on my freedom. I can't even take Hana to the hotel to keep her safe until this is over."

Bodie shrugged and his jawline hardened. "Likewise. Can you imagine how much trouble your phone call caused me? Odering got a transcript of the whole conversation and I thought I'd get busted down to bloody janitor!"

Logan ground his teeth but resisted the urge to apologise again. He sensed Bodie liked feeling hard-done-by and figured if he feigned a headache, Bodie might develop a worse one. "I should head back to work," he said, standing and pushing his chair under the table. "Thanks for brainstorming. I hope you find the car. I don't think you'll get Laval that way though."

"Why?" Bodie stood and matched his movements.

Logan paused with his hand on the doorhandle. "Because there are two factions in play here. I think Laval and the blonde man are separate."

"Na." Bodie's tone sounded dismissive. "Flick works for Laval. Odering has good information on him."

"Whatever." Logan shouted his farewell to Jas and left before the child ran along the hallway and kicked up a fuss. He heard small fists pounding on the back of the door.

"I wanted him to play with me!" the voice squeaked in temper.

"I'll play with you," Bodie replied, failing to make himself sound like an attractive alternative. His phone rang and he answered it as Jas continued to rage against the wooden door.

Logan climbed into the Honda and drove away. Hana's son might prove an excellent cop but as a father, he occupied one slot above useless. Right below the one pegged as disinterested.

Chapter 5

"I need a favour." Logan kept his tone clipped as he navigated away from Amy's street, hearing the man's rapid Chinese relaying his request to someone in the background. The new phone bounced in the cradle and Logan wondered what possessed him to buy such an expensive one on impulse. Another voice spoke from the handset and Logan winced as a natural reaction. Dealing with the devil never seemed to get any easier.

"Du Rose." The voice sounded smooth like syrup, an impeccable English accent masking an Oriental twang. "I owe you thanks."

Logan inhaled and made the turns to take him away from the Claudelands area, his mind elsewhere. The Chinese man's face drifted across his inner vision and he shuddered. "It's nothing. I'm glad everything turned out okay."

"Better than okay, Mr Du Rose." The man made a breathy sound. "Mrs Che is very happy. She says thank you."

"It's no bother. Really." Logan inhaled. "I need some information, please Mr Che."

The brief conversation yielded little, but set certain Auckland wheels in motion. After disconnecting, Logan rang a Du Rose family member. "Hey, Alex," he said, relief in the momentary shuttering of his eyelids. "How's it going?"

"Good, partner," his cousin replied. "Cafe renovations are going well. I heard you got married, man. Did my invitation get lost in the post?"

Logan snorted and allowed himself a smile. "Mum dealt with it all very last minute. It meant she got to pick the guests."

"Ah." Logan imagined Alex's sage nod. "So only half the whānau received the royal summons then?"

"Something like that. I'm sorry." Logan wrinkled his nose on one side and regretted letting Miriam have control. "I'll bring Hana for dinner when you've got the restaurant up and running. You can meet her then."

"Sure thing, bro'. Why you ringing? You know your investment is sound."

Logan laughed. "Yeah, because I do the books. No, it's not that. I'm asking around about a guy named Laval. I think his first name is Michael. You ever come across him?"

"Not me. But the cousins might have. It sounds familiar, but that name doesn't have good vibes."

Logan raised an eyebrow. "In what way?"

"Just whispers really. Nasty piece of work. Money lending and an art heist last year. He has links to gangs and drug trafficking."

"Okay." Logan shook his head to dispel his confusion. There seemed more to the white haired old man than he believed. He'd underestimated him. "Put the word out, Alex. But don't forewarn him."

"Oui, mon frère." Alex Du Rose answered in French. Like each of the generations, English came third after Māori and the colloquial form of their ancestors' language.

"Sweet. Thanks for that. I'll talk to the cuzzies and see what I can find out. Au revoir." Logan squeezed the bridge of his nose between finger and thumb and let out a sigh of exhaustion as Alex ended the call. Many of the Du Rose businesses owed their early survival to Logan's generous investment. It gave him the ability to move throughout the myriad complicated circles without guilt. Nobody else boasted such ease of passage.

He pulled over into a side road to make the second call, the phone number dredged from the annals of his photographic memory. Logan blew through pursed lips as the call connected.

"Hello, Du Rose Interior Designs. How can I help you?" The woman's voice conjured a memory of an attractive, dumpy cousin and Logan relaxed.

"Hey, Calli. Is Uncle there?" He watched the unmarked cop car slip past him and shook his head in disgust. Amateurs.

"Hey, Logan. How's my favourite cousin?" Her voice softened and he smirked.

"Married, babe. You're too late."

She snorted. "Still an arrogant sod then? No change there. Yeah, Uncle's here." She put her palm over the office phone but Logan still cringed at her shout. "Uncle! It's Logan. He wants you."

The sound of shuffling preceded the old man's journey to the telephone. He grumbled all the way. The phone clattered as he fumbled to put it to his ear. "You want yer money back?" he demanded with a cackle.

"No, thanks. The dividends are too valuable."

"Pity. I'm selling up at the end of this year."

"Yeah, yeah. You've said that for the last decade." Logan rubbed his eyes. "You're enjoying yourself too much. The millionaire homeowners on the north shore want your brand of Hollywood in their master bedrooms, Uncle."

"What do you want then?" his uncle bit, stifling a sickening sounding cough.

Logan inhaled. "What do you know of a man called Michael Laval?"

"Enough. Stay away from him, Logan."

"I can't. He went after my new wife and made it personal."

The old man tutted and blew his nose. "What did Che say?"

"He's asking around but I don't want to involve the Triads. I need to break away from all that now I'm married."

"I heard." His uncle lowered his voice. "Word around town is that you're gonna be a father."

"Yeah." Logan couldn't keep the smile from his voice. "January."

"Congratulations." The cough came again. "It's about time. There's no room in a father's life for the Auckland underbelly. Clean up your act."

Logan blinked at the rebuke. His uncle's innocent looking shop front was the place where Logan first encountered the Chinese Triad gang. He'd entered a world not previously acknowledged. Wiping out the foot soldiers collecting protection money, he earned respect and a relationship with the formidable Mr Che. They'd called a truce and the interior designer received twenty years of protection for free.

"That's unfair!" Logan grumbled and heard his uncle laugh.

"Don't behave like a baby," the old man cackled. "It's time for many things to change." He scolded someone with his hand over the receiver. "You know some of these people I employ don't actually know what they're doing!"

"I'm the last person you should admit that to." Logan sniffed with irritation. "Seeing as you owe me such a lot of money."

"Ah, whatever!" the eighty-year-old man scoffed. "I'm your favourite uncle and I make you a fortune. When do you want the renovations to the motel units to start? I need to book it in. This designer is so good, I have to timetable her months in advance."

"Summer," Logan replied. "But if you're quitting, don't leave me high and dry, thanks. I'll still expect the same level of service." The old man said a filthy English word which made Logan recoil in the driver's seat. "Geez Uncle! Stop listening to those grandkids of yours. You don't know what you're saying, man!" His uncle laughed and Logan shook his head.

"Who says I don't know what it means?"

Logan shuddered. "Gross, old man. I don't know how you get away with talking dirty to millionaire's wives!"

"Well, not for much longer," his uncle cackled. "Did you speak to Che?"

"About Laval? Yeah."

"No. About those assets you have in the city. He wants to make you an offer."

"Na, I'm not selling." Logan squirmed at the thought of the envelope Hana found. "I'm not ready." He rang off as a peel of laughter broke out in the workroom behind the old man and he let out a guttural wail of anger. Logan smirked to himself. Uncle liked to lean against the work benches to talk on the phone. Someone often stitched his shirt tails to a random piece of material on purpose.

Logan made more calls from the layby as he watched the digital clock display click through an hour. Without even disturbing his immediate family, he flushed out Tama with frightening ease. Through the most reliable branches of the family grapevine, he arranged to meet the teenager at a cafe on Wellington Street Beach.

Tama stood on the curb at the allotted time, looking shifty and flush. Both signs represented trouble to Logan's experienced mind. He gritted his teeth and pulled up alongside the teenager. Then he leaned across and opened the passenger door. "Get in!" He rapped out the order with confidence and Tama jumped.

The boy pointed back at the cafe as though hoping Logan might take him for afternoon tea. "I need to stay here." He stepped forward and poked his head into the car. "I'm working now and my partner is picking me up at five."

Logan's eyes narrowed to take in Tama's new jacket, trousers and shoes. His regulation school-short-hair grew into wavy curls not unlike his own. He looked smart. And full of himself. "Get in the car or I'll make you," he growled through gritted teeth.

Tama swallowed and Logan watched doubt creep across the handsome olive face. "Okay," he conceded. "But I need to get back here before five." He climbed into the vehicle and fastened his seatbelt, not commenting as Logan pulled away before he'd closed the door fully.

Logan headed south, comfortable with the ominous silence. The teenager shifted in his seat and tapped an irritating beat on the sill of the passenger window. They travelled out the bottom of town and into the back roads. "What's this about, Uncle Logan?" Tama's wide eyed glances communicated the truth to Logan louder than if he spoke it and the older man battled his temper. He pulled into a layby which the council used for storing grit and sand. Nosing the Honda between two large mountains of grey metal stone, Logan felt confident they were sheltered from view of the deserted road. He killed the engine and turned sideways in his seat.

"You know what this is about." He kept his tone relaxed and observed Tama's discomfort with a detached air. The young man squirmed like a coiled spring, looking shifty and nervous as he reached for the door handle. He gave it a tug, hearing the clunk as Logan activated the central locking.

"No, I don't. I don't." Tama grappled at his crotch in a childish action and amusement crossed Logan's face, a dark cloud scudding across his expression. "I need to go," the teenager squeaked and jerky head movements betrayed his fear.

"Do you?" Logan took a long hard look at his watch and Tama's remaining resolve crumbled. He thought he knew what it felt like to play with the big boys. His uncle's glowering eyes told him he'd over reached himself way too far.

"I got a job," he babbled. "I'm collecting debts and it pays well." His brow furrowed. "It's not like I've many options left."

Logan sighed. "Who's your boss, Tama?"

The young man swallowed. "Nobody important."

Logan snorted a sad laugh and raised his right eyebrow into a quizzical expression. "Will I tell him that?"

"No." Tama shifted in his seat and resumed his nervous tapping on the sill. "I didn't know one of the debts was Mr Lomax. My boss told us to collect. The other guys set me up and I needed to follow through."

"Or what?" Logan leaned forward. "Just clarify this for me. You needed to break the bones of a man you knew, or what?"

Tama blew out through pursed lips. "The last guy quit because his girlfriend got pregnant. The guys busted him up pretty bad." His wide eyes roved around the interior of the vehicle, unseeing.

"How did you get involved with Larne?"

Tama winced. "I went to school with his son, Derek. When Anka left me I didn't have a choice. I'm sleeping on the floor of Derek's rental. I need to pay my way."

Logan looked through the windscreen into the grit mound, the shake of his head slow and pronounced. "Tama, Tama, Tama," he said. "Did it not occur to you to go home?"

"To Kane? Are you serious?" He pouted, his full bottom lip protruding like a ledge. "He beat me up last time I went home. Poppa Reuben's no use to anyone at the moment. He used to protect me, but he's got his mind on other stuff at the moment."

Logan gritted his teeth and contemplated the precious section of stolen land as acid rose into his gullet. "I bet," he spat. His gaze moved to Tama's twitching fingers. "Why did you sell my wife out?"

Tama gulped. "Who told you?"

"Che."

The teenager's eyes grew so wide that the whites overshadowed his grey irises. "How does he know?"

"He knows everything. And after what happened, my enemies are his."

Tama screwed himself back against the seat. "Help me, Uncle. Please."

Logan shook his head. "I already have. I paid your school fees for years and tried to set you up for a good life. Angus didn't want you in the school boarding house and I persuaded him. What did you do? Told a load of crap to a mate's mother, laid her and then screwed up everything." He gritted his teeth and the bones dug through his jaw. "You almost took me down with you."

Tama's expression grew hard, his features becoming chiselled and angular. He balled up his fists, hissing through his teeth, "I loved Anka. I wanted us to get married and have a happy-ever-after. It's not my fault it didn't work out."

"You're never to blame, are you?" Logan considered the young man with narrowed eyes. "You're a bad investment and it's time I sold my shares."

"Screw you!" The pain in Tama's heart vented outwards as rage and he took a swing at Logan. Half-hearted and pathetic, it bounced off a strong, cupped hand which deflected the blow.

"Are you sure you don't want to come at me from behind like the pussy you are?" Logan taunted. "That's how you roll now, bro'. Attacking me and then Boris. That's how I knew. When the cops said someone hit him from behind, I wondered what the odds might be that you got involved with Larne."

Tama launched again, harder this time. Logan seized the scrawny wrist in the fingers of his right hand, squeezing until it deadened the nerves and affected Tama's circulation. He deflected the other flailing arm. "Let go!" Tama screamed, his voice high and girlish.

Logan laughed. "Why don't you pull my hair and scratch me, baby? You fight dirty like a girl so why not do the whole act?"

Logan's face didn't alter from its dispassionate, blank stare. His grey eyes bore into Tama's, flickering as they hardened to the colour of the grit piles surrounding them. Tama squirmed against the pain and tried to free at least one of his hands. "Let me go!" His voice broke, reducing him back to his childish status and Logan relented.

"Just get out," he said, turning to rest his hands on the steering wheel.

"No! Drive me back to town," Tama protested.

"Get out."

"No!" Hysteria commanded Tama's senses and he took an ill-advised shot at the side of Logan's head. His uncle's reflexes proved quicker than he remembered and he found his spine pressed against the passenger door handle. The hard metal jabbed into his back as Logan lay sideways across the centre console. They tussled and Logan turned Tama's fist into his own face, drawing blood from his eyebrow and nose. Giving a final shove, Logan sat up and leaned back in his seat.

"If you get blood in this car, there'll be trouble. And if I have to give you another slap, I'll make it count!"

Tama's eyes filled with tears and his apologies fell on deaf ears. "But I'm whānau! I'm family. Uncle Logan, I said I'm sorry." His upper lip curled back and his mind drifted to Hana. "I'm family, not her. Blood's thicker than water."

Logan made a disparaging snort and shook his head. "People always get that saying wrong, Tama. It doesn't mean what you think. The water of the womb relates to family. The blood means agreements formed through blood mingling." He peered down at his scarred palms and his expression became wistful. "I get more loyalty from friends like Che than I ever will from my own family." He turned the key and the Honda's engine made an eager roar. "Stay away from me, Tama. Don't use my name anymore. You don't deserve it."

Logan ejected him from the vehicle without laying another hand on him, intending to leave the boy to walk the five kilometres back to town. Winding the window down and ignoring the devastation on Tama's face, he issued his final threat. "Bring them near me or my family, Tama and I will find you and kill you myself! I don't want to see your face again." He drove away with a heavy heart but no backward glance. "Stupid boy!" he exclaimed to the empty vehicle. "You sure bit the hand that fed you this time."

Tama stumbled back to town, a broken man. He used the last of his phone data to ring his grandfather. "I screwed up, Poppa," he sniffed. "I got a job as a debt collector and beat up a friend of Logan's." He heard the deep male voice let out an exclamation and waved his other arm in distress. "I know, I know. He's cut me off, Poppa. I didn't realise it was all about my new boss finding out where Logan's missus lives. Now Uncle hates me. What should I do?"

He sensed he'd end the call no wiser. Rueben's slurred voice and the clink of a beer bottle in the background chilled him with an icier blast than the Antarctic wind. "Stupid little punk!" Reuben drawled. "You've made things worse!"

Tama killed the call and spared himself the rest of the drunken rant. "What's wrong with you lately, Poppa?" he sniffed, wiping his eyes on his sleeve. A streak of blood ruined the new fabric and he cursed.

His footsteps sounded heavy against the gravel bleeding into the grass verge, grey grit marring the healthy green strands. "Logan doesn't trust me enough," he complained aloud as darkness descended around him. "But I'm family!" The memory of his whānau burned into his soul. Michael despised him, Kane used him as a punch bag and Logan felt betrayed enough to cut him off like a withered branch.

As Tama crunched along the rough verges back to town, the mud crept up his new trousers and stained his shiny shoes. Hot tears leaked from his eyes as Logan's words cut him deeper than he would ever admit, even to himself. The roll of cash that felt so good in his wallet earlier, burned into his hip. He felt dispossessed and ripped up from the root. Tama spent a lifetime looking up to Logan Du Rose and grief bit at the fringes of the young man's jaded heart. "We're not done," he sobbed. "We're not."

Logan's words echoed and repeated themselves in his head as he tramped along Cobham Drive. He taught Tama to ride, shoot and muster the stocky white cattle from the mountains. When he struggled in school, Logan gave him extra lessons and then he sent him to one of the best private schools in the country; no expense spared.

Losing Logan's favour cut Tama to the bone. The Du Rose name seemed the only good thing in his short life and Logan's withdrawal of it caused a physical pain in the young man's soul. He wiped his nose on his sleeve again and pondered on the origins of his name. Tama meant son. "I'm nobody's son," he sobbed, his chest heaving. When he stumbled, he collected himself and straightened his spine in response. "I'll show you, Logan Du bloody Rose," he vowed.

At the start of the city limits, Tama picked up his speed to a steady jog. Each step forward strengthened his resolve and hatred boiled up inside him. By the time he got back to the cafe he'd made his plan.

The BMW waited for him, the Chinese driver flicking the lid of a Zippo lighter open and closed. "You're late!" he growled as Tama clambered into the vehicle. He jammed his foot on the accelerator and the car glided away from the curb. Tama licked his lips and nodded, dragging his foot into the interior before the door slammed with the pressure of the sudden forward movement.

Chapter 6

Logan waited in the front car park for Hana to finish work. He kept the radio on but didn't listen to the blather of the guest speaker. The unmarked cop car slid past the gate and Logan raised his middle finger at the face peering at him from the passenger window. It didn't reappear. Running a tired hand over his stubble, his mind switched to memories of a skinny, olive toned child who had crumbled beneath the odds stacked against him. "Geez, Tama," he breathed. "Why am I surprised?"

Reaching for his phone, he dialled Liza's number. She answered on the first ring. "What's happened?"

He sighed. "Tama hurt Boris. Stupid kid."

"Ah well. Michael isn't gifted in the common sense department so he's inherited his father's idiocy. Sex and money are popular vices in our family."

"It's not funny. He put Hana in danger without a second thought."

"You think he knew?"

"Not at first. But he does now."

"Will he turn himself in?" Liza made slurping sounds as she sank a double espresso between meetings. "I'm not representing him. This week is booked solid for me."

"I didn't ask him to." Logan winced and watched dark clouds drift across the sky.

"Then you're an idiot, Logan. He doesn't care about you. He'll see you standing before a judge with a clear conscience as long as he wriggles off the hook. Let that lanky cop loose on him."

"Not yet. But please can you get one of your menials to freeze my last will and testament? Draw me up a new one."

"He shouldn't even be on any will of yours and I told you that when you signed it. He's not your kid."

"I felt sorry for him and he grew on me."

"Yeah, like a wart." Liza took another slug of her coffee. "I guess that means you're signing your empire over to your little English doll? You needed a pre-nuptial agreement, but you don't listen to me anymore."

Logan sighed. "Just get it drawn up, Liza. You can forge my signature. You've done it before."

"Sod off, Logan." Liza paused. "What's the rush? Are you planning to die soon?"

"Not on purpose." Logan chewed his lower lip and considered his words. "There's something going on here. I'm under a lot of pressure. If anything happens to me, make sure Hana gets taken care of."

"Geez, Logan! Level with me or I won't help you."

"I need to go. Just do your job or I'll find someone else who will."

"Whatever!" Liza retorted. Her final question hit Logan in the guts for a different reason altogether. "Did it go okay this morning?"

"What? I didn't get fired."

"Signing in at the police station. How did it go?"

Logan closed his eyes and banged the back of his head against the seat. "Fine," he lied. "I need to go now." He rang off and threw his phone onto the passenger seat. "Bloody idiot!" He smacked the steering wheel, making the Honda shudder. "How could you forget? Give Odering an excuse to get a warrant why don't ya?"

Hana emerged from the main doors. The classy cashmere coat she borrowed from Sheila mid-morning, flapped around her calves in the gathering wind. Her small baby bump protruded from beneath the file boxes in her arms. The cast looked clumpy on her delicate right arm, but she used it with more ease. Logan leapt from the car and took the files, laying them on the back seat and giving her a lingering kiss. Her lips felt cold against his and he put his hands either side of her face. Liza's allusion to death seemed to hang above them in the wintry air. Logan pulled Hana into his chest and held her, feeling her heart beat against him. He knew in that moment that he would die for her. He also hoped he wouldn't need to.

"I love you, Hana Du Rose." He smiled and rubbed her cold fingers in his. "Let's get out of here."

Logan pulled away from the school and turned right instead of left, heading into town. Hana looked at him sideways and her brow knitted. She opened her mouth and then closed it again. Logan's heavy mood acted as a deterrent for conversation. He pulled up outside the police headquarters in town and Hana pursed her lips at the sight of the ugly concrete monstrosity. Functional and unattractive, it screamed the reality of sick-building-syndrome. Logan turned to face her. "Don't worry," he said, forcing a fake smile onto his lips. "I need to check something."

Hana waited in the car, locking the doors for her own peace of mind. She watched the rush hour traffic stream by, car headlights bouncing in protest at the unevenness of the road surface. Her fingers strayed to her stomach and she caressed the essence of the tiny being inside. An image of Caroline rose to the fore again and she focussed on controlling the tightness in her chest. Logan denounced the child and denied its making with just as much vehemence. Yet the rumours at school continued behind shielding hands. "My pregnancies are doomed to be troublesome," she whispered. "I've often wondered if Bodie's issues began there." She stroked the firm bump and prayed this baby could resist all outside influences and arrive with a cheerful disposition.

A group of men passed the car and one glanced inside. His smart business suit meant Hana dismissed him as a carjacker or thief. But he stared for too long and she grew uncomfortable. His lips raised into a grin and he nodded his head once at her. Swallowing, she forced a smile onto her face and felt her body stiffen. The men walked on and Hana released the held breath. She watched in her vanity mirror as the man shoved his hands deep into his trouser pockets and didn't look back. His blonde hair bounced on his head as a breeze snatched at the longer layers. His momentary connection with Hana left an unsettling foreboding in her chest. Something passed between them, yet she didn't know him.

The man's slender build reminded her of her brother and she gave herself a shake. She'd trained herself never to think of Mark McIntyre and even his name brought a drop in temperature within the car. Drumming her fingers over her stomach, she felt the baby move around and she tried to drag her thoughts away from lost family. But the residue remained and as Logan stayed within the bowels of the concrete maw, they returned to tease her.

Hana forced herself to recount the dreadful train ride from university to see her family, her memories taking charge. Judith looked so frail that day, her flame-red hair laying over thinner shoulders like a carpet. Hana didn't bank on her brother Mark visiting from London with his perfect wife and perfect children. She almost ran away when she saw the expensive car parked in front of the vicarage. Vik forced her up the front steps and onto the porch but when the men saw her rounded belly, the sense of surprise turned to horror.

She heard Mark's voice calling Vik a darkie and saw him shove him against a dresser. Crockery tumbled around them as Mark rained blows on Vik's dark head. Their father hauled him off, Robert's clerical collar glinting against the sunlight streaming into the kitchen. The vicar didn't help though. He shoved them both through the hallway and onto the flagstones in the front garden, expelling Hana and Vik from his home and his life. She landed on her knees and a bleeding Vik hauled her to her feet. "Whore. Slut." Hana repeated the words to the darkness and their sting caused physical pain.

Hana sat in the car and swiped stray tears from her cheeks, determined Logan mustn't see. Because the memories always ended with Judith's distress. Deaf and not understanding the violence, she howled in a disjointed voice which never formed complete words. She held her arms out to her daughter, but Robert pushed her back inside and slammed the door against Hana. She never saw Judith again.

Hours after breaking the news to her family and moments after leaving Logan on the train, Hana had faced Vik's parents. Stunned and disgusted, still they unpicked his arranged marriage at great cost and embarrassment. An innocent girl had expected to marry the handsome Sikh since the age of thirteen and around the time her teenage world collapsed, the poor child sat her most important exams. One drunken fumble after a party ruined so many other lives. Including their own. Hana wondered about the little Indian girl. She hadn't thought of her for years. A filthy white slut ruined the poor girl's plans and forced her into a Plan B life. Hana swallowed at the legacy of guilt. No wonder Bodie ended up so jaded.

It seemed bizarre that Hana's memories of the train ride to Aldgate included Logan now, when they never did before. It felt as though an artist lifted him from the background in the portrait in her mind and defined him within the scene. Hana swiped more tears away, seeing the grey eyes study her from across the train. Thoughtful, angry grey eyes. They stared into hers and something scorched her soul as though the boy projected some thread of his consciousness into hers. The intimately searching look made Hana feel powerful in a way she knew she didn't deserve. The teenage Logan smiled that lopsided, wistful look, which twenty-six years later gave Hana lifeblood. Embarrassment forced her to blur his image.

Grappling in the pockets of Sheila's coat for a tissue, Hana found nothing. It formed a stark contrast to that other day, twenty-six years ago. Miriam's kiwi handkerchief sat in the drawer at Culver's cottage, faded but still evidence of a stranger's generosity in the face of human frailty.

Logan said he fell in love with her that day, the worst twenty-four hours of her life. He knew she was his soulmate and safeguarded their future. But did he? Or would Caroline succeed?

Hana felt Logan's baby move beneath her hand as he appeared from the front doors and strode towards the car. The child knitted her past and future together and promised to make her whole. Miriam's kindness on the train seemed to offer a proxy for Judith and despite recent events with the Du Roses, Hana craved the maternal contact.

"What's wrong?" Logan asked, waiting for Hana to unlock the doors. "Did something happen?"

"No." She shook her head and felt the wetness on her cheeks. "Just thinking about our first meeting."

His expression grew soft and his smile looked sincere. "My girl on the train," he said with a sigh. "I loved your yellow dress. It made your red hair stand out like a flame."

Hana shrugged. "It didn't fit anymore. I couldn't breathe. I never wore it again because it reminded me of something bad."

Logan leaned across and kissed her temple. His brow knitted at the feel of tears as he cupped her chin in gentle fingers. "I'll get you another. We'll rewrite history. I met you that day and that experience kick started my life."

Hana shook her head and snuffed out a tired laugh. "You're an idiot. I don't need a yellow dress."

"You can have whatever you want." He winked and squeezed the back of her neck, pulling her into his chest. "Hey, I'm paying."

"Okay, Casanova." Hana feigned reluctance. "I'll sleep with you. If I must."

Logan snorted and removed his arm from around her shoulders. The engine fired to life and he gunned the gas. "I'll hold you to it."

Hana shifted in her seat as Logan sought a gap in the traffic and her voice wavered. "After the expo, please can we drive up and tell your parents about the baby?"

"Yeah." His eyes widened in surprise. "I'd love that." He indicated and pulled into the traffic, not noticing the audience of one who studied his progress with interest.

Hana watched Detective Sergeant Odering give a slow shake of his head as they passed. He slapped his thighs as though in frustration. Hana quailed at the look of malice in his expression as their eyes met. He hated Logan's guts and the realisation made fear prickle in her chest.

Chapter 7

After a sleepless night with indigestion and an exhausted collapse onto the sofa in the early hours, Hana overslept on expo day. She rushed around the house like a maniac, showered in record time and sent her blood pressure skyrocketing.

"Slow down!" Logan insisted, catching her around the waist as she sped past him in her bra and knickers. "You'll slip and then you won't go anywhere today."

"It's all going wrong," Hana groaned, rubbing her eyes with her left hand. "I'm sick of my cast. I want it gone."

"Yeah, I hear ya." Logan massaged her shoulders and kissed her forehead. "What can I do to help?"

"Help me get dressed." Hana's eyes narrowed at the smirk in his eyes. "No, Logan. I don't have time."

"What?" He feigned innocence and gave her shoulders a gentle shake. His eyes crinkled at the corners.

Things went from bad to worse as the designated outfit refused to fasten around Hana's bulging stomach. "What happened?" She stood in front of the mirror in disbelief, hauling the buttons across her torso and trying to squash her belly in.

"Geez, Hana, you can't do that. You look like Santa!" Logan pushed her hands away. "I don't want my baby born with buttons indented in its forehead!"

Hana's eyes narrowed and she turned her venom on him. "This is your fault! You and your damn Du Rose genes!" Buttons popped as she ripped the dress off and hurled it onto the bed. She folded her arms across her chest and peered down at her swollen breasts. "It's happening everywhere!" she wailed. "What am I going to do? I can't go to the expo naked."

"You must have something left." Logan wrenched open the wardrobe door and poked his face into the mass of hanging fabric. Hana's scent wafted around his head and he closed his eyes and inhaled. "I love your smell," he sighed.

Hana jabbed him in the back. "Logan, stop! This is serious."

"I know." He withdrew his face and retrieved the previous day's leggings and sweater from the bedroom chair. "Can you wear these again?"

"Not to the expo! I wear them all the time." Hana's fingers fluttered near her breasts. "Why is this happening to me?"

"I can draw you a picture." Logan wrapped his arms around her and rested his chin on her head. "Look, wear yesterday's stuff and I'll nip out during my free period and see if I can grab you something nice."

Hana pulled back and eyed him with suspicion. "You haven't bought clothes for me before. I'm nervous."

Logan shrugged and pushed the leggings at her. "Then wear these for the expo, Hana. I can't whip out a sewing machine and rustle up something frilly for special occasions." He smirked. "Not without more notice."

Hana's face creased with conflict. "Okay," she ventured. "This can be a test of our relationship. If you get the perfect outfit, I'll continue sleeping with you."

"If I don't?" Logan raised a speculative eyebrow and Hana gave a beatific smile.

"Do you wish to find out?"

Logan caught her around the waist and hauled her into him. "Don't make me go caveman on you, wahine. You'll do as you're told."

Hana giggled as his rough chin grazed the tender flesh above her collar bone. "Fine," she conceded. "Please help me into the boring sweater."

Logan left Hana to slap on makeup using her left hand and retreated to the kitchen. His phone vibrated in his pocket and he dragged it out and answered it. "Mr Che," he said with deference, lowering his voice and pushing the door closed behind him. "How can I help you?"

"You are rippling the waters, Du Rose," the clipped voice replied without preamble. "Is that your intention?"

Logan sighed and leaned back against the counter. "No. I tried to take care."

"Not enough." Che chuckled. "The old man obtained a favourable last will and testament, accompanied by an engineering report for a section of land in the north." The triad king's English sounded impeccable. "Your wife is in danger."

"I know." Logan pursed his lips. He wouldn't tell Che that he'd handed the documents over to the cops. He swallowed. "I have nothing to bargain with."

"Laval needs the document to enforce his claim on the land. This is the big one of his career. He won't stop until he gets it." Che sighed. "You should have come to me sooner, my friend. We would have sorted this little matter out in an instant."

Logan laughed, the sound hollow. "Yes Mr Che, but then I'd owe you a debt bigger than I'm willing to pay. And I'd quite like his head left on his shoulders."

The Chinese patriarch tutted. "You are a son to me, Logan. Such a debt will never happen. I value your friendship and business sense. In that, we are equals. As to Flick and his compatriots, yes, you may be right. Sharks can be hungry this time of year. Concerning Laval, I'm not sure I could get access to him." The clipped accent disappeared in a hail of quick fire Chinese at someone in Che's vicinity. Logan waited. "Ah, Du

Rose, an interesting fact which may alter your perspective. Your name came up in our enquiries. It's no longer about whatever your wife stumbled over. This is very much about you. Watch your back."

"What?" Logan sank into a kitchen chair. "That doesn't make sense. Hana's troubles began before we started dating." He ran a hand over his face. "Are you saying her problems track back to me?"

The Chinaman sighed and Logan tensed. Che never got information wrong. "I'm sorry to bear bad news," he said. "But yes. Somehow the focus has changed to you. Call me if you need me. I am always here for you."

"Thanks Mr Che," Logan said with gratitude. "Zàijiàn."

"Zàijiàn, Du Rose," Che returned the colloquial goodbye and ended the call.

Logan used his Auckland contacts to send a crystal clear message back along the wire, borne by his informants and aimed at the centre of Laval's empire. "You want me to say what?" the gruff voice growled down the phone. "You want me to say, 'You're messing with the Du Roses. Think again.' That's it?"

"Yeah." Logan's eyes narrowed. "It's worked before. Is there something you want to tell me?"

"Yup. You're making a big mistake." The man disconnected the call and left Logan in confusion. He shook his head to clear his thoughts, but an unease settled on his shoulders.

Little scared Logan Du Rose. He hadn't risen to lofty heights by soiling his pants when the big players shouted. Clever, calculating and shrewd, he invested with care and recouped when it suited him. Occasionally he crossed the line, sashaying through legal boundaries with his astute sister covering for him. Not one of Che's men would take him on in a fist fight.

Logan possessed mana and the charisma to match. Mana indicated power and influence for Māori and he'd never known life without it. His paternal grandmother recognised and cultivated that quality in him. The daughter of a rangatira, a tribal chief by birth, she saw that same essence pass through her blood into her favourite son and then her grandson.

Logan's heart clenched at the thought of his tupuna wahine Du Rose. "There's so much I need to ask you," he whispered to her imagined ghost, sadness blossoming in his chest. "So much you could have helped me with. What have I missed, Kuia? What am I not seeing here?"

"You said you'd help me." Hana pouted in the doorway with a high heeled boot in her hand. She listed, standing on the already booted foot. "Are you talking to yourself?"

"Just to my kuia," he sighed and stood. Hana eyed him sideways.

"You know she's not really here, right?"

"So you say." Logan took the boot from her hand and unzipped it. He dropped to his haunches and fitted Hana's tiny foot in and pulled up the zipper. His fingers against her calf made the action feel erotic and she shivered in anticipation.

"You're a bad man," she sighed as Logan brushed his palms up her legs and clasped her around the waist. "You turn my brain into candy floss."

"Nice." He pushed his face into her neck and breathed in her scent. Midnight orchid assailed his senses and he tugged her sweater aside and trailed his lips along her collar bone. Hana groaned and leaned into him, holding her breath as the kisses turned to the gentle pressure of sucking.

"Logan, don't." Her voice sounded strained. "Don't leave a mark, please."

"Can't help it." His eyes looked glazed as he found her lips. Hana came to her senses first and placed her left hand against his chest.

"You need to help it," she whispered, giving him a persuasive shove. "Please don't mess this up for me."

"Okay." Logan turned away and cleared his throat. Fear mingled with lust as he gave himself a shake. It drove his desire to take Hana to bed and keep her there in safety and distraction. He swallowed and licked his lips. "You ready?"

Hana winced. "Not really." She looked down at her leggings and frowned. "These feel too tight."

Logan blinked. "They aren't yesterday's."

"I changed them." Hana pouted. "But these hurt more." She reached behind her and yanked the seam from her bottom. "Real bad."

"Then change back into those other ones."

"No! I spilled tea on them yesterday. I forgot until I spotted the stain."

Logan exhaled, a sound of pure exasperation. "Geez Hana, you're a worry, wahine!"

"Sorry." She grappled behind her again and a grimace of discomfort overtook her expression. "I'm in them now. Let's go."

Logan dropped Hana at the front entrance of the school and drove to the staff accommodation near the boarding house. He hid the Honda on a narrow access road outside a colleague's unit.

"You're early." The boarding house chef stepped from the dilapidated unit and closed the front door. It rattled on its hinges and Logan gave the man an upwards nod.

"Hey, Simon. You sure this is okay?"

"Yeah, for certain. My car's still in the shop. Why don't you park in Hana's space? I don't think I understood the reason."

"She let a student teacher use it," Logan lied. "I just need it here for the expo tonight."

Simon waggled his eyebrows. "Ah yep. All good."

Logan locked up the car and they walked towards the school together. Conversation turned to the boarding house and Logan listened as the other man extolled the virtues of living on site. "You should apply for the job of boarding house manager," Simon said, jerking his head towards St Bart's.

"Nah." Logan eyed the leaded windows of the old building and imagined Laval gaining permanent access to Hana. "We like keeping home and work separate."

Simon shrugged. "True. But the job is up for grabs, anyway. Angus can't seem to keep anyone in post for more than a few months."

"Why are you leaving?"

Simon scratched his forehead. "My parents are in Christchurch and Dad was diagnosed with a brain tumour last month. I want to stay near them for a while. I can cook anywhere, but I've enjoyed working here."

"Sorry. About your father." Logan swallowed and imagined receiving news like that about Alfred. A peculiar detachment blocked any sense of horror and he pushed it away in surprise.

"Good luck with the expo tonight."

"Thanks. See you in briefing in a minute." Logan drew his buzzing phone from his pocket and peered at the screen. He turned his back as Simon strode up the steps into the main building. A single text sat in Logan's inbox and he chewed his lower lip.

'Done.'

Logan ground his jaw and pushed his phone back into his pocket. A sense of foreboding seized his heart and his fingers shook with uncharacteristic fear. Boys poured into the buildings around him and he stood and watched. The expo promised to leave the school wide open to the public. And Hana vulnerable to Laval. Logan hoped the warning might buy them time, but something told him it wouldn't.

"Those women are rabid!" Peter North complained as he took refuge at the back of Logan's classical studies class half way through the second period. "Sheila thinks I'm her slave. I hate expo week. It sucks!" He guffawed at the sexual imagery in one of the texts and then fell asleep at his desk.

Logan taught for three periods and then nipped out to honour his promise to Hana. He lifted Pete's car keys from his pocket as he slept and left him locked in the classroom. After a five-minute drive, he found himself at the Five Crossroads shopping centre and strolled into a women's wear shop.

"Can I help you?" the shop assistant asked. Her eyebrows rose in suspicion as Logan poked around in a rail of dresses.

"Yes, please. I need a dress for my wife. It's urgent." He winced, discomfort oozing from every pore of his skin. The woman's narrowed expression made him nervous. He imagined she suspected him of cross dressing and the thought haunted him as she eyed him from head to toe with a speculative air.

"What size is she?" she demanded, with exaggerated politeness. Logan dangled a dress from a hanger in front of him and held the shoulders up to his chest.

"About this big," he answered.

The assistant looked confused. "Really?"

"She's a real woman." Logan's brows knitted into a dark line. He dangled the dress in front of him again. The long swags of fabric trailed along the carpet. "But she's tiny. I need something smaller than this."

The assistant's posture relaxed. Beneath her heavy covering of makeup, her features sagged with relief. "Okay. That's great. Do you know her dress size?"

"No." Logan's shoulders deflated and he replaced the hanger. "But I promised I'd take something back with me."

He put his hands around his waist and held them out about ten centimetres to the front. "She's this big around the middle." He cocked his head in concentration and then nodded. "Yeah, about this much."

The woman's eyes bugged. "So, very small and quite round?" She cleared her throat and reached for a dress which dribbled in swags from its hanger.

Logan ran a hand across his face and heard the bristles work against his palm. He started to back away, imagining Hana's expression when he presented her with an Ethel Bowman type dress. "No. That's not right. I'm not good at this." He kept backing away from the flowery tent, shaking his head for emphasis. "She isn't fat. She's pregnant." He pointed at the dress. "And she'll kill me if I give her that."

"Ohhh." The shop assistant dragged out the sound and her expression softened. She beckoned Logan with a long, manicured finger and her eyes twinkled.

He emerged from the shop twenty minutes later with sweat beading on his forehead. His fingers clutched a branded paper bag and a credit card requiring resuscitation. Grabbing drinks and sandwiches from a nearby dairy, he shook his head in disbelief.

"You okay, bro'?" the cashier enquired.

Logan nodded with uncertainty. "Yeah. I think the woman next door just mugged me."

The man put his dark head back and laughed. "I bet. She only needs one customer a week to pay her overheads."

Logan puffed out a breath and leaned back against the counter while the man made his coffee and a hot chocolate for Hana. "I walked in wanting a dress for the wife and came out with a mortgage."

The man grinned. "Yeah, but she sells one off stuff, man. She's the designer and seamstress. Your wife will love whatever you got because there won't be another like it."

"Really?" Logan lifted the bag and peered at the logo on the side. His shoulders lifted. "Cool. So, I get points for effort then?"

"Effort and achievement." The man shoved the drinks into a cardboard holder and added the sandwich cartons to the top. "And sexual favours for at least a year."

"Thanks." Logan collected the goods and balanced the bag over his wrist. He jerked his head towards the man with a grin. "For the kai and the advice."

"No problem." He waved and went back to reading his newspaper. "Anytime."

Logan took his wares back to work and climbed the stairs to the student centre. His credit card recovered in his wallet and he dangled the clothes bag from his fingers. Pete eyed the sandwich with delight as he stepped over the threshold. "Is that for me?"

"No. Thanks for the use of your car."

"What?" Pete stood up and felt in his pockets. His eyes narrowed in disdain. "You git! I banged on the door for twenty minutes before someone came with a key to let me out."

Logan threw the keys onto his desk. "Where's Hana?"

Pete slumped into his chair and pouted. "It'll cost ya."

"What? A black eye? Yeah, sure. I can give you one of those."

Pete exhaled and looked at the dress bag. "What's that?"

"A dress for Hana. For tonight."

"Will it stop her squeaking and hauling her pants out of her ass?" Pete smirked. "Logan Du Rose buying dresses? Just wow."

"Shut your face or I'll hurt you."

Pete chuckled. "What did you get?"

Logan reached into the bag and the soft fabric fluttered from his fingers. Smoke grey in colour, it boasted three pieces. A flared skirt and simple V-necked top complimented a laced over-wrap which reached almost floor length. "Hana put boots on this morning. The shop assistant said it goes great with boots."

Pete gripped his stomach and squawked with laughter. "You've gone soft!" He cackled and bent double.

Logan dropped the clothes into the bag and stood. He reached Pete in two strides and grabbed him by the head. Pete squealed and they tussled like boys. They only stopped when Sheila blasted into the office and glared at them. "I can give you both jobs if you're bored!" she snapped, standing before them with her hands on her hips.

Logan stood and smoothed down his ruffled hair. He swallowed and tried not to laugh at the expression of indignation on Sheila's face. Nudging Pete with his foot, he hissed at him, "Get up, idiot."

Pete hauled himself to his knees and slithered onto his chair. He rubbed at a sore spot on his ribs. Sheila stomped into her office and out again. She brandished a heavy duty stapler in her hand. The smile disappeared from both men's lips. Logan tucked his shirt in and sobered. "Sorry," he said, affixing an appropriate degree of shame on his face. Sheila marched from the room, clicking the stapler over her shoulder. Logan snorted with laughter once the doors to the bridge slammed shut, but Pete kept a cautionary hand over his groin.

"I'm hungry," he whined, eyeing the sandwich on Hana's desk.

"Don't even think about it," Logan warned.

"Give me some money then and I'll go to the tuck shop." Pete narrowed his eyes. "Or Hana will never know you visited."

Logan whistled. "Man, that's one big death wish you've got right there." He grinned and reached into his trouser pocket for his wallet. "Here's five bucks. Pay me back tomorrow."

Pete gave a toothy grin of victory and snatched the note from Logan's fingers. His eyes acquired a glossy sheen as he dreamed of his next pie. "Thanks," he murmured.

"Why are you always broke when you have so few expenses?" Logan asked as he put his wallet away. "Where do your wages go?"

Pete's face blanched and Logan's sixth sense flicked on. "I'm paying off a debt," Pete replied. He bent the note back and forth in his fingers but his stiffened body gave off distress signals.

"The tuck shop debt?" Logan watched his friend's face, knowing he'd paid off nothing and was banned from asking for credit there.

"Yeah." Pete swallowed. "That one."

"Liar." Logan's eyes narrowed. "What debt, Pete?"

"Garage debts." Pete shifted on his seat in discomfort and the wheels gave a wretched squeak.

Logan snorted. "Your car is a write-off on wheels. I'm asking you one more time. What debt?"

He sighed and closed his eyes as Pete dragged a shaking hand across his face. The bank note fluttered onto his desk, no longer sought after. "I didn't want you to find out."

"The gambling syndicate Boris joined. Were you in it too?"

Pete shook his head and then thought better of lying to someone who would know before the words left his lips. He tapped his skinny fingers on the top of the desk. "I joined before him, but I got out of pocket real fast. Henrietta found out and made me leave the syndicate, but Larne didn't like it. He sent his boys after me for my share. When I couldn't pay, he wanted me to do jobs for him. That's what those other two guys were doing at Hana's place. He lets you pay off debts by working. I owed a few hundred and Henrietta bailed me out." He groaned. "I still owe her. She almost dumped me over it."

Logan shook his head and turned to leave. Pete leapt to his feet. "Say something, Logan. Hit me or something, but get it over with."

"No." Logan shook his head. "I don't want to be near you."

"I didn't tell him about Hana! He thought I worked at the university so he didn't ask. I told Boris not to say he taught here. I didn't know the name Laval until you said it. How could I know he gives Larne credit?"

Logan shrugged. "We both know why I'm beyond furious, don't we Pete?"

"I couldn't help it." Pete grabbed the note and held it out towards Logan's retreating back. "It's not like last time. I'm okay."

Logan stopped with his hand on the door handle. "How much did you lose?"

Pete threaded the five dollar note through his fingers and back again. "Just over five hundy."

"And what did it amount to?" Logan's tone sounded sharp and his knuckles shone white on the handle.

"Couple of thousand." Pete fixed his gaze on the cash in his hand as though it held part of the blame. "It kept doubling and I couldn't keep up. I got scared. It's like, you get in and then can't get out."

"What happened when you paid it back?"

"We paid cash." Pete's hoarse whisper contained shame.

"We?"

Pete swallowed. "Henrietta met them inside the Gordonton Arms. She wouldn't let me go in with her."

Logan recoiled in horror. "You let your chick fight your battles?" His upper lip curled back in a sneer. "You make me sick! When will you learn, Pete? When?"

"I'm sorry, I'm sorry. It won't happen again." Pete ran towards him and Logan backed away.

"No, it won't. Because we're done. I warned you last time." Logan shuddered as though an old adversary stepped across his grave. He swallowed and severed their age old friendship with a shake of his head. "Never speak to me again."

"But I didn't know," Pete whispered. Tears sprang into his eyes. "I didn't know Larne was connected to all that stuff happening to Hana. I promise I didn't know."

Logan closed his eyes and when he opened them, a cold, grey sea swirled in his irises. His jawbone poked through the skin as he ground his teeth and he flung the door open, leaving it to bang on the radiator. He ignored Pete's agonised shriek behind him and kept walking towards the bridge and the safety of the English department.

He taught for two more periods after lunch, using the mental gymnastics of switching from year group to year group to numb his senses. Moving from Shakespeare to creative writing, he expelled the anger leaving disappointment in its place.

After school, he drove to the police station to sign in, but the desk officer refused to let him. "Detective Sergeant Odering wants to see you," he said, reaching for the telephone.

Logan shook his head. "I don't have time for his games today. Just let me sign in."

"No," the officer repeated. "You can't sign in until he's seen you."

Logan swore. He shook his head. "Tell him the answer is still no. I've too much to lose. Please let me sign in." He looked at his watch and panic gripped his heart. The stallholders for the expo would arrive any minute. Laval or Larne's men could stroll through the open building and snatch Hana within seconds.

Logan backed towards the front door. "I'm not waiting around," he said. "Tell him I came in willing to sign. I don't want my non-compliance to come back to bite me later." Sarcasm dripped from his tone and the desk officer's fingers punched a number into the phone.

"He needs to see you, son. You can't want him to send a car to pick you up. It's less trouble for you to just wait here for him."

"No. Tell him I'm not doing what he wants. I'm telling my lawyer and he can go screw himself. Do you need me to spell any part of that for you?" Logan heard the sliding doors swish open behind him and cold air filled the reception area. He produced a suitable gesture for the benefit of the overhead security camera and took a phone snap of the desk sergeant sat beneath the clock. It showed the time and date in blocky digital characters; his evidence, in case something brown and sticky hit the fan. Liza warned him to be careful with Odering. He turned up to sign in and his phone contained the proof. Reaching the fresh air, Logan turned off the voice recorder and saved the conversation with the desk officer to his sim card.

He drove back to school and found his parking space taken by someone else. Cursing, he dumped the Honda on the lawn behind the boarding house and jogged to the main building. Hustling into the hall, he located Hana with ease. She stood in the centre of the huge space, pointing like an air hostess at various pitches as presenters dashed to claim tables. The grey fabric floated around her, displaying the rounded arc of his child. The sight made his chest clench. A cream scarf pitted with tiny rosebuds finished the effect, Logan's addition under the approving eye of the assistant.

"You seen what they've done?" The head groundsman stamped towards Logan, shouting. "See what your wife did?"

Logan tensed and balled his fists at his sides. The man prodded him in the chest, alarmed when Logan grabbed his finger and bent it forwards into his palm. Logan's expression remained impassive and he lowered his voice to a whisper. "Shut your face, man. Your grammar sucks!" He continued to bend the bony finger and the groundsman's face turned an alarming shade of puce as his nail dug into the soft flesh of his palm.

"Touch me again and I'll snap all ten of them," Logan hissed. "Do you understand?"

When he let go, the groundsman backed away at speed, nodding his head like a clockwork toy. He pointed to a series of notices taped to the parquet floor. "Your wife taped the signs down. I polished that floor in the holidays and the tape's gonna mark."

Logan shrugged. "And it's my problem because why?"

"She's your wife!" The man's eyes bugged. "Can't you control her?"

Logan glanced across at Hana. She looked amazing, the grey fabric swirling around her calves. Ignoring the angry, bouncing man he strode across the floor towards her. He halted as she greeted an austere looking woman carrying a data projector and balancing a box. Hana pointed and the woman gave a curt nod. Logan set off towards her again, exasperation budding in his chest as another arrival hijacked her.

The hall became a hive of activity as data projectors hummed to life and screens popped up alongside brochure stands. People swarmed everywhere in a confusing jumble of bodies. Logan attached himself to Hana, helping out with small jobs but careful not to take on anything that might prevent him shadowing her. He switched into defensive mode, watching entrances and exits for anyone looking out of place. The task seemed impossible. Someone flung the fire doors wide open for presenters to unload their vehicles and carry their gear in. Logan's neck ached with the effort of swivelling on the spot to monitor the numerous open doors.

"Excuse me. Please can you help?" A Northland college presenter indicated her intricate brochure rack leaning at a jaunty angle. She twinkled red painted nails against Logan's chest. "I think I've put this together wrong." Long eyelashes fluttered and she smiled seductively through red, glossy lips. Logan hesitated, darting a concerned glance towards Hana. She stood near the fire doors, fanning her face with a brochure and speaking to a dumpy woman pulling a laden trolley.

"I'm helping someone else," he said, turning his body sideways to demonstrate his reluctance.

"Can you hold it while I screw it?" she asked, tittering at her intentional double meaning. Brandishing a screwdriver in her manicured fingers, she jutted out a slender hip and narrowed her eyes.

Logan saw a woman used to getting her own way and felt the tightening of revulsion in his gut. Loose women never entertained him and he gave an upward tilt of his head. "I'll find someone for you."

"Oh, come on," she entreated, her tone enticing. Glancing at his wedding band, her eyes narrowed in challenge. Logan hardened his jaw, knowing how it felt to be on the receiving end of a serial cheat. He glanced behind him and spotted a prefect wandering across the space. His upper lip curled in a sneer and he looked forward to offloading the woman onto the spotty teenager. The prefect diverted his trajectory as Logan beckoned and he stumbled over the splayed legs of the stand. The structure tumbled sideways, sending brochures scattering in every direction. People moved aside and watched the mess. The boy swore and then winced as Logan raised an eyebrow in rebuke.

"Now you must help," the presenter said, squatting to gather up the mess. She flashed an impressive cleavage as she stretched forward to claim the pile nearest his feet. Logan edged his cowboy boots backward and jerked his head towards the teenager.

"Help her," he ordered and the boy dropped to his knees.

It seemed only a second's worth of distraction but when Logan sought Hana in the crowd, he didn't see her. A broad-shouldered man with thinning hair stepped through the fire exit, a cumbersome oblong case in his hands. Logan spun on the spot and sent leaflets scattering around him as he searched for his wife without success. The fire exit doors banged as the wind caught them and Logan's gaze raked every square metre of the room. She'd gone.

Ignoring the leaflets underfoot, Logan snatched a programme from a nearby table and scoured it. He gave himself a mental shake for not getting one sooner and familiarising himself with the locations in use. Hana had chattered for weeks concerning the problems with rooming and issues with power sources and capacity. He'd nodded in the right places but allowed his mind to wander, not caring who ended up where. His grey eyes roved over the tops of heads and stands and he forced himself to wait a few minutes in case Hana settled her guest and returned. Running around the busy corridors like an idiot served no useful purpose. "She's fine," he muttered to himself under his breath. "She's fine."

When she didn't reappear after five minutes, Logan carved up the site into search areas before setting off at a jog. His heart pounded in his chest and awful possibilities ran before his vision like a film roll. Larne's men and Laval's didn't care if they hurt her. They already had.

Sheila's publicity backfired on Logan as he ran from room to room and people poured in from every open access. Doorways bulged with bodies, making it hard for him to move against the flow and corridors swarmed with milling families. It provided a perfect opportunity for someone to enter the property and take a good look round without raising suspicion. Hana didn't understand how vulnerable the event made her.

Logan shoved his head through each classroom door on the ground floor of K Block as he passed. A life-sized cow greeted him inside one room, complete with udders and grass in its mouth. He waved to a man erecting a model of a milking machine on a nearby table. "I'm looking for Hana," he said. The man shrugged and jabbed his foot in the thigh of a colleague plugging in a data projector beside him.

"What?" he said, without looking up.

"Hana. The woman who unlocked the door for us, have you seen her? This bloke's looking for her."

His colleague stood and brushed dust from his trousers, taking his time before answering. "No," he said after a painful pause. Logan fought the urge to hurt him.

As he pulled his head from the doorway and whirled around, Logan heard his name called from a distance away. Panic made him pleased to see his stepson and he jogged the length of the corridor towards him. Bodie raised an eyebrow and gave him a playful reprimand, "Don't run in the corridor!"

Logan's stiff body language wiped the smile from his face. "I can't find Hana!" he said, fear edging his voice. To his surprise, Bodie rolled his eyes. Dressed in his formal uniform with shoes which gleamed under the strip lights, he gave Logan a look of disdain.

"You won't find her at one of these things." He raised his hat and scratched at a tuft of dark hair on his crown. "She's everywhere and nowhere all at once." His lips quirked upwards. "I endured years of these things. Can't imagine why I'm back in an official capacity. At least I don't need to stay and help clean up afterwards."

Logan shook his head. "You don't understand. I checked all the rooms on the programme. She's not here."

Bodie's eyes widened. "Laval?" He stepped closer to Logan. "I told her to go into witness protection."

"Odering won't let us." Logan lowered his voice to a hiss. "It's not part of his grand plan."

"But if she's in danger, he can't stop her." He blinked and his eyes narrowed. "What are you saying? She's bait?"

Another head poked from a nearby door. It wore a smart uniform hat and as the rest of the body followed, showed a dress uniform complete with a lapel laden with medals. "Johal?" The police superintendent narrowed his brows at Logan and then his gaze passed over him and rested on Bodie. "Get back in here. You're doing the speaking." The head withdrew.

"What? No!" Logan's eyes grew round and his grey irises stood out. "I thought you came to help protect Hana, not get trapped in a classroom for two hours."

"She's fine." Bodie took a step backwards and turned on his heel. "Flick won't dare show up here. You're worrying over nothing. It's always like this on expo night." Logan shook his head and ran a hand through his dark hair. He experienced a moment of surprise as Bodie halted and threw a comment over his shoulder. "Text me when you find her."

"Okay." Logan forced himself to relax. "I'll check her office." He rolled his eyes at Bodie's casual wave and walked to the end of the corridor. Then he took the stairs three at a time. "Where are you, Hana?" he hissed on the landing as his heart rate increased again. A sensor picked up his movement and the light flicked on overhead. He stood in the open area alone, no one else on that level. Lifting his phone, he dialled Hana's number, cursing when it went straight to voicemail. Dusk had arrived at five thirty and night hurried in after. The sky wore its darkest navy outfit and lights blazed throughout the site. Logan stood by the window and peered outside, stilling his body as the light went out so he didn't reactivate it. A buttery glow poured from the arts' block as groups milled around, peering in external windows and stopping to glance at programmes. They swirled like water, altering their direction with each change of heart.- Huddling in bunches, they drew winter clothing more tightly around them and hovered outside packed classrooms. Logan jogged across the bridge to Hana's office, blinking as lights flared overhead. He tried both doors, but the room remained in darkness. Dashing through the staffroom, he poked his head into the ladies' toilets. Desperation drove him to extreme lengths. "Hana? Are you in here?" Nothing.

He backed out and used the rear stairs, looping round to the hall. He saw a lab assistant emerging from another set of toilets and hurried over. "Is Hana in there?" he demanded, blocking her path.

She shook her head and narrowed her eyes in suspicion. "Sorry, no. I just got here."

People swarmed everywhere. Bodies poured through doorways until the school heaved, then still more arrived. The school's success proved to be Logan's personal nightmare.

A bell sounded, a single quick, deafening blast which cut across voices and the sound of shuffling feet. The effect resembled the pulling of a sink plug. Crowds swirled and dispersed, filing into the hall and outside on cue, heading to whichever talk they travelled to hear. Logan held his breath, searching for Hana in the constant movement. As the surrounding floor cleared, he waited, hoping to use his height to locate her. His quest took him into the hall and he lurked along the back wall near the doors.

"How long is each talk?" he hissed to a nearby prefect and the boy leaned sideways to answer in a whisper.

"Thirty minutes. They'll repeat it three times and use the last half an hour for exhibiting and questions."

"Thanks." Logan raised himself onto his toes and scanned the room for a tiny woman in a grey dress. "Have you seen my wife?"

The boy shook his head and shrugged and Logan sighed. "She was Mrs Johal."

"Oh? Congratulations." The boy's cheeks flushed with awkwardness and he gave a rapid succession of blinks.

"Have you seen her?" Logan repeated, his voice louder.

"Not for ages." The teenager swallowed and moved away from the anxiety radiating from Logan. As the speakers got into their stride, Sheila glared across at him, not appreciating his distraction. Ignoring her silent rebuke, he left the hall and stepped outside into the lobby. Forcing himself into a calmer state by a sheer act of will, he sought the source of the crisp air from the doors open to the night. His ragged nerves responded and his tall frame burst out into the cold, dragging in gasps of the bracing atmosphere. Bending double and resting his palms on his knees like an exhausted runner, Logan forced himself to think. Light flooded the steps around him and his grey eyes adjusted to the darkness beyond with practiced ease.

A line of wooden benches surrounded the courtyard, fixed to the walls as seating. His gaze raked the area, sifting through family groups running late and a little knot of students using the open grounds as somewhere to hang out.

A flash of something caught his keen eye, over near the path leading into the gully. Logan walked towards a tiny patch of reflected light, breaking into a run as he recognised the scarf he picked out with such care. Hana sat on a bench alone in the darkness, the scarf clutched around her neck. Her forehead appeared grey in the dim light and her closed eyes made him panic. "Hana!" His half shout made her jump and she let out a scream. He thudded next to her on the bench, making the wooden slats bounce. The hard embrace he subjected her to communicated his fear and exasperation. "Geez woman! I've searched for you everywhere!"

"Sorry," she breathed, her voice muffled against his jacket. She sounded sad and distant. "I took the engineers to their room and then felt strange. I thought the fresh air might help. It became stuffy inside with all the people." She pushed against Logan's chest as his crushing embrace hindered her breathing. Suspicion laced her voice. "You're trembling. What's happened?"

"Nothing, it's fine. Nothing."

Hana ran a hand across her forehead, snagging her eyebrow on her cast. She gave an exasperated huff. "I put my phone in this little bag but it's too hard to get in and out. The midwife thinks putting it down your bra causes breast cancer. Please can you get it out for me? I suspect I've missed some calls."

"Out of your bra? Sure. I can look for it." Logan made the joke but his fingers shook as he pulled her closer into his chest.

"No, silly. Out of this daft bag." Hana wriggled free and flapped the small handbag at her side. "This one."

"Yeah, you missed some calls. Mine." Logan hauled the phone out and peered at the screen. He deleted three from him and one from Bodie. The latter made his left eyebrow rise in surprise. Bodie called his mother and then texted her moments after they parted in the corridor, belying his casual air. "Your son texted to see if you're okay and one of your presenters got stuck in traffic on the expressway."

Hana's brow knitted. "Oh, that explains why the dairy guys arrived late." She exhaled. "I'm having lots of problems with my phone at the moment. It doesn't seem to work in the main building."

Logan shrugged. "Angus talked about a device that jams the signal and stops the boys getting messages in class. He's sick of them using their phones instead of learning."

"You think he bought a signal jammer?"

"No." Logan shook his head. "He would have said."

"Yes, because half the boys use their phones to screenshot the whiteboard or make notes." Hana shook her head. "Do you think he's trialling it without us knowing?"

"No." Logan stared around them at the probing darkness and shivered. Doubt nibbled at the edges of his certainty and he wavered. "Who knows with Angus? He does what he likes. Let's go inside. Can we leave soon?"

He felt Hana shake her head against his shoulder as they stood. "No. I need to walk around taking photos. There's a supper in the staffroom for the presenters afterwards and Sheila asked me to heat the savouries, serve drinks and clear up. Then we can go."

Logan groaned and did the maths in his head. One hour and fifty minutes until the students filtered home, then another hour for the supper and the clearing away. He released Hana as they walked towards the foyer steps and the bright yellow glow of the main building. "Why don't we stand on the balcony above the hall? It's a great vantage point to take pictures."

"Genius!" Hana gave a tired smile. "Then I can sit on the chairs if I feel funny again."

Logan nodded. "Do you want to talk about this feeling faint thing? We can call the midwife."

"No, it's fine." Hana's fingers fluttered to her chest. "It's nothing I haven't had before. Probably blood pressure related."

Logan eyed her sideways and gave a reluctant nod. "Don't ignore it, Hana."

"I won't," she assured him, giving him a disarming smile as they walked into the lobby. Logan reached for her hand as they climbed the back stairs to the first level, ignoring the amused expressions of a group of prefects. From the cavernous, wooden panelled hall, came the steady hum of the presenters as they spoke to groups of between ten and fifty people. Their audience collected around them in multi-coloured arcs. Some looked interested and others counted the minutes until they could extricate themselves and dash to hear someone else.

In front of the double rimu doors to the balcony, Hana realised she didn't own a key to unlock the mezzanine. "I've never had one. I'm not important enough," she griped.

Logan shuffled through his bunch and gave her a mischievous grin. "Good job you're married to someone who is then," he joked.

Hana narrowed her eyes. "Liar. You inherited them from the last head of department. I bet you don't know what half of them open."

"True that," Logan admitted. He slotted the keys into the lock one at a time. Some refused to fit into the designated hole. Hana reached out and took them from him, isolating a smaller one with an ornate stem.

"This one," she said, victory in her tone. She fumbled with the bunch one-handed and Logan retrieved them and fitted the tiny key into the lock. The satisfying click sounded as the mechanism responded. He closed the door behind them and pressed a finger to his lips as Hana turned towards him to speak.

"It echoes," he mouthed and she nodded in understanding.

The wood panelled balcony towered over one side of the Great Hall, running lengthwise above the room. A 1990s addition, it robbed the hall of its openness and obscured the ornate, vaulted ceiling. Marring what had once provided a space for the early chapel services, it never received its planned partner opposite. Horrified, the local council listed the building to protect its character from further blight and halted the plans for an identical mezzanine monstrosity.

Wide steps led down to a solid viewing rail and Logan held Hana's hand as they headed there. He jerked his head towards the seating and she nodded and planted herself on the front row. Logan stood at the rail and looked over. From above, the masking tape boundaries denoting stall areas resembled a playing field. Hana peered over and winced at the wonky bits where she struggled to crawl around on the parquet floor. Logan pointed to a polytechnic presenter standing in the centre of a rhombus, which explained why he'd failed to line up his stand and table.

Hana shrugged. "Should've got you to do it," she whispered and saw his irises flash. Nothing short of perfection ever satisfied him and she imagined him planning out such a feat with a tape measure and protractor. The idea amused her.

Logan leaned on the rail and his body stiffened. Hana watched the muscles flex in his spine and knew his gaze raked the room below. She yawned and fought the zipper on her handbag, retrieving the digital camera from its folds. Standing, she stood on tiptoe and snapped one-handed pictures of the event.

She spied some people she knew and waved, but nobody looked up towards the ceiling. They concentrated on the presenters or read leaflets. Looking back through the photos, she tutted with displeasure.

"What's wrong?" Logan whispered.

"Too shaky," Hana mouthed and he took the camera from her. He wrinkled his nose and nodded at the indistinct images. Without speaking, he focussed the lens and took a few quick snaps. He showed her the result and she beamed with enthusiasm.

The humid air from below seemed to clog her lungs and Hana stepped away from the rail, sinking into a chair and flapping her hand in front of her face. Logan turned and his expression screwed up in alarm. Hana shook her head. "I'm fine. Just hot," she whispered.

Reassured, he continued snapping a visual record of the scene below. Hana admired his neat backside as he bent to get an excellent shot of Peter North picking his nose and eating it. Logan scrunched up his forehead in disgust and held the camera in front of her. Thinking she may vomit, Hana shuddered and turned away from the nasty frame of Pete admiring his bogey. Logan noticed Pastor Allen standing near a polytechnic presenter and zoomed the camera lens onto him. Leaning down to whisper to his eldest stepson, Allen cradled a wriggling baby over his shoulder. He looked like an image of the perfect father until the baby projectile barfed over the people sitting nearby. Logan caught the shot and grinned to himself.

Hana slapped him on the bum. "You're not meant to stalk people," she complained in a loud whisper. "Take some proper photos or Sheila will get mad at me!"

Chastened, Logan changed the camera angle and took shots suitable for the following year's publicity images. "Are these okay?" he whispered, sitting next to Hana and handing her the camera.

"Yes, you're amazing." She gave a sigh of relief and reached up to kiss his cheek. "I love you."

Logan capitalised on her gratitude, pressing his lips against hers. Strawberry scented lipstick assailed his senses and he tasted the sweetness of Hana's tongue against his. His hand fumbled the camera onto his knee so he could continue the kiss and his hand snaked around her waist. The grey fabric slithered beneath his fingers and Hana pulled away with a gasp. "Here?" she mouthed and looked horrified at the mischief in his eyes.

"Why not?" Logan replied, pulling her closer. As the kiss heated up, he felt the weight shift on his knees and the expensive camera slipped into mid-air. He scrambled, but failed to stop it hitting the floorboards with a dreadful clang. The sound echoed around the cavernous hall and Hana clapped a hand over her mouth. Logan's eyes widened as the drone of voices stopped and his lips curved upwards into a grin. Hana shook her head in horror. He waited a heartbeat before sticking his face over the rail and raking the area below. "It's fine," he reassured her, sitting back down.

"What about the camera?" Hana's eyes widened and Logan retrieved it, testing the zoom and checking the outer casing.

"It's okay," he whispered, pointing to a slight scuff on one corner. "I can clean that off."

Hana nodded and swallowed. Neither of them resumed the fated moment of passion. Seriousness descended over them like school children caught by a parent, but Hana noticed the amusement gleaming in her husband's eyes.

Logan stood and continued taking photos, checking the quality after every set of ten. Attempting to zoom in and snap a close up of a university brochure stand with the speaker in full pitch, he noticed the fire doors swinging open behind her. "That's weird," he muttered.

Hana sighed. "It is." He narrowed his eyes and glanced back at her in surprise, certain she couldn't see the open door from her sitting position. He saw her holding her phone on her palm. "Look," Hana said. "My phone's vibrating by itself. Do you think it's broken?"

Logan blinked. "Maybe." He turned back to the scene below, watching the tell-tale open doors. A breath lodged in his lungs as a slender man with Chinese features positioned himself in the exit, like a bodyguard. A woman carrying a grizzling toddler navigated towards the doorway, hoping to escape before the open mouthed child let loose and disturbed hundreds of people. Logan watched as the man held his ground, scrutinising her with avid interest. The woman spoke and he stepped aside and let her pass. She demonstrated her discomfort by looking back at him several times from the steps and clutching her son closer to her body. Logan gritted his teeth and scoured the rest of the room. Ill intent spewed from the man in waves. "I knew you'd come," Logan hissed under his breath.

Laval's heavies travelled in pairs and Logan searched from above, looking for another man who appeared to work the room. Hana popped up next to him at the rail and he shook his head and pushed her away. "Sit down," he hissed. "You look pale. I don't want you fainting up here."

Shock spread across Hana's expression and she took a clumsy step backwards. Logan's heart clenched at her distress. "I'm sorry," she muttered and he let the moment go with a curt nod of approval as she sank into a seat.

She concentrated on controlling her breathing, forcing her heart rate to slow by degrees. Caroline's spectre rose to taunt her, increasing her insecurity and helping her to convince herself Logan grew bored of her. Hana stroked her chest to hide the painful thudding and swiped away ready tears. His sharpness shocked her but she couldn't let it lie. Tugging on his shirt to grab his attention, Hana saw the irritated set of his jaw. "Are you sick of me?" she whispered, her tone pitiful. "Is it because I'm struggling with this pregnancy?"

"What? No!" Logan's eyes widened and he withdrew his attention from the scene below. His body twisted so he faced her, the arm containing the camera resting on the rail.

"Is it Caroline? Do you think you've made a mistake?" Hana stared at the edge of her cast, wishing she could strip the cumbersome weight off. It compounded the heaviness of her body as foreboding settled on her shoulders. Her fingers shook.

"No!" Logan thudded next to her, Laval's men forgotten for the moment. "Geez, Hana. Why would you say that?"

She shook her head and wiped her cheek on her sleeve, leaving a streak of mascara on the grey fabric. "I'm feeling insecure," she admitted. "People still talk about Caroline behind their hands. They think I don't hear but I do. I suppose when her baby's born, they'll report back how much like you it looks and I won't know what to think."

Logan shook his head. "We'll do DNA, Hana. I'll get Liza to force her."

Hana swallowed and it sounded like she choked. Her nod appeared unsure and Logan crushed her to him. "I didn't think about DNA," she said. "What if she won't agree?"

Logan snorted. "Are you kidding? All she wants is cash and if she agrees to the test, I'll pay her to go away."

Hana counted up the remaining time on her fingers and sighed. "So, only another few weeks to wait, then."

"No, Hana." Logan tipped her chin up with his index finger and his mouth conveyed his sadness through its downward tilt. "I've told you numerous times, it's not my baby. You don't need to wait for it to be born to know for sure. I'm telling you."

Hana sighed and looked away, unable to face the betrayal in his sparkling grey irises. "I'm sorry. I believe you in my heart, but then they start talking and I feel a pain here." Her fingers fluttered over her chest and Logan covered them with his strong hand to still their frantic action.

"I know. If I'm honest, it disappoints me that you don't back me on this." His words cut her.

"I do. I protest your innocence to anyone who will listen but then I remember what she said, or I sense you're fed up of me and the doubts creep in."

Logan nodded. "Hey, you're doing better than I would in your position. I'm the most jealous person I know and I'd go out of my mind over less than this."

Hana nodded. "I do love you, Logan."

"I know." He kissed her temple and his gaze strayed back to the balcony rail. "Hana, there's a more pressing problem right now."

"What?" Her eyes widened and she jumped backwards. "What did Pete do?"

Logan flapped his hand to silence her and put a finger to his lips. He leaned close to her ear. "Nothing. But Laval's men are here."

Hana clapped a hand over her mouth to prevent the wail escaping. Logan placed a reassuring arm around her shoulder. "Don't panic," he whispered. "I thought this might happen. It's perfect. I intend to find out what they want."

"We know what they want!" she squeaked. "They want the box and Odering has it."

"It's okay, it's okay." Logan stroked her hair. "Hana, I need you to trust me now. More than ever before. I won't let you down."

Hana nodded, a jerky, uncontrolled action. She watched with huge green eyes as Logan stood to survey the hall below. He leaned on the rail and took a couple of photographs, tracking the blonde man as he appeared from beneath the mezzanine. The Chinese man remained on door duty but Flick strolled around the crowd. Logan sat down to show Hana his evidence.

Her head nodded up and down with certainty. "Yes, that's the man who gave the orders when they forced their way into Achilles Rise." She swallowed and cocked her head as Logan scrolled to the next picture. Identifying the Oriental looking male didn't send her into quite such a panic as observing a still of the blonde man's face. She exhaled in a rush and swivelled around, seeking escape. "He's here? I need to get out." She tried to stand and Logan grabbed her around the waist and hauled her back to a sitting position.

"No, don't run, Hana. That's what they want." He stood again and stared over the balcony, watching as the blonde man worked the room and his companion guarded the exit to the outside. Returning to her side, he held onto her wrist and massaged the back of her hand. The promise of revenge glinted in his grey eyes and his face looked angular in the light of the overhead chandelier. "I need you to stay here and keep out of sight." When Hana protested, he lifted her cast up and forced her to look at it. "This should have come off yesterday, Hana," he reminded her. "But it's not healing. I don't want anything else to happen to you." Then he looked at her stomach and frowned. "I need you to protect my baby!"

Hana conceded. She could disregard her own safety, but her unborn child deserved better. Logan's choice of words turned her into a caretaker and affected her like a guilt trip. She squared herself on her seat. "What shall I do?"

"Good girl." Logan hugged her, reassuring her before outlining his plan. He dug in her handbag and retrieved her phone. Fiddling around on the screen, he entered a phone number but handed it back without starting the connection. "As soon as I leave, lock yourself in here and let this number dial. It's Odering's direct number. If he acts difficult, hang up and dial 111 for emergency. Tell them you're pregnant and scared and Flick is here with his sidekick. He's wanted for breach of warrant so they'll come. But Hana," he looked at her, his eyes full of seriousness and concern. "If you need to dial emergency, it'll cause mayhem here. The cops will crawl all over this expo and Sheila will die of shock. It would be better if Odering deals with it."

Logan grappled in his jacket pocket for his own mobile phone. He took it out and located the contact he needed. He sent a text as fast as his fingers could fly across the keypad while whispering an explanation to a frightened Hana. "I've texted Bodie. He's downstairs in the police presentation. He might struggle to get out, but he's here and I know he'll come when he can." Logan stood, taking the wide steps two at a time. He looked back at Hana, surprised she didn't match his speed. "Come on Hana, lock up behind me and only let Bodie in."

She stood with frustrating slowness, moving up the stairs in a way which made him want to scream. "What will you do?" she asked, her voice forced. "And why do you have Odering's direct number?"

Logan shook his head. He reached down and kissed her on the lips without answering. He pulled the door open and slipped through, waiting on the other side until he heard the turn of the key. "I won't be long," he promised, crossing his fingers behind his back. He heard Hana's skirt swish across the door as she turned away.

Logan ran down the stairs, using the bannister rail to suspend him in a haphazard descent. He opened a fire door to get outside, pulling it closed behind him and hoping the stiff breeze didn't make it bang. Freezing temperatures bit at his lungs as he slipped around the outside of the hall, skirting the building until he reached a suitable viewing point. The man with his back to the doors stood with his arms folded. He cut an imposing figure and Logan cocked his head to one side. He'd met him before. His lips quirked upwards in a smile and he gave a satisfied nod. Easy.

His watch revealed fifteen more minutes before the bell sounded and the whole room began moving like a game of musical chairs. The high windows provided no opportunity to see anyone walking towards the exit and Logan took a chance and snuck closer. The man's squat body kept vigil in the doorway, making it impossible for anyone to pass without scrutiny. Logan weighed up the pros and cons of taking the man down where he stood, dismissing the idea instantly. Too many witnesses. He needed to give him a reason to leave his position. Alone.

It proved as easy as walking up behind him and tapping him on the shoulder. The guy spun around and saw Logan retreating to the bottom of the steps. Without thinking, he gave chase. His Oriental features looked ethereal in the half-light. Beautiful toned skin and delicate bone structure offered a modelling opportunity. Instead, the man employed his brawn and chose a different lifestyle. Logan backed off further, drawing his opponent away from the massive audience. The man followed, the idea of capturing Logan greater than any other consideration. Down the steps he came and out into the courtyard, fists clenched in front of him. His vehemence took Logan off guard. He'd expected to entice him with a promise of access to Hana, but the man kept coming, knowing Logan's identity and hungry for capture. His expression showed an anticipation of enjoyment of the frenzied, sadistic kind. Logan changed his plan when he saw the determination in the way his opponent cracked his neck from side to side. He switched to the slam-dunk approach.

The man misunderstood Logan's retreat as defeatist and let it afford him a false sense of superiority. He increased his speed, fists ready and his right arm already drawing back as he moved. Logan halted his progress, seeing surprise in the other man's eyes. He used his opponent's stance against him, forcing his own weight onto his rear foot as he prepared a killer slam with his leading heel. It contacted the man's leg, driving his knee cap the wrong way. Logan heard a sharp intake of breath as the joint gave and his own weight crushed the ligaments inside.

Pure agony dropped him forward and Logan gave him a right hook in the face to prevent further noise. A fighter's trick, it bent his nose sideways before the cartilage twanged. "Let's go for a little chat somewhere quiet," he hissed. He fixed one hand over the man's spluttering mouth and the other around his chest. Hauling him backwards, he headed for the other side of an adjoining building.

Once out of sight of anyone leaving the hall, Logan dropped him to the ground. The man groaned in pain as Logan used his limp feet to drag him through the narrow alley between F Block and the gym. Neat black shoes glinted in the moonlight and Logan narrowed his eyes. "Nice shoes," he whispered. "I complimented you last time I broke your leg. Remember?" He shrugged. "You didn't say thanks that time either."

The man gargled something unintelligible through the blood in his throat and Logan kept pulling until they reached the end of the alley. Trapped between the two tall buildings, Logan leaned over the stricken male. Blood and air bubbles ran down his broken face and into his ears and his breathing sounded laboured. Logan turned him onto his stomach. "Hey, don't drown, dude. That's not part of the game, is it?"

Logan frisked him with expertise, finding a phone and wallet in his jacket pocket. He flicked through the wallet, ignoring the cash and cards until he came to the driver's licence. "Interesting name, Huang," he mused. "I heard that name only a few months ago. Mrs Che was missing a security guard named Huang. Maybe I'll tell her I found one. Maybe I won't."

The man squirmed and writhed on the ground, spitting blood onto the concrete slabs. Logan lifted the phone and pressed the buttons, seeing the screen flash up a message demanding a code. He turned Huang onto his side and forced the phone into his hand. "Unlock it."

He struggled with the buttons and Logan heard a satisfying beep as the screen lit up. Huang pushed the phone away and lay face down on the floor, panting from his mouth. Logan yanked his head, holding him by his spiky dark hair and thrusting the phone into his face. "Who's your mate?" he demanded.

"Flick," Huang coughed and Logan slapped his crown so his face hit the floor.

"I know that already. But what's he called in your phone?"

"Flick!" he groaned and Logan snorted.

"Geez, you're an amateur." He scrolled through the contacts until he found the right name. "The cops are on their way. I'm sure they'll take good care of you." Logan stood, towering over the fallen man. "I hope they find you before Che's wife. Sorry about your leg and all that, but you didn't give a stuff about my wife."

Grit moved under Logan's heels as he surveyed the area. Huang's location remained hidden, making it difficult for him to receive medical help. He contemplated tipping Bodie off, but figured his stepson might go purple with rage only seconds before he lost his job. "You'll have to take your chances," Logan remarked, nudging the stricken man with his boot. "Or you can try crawling."

Huang made a sound like a growl as Logan moved away with the phone. He paused for a second. The men had abandoned each other before under pressure. He had no evidence to suggest one would come to the aid of the other this time either. Logan brought up the text box and entered a message. The keys clicked as he typed. He turned to Huang. "You know my name, but does Flick?"

"Yes," he replied.

Logan stepped towards him and raised his boot above Huang's dislocated knee. "You lying to me, bro'?"

"He knows your name," the man groaned, covering his limb with fluttering fingers. "Laval wants to deal with you himself."

Logan snorted. "Whatever. I don't know him."

"Well, he knows you." Huang tipped onto his side and panted into his shoulder. Logan shrugged and sent a text to Flick. '*Got him. Bringing him to rear doors. Wait on the steps.*'

It felt like a long shot but anything more specific would raise suspicion. Huang didn't waste words, so Logan didn't either. A loud peal rent the air like a scream. The bell indicated the end of the first talk. Logan paused as it went on longer than usual and he remembered Sheila coercing two of his Year 10s into operating it manually from the box behind the receptionist's office. He shook his head, picturing their glee as they deafened the school population.

With a last look at Huang, Logan used the cover of the bell to slip into the darkness. He retraced his steps, giving himself a minute to get back to the hall door. In the seconds after the bell stopped ringing, he heard no other sound. Then pandemonium broke out. The scraping of chairs dragged against wooden boards, joining the sound of shuffling feet. The noise level trebled in the space of a second. Logan cursed, wishing he'd got into position before sending the text. A public showdown wasn't on his wish list. Witnesses wouldn't be great either.

He covered the remaining distance across the rear of the gym, clutching the stolen phone in his hand. A column of people moved by in either direction, parents discussing their son's career choices. The boy slouched behind them, listening to music in hidden earbuds. With a five minute break between sessions, people pushed and shoved to get into place in front of the next speaker of their choice, but hundreds of other bodies required navigation first. A steady stream of people ambled across the lit courtyard towards Q Block where the big tertiary players waited to make their pitch. Logan watched the classroom windows leak bright yellow light into the darkness. The classrooms filled until it left standing room only. Latecomers lined the windows outside, hiding from the cold beneath the inadequate porch. Body heat rose from the packed rooms like white haze. Witnesses everywhere.

Logan ran a nervous hand over his face. The blonde man would guess. He wondered if Huang neglected to give him a code word but doubted it. He'd already exhibited no class. The doorway remained packed as people pushed through and hurried away. Logan estimated the time it should take for the blonde man to leave his previous location and move through the crowd to the door. He flexed his fingers in anticipation and shoved Huang's phone into his pocket.

The man appeared on cue, standing on the steps and blocking the exit. A disagreement sparked between him and a hurrying family, but he stood his ground. The crowd dispersed around him and the next bell pealed into the night.

Logan made his decision and the process revived an old sense of thrill. He'd forgotten the satisfaction of bending others to his will. The stakes were higher now though. He had more to lose.

Logan used the lights behind him to silhouette his outline. He hunkered down to represent the Chinese man's height and peered around the corner of the building. Shuffling his feet disturbed the grit beneath his boots and Flick's head jerked towards him. Logan leaned forward and beckoned with his arm, making the action look urgent. He held his breath, knowing surprise formed his best asset.

Flick moved off the steps with caution, his body tense and his shoulders squared. Logan created more shuffling, creating the illusion of two people struggling. He prayed to Hana's God, understanding the unlikelihood of his prayer receiving an answer, not when he planned to cause someone else deliberate physical pain. As Flick grew nearer, Logan took off running and covered the entire length of the gym before the other man reached the first corner. Hearing quick footsteps, Flick bowed to his innate desire for the chase just as Logan expected. Heavier footed, he pounded after him.

Logan scrabbled to a halt, using the wooden struts of the weatherboard corner to spin himself. He registered the pain of a rotted splinter entering his palm, choosing to ignore it. Readying himself for impact, he braced every muscle and Flick flew around the last corner and straight into Logan's bunched right fist.

Logan estimated the point of contact, hoping to break Flick's nose and bend him double for another knee to the face. His calculations failed him. Instead, his fist ploughed into Flick's throat, knuckles first. His opponent dropped like a stone to the gritty surface, gasping and spluttering.

"Bugger!" Pain shot through Logan's finger joints and into his right shoulder. The ruthless punch proved ill-timed and aimed like an amateur. His school boxing coach would roll over in his comfy plot in the urupa. Logan hissed another raft of worse swear words and tested his fingers for movement. Two joints ground as they started to swell. He felt in his pocket for his prescription spray, knowing it wasn't there even as his fingers scrabbled. "Too bad," he hissed to himself and kicked Flick's thigh in frustration. A bead of realisation budded into a satisfied smile. He'd instinctively protected his weak dominant arm.

Logan knelt next to the man on the ground and turned him over. "You don't deserve this," he commented, rolling him into the recovery position. Flick's breathing sounded less constricted as he gulped cold air. Logan jabbed him in the spine. "Your wee mate is in a similar mess." His tone sounded casual. "And the cops are on their way." He shoved Flick's temple and heard his face contact the ground. "Get talking. I want to hear all about your attacks on my wife."

Flick spluttered a curse and Logan shifted his weight. The recovery position left the man's left arm sticking out behind him, intended to stop him rolling onto his back and choking on his tongue. Logan used the trapped limb as a lever, pressing his knee into the elbow joint. Flick cried out in agony. Leaning down, Logan hissed into his ear. "I don't have time for this. You must know my stepson's a cop. You've hounded his mother. You broke her arm and karma's a bitch."

"I didn't do that!" Flick pulled his head back in a swift, practiced movement. He caught Logan across the bridge of the nose and scrabbled to release his arm. Eyes watering, Logan used the heel of his hand to crack the back of Flick's head and his face hit the concrete beneath. He heard him eat grit. "Geez, man! That bloody hurt." Flick coughed and his voice sounded strained.

"Yeah." Logan pushed him onto his face and sat on his back, hearing the air whoosh from the other man's lungs beneath him. He kept his left hand clamped around the back of his neck and used the other to squeeze the painful bridge of his nose between finger and thumb.

"Okay, okay!" Flick conceded. "I'll tell you, but no cops."

"Whatever!" Logan shook his head to clear his watering eyes. He slapped him on the back of the head again and heard him grunt as his forehead hit the floor. "You're done bargaining."

"Your wife has something my boss wants," Flick rasped, anticipating more pain as Logan paused in the process of lifting his hand for another slap. "Something he needs."

"A box," replied Logan, sounding bored. "A box with papers in it. Yeah. You're too late. The cops have it."

Logan heard the skin of Flick's face moving in the grit beneath him as he wriggled, but the fight left his body in a whoosh of expelled air. He lay still. "Keep talking." Logan slapped him again. "I didn't say you could stop."

"It's pointless." Blood dribbled from Flick's mouth and he lay prone beneath Logan. "It's over."

"Why?" Logan cocked his head, curiosity stiffening his muscles.

"I needed it for someone. If the cops have it, it's safe."

Logan laughed, the sound echoing off the surrounding brick and weatherboard. "Is this where you tell me you're an undercover cop? I don't think so."

"No. But I needed to stop my boss getting the deeds in that box. The family doesn't want him to have them. Now he can't." Flick coughed and spluttered, his body rocking beneath Logan. Sensing the man beaten, Logan climbed off his body, allowing him to catch his breath. He knelt next him, his left hand on the back of Flick's head to prevent another counter attack.

"The deeds showed a tract of land in Northland. Why did a crappy little farm become this important?" When Flick didn't answer, Logan pressed on his elbow with his knee again. His opponent used a paroxysm of coughing to avoid the question and Logan increased the pressure. He heard the grit move beneath and felt the muscles strain in the upper arm to resist breaking point. Flick expelled a wail.

"It's land with oil. They found oil about ten years ago. Laval wants it. He's got a buyer. It's worth a fortune. The papers under your wife's car protected the family and Laval needs to destroy them to validate his claim."

"What's your angle?" Logan removed his knee from Flick's elbow and squatted next to him. He heard his knee joints crunch and sighed. "I'm getting too old for this."

"You and me both." Flick rolled onto his back, but held his hands out in front of him. "I'm done, dude. We're good."

Logan snorted and his face hardened. "We are. Because my next hit knocks you unconscious with a reasonable degree of permanence."

Flick sighed. "Yeah. I know your reputation. I figured the box was safer with you than me. That's why I made a show of looking but didn't collect."

"Really?" Logan's disbelieving tone and the way his fists balled made Flick wince. He raised his hands again.

"I won't take you on, Du Rose. And I didn't mean to hurt your wife, okay? It was for show."

Temper gripped Logan and he seized Flick's chin in his hand. He twisted his face until he'd screwed the man's neck sideways. "Are you kidding me? A sprained wrist, a cut hand and a broken elbow say different!"

"I didn't break her arm!" His tone held vehemence. "I bloody didn't! The other stuff was just work. Then Huang mentioned your name and I backed off."

"I asked what your angle is!" Logan spat and Flick lay inert for a second, his head twisted at a dangerous angle.

"I work for Laval," he said, strain in his voice. "But I have a vested interest in the box. I need to keep it out of his hands."

Logan sighed and let go of Flick's chin. The other man put a hand up to his painful throat and Logan let him. He concentrated on the swollen fingers of his right hand, shaking his head as they refused even to bend anymore. "Does Laval know you've got a different agenda to his?"

Flick pushed himself into a sitting position. He rubbed his sore larynx and kept a wary eye on Logan. Upright, his breathing sounded easier and his voice less hoarse. He leaned against the weatherboard and bent his knees. "He didn't until recently. Someone tipped him off. Huang got an extra order tonight, outside of this. There's a pistol in the car and he's spent more time watching me than you."

Logan's eyebrows knitted together in the darkness. "Huang planned to take you out?"

"Hell yeah!" snorted Flick. "He needs to prove himself. He'll drop me in the Waikato River and let some kid with a fishing rod find what's left. Easy. That's what he did with the old lady." He blew out through pursed lips and Logan's instincts vindicated themselves.

"I knew it!" he hissed. "None of this added up."

Flick swallowed, distress ranking higher than pain in his crestfallen stance. He ran a hand over his face. "Well, aren't you the clever one, then?"

Logan ignored the slight. "So, your employment is terminated as of tonight?"

"Yeah." Flick's heels moved in the grit. "Laval found this flash young idiot to do his bidding and he gets him to collect Larne's debts as a sideline. My replacement."

"I saw." Logan nodded and pushed thoughts of Tama away. The blonde man stared at the ground, his psyche projecting a deep sense of failure. He rubbed a hand over his eyes and licked his lips. Logan narrowed his gaze and touched Flick on the shoulder. "Who owned the copy of the deeds stuck under Hana's car?"

Flick's shoulders slumped. "Deeds, an engineer's report and a last will and testament. My stepmother wrote the will to protect the family after Laval tried to con her."

Logan gave a slow nod and sucked on his bottom lip. "Whose copy, Flick?"

The man tipped his head back and his eyes raked the heavens. The Milky Way spread out overhead in a cloudless sky. He took his time to answer, but Logan already knew. "Mine," he said.

Chapter 8

Bodie smiled as he walked towards Logan, unnerving him with his apparent calm. "So, you found Mum, then?" His voice held suppressed laughter and he looked around him in anticipation of an audience in the empty corridor.

Logan stopped and narrowed his eyes. "Where is she?" His hard tone pulled the young man up short.

"What? You didn't find her?" His expression fell. "What about the text?"

Logan gave a series of blinks and winced as the bridge of his nose ached in remembrance of Flick's counter attack. He put a hand up to his face and Bodie noticed the blood on his sleeve. "Forget it!" Logan snapped. "She must still be on the balcony."

"Whoa! What are you talking about?" Bodie raised his voice and then looked back at the classroom door behind him. The sound of his superior's voice droned in a monotone. "I told him I needed a drink of water so I could get out for five minutes. Where's my mum?"

Logan blew out through pursed lips and shook his head. The action hurt. "I texted you, man!" He spoke through gritted teeth and Bodie took an instinctive step backwards. "I told you Laval's guys turned up and to take care of Hana." Turning on his heel, he strode away.

Bodie ran after him and yanked on his jacket sleeve. He fumbled in his smart uniform pants and retrieved his phone. "No, you didn't. Look."

Logan peered at the screen, squinting to make out the type. '*Got fleas. Help Hana.*' His lips moved as he read the words and then cursed. "Flick!" he snapped. "Got Flick!"

Bodie smirked. "Predictive text, by any chance? I'm not quite sure I can help Mum with your itchy problems."

Logan shook his head and gave him a filthy look filled with malice. His upper lip curled back in a sneer. "And you didn't think that might be odd?" he demanded. "You didn't question something that random?"

"Yeah." Bodie pouted. "That's why I came out to look for you. What happened to your hand?" He tilted his head back to inspect the bridge of Logan's nose. "Why do you have bruising starting under your eyes?"

Logan let out a hiss of annoyance. "Why do you think?"

"So, they're really here?" Bodie cleared his phone screen and started pressing numbers. "I'm calling Odering," he said, excitement making him tumble over his words.

"Hana's already done it!" Logan snapped and set off jogging up the steps. "Just go back to telling kids how a big, brave cop behaves."

Fighting the desire to be physically sick, Logan knocked on the balcony door and called Hana's name. He heard a noise on the other side of the door like cloth brushing up against it. "It's me, Logan. You can unlock it now, babe."

The lock ground and the handle turned from inside. Hana's face peeked out and Logan pushed his way in, careful not to clatter her with the door. "Sweetheart! What happened?" He cradled her in his arms, alarmed when her body rocked with sobs against him. Sweat beaded her skin and mascara covered her cheeks.

"I'm sorry," she sniffed. "I'm sorry."

The murmur of voices from the hall below made Logan press a finger to her lips. He jerked his head back towards the door and they slid out into the deserted corridor. "Tell me what happened?" he demanded, holding her by the shoulders.

Hana turned her mobile phone to face him, her fingers shaking. "Every time it connected to the police station, it cut out." Her lungs hitched. "I couldn't get help. I tried 111, but it wouldn't work. It's broken."

Logan closed his eyes and pulled her into his chest. "Oh, Hana! I'm sorry. Everything's okay. It's all fixed."

"I didn't know what to do." Her body felt overheated against his and he sought to calm her.

"It's okay." Taking the useless phone from her hand, he looked at the network connection. "Something's weird with cell coverage up here." He pushed it into his pocket.

"But I failed again," Hana sniffed. "I needed to call help and I didn't know what happened to you and I felt so useless." Her fingers fluttered over her heart. "I can't stand this, Logan. We can't live like this anymore."

"We don't have to." Logan pressed his lips to the side of her head and waited for her to calm. "It's gonna be okay."

Hana blinked as another black line of mascara tracked down her cheek. She reached up with her good hand to touch the darkness beneath his left eye. "Something happened to you. Logan, tell me!" Her voice hiked up again and he shook his head.

"Later, Hana. I promise. Later. I'm fine, you're fine and the guys are dealt with." He gritted his teeth. "And your son's hilarious."

She sniffed at the sound of her son's name. The hopefulness in her face sent a spark of irritation into Logan's psyche. "Did Bo help?"

He heaved out a sigh and picked his words with care. Turning Hana's body to face the corridor leading to the staffroom, he nudged her forward. "Let's get you cleaned up, babe. You'll need to serve supper in about forty minutes."

Hana glanced back at him, the childlike innocence in her expression making his chest hurt. "Do I look like I've been crying?" she asked, hiccoughing against another spasm in her lungs.

"No, babe," he lied. "You just need more lipstick."

Clasping his fingers over her shoulders, he pushed her forward in the direction he wanted. His bloodied knuckles oozed and he frowned with irritation.

As the second bell pealed through the building, they reached the staffroom level and Logan unlocked the darkened post room next door and pulled Hana into it. "Why are we in here?" she whispered, peering through the glass into the empty staffroom. He ran his hands through his hair and she noticed his knuckles and the oozing gash in his palm. Panic returned the shadow to her face and taking his hand gently, she inspected at the damage. "What happened?" Her pupils looked huge in the reflected glow from the staffroom lights. The buzz downstairs became deafening as people moved around in their game of careers-musical-chairs for the second time.

"I found Laval's men and I took care of them." He licked his lips. "And you know when I said you didn't look like you'd been crying?" Hana nodded, her eyes dark voids in her soul. "I lied. Your makeup is all over your face. I didn't want people to see you."

Hana swallowed and nodded. "Did you kill the men?" she asked, jumping as Logan recoiled.

"No!" Scorn and anger crossed his features like a scudding rain cloud. "What do you think I am?"

Hana's mouth opened and closed and a pink tongue moistened her lips. "What did you do to them?"

Logan set his jaw in a hard line. "Do you trust me?" he demanded. The loaded question hung in the air between them, choking and unwieldy. Each word assumed more power than it deserved.

The school grew silent as another talk began, yet time slowed for Hana. She sensed the frailty of trust within their marriage, but no solution rushed to rescue her. The lies of her first marriage stained her heart and she craved truth and honesty. Staring at Logan brought no clarity and she realised the root of her fear lay in her inability to read him. Taking a deep breath, she wiped her wet cheeks with the palm of her left hand and bought herself a moment of recovery.

Logan's grey eyes bore into her as he waited for her answer. He schooled his reaction before she spoke, watching her wrestle. "I trust you with my safety. I think I trust you to do the right thing. But you have secrets, Logan and that makes me doubt you."

Logan jerked in shock at her perception. He looked down at the floor and then forced himself to meet her gaze. "Okay." He sighed. "Fair enough. Please just trust me for tonight?"

Hana nodded, a bobbing, stilted action. Logan pulled the door ajar and peeked into the corridor, his shoulders relaxing when he found it empty. Looking back, he opened his mouth to usher Hana out, but found her poking into her tiny handbag. She sniffed and he saw her pull out a ratty, balled up tissue. He sighed and reached in his pocket for the clean handkerchief he always carried. He offered it to her and she accepted it, shades of their teenage meeting in the backs of both their minds. Hana gave a tight smile. "Thank you."

They'd reached an understanding. The handkerchief served as a white flag, not of surrender but negotiation. It offered a starting point.

Their fingers touched and Hana put the cloth up to her nose, sniffing Logan's familiar scent. Ironed into a neat triangle, the handkerchief bore a small bloodstain at the corner and Hana frowned. "Your hand is bleeding." She narrowed her eyes in concern. "Do you want me to check it?"

"No." Logan shook his head. "I'm good." He held his hand out to her and beckoned. "Are you ready?"

Hana nodded and put the handkerchief beneath her nose. She intended a dainty wipe but distress made her sinuses feel blocked. Instead, she blew. The honking sound echoed around the post room and Logan jumped in shock. "Geez woman!" he exclaimed. Then he laughed and Hana giggled into the handkerchief in response.

She used the staff washroom upstairs and Logan leaned against the wall outside. It took a while to clean up her face and reapply enough makeup to disguise her swollen eyes and red nose. Emerging with her tiny handbag at her side, she saw Logan in his usual stance with one leg bent and the sole of his boot on the wall. Hana pointed to the imprint of a foot on the paintwork behind him. "He'll know that's you. Nobody else wears cowboy boots. He'll come after you."

Logan raised an eyebrow in challenge and Hana shook her head. He spoke into his mobile phone, his voice low and his speech clipped. Hana failed to translate the Māori words and wrinkled her nose. "Who are you speaking to?" she demanded, pressing her chin into his chest.

"Nobody." Logan disconnected the call and shoved his phone in his pocket. He kissed the end of her nose. "Nobody for you to worry about, anyway." He raised an eyebrow at her pout and bit the soft skin beneath her earlobe. "The food just arrived," he said. "I nipped into the staffroom and turned the oven on. The chef said to keep the savouries hot."

"Cuddle me," Hana demanded like a petulant child and Logan wrapped his strong arms around her. His chin rested on the top of her head and he bit his lip in thought. "You're doing it again," Hana grumbled, digging her fingers into his ribs.

Logan jumped and released her. "Doing what?"

"Keeping secrets." Hana pursed her lips and a frown caused furrows in her forehead.

"Come on," Logan urged, ignoring her accusation and tugging her towards the staffroom. "Let's put the food in the oven and get this stupid night over with." He towed her through the double doors, terminating their conversation.

A sense of foreboding settled over Hana and soured her sense of survival. Instinct told her that her husband was up to something. Logan denied her the opportunity of challenging him further, busying himself with loading trays of bite sized pies into the dirty interior of the oven. "This is foul," he grumbled, a familiar clean freak expression shrouding his face. "I'm not eating anything from here."

Hana settled in a chair to watch him. Any one-handed attempt to help pointed towards disaster. Logan gave nothing away apart from his disgust at the filthy oven and she distracted herself with the camera. Flicking through the array of photographs, she saw the images of the blonde man and his companion. She skipped over them and examined the other pictures. The scene from the balcony made an impressive image and Hana sighed with relief. It looked cheerful and engaging, but the photos of her attackers left her chilled to the bone.

Logan stood up from loading the oven and rolled his shoulder. Hana watched his movements with suspicion. He used a piece of toilet roll to dab at the gash on his palm and dark bruising grew beneath both eyes. A welt along the bridge of his nose gave him the look of a man fresh from a rugby scrum and Hana licked her lips. She almost burst with the effort of not questioning him until she possessed the whole story. She'd promised to trust him, but hadn't imagined how hard it might prove.

Hana sighed and rested her head on her left arm. It felt as though Logan demanded more trust than he gave. *Trust me, trust me.* Hana squeezed her eyes tight shut. The last man who asked that of her blew her world apart.

The rest of the evening sped by. Hana took more photos and Logan accompanied her across the dark courtyard to the remote classrooms in use. Sheila buzzed with the success of the event, enjoying the congratulations and the applause. The evening finished with a supper in the staffroom to give Angus an opportunity to thank the presenters. Prefects arrived to take over the serving role with efficiency and before long, everyone clasped a glass of wine or mug of coffee in their hands.

"Sheila said I can go soon," Hana whispered as Logan joined her at the back of the room. He searched the room for Hana's boss until he found her flirting with the representative of a south island university. He nudged Hana and jerked his head towards them.

"Looks like her relationship hiatus is over," he whispered and Hana giggled.

"I saw. She looks quite smitten."

Logan snorted. "In a cougar kind of way."

Hana exhaled and elbowed him in the hip. "Give her a break, Logan. She deserves some fun after Martin's antics."

He murmured something unintelligible and Hana rolled her eyes. "Hey!" He reached out and grabbed the sleeve of a passing prefect. "The food is for the guests, gobshite, not you lot."

The teenage boy swallowed, a look of pain in his eyes as the red hot pie made a hasty exit into his gullet. A prefect next to him shoved a bacon and cheese quiche into his mouth whole and tried to look innocent. He chewed like a cow, his mouth decorated with acne and braces. Logan's expression projected his disgust. "Bloody hell!" he hissed. "Did you even wash your hands?" The boys moved away and Logan shook his head. "That's nasty!" he grumbled. His eyes strayed to the school staff who stayed behind to help with the expo. They gathered around platters and filled their faces like they hadn't eaten for a month. "No guesses where the boys get it from," he sighed.

Hana grinned at him in amusement and gravitated towards Bodie. Logan tried to head her off but failed. He produced the digital camera from his jacket pocket and handed it over in a slick movement. "You left this on the table," he said, waiting until she took the weight to let go. Hana looked up in surprise as Logan spoke to Bodie first. "Please can you give your mum a ride home?"

Bodie smirked. "The pest clinic won't be open this late."

Logan grimaced. "Predictive text mate. Not even funny."

"What's this?" Hana looked up from the camera and sensed she'd been played. "What text? And why can't we go home together?"

"I need to sort some stuff out. I'll be a couple of hours." Logan turned towards Bodie. "Stay at our place tonight if you want." Logan kept a straight face as Hana blinked at his sudden change of heart towards her son.

Bodie shrugged. "Guess so. I've still got clothes at yours."

Relief flooded Logan's face and Hana's eyes narrowed. "Where are you going, Logan?" Her bottom lip puckered in fear.

Logan turned and held her gaze. He observed her efforts to trust him and saw how much it cost. Her green eyes widened in fear and she struggled with her doubts as though drowning.

The sound of Angus clearing his throat cut through the room. "I'd like to thank my wonderful staff for making the event happen, Sheila and Hana." He beckoned the women forward so they could savour the appreciation of the gathered crowd. Hana resisted but Sheila dragged her forward to the sound of applause and wolf whistles. Angus presented them each with a box of chocolates and an air kiss, causing Hana's cheeks to redden with embarrassment.

Hana felt embarrassed when everyone turned to her and clapped, her cheeks reddening in discomfort. But by the time the noise faded away, Logan had already pushed through the crowd towards the nearest exit. Hana watched his tall frame move through the door, his dark, wavy hair fluttering against an air current. Her eyes widened, willing him to look at her. "Don't go," she murmured as the gathered crowd laughed at one of Angus' anecdotes. "Stay with me."

Logan's grey eyes flicked up as he reached the top of the stairs and his gaze locked on Hana's. Her lips parted and she took a step towards him. The smile didn't reach his eyes as he disappeared down the stairs and out of sight. Hana ran to the window and put her palms against the glass. Darkness crowded against the school buildings and denied her any view of her husband. He'd gone.

Chapter 9

Hana didn't speak as she walked to Bodie's car. He carried her bag of work clothes and dumped it in his boot. Despite knowing she wouldn't find it, Hana looked around for her car. She no longer knew where Logan parked and her old space looked grey and empty in the hazy lighting. Hana stared at the concrete, wondering if she stood in her parking space she might gain some supernatural insight into her husband's urgent business. Perhaps even into Logan himself.

"Mum, get in, it's freezing!" Already in the driver's seat, Bodie turned the heat up, rubbing his hands together in front of the tepid warmth as the engine fought to thaw the interior. Hana slid into her seat, feeling an ache in her heart to match the ones in her body.

Bodie concentrated on the dark road ahead, pressing numbers into a digital display on his dashboard. The sound of ringing burst into the silence as the call connected through his phone. "Just ringing Odering," he said and glanced across at Hana. "I'm surprised he didn't look me out when he arrested Laval's men. What time did you call him?"

"I didn't." Hana gulped. Bodie's fingers jabbed at the screen to kill the call.

"You what?" His eyes bugged in accusation and for once, he appeared speechless.

"I couldn't make the call." Hana's voice wobbled as her excuses tumbled out. Bodie shook his head and slammed his hand against the steering wheel.

"I don't believe this," he muttered over and over.

At the end of River Road, the traffic lights with Wairere Drive shone red into the night sky and Bodie skidded to a jerky halt. Hana burst into tears. Chastened, Bodie reached his left arm towards her, finding her fingers poking from her cast. "Where's Logan gone?" he asked, his voice more gentle.

Between sobs, which punctuated her words with hiccoughs and sharp intakes of breath, Hana stuttered, "I think he killed them. Now he's getting rid of the bodies."

The car behind Bodie pipped its horn as the lights turned green and he failed to move. He stared open mouthed at Hana instead. Pressing the gas pedal with shaking legs, he lurched at the open junction and left skid marks on the road. They reached River Road northbound and Bodie screeched into the first bus stop he came to. The other car cruised past them as they sat in silence with the engine still running. Bodie kept his hands in his lap and even in the darkness Hana saw them writhing. "I knew it!" His teeth made a noise as they ground together. "I bloody knew it!"

Hana wiped her eyes with the back of her hand and turned her body to face him. "They came for me. He went out to find them and came back cut up. He asked me to trust him."

Bodie put his hand in front of her face as though warding off something nasty. "No!" he yelled. "No more! Don't tell me anything else, Mum. You seem determined to wreck my career. Why did you marry him? I warned you. Geez, I'm finished." He ran a shaking hand over his face.

Shocked into silence, Hana felt dismay merge with resentment. She threw herself back against her seat. "It's all about you," she breathed. "It's always about you." Her heart formed a solid lump of lead in her chest and the effort of sitting upright hurt with its mass suffocating her.

"It's not about me." Bodie indicated and pulled the car back onto the road. "I'm worried sick for you. You're in way over your head."

Hana gritted her teeth and maintained a determined silence. Brightly lit houses slipped by, painting a picture of other people's cosy, domestic bliss. She reminded herself it was an illusion and she could still possess such happiness. She just needed to get home to Culver's Cottage, close the door behind her and wait for Logan.

"This whole thing's a bloody mess," Bodie fumed. He tapped a finger against the steering wheel and shot nervous glances at her. "I should take you down to the station."

"Don't!" Hana kept her eyes facing forward and ran her good hand over her abdomen. "Take me home."

"He's a violent thug, Mum! And now he's a murderer. Maybe he tried to kill Boris."

"He didn't! Boris told Angus he didn't." Hana swallowed the lump in her throat, feeling her heart pound through her chest wall. "Just take me home."

"I can't believe you've done this to me. Years of building up a career for you to ruin it."

Hana forced her eyes sideways and looked at her son. Really looked at him for the first time. Selfishness oozed from every pore and something snapped within her. She saw her life mapped out behind her like a smudged painting and saw guilt running through it like a bloodline. This is what parenting through guilt produced. The shock and unexpectedness of her teenage pregnancy and the trouble it caused made her wish it never happened. When the tiny, squalling, olive skinned baby arrived, she felt nothing but guilt for her wicked thoughts because she loved him after all. And her guilty conscience made her soft and malleable to a strong personality like Bodie.

Hana Du Rose shook her head. No more. She'd paid her penance many times over.

Bodie activated the gate for Culver's Cottage and his car slipped up the driveway. He pulled up on the flat section outside the house and switched off the engine. Hana shot from the passenger seat and bent down to speak to him through her open door. "Thank you for the ride Bodie. I don't need you to stay." She closed the door, careful not to slam it.

Bodie clambered out and ran around the bonnet towards her. "Look, Mum, sorry, I didn't mean it. We need to sort this out. Tonight. I should call Odering."

Desolation churned deep within Hana's spirit. So many times Bodie placed her in difficult situations as a schoolboy. So many times as an adult too. Her gaze took in his father's arrogance and the firm jut of his jaw. He threw things at her and expected her to deal with it without fuss. Like Jas. And she behaved as he wanted because it promised to take her through the course of least resistance. "Do what you like," she said, moving past him. "You always do."

"You said he killed someone!" Bodie slapped his thighs in frustration.

"I believe you misheard, officer," Hana replied. The porch steps loomed like a mountain range and she forced herself onward.

Bodie's footsteps followed and Hana tensed. "I need to come in, Mum. I have to see Logan."

Hana turned and shook her head. "I don't think so." Bodie recoiled at the hardness in her eyes. The porch light threw glittering embers into her emerald irises.

Bodie held his ground and a crease appeared between his eyebrows. "Why?"

Perhaps it was the plaintive tone of his voice which acted as a match, lighting the blue touch paper on a firework because Hana exploded. "Why? Because I'm tired of being your fall guy, Bodie!"

"I don't understand." He watched her unlock the door and moved up a step. Hana reappeared after deactivating the burglar alarm.

"You wouldn't," she said, her tone sad. Exhaustion forced her shoulders into a slump of defeat. "You can have your life and throw your problems my way whenever you wish. But if I find just a tiny piece of happiness, you wreck it without a flicker of conscience." Her fingers strayed to her baby bump and she watched Bodie recoil.

"Well, that's disgusting!" he spat. "I'm twenty-six and my mother is pregnant."

Hana shook her head. "No, your mother found love and is having your brother or sister."

"Love!" Bodie spat the word. "He's bad news, Mum. You'll see."

"They always are bad news to you, Bo. I think we've had this conversation one time too many, don't you?"

Bodie swallowed. "That was different. The guy was a loser."

"Yeah? Well, I liked him." Hana set her jaw and turned away. "You're determined to see off anyone who makes my life a little more pleasant. Not this time, Bodie. It's okay for you to have affairs with married women and father children. You can throw that at me and I have to accept whatever comes. But you don't return the loyalty."

Bodie shook his head. "I can't believe you're still harping on about Graham!"

"He was a friend!" Hana shouted. "Someone to go to movies or out to dinner with. We liked each other and you ran him out of town. He told me what you said to him. And all the time you were wrecking my life, you were having an illicit affair with Amy!"

"Why are you bringing this up now?" Bodie shouted, his face a dark mask of anger.

"Because you make everything about yourself," yelled Hana. "I am sick and tired of it. Logan will never be good enough for you because he's not Vikram bloody Johal!"

Bodie jumped back as though shot and lost his footing on the step. He staggered backwards into the gravel before righting himself. Silence filled the air between them and Hana regretted taking her dead husband's name in vain. It acted like a bucket of cold water over them both and she shivered. Her secret bubbled onto her lips and she swallowed it down in a painful gulp. Not the time or the place.

Bodie balled his fists and skirted the mention of his father, leaving the dark spectre hanging there unacknowledged. "You just told a serving police officer your mafia husband killed two people tonight and is right now hiding the bodies!" Veins stood out on Bodie's neck and his eyes widened in mock disbelief.

Hana swallowed, remembering her promise to Logan. Her fingers caressed her child in a guilt reflex. "Don't be ridiculous," she said, biting back the rising panic. "Go home, Bodie. We can't fix this tonight."

She made her choice, the sensation unpleasant like something cold and slippery dropping down the back of her neck. Blinking, her voice emerged as a whisper. "Please go, Bodie. I won't do this right now. And never ever call my husband that again!"

Bodie opened his mouth to speak and then thought better of it. The night felt unreal and he sensed the relationship with his mother riding a new course over which he had no control. As Hana turned away, he reached out his hand and implored her with his eyes. "I don't know what to do!" he called, seeing Hana's pale face turn towards him, grey in the half-light. "Everything's a mess, Mum. I can't move forward with Amy and I'm struggling to know what the hell to do with Jas."

Hana shook her head and sighed. "It's always all about you," she whispered. The front door closed behind her.

Bodie gulped and waited for her to relent, realising as he shivered on the driveway that for the first time in his life, she wouldn't. He retraced his steps to the flash silver car which reinforced his superiority, finding the sense of pride unusually absent. Starting the engine, he careened down the long driveway, pausing at the gate. Hana activated it from the house and the barrier slipped open without a sound, demanding his exit on her behalf. Bodie drove through and watched it close behind him, sickness snaking into his gut like a hand clenching his insides.

Hana sat at the kitchen table and cried. Her boots squeezed her feet and her handbag strap dug into her ribs. "What have I done?" she sobbed and the cat responded, winding his furry body around her calves. She'd made a dreadful decision and thrown everything into her relationship with Logan. Her heart rejoiced, but her head screamed warnings and misgivings until it throbbed and ached.

The camera dug into her side through the thin leather of the handbag and she fumbled it out one-handed. Amidst snot and tears, she flicked through the captured scenes to relive the awful evening. The photograph of Sheila with the university rep bore a dreadful case of red eye. It made her resemble a vampire about to eat him.

Hana flicked through all the photos again, dread making her nauseous. "Oh, no," she whispered, searching back and forth. She scrolled past the close up of Pete, cross-eyed as he stared in delight at the bogey on his finger, then back to vampire Sheila. "They're gone," she breathed into the silence. The camera contained no images of Laval's men. Hana opened the recycle bin on the menu screen where she expected to see the photograph of Pete's tonsils, which she deleted that afternoon after confiscating the camera from him. Nothing. The bin glowed green to highlight its empty state. Someone went to a lot of trouble to get rid of the evidence. And Hana knew who.

She sighed and rested her head on her forearm, leaning the heavy cast in her lap. The baby decided to have playtime and Hana grimaced in discomfort while it danced on her bladder. Despite the distraction, her eyelids drooped and she slipped into a heavy sleep. Exhaustion claimed her and numbed her to the unnatural position of her body or the antics of her child.

Logan arrived home in the early hours of the morning. He pulled his cowboy boots off tired feet and stood them against the skirting board. Yellow light streamed from the kitchen and he saw Hana collapsed in her chair, her cheek about to slide off the table. Standing in the doorway, he watched her for a moment, drinking in the swell of her stomach and the sheen of the overhead bulb which returned her hair to its natural red. He ran a hand through his tousled hair and down his face. His fingers contacted dark stubble which prickled from his skin into a rough beard. Grey circles ringed his eyes and he carried his right hand with care, pain etched across his face. The index and middle fingers resembled bananas, swollen and bruised. Stress, altitude and the head butt conspired to give him a nosebleed as he went over the mountains and drops of blood coated his white shirt like rain drops.

Tenderness filled his expression, softening the hard edges as he ran a hand across his sleeping wife's shoulders. "Come on sweetheart," he whispered into her hair, peeling her from her seat and picking her up like a child. She stirred and murmured something unintelligible, recognising his scent and snuggling into his chest as he carried her down the hallway to the bedroom. His fingers throbbed as he fumbled with the delicate buttons and removed Hana's outer layers. He left her in her bra and knickers and covered her with blankets.

Logan moved around the house with quiet steps. Tiger milled about, winding around his legs and almost legging him up on his way to the bathroom. Pouring himself a glass of water, Logan stared at himself in the mirror while he drank. A bone wearying, miserable, soul and spirit kind of ache blossomed deep inside his core. He glanced at the shower and wondered if he could be bothered, despite feeling filthy.

The water revived him, running over his body and washing away sweat and the day's dirt from his hair. Logan wished it could wash away his problems with as little effort. He turned the water onto the cold setting, shocking himself awake. It eased the ache in his forehead and fingers and he leaned his head against the tiled wall. The water mingled with drops of blood from his nose, creating a spattered art work on the floor of the bath.

The nasal spray helped with the bleeding. Logan jabbed cotton wool balls into his nostrils to stop the mess and allow the spray to work. Then he used Hana's first aid kit to strap his painful fingers together, winding plaster around all four to form a natural splint. He admired his handiwork and downed painkillers and anti-inflammatories, pushing the dosage higher than he should in desperation.

He made whispered phone calls, speaking to his father and then his head stockman. Alfred sounded rattled. "You didn't just open a can of worms, son," he bit. "You bloody shook it first! Did you think we didn't have enough problems?"

Logan turned his phone onto silent mode and slumped in his chair. His body ached and age seemed to creep into his bones. Flicking out the kitchen light, he walked through the lobby and into his marital bedroom. Hana's light snores came out of the darkness and relief washed over him. Tomorrow he'd tell her what he'd done.

Chapter 10

The sound of a buzzing alarm broke into Hana's sleep, creating a sense of irritation in her consciousness. It roused her, forcing her to a surface she didn't want to visit. She lay still, squeezing her eyes tight shut and hoping sleep might reclaim her.

"Freaking hell!" Logan's groan sent her shooting upwards, following the agonised sound until her hands found his body in the darkness.

"What?" she demanded. "What's wrong?"

"I think I broke my hand last night," he moaned. Hana heard a twang, followed by the sound of breaking plastic as he threw the clock radio against the wall to silence it. She drew back in shock.

"Logan! Now you broke the clock. And probably pulled the plug socket off the wall."

"Sorry," he replied, his voice sleepy and laden with discomfort. "The buttons are fiddly and my fingers won't bend."

Hana snuggled into his shoulder, reaching for his hand beneath the covers. "Want me to have a look?"

"It's dark." He sounded sulky and Hana nudged him. "I meant with the light on. Why am I in my undies?"

"That information is classified." Logan's voice drawled with sex appeal. He turned to face her, his features screwed up in a look of teasing. The dawning light displayed the state of his nose and Hana jerked backwards. A long, blood-stained piece of cotton wool protruded from each nostril.

Hana sighed. "I'd remember rampant sex with a walrus." She pushed her face into the warmth of her pillow and then groaned. "Oh, no. I do remember last night. What a mess!" The weight of the previous evening hit her like a moving truck and her heart filled with dread.

Logan narrowed his eyes and turned on his side. "Now I'm nervous. What did you do last night? I thought I sent you home." His lowered voice held shades of accusation. "Bodie's car isn't here and nor is he. What happened, Hana?" Misery crossed her face and pooled in her green eyes. Logan reached out to stroke her face but drew his hand back. Broken fingers and lack of dexterity meant he'd probably poke her in the eye instead. He waited for her confession with the patience of a horse trainer. When she didn't prove forthcoming, he turned onto his back and sighed. "You told your cop son I went on a killing-and-burying-spree, didn't you?"

Hana squeezed her eyes shut tight and buried her face in the pillow. "Not exactly," she mumbled. "There's more to it."

Logan rolled his eyes and watched daylight increase across the ceiling. "You finally realised that his tendency towards self-preservation borders on selfishness?"

Hana's eyes snapped open and she pushed herself onto one elbow. "Something like that." Her brow furrowed at Logan's astuteness.

Her husband shrugged. "He'll come around," he encouraged, forcing optimism into a lighter tone.

"No, he won't." Hana rubbed her eyes. "He can be vicious. I can't believe I let him dictate my life while he messed around with a married woman."

"I know a married woman I wanna mess around with." Logan slipped the fingers of his good hand under Hana's bra strap.

"No!" She batted him away, her face drawing into a scowl.

Logan pinged her bra strap and crinkled his nose at her expression of venom. "Not attractive, babe." He shook his head at their predicament. "Two broken fingers and one broken elbow between us. We don't even make up a complete person." He caught her as she wriggled away from him, wrapping his arm around her and hauling her into his side. "I refuse to get in the middle between my wife and stepson," he whispered. "Wisdom tells me I'll be the loser." Logan sighed with satisfaction as he popped the catch one-handed and released Hana's breasts. Bowing his head to kiss the column of her neck, he muttered softly, "And I'm no loser."

Hana pushed herself closer, savouring Logan's warmth and running her hand over his muscular back. She kissed his chest and slipped a tentative finger into the waistband of his boxer shorts, feeling the soft skin over his hip. Logan stilled, waiting. When he felt the tug of the material sliding down, he moaned and rolled Hana onto her back. His broken finger joints ground as he attacked her remaining underwear, but somewhere in his subconscious mind, it seemed worth it.

"You don't take no for an answer, Mr Du Rose," Hana purred in his ear.

Logan smiled and pressed his lips over hers. "I know when you mean it," he replied. Her answering kiss silenced him.

The first opportunity to discuss Logan's injuries came on the way to work. "The car's filthy," Hana complained. Her lips curled back in a snarl of irritation at the old, tatty pair of leggings working their way up her butt. The worn elastic rolled them down her belly without warning, creating a crawling sensation and making her jump. She wriggled like she had fleas and gave an unexpected shriek.

"Stop woman!" Logan exclaimed, swerving as she grappled around behind her.

"Sorry! If your pants kept going up your bum, you'd feel miserable."

"You crack me up, wahine!" Logan shook his head and tried not to laugh.

"So, why are your fingers broken and what's with the black eyes?" She grunted as she gripped the seat of her leggings and held on while Logan steered the car around a roundabout.

"I certainly didn't murder anyone." Logan smirked. "I knew you'd think it though."

Hana cringed, regretting the lack of trust her conversation with Bodie proved. "Your whole body looks sore," she said, injecting sympathy into her voice and suppressing the selfish, physical discomfort of her wedgie.

"My nose hurts more than my fingers," Logan said.

"It looks raw."

"I spent several hours wiping it on my cotton sleeve, which didn't help. Silly bugger head butted me. I'm hoping it isn't broken inside. Again!"

"What happened after you left the staffroom?" Hana asked, her face a mask of worry. "Did the men attack you again?"

"No, babe, no." Logan reached out his left hand and rubbed Hana's thigh. "It happened earlier, but the altitude made it worse. For what it's worth, he seemed sorry." He took his hand back to turn the steering wheel.

"Where are Laval's men, Logan? I can't imagine the blonde man sorry for anything. What's stopping them coming after me when you're not around?"

"I won't give you details." Logan sounded stubborn and Hana watched a frown settle over his face. "You're safe. I killed no one, but it's best you know as little as possible, especially with Bodie on my case. Flick and his mate won't come after us again, but they're alive and breathing."

Hana opened her mouth to complain and then closed it again. "Oh, for goodness' sake!" she shrieked and Logan almost rear-ended a logging truck.

"What the hell?" he demanded, shooting her a sideways glare.

Hana jiggled on the seat with a pained expression on her pretty face. "I'm sure half the value of these leggings are stuck up my whatsit!" she wailed in frustration.

"Well, ask for your bloody money back!" Logan retorted with irritation. "And stop jumping around!"

"Ignore Bodie." Hana settled herself in the seat but the pained expression remained. "I want to know what happened last night."

Logan winced as he steered with his painful hand. "Fine. But if your son whines it out of you, don't blame me."

"He won't," Hana promised.

Logan rolled his eyes and bit back sarcasm. "I dropped Huang near the emergency department of the Waikato Hospital and watched him crawl inside. He's an ex-Triad, so I figured he'd get first aid and then disappear."

"What about the blonde man?" Hana's eyes widened as she conjured up an image of his face.

"Huang had orders to get rid of him. There's no guarantee he won't still try once he's fixed up. So, I took him somewhere he can hide out for a while."

"Hide out?" Hana's lips formed a circle of displeasure. "I don't believe this."

Logan exhaled in irritation. "I took care of it, Hana. That's what I promised I'd do."

"Where did you take him?" Her eyes narrowed and she inspected the seat beneath her. "I can't believe you let him sit in my car!"

Her husband sighed. "It's not nice to put passengers in the boot."

"He's not nice!" Hana snapped and a warning vein began a steady ticking in Logan's neck. She sulked all the way to work and he enjoyed the peace. His mind worked through problems like an accountant weighing risk. He dropped Hana at the main gate and drove around to the chapel car park where he reclaimed her original spot. His phone chirped as he exited the car.

"Yeah." Logan exhaled and waited for the caller to speak.

"What do you want me to do with this dude?" Toby sniffed and Logan's jaw tightened at his head stockman's lack of finesse. He heard the young man spit in the background.

"He goes nowhere until I say so," Logan snapped. "Keep him at the bunkhouse and don't let him out of your sight."

"I don't have time for this." Toby's voice rose an octave. "One of the boys can trail him around the mountain with them."

"You do it." Logan gritted his teeth. "This guy's tricky. Don't let him near any vehicles, hotel guests or family."

Toby sighed and spat again, this time in disgust. "Who is he, Logan?"

"The dude who attacked my wife."

"You're kidding?"

"Damn straight," Logan bit. "I haven't decided what to do with him yet, so you watch him, Toby. Understand?"

"Geez, boss!" Toby's exasperation crossed the kilometres between them. "Thanks for putting him in the bunkhouse with me!"

Logan waited for a school bus to pass before stepping across the narrow arterial road towards the English block of classrooms. "Na. I banged his throat up enough for him not to get up to much over the next few days. Get Jack to watch him if you can't. Not much he can get do around horses he's probably scared of."

Toby exhaled. "So, put him with a deaf man?"

"Jack's fine." Logan's brow creased at the memory of the old man's cunning left hook. He rubbed his ear without conscious thought. "He misses nothing. And he packs that old pistol down the seat of his pants. Put Flick with him for the next few days while he's still sore. After that, he's your responsibility."

"So, he hurt Mrs Du Rose?" Toby's voice held a faint thread of threat.

"Yeah. Don't ask why I'm giving him house room. It's complicated." Logan inhaled through his painful nose and blinked as his eyes watered. "And it's temporary."

"Okay." Toby spat again, this time with more disgust. "He might get a bit hurt up here, boss. It's not the life for woman bashers. Jack might bend over and accidentally blow the dude's brains out."

Logan snapped the phone off without replying. Toby's loyalty gave him a sense of satisfaction and he harnessed the emotion as he changed hats and dropped into his teacher role. Hana noticed he appeared happier when she ran into him in the staffroom at interval. "Sorry about earlier," she whispered as they danced around each other to get to the hot water heater on the wall.

"Not your fault." Logan leaned in and kissed her temple. "I'm tired and grumpy." He showed her his fingers. "The school nurse strapped these for me. It's helped."

"But your nose is still bleeding." Hana's brow narrowed in concern as Logan dabbed it with a stained handkerchief. "What did she say about that?"

He shrugged. "Nothing, Hana. I used my spray and it'll stop, eventually."

"What about the rest of this mess?" Worry created a vertical line through her forehead. "Laval will send other guys. He'll get them from Larne, like before." Her fingers fidgeted behind her, the pained expression more to do with her clothing than her precarious safety.

"I don't know what more I can do." Logan ran his left hand over his face and moved aside for other staff to fill their cups with boiling water. He leaned against the sink and lowered his voice. "I'm tired, Hana. If the cops lock me up or Laval takes me out, I get to lie down and sleep. Either seems like a great idea at the moment." His chest pricked with guilt at the alarm which crossed Hana's face at his casual dismissal. He reached out to touch a strand of her coiled hair. "It won't happen, Hana. Let's get through today, huh?"

She nodded and they walked to the common room together, dodging boys as the bell sounded for the next lesson. Hana kept her eyes on the worn carpet as Logan said goodbye. He paused before walking across the bridge towards his classroom. "What?"

Hana shook her head. "Nothing."

Boys surged around them like a stream circumnavigating a landslide. "Liar." Logan tilted his head and blood dripped onto his sleeve.

"I love you, Logan Du Rose. Please never leave me?" Pain and fear back-lit her eyes as Hana's question tumbled free.

"I'm going nowhere, babe." Logan crushed her into his chest and kissed the top of her head. A tennis ball bounced perilously close and he shot the owner a warning look. Responding to his indefatigable authority, the boy retrieved his ball and moved away.

In the office, Sheila buzzed like an electric eel. Wired from the success of the previous night's event, she surged around issuing orders. "Photos, Hana?" she demanded, holding out her hand. "Did you get good ones? How many did you take?"

Hana groaned at the memory of the camera still sitting on the kitchen table amidst the morning's abandoned toast crumbs. "I'm sorry. I forgot to bring it." Her voice held tiredness, but Sheila huffed and puffed with annoyance. She turned her attention to Pete, sending him on countless retrieval errands and pecking at anyone who entered the student centre.

"Has anyone collected the extension cables from the hall?" she demanded, knowing they hadn't.

"You said you'd get them last night." Hana sank into her chair after a trip downstairs to reception and a long trek over to the gym to peel sticky tape off the sprung wooden floor. She sighed. "My feet hurt. The groundsman stood over me while I picked the tape off the floor. He sent a message for you but I can't repeat it."

Sheila winced. "It's still on the hall floor too." She brightened and patted her swinging bob. "You can peel it off now assembly is over. You can collect up the extension cables while you're down there?"

Hana swivelled in her chair and put her head on her arms as Sheila rushed from the room on an unnamed errand of some magnitude. "Pete?" she called, her voice muffled through her jumper sleeve.

"No," he replied and she heard the soft shuffle of his tracksuit as he bit into his pie.

"Please help me collect stuff up?" Hana groaned. "I feel like I'm going to die."

"Really?" His uncharacteristic concern made Hana squint at him over her arm.

"I don't feel great." Foreboding settled over her the moment Logan mentioned the possibility of arrest or death. It stuck with her, sapping her energy. His death, not hers. She sensed something badly wrong but couldn't work out when the focus changed to include him.

"If I help you, can you tell me something?" Pete swallowed and lowered his voice.

Hana sat up and gave a shallow nod. She worked out how much cash might still be jingling around her purse and figured it added up to at least a custard slice. "Yeah, sure. Can we start walking now though? Before you change your mind."

They slunk through the back door, Hana wielding carrier bags to transport the cables back to the office. As soon as they reached the bridge, Pete turned towards her, his eyes huge in his pale face. "Why did Logan put a dead Chinaman into the back of your car last night?"

Hana stopped dead, colour draining from her cheeks. "What?"

"I saw him." Pete looked around them to ensure privacy and then leaned closer. Hana caught a waft of his vapid breath and stopped inhaling until it passed.

"He didn't." She brushed off his accusation with stellar effort and picked up her step. "You got it wrong."

"You said you'd tell me." Pete's ugly face crinkled to gargoyle proportions. "Or I'm not helping you with the hall."

Hana shrugged, tamping down the panic in her breast. She wasn't sure which she feared most, Logan as murderer or Pete as chief witness for the prosecution. "Help me with the hall, Peter North, like you promised. Or I'll kill you and bury the body." She kept walking, hearing Pete's exhale of disgust.

"Now you sound like him!"

"Well, you witnessed the marriage." Hana picked up speed, hearing Pete's laboured breath as he broke into a run.

"I want to know what he was doing!"

"No, you really don't!" she retorted. "Shut up about it!"

"I need to know."

"So, ask Logan!" Hana snapped and Pete gave a sharp intake of breath. She stopped and spun around to face him. His expression stopped her making further threats.

"You know he's not talking to me." He gulped and Hana saw tears spring into his eyes. "Will you speak to him for me?"

"He won't tell you what he was doing, Pete. It'll make no difference."

"Not about that." He sounded pitiful, picking at a scab on his chin. "Will you talk to him about being friends again?"

Hana sighed and exhaustion shrouded her like a blanket. "You're not four years old, Pete! Talk to him yourself. I don't even know what this is about."

They reached the hall and retreated to separate corners, peeling sticky tape from the polished floor. Hana muttered to herself, doing an impression of Sheila for her own entertainment. "Yeah, of course it'll come off, Hana. It's only sticky tape." The seam of her leggings became part of her body as she crawled around the floor. Abandoned extension leads littered the edge of the room, shoved there by boys sitting down for assembly earlier. Kneeling up to wind another lead into the carrier bag, Hana jumped as Pete whispered behind her.

"Nice bum," he hissed.

"You're pushing my patience!" she snapped, flapping behind her with the next cable and trying to whip it against Pete's shins.

Still plugged in, it refused to conspire with her in revenge and stayed attached to the wall.

"I'm only saying!" Pete bit. "It's a compliment for a woman your age."

Hana gave the cable a tug and pitched over backwards as it pinged from the wall. A loud bang terrified her further. Pushing herself up like a skittle, her heart sank at the devastation. Chunks of plaster decorated the wooden floor and the facia board of the plug socket clung to the end of the cable. Wiring spewed from the hole in the wall.

Pete appeared from beneath a chair, edging towards the mess. He pointed a shaking finger at Hana. "I'm telling. You did that, not me."

Hana inhaled through her nose, feeling her blood pressure hike to near boiling point. She sucked in her chest and her eyes bulged. Then her leggings disappeared up her bum again and her whole world ended. "Aarrgghhh!" She yelled at the top of her voice and grappled behind her. Pete jumped back at the fury in her face. Hana made it onto all fours, her belly protruding from between her legs. "Get the groundsman!" she shouted at him. By the time her voice finished echoing around the cavernous hall, all that remained of Pete was his empty carrier bag and a pile of sticky tape.

Hana hauled herself onto a stack of chairs leaned against the wall. Her whole body ached for the comfort of her squashy dressing gown. She sighed and pulled her leggings out of her ass. The electrics spewed from the wall like a silent accusation and Hana closed her eyes to avoid looking at the mess. She concentrated on the deep breathing exercises the midwife taught her and groaned as the elastic waist of the leggings crawled down her swollen belly like a stealthy insect.

"Hana, I'm coming!" Sheila's screech entered the room before her frantic footsteps and Hana looked up in alarm. Her lips parted at the sight of her boss jogging in four-inch stilettos, a guilty looking Pete scurrying behind. "I'll call an ambulance,"

Sheila puffed, dragging her phone from her bra. Pete's eyes bugged in surprise as she released it from its comfy nest.

"I don't need an ambulance." Hana ran a hand over her face. "I just want to get naked."

Pete's jaw dropped as Christmas came early and his eyes glinted with sleazy pleasure. "Together, or just you?" he demanded, a peculiar hitch in his voice.

"Shut up, Pete!" the women chorused.

"You're not in labour?" Sheila demanded and Hana shook her head. "And you weren't electrocuted?"

"No." Hana sighed. "But I've had enough. I want to go home."

Relief crossed Sheila's face and she climbed onto the stack of red chairs. "I'm such an idiot," she breathed. "You shouldn't be here, not after all your hard work last night. I'm sorry, Hana." Sheila's voice wobbled. "I'll drive you home right now."

"Thanks." Hana slid down the chairs until her feet touched the floor. Sheila put out a hand to steady her before loading her venom onto Pete.

"Why did you make Hana crawl around the floor?" she demanded. "This is your fault too."

Pete swallowed and glanced across at Hana. "Logan doesn't have to know about this, does he?"

Hana exhaled, her mind playing tricks on her. The floor seemed to lurch away as she put one foot in front of the other. Pete tapped her on the shoulder. "Please, don't tell him."

"It's nobody's fault," Hana breathed, gritting her teeth as the leggings made another journey north. Sheila grabbed her good arm in a death grip and despatched Pete to fetch their handbags.

"Do you have a door key?" she asked, her eyes darting around with a nervous glimmer. She lowered her voice. "Or must I get some from Logan?"

"I brought my own." Hana bit her lower lip, knowing why. She half expected Odering to come for Logan and knew she couldn't rely on her son anymore.

Sheila brewed tea at Culver's Cottage while Hana discarded the offending leggings. Her phone rang in her bag as she slipped into her dressing gown and savoured its fluffiness. Her fingers fumbled the keys as Logan panicked from outside his English class. "Where are you?" he demanded. "What the hell happened?"

"Nothing." Hana sighed and slumped onto the bed. "I'm just tired. Tomorrow's another matter. When Larry Collins sees the state of that floor and the hole in the wall, he'll slam my head in the trophy cabinet."

"So, you didn't go into labour?" Logan heaved a sigh. "Bloody hell, Hana. The gossips in this place had you birthing triplets on the tennis courts."

"Sorry. I'm fine. Sheila drove me home. I need a hot bath and an early night."

"Yeah, me too." Logan's tiredness crossed the distance between them and Hana heard the defeat in his voice.

"Don't forget to sign into the police station before you drive home," she reminded him. "Don't stay late, Logan. We need to talk."

"Okay." He sounded so non-committal that Hana sighed and hung up.

Sheila stayed to drink her tea and then left, the camera clutched in her eager fingers. Hana took a sandwich into the bath but dropped off to sleep and drowned it. Swilling wet breadcrumbs off herself with the shower head, she pondered on Logan's curious change in emphasis. He seemed to think Laval no longer wanted her. The danger had somehow shifted to him without her noticing.

Her brain complained at the forced activity and sitting on the bed in her towel, sleep proved too tempting to resist. Logan arrived home to find her snoring on top of the covers. He slumped next to her fully clothed and didn't wake again until the early hours. Covering them both with the blankets, he drifted back to sleep.

Chapter 11

"I didn't know you trained as a hairdresser." Hana sat on a stool in the bathroom at Culver's Cottage with a towel around her shoulders. Amy snipped away behind her with sharp scissors.

"Yep. From school until my twenties. Then I joined the police force."

"Which do you prefer?" Hana watched Jas run around her feet with a dustpan and brush, trying to catch the hair before it fell to the floor. He giggled himself into a stupor and collapsed, his face alight with mischief.

"I'm not sure sometimes." Amy sighed. "Hairdressing is easier when you're a mother. More flexible." She paused and humour laced her voice. "I sometimes wish I had my scissors in the watch house."

Hana laughed and her hair swished across her shoulders. "I bet. Some of Bodie's stories make me wish he'd done something different."

Amy's exhale betrayed the awkwardness in her relationship with Bodie. "Has he said anything about me," she asked, sounding tentative and anxious. "Does he talk about me and Jas?"

Hana snorted and a steady throb of regret budded in her chest. "He doesn't talk to me at all, Amy. I haven't seen him since he dropped me here and we argued. He hasn't replied to my texts either."

"I never know what he's thinking." The scissors snipped away, as though possessing a life and intuition of their own. "I can't read him."

"You and me both."

"I can read him." Jas sat up, a finger raised. Hair dusted it and he'd created a pattern on the floorboards. He jabbed the hairy finger at Hana. "He loves you but he's scared because you love Poppa." Jab, jab at Amy. "And he loves you and wants to do kissin' but he's real scared of you."

"Why?" Amy demanded and her snipping stopped. Hana watched in the mirror as she put her hands on her hips.

"You're very scary, Mummy. Even I'm scared of you." His eyes bugged wide and he messed up his hairy sketchpad and began again.

"Well done, Hana." Amy combed through the longer layers and moved around to her fringe. "You raised a sooky baby. Congrats."

Hana gave her a wan smile and pondered on Jas' astute summary. Commitment wasn't Bodie's strongest suit and it baffled her. She thought she'd modelled a good example, but her allegiance to any man other than his father reached beyond her son's tolerance. Shutting down thoughts of Vik, Hana watched her reflection change shape.

Amy used two packets of dye on Hana's long hair. She mixed it up and spread it onto her head. "What colour is it?" Hana asked again and Amy jabbed her in the back.

"You'll see," she replied. "Stop asking."

"It's purple," Jas interjected, reaching for the box. Amy shrieked and made him jump. The box and discarded bottles clattered to the floor.

"It's permanent!" she barked at him. "I told you not to touch."

"See!" His dark brow furrowed into thunderous lines and he put his hands on his hips. "I did all that sweeping up and you just treat me like this." Hana turned her face away from his indignation and forced the laugh back into her chest. He sounded like his mother. "This is why you're a scary mummy!" His tiny finger prodded in her direction and Amy pointed towards the door.

"Thank you for your help. Please leave me to finish the messy bit."

He reverted back to his childlike state in the blink of an eye. Raising his thumb and finger to accentuate his point, his face became pleading. "One little bit," he begged, pointing at the brush. "Let me paint the teeniest tiniest bit of Hanny's head."

"No!" Amy replied and pointed to the door. "Find Logan."

Jas stomped from the bathroom and Amy sighed. "See what I'm up against?" Her eyes appealed to Hana's reflection for wisdom and relief.

"I'm sorry, but he's the image of his father." Hana bit her lip. "He thought he could do everything and never respected the word no. One time, he cut Izzie's fringe with the kitchen scissors. He left it so short, it stuck out at right angles from her face. She looked like a daisy." Hana gazed down at the floorboards as the memories flooded back. "Vik blamed me."

"Why?"

Their eyes met in the mirror and Hana's tongue moistened her lower lip. She swallowed. "Because he could."

Amy leaned closer. "Was Bodie's father violent?"

Hana looked away and shook her head. The sound of her heartbeat raced in her ear drums. "No." She swallowed. "Just a strong personality. Life didn't turn out how he expected."

Amy cocked her head. The gate alarm sounded from the lobby and subverted her next question. Hana tensed. "Someone's here!" she hissed. Her eyes widened and she whipped around on the stool. Hair dye adorned her head and Amy jerked the brush sideways to avoid coating Hana's cheek.

"It's okay," she soothed, her eyes narrowing in concern at Hana's distress. "I'll take care of it."

Hana breathed out through pursed lips and flapped her hand in front of her face. Blood surged into her stomach and the baby grew fractious.

"I'll get it!" Jas yelled from the lobby and his feet pattered across the floor.

"No!" Hana shot to her feet. Her eyes implored Amy to intervene. "Don't let him open the door!"

"I'm back," Logan called and Hana's breath heaved with the adrenaline rush. "I picked up a movie for Jas and heaps of bad food."

"Fantastic!" Amy shouted through the door, not sounding as though she meant it. "When did you leave?"

Logan's voice sounded muffled through the wooden door. "Twenty minutes ago. I did shout, but you were making heaps of noise."

Hana sat back down and waited for the blood to stop pounding into her chest like a jack hammer. Amy covered for her. "Okay, thanks."

"Hanny's getting blue hair with yellow spots." Jas feet thudded against the floorboards as he hopped up and down.

The women heard Logan snort. "I hope not. My mother will hate it."

"Does that mean you might like it?" Amy called.

"No!" Logan replied. "If you turn my wife blue, I'll turn your son green." They heard the rustle of food packets. "And I'll time it so he pukes on the way home."

"Whatever!" Amy laughed and screwed up her face. Her brow knitted at Hana's bowed head and the way she patted her chest as though struggling to breathe. "It's okay," she whispered. "You said Logan saw Laval's men off."

Hana nodded and caught sight of her grey complexion in the mirror. "He'll get more men. He wants the box and he's gone to long lengths to get it."

Amy looked at the bottle of hair dye in her hand and her resolve failed. Her lips parted to admit she'd made a terrible mistake and then closed again. Hana's fingers shook as she dragged them across her face. "What is it, Hana?"

Hana whipped around on the stool, her eyes wide and her irises an ethereal green in the sunlight from the window. "Something's changed," she whispered. "And I don't know what." Amy crouched next to her to listen, her body rigid and alert. "Logan said something so innocuous I almost missed it." She swallowed. "I think it's become personal. Taking Laval's men out of the equation put the spotlight on him. He thinks he's in danger."

"What kind of danger?" Amy whispered. "And how serious?"

Hana's face paled and she gnawed on the inside of her cheek. "He made Maihi witness his signature yesterday and acted real odd when I walked in on them."

"What was it?" Amy leaned closer.

"Maihi said it was his last will and testament," Hana breathed and her eyes filled with tears. "It's not over, Amy. He thinks Laval's going to kill him."

The women stayed in the bathroom for an hour and a half, spreading the dye, waiting for it to work and then washing it off. Amy tried to allay Hana's fears without success. As the subject caused her so much anxiety, she dropped it, powerlessness forcing lines into her forehead.

Hana saw the mahogany-red dye flow into the bath as she bent over for Amy to run water through her cascading curls. She resigned herself to going back to square one. The little shower attachment stretched to its limit as Amy leaned over Hana, shampooing and washing until the water ran clear. Then she reached for a bottle of ordinary hair conditioner and squirted some into her hand. She spread it through Hana's hair, concentrating on the ends. "Style it like this after your shower each morning," she said, the timbre of her voice changing as she exerted herself. "Turn your head upside down and spread a tiny bit through the curls. Then let it dry and don't touch it. Your curls are gorgeous and you won't have time for straighteners when you're managing a newborn."

Hana leaned over the bath, her chin resting on the hard surface as Amy wrapped her hair into a towel and piled it on top of her head. "It's very red," she said, her voice sounding dull.

"Yep," Amy replied. "You're a redhead, Hana. Rock it."

Hana stared at her reflection in the mirror after Amy left her to clean up. The tumbling curls and vibrant red stripped years from her age, but left her feeling naked and exposed. Hiding became second nature and she doubted her readiness to step out into life again. She regarded the image of her eighteen-year-old self, a host to riotous curls which invited the sunlight to dance on their highlights. Reaching out, she touched the face framed beneath them, feeling the cool of the mirror against her finger. "I went into hiding that day," she whispered. "I'm not ready to come back out."

Hana took a long time to emerge from the bathroom. She smoothed out the anxiety on her face with makeup and cleaned every surface of the room to Logan's exacting standards. Her hair dried and hung down her back, taking on its rightful role as a defining characteristic of an ordinary, but beautiful woman. She stayed in the bathroom until Amy hauled her out. "Come and look at this," she demanded, her fingers straying to tease strands of Hana's fringe. She smiled with satisfaction at her creation, ownership in her gentle touch. "Look at the boys."

Hana halted in the lounge doorway. Logan and Jas lay on the sofa and faint sounds of snoring came from the bodies twisted together into a heap. The fire sent a wall of heat into the room and a rented copy of Lion King played to itself on the television. Logan held Jas to his chest in a protective wrap and the boy sucked his thumb, his little world at peace.

"Cute, hey?" Amy whispered as Hana watched. She nodded and ventured into the room, emotion rising into her chest. The terror of losing this man, who'd strolled into her life and provided a powerhouse of emotional fulfilment, sent her heart thudding in an unhealthy rhythm. She reached for the remote and turned the volume down as the wildebeest trampled Simba's father.

Jas rose from the sofa like a ghoul, his dark hair tousled in a halo over his head. "No Hanny. We was watching it!" he complained. His brow furrowed as he took in her altered appearance and he clambered over Logan to get to the floor. "Wow! Youse a red, poofy Hanny!"

Logan roused from his doze and Jas patted him on the forehead without taking his eyes off Hana. "Look Poppa-Logan. Wake up. Your Hanny's bootifool."

Amy smiled from the doorway and retreated to the kitchen. Logan sat up and rubbed his eyes, the fog of daytime slumber still clouding his vision. "I'm awake, I'm awake," he promised as Jas' fingers strayed near his eyes with his absent patting.

"About bloody time," Jas replied. His ears caught the clatter of crockery in the kitchen and the prospect of food distracted him.

"Hey, language dude," Logan rebuked, his words wasted as the child followed the leading of his stomach towards the kitchen.

Logan rose to his feet and studied Hana. He pulled his shirt down to meet his pants and chewed the corner of his lip. His scrutiny rendered her emotions to feelings of girlishness and she cringed before his attention. "You look unchanged," he breathed. "It's exactly how I remember you."

"I'm not sure I like it," Hana whispered, her voice wobbling. She clutched the remote in her hand as Simba mirrored her grief on screen. "I've spent years straightening it and adding blonde highlights. So much went wrong around that time. I changed everything to leave it behind."

"I know." He held her, smelling the freshness of her scent and revelling in the feel of her slender frame in his arms. Something clicked in his heart as the teenage boy caught up to the man he had become. Full circle, like a neat ending. Contentment flooded him and Logan savoured the moment, sensing it couldn't last and already regretting its loss. "I've loved you for so long," he breathed and closed his eyes against a tumult of conflicting emotions.

Chapter 12

They left work as soon as the last bell rang, driving straight up to the hotel in the mountains. "It feels good to leave the city," Logan sighed as they blasted up the highway.

"You already left the city," Hana replied, watching shades of spring scenery pass the windows at speed.

"Yeah, but Odering doesn't know that." Logan smiled with mischief in his eyes. "I meant legitimately leave."

Hana nodded. "I'm relieved Odering dropped the charges." She examined the skinny wrist of her right hand and flexed the weak muscles. The cast left her arm atrophied and she crinkled her nose in irritation. "Angus said Boris flew back to Germany." Her gaze tracked towards her husband as his body tensed. "Is that where you went yesterday? To say goodbye?"

Logan snorted. "No, Hana. The only goodbye he'd get from me is a kick in the head."

"Don't joke!" She pushed herself back in her seat. "It's not funny." Her fingers strayed to her wrist again and she rubbed at the pale, wasted skin.

Logan gritted his teeth and thought of ways to steer the conversation away from Boris or Odering. "The phone coverage at the hotel is limited." He tapped his top pocket. "I'm looking forward to it."

"Why?" Hana narrowed her brow and he realised his mistake. "Who don't you want to hear from?"

He sighed. "Nobody, Hana. I just want a break from Hamilton in general. It's a chance to spend time with you." He reached across and stroked her thigh, glancing at her writhing fingers. "Leave it alone. Do the exercises the physio gave you and moisturise your arm heaps. It'll be okay."

"My whole arm's weak," Hana grumbled. "I hate it."

"It comes right." Logan flexed his left bicep and waggled his fingers. "Work at it every day and it should get better by the time you're lifting the baby."

Hana peered at her arm and wrinkled her nose. "I hope so." She jerked her head towards the strapping on Logan's right hand. "The doctor wanted to x-ray that. He wasn't very happy with you."

"Don't care. I'm the customer. I know they're broken, so why pay for an x-ray just for him to look and confirm they're broken? I needed him to splint them together like I wanted and the school nurse refused."

"You're not meant to go to her every day," Hana replied. "She's not allowed to deal with breaks, especially on haemophiliacs. And you frightened the doctor. Poor man. I'm not coming with you again."

"I was authoritative. It's different."

"Well, he didn't appreciate it."

"Nope. But his strapping worked. It's heaps less painful." The vein in the side of Logan's neck throbbed, warning Hana to stop picking at a closed subject. She turned her face towards the window and remembered her commanding husband standing over the snippy doctor, oozing mana and power. He got what he wanted and left the medic in his wake. She leaned her head back and sighed, darts of pleasure shooting through her stomach. Authoritative. The word snaked through her brain, invoking a sense of safety and security. She clung to it and allowed herself to relax.

The weather improved across the borders of the Waikato. Sunshine sneaked from behind picturesque clouds and the hunting ground of Logan's youth opened up before them. At the turn towards Rangiriri, Logan stopped outside a restaurant off the beaten track. Hana peered through the window and curled her top lip back. "You brought an Englishwoman to a French eatery?" She raised an eyebrow.

Logan laughed and held her door open, offering his hand as she stepped off the side rail. "You married a Frenchman, babe. It's a bit late to reject my heritage now."

"I choose to see only your Māori half. I ignore the rest of you." Hana glared at him and he threw his head back and laughed.

"The best bits of me are French." He raised his eyebrows and she gave in to the smirk budding across her lips.

Logan squared his shoulders and led Hana into the restaurant, knowing he courted disaster. One wrong word and Hana would know everything. He chewed his bottom lip and worry vied with relief as his subconscious revealed its hand. He wanted her to find out.

A waitress seated them by a stained glass window and handed them menus. Within minutes, the owner appeared. Logan rose to greet him and the man clasped him in a bear hug. "Hey, cuzzie, kia ora!" They pressed noses and Hana's brow knitted at the familial similarities in their bearing. Dark and swarthy, the restaurant owner carried too much weight which obscured the distinctive Du Rose looks. But his grey eyes twinkled as he turned to greet her.

"This is Alex." Logan introduced him with a nudge to his cousin's ribs. "Alex, this is my wife, Hana."

"Ah, the elusive missus," Alex replied, drawing Hana into a fleshy embrace. Mischief lit up his face. "Apologies for not making your wedding. I wasn't invited."

Hana swallowed and looked towards Logan for help. His eyes darkened and she sensed his conflict. "I wasn't invited either." She qualified, "I didn't know about it."

Alex jerked backwards and his jaw dropped open. "Sheesh!" he exclaimed and jabbed Logan in the shoulder. "You dirty dog!" His eyes roved to Hana's full stomach and he waggled his eyebrows. "Youse been a busy boy."

Hana exhaled as she realised the inference. Another person painted a shotgun over their marriage. It seemed pointless to correct him and so she sank into her seat as heaviness filled her chest cavity.

Logan saw and narrowed his eyes. "Just here to sample the food, Alexandre," he said, using his cousin's full, French moniker.

Alex furrowed his brow and understood the overt signal. "Okay. Enjoy your dinner. It's on the house, bro'. You on your way home?"

"Yeah." Logan nodded. "We are." His grey eyes flashed in warning and Alex snorted.

"Too late, cuz. Them jungle drums is already beating."

Logan exhaled and took his seat, his shoulders slumping. Alex strolled across his restaurant and spoke to the head waiter.

"What did he mean?" Hana whispered and Logan shook his head.

"Nothing."

"He's not scared of you, is he?" She watched Alex glance back several times and appraise her with open curiosity.

"What are you talking about, wahine?"

"You know what I mean!" Hana watched the corners of Logan's lips curl upwards. "You're intimidating. And you know it. Everyone's scared of you."

"Except you." Logan sipped his water and smirked. "You never do as you're told. Isn't it meant to be love, honour and obey?"

"That goes both ways," Hana retorted. She smoothed her hand across the pretty green fabric covering her baby bump, conscious of Alex's interest from the other side of the room. Logan reached for her fingers across the table. "What's wrong? I thought you liked the dress."

"I love it, babe." Hana held onto him like a lifeline. "I can't believe you went back to the same shop and got three more dresses for me. You left the price tag on one of them though. I'm surprised your credit card didn't melt."

Logan snorted. "Who says it didn't?"

Hana glanced across at the staff converging near the serving hatch, heads bowed in conspiracy. "I just feel self-conscious." She leaned closer and dropped her voice to a whisper. "I should have listened to you months ago and let you tell your parents about the baby. Now I feel like an old person dressed as a pregnant woman." Hysteria bubbled beneath the surface of her panic and Hana bit her lip to stop it tumbling out. "I'm terrified of seeing their shock. They needed time to get used to the idea and watch me turn into an Easter egg. This feels horrible." She ran a shaking hand across her face and poked herself in the eye. "Bloody arm!" she hissed.

Logan reached across and took her chin in his fingers. "Hey! None of that!" he soothed. "I tell you every day how beautiful you are and it's what I think that counts. You carried another man's child when I fell in love with you. I love you even more now you're pregnant with my baby." He squeezed her fingers and narrowed his eyes. "Stop fretting, wahine. For once, do what your tāne says."

Hana nodded and forced a watery smile onto her lips. A niggling anxiety remained in the back of her mind, a tiny voice whispering doom and destruction. It plagued her even in her happiest moments, robbing her peace and promising she may never be safe, despite Logan's dismissal and assurances.

Logan stared at the menu as his first memory of Hana thrust itself forward. Despite the cruel and intervening years, he remembered the tears which coursed down her cheeks. He ached to step back through history and wipe them away, to snatch her up and offer rescue from the cold man at her side. In his memory, Vik ignored the distressed girl in the yellow dress, dabbing at cuts on his face with a dirty tissue.

"What shall I do?" Hana's comment dragged Logan into reality. She wiped her cheek with her wrist and her characteristic anxiety-tell sent a jolt through his heart. Had she guessed any of it?

"Sorry?"

"What can I eat?" She touched her belly. "I'm not allowed a lot of this. I don't speak French and I'm scared of ending up with frogs' legs or snails." An involuntary shiver shook her body and Logan released his held breath.

"Is that what you're worrying about?" he asked and she shrugged.

"Amongst other things."

Logan inhaled. "I'll order for you," he said and gave her a reassuring smile.

Alex hovered in his chef's whites and Hana ate with an audience. The younger staff stared holes in her and her confidence sank further. "I don't think I'm popular," she mused as a waitress took her plate towards the kitchen. The delicate potatoes sat like a wedge in her gut. Logan cocked his head in confusion and Hana qualified her statement. "The best looking Du Rose is off the market," she whispered and Logan laughed.

"Yeah, whatever."

"I'm serious!" Hana rolled her eyes. "Your fans are displeased. This is awkward."

"You don't want dessert?" He looked disappointed and Hana licked her lips, acid rising into her throat.

"Do you?"

Logan saw her distress and shook his head. "No. Let's get home before dark." He rose and waited for her to stand, holding her hand as they approached the exit. They circumnavigated tables which filled in rapid succession. "I'll settle up now," Logan said to the man working the bookings and cash register.

Alex appeared like a genie. "No, man!" he insisted. "You're my guest. Put your moni ukauka away, I insist. Go home to aunty. I bet she's dying to see you." He led them to the front door, grinning at Logan's narrowed grey eyes and sadistic glare. Hana followed, clinging to Logan's hand like a drowning woman. A drowning woman of Easter egg proportions.

Alex held the front door open for his major shareholder and walked outside, blinking against the striking colours of the setting sun on the mountains. "This yours?" He waved his arm at the Honda after looking around the car park. "Nice."

"It's Hana's." Logan made the distinction and held the door for her to get into the passenger seat.

"Nice one, bro'. See you around." Alex slapped him on the shoulder and turned back to his restaurant.

Logan tutted and shook his head. "You just couldn't help yourself, could you?"

Alex glanced at Hana's face through the passenger window. "Not me, man." His eyes sparkled before growing serious. His face hardened to the classic Du Rose angles. "Did you sort out your problem?"

Logan swallowed. "Yeah. Kind of." He shot a nervous glance towards the car and lowered his voice. "I sold my soul to the devil."

"Oh." Alex took a step back. "Doesn't sound good." He whispered something in Māori and Logan nodded. They parted with a last embrace and Alex watched them drive away. He dug his chubby fingers into the front pocket of his apron and shook his head.

Logan made the route through the mountains interesting, distracting Hana from her worries. He retold the whispered stories of his grandmother, pointing out landmarks as familiar to him as his own palm. "Do you understand what the tangata whenua is?" he asked, rounding a bend and beginning the descent into the valley.

"Are they the people of the land?" she replied, her fingers writhing in her lap. She trotted out a trite explanation and Logan sensed no understanding behind it.

"Yeah," he agreed. "But it's more than that. My family members have lived and died here. A newborn's placenta is buried on the land and when the adult dies, their body completes the circle. The concept is of belonging to a land or people." He silenced as his mind wandered to another time and place, collecting his uncle's ashes and fighting to return them home. His voice faltered. "When you're linked to the land, it calls to you." A hush settled over the car and Hana sensed the weight of the sentence. Her body tensed as she absorbed the underlying message.

"Does your mother know we're coming?" Her voice wobbled as she fought to change the subject. Miriam's unpredictable nature rose like a threat.

"I didn't tell her." Logan grimaced at the stupidity of eating at the restaurant. He let pride overrule common sense and Alex's smirk showed he recognised that fact. Maybe Miriam stepped outside for one of her constitutional walks and missed the revealing phone call.

"Where will we sleep if there isn't room?" Hana asked, pulling Logan from his private thoughts.

"My room's always free."

"What if it's not?" Hana persisted and Logan bit his lip, forcing irritation under control. She couldn't understand what she didn't know.

"It will be. It's my room." His words betrayed ownership and he opened the window to breathe in the fresh mountain air. He inhaled and glanced across at Hana as the whenua fortified him. "Do you miss England?" Air whooshed from his lungs as he grounded himself in the mountain. "I never asked you that."

Hana shrugged. "I miss the people." Her fingers linked and released, linked and released. "But they aren't there anymore. I never went home again so I've forgotten what it's like. People say it's changed and I think I wouldn't like what it's become." Her eyelashes fluttered. "I'm not good with change."

"I liked London." Logan leaned his elbow on the windowsill and drove one handed. "I found a world of opportunity for a Kiwi guy eager to learn."

"You taught there, didn't you?" Hana turned in her seat, interested in his history and unused to his candidness.

"Yeah. In a dirt poor inner city school."

"Why London?" She cocked her head as though striving for a thread of consciousness she couldn't reach.

Logan's brow furrowed and he turned to her in surprise. "For you, Hana. I searched for you."

She gulped and her lips opened and closed without sound. "But millions of people live in London. How could you hope to find me?"

Logan's nose wrinkled. "I figured I'd get lucky. I didn't." He reached out to clasp her fingers, switching his right hand onto the steering wheel. "I lived near the tube station where you got onto the train and watched for you all the time. I rode the train at weekends from one end to the other. Do you know how many redheads live in or visit London?" Hana shook her head. "My original plan was to go straight to a London university after school, but I couldn't scratch the money together in time. I tried."

Hana stroked his scarred fingers and found no words to describe her depth of emotion. She lifted his hand to her lips and pressed a kiss over his knuckles. Logan turned towards the steep downward road, following its twists and turns with confidence. He didn't remove his hand from Hana's grasp as she closed her eyes and rested it against her cheek. His mind filled with memories of a former life where he treaded water and watched his purpose trickle through his fingers. A love of mathematics led him to fill his evenings with night school classes. Maths degree papers became accounting qualifications and then stock market gambling. A few hundred sterling became a few thousand. Then millions. Losses acted as fuel, driving him to learn the market as well as the face of an old friend. Like legalised gambling, it invoked the same thrill and buzz. His pet stockbroker entertained him at posh restaurants before staggering home to his luxury penthouse in Kensington. After each meeting, Logan caught the underground train home to his grotty bedsit.

Logan Du Rose bounced money around the globe like a tennis ball around a court, sending it home to New Zealand where it awaited his return. Recession hit Britain hard and fast, stalking in like a thief during the night. Logan saw it coming, cashed in his assets and booked his ticket home. He left his foolish dreams of Hana on the tarmac at Heathrow Airport. The plane rose into the air and banked towards Dubai as his stockbroker flipped open his morning newspaper. The headlines hit him between the eyes as his greedy hedge fund trading colleagues detonated the global market from the inside. He ate his own words along with his cereal as he recalled his last conversation with Logan just a few months before. "You're an idiot," he'd said as his best client instructed him to sell everything. The grey eyed man had just smiled. Perfect teeth and a scar in his cheek which dimpled when he stretched it into a good natured grin.

"Whatever," he'd replied. "Just do it."

Hana moved and muttered something, starting Logan from his reverie. "What did you say?"

"I asked what you were thinking about." she replied. "You looked pensive."

Logan smiled and squeezed her hand. "Remembering when I saw you again for the first time," he lied. "All those years searching Britain and you were here in New Zealand."

Hana grimaced. "Grovelling on the floor of the car park looking for a lipstick. Nice."

"Stunning." Logan's grey eyes misted. "Bloody gorgeous." His eyelashes fluttered at the memory, recalling at will the sounds and smells of their first meeting. Her unexpected presence stunned him into silence. A spell consumed him, threatening to break if he so much as exhaled. The little voice in his head taunted him like all the other times. The little voice was wrong.

Hana pinched his thigh and Logan jumped. "If you tell our baby that your first view of me included my upturned ass, I'll hurt you."

Logan laughed. "Hey, sweetheart, that's the best view." He dodged another pinch and swerved the car. "Stop! You'll make me crash! It wasn't the first view. You sobbed through our first meeting and this bead of snot dangled from your left nostril." He flapped his fingers near his nose and Hana shrieked.

"Did not!"

Logan grinned. "I'll write a waiata and sing it to our children. I'll call it The Fortuitous Bogey."

Hana groaned and threw her head back against the seat. "Don't, Logan!" she begged. Her face clouded. "You said children." She released his hand and turned to face him and her fingers strayed to her bump. "I can't do this again, Logan. Do you understand?" She swallowed and anxiety flooded her face and revealed itself in the downward contour of her lips. Her voice dropped to a whisper. "I'm not through this pregnancy unscathed yet."

Logan shook his head and took a sharp right turn off the main track. He readied his next sentence as the Honda nosed through encroaching bush and scrabbled up the climb. At the top of a rise, he bounced over rock and loose soil to park on a flat outcrop. The valley opened before the windscreen, lush and secluded. Mountains crowded around the hotel at their feet like children admiring a kitten. Logan engaged the handbrake and switched off the engine. Darkness moved across the sky, chasing the setting sun as it snuggled into the earth. Hana watched as he left the vehicle, spinning in her seat to see where he'd gone. A small moan passed over her lips as she saw him walk towards the edge of the precipice and dig his hands into his pockets. His shoulders squared as though fighting a war she couldn't see.

The door clicked but didn't close as Hana left the vehicle. The hem of her dress fluttered in the light breeze and she hesitated to touch Logan's arm. He heard her approach but didn't face her as she stood next to him. His gaze appeared faraway and his sigh came from the soles of his tan cowboy boots.

"I'm sorry." Hana pursed her lips and swallowed down her fear. "I didn't mean to burst your bubble."

Logan turned to face her and ran a shaking hand through his dark hair. The fringe flipped forward over his eyes and rippled with the movement of his lashes. "You don't understand, Hana. Everything we have right now is more than enough. I want to stay trapped in this moment, you, me and our baby. If we come through this unscathed, I'll do whatever it takes to show my gratitude." He rubbed his eyes. "Maybe I'll go to church."

Hana smiled and slipped her hand through his crooked elbow. "Steady on, Logan. Is this you acknowledging God?"

Logan shrugged. "I dunno, Hana." He wrapped his arms around her and pulled her close, breathing in the essence of her and knowing it would never be enough. "I feel so powerless."

Hana winced and closed one eye as the child shifted in her womb, pressing a tiny hand through the tight skin. "We're nearly there," she whispered. "Almost home and dry."

"And you're doing great. One tamariki is more than enough for me, babe. We can build a legacy on that."

Hana nodded against his chest. "You'll have to. Promise you won't leave me?"

Logan cupped her cheeks in his hands and ran his thumbs along the delicate underside of her jaw. "I promise," he whispered. Pulling her onto the ground, he pressed his lips against hers, heating up the kiss as she gasped for air. His fingers moved to the hem of her dress and slid along her thigh.

"You are such a chancer," she giggled, pushing his hand away. "Where's your off button?"

"Same place as your mute button." He trailed his lips along her collar bone and resumed the gentle stroking against the elastic of her knickers. Hana inhaled with indignation and Logan stopped all further conversation, pausing the kiss as he dragged his tee shirt over his head. His eyes danced with risk and excitement and Hana conceded defeat even before he pushed the button of his jeans open. Her red hair danced in the last of the sunlight, shrouding her head like a fiery halo.

Chapter 13

They sat on the ridge overlooking the hotel until the sun slithered down behind them. Logan pulled Hana in close and kissed the side of her face. His fingers twisted a stray curl, fascinated by the red glow coaxed out by the dying sun. "I love it up here." His voice sounded husky and contented as he sighed and rested his chin against Hana's cheek.

"Mmnn," breathed Hana. "It's quite gorgeous." She sounded so English it made Logan smile.

"I'd like to come back one day. For good," he murmured. He felt her stiffen and bit his lip. Hana sensed the cry of his heart, hearing it call from deep inside him and reverberate in the sad depths of his sigh.

"What about Culver's Cottage?" she asked.

"I don't know." Logan shrugged. "I haven't thought that far ahead."

"Is the land pulling you?"

Logan jerked backward and his lips parted in surprise at Hana's astuteness. He considered his response with care before moving his head in a slow nod. "Yeah. For a long time now. I can ignore it while I'm in Hamilton, but it's grown stronger since our marriage."

"I get that." The fingers of her left hand played with the fabric of her skirt. "I feel this hard knot in my chest whenever I think about England." She turned to face him. "So, I stopped thinking about it."

Logan's brow furrowed. "You said you didn't miss it. I knew you lied."

"Not lied exactly." Hana scrounged for suitable words and then abandoned the quest. "Just confused, even after all this time."

Logan's answering nod gave her confidence. He understood and she sought to meet him half way. "I might like it here," she agreed. Then her expression clouded. "But I'd need space and privacy." Her gaze strayed to the hotel in the lea of the mountain range, a child's toy on a speckled green mat. She shivered at the awkward conversation ahead of her and her hand strayed to her stomach. Logan saw.

"We should go," he said and Hana gave a nervous swallow.

The breeze picked up and rustled the grass around them. Logan got to his feet and hauled Hana up next to him. She peered over the ridge and her eyes narrowed. "You're still not forgiven though," she announced, her voice barbed.

"I said I'm sorry!" Logan tamped down his laughter, but failed to dispel the lingering smirk.

"No you're not!" Hana bit. "You lost my knickers over the side of the cliff! I'm about to meet your mother commando! I'm pregnant, Logan. I'm supposed to have dignity."

Logan snorted and Hana stomped towards the car. "I want to find them. They might be on the road, down there." She jabbed a finger at the cliff.

"It's windy, babe. They're gone." He turned away to avoid her seeing his mirth. She noticed the shaking of his shoulders and stamped her foot.

"Get me some from the suitcase."

Logan fixed a blank expression on his face and stared at the rear door of the Honda. "You're kidding! The suitcase is under everything else you packed. I'm not getting that out and putting it back again. It's getting dark. Please Hana, let's drive down to the hotel and sort it out. Five minutes, that's all."

Hana grimaced and channelled disgust. Logan glanced at her long tan boots, biting his lip at the thought of the bare legs beneath her dress. He swallowed. "Can we stop talking about this now? Unless you want to come back here and lie down again."

"Please find my knickers?" Hana begged and Logan shook his head.

"No, I don't even want to think about them." He climbed into the driver's seat and paused. "They looked nice though. I loved that black lace. Do you have any more in your suitcase?"

"Logan! I owned three pairs that didn't roll down my stomach every time I sit. Now I have two."

"Sorry." Logan's lips turned down in an impression of apology. The knickers played on his mind way too much for a man about to walk into the dragon's den. "We'll sneak into the hotel and go straight upstairs, I promise."

"I'll go upstairs. By myself!" Hana narrowed her eyes at him and Logan smirked again.

The mountain road wound below them and Logan bounced the car over the rugged track. Washouts produced huge bites in the sides and he shook his head. "Nothing's permanent, is it?" he sighed. "As fast as I repair this road, nature steals it away from under me."

Hana's brow furrowed. "I haven't seen you with a shovel and a pile of grit," she commented. Logan's tongue poked over his lower lip.

"Figure of speech, wahine," he joked.

Hana pondered on his words, distracting herself with thoughts of her own life. She had learned the fragility of permanence to her cost. One dead husband proved enough for anyone. She reached across the car and touched Logan's thigh. His muscle felt taut and powerful through his jeans as his body shifted with the turns in the treacherous road. He glanced at her sideways. "Are you sure I can't help you with your underwear?" he said with a smirk.

The way Miriam flung herself down the stairs appeared suspicious. The Honda ground to a halt as she wrenched Logan's door open. "Son!" she wailed, tears in her eyes.

"Jungle drums," Logan hissed under his breath as Miriam wrapped herself around his neck. Hana tensed in her seat and felt herself withdraw. They pressed noses in a hongi and Hana's exclusion increased with their whispered Māori. She jumped as Miriam darted to her side of the car and wrapped her into an embrace. Her fingers strayed to caress Hana's bump and the child lurched within her. Unused to such familiarity, Hana faked acceptance and forced a cringing smile onto her lips.

"A grandbaby," Miriam whispered, pressing her fingers over her mouth as though fighting to suppress an avalanche of emotion. "For me."

Hana sought reassurance as she followed Miriam up the wide front steps. Glancing back at Logan, she saw him grab their bags from the car and hurry after them. An aura of pride clung to him as he buzzed beneath his mother's admiration. Ready laughter lines emerged in the corners of his eyes.

"Sit, sit!" Miriam insisted, pushing Hana into one of the comfy armchairs in the reception. The girl behind the main desk lifted her chin to peer at the spectacle whilst speaking to someone on the phone. Hana swallowed down her anxiety and felt it lodge in her chest. The lack of underwear beneath her dress seemed to translate into visible nakedness. Mid-forties and pregnant; she'd become the family freak show.

Miriam fussed and hovered, her eyes barely leaving Hana's stomach as she rambled and fluttered her fingers. Logan's grey eyes sparked with understanding and he sat on the arm of Hana's chair, screening her from his mother's intensity. "I'd love some coffee, Mum. I'll take Hana and the luggage up to my room and we'll talk in the kitchen in a while."

Miriam looked like she might insist on accompanying them and Hana's toes curled high in her boots. The old lady hovered on the edge of the rug, wringing her hands as though concerned Logan and his unborn child might disappear in a misty haze. Trapped between the women, Logan struggled to keep a balance between his wife's sensibility and his mother's insanity. "Are you only here for tonight?" she asked, her eyes narrowing. "You never stay anymore, son."

Logan rose and drew his mother into his chest. "We'll stay for a few days, Ma. Don't worry."

Hana gritted her teeth and kept the biting comment to herself. The war for possession of Logan sapped her energy and left her ragged. She concentrated on Miriam's positive reaction, comparing it to her father's rage and the disappointment of Vik's family twenty-six years earlier. Deep in her soul, she ached for her own mother and thoughts of Judith's death revived an old, buried grief. She held Miriam responsible for filling the void, yet the task proved outside the woman's mental or emotional scope. Hana watched Logan soothe his mother and send her off towards the kitchen and tried not to dwell. She was the victim of her own dreams and expectations and it soured her mood. The peace and hope of earlier dissipated like an ethereal smoke. Logan dug his hands in his pockets and squared his shoulders, watching his mother walk down the long corridor to the kitchen. Hana saw the slight shake of his head.

"Right, Mrs Du Rose." He turned to her and his grey eyes glinted with anticipation. "Best get you upstairs and sorted out."

Hana opened her mouth and then closed it again. Experience dictated she should make the most of time with Logan here. Miriam's influence stretched from the kitchen, already clawing him to her bosom. Hana shot him a sideways look and shook her head. "Not appropriate, Du Rose," she murmured. He smirked in reply.

Hana turned towards the main staircase and Logan shook his head and tugged on her arm. "This way," he said. Hefting both bags into one hand, he led her through a narrow corridor marked with a sign declaring it private. He pulled an ornate rope aside for her to pass through and then went ahead.

"Where are we going?" Hana demanded, trotting behind him. Her feet pattered against the quarry tiled floor. "I don't know this wing of the house."

"I'm taking you upstairs," he replied over his shoulder. "This is the quick way."

Dark rimu panelling betrayed the age of the house as Hana followed her husband into its bowels. "What's this part used for?" she asked, walking close to his heels.

"It's the old servants' wing," Logan answered over his shoulder. "This way." A sharp turn took them to the foot of a staircase which rose above them in a spiral. Light filtered from the top and dust motes danced in the curve of the void. "Just watch your footing." Logan glanced down at her boots as though to reinforce his instruction. "Would you rather go first?"

Hana shook her head and moved behind him, watching as he put his foot on the first step. His sole pressed into the worn wood where his ancestors climbed before him. Generation after generation of Du Roses took the back stairs to their lofty heights and this Du Rose son followed. Something about it seemed poignant, but the thought drifted away before Hana could grasp it.

Logan waited for her as the steps arced left and she climbed, sensing the feet of people long gone. Their influence pressed in on her, so she appeared at the top with a heady breathlessness making her pant. Logan put the bags on the floor and reached for her. "Sorry. It misses out the first floor and brings us straight up here. Is it too steep?"

"No." Hana's emphatic shake of the head felt overdone. "It's quirky. There's so much to learn about this house."

Logan smiled. "We can take the lift back down." He picked up the bags and strode towards his childhood bedroom, a spring in his step and a sense of homecoming about the tilt of his head.

"Great," Hana sighed to herself and followed.

In the bedroom she removed her boots and stretched out on the bed. Logan surveyed his kingdom through the wide windows and glanced back at her. "She's expecting us downstairs," he said, quirking an eyebrow.

Hana's face broke into a smile and she shook her head. "You're terrible," she whispered.

"What?" His feigned innocence dragged a chuckle from her and he used the advantage, bumping down next to her and shaking the mattress. He shifted to trap her, fixing a long leg across hers. "You make me crazy," he whispered, smoothing her fringe from her eyes. Soft kisses along her neck drew a moan from her lips. When his fingers strayed beneath the dress and rose higher, she let out a protest.

"Don't, Logan! Your mother will come searching for her favourite son and the illusion of your perfection will tarnish."

Logan snorted. "I'm certain she's seen worse."

Hana pushed him off and rolled away. "Charming. I don't wish to sleep in a bed you've entertained in."

"I haven't." He sounded hurt but Hana kept walking towards the bathroom. "I meant my horny brother."

Hana locked herself in the bathroom with her overnight bag, freshening up and replacing her underwear. A lack of towels hindered her. She peered at herself in the mirror and squared her shoulders against the coming storm. Miriam's reaction to the baby seemed odd, acknowledging it in a way that obscured Tama. She behaved like Hana carried her first grandchild. "No wonder he's messed up," she sighed, reaching for her lipstick.

"I'm not messed up." Logan's hands snaked around her waist and he rested his chin on her shoulder.

"Those who listen at doors will never hear good about themselves," Hana growled, pursing her lips to stain them with matte lipstick the colour of mahogany wood.

"I didn't listen at the door." Logan pressed his face into her hair, his body moving with hers as she reached for her makeup bag. "I stood behind you."

Hana turned in the small space between his arms and looked up at him. "When I lock the bathroom door, I want privacy," she said, warning in her eyes.

Logan's lips curved upwards on one side. "And when I unlock it, I want company."

Hana ducked under his arm and wagged her finger over her shoulder. "That will get old," she warned. "And one day, I'll take exception."

Hana pushed her feet into slippers to protect her against the cold, tiled floor downstairs and Logan slipped a hand up her dress and touched the red, lacy briefs with tentative fingers. He groaned. "You're such a tease," he complained.

Hana laughed and slipped through the door onto the landing, waiting as he closed it behind him. "I never imagined you'd throw my knickers over a cliff," she retorted. "Keep your hands off this pair."

A throat cleared behind her and a maid picked up the towel she'd dropped. Colour flushed into Hana's cheeks as a riot of blotchy red. A laundry cart sat outside their room and the woman held out a stack of towels. "Sorry," she stammered. "Mrs Du Rose sent these."

"Thanks." Logan took the bundle and pressed numbers into the keypad, waiting for the door to click before he pushed into the room. Hana gnawed on the inside of her lip, studying the awe in the woman's face and adding jealousy to her embarrassment. Both women watched his tall, angular body emerge and he blinked at them both in surprise. A dark curl bounced against his eyelashes.

"What?" he demanded and the maid scurried away.

He raised his eyes at Hana and she sighed and shook her head. "Nothing, Logan." With a nonchalant shrug, he linked his fingers through hers and led her towards the lift.

Miriam paced the industrial kitchen from end to end. She looked at the clock, barked orders to the kitchen staff and wrung her hands. Anticipation oozed from every pore and the women bunched at one end of the room to avoid her. They sent nervous, covert glances her way.

When the door opened and Logan walked in, the younger girls forgot Miriam and concentrated on him. One jabbed another in the ribs and they feasted their eyes. Miriam caught them staring and flapped a hand in their direction, barking an instruction in Māori. Chastened, they looked away. Hana sensed the leaden atmosphere as she stepped across the threshold and her heart sank. All eyes turned to her and her burgeoning stomach and she tensed.

"Sit, sit!" Miriam ordered, tugging her arm and pushing her into a kitchen chair. "You won't want coffee. I'll fetch tea." She sprang to the other side of the large room, shouldering staff aside as she laid out china cups and saucers. "Get on with your work!" she snapped at a woman peeling potatoes and Hana cringed.

She sipped her tea, feeling like a circus freak. Dragging her chair under the table to shield her bump from overt scrutiny seemed to hike the curiosity further. Hana concentrated on breathing and sipping and formulating valid excuses to escape the intensity of the room's occupants. Logan seemed distracted, missing her cues of distress as his eyes followed his mother's frantic movements. The women left together, armed with cutlery for the dining room. As the door closed behind them, Logan stood and strode towards a cupboard near the sink. Reaching inside, his fingers withdrew a metal box and he opened the lid and peered inside. Hana watched his shoulders slump.

He caught Miriam's arm as she bustled past with a plate of biscuits and Hana watched a chocolate covered slab smash on the tiles. "Mum!" he said, his tone betraying the tension in his body. "How long?"

Miriam shrugged off his grip and dumped the plate on the counter. She searched in another cupboard for a dustpan and brush and cleared up the mess. Hana shrank lower in her chair and wished she could teleport herself back to the safety of the bedroom. Logan's fingers rustled through the box's contents and she held her breath. He pulled out a white blister pack and held it up, shaking it back and forth in his fingers. "You must take these," he said, his voice sounding urgent. "This is over a month's worth of tablets. How long, Mum?"

"I don't need them." Miriam jutted her chin upwards. "They make me groggy and confused. I want to be myself, Logan."

Hana observed the rigidity of her husband's back and heard him grinding his teeth. She tensed and pushed her cup away, her gaze already flicking towards the door. Logan took a step forward and raised the blister pack in Miriam's face. "Take the pills, Mum. Take them or I walk away for good. I can't keep doing this. Do you understand, Mum? I'm over it. It's not a game."

Hana pushed her chair back with deliberate slowness, desperate for escape. The rawness of Logan's emotion and the private nature of the exchange filled her with discomfort. The chair squeaked against the tiles and Hana ceased her backward movement as Miriam looked across at her. "You won't take my mokopuna away," she said, warning in her voice.

Logan leaned into her face. "She will if you don't take your pills."

Hana swallowed and her eyes widened. "Please don't make me part of this," she hissed. "It's nothing to do with me or our baby." The chair scraped back with force and she stood.

"No!" Panic crossed Miriam's face and she raised her hands as though in self-defence. "Don't go. Please don't take him away from me." The wildness in her eyes seemed dark and foreboding and Hana froze, protecting her child with a cupped hand. "I'll do it. I'll take them."

Hana opened her mouth in protest. "You can't blackmail someone to take medication, Logan," she said, her brow furrowing. "It's her choice."

"I'll do it, I'll do it," Miriam begged, snatching the pack and popping open blisters. White tablets skittered across the tiled floor before she pushed one into her mouth and swallowed.

Logan shook his head and defeat showed in his darkening eyes. "I can't keep doing this," he said, his tone sad. "I just can't."

"I'm sorry, I'm sorry." Miriam clutched his sleeve and gave his arm a shake. "I won't do it again."

Hana inhaled and Logan darted a warning glance in her direction. The vehemence in his eyes silenced her. He pulled his wallet from his trouser pocket and Hana watched as he gave his mother the smallest glimpse of something inside. Miriam's eyes widened and she seized another tablet. "Later." Logan pulled it from her palm and threw it in the sink. "Take another one later. You can't overdose, Mum. That's going from one extreme to the other."

Miriam cupped her hand beneath Logan's wallet and Hana bit her lower lip. The woman looked pitiful and naked, an expression of desperation like a recovering addict facing their drug of choice. Logan's fingers shook as he withdrew the baby scan photo and placed it into his mother's palm.

Her hand closed around it as though it might break. She stared at the image and a gnarled finger stroked the glossy surface. "A boy," she breathed. "I hope it's a boy. He'll look just like you."

Hana cringed and closed her eyes. Sickness roiled in her gullet and she yearned for escape. Her stupid idea to come to the hotel backfired in her face and she wished for the peace and safety of Culver's Cottage.

Boot soles clattered outside the door and it opened with a creak. Alfred's tousled head pushed into the gap. "Toby said you came." He ventured inside, horse hair coating his lower legs. Mud speckled across the tiles behind him and he approached Miriam with care, his eyes never leaving Logan's face. "You got my message?"

"That's not why we're here." Logan pointed towards Hana and Alfred's eyes widened at the sight of her stomach. Hana watched him swallow and a dark shadow passed across his expression. Gone as quickly as it arrived, he grinned, banishing it.

"Congratulations, kōtiro," he whispered. His gaze flicked from her stomach to her face and back again. "We'd given up."

Hana sank into her chair and fixed a wooden smile on her face as Alfred wrapped his arms around her and kissed her temple. She accepted his enthusiasm and allowed it to distract her, perplexed by the scudding darkness she knew she'd seen. The moment felt unreal and she stopped trying to rationalise it. Thoughts of Caroline tortured her. Perhaps they knew of her claims and already planned to shower their love on that child instead. Hana bound herself into a protective bubble and worked hard to sustain the remnants of her fragile confidence. Around her, the family celebrated and she relegated her role to surrogate host.

"Drink your tea." Logan extracted himself from his parents' bubbling chatter and reached out to touch the cup. "Oh, it's cold." He snagged it with a clatter and ditched the contents in the sink. Then he poured her another.

"I'm not thirsty." Hana's words tumbled free and his brows knitted.

"Sorry about this," he breathed and licked his lips. Hana sensed his embarrassment at the spectacle and she shook her head.

"I'm just tired," she lied.

"Okay." Logan glanced back at his father as Alfred leaned against the kitchen counter. The women swarmed back with empty cutlery trays and the room grew busy. "One second," Logan promised and lifted his index finger.

Hana watched him stride to his father and lean down. Whatever he said in Alfred's ear made the old man's complexion pale. Alfred swallowed and nodded and Logan squeezed his shoulder.

Miriam returned to her role of ordering the women around, dropping into it with a snap. She placed the baby photo in her apron pocket like a marsupial resettling its roo. Clapping her hands together, she sounded businesslike and clipped. "Right. Party of forty is due in half an hour."

Logan nodded to Alfred and jerked his head towards the door. "We'll get out of the way," he said.

"Do you need some help?" asked Hana, hating herself for feeling the need to offer. The women tittered and Miriam shook her head.

"Maybe one day," she answered, reducing Hana to a child offering to wash knives. "You get your rest today." She patted her own stomach and Hana seized her cue to rise. The exit seemed to hold a magical allure as she strode towards it with gladness.

In the corridor, she stopped and leaned her spine against the wall. Her heart pounded and she rested a palm against her breastbone.

"I'm sorry," Logan said, his tone dull. "I should have guessed she'd stopped the medication." He exhaled and shook his head.

"It's okay." Hana pushed herself into a walk, heading away from the bustle of the kitchen. "It explains a lot."

Logan took her exploring, aiming to banish the strange heaviness which hung over them. He showed her passageways and rooms she hadn't known existed. "My kuia loved this room," he said, pushing open a door. "She let me light the fire here and told me stories. We keep this wing of the house for the family."

Hana walked into the room first, its homeliness wrapping around her like an embrace. Old fashioned leather sofas sat at angles in the wide space, crowded around an open fire. Ash decorated the grate as though the occupants sat there recently. "My parents use this room as a lounge when they finish work," Logan said, his fingers caressing the back of a worn sofa. "We used it as a family room after kuia died, but it was her bedroom before that." His eyes strayed to a battle scene above the fireplace. Half naked Māori warriors battled English soldiers, their te rākau bats futile against guns. Despite the awfulness of the depiction, it held a grace which contrasted the sense of futility.

"It's nice." The words sounded pathetic and Hana sank onto one of the sofas. Exhaustion beat her back against the cushions. "Let's stay here for a while."

Logan set to work on the grate. He raked through the ash with brass tools and scooped it into a bucket. Then he built a fire made of newspaper, delicate sticks and logs from a basket on the hearth. Hana watched his steady movements, their familiarity a comforting reminder of home. "Want some help?" she asked, the insincerity of the offer highlighted by her kicking off her slippers and drawing her legs onto the sofa.

"No." Logan glanced sideways and snorted. "I've given up trying to teach the city girl to light fires."

Hana pouted. "I can't get the hang of it. And it's easier to wear a coat over my dressing gown." She yawned and he laughed.

"So I've noticed."

"Vik let Bodie light the brazier on his ninth birthday. How old were you when you made your first fire?"

Hana watched Logan's body tense at the mention of her former husband. She wondered if it would ever change. "Five," he grunted, poking kindling into fiery orange gaps. "Outdoor fires are harder for a kid, but Jack taught me. Once I grasped the rudimentary principles, I stoked the family room and kitchen fires every morning. The kitchen fire heated all the water for the house. If I didn't get it right, I got into trouble."

Hana pressed her head against the arm of the sofa and closed her eyes, imagining a younger Logan bowed down by responsibility. His face drifted across her inner vision, fourteen and already care worn and wary. "It sounds like a hard life," she mused.

"Yes and no." Logan sat back to admire his handiwork. The fire crackled and blazed and he waited until sure it wouldn't flicker out. He knelt in front of it like he did at home, hands resting on his thighs and the orange light dancing in his irises.

"Is it depression?" Hana asked, her voice soft. "Your mother's condition."

Logan nodded. "Bi polar disease. Ever since I remember." He sounded sad. "She's manic but I got busy and didn't see the signs soon enough." He bit the inside of his lip and then stopped himself. Pushing upright, he inspected his hands and satisfied, gave them a wipe along the front of his jeans. "Move over," he said, waiting while Hana sat up before sitting next to her. He patted his stomach and she lay back down. He lifted his feet and planted the heels of his cowboy boots in the well-worn grooves of an oak chest used as a coffee table.

They sat in silence while an antique clock on the mantelpiece marked time in soft ticks and clunks. Peace surrounded them and Hana drifted in and out of sleep. Darkness clothed the hotel and stretched its tendrils outwards from the corners of the room, vying with the yellow glow of a lamp. Logan's fingers toyed with a long red curl and his body moulded itself into a perfect pillow. "Let's stay here forever," Hana sighed, closing her eyes again. "I'm so comfy."

She woke an hour later, hot and disoriented. A cushion replaced Logan's perfect abdominal muscles and Hana found herself stuck in the depression between the seats. Her neck ached and her cheek felt wet. The sofa she admired so much kept hold of her as she tried to rise, sucking her into its folds like an over enthusiastic aunt. "Logan?" She spoke his name into the empty room, fear prickling its way up the back of her neck when he didn't answer.

Hana waited, imagining he'd stepped out for a moment and would return soon. When he didn't, she grew anxious and contemplated finding her way upstairs to their room. She doubted she'd locate the spiral staircase without his direction, but if she kept walking guessed she'd discover some recognisable landmark. As she opened the door, cold air rushed in as though waiting for admittance. The corridor outside looked gloomy and foreboding in the light from the room's single lamp.

Hana wrapped her arms around herself and stepped over the threshold, her ears straining for the sound of other human life. She took a step forward and then another, peering into the darkness and deciding on a direction. Remembering how they turned right into the room, she went left, hoping to end up back where they started.

After five tentative paces, Hana heard the door click behind her and all light disappeared. She whirled around and her thigh hit a dresser, disorienting her further. Her seeking fingers found a wall with peeling flock wallpaper and the edge of a hard surface. An ornament rocked and she stepped back, waiting for a crash which didn't come.

With her arms held out either side of her, Hana crept along the passage. She contemplated screaming into the darkness but her imagination ran riot, producing scenes of chaos and embarrassment. "I can do this," she whispered into the blackness. "You're being ridiculous." Her hands stroked the wall to her right, searching for a light switch at chest height. Her thighs bumped against solid tables and antique chairs which lined the corridor, but no switch passed beneath her fingers. Doors came and went and Hana tried not to panic as each handle resisted her. Locked. Every one. After a few minutes she turned a corner, clattering with another surface and hearing a heavy book fall over with a muffled whump. A streak of light glowed from beneath double doors ahead.

Hana picked up speed, rehearsing the awkward conversation with a stranger as she explained her presence and asked for directions. Her fingers contacted a knobbly switch located next to the architrave around the doors and she hesitated. The possibility of setting off a fire alarm filled her with horror. A flush rose to her cheeks and warmed her. Instead, she ran her fingers down the crack between the doors and felt for a handle. "Knock first," she admonished herself and raised her knuckles.

"You need to take care of it," a male voice said and she halted, her hand raised.

"Can't you just speak to him?" another man implored and Hana heard a snort of derision.

"I'm done talking. I got a brandy bottle thrown at my head last time."

"There are things you don't understand." Hana heard a chair scrape against wooden boards and her eyes widened. The desire to hide overtook the need to find her way out.

"I'm liquidating my assets," Logan said. "Everything's changing. For what it's worth, I'm sorry. It's nothing personal."

Hana heard the other man's voice change, becoming beseeching, like a low whine. She didn't hear what he said.

"Circle Line is not a lolly jar!" Logan snapped. "I owe you nothing!"

Hana heard more movement inside and looked around her in panic. The occupants walked towards the door and she spun around to the right. With her arms held out in front of her, she scurried away, falling over an armchair and occasional table. Her blindness sent her at an ill-advised tangent towards the far wall like a pinball and she bounced off and kept going. Another right turn took her towards light and she picked up speed as her pupils adjusted.

"There you are." Miriam met her in the corridor outside the kitchen, narrowing her eyes at Hana's flustered expression. "You want some kai?" She placed gnarled fingers over Hana's wrist and tugged.

"Dinner? Yes please." Hana tried to control the trembling of her hands, knowing Miriam sensed it through the contact. She jerked her head back the way she'd come. "I fell asleep in a lounge and Logan left me. I got lost."

Miriam accepted her gushing explanation with a nod. "This place is a maze, but it's home." She smiled and gave Hana's wrist a gentle shake. "You'll get used to it once you're here full time."

Hana's jaw dropped open in surprise and Miriam shuttered her emotions in an expression reminiscent of Logan. The same portcullis crashed down over her soul. "What do you mean?" Hana asked in a hushed voice and Miriam tightened her lips.

"Logan's in a meeting," she said, ignoring Hana's question. "He won't take long."

Hana followed her mother-in-law into the bright kitchen, blinded by the glare which rebounded off the stainless steel surfaces. A mystery nagged at her brain as she sank into a kitchen chair and stared at the macaroni cheese piled into a dish before her. "Circle Line," she mouthed, making links and connections as she pushed her fork into the melting cheese.

"What?" Miriam's brows knitted as she dumped a teapot in front of Hana. "Don't you like it?"

"Yes, it's lovely." Hana fixed a smile on her lips. "Very nice. We first met on the Circle Line in London, didn't we?"

Miriam's face clouded. "Yes. My brother died. Logan wouldn't get off the train." The sound of giggling distracted her as the man washing up pots in the huge sink dropped a heavy pan with a splash. Water soaked the front of his apron and the women laughed. Miriam turned back to her work like a commander to a rebellious army and Hana exhaled in relief.

Her brain did the final piece of maths and she watched her fork sink into the pasta without rescuing it. Circle Line. CircleLine Holdings Ltd. The letters she'd spent months returning belonged to her husband.

Chapter 14

The industrial dishwasher gurgled and the last of the huge pots clanked as the women stored them away. The chiller door opened and closed behind Hana with a hiss, disgorging plate-laden women with leftovers from the guests' meal. Miriam wiped down the steel counters around the sink and the staff filtered home.

Hana looked away as Miriam paid the women in crisp bank notes and tried to hide as much of the macaroni beneath her fork as she dared. The last member of staff nodded to Hana and her lips quirked upward in a smile. An older woman, her olive skin crinkled like a worn tissue, but her acknowledgement radiated genuine kindness. "I'll get off home," she said. Her gaze strayed to Hana's belly and she winked. "You're eating for two," she whispered, leaning closer and watching Miriam through the corner of her eye. She pointed at the plate. "Don't play with it, girly. She'll take offence."

"I know." Hana swallowed and picked up her fork again. "But I'm not hungry."

The woman flared her nostrils and hitched up a sagging breast. Her brown eyes fixed on Hana with concern. "I'll take it," she whispered. She scooped up the plate and slung the waste into a nearby dustbin, opening the dishwasher while it gurgled and dumping Hana's plate and cutlery inside. The lid closed with a clang.

"You can go, Leslie." Miriam's bark made Hana jump and her saviour shrugged and returned to Hana's side.

"Just finishin' up," she retorted. The dynamic between the two women bordered on antagonistic and Leslie squared her shoulders in defiance. "Talkin' to youse daughter."

"Well, don't!" Miriam snapped and her grey irises darkened. She moved to put herself between Leslie and Hana, forcing her body into the small gap. Hana leaned back in her seat, fearful that Miriam might end up on her knee. She pushed her hands forward to cover the baby just in case.

The door burst open and Alfred appeared like a tall, thin tornado. His dark wispy hair stood on end and his fluffy socks flapped empty at the toe without his boots. "I took my shoes off," he announced, looking pleased with himself. He stared at the women bunched around Hana and his brows knitted. "What's happening? Is she sick?"

"Yes!" Hana seized her moment and called from behind Miriam. "I don't feel well. I need to get out of here."

Leslie jumped back in guilt, giving Miriam room to turn and Hana found herself face to face with her mother-in-law. "Is it the baby?" she demanded and Hana shook her head.

"No, it's air. I just need some air."

"Move back Leslie!" Miriam snapped, almost falling over the larger woman as their feet tangled. Alfred's fingers closed around Leslie's wrist and he led her sideways to safety. Hana watched hysteria work its way across Miriam's face and her heart rate increased. The lie became truth as she desired freedom above anything else.

Strong hands rested on her shoulders and Logan's voice came from behind. "Sorry, babe. I got caught up in something." He kissed the top of her head and his fingers tightened as he felt her shake beneath him. "You okay?"

"Fine." Hana turned and shoved at his firm chest wall. "I want to go upstairs now. I'm tired."

Logan nodded and his eyes narrowed. He acknowledged Leslie with an upward jerk of his head. "Thanks for your help," he said, running his tongue over his lips. "We're good now."

"Bye Mr Logan." With a last look at Miriam, she let herself out of the kitchen.

Logan waited for the door to click behind her and then looked from one to the other. "What's going on?"

"Nothing!" Hana heard her own desperation and shoved his chest again. "Excuse me, please?" she implored.

Logan stepped aside and Hana almost plunged forward, catching herself on the table. She steadied herself on Alfred's arm and squeezed through the gap. Logan spoke behind her. "Did you take your second tablet, Mum?" he asked, his voice hard.

"I'll sort it. You get your wahine settled," Alfred muttered. Hana noticed Logan's raised eyebrow as he formed the silent question and his father nodded. "I'll do better, I promise."

Hana slipped from the room and let the door close behind her. She used the main staircase to the second floor and gained entry to the bedroom after three mistakes with the keypad. Logan appeared as she removed her slippers and flopped backward onto the bed. Her rounded stomach poked up like a small hill and she fought the need to find a comfier position.

"What was that about?" Logan demanded as he kicked off his boots. He laid them side by side like sentries and climbed onto the bed.

"No idea," Hana admitted. "The kitchen lady came to speak to me and your mother boxed me in. You could cut the atmosphere with a knife." She ran a hand over her belly and closed her eyes.

"Sorry." Logan's resignation suggested an old dilemma. "I sometimes think they're all tapped in the head."

Hana snorted. "You'd know, babe." Her brow furrowed. "They scared me. I didn't like it."

Logan exhaled and took a lock of her hair, twisting it in his fingers. "She needs the meds to kick in, then she'll come right," he said, sounding unsure.

Hana watched his fingers twirl the strand into a tight ringlet. "I took antidepressants after Vik died. I remember emerging from a dense fog one day and realising I could cope after all. It felt like coming up for air after drowning for a long while. I came off them and managed okay. Maybe she thinks she can cope."

Logan's brows moved together and he chewed the inside of his cheek. Hana watched from an upside down position and licked her lips. The desire to kiss him began as a flower opening in her gut and she gave in to it, clambering into his lap and holding his cheeks in her soft palms. Her first tentative kiss met with an avalanche of passion which left them both breathless. "What if there's someone next door?" Hana gasped as his strong fingers pulled her dress over her head.

"There isn't," his breath felt seductive on her skin. "I checked."

"Liar!" she squeaked as a tearing sound bit into the silence. "Logan, don't!" Her second pair of knickers spun over her head and landed on the floorboards next to the bed, one leg detached from the gusset.

Logan groaned into her neck. "Lace knickers on pregnant women. I never knew it looked so hot."

Later, Hana lay in the big double bed, her head across Logan's upper arm and chest. The portable television played to itself in the corner and he dozed beneath her. "One remaining pair of knickers for three days," she murmured. "Just my luck."

Logan made a small sound, halfway between a sigh and a purr. He turned his face sideways and blinked eyes filled with lust. Hana pulled herself free. "Don't even think it!" she threatened. "I can't risk my last pair."

"When you run out, will you stop wearing any?" His hands roved over her naked body, settling in the places he had grown to love. Hana pushed his questing fingers away.

"No, it means I start wearing yours."

Logan wrinkled his nose. "That does surprisingly little for me."

"Good!" she bit. "I'll try it." Leaning up on one elbow, she studied his face to gauge his reaction when she detonated the proverbial hand grenade she held. "What's CircleLine?" she demanded.

Logan behaved as though shot, jumping and then tensing. His face became blank and he balled his fists beneath the sheets. "That's a low blow." He pushed his tongue into his cheek while he looked for a suitable retort. "Wait until I'm vulnerable and then interrogate me."

Hana shook her head in disbelief. "Grow up, Logan. You knew I'd find out eventually. I'm not stupid."

He swallowed and she sensed his desire to run. His jaw worked in his cheek and his lips moved without sound. "Well played," he conceded after some effort. "I underestimated you."

Hana's chest tightened. Her bluff came back to bite her and she couldn't allow him to know how little she understood. She waited as Logan shifted in the bed and bought himself thinking time. The urge to pee sent warning signals to her brain and she sighed in defeat. "Fine!" she snapped, pushing the covers back. "I'm over the lies, Logan. I refuse to live like this anymore."

Hana used the bathroom and slipped a robe over her nakedness. Logan appeared as she washed her hands. He wrapped a towel around his waist and sat on the side of the bath. He looked wrong-footed and awkward. "The Circle Line is the London Underground train line I first met you on."

"I remember," she said. "Like I said, I'm not stupid. My crime is trusting you."

"Don't say that." A line appeared on Logan's forehead, bisecting his brows. "I want you to trust me."

"Yeah, you say that a lot but I don't see it going both ways." Hana sighed and poured water into a glass.

Logan swallowed. "I own a company called CircleLine Holdings Ltd. I named it after our first meeting."

Hana turned to face him, leaning her bum against the edge of the sink. "The letters which came to the house were for you."

Logan nodded. "I said I'd take care of it and I did."

Hana snorted. "You know that's not what you meant."

"It's not your understanding of what I meant."

"Don't split hairs." Hana forced the robe closed and tied the cloth tie. "What does the company do?"

Logan gritted his teeth and tried not to lose patience. She watched him struggle. Angus' face drifted into his inner vision and his employer's unanswered question hung in the air. 'Planning on going somewhere, Mr Du Rose?' He'd witnessed Logan's last will and testament with a dramatic flourish of his ink pen.

Logan held Hana's gaze, his grey eyes watching every movement for a reaction. "It was an investment company I started years ago."

"Was?" Hana cocked her head. "You're winding it up?"

Logan nodded. "It's equity rich, but cash poor. I want rid of it and it's difficult to unravel at speed. The money is more use to me now in my hand."

"But someone owes you?" Hana watched the recoil in her husband's eyes. "I heard you Logan. I tried to find my way to the kitchen in the dark and heard you arguing."

He nodded and jerked his head sideways in concession to the truth. "I loaned money to Tama's grandfather and it backfired."

"Isn't Alfred his grandfather?"

"Yeah." Logan pushed himself upright and glanced back at the bed as though it might provide an escape. "But my uncle raised him so he earned the title. He used my cousin, Nev as the go-between. The bailiffs paid them a visit about two years ago and I lent them enough to buy some time. They made no repayments and Nev said they can't pay."

Hana groaned and rubbed her eyes. "Oh, Logan! Money and family don't mix. It never ends well."

Logan pursed his lips and stared at the skirting board. "This ending will be really bad, Hana. Not satisfied with taking two hundred grand from me, the old man conned my father out of my inheritance."

Hana stood up straighter. "That land on the mountain? You got upset about it when we went riding and I thought you didn't like me anymore."

Logan's expression shuttered and he shook his head. "Right moment but wrong conclusion. You did nothing wrong, but I didn't know he'd started developing the land. Yeah, it hit me hard."

Hana shrugged. "What can you do? Did you draw up contracts for the money you lent him? People often don't with family." Her eyes widened. "That's a massive loan, Logan."

He exhaled. "I've got paperwork, Hana. I'm not an idiot. He just doesn't think I'll go after him."

She shook her head as though trying to place an awkward puzzle piece. "How could he steal your land and not expect to give it back? It makes no sense."

Logan licked his lips and she saw his entire body tense. "Caroline is his foster daughter. I thought you knew."

It seemed as though her subconscious always knew it would upset her and hid the knowledge away. "You grew up with her?" Hana's top lip curled back in dismay. "She made that mark on your side?"

Logan's fingers twitched as they strayed to touch the rough ridge of skin. His complexion paled. "Not quite. She told my cousin and brother to do it."

Hana blinked. "And after that, you thought to yourself what a great marriage prospect she might turn out to be?"

Logan ran a hand through his hair and left it sticking up. "No. You're twisting things, Hana. It wasn't like that." He sighed and the action rocked his whole body. "It's about the money, not Caroline."

"Don't say her name!" Hana warned through gritted teeth. "I mean it!"

Logan took another look at the bed and then padded towards it. He crawled under the sheets and put his arms behind his head. "I knew this would happen," he grumbled.

Hana approached him, her hands balled into fists. "So explain!" she spat. "Explain how that woman gets yet another route into my world."

Logan rolled his eyes. "She jilted me at the altar and my uncle went to Dad and said I owed money for the wedding." He sighed. "He named a sum he knew would scare him and then bartered it down to the price of the land. The stupid fool signed it over to him."

"You can't sign over land you don't own." Hana pronounced each word, betraying her ire. "It's not legal."

"I know that!" Logan hauled himself up onto his pillows and locked his hands around his knees. "But he let a developer in to create an access road up the mountain and made a fortune. They got plans approved by the local council and sold house and land packages to families. It's complicated. It's a legal fricken nightmare."

Hana cocked her head. "It makes your wedding sound like a ruse," she said, her brow knitting. "Do you think she knew?"

Logan shrugged and wouldn't catch Hana's eye. "I don't know, babe. I don't know anything anymore."

"What will you do? If he got paid by the developer then he must be able to pay you back. Perhaps you could take back the debt and extra to cover the land."

Logan's nostrils flared and he gnawed on his lower lip. "You don't understand, Hana. That land is the only thing left of my kuia. She named me in her will and left that section to me."

Hana swallowed. Everything in her wanted him to let it go. She needed Caroline out of her life forever and getting into a legal wrangle with her family wouldn't achieve that. Her fingers wrung against the robe and she couldn't stand still. "What will you do?" She repeated the question even though the darkness in Logan's eyes told her the answer.

"You won't let this go now, will you?" His irises flashed the colour of storm water.

Hana fixed her hands over her hips and her posture betrayed her distress. Gritted teeth framed her words. "I'm surprised you expect me to, Logan. Have you forgotten she's due to give birth to a child she claims is yours? Now you're telling me you're involved with her financially too." Hana released her hands and they slapped against her thighs. "I can't do this, Logan. Everything she touches is poisonous and it follows me everywhere." A shaking hand covered her eyes.

"Hey, hey," Logan soothed. He slipped from the bed and wrapped his arms around her. The towel slipped and puddled around his feet and he ignored it. "I'll keep it away from you, I promise. For once, she didn't do this, Hana. I'll deal with it."

Hana squeezed her eyes tight shut and willed Logan to stop. Ignorance called to her with its blissful oblivion and she wished she hadn't trespassed into his business world. Caroline mocked her even when absent and the spectre of her illegitimate child hung over Hana's head.

"I didn't do it, by the way."

Hana started and a cool draught pressed around her legs. She extracted herself from Logan's embrace and crawled into bed. "Do what?"

He turned to face her, tall, imposing and formed by a god with an eye for perfection. Conflict burgeoned in Hana's heart. "I didn't leave a bill unpaid. It's not what I do, Hana. I always settle my debts. Uncle Reuben made it up."

"And Alfred believed him." Mention of Logan's fancy wedding to another woman curdled the macaroni cheese in her gut. Hana rested a hand over her bump and snuggled into the sheets. The child turned somersaults inside her, providing a ready distraction.

Logan crawled in next to her, his skin warm against her chilly feet and hands. "Dad hates Reuben. They don't speak. I'm amazed he let him visit at all, but he'd do anything to get rid of him."

"Why?" Hana closed her eyes and leaned into the pain of Caroline's most recent invasion of her peace.

"No idea." Logan sighed. "Been that way as long as I can remember. They used to all live here in the house together. Some big fall out happened and my kuia threw Reuben out. She gave him that small section of the mountain to the east and our families remained enemies even after her death."

"I'm sorry." Hana pushed her face into the pillow and sighed. "Family stuff sucks." Her mind strayed to Bodie and their lack of communication.

Logan's fingers stroked her hair, smoothing from her crown and following the curls to the middle of her back. When she looked up at him, his serious expression lit a fire of anxiety in her soul. "How will you resolve this?" she asked, worried about the reply before it came.

"Court." Logan blinked, shuttering the darkness behind his eyes. "It will ruin them though. They won't come back from it."

"Do you care?"

Logan inhaled through flared nostrils. "Yeah. Whānau ties make it impossible not to. It will rock this mountain and the town like nothing else ever has."

"Then what?" Hana reached out to trace the scar beneath his right eye, focusing on the knitted skin and the white line it created in his olive face. "When they're ruined, what happens afterwards?"

Logan shrugged. His biceps flexed as he put his palm in the small of her back and hauled her closer. "Then I see the developers off and restore everything back to the way it should be." His lips pressed over hers as he sought to tame her and stop her ready flow of questions. All sensible thought vacated Hana's brain as Logan's fingers released the knot at her waist and pressed the robe aside.

Logan woke to the vibration of his phone on the bedside table. Padding into the bathroom, he closed the door and switched on the light over the mirror. "What?"

"Don't you snap at me, egghead!" Liza bit. "You left a message and I'm returning it."

Logan avoided his reflection in the mirror and instead, faced his immediate problems. "Yeah, thanks. I've decided how to proceed with the land theft. Get something lodged with the local council by Monday and I need to see the ball rolling with court action. I'll recoup the two hundred thousand I lent Reuben without interest and take the land back."

"Logan, that's massive. Why don't you make him pay you out on the land? I bet the developers will come to the party and help him out. They're advertising their flash mountain retreats all over Auckland."

"No." He set his jaw and leaned against the warm towel rack. Electricity hummed through new wiring and drove the chill from his heart. "Kuia gave that land to me and I'm keeping it. No amount of compensation will make up for its loss. It's tapu, sacred."

"I know what tapu is, Logan." Liza's sarcasm made the distance between them feel like millimetres. "This will detonate the family, bro'. I need to caution you not to do it. You'll open up old closets that can't be closed afterwards."

"I don't care." Logan's gaze strayed to the mirror and his pink scar stood out in the fluorescent light. It snaked around his ribs like a mountain contour and he gritted his teeth. "They've taken enough from me. It stops here. Their fight with my family has nothing to do with me. I'm tired of paying for it."

"It has everything to do with you, Logan!" Liza's temper flared. "Please, don't do this, Logan. Let's find another way. Beat someone up. It's what you usually do."

"No." His resolute determination crackled down the connection. "This way. And if you don't have a suitable lawyer in your armoury who can get it done, I'll find someone else."

Liza groaned. "I do have someone, Logan. But he'll cost you big time." Logan heard the faint strains of possession in her voice and capitalised.

"Give him my number. I'll expect his call tomorrow."

"It's the weekend!"

"And I'll pay him to work weekends. I want it done before the baby's born."

"Baby?" Liza grew silent. "You didn't hear. I'm not surprised. I think she hushed it up."

"What?" Logan's gaze flicked to the ceiling and then the mirror, seeing the distaste in his expression. His lips curled back in a snarl. "Not her baby, Liza! It's not mine. I should have guessed you'd believe your little mate over me. I'm talking about our baby, Hana's and mine."

"Oh, that baby. I didn't realise your little English doll was still cooking it." She snorted, the sound derisive. "Good on her."

"You're such a bitch." Logan closed his eyes and tried to distance himself from Liza's hatred. He understood her because he'd provided her only comfort during the worst week of her life. Yet her spite against Hana seemed unnecessarily cruel. "Back off my wife."

Liza sighed as though bored, the sound like an Appaloosa's warning snort. "You don't need to worry about Caroline anymore. I met with her yesterday."

"And?" Logan snapped. "This concerns me why?"

"Because she lost the baby."

Logan pushed the lid down on the toilet and sat on its smooth surface. The plastic felt cold against his thighs. He knew he should feel relieved, but didn't. Caroline used a vulnerable child as a weapon and its escape should have made him glad for it. He breathed out through his nose and tried not to project concern onto the child in Hana's womb. Their baby would live. It would thrive with Hana's strong genes and not carry haemophilia, the Du Rose punishment for inbreeding.

"Are you okay?" Liza at least sounded concerned for someone other than herself.

Logan sighed. "I'm fine, Liza. I'm sorry for her but it wasn't my child."

"I know." Contrition snaked through her words. "She admitted it."

"Finally." Logan shook his head in the empty bathroom. He pinched the bridge of his nose between thumb and forefinger, making his eyes water. "The damage is done. She slurred my character at work and in my marriage. I should sue the ass off her for defamation."

"Maybe." Liza sounded tired and her attention wandered. "When did it happen?"

"A month ago. Full term but stillborn. She's devastated."

"Yeah." Logan swallowed and a piece of him still ached for a mother with empty arms. He wanted to ask if she'd been alone but didn't want to open a door to emotions he didn't need. They'd both been alone and messed up. Shared rejection formed a dreadful basis for a long term relationship. His brow furrowed. "Not full term. It must have come early."

"Nope." Liza yawned, feigning boredom in the subject. Logan winced, knowing the extent of the fake. "She got pregnant in Fiji to some married guy she met there. You forgot to cancel the honeymoon, so she used it. Hell of a present to give yourself."

"Boy or girl? The child."

"It doesn't matter!" Liza exploded. "It died, Logan. I don't wish to discuss this anymore. It was hard enough to listen to her rambling on and sobbing. She didn't even pay for her own bloody coffee as usual. I'm done with her."

"Don't be callous. She needs a friend right now." Logan surprised himself in Caroline's defence, regretting his interference as Liza loaded into him.

"Yeah, because I really need to hear another woman's labour horror stories, don't I Logan? Grow up man!"

"Sorry." Reduced to the role of younger brother, Logan bit at a hangnail on his thumb. He forced himself to a standing position and readied his finger to end the call. "I expect to hear from your latest hotshot by tomorrow then." His eyelashes fluttered against his cheek and a smirk curved his lips. "Wake him up and give him the good news."

"You're a bastard!" Liza bit and Logan laughed.

"And you should stop banging your juniors. It's not a good look for a judge." He hung up, missing Liza's midnight rant which woke her latest conquest from his exhausted slumber. Logan pursed his lips and leaned his cheek against the cold shower glass, his phone dead in his hand. "Fraud lawyer," he muttered. "At least this one might prove useful."

Chapter 15

L ogan took Hana breakfast in bed so she could avoid the chaos of the kitchen. He ran the gauntlet of his mother alone as she demanded Hana's presence. "Take your pills," he told Miriam, leaving with a laden tray and the kind of deep-seated exhaustion which came from fighting the same endless battle on a loop.

"This is sweet," Hana said with a yawn. The jam knife slipped through clumsy fingers and spread strawberry stains along her naked stomach. Logan swallowed and looked away at its likeness to blood.

"When you're dressed, we'll ride up to the top of the mountain." He rested his forearm against the window and pressed his head against it. Mist coated the scene outside, blanking out the surrounding hills as though they didn't exist. His memory painted them back in, fine, exacting detail borne of experience and familiarity. "I love this place so much," he whispered, his breath fogging up the glass.

Hana showered and dressed, meeting him on the front steps. She looked anxious and clasped a jacket in front of her stomach. Logan shook his head and looked up at the blue sky. "You won't need a coat," he said. "The mist is burning off and it's warm. By the time we get up there, it'll be baking hot."

Hana shifted in discomfort and waited for a group of new guests to file past. Then she pulled the jacket aside to reveal the open zipper of her jodhpurs. Her stomach hung over the top of the waistband like an old man's beer belly. "I borrowed your sister's pants. They won't do up."

Logan swore and put a hand over his mouth to suppress the laughter. He saw Hana's expression darken and bit down on his lip. "Sorry," he said. "We'll go up on the quad bike. I should've said."

"Yeah, thanks for that!" Hana snapped. She reached behind her to hook the seam from her ass.

The quad bike took two riders side by side. Instead of handlebars, a steering wheel directed four, heavy treaded tyres. "I've never seen a machine like this before." Hana clung to the edge of the window and bounced in her seat. She shouted over the sound of the motor.

"I know." Logan gave her a sideways smirk. "My poppa built it after the war. He cut down the chassis of a jeep and shoved a truck engine under the bonnet. It can go anywhere."

Hana tightened her thigh muscles against the bench seat and braced herself as they mounted a shallow ridge. Logan placed his left hand at the back of her neck and drove one handed. "Sorry," he called. "It gets easier up ahead."

Hana closed her eyes as the strange contraption got airborne over a rut and chewed up the ground beneath them. She decided she'd rather climb the mountain on horseback, belly overhang and all.

At the top of the ridge, Logan unlocked the gate and drove the quad through, parking at the edge of a cliff. Port Waikato spread before them like a speckled handkerchief. "Wait a second," Logan said, bouncing from his seat and walking behind. From a truck bed welded to the rear, he pulled a rucksack and blanket. He winked at her as Hana wrestled her heart rate back to within normal levels and contemplated the warning signs from her bladder.

Logan took extra care laying the blanket on the ground. He squatted down with his back to her and Hana heard the clink of glasses and the rustle of packets. She waited for her husband's steadying hand before testing her legs. "Thanks," she said, peering around him at the picnic. Her face broke into a delighted smile. "This is like our first trip up here," she said, her green irises dancing in the sunlight.

"Yeah." Logan bent to kiss her temple and led her towards the blanket. "I thought you'd appreciate the view."

He'd substituted grape juice for wine and they lay in the sunshine and talked about nothing important while they ate. Hana rested on her back with her legs bent and her eyes closed. "Did you see Jack?" she asked, hearing Logan's grunted reply. "When we got on the quad, he kept pointing to my stomach and gave me a thumbs-up. He looked so happy, I thought his face might split." Hana rolled onto her side. "Aren't you embarrassed everyone knows we've had great sex?"

Logan snorted. "Can't you get pregnant from rubbish sex?"

Hana pursed her lips and thought about Bodie's conception. A drunken fumble she hardly remembered resulted in a difficult, obnoxious adult male. She grieved for the happy boy he'd seemed until the last year before Vik's death. "I guess," she conceded. "Maybe you just don't get nice babies."

Logan shook his head and Hana saw dried grass clinging to the ends of his hair. "I think Jack felt happy about the baby, rather than the sex."

"Maybe." Hana wrinkled her nose. "I can't get used to everyone staring at the one part of me I've spent the last twenty five years trying to hide." She groaned and Logan reached for her hand. His fingers felt warm.

"Idiot! You're beautiful."

The sun warmed their faces and the click of the quad bike's cooling metal lulled Hana into a doze. She started as Logan broke the silence. "We should call this place, Serious Hill." His voice rumbled against the backdrop of bird sounds and moving grass.

"Why?" Hana gave a lazy sigh.

"Because I always have something serious to tell you when we come here," he replied. Hana pushed herself into a sitting position and faced him with her legs curled beside her.

"Uh oh," she breathed. "I don't like the sound of that. I always think of it as Horny Hill because it's where you get rampant."

Logan smirked at the alternative name. "Okay, we'll leave it at Horny Hill then. But I do need to talk to you."

Hana steeled herself, but didn't expect the first of his sentences to hit her so hard. "Caroline lost her baby." Her hand strayed to her stomach where the child rebelled against the gurgling of her sandwich and the packet of cheese flavoured puffs. She pursed her lips and willed herself not to feel. Logan reached for her hand and squeezed. "Don't dwell on it, babe."

"Does Boris know?"

Logan sighed and rolled his eyes. "The baby wasn't his." He watched her shutter her emotions and raise an internal shield to protect herself from pain. "It wasn't mine either, Hana. I promised you. She admitted to Liza that she fell pregnant on our honeymoon. I didn't cancel it and she went by herself. She met a married Fijian guy."

Hana's wooden nod conveyed only acceptance and she hid all other emotion. "Is she okay though?" she asked. "It's a mother's worst nightmare." Her jaw flexed with the effort of gritting her teeth and she struggled with the strain of not crying. The child in her womb stuck a tiny hand through the skin housed beneath the jodhpurs as though highlighting the constant threat of disaster to her pregnancy. Hana licked her lips and watched surprise filter through Logan's expression.

"I can't work you out," he sighed. "I didn't expect you to care." He swallowed and reached for his cowboy hat, sitting it on his head as he sat up. "Liza thinks she's okay," he lied. "Who knows?"

Hana nodded. "I hate her but it still touches me. A child died. Babies can't help who or what their parents are."

Logan felt a prickle of discomfort in his soul. Something about Hana's words hung in the air above them, readying themselves to reverberate much louder in the coming months. Logan shook his shoulders to release the awful sense of foreboding. His voice grew quiet. "I've instructed a lawyer to go after the money my uncle owes me. He'll issue a trespass order on the land too. I need you to understand how messy this will get. My uncle's up to his ears in debt and Nev doesn't know where it's going. Their farm is haemorrhaging cash somewhere so I'm certain they'll go bankrupt."

"Oh." Hana absorbed the information and watched her husband's stress tell. The vein pulsed in his neck below his open shirt collar and she distracted herself by concentrating on a tantalising line of downy hair. "How will your parents take the news?"

Logan inhaled. "I heard a rumour once. About my mother." Hana narrowed her eyes and watched his face muscles tighten. "She slept with my uncle and I always suspected Barry was the result." His nostrils flared and his fingers strayed to the ragged scar beneath his shirt. "He was twisted enough."

"Do you think that's why your family split?" Hana asked. "Infidelity."

"Yeah. Maybe." He sighed and his shoulders bowed beneath the weight of the world.

"Why do this, if it promises to cause so much damage? Can you live with yourself if they end up homeless and your mother never speaks to you again?"

Logan lay back on the blanket and studied the clear blue sky. He thought hard about his answer but when Hana heard the words, she knew he'd set his decision in stone. "My ancestors were good people, Hana. Full of mana and honour. Something happened with my parents' generation and they've dishonoured our traditions and dirtied the land. They spat on the Du Rose name repeatedly and reduced it to something only worthy of sneering at." He turned to face Hana and his grey irises swirled with the power of recollection. "I remember my grandmother. She was an amazing woman. She possessed more mana in her baby finger than any of the people who carry her name. She would turn in her grave if she saw what's become of the family now." He sighed. "I think she sensed it coming. She gave me a task and I think it's time."

Logan stood and held his hand out to Hana so he could pull her up. They stared over the lime green pastures, interspersed with areas of dark green native bush. The Tasman Sea swirled beneath, providing an aqua backdrop. "This belongs to me, Hana. One day, I'll gift it to our child. It's not about land, though. It's principle. Rueben attacked my birthright and I believe he knew what he was doing. If I don't fight for this, I'm not the Du Rose my kuia believed me to be." Logan drew in a breath and held his head high. His grandmother's words floated back to him on the sea breeze. "The Du Rose house will be swept clean, Hana. It's time."

Logan kissed her, impassioned by the swirl of emotions seizing his heart in a death grip. He took Hana's breath away and she hungered for him, always wanting more. They stripped in the open air and he made love to her in a bed of downy grass. A black tui bird adjusted his white bib in the branches of an ancient kauri tree. He poked out his beak and squawked a warning as they wrapped their bodies around one another.

Logan's ancestors groaned in agony at the coming storm, knowing the legacy would reveal itself and burn everyone who got in its way.

Back at the hotel, Hana sat on Logan's bed and pretended to read a book. In the family room downstairs, her husband revealed his plans to his parents. She shut her book with a slap of filmy pages. "You should be with him," she rebuked herself. "He needed your support. You're a doozy, Hana Du Rose. A complete coward."

Chastened, she pushed her feet into slippers and padded to the door. She used the main staircase to access the lobby, nodding to the receptionist on her way past. "Everything all right?" the woman asked and Hana stopped and turned.

"Yes, thanks. Please can you point me in the direction of the family room? Logan's parents use it as a sitting room."

Looking relieved at the simplicity of the request, she unplugged her headset and stood. "I'll show you," she said. She flipped a notice on the desk to advise guests she would be back soon and pointed towards the passage to the kitchen. "This place is a maze," she commented as she led Hana further into the house. At the end of the corridor they turned left, then left again. She flicked light switches as she went and Hana concentrated on remembering furniture landmarks beneath the yellow glow of ornate chandeliers. They passed the double doors where she overheard Logan's conversation with Neville Du Rose and Hana stroked the wood.

"What's this room?" she asked. The girl halted and gave her an odd look before fixing blankness over her surprise.

"Mr Logan's office," she said. Her eyelashes fluttered and she glanced at Hana's protruding belly and back at her face. Hana read the implication there and colour flared into her cheeks. The woman plastered a smile on her face. "The sitting room is there," she said, pointing towards the oak framed fire door. "Would you like me to knock?"

Hana shook her head. "No thanks. I'm fine." With a shrug, the receptionist turned and walked away, rounding the first corner on soft soled shoes. Hana stared at the knots in the mahogany stained doorframe, counting the lines to distract herself. Her heart pounded and it occurred to her that her appearance may prove unwelcome. She glanced at the corridor and imagined stalking past the receptionist with her tail between her legs. A violent cringe shook her body and drove her backwards into an ornate French styled chair. She blew out through pursed lips, ruing her poor decision making.

Voices rumbled from inside the room and Hana jumped at the sound of wailing. "No, no, no!!!" cried Miriam, her voice muffled through the wood. "You'll start a war!"

Logan's voice rose over it. "When he chose to take my money and cheat my father, he started it."

Hana heard a crash and the tinkling of breaking china. She rose from the seat and stared around for somewhere to hide. Miriam's agony filtered through the door as deep, painful groans. "You don't understand!" she implored. "You don't know what you're doing!"

"Pa." Logan appealed to Alfred and Hana listened for a reply. She heard only Miriam's sobbing. Footsteps moved towards the door and Hana panicked. Like a fully fledged coward, she bolted towards a nearby alcove. Her fingers grappled to switch off the lights as she dived behind an armchair. The door opened and Hana peeked from her hiding place, seeing Alfred's bent shape silhouetted in the light.

"Shut her up," he snapped, raising a gnarled finger and pointing back into the room. "I can't take anymore of her hysterics. I've endured a lifetime of them and I'm done."

"Don't say that." Logan appeared next to him, his forehead lined with strain. "She's upset."

Alfred shook his head and stepped into the corridor. "I support you, son. I'm satisfied that you'll do the right thing. You always do, Logan."

Miriam appeared in the gap, clutching at Alfred's arm as her body went into a paroxysm of shaking and twitching. "Foolish old man!" she screamed. "He's your brother? You would stand by and see him ruined again? Hasn't he suffered enough?" Her voice sounded shrill and piercing in the stillness and Hana's fingernails dug into the fabric of the chair. Miriam pointed at her husband with jabbing movements, forcing Logan to reach for her hand as she prodded Alfred in the chest so hard she almost overbalanced him. "Stop him, Alfie, I'm begging you. Not this way, not by the hand of one of your sons. It's cruel."

Logan pulled her hand away from Alfred, clasping her fingers against his chest. "Quiet, Ma. The guests will hear you." He muttered something in Māori and Miriam squeezed her eyes closed and shook her head.

"Don't bother, Logan." Alfred turned and Hana saw an uncharacteristic hardness to his wrinkled face. "We reap what we sow in this life." He spun to face Miriam and his words struck lead into Hana's chest. "Not by the hand of one of your sons, wife?" His head shook in a slow movement and Miriam ceased her thrashing. Her hands pressed against her lips and her eyes widened.

"Don't, don't, don't," she whispered.

Alfred's stooped back straightened until he towered above her, revealing something of the tall, imposing man he once was. "One of my sons, Miriam? We both know there's only one."

Hana clapped a hand over her mouth as Miriam launched herself at him. Logan restrained her with his arms locked around her torso, but Hana saw him take several kicks to the shin. Alfred stalked away without looking back and Logan pulled Miriam into the room and closed the door with his heel. Hana crouched in the darkness and listened to her muted wailing and Logan's attempts to comfort her. Her mind raced with the revelation and puzzle pieces tumbled into place. Not Barry, but Michael fell from the wrong branch of the Du Rose tree. The explanation felt right and Hana remembered the gossip about Reuben refusing to let Tama's young mother take him when she returned. She racked her memory, trying to recall where she heard the sorry tale. If Alfred denied him access to Michael, his revenge deprived him of a grandchild.

Hana rose from behind the chair and fought her way onto the narrow strip of available walking space. She felt her way along the wall, wishing she'd stayed upstairs and not ventured down to help. Her fingers froze above the flock wallpaper as an eerie noise registered in the distance, faint but unmistakable. Alfred's uneven footsteps turned the second corner towards the kitchen and as he progressed further into the annals of the old house, his laughter echoed around the walls.

Chapter 16

"How are you?" Hana jumped as Logan unlocked the door. She sprawled sideways on the bed in her monkey pyjamas, trying to find her equilibrium after a frantic dash up the main staircase and a speedy change of clothes. Guilt snaked around her heart as Logan ignored her. He pushed into the bathroom and closed the door.

She heard him retch and lose his dinner. Her fingers fluttered over her mouth as she slipped from the bed and padded towards the door. The new situation fazed her, leaving her unsure how to react. She waited until she heard the toilet flush and then pushed the door open.

Stepping over Logan's legs, Hana filled a glass with water and held it out to him. "Here," she said, her voice soft. "You've done it for me often enough." Logan took the glass from her fingers, spilling it up his wrist. The rivets in his jeans made faint, scratchy sounds on the tiled floor and he leaned his head back against the shower cubicle. Hana watched him sip the liquid. "That awful?" she asked in a whisper.

"Worse," he replied. His eyelids fluttered closed. "Much worse."

Hana ran a facecloth under the cold tap and squatted, her rounded belly jutting between her legs. She pushed Logan's hair back in a tender movement and used the cloth to wipe the beads of sweat from his brow. Logan studied her expression. He knew every freckle, every mark and every curl which tumbled down around her porcelain face. He reached out and fingered a ringlet which fell near her left shoulder. It twisted between his thumb and forefinger, the softness running over and over his flesh. It gave him clarity. "I haven't changed my mind," he said, blinking against the coolness of the facecloth. "I need to see this through."

"I understand," she replied. "I'll support you."

She tried to help him from the floor in the small space, giggling when he almost pulled her down with him. Some of the colour returned to his cheeks and he cleaned his teeth. They took a shower together, fooling around and staying under the water until it ran cool. The lead weight in Logan's heart lifted as Hana distracted him, but returned straight afterwards.

He knelt behind Hana as she sat on the bed, his fingers drying the ends of her hair with a clean towel. Her auburn curls cascaded to the middle of her back and he twisted it into a half-decent knot. Hana reached up and snapped a clip over the loose tendrils. She turned to look at him. "I can see your brain working," she sighed. "Your ears are steaming."

Logan stuck his tongue out and climbed off the bed. He boiled the kettle and pushed tea bags into a pot. He faced the wall, concealing the haunting misery in his eyes as the tea steeped. Hana watched the set of his shoulders and ached for him. "Telly's rubbish," she announced, fingering the remote and screwing her nose up at the pictures on screen. "Do you have any movies up here?"

"Yeah. Some old serials." He bent to grapple around in the cupboard beneath the television, retrieving the dusty offerings. He brushed them clean over the sink. "American cowboy serials," he said, smiling at the memories. "I owned the videos and Jack recorded them onto DVD about ten years ago." He shrugged. "We can watch something else if you'd rather."

"I don't care." Hana shrugged and climbed into the wide bed. "We can talk."

"Na, I'm good," Logan lied and another fragment of her trust died.

The atmosphere in the house seemed unstrained the following day. Hana kept waiting for the axe to fall but it didn't. Logan's parents behaved as usual and it served to make her feel even more excluded from their world.

"You're not listening, are you?" Logan said, pausing as jam dripped from Hana's toast onto the plate. She looked down at it and gave an involuntary shudder. Miriam's back looked ramrod straight as she flipped pikelets in a pan on the stove.

"What? Pardon." She gave him a smile, her mind elsewhere. "You said we're going to lunch with a friend of yours."

"No." Logan shook his head and his brow knitted. "I didn't, Hana. I knew you weren't listening." He threw his napkin onto the table and sighed. "I'll cancel."

"Don't!" Hana grabbed his wrist, feeling the knotty bones beneath her fingers. "I'm sorry. Wear a dress and keep my mouth shut. I heard." The words sounded odd on her lips and she frowned. "That is what you said?"

Logan gave an irritated inhale. "Not quite, but it will do. We'll leave in half an hour."

Hana found herself unprepared for the lavish Sunday luncheon, served to her before noon. The Chinese restaurant on Auckland's north shore looked open for business, but the door remained locked and a closed sign swung behind the blinds. A greying man of Chinese descent greeted Logan like a long lost relative and bowed to Hana. The stripes on his expensive suit blurred her vision and she gave him a nervous smile. "This my wife," he said in clipped English, introducing a tiny thin woman with black hair scraped back from her face. His voice echoed in the empty restaurant and Hana acknowledged the woman with a nod.

Logan looked uncomfortable and Hana caught him tugging his tie away from his throat. His unease communicated itself to her and she grew clumsy with nerves. The walls and décor provided a riot of red and gold. Hana swallowed and shot anxious looks towards her husband, hoping he sensed how expensive a luncheon for four might become. The tables lay waiting, already dressed with cutlery and sumptuous serviettes as though unseen customers might arrive, but the door remained locked.

"Mrs Che runs a security business," Logan said, inclining his hand towards the woman. Her gimlet eyes narrowed and she turned towards Hana.

"Nice," Hana replied, knowing straight away she'd said the wrong thing. A tiny flick of Mrs Che's eyebrows expressed the woman's veiled dislike.

"Sit, sit!" Mr Che ordered, pointing towards seats like an orchestra conductor. He placed himself and his wife between Hana and Logan, forcing her to look at the side of her husband's face without being able to communicate. A shiver ran along her spine and instinct made her cover her bump with her fingers.

Four place settings occupied the table. Mr Che sat at one end with Logan to his left. Hana faced him and he eyed her frightened movements with interest as his wife thwarted her safety. Waiters scurried to the empty side of the rectangular table and bowed, awaiting instruction. Unable to read the menu thrust in front of her, Hana concentrated on breathing and calming her nerves.

Kitchen sounds issued from behind them, the noise of metal clanged against a stainless steel surface. It echoed around the room and caught in the vaulted ceiling, forcing Hana to mishear Mrs Che's question. "Pardon?" she asked, leaning forward. Mrs Che jerked backwards as though bitten and colour flushed into Hana's cheeks. She felt like a leper.

Mrs Che breathed out through her nose, the whole debacle clearly not to her taste. "When is your child due?" she demanded.

Hana's gaze flicked to Logan and she saw him in deep discussion with Mr Che. Waiters delivered pots of tea and a tray of cups. "January, we think." she replied. She reached for a conversation piece and regretted it seconds later. "Do you have any children?"

The woman's face curled into an ugly lemon-sucking-mask and she spat her answer. "No!"

Hana choked on her next sentence, the menu bouncing in her shaking fingers. Wishing she'd listened harder to Logan's careful instructions, she shot him a look of desperation. As though pulled by an invisible thread, his face turned towards her and he bobbed his head forward to get eye contact. "Mr Che," he said to the man pouring tea into a tiny cup and saucer beside him. "My wife accompanied me to the hotel for the weekend. Our baby's due in January."

The man tilted his head sideways and lifted the teapot in salute, a smile breaking out across his face. "Ah, congratulations," he said. "May I pour you some tea?"

Hana nodded and took the tiny cup with care as the waiter handed it from Mr Che to her. She peered into the dark, black contents of the smallest teacup she'd ever seen. As she held the delicate china in her hands, she felt Mrs Che's eyes burning holes in the side of her face. Her fingers shook and she placed it back in the saucer, fearful of dropping it in a fit of clumsiness. Mr Che clapped his hands and the waiters skipped away to the kitchen. With feverish accuracy they returned to load the table with platters and dishes, more than four people could ever eat. Hana struggled to keep the trepidation from her face. She recognised little of the food and worried it contained all the items denied a pregnant woman. "Is that chicken?" she whispered to a waiter, pointing to a tray of white meat near Logan.

"Baby octopus," he replied. Hana swallowed as Mr Che used chop sticks to select one of the small white bodies. He lifted it high into the air and tentacles dangled either side of the utensils. She inhaled and held the breath, pinching her thigh to stop herself throwing up at the sight of the tiny creature disappearing into his mouth.

Hana's fragile hold on her sanity became shakier as the meal progressed. She battled a sense of ineptness, out of her depth and terrified. The distance between them made it impossible for Logan to bail her out. Every move she made drew sighs of irritation from the severe woman to her right. Fear of causing offence made her clumsy and afraid. Sideways glances at Logan found him collected and easy in his movements, dishing food onto his plate as though familiar with the process. Snippets of overheard conversation told her she'd trespassed into a business meeting as the men discussed stocks and shares. She wracked her brain for Logan's earlier direction, but a fog descended over her mind and she couldn't remember a single word. Heat crawled over her flesh and she felt herself undeserving of Logan's faith in her.

"I can't do this," she breathed as the woman next to her crushed the head of a prawn. Mrs Che turned gimlet eyes in Hana's direction.

"What?"

The desire to escape consumed Hana's consciousness and her blood pressure climbed to dangerous heights. Failure laughed through its viewfinder as she proved her lack of worth as Logan's mate. Faking sick removed itself as a viable option, leaving her with no exit strategies at all. The desire to fake sickness disappeared as the real kind replaced it. The child lurched in her womb, reacting to the spike in her blood pressure and adding guilt to the growing pile of her failures. When it kicked her hard in the ribs, Hana let out an involuntary groan and grabbed her side.

Mrs Che narrowed her dark gaze and the men stopped talking. Logan's grey eyes pierced her soul. Alight and sparkling, they looked more animated than she'd ever seen them. He resembled a moth which deliberately flies too near a flame, thrill seeking. "Hana?" His left eyebrow rose in question.

"Just a kick," she replied, rubbing at her ribs. She picked up a knife and fork and the moment ended. Logan recommended two dishes and Mr Che a third. Hana spent the next fifteen minutes chewing fried seaweed and chicken in a rich, salty sauce. Logan wielded his chopsticks like a professional, compounding Hana's inadequacy as she manoeuvred her knife and fork.

The nourishment lifted her spirits as well as her blood sugar. Mrs Che gave her sly, sideways glances, causing Hana's appetite to dry up long before anyone else's. She used the cover of sipping her tea to survey her surroundings. Eight waiters stood nearby, all paid Sunday wages to serve their private party. An air of fear clung to them as though an error might lead to terrible consequences.

Mirrors decorated the walls between the ornate windows. It gave an illusion of grandeur and extended the visual appearance of the restaurant's size. Hana sipped and watched the kitchen reflected in the mirror opposite her. Stainless steel and high tech, it housed chefs in tall hats. All male, they exercised frantic activity. As her gaze strayed to the right, the neon sign for the bathrooms seemed to call her. Hana peered into her teacup and held onto the groan of dismay. Seeing the sign set off a chain reaction of wanting and then needing the toilet. She looked away, but a movement through the corner of her eye caught her interest.

A bulky man stepped into the passage between the restaurant and the bathroom. The kitchen door swung on its hinges and he wiped his lips with the back of his hand. His eyes darted to Mrs Che's reflection in the mirror and he swallowed the object swilling around his mouth. An Adam's apple bobbed in his throat as he stifled a choking sound. Oriental like the Che's, he carried a much heavier body on short, stocky legs. His black suit looked recently pressed and a white shirt collar glinted over the top of his lapel. Sweating in the heat from the kitchen, he stuck a pudgy finger into his collar and pulled, loosening it as he twisted his head from side to side. He grappled in an inside pocket for a white handkerchief and turned aside to mop his brow, his gaze never leaving Mrs Che's face. As he turned back, Hana saw the gun holstered beneath his left arm.

The teacup clattered against the saucer and she cursed the attention it drew. Forcing a smile onto her lips, she dipped her head and gave Mr Che a winning smile. He narrowed his eyes and raised his chopsticks in salute, turning back to his conversation with Logan. Hana swallowed and allowed herself to study the man blocking her route to the toilet. Her mouth felt dry and uncomfortable and silent appeals to Logan went unanswered. She felt her chest tighten at another glimpse of the gun. The man settled his handkerchief back in his inside pocket and buttoned his jacket. By the time Mrs Che looked up and got eye contact with him, he was collected enough to offer the slightest of nods in sinister acknowledgement. Hana inhaled through her nose and considered the gun. Dull black metal with a patterned handle, it resembled something from an American cop show. The tiny pistol Logan used to teach her paled in significance next to its bulk.

"Eat!" Mrs Che snapped under her breath. She inclined her head towards Hana's bulky knife and fork and waved her chopsticks. "Good food."

Hana plastered a smile onto her face, wondering when the nightmare might end. "Tell me about your work?" she asked, grasping for conversation to distract herself from the need to use the bathroom. "Security sounds interesting." In the corner of her eye, Logan devoured rice with enthusiasm, waving his chopsticks like a wand in animation. She heard the delicate squelch of another baby octopus beneath Mrs Che's razor sharp teeth and concentrated on the hilarity of the noise, rather than what it signified. The woman swallowed and replied in stilted English, "I take care of personnel and security for family business." Her accent caused the words to fire like missiles. Hana got it. The man with the gun belonged to her.

"I work in a school," she ventured, unable to think of anything interesting to make of that snippet of information.

She fumbled the tiny cup of tea, finding it empty and unable to alleviate the dryness in her mouth.

Mrs Che leaned in towards her, the proximity uncomfortable. Hana smelled the seafood on her breath and thought of death. "I know all about you, Mrs Du Rose." she whispered. "There is little I do not know." She gave a satisfied nod and her lips quirked upwards in a cruel smile. "I know your son is policeman." Her voice became sing-song, as though she spoke to a small child playing hide and seek. "I know where his small son goes to playschool."

Hana glanced across at her husband for help, but Mrs Che's head blocked her view. Brown slanted eyes drilled into Hana's face. A sense of abandonment washed over her. Deciding to remove herself from the situation, she scraped her chair back over the tiled floor, making a screeching sound in her haste. Without speaking, she tottered towards the passageway and the relative safety of the toilet. Half way there, Hana realised her mistake as the gunman snapped to attention and fixed dark, beady eyes on her progress.

Her legs wobbled like jelly and she forced herself to glide across the tiles in high heeled boots. Logan rose to his feet as she passed, his lifted eyebrow enquiring. Hana fought the urge to slap him for putting her and their baby in a situation he couldn't control. The tell-tale vein ticked in his neck, belying his relaxed air. Hana ignored him and willed herself not to run as the guard stepped neatly sideways to allow her into the passageway. The bathroom sign called to her from the door at the end.

Once inside the tiny cubicle, Hana leaned against the wall and placed a hand over her chest. Her heart beat like a jack hammer and she breathed through pursed lips. "Damn you, Logan Du Rose," she hissed. "Damn you!" She used the toilet and wasted time sizing up the small window above it. A laugh bubbled onto her lips at the thought of crawling out onto the street with her bulging stomach and high heels. Fear and nerves drove the sound from her as hysteria threatened. "Where would you run to?" she demanded of the empty space, leaning her hot forehead against the tiled wall.

Hana jumped as a dish clattered in the kitchen. The realisation that Mrs Che might come to find her filled her with terror. Bad enough to endure the woman in an open space, but to find herself in close proximity without escape was more than she could bear. Her implied threats told Hana these were bad people, very bad people. Logan's secrecy acted against him and doubt snaked its fingers around Hana's throat. She contemplated Bodie's frequent warnings and pressed her fingers to her lips.

Hana felt sick and willed herself to repress the acid churning tea and seaweed into an unhealthy mixture in her gut. Her skin appeared waxy and pale under the expensive chandelier. It seemed ironic that she'd craved Logan's honesty and when he drew her into his other world, she couldn't handle it.

With a huge act of will, Hana forced herself back to the table although she didn't speak to Mrs Che again. She picked her way through an exquisite watermelon sorbet and hung out for the moment when they could leave. The staff made no comment about her lack of appetite as they cleared away the dishes, almost invisible in their swift movements. The men appeared twitchy around Mrs Che and Hana observed one of them quail beneath an icy stare. She glanced at the waiter in sympathy, recognising her own reaction to the woman's severity. She knew how he felt.

Logan rose from his seat at the same time as Mr Che. The small man put his arms around him and the tight embrace contained a squeeze of affection. Hana took a sharp intake of breath and prayed Mrs Che wouldn't expect the same of her. She didn't, inclining her head with feigned politeness and smiling with her lips only. In the last moment of defiance, Hana refused to bow her head, giving an acidic smile and clattering towards the door on her heels.

Logan raised his eyebrows at her in surprise as she jogged towards the passenger door of the car. She yanked on the handle before he deactivated the central locking and caused confusion with the electrics. "Steady on," he rebuked, his eyes narrowing as Hana wrenched the door open and hurled herself into the seat. His lips turned down as she locked the door behind her.

His fingers seemed slower than usual slotting the key into the ignition and every moment of delay increased Hana's sense of terror. "Hurry up!" she breathed, glancing back to the restaurant.

The engine fired and Logan checked the road behind them before pulling onto it. "I wondered if you wanted to go to the beach. Devonport is gorgeous on a clear day like today."

"Take me home!" Hana's white face set in a grimace, her top lip pulled back from her teeth. Shaking fingers fluttered to wipe sweat from her hairline.

"Are you ill?" Logan's hand reached out to clasp hers and Hana shoved his fingers away.

"Don't speak to me," she hissed. "Just drive." She turned her face aside and avoided his gaze. Her lips pursed shut, unable to regulate the cruel words threatening to burst free.

Traffic built on the Harbour Bridge and Logan pointed over the steering wheel at the Sky Tower soaring high above the city. An azure sky made an impressive backdrop. "Would you like coffee in the revolving restaurant?" he asked, his voice tender and cajoling.

Hana exploded, a detonation of pent up fear and disappointment. "No!" she shouted. "I want to go home."

Logan's jaw set in a hard line, unnerved by her unusual anger. He watched fear take hold of her, spreading like a black stain over her chest. "What happened?" he asked, his tone dull. "What did she say?"

Hana snorted in reply, a harsh, ugly sound. "Like you don't know!"

"I don't." He sighed. "That's why I'm asking."

Hana shook her head and closed her eyes against the irritation she heard in his voice. She didn't feel safe and the sensation rose around her like a cloak. Laval had proved quiet enough of late with his men gone for her to begin to feel normal. Mrs Che's sideways comments revived the gnawing feeling in her stomach and it overpowered her.

In downtown Auckland, the sea sparkled and blinked beneath the glare of the welcome spring sunshine. The seatbelt trapped Hana in place and the unwelcome restriction acted as a trigger for fear to morph into terror. As the car slowed for a traffic light, Hana flailed at the door handle.

"Hana!" Logan shouted, activating the central locking as she unlocked her side. The mechanism's soft clunk thwarted her escape and panic rose into her breast and drove the irrational desire to dizzying heights. The lights changed and Logan pulled the car away from the junction, shooting concerned glances across at his wife as she tugged at the door handle. He indicated left and spun the car around a sharp corner, jamming its front wheel into the side of the curb. "What the hell?" he demanded, lurching for her dress as she got the door undone and pitched forwards.

Hana's feet touched the footboard and she reached sideways for her handbag. A plan without definition swirled in her head, urging her to run to a hotel and hide from Laval and Mrs Che. She heard Logan swear and felt a tug on the hem of her dress, accompanied by an unhealthy tearing sound. Glancing back as she slapped at Logan's hand, she saw him turn his body to look through the rear window. He swore again and grabbed at the wrist of her right hand.

Pain shot through the weakened elbow joint and she cried out in pain. Logan held on, his grip leaving raised, red marks on her tender flesh. He leaned towards her and hissed, "Get in the damn car, Hana. Now!"

She gasped as he reeled her in, his grasp straying into the realms of deliberate pain. "Get off me!" she sobbed, crying out again as he shook his head and pulled her onto her seat.

"Stay in the bloody car," he replied through gritted teeth.

Hana lost the tug of war and fearing her bone might snap again, let out a gasp and a wail. Logan looked down and shock crossed his darkened features. He let go. Hana pitched forwards onto the grass verge and bent from the waist. Lime green grass spiked beneath her boots, the blades waving in the breeze from the Pacific Ocean.

Logan's arms wrapped around her shoulders and he pressed her face into his crisp white shirt. The buttons dug into her cheek. "Sorry, sorry," he repeated. "I forgot about your arm. I'm sorry."

Hana pulled herself free and this time, he let her go. Tipping forward, she threw up into the gutter as herbal tea chased fried seaweed into the ecosystem.

"Are you all right, dear?" A lady walking her dog stopped on the pavement as Hana puked on the fringes of a pristine grass verge outside an expensive Auckland home.

Logan nodded and his fingers pressed into Hana's shoulders. "It's just the baby," he said.

The woman raised an eyebrow and stared at Hana's bulging stomach. "Are you sure, dear?" she demanded, not moving on without definitive confirmation. "Do you want me to get help?"

Logan's teeth ground in his jaw. He knew if he became objectionable, she'd call the cops. Bodie's sanctimonious grin slid across his inner vision and he rubbed Hana's shoulders and watched the road with a series of quick glances. Hana sensed he waited for her next move and power reverted back to her a little more.

She stood up and ran a hand over her forehead. "I'm fine," she panted, embarrassed by the mess at her feet. "I'm sorry about your verge."

The woman's brows knitted. "Don't worry about it. Are you sure you don't need help?"

Hana shook her head and forced a weary smile onto her face. "I'm getting too old for this," she said, running her left hand over her pregnancy. The words held a latent warning for her husband and she felt his fingers stiffen against her shoulders. Too old for the life she'd ended up with, a life filled with intrigue and danger.

The woman moved away and Hana breathed in lung fulls of oxygen. She jumped as Logan leaned forward. "Get in the car, Hana. It's not safe."

"We're never safe!" she hissed. "I'm never safe."

"Just get in the bloody car!" Anxiety laced his voice and the urgency broke through her self-pity. At her look of scorn, Logan pulled her face toward him. "Mrs Che had us followed, Hana. Get in the bloody car!"

"Or what?" she spat. "Or she'll hurt my cop son or me? Perhaps she'll come after us both. Or Jas? Is this the company you keep, Logan Du Rose? Is this who you really are?"

Rage flickered across Logan's face, building from somewhere deep in his chest. "How dare you!" he snapped, gripping her above both elbows and steering her back to the car. "You don't like secrets but can't handle the truth. I don't know what you want from me, Hana." He pushed her into the passenger seat and slammed the door as though wanting to slam her out of his life.

Back in the driver's seat, Logan started the engine and drove away without fastening his seatbelt. He drove in silence, his world crumbling around him and Che's bodyguards visible in his rear view mirror.

Chapter 17

Hana opened her eyes as they passed the Rangiriri turn. She watched Logan drive through the corner of her eye. He headed south towards Culver's Cottage and home, their suitcases already in the back of the car. She hated how much she loved him and the devastating effect his scarred hands produced on her body. Her lips craved his and her palms ached to trace the shape of the muscles which bulged either side of his spine. Hana sighed and watched the Kaimai ranges spin past in the east as the motorway carried her south.

Logan chewed his lower lip, an action he'd regret later when it still bled hours after. It demonstrated his level of angst and Hana avoided his sideways glances. She'd wanted to know more about him. Now she did. Logan honed himself into a programme hard wired to recognise rejection and Hana knew it oozed from every pore of her body. She didn't want what he'd brought, sinister women with whispered threats and gun toting bodyguards. She wanted peace, security and a gentle, lyrical existence in which to raise her baby. Everything she'd built with Logan rested on a farce, a smokescreen for danger to lurk behind. Hana sat up straight and faced her husband. "You brought all this mess with Laval into my life, didn't you?"

"What?" he jumped in surprise and his jaw slackened. "You can't seriously believe that!"

Hana jabbed a finger at him, her lips curling back in a snarl. "My life was a picture of order and calm before you stepped into it. I'd never heard of Michael Laval or nasty men called Flick. They're from your world, Logan! Not mine!"

Logan swallowed and ran a shaking hand across his face. "Great," he said. "Just great."

"Oh, it's fantastic!" Sarcasm dripped from Hana's tongue. "Thanks for inducting me into your nasty little group of friends. Could Laval not make it to lunch today? Mrs Che proved an absolute delight. She knows everything about me, Logan. She knows where I work and the fact my son's a cop. I wonder if she wants a copy of the power bill for my house. I can't bear to think there might be gaps in her knowledge."

Logan banged his hands on the steering wheel. "Hana!" he exclaimed. "I told you not to give personal details."

"She already knew!" Hana's voice rose to a high-pitched scream. "She knew everything!" Distaste crossed Logan's face and anger infused her bones at his reaction. She felt herself diminish to the level of screechy woman in his eyes and hopelessness washed over her like unrelenting surf. Hana inhaled, disliking what she'd become. "I can't do this anymore," she blurted. "I can't do any of it." Tears rolled down her cheeks and she grasped at straws. She needed to regain control of her life as a train wreck loomed ahead. "You have to go. I need you to leave." The second the words left her mouth, Hana regretted them. Stubbornness and desperation prevented her taking them back.

Heat flushed up Logan's neck and his teeth worked in his jaw. His knuckles showed white through his skin on the steering wheel and his eyes glistened as though tears pricked behind his dark lashes. Hana longed to take back the foolish command, but she didn't know how. "Fine," Logan replied and he kept his eyes fixed on the road ahead.

He flung the car up the slope to the house, almost hitting the gate as it eased open with painful slowness. Hana's misgivings met her on the front step as she clambered from the car and made her escape. She unlocked the door and deactivated the burglar alarm, nerves making her fingers shake. "What have I done?" she breathed, leaning her forehead against the wall.

She willed Logan to bounce up the steps ready to talk it through. She needed him to justify and explain so she could forgive him. Loneliness and isolation crowded in, threatening her with the life Logan's presence banished. The scent of soup summoned her to the kitchen where one of Maihi's delights sat ready and waiting.

The garage door rose and its vibration rumbled the foundations of the house. Logan's footsteps sounded on the back stairs and Hana tensed, ready to back down from her rash standpoint and issue ultimatums in her favour. He walked into the bedroom and she waited, leaning with her back against the counter. The fingers of her left hand caressed the painful joint his iron grip upset. She planned her words. Her lips formed the sentences to dictate terms and still she waited.

Logan's footsteps moved away, clattering down the stairs to the garage. Hana heard an engine start and the garage door close. She gasped in disbelief as Logan's truck flew past the front window and crested the rise. A single blink and he'd gone, driving out of her life as instructed. And without a fight.

Hana walked to the bathroom in her shoes and coat and found a new toothbrush in the cupboard. She cleaned her teeth and rid herself of all traces of sickness. Her overnight bag sat on the bedroom floor where Logan left it. She kicked him out and he still carried her bag upstairs. Hana pressed her fingers to her lips and Caroline's image taunted her. Despite everything, would he run to her?

Hana sat on the bed and cried for a long while. The temperature of the house dropped and the seeping cold drove her into her monkey pyjamas and dressing gown. Logan's aftershave mocked her from the dresser where he left it before work on Friday, reminding her of her aloneness. Her arm ached and the lounge fire defied her pathetic efforts. Dropping the poker onto the hearth, Hana stood up and wondered how she might take the pain away. "Not like Vik," she breathed. "It's not like that."

Hana bowed to her English roots and made a pot of tea. She heaped sugar into the cup, her mother's cure for all ills. Maihi's pumpkin soup looked delicious but her stomach roiled at the thought of food. In the hallway, Hana paused by the telephone. It seemed rude not to make the call.

Maihi answered on the first ring and a game show played in the background, complete with studio audience laughter. Hana stammered over her words. "Thanks for the soup," she said. "And for feeding Tiger. I haven't seen him yet."

"Ah, he followed me home," the old lady chuckled. "He likes my old moggie a bit too much."

"That's okay." Hana drew her dressing gown cord tighter. "As long as he's fine."

"He is." Maihi lowered her voice. "You don't sound so good."

Hana shook her head but the lump in her throat remained. "I'm just tired," she lied and disconnected the call.

Unable to face her marital bed, she curled up on the lounge sofa, the cold, dark grate mocking her as she snuggled beneath a throw blanket. Logan's scent rose around her like a painful reminder and she buried her nose in her sleeve. Her disturbed dreams contained a faceless Laval and Mrs Che. They combined to hunt and torture her with accusations she didn't understand. She cried for Logan, but he didn't save her.

The rough shake against her shoulder sent Hana scrambling from sleep and the blanket tumbled to the rug. Cold air rushed to attack the parts of her not covered by clothing. "No!" she screamed and jerked back against the sofa. "Don't hurt me."

"Hana." Maihi's gentle voice broke through the panic and Hana pressed a hand to her racing heart. "What's happened, girly? Who wants to hurt you?"

Hana groaned and pressed her face into her hands. "Nobody. Everybody." She didn't sound sure of her answer and Maihi squatted next to her. Windswept hair and a reddened nose made the old woman look crazy. She tutted at the empty grate and pressed the blanket over Hana's legs.

"Talk to Maihi," she instructed, nudging Hana over so she could sit next to her. She got the whole miserable truth, with nothing held back. Hana experienced a sense of catharsis, allowing her redemption through confession. "I blamed him for everything," she concluded with a sniff. She rubbed her nose on her pyjama sleeve. "It wasn't true. I had problems with Laval before Logan arrived. It felt easier to make it all his fault, so I did."

Hana exhaled, empty of tears and exhausted. "Logan took me to lunch with these scary people. I think they're Triads. That world is alien to me. I'm a small town girl from a village in England. I can't cope in his world so I sent him away and he left. They always leave me, Maihi. Why? What's wrong with me?"

A sharp jab in her stomach reminded her she had bigger problems and she rubbed a hand over her belly. "I can't do this again, Maihi. Not alone. I've messed up once already. It's just not fair."

"What's not fair girly?" Maihi stroked her hair back from her forehead with gnarled fingers, crooked by age and arthritis. "What happened with your first marriage?"

"Nothing." Hana's eyes widened and she withdrew inside herself. "I'm tired and talking nonsense. The idea of parenting solo just wears me out. I don't have the energy and I'm too bloody old." She scrubbed at her eyes with her sleeve and Maihi tugged her wrist away so she'd stop.

"You're not alone," she soothed. "You have me."

Hana swallowed and nodded. Her swollen eyes blinked. "Just as well," she said, sounding desperate. "I sent my husband packing."

Maihi stroked her cheek. "Go to bed and try not to think about it tonight. You can't make good decisions in the midst of such emotion."

"I might go back to England." Hana sniffed and set her lips in determination. "My son doesn't speak to me, Izzie will visit wherever I go and I can start again with nobody knowing what a fool I've been." She swallowed and gave a nod. "That's what I'll do."

The determination in her voice alarmed the old woman. Maihi placed her hand over Hana's as it rested on her stomach. The intimate gesture, kindly meant almost unpicked Hana from the inside. "You are whānau. Family. You will never be alone. There's no need to run away."

"Thank you Maihi," Hana whispered. Her eyelashes fluttered and Maihi sensed depression and resignation rearing their ugly twin heads. She tugged at Hana to get her moving and led her to the bedroom. Hana baulked at the door, but Maihi forced her to climb into the wide bed, pushing her down between the covers.

"It'll turn out fine, child. He loves you. Anyone can see that."

"No," Hana replied, shaking her head. "I behaved like Caroline, pulling and pushing so he doesn't know where he is. I love him so much, Maihi, but I'm not sure I want what he's offering. He's in business with that terrifying woman and her husband." She sighed. "I've done it now anyway and he's gone. He didn't even put up a fight." Hana lay down in the huge empty bed and shut her eyes. "I'll make my own decisions from now on."

Maihi drove back across the fields on the quad bike, the same way she arrived. She opened and closed the gates her husband installed while the cattle grazed Hana's paddocks. The chill air snatched at her clothes as she rode standing up. A movement on the bush line caught her eye and she pulled up with a squeal of brakes. "You're out late, Aunty. Everything all right?" The man stepped from the undergrowth, a shotgun slung over his shoulder. His camouflage jacket and pants helped him blend into the natural background.

"No, Nephew," Maihi replied. "Stay some more. She's all on her own for a while. Stick close and don't take your eyes off her place. She's a good lady and we owe her a debt for the grass."

The figure nodded and blended back into the bush. Maihi drove home, cursing the gates and latches as she went. She parked the quad bike inside the shed and kicked her gumboots off on the porch. Her husband and his guest watched a rugby game and sipped cans of beer. Hemi shook his fist at the television, but his companion stared at the scene through the darkened window without seeing.

"Hey, wahine," Hemi said, waving his arm at the picture on screen. "These jokers can't score tonight."

Maihi jerked her head upwards and closed the back door behind her. Temper got the better of her and as she passed behind the sofa, her hand shot out and slapped their houseguest around the back of the head. His drink wobbled and beer slopped onto the rug. He rose in an instant and whirled around to face her. "You stupid man!" she shouted at Logan. "You are a foolish, foolish idiot!"

"Maihi, Maihi!" Hemi stood and reached for her arm. She gave him a look of disgust and shook him off.

"What the hell?" Logan demanded, raising his voice. Hemi tapped him on the shoulder in warning.

"No, man," he cautioned. "Calm it."

Logan's jaw worked as he struggled to control his temper. Maihi's slap to the head hurt and he rubbed the area with bunched fingers, knowing she left a bruise. "What did I do?" he demanded, spreading his fingers in bewilderment.

Hemi shrugged and sat back down, but Logan waited for Maihi to answer. When she didn't, he shook his head and gritted his teeth. "I'll get a motel room," he said and bent to pick up his jacket.

"That would be dumb," Hemi said, without looking away from the television.

Logan felt anger building in his chest. He shook his head. "Na. Coming south was dumb. Thinking I could find happiness with Hana was dumb." He shucked his jacket over his broad shoulders. "I need to get back to what I know and that's not here." He inclined his head towards Hemi. "Thanks for the hospitality, man. I appreciate it."

"Always here." Hemi waved a hand in a casual movement.

Maihi intercepted Logan, body blocking him near the back door. She reached out a hand which had seen hard work in her lifetime. Out of respect for an elder, Logan stood back, waiting for her to speak. "You're not who I thought you were," she whispered. "Youse like all the others. What about that baby you're walking away from?"

Logan closed his eyes and when he opened them, his irises twinkled grey as storm water. "I'm not walking away from my child and nobody can make me."

Maihi dug a bony finger into his hard chest. "You think you can have it all your own way, don't you?" Logan gritted his teeth and his composure slipped. "You've destroyed her world today. Just like that!" Maihi's fingers clicked in front of his face to emphasise her point. "Now you will just leave, yeah? Like a coward at the first sign of trouble."

Logan glanced across at Hemi for help, but the other man watched the television with his arms folded and his face blank. He stayed quiet and if Maihi saw the vehement danger in her husband's eyes, she chose to ignore it. Logan shuttered his emotions and reached down for his boots. "Hana doesn't want me anymore. She doesn't like what I bring and asked me to leave. She made the choice for both of us."

Maihi stamped her foot and made a sound like a growl. "She deserved better than this! A man who loved her for years, but isn't willing to work through the hardships. You wanted a fairy tale and they don't exist!" Maihi spat the last two words and Logan felt her spittle hit his cheek. He resisted the urge to wipe his hand across his face.

"I don't beg women for chances," Logan replied, his voice hard and cold. "She made her choice."

"Do you know what she said to me?" Tears glinted in the corners of the old woman's eyes and she drew herself near to Logan, as close as she dared. "She said she can't do it alone and she meant it!"

Logan blanched. His face paled so his eyes stood out vivid grey, the firelight reflected as flickering flames in his irises. "What did she mean by that?" His lips curled back into a snarl and hatred brimmed near the surface. The power of it knocked Maihi's breath from her lungs.

"Desperate women do desperate things." She raised her voice to match his. "It hangs over them like a shroud. So. Don't. Make. Her. Desperate!" She dared to punctuate her last words with a succession of prods to Logan's hard chest and he took a step back, his face unreadable.

He shook his head in denial of something unforeseen. "What did she mean, Maihi? Tell me. Will she hurt herself or the baby?" Latent fear clouded his view and Miriam's face drifted through his memory. Manic and unpredictable, only medication sedated her in her worst moments. "I need to go home." He turned for the door and Maihi shifted to cover the handle with her fingers.

"No. I settled her for tonight. Leave her to get some rest."

Logan shook his head. "Please get out of my way."

"No. See her tomorrow when she's calmed down." She placed a finger over his lips and watched him struggle not to recoil from her touch. She spoke to him in Māori, soft and lyrical like his grandmother's steady cadence. Not Te Reo but the old Māori, unwritten, handed down as a taonga, a treasure. It washed over him like a breath of wisdom. "Your todays will shape all of your tomorrows. Shape today well."

"Will she hurt herself?" He sounded calmer and Maihi took her finger away. She listened to Logan's exhale.

"Never," she breathed. "But she might buy a one way plane ticket. Right now, go to bed." Her tone held authority. "Talk tomorrow."

Logan resisted for a moment before kicking off his boots again and moving towards the stairs. Maihi glanced across at her husband and saw him give a slow shake of his head. "I don't think he'll still be here in the morning," he said, raising an eyebrow. "You changed nothing, woman."

"I had to try." Maihi's hands fluttered across her top lip, demonstrating the extent of her emotion. "She deserves it."

Hemi rose and his long legs took him across the room to her. He knew how Maihi's past, like everyone's, forced its way into her present with amazing power and not always for good. He wrapped his arms around her and kissed the top of her head. "She's not you," he breathed. "Your circumstances were different."

"He still walked away." Her voice sounded muffled in his shirt. "He left me with a baby."

Hemi patted her back with his tender paws. "And I'm glad the jerk ran because you wouldn't have looked at me twice otherwise."

Maihi slapped his chest. "I should have met you first, Hemi. Could've saved myself a heap of trouble."

Hemi inhaled and his lips curved upwards into a smile. He ruffled her hair. "Ah, the burdens and baggage we carry, it's a wonder we ever get anywhere." He squeezed Maihi's shoulder. "You go too far sometimes, woman."

Maihi's brown eyes glistened with tears and she nodded in agreement. "E tohe i ngā tohe a Pōtoru," she sighed. "Stubborn as the stubbornness of Pōtoru, a man who rushed to his own destruction."

Hemi glanced up the stairs to Logan's door and shook his head. "Him, wahine? Or me?"

Chapter 18

Logan's feet hung over the end of the bed, poking through the blankets. He rose and slipped his socks back on. The image of Hana alone and frightened next door made him want to go to her, but Maihi's voice rose downstairs. He doubted she'd let him go tonight. "Geez, Du Rose," he sighed into the darkness. "Are you really that scared of an old kuia?" The question remained rhetorical. He'd sensed her wisdom and suspected another argument with Hana wouldn't stop her climbing on a plane back to her homeland.

He tossed and turned in the tiny space and tried to keep his past from haunting him. Memories of Caroline's abortion returned, giving him a pain in his head. "Some twenty first birthday present," he muttered, his voice muffled beneath the blankets. He recalled the angry exchange with his brother, a fight which destroyed their relationship once and for all. 'It's not your kid, dumbass,' Michael had laughed. 'She's been coming to me for months. Did you not notice you weren't getting any?'

He'd broken Michael's nose but not wiped the smile off his face. Logan caught the next flight from Auckland International and barely looked back. He missed graduation but didn't care. His life's goal was to find Hana and all he'd done was brought the start forward. Michael visited him in London many years later to apologise, but the trust had gone.

Logan turned over and groaned as the blanket slid to the floor, uncovering his back. He sensed Maihi owned better offerings, but freezing him to death served as a suitable punishment for hurting Hana. In covering his back, his feet protruded from the blankets again. He threw the whole thing off in temper and curled into a ball. It reminded him of his childhood in the dilapidated hotel with moth eaten sheets and a hungry belly.

A light knock on the door sent him scrabbling for the blanket to cover himself. Hemi stuck his head through a narrow gap, back lit by the light from the hallway. "Guessing you're still awake," he whispered.

"Yeah." Logan hauled the tiny blanket closer and sat up, leaning against the cool plaster behind him. "Come in, man."

Hemi pushed his way inside and closed the door, snapping on the overhead light. "I'm not meant to molly coddle you," he said, his eyelashes fluttering with sheepishness. "But I thought bugger it."

Logan snorted. "Brave man. I'm laying here with a tea towel over my bits because I'm too frit to ask for more blankets."

Hemi wrinkled his nose and reached behind him. Cracking a wardrobe door, he produced a warm duvet and extra pillows. "Don't tell her, ay?"

"Why is it always my fault?" Logan demanded, covering himself in warmth. "She didn't even ask what happened."

"Womenfolk." Hemi leaned back in the bedroom chair and his long legs covered the space between them. "I'm asking now."

Logan rested his crown against the wall. "Long story, mate. The short version is that I took Hana to meet some business associates and she freaked out. Said we're done and kicked me out."

"That don't sound like her." Hemi cocked an eyebrow. "Who are these business associates?"

"Triads." Logan pursed his lips. "But more than that. They've behaved more like family than my own blood. I owe Mr Che a lot."

"Does Hana know that?"

Logan inhaled and examined a ratty thumbnail. "I tried to tell her but I don't think she understood. On reflection, maybe I didn't try hard enough to spell it out. It didn't help that Mrs Che's bodyguards followed us to the city limits. I assumed the final meeting would be different."

"They followed you?"

Logan bowed his head in a nod. "Yeah. They always do. It's an ego thing and I've never challenged it. It rarely matters and as it turned out, today wasn't the day to start."

"Did some part of you want Hana to reject you?" Hemi leaned forward and balanced his elbows on his knees.

"No!" Logan jerked backwards and banged his head on the wall. "Course not!" The thought drummed in the back of his brain somewhere and resonated with truth. He shrugged. "Ah, maybe I expected her to. It didn't come as much of a surprise."

"So, you left without a fight."

Logan wrinkled his nose. "I guess."

"Then you're a dork." Hemi rose. "Get a good sleep and it'll make more sense in the morning."

Logan pushed himself under the covers and drew his feet up. "If she's still here."

"She will be." The door clicked closed.

The weekend's events invaded Logan's thoughts and sadness washed over him. Alfred's revelation clouded his mind. He lay on his front and pulled the pillow over his head to block out the world. His thoughts turned to Hana again and his heart yearned to go to her like elastic pulling him back. He offered his love and loyalty to people and they always stamped on it, broke it into a million pieces. With her, it seemed different. He went over and over the awful conversation in the car, trying to drum up the anger and bitterness again and ride on the easy tide of it, but it wouldn't come back. Just an all-pervading sadness remained.

He recalled the pain in Hana's expression as he pulled on her broken joint. Turning onto his back, he punished himself for his neglect.

Darkness deepened as he concentrated on identifying the night noises issuing from the dense bush behind the house. He wondered if Hana listened to the same sounds. Shame blossomed in his chest at the memory of her discomfort during the luncheon. He should have intervened and regretted not doing so.

A quiet prayer issued from his moving lips, imploring a God he rarely considered. He asked for help to mend today so he might have good tomorrows. "Can you help me?" he whispered. "I don't know what to do."

No crack of thunder or vivid, glowing words appeared on the wall opposite to tell him what to do. He pulled the duvet around himself and sulked. "Thanks for nothing," he muttered, knowing he didn't deserve much help, anyway. He pictured the strip of land reaching high above the hotel and scented the ocean in his mind. His grandmother's words drifted back on an imaginary breeze.

'Remember tangata whenua my grandson, Logan. They will help you rebuild our house.'

Her insight struck him with fresh understanding as he curled in the tiny bed, the springs creaking every time he moved. She didn't mean his whare, the physical house, but his whānau, the family. Rebuild the Du Roses.

Logan hugged his knees. A wave of optimism swept over him. The kuia's words haunted him like a coded cipher for decades and yet seemed ridiculously obvious. Rebuild the family and those who had gone before, would help.

"I can't now!" Logan grumbled, lying down. He fitted his hands behind his head, his muscular arms prickling with cold in the freezing air. "Hana kicked me out, Kuia. I blew it." The old lady's scent drifted over him in a comforting memory of lavender and kowhai, settling his nerves and bringing him peace.

Sleep came with it and the sense that everything would turn out okay.

Logan relaxed beneath the divine grace summoned to soothe his troubled soul. He couldn't name its source because he didn't know the author, but felt the gentle hands and let go of his angst.

Maihi woke Logan while it was still dark, slapping his head with the flat of her hand. He startled awake as though doused with freezing water and struggled to contain his lethal defence reaction. Maihi jumped back as he balled his fists, knowing he might be defensive but surprised at the voltage of it. Logan bounced to his feet and rounded on her, all hard angles and muscular definition. His top lip curled back in a snarl. "Don't do that!" he exclaimed.

Maihi faltered. "Get up bro'. Go get your life sorted. Mend today."

"Piss off!" Logan's heart raced with the shock of the rude awakening and his body shook as adrenalin dispersed itself through his blood stream. Maihi left the room as fast as she entered, blinding him by flicking on the light switch. "Bloody woman!" Logan hissed as he dragged on his suit trousers.

"I heard that," she shouted from the stairs. "Respect for elders, taitamaiti. Youse not too big for another slap!"

Logan smirked and reached for his shirt. Some Māori women possessed more balls than their men.

Chapter 19

Hana's sleep offered no rest. She jumped awake at every creak and groan of the old house. Peering through the window in the early hours, she spotted light in the canopy high above the house and feared a bush fire. The orange glimmer looked distant and she fumbled for her phone. In the darkness she missed it and the handset skittered down the back of her bedside cabinet with a clunk. Hana groaned. "Bloody marvellous!" More awake than before, she checked the flickering light again and abandoned her attempt to mobilise the local volunteer fire service. "Oh what the heck," she grumbled. "I'll burn in my bed if it gets out of control. It's what I deserve, anyway."

The baby kicked her in rebuke as Hana clambered back into bed. She groaned, placing her hand over the tiny foot digging into her ribs. "Shh baby," she soothed. "I don't want to think about you right now. I don't want to think about anything important."

Hana settled down in the cold bed and tried to sleep. She woke around six, aware of a presence in the room with her. The hair rose on the back of her neck in a prickling sensation and she held her breath. Mrs Che's veiled threats returned to heighten her fear and Hana's body trembled in the large bed. "What do you want?" she snapped, expecting to hear a reply in the woman's broken English. She pushed herself upright and her head swam.

"It's just me." Logan stood next to the bed and sat down as soon as he saw Hana surface from sleep. She felt his weight depress the mattress and resisted the natural tilt towards him. He looked a mess, his hair tousled and beard growth on his cheeks and chin. Yet his eyes sparkled with life, a sharp paradox to the rest of him. "I'm sorry," he whispered. "Yesterday didn't go as I planned."

Hana felt fury build in her chest, coming from nowhere and consuming her. "Sorry doesn't cut it, Logan." She shook her head without compromise and shoved her foot against his leg. "You left me here."

Logan gaped. "You told me to get out!" The new game confused him and he played it without skill.

"I didn't mean it!" Hana's lip curled back in a snarl. She saw Logan's jaw tighten and realised if he walked away again, she couldn't handle it. Her resistance foxed her and she scrabbled in her mind for answers. If she didn't understand herself, she couldn't expect him to. The words tumbled from her mouth and she heard them as though from the lips of a stranger. They contained the cry of her heart. "You'll go eventually, everyone always does. I'm the one left to pick up the pieces every time."

The sentence spewed out, words filled with grudge and self-pity. They tumbled free, falling over each other like foundation stones. Logan let out a sigh of realisation and his eyes narrowed. Something didn't sit right. "I'm not Vikram Johal, Hana." His tone sounded leaden and severe. "Stop blaming me for whatever he did."

Hana swallowed and bit into her bottom lip, knowing she'd said too much. "He did nothing." She heard the hysterical strains and held her breath.

"Hana listen." Logan grasped her shoulders in his hands. Her slender fingers pressed his chest, pushing with futile bursts of pressure. Tears of confusion spilled from her eyes and coursed down her cheeks. Logan shook his head and bent to kiss her. She pushed him away. "Go, go away."

"No!" He set his jaw with determination, a light glowing from behind his eyes. "Not this time. You can't get rid of me, Hana."

"I want to," she wailed and he shook his head.

"No, you don't. I won't make that mistake again." He swallowed and caught her to him, crushing her into his chest to prevent her aimless thrashing. "We have bad history, babe. You're right. I do always run but that doesn't make it right. It's just what I've learned to do. I'm sorry that it repeated some kind of pattern for you, but let's end it right here. I'll stop running and you stop pushing me away. We need to learn to trust each other."

Hana ground her teeth and the anger subsided, slithering back into the cage in her heart. "What if I want to run?" she mumbled.

Logan cocked his head and made her look up at him. Her irises swam with more tears. "To England?" He wrinkled his nose. "What would you run to, sweetheart? There's nothing there for you."

She closed her eyes against the cruelty of his words but the truth shone through like a sunbeam. Someone else torched that bridge for her long ago. "I don't know," she breathed, her body limp with exhaustion. "I don't know anything."

"You don't need to." Logan stroked her hair back from her face and his pupils dilated. "Let me take care of you, Hana. Stop fighting me." His body twitched as her vulnerability pulled at the core of him. He pressed his lips against hers, groaning as she bit him. The pain spurred him on and a ripping sound cut across the silent bedroom as the monkey pyjama top ripped up the side seam. "I bloody hate these things," he gasped, hurling the ruined shirt to the floor.

"This won't make it better." Hana splayed her fingers against his chest and Logan ignored her, yanking his shirt over his head.

"I don't care." He stood and unbuttoned his smart trousers, kicking off his boots and clambering back into the bed.

Hana felt the intoxication of his maleness sweep over her, dominating and subduing her anger. It felt right and yet she resisted, afraid of afterwards when their blood cooled and awkwardness descended. "You'll leave me," she whispered, wrapping her arms around her torso to cover her nakedness. "Right when I need you most, you'll go."

"No, I won't. Trust me." Logan's lips covered hers and his authority threaded itself around her, bowing her back into the pillows and urging her to give in. Hana succumbed without another protest, sliding her fingers down the back of his shorts and stroking the bunched muscle of Logan's firm butt. She shuttered the nagging anxieties and let him love her, banishing the image of Mrs Che from the bedroom. Yet Michael Laval's ghostly presence remained, wrapping its influence around her life and getting ready to squeeze.

Logan held Hana as daylight increased in strength, permeating the room through a crack in the curtains. He felt her shift and held tighter, knowing words could break their uneasy truce. He took a deep breath and sensed her tension hike. "I don't want to talk!" she gasped. He heard the panic in her voice. "Don't ask me anything."

Logan sighed and his fingers strayed to her hair. He wrapped his other arm around her and pressed her closer. "Let's forget yesterday," he soothed. "It suits me. But we can talk about today and tomorrow. I'm in this marriage for life, Hana. But just remember that my default is to run, so don't push me away." He kissed her. "Agreed?"

Hana nodded. "I'll try," she whispered. "I don't know why I said it. I figured you'd go one day anyway so I might as well get it over with. Those Chinese people terrified me. The woman fogged my head and made me want to hide in a very dark place."

"I know, babe. I tried to warn you but not hard enough. I won't see them again now. It's all done. I've a few more interests to get rid of and then CircleLine is finished. But we need to work harder to trust each other, Hana. Both of us, yeah?"

"Okay." Hana pushed her face into Logan's downy chest and sighed, satiated by sex and exhausted from her disturbed night. She closed her eyes, resenting the intrusion of hastening daylight. "I don't want to go to work," she grumbled.

"Tough." Logan pushed her into a sitting position. "I'm not leaving you here, so get up and get a move on." He refused to bow to her tantrum, pulling the sheets all the way off the bed and letting the cold air wrap itself around her. She got up and examined the ruined pyjamas.

"Poor monkey," she sighed, frowning at the rumpled brown face and detached sleeve. While she showered. Logan confiscated them, balling them up in the dustbin in the garage and making sure they sank to the bottom.

"See ya!" He used a piece of firewood to plaster the petulant monkey faces into the mouldering remains of a spaghetti Bolognese and slammed the bin lid. Another vestige of Hana's former life as Mrs Johal awaited the refuse collectors. Logan stared at the mountain and sighed. Vik's legacy remained in the form of his arrogant son and whatever damage Hana seemed to harbour. Suspecting it ran far deeper than she would ever admit, he raised his middle finger in an ugly gesture at the dustbin and climbed the steps to the main house.

They readied themselves for work, Hana dragging her heels at every opportunity. She used each complaint she could think of to avoid getting in the car. "My tummy feels odd," she said, rubbing at the space beneath her bump.

"Get in the car. If you think I'm leaving you here with your imagination, you're kidding yourself." Logan jabbed his finger at the front door. "Out."

Hana clattered down the steps whilst spewing a constant stream of grumbles and he followed, his finger hovering over the keypad for the burglar alarm. A picture of a crucified Jesus hung on the wall next to it and he bit his lip. He'd trailed Miriam's odd Catholic icon all over the globe, scared she'd sense if he got rid of it. Hana found it and stuck it on the wall. His mother's words returned and he remembered her shaking hands as she handed it over decades ago. 'It hung in your kuia's room. She liked all that Atua stuff. God never did much for me, but he might for you.' The Rabbi's face held tenderness amidst the suffering beneath the ethereal glow of his halo. Logan studied it for a moment, seeing it as though for the first time. He twisted his lips into a grimace, remembering the peace of his night's sleep. "Maybe there's more to you than I thought," he said with a sigh.

Hana watched him from the front steps, impatience in her expression. Logan gave her a smile and slammed the front door behind him.

Chapter 20

Work tired Hana so much, she struggled to reheat Maihi's soup and stay awake long enough to eat it. She disappeared to the bedroom and Logan found her rummaging beneath her pillow. "What's up?" he demanded, watching her pull the bed apart in her bra and undies.

"I can't find them!" Hana exclaimed. "I just want to go to bed."

"Find what?" asked Logan. A flush of guilt crept up his throat.

"My jamas!" Hana got onto her hands and knees to look under the bed.

Logan stifled a snort. "I chucked them in the rubbish, babe. They're knackered."

"No! How could you?" Hana narrowed her eyes and her face lit with a redhead's determination. Logan intercepted her at the bedroom door.

"No you don't." His laugh sounded forced and he held onto her, wrapping his arms around her wriggling body. "I hate them. That damn monkey gives me the evils every time I come near you. You're my wife, not his."

"I liked them! I'm getting them back. They can soak overnight to get any stains out."

"Not these stains!" Logan kept hold of her. "Tea bags and cat sick. Ils sont irrécupérables, mon amour."

Hana glared at him. "You should know better than to speak French to an angry Englishwoman and Tiger has never yet puked in the bin. I want my pyjamas! You ripped them on purpose!"

Logan pouted but didn't deny it. "Wear some of your nice ones," he soothed, letting go of her flailing arms so he could peer into the drawer where she kept night wear. He prodded about in the swathes of silky fabric. "These."

"Don't fit!" Hana answered, sitting on the bed and wrapping her arms around her cold torso. Logan ignored her. He pulled a red silky number from the drawer and held it up against her.

"Liar. I bought you this. You look really ooh la la in it." A glint lit his grey irises and Hana pouted.

"Stop with the French!" She snatched the silky negligée from his hand and flicked him with it. "Stop that too!" She jabbed a finger at the expression of desire on his face. "Fine, I'll prove it." Logan groaned under his breath as Hana slipped off her bra. She found the neck of the nightdress and pushed her head through, colour lighting her cheeks with the effort. The soft material slithered provocatively over her breasts and down her waist until suffering a silky traffic jam over her stomach. Logan's brow knitted in understanding but undeterred, he tried to yank it further. His enthusiasm produced a rotten tearing sound and he stepped back in horror.

"Happy now?" Hana griped. She stood and spun on the spot, stuck inside the garment. Logan snorted at her hopeless actions and she gave him a shove. "Stop laughing!" she shouted. "And don't say you're sorry because I can see you're not!"

Logan removed the amused expression with difficulty and helped her extricate herself from the nightdress. He eased it over her head, rolled it up and fitted it back into the drawer. Then he poked around looking for something else while Hana shivered on the bed. "They were elasticated," she grumbled. "And comfy."

"They reeked of your old life and I hated them." A quick glance at Hana earned himself a glare and a retort.

"Don't you dare look at me with that glint in your eye!" she threatened him. "I'm freezing because of you. You're not coming near me!"

Logan sniggered and pulled open the door to his wardrobe. His hands rested on an old shirt hanging near the back. "What about this?" he asked. Almost threadbare from his work on the farm, it made a sorry picture alongside the designer shirts. Logan pulled it off the hanger. "You borrowed this when Odering locked me up."

Hana's face brightened. "Yeah, this one," she said. She dropped her arms and ran to collect it, her face innocent and guileless like a small child. Her rounded breasts bounced as she lifted the shirt over her shoulders and Logan blew out a pursed breath. Hana buttoned all but the top three and twirled on the spot. "I like it," she said. Her fingers moved behind to pat the flap which dangled to her thighs. "I'll need to wear knickers to bed though."

"Believe me, you won't," Logan mouthed, feeling the tension in his chest hike. "Geez, Hana. This is a terrible idea."

"No, I like it." Hana grinned. "I forgive you now. I like this much better."

"It's too damn sexy," Logan breathed. "I can't cope with seeing you in this. It's gonna have to come off!"

Hana squealed as he hoisted her into his arms. "That's the worst pick up line I've ever heard. Have you any more of those little gems tucked inside your egotistical Māori book of how to bed babes?"

"Plenty. And they all work." Logan bit her neck and laid her on the bed, popping the next three buttons with little effort.

"Logan, stop. I only just got it on!" Hana shrieked.

He buried his face in the soft skin beneath her hair and inhaled her jasmine scent. "It doesn't look right. It's coming off."

Hana resisted long enough to hear the small tearing sound from the seam beneath her armpit. "Don't you dare! Not again!"

"Do as you're told then, woman." Logan's voice sounded husky and he worked his fingers beneath the edge of her underwear. "Mmnn, I love the easy access," he breathed.

"Do not rip another pair!" she grumbled and eased them over her hips.

Hana climbed back into the shirt later, despite Logan's best efforts. "Stay," he pleaded, wrapping an arm around her swollen stomach. His fingers slid upward and he cupped a full breast in his scarred palm. "Geez, I love you pregnant, wahine. You're gorgeous."

Hana giggled and turned away, the smile fading from her lips at the sound of the gate alarm buzzing in the lobby. She panicked, her chest freezing mid inhale and her eyes widening. Logan shot from the bed and grappled for his nearest pair of jeans, hauling them from the drawer and stuffing his feet into the legs. A proliferation of swear words spewed from his lips.

Hana swallowed. "It must be Bodie," she stage whispered. "Nobody else knows the number."

Logan halted, his jeans half covering his naked butt. "What the hell are we doing? This is our house!"

Hana giggled. "Fine! Go out in your undies and say howdy!" She threw herself against the pillows and raised her arms, watching him grind his teeth and look conflicted as she displayed her naked torso against the creamy white sheets. "Say hello from me."

"I'll get you for this." Logan narrowed his eyes and exited the room, jerking his head in her direction. "I'll get rid of him and then you'd better watch out."

Hana's smile slipped from her lips as the door closed behind him. After weeks of no contact, it seemed typical that Bodie would just walk into her home like nothing was wrong. She heard Logan intercept her son at the front door and reached for the shirt, slipping it back over her shoulders. Tempting as it felt to ignore him, Hana pulled on her dressing gown and knickers, complimenting her outfit with a pair of Logan's woolly farm socks.

Bodie swallowed as Hana strolled into the kitchen, her hands pushed deep into her robe pockets. He recognised the bloom of sex in her twinkling eyes and she saw him recoil in disgust. Logan turned his back to fill the kettle and Hana watched her son study the awful scarring on his muscular torso. His eyes sparked with a policeman's curiosity and he winced. "Tea for me, please." Hana ran a finger down the ugly ridge of knitted skin on Logan's side and gave her husband a sweet smile. The awkwardness in the room felt tangible and she allied herself with him before turning back to her son.

"To what do we owe this unusual pleasure?" she demanded, her tone harsh. Logan's lips pursed in amusement and he leaned against the counter and observed the scene playing out, his arms folded across his chest.

Bodie sat at the kitchen table, not quite sure where to look as he poked around with a crumb of toast forgotten in the teatime clean up. "Just wondered how you were," he lied. His eyelashes flickered and Hana felt a stab of satisfaction in her chest at her recognition of the old tell.

"How's Amy?" she asked, trying to steer towards neutral territory.

"Don't know." Bodie rolled the crumb against the wooden table without looking up. "I pick up my son and hand him over to the woman you met. Haven't seen Amy for weeks." He rubbed a hand across beard growth which looked day's old. Unkemptness surrounded him in the form of stained track pants and a white tee shirt which had become grey through washing.

"Do you want to see her?" Hana pursed her lips, not surprised when Bodie gave a jerky shrug.

Logan clattered around on the counter top with the teapot and coffee. He glanced back at Hana, catching her eye and jerking his head to indicate he would leave them alone. Hana shook her head and screwed up her face with a silent plea. Bodie's problems presented a rabbit hole she'd negotiated before. Her own complicated life dictated she leave well alone this time.

If Bodie expected his mother to probe and give him the pleasure of shutting her down, he found himself sadly disappointed. Hana changed the subject. "I heard from Izzie on Saturday," she said, rising to fetch a packet of biscuits from the pantry cupboard. "She said she looks like the side of a barn. Marcus has to help her put socks on."

Bodie nodded and a flicker of a smile raised his lips. The crumb refused to roll beneath his finger anymore. Hana slapped the packet of biscuits in front of him and sat back down. He reached for one as though starving and began munching as Logan placed the teapot on the table. Logan hovered for a moment, trying to catch Hana's eye and failing. Making a decision, he excused himself. "I'm nipping to the bathroom," he muttered as Hana mentally labelled him a coward. She pulled a snarky face at his retreating back.

Bodie looked up as Logan left the room, waiting until he heard the bathroom door click. "Do you know he does business with the Triads?" he hissed, launching into his hate campaign. "He's like a son to their head guy. I knew there was something off about him!" The victory in Bodie's voice made Hana's stomach churn.

Her brain recalled the security detail, the private meal and the gun. She swallowed, knowing she'd already pledged herself to Logan. Turning determined green eyes on her son, she replied, "I know who my husband is and we enjoyed a lovely meal with the Ches on Sunday. I tried crispy fried seaweed for the first time and liked it." She didn't add that it tasted different the second time around.

Bodie's gasp saved her the trouble of adding anything else. "Mum!" He glanced at the doorway before lowering his voice again and adding a beseeching tone. "These people are felons. You talk about lunch with the Triads like it's a normal thing! Has it not occurred to you that all your problems started when you met Logan?"

Hana rose and her jaw worked in her cheek, making her head swim. She reached for the teapot and poured with shaking hands. His accusation echoed her own and guilt made her spiteful. "Just because your life isn't going how you thought, don't start picking holes in mine!" She dumped a mug in front of Bodie, regardless of whether he wanted it. Liquid slopped over the side. "My problems began long before Logan came on the scene, but you wouldn't know that because you drop in and out of my life when it suits you." She thumped the milk jug in front of him before sitting down again. He looked confused at her sudden ability to defend herself. It wasn't what he expected.

"I'm trying to protect you," he began, spreading his hands in placation. "Dad would expect me to."

Hana felt herself withdraw at the mention of her former husband. An uncharacteristic hardness crashed over her slender features. "Bodie, the night you dropped me home after the expo, your main concern was for your career. I don't blame you and I'm telling you it's fine. But don't turn up weeks later to put me straight because you've done some digging and wish to brag about your latest find." She took a sip of her tea and found it hot enough to burn her lips. She raised an eyebrow and fought irritation. "I thought doing background checks on people without good reason was a dismissible offence. Won't you get into trouble?"

Bodie chewed his lip. "I didn't do that!"

"No?" Hana countered, pushing her mug aside. "Then you've found a ready informant. Lucky you. Bo, why don't you stop making out my husband is a career criminal and do something useful? Put your efforts into finding Laval, so people like me and Mrs Bowman can stop looking over our shoulders.

She and I are the victims, not you!" Hana ran her hand over her stomach and sat up straighter. She realised she didn't hear the toilet flush and wondered where Logan got to. He appeared in the kitchen after an awkward, protracted silence which Hana thought might never end. His hair hung limp and wet and the scent of coconut shower gel hung around him. Jeans clutched his buttocks but his bare torso held a damp sheen.

"That's better," he said, giving Hana a smile. "I grabbed a shower and set the washing machine off."

"Thanks." Her heartbeat skipped and then levelled with his calming presence. Logan retrieved his coffee from the draining board before sitting down at the table. He seemed adept at ignoring loaded atmospheres as he slid the biscuits away from Bodie and poked around in the packet. Hana watched him wrinkle his nose and push it away, withdrawing empty fingers.

Leaning back in his chair, he lifted his hands to cup the crown of his head. His scars looked intimidating and accentuated Bodie's impression of a gangster image. "Pointless going to the gym and running up that hill if I'm gonna eat crap!" Logan patted his six pack and winked at Hana. "Gotta think of next year's soccer season!"

Hana smiled, but Bodie didn't. "What happened at the expo?" her son demanded, looking at both of them in turn. His gaze strayed to Logan's scar and then away. He slapped the table with his palm. "I know something happened! I'm not stupid."

Logan's grey eyes studied Bodie with veiled dislike. Hana saw distaste peeking through the cracks she'd learned to look for. "Laval sent two guys to find Hana because the school was wide open. They found me instead."

Bodie shook his head and shrugged, raising one shoulder in question. "And?"

Logan heaved out a sigh of irritation. "And they left. Look bro', with the greatest of respect, how far into this do you want to go? You're a serving officer as you keep reminding us. Aren't there some things you're best not knowing?"

Bodie swallowed and conflict shrouded his expression of curiosity. He gritted his teeth and Hana saw amusement light her husband's lips. She stretched out a hand and rested it on his thigh in warning. "You should tell me," Bodie said, a nervous swallow sending his Adam's apple bouncing in his throat.

Logan looked to Hana for advice. "What should I do?" he asked.

"I don't know," Hana whispered. She ran a shaking hand over her eyes. "Tell him the truth?"

Logan inhaled through his nostrils like an angry horse. "I had a scuffle with both of them. I dropped the Chinese guy at the hospital for treatment to a knee injury and left Flick alive, but bruised. It appears Laval put a price on Flick's head that night, so I'm picking that neither will come after Hana anytime soon. They have their own issues to keep them busy."

"Thanks," Bodie said, his voice quiet. "I needed to ask because a Chinese illegal by the name of Huang was found in Manukau Harbour in the early hours of this morning. He's been on the immigration radar for a while and they tracked him to the Waikato Hospital. Surgeons gave him a knee replacement before discovering his medical number was fake and he wasn't entitled to healthcare. He left the hospital before officers arrived and disappeared. A truck driver picked up a hitchhiker in a lot of pain on State Highway 1, going northbound on Saturday morning and dropped him off downtown. He washed up on the beach this morning around six. The coroner identified the body by the serial number on the new knee joint."

The kitchen remained silent and Hana watched the warning vein tick in Logan's neck. He kept his composure beneath Bodie's avid scrutiny, affecting an air of casualness. "This will come back to you." Bodie said. Hana's heart lurched at the challenge in his tone.

Logan leaned forward in his seat and fixed Bodie with a hard stare, his voice stilted and jerky. "Where is your evidence?"

Bodie shook his head and raised his voice to make the point. "There's always evidence! I'll get a warrant and seize that Toyota four wheel drive you run around in."

Logan snorted. "Fine, do it. Take Hana's while you're at it. In fact, search the house, Bodie. Knock yourself out."

Bodie looked like a man on a winning streak in the moments before he realised the game may not be played as he thought. "Do you think I wouldn't?"

Logan snorted. "I think you'd sell your own granny for a win, mate. Cops like you get a scent and just keep going, even if it takes you in the wrong direction. Then you fix stuff to validate yourselves. Do whatever will advance your career and good luck to ya. But just remember this, son. Hunger for success is a cruel mistress. She puts you on a hamster wheel and never lets you off." He rose and pushed his chair under the table. Standing behind Hana, he rested his hands on her shoulders in a show of possession.

"You're going to jail, you know that?" Bodie shouted.

Hana tilted her head back and fixed her eyes on the underside of Logan's jaw, watching his lips move as he spoke. She couldn't look at her son. "You've formed an opinion of me and nothing I do will change that. What do you want Bodie? To be the cop who gets promotion fitting up a family member? Is that how you want to make a name for yourself?"

"I don't." Bodie stood and balled his fists by his sides, his face a mixture of pain and regret. "I don't want to believe the worst. I want my mother to be happy, don't you get that?" He moved towards the doorway and turned to jab a finger in Logan's direction. "Promise me that nothing you're involved in will burn me or my family?"

Logan nodded. "I give you my word. I'll protect Hana with my life." His eyes narrowed. "You? You're fair game, officer."

Bodie jerked his head once in response, pulled on his trainers without lacing them up and left, running down the front steps to his car. Logan locked the door behind him while Hana grappled with her shock reaction and forced her hands to stop shaking. She heard Logan snort. "He's a brat, Hana!" he snapped. "He left his keys like a spoilt little boy." Hana heard the cupboard drawer open and close and a jangle as metal dropped into it.

When he returned to the kitchen, he noticed Hana's ashen expression. "The Asian man died!" she whispered in bewilderment.

Logan's brow knitted and he kissed the top of her head. "It's not a nice world he got messed up in, Hana. Triads don't leave and go to work for someone else. There's only one way out and he knew that."

Hana shook her head as though trying to clear space for the information to fit into. "I knew nothing of this world. It's never touched me before."

Logan sat down next to her and laid his hand over hers. "It's always been there," he said. "The Ches of this world are as well rooted as the kauri tree. People don't see because they don't want to."

"Where do you fit in with that old man and his hideous wife?"

Logan exhaled and leaned forward so one elbow rested on the table. He fiddled with the strapping around his fingers, pulling at a loose thread. Then he smiled. "We crossed paths about sixteen years ago. He ran a protection racket in the city. I came home on a visit with cash to spare. I floated an uncle who owned an interior decorating business. He wanted to move it out of his garage and we found a vacant shop in a great location. Che's men visited just after we moved everything in. The paint was still drying on the walls. They said they'd burn the place down if Uncle didn't pay their fee every Friday. He said he'd speak to his business partner and gave them a time to return for their money. I got the whānau together and we broke some bones in the alley behind the store. I spent a week camped out in the back of the shop and we rigged the alley so we could see them coming. Every time a new face showed up, we nailed them. But they just kept coming anyway. The day my flight left for Heathrow, I went to see Che. I didn't think I'd get near him but he was keen to meet."

Logan stood and emptied cold tea from the pot into the sink. Hana waited, wondering if he'd finished his story. She jumped as he turned to face her. "Che said he liked my spirit. He offered me a job and I turned him down. His guys protected the shop from that day to this and Uncle paid nothing for the service. We enjoy a mutual understanding and I've grown to like him. He's proved a wealth of knowledge and always knows what deals to back and what to leave alone. I did him a huge favour once and he can't repay the debt. He treats me as an equal."

"Weren't you scared?" Hana swallowed and stared at the tiled floor. "Couldn't they have killed you?"

Logan nodded, but a depth of hopelessness lurked in his grey eyes as he trawled the darker times of his past. "You don't understand, Hana. Until I met you again, I didn't care what happened to me. I had no reason to stay alive. Time was just something to kill."

Not for the first time, Hana felt appalled by her husband's lack of regard for his own value. She didn't know how to answer, but his words struck fear into her heart. "Today I live, tomorrow I die."

Logan shrugged. "Isn't life like that anyway? We have no guarantees beyond our current breath, Hana."

Hana nodded. She knew that better than anyone. Her husband kissed her goodbye in the morning and drove beneath the wheels of a truck. He left a mess in her life she'd never finish clearing up. "Did you tell Che yesterday about the Asian man you injured?" He heard her voice quake with dread. "It would be a good way of getting rid of him permanently."

Logan snorted. "I must admit I thought about it. Che's wife does all the heavy lifting. She stepped up after his heart attack a while ago but she's more lethal than he ever was. No, Hana. I didn't turn Huang over to her. I knew what she'd do."

Hana thought about the woman's death-stare and the small black, beady eyes boring into the side of her face. Her stomach gave a lurch of sympathy. Hana turned Logan's hand over and studied the back of it. His olive skin contrasted against her pale palm. She linked her fingers through his and turned his hand back over, aware of the tension in his body. "What was Sunday lunch about?" she asked. "I heard you talking about stocks and shares."

Logan rubbed his thumb over hers. "It was a hand-over." He bit his bottom lip as he sifted through a choice of words. "I owned some long term investments you wouldn't approve of. Che bought them and paid me out. There are a few more assets I want to release, but they're taking longer. I'm using one of Liza's lawyer associates to mop up the legal ones." He pursed his lips and Hana watched a smile creep into his eyes.

She screwed up her nose. "That's why I suffered that awful woman? So you could offload a few thousand dollars in bad debts?"

Logan sat back in his chair and his eyes widened in surprise. He ran a hand over his face and through his hair. "Hana," he said, his voice level. "Che paid four million dollars into my CircleLine business account last night at midnight. There are more than a couple of boards who will discover I'm not at their next meeting. They won't much like the guy who goes in my place."

Hana's jaw fell slack and she forced her mouth to close. "You became a millionaire yesterday and didn't tell me?"

Logan winced. "Hana, I've been a multi-millionaire since I was twenty-five." He watched disbelief crawl across her expression and cocked his head. "I knew you wouldn't marry me if I told you."

Hana recoiled in shock. "Damn straight I wouldn't!" Her chair legs ground across the tiles as she pushed herself back. "No wonder your sister thinks I'm a gold digger. Bloody hell, Logan!"

Logan gave her a sad smile. "I didn't tell you because you're convinced you're not good enough for anyone and you have this massive chip on your shoulder about paying your own way. You'd have run a mile and we both know it."

Hana swallowed and set her face in a look of stubbornness. "I dislike owing someone else. What's wrong with that?"

"Nothing, sweetheart. Nothing at all. I'm sorry you had to find out like this but it changes nothing. What's mine is yours and always was." He reached for her balled up fingers. "My family treat me like an open wallet but you never have."

Hana swallowed. "You own your parents' hotel don't you? Outright or just shares?"

"Outright," Logan admitted. "About three quarters of the mountain. Reuben owns the other quarter and there's a bit near the road I don't own. I only inherited the part my kuia left me. I worked hard, Hana, buying it up piece by bloody piece to stop my father losing it all."

"Who owns the piece by the road?" Hana clenched her teeth. "Caroline?"

"No!" Logan recoiled in horror. "She's not a Du Rose." He set a blank look in place and met Hana's gaze. "There's a few hectares by the front gates which I lease through a property lawyer when we need it. I could never find out who owned it, otherwise it would be mine. I promise it's not Caroline. Whoever owns it has done so for the last fifty years or more." He shook himself and stood up, pulling Hana with him. "Get into bed and I'll bring you a drink. It's getting late."

She nodded, but pulled his hand towards her heart. "Why did you get so angry before when I noticed you ran things at the hotel and challenged you?"

Logan bit his bottom lip. "Fear. I thought if you knew everything, you wouldn't stay with me. I couldn't risk that."

"You think I over analyse things?"

He cupped her chin in his hand and kissed the end of her nose. "Hana, I grew up in a family where emotions got the better of them and ruined most of what they built. They took what they had no right to touch and my generation is still paying for it. I learned not to run on feelings and it makes life a whole lot easier."

Hana grappled to understand. She tried hard, but each foray into the rabbit hole left her more confused than the last. She let Logan kiss her again and walked towards the lobby, the porch light shining through the glass. She turned, her body stiff with shame. "Logan, I would have told Mrs Che about Huang. Does that make me a bad person?"

He exhaled and stuffed his hands into his pockets. His pectoral muscles bulged with the action. "Hana, you're the least bad person I know. What is it your pastor guy always says? 'God looks at the heart of a man, not at what's on the outside.' You're human, babe, just like the rest of us. My outside is the best fake I ever created and I don't think the inside is too flash. If God doesn't give a shit about you, there's not much hope for me."

Chapter 21

The next few weeks passed without incident and Hana grew lax about her safety. The September holidays loomed in the distance with the promise of spring on its tail. Her pregnancy progressed well although her age meant she struggled more than she remembered. The five-month marker came and went, including another scan showing a small child sucking its thumb amidst a rolling sea of black and grey clouds. Logan's childish excitement reduced her to tears as he purchased copies of scan photographs in the antenatal clinic. "I didn't expect to see so much!" he gushed. His eyes glittered with life and he dragged Hana's body against his in the busy walkway. "I'm so proud of you," he whispered into her hair, his voice quaking with emotion. "Thank you for this."

Logan's gratitude increased Hana's sense of inadequacy. She produced two perfect children for Vik, who showed nothing like the same level of excitement. "I don't deserve you," she sobbed into Logan's chest in the middle of the car park. Afterwards she blamed the pregnancy hormones.

Logan spent long evenings away from home, leaving Hana to go to bed alone. She knew he travelled to Auckland, but her questioning returned minimal details. "I'm meeting the lawyer," he sighed with irritation as she asked again. Hana ran a hand over her stomach and pursed her lips.

"I didn't marry you so I could spend every night by myself," she grumbled.

"It's not every night!" Logan ran a hand through his hair and licked his lips. The vein in his neck ticked and Hana gritted her teeth.

"Why must you see him so often?"

Logan heaved out a sigh. "I'm signing papers, Hana. I explained what I was doing last time you asked."

"Why can't I come?" she demanded. "I don't want to stay here alone."

Logan snorted. "You want to ride up on the back of my bike? I don't think it's legal."

"You can take the truck, or my car." Her fingers wrung behind her back as nervousness took hold. "Unless you're seeing Caroline. Then I guess you wouldn't want me there."

Logan closed his eyes and huffed out an irritated breath. He dumped his mug into the sink. "Not that again, Hana!" He shook his head. "I'll see you at work."

"No!" Hana blocked the kitchen doorway and stood her ground. "I want to go together. My back hurts and I don't want to drive."

Logan observed her with a steady gaze, assessing and reassessing her truth. "Fine. Pete can drop you home after work."

"You're going out again tonight?" She took a step back, her mouth hanging open.

Logan winced. "I'm driving up to the hotel after the departmental meeting. I'll be back before work tomorrow." He reached out to stroke her cheek and Hana jerked her head backwards, banging it on the doorframe. It hurt and her eyes welled in pain and disappointment.

"Why?" She shoved his fingers away but remained planted in the doorway, knowing he wouldn't shove past her.

"I just need to."

"Then take me with you."

"Hana, this is boring."

Hana swallowed. "Okay." She moved aside and watched his pupils dilate at the prospect of freedom. "Then stay there. Don't come back here. I didn't realise I married the invisible man."

"Hana!" Logan's leather jacket crinkled as he moved and he shifted from boot to boot in obvious discomfort. "You don't mean that."

She turned her back on him and ran water into the sink, squirting way too much liquid into the bowl. Logan called her name again and she ignored him. "Hana!"

"Bye Logan."

He sighed and she heard his footsteps move across the kitchen. His hands squeezed her shoulders to turn her around. "Flick's at the hotel."

"What?" Dishwashing bubbles floated from her fingers and coated her bump like a foamy ledge. She swallowed. "When? How?" The colour drained from her face and she felt faintness creep into her brain.

"Since the expo." Logan watched her reaction.

"That was ages ago." Hana shook her head to clear it but failed. The fear gripped her heart and squeezed.

"He's working for Jack. Dad keeps a very tight rein on him, but I need to maintain a presence. Just in case he decides to kick off."

Hana shook Logan's hands from her shoulders. "So let me get this right. You gave sanctuary to a man who stalked and injured me and you've kept him at your hotel?" Her eyes widened in anger, flashing a deep green. "You didn't say you kept him there."

Logan shrugged and refused to take the bait. "Yeah, but he's turned into a decent worker. I need to leave, Hana. Get in the car."

"Not with you! Traitor!" She slapped his hands away. "Well, I'm speechless!" she added.

Logan smirked. "Apparently not, because you obviously have lots to say."

"Not only do you leave me here alone most nights, you're visiting the felon who bashed me." Hana threw a plate into the sink and heard it crack. It offered little satisfaction. "Nice. Bloody nice."

"I'm leaving." Logan strode from the room and snatched his motorbike helmet from the cupboard in the lobby. Hana listened to his footsteps run down the back stairs and the roar of his motorbike starting.

"Damn you, Logan Du Rose!" she shouted, slamming her hands into the water. She spent the next half an hour fixing band aids over the cuts to her fingers and arrived at work both flustered and late.

Logan refused to engage in an argument at work and Hana buried her frustration until she saw him next. It brewed like bad ale in her guts and she decided to use manipulation to achieve her goal. She'd grown sick of butting her head against Logan's iron will and settled on other negotiation techniques. The next morning provided her first opportunity as he reached out to stroke her leg as she passed.

"I can't sleep with you. I feel too betrayed." Hana fingered the bottom of her nightshirt, exposing a decent amount of leg. She felt as sexy as an Easter egg, but the tension in the room hiked as Logan's interest piqued. Sitting in the kitchen in crumpled work clothes, he let the front legs of his chair clump to the floor and put his hands on the table. He looked wrecked, black shadows beneath his eyes and his hair sticking up on end. She didn't remember him returning and suspected he just arrived home. Hana took a step back and put herself out of range. She lifted the checked material higher and watched his pupils dilate. "You should have warned me. We went to the hotel a few weekends ago. What if I ran into him?"

"How? I kept you with me the whole time. He won't touch you. Apart from the fact he knows I'd kill him, the box is with the police and that's all he wanted. Dad says he's behaving himself. I think he likes the peace and quiet."

"I feel my trust has been violated," Hana said with real feeling. She knew she'd pushed it too far when she flashed the side of her skimpy knickers. Logan stood, a predatory look in his eyes. He beckoned to her with his finger crooked.

"Come here and I'll make it better."

"No!" Hana made her reply sound cross. "I'm never coming near you again!" She placed a hand over her heart. "I just can't."

Logan bit his lip and his long lashes brushed against his cheek. He fixed stunning grey eyes on Hana. She mapped out her escape into the hallway, hating how nothing ran to plan with Logan Du Rose. He watched her brain working it all out and gave a veiled smirk. "I said come here, babe. I'm sorry you're upset. Let me show you how sorry I am."

Hana moved at speed, but she didn't quite make it. Logan caught her in the lobby, lifting her with ease beneath her thighs and back. His biceps bulged through his work shirt, his tie hanging loosely on his neck. "When are you going to learn to trust me, woman?" he whispered and the question sounded serious, despite his sparkling eyes.

"Maybe one day," she replied, squirming in his arms. Logan nodded.

"I can wait." He carried her to the bedroom and showed how sorry he could be. It left her resolve in tatters and she learned nothing.

On the last Monday of term three Hana finished early, aching for the well-deserved rest during the two-week holiday approaching. Sheila pointed at her bulging stomach. "Are you struggling?" she asked, her face softening in sympathy.

Hana nodded. "I'm just fed up," she admitted. "My back aches, my skin looks like a wrinkled stocking and this child just doesn't sleep anymore." She slipped her jacket over her shoulders and sighed.

"Want me to call Logan?"

Hana shrugged. "No point. I drove and he came on the bike again. I'll see him at home later after his meeting."

"You don't sound very happy." Sheila cocked her head and Hana sensed Pete turn in his seat. She hastened to smooth the troubled waters she'd created.

"We're fine," she gushed. "I just need a good night's sleep."

Sheila nodded and retreated to her office. Hana snatched up her handbag. "Hana?" Pete turned towards her, an index finger planted in his right nostril.

"Not now, Pete. See the nurse if your finger's stuck."

"It isn't." He pulled it out with a pop. "Look."

Hana inhaled and walked towards the door. "No thanks. I don't want to see your latest find. See you in the morning."

"But Hana!" he protested. She slammed the door behind her, knowing he'd prove too lazy to pursue her.

Trotting out to the car in the chapel car park, Hana felt her body relax at the thought of approaching summer. She fumbled with her car keys and deactivated the central locking. It took a moment to squeeze between the cars and shove her handbag into the space behind her seat. She worked hard not to bang the wing mirror next to her as she manoeuvred into position. The key fumbled into the ignition and Hana sat up, brushing her hair back from her face. The click of the passenger door made her look up, expecting to see Pete or Logan.

Tama faced her, his grey Du Rose eyes drilling into her face. He'd filled out in the last few months, his face acquiring a sullen hardness. He settled in the seat and ran a fingernail over a smudge on the dashboard. His ice cold gaze resembled the still water on a lake and he gave a small, lazy smile. "Hey Miss," he said, the ex-student still speaking to a school adult. "How's it going?"

Hana swallowed and remained quiet, her mind turning somersaults at what this dangerous man-boy might want from her. She felt the thud of her heart in her chest and her blood moved too fast through her stomach, raised blood pressure bombarding her child. The baby stilled against the change and

Hana felt sickness rising. "What do you want, Tama?" She tried to make her voice sound strong, but failed as the words squeaked out.

"Well, Miss." He relaxed back in his seat, as though about to give her a synopsis of his dreams and desires. But the answer emerged short and to the point. "Tell Uncle Logan, if he doesn't stop with the lawyers on my family, I'll tell my employer something he doesn't know."

The puzzle evaded Hana's frazzled brain and her fingers shook as she gripped hold of the steering wheel. Fear increased the fog. "So, you'll tell your employer something Logan doesn't know?" Her voice shook and betrayed her terror. Tama leaned forward, gripping her chin in his fingers. His voice oozed out with menace.

"I'll tell my employer something Logan doesn't want him to know!" He gritted his teeth. "Geez, I didn't expect someone like Logan to marry such a bimbo."

Hana pressed herself back against the driver's door, aching to escape Tama's proximity. His grip on her chin hurt. "Tell me again?" she stammered, knowing the panic in her brain had already overwritten the message. Tama snorted with derision and hauled her towards him. He put one hand behind her neck and forced her forward. His kiss felt rough against her lips. She pushed her palms against his rock hard chest and squirmed her face aside. He let go and the unexpectedness of it made her recoil and bang her head on the window. Tama turned to exit the car, taking one last sneering look back at her as she put her hand up to the back of her head.

"I don't understand what Logan sees in you," he said spitefully. "He won't stay, so don't get comfortable."

The instant the door clicked behind him, Hana fumbled for the switch to activate the central locking. White dots raced in front of her vision and her hands shook in crazy arcs as she turned the ignition key. Her flight instinct overrode any need to wait until the wave of nerves subsided. She gunned the engine and pulled onto the main road in quick, jerky movements without looking properly. It drew an angry horn blast from the lorry she cut up. Hana tried to breathe through pursed lips to regain control and by the time she passed Chartwell, she felt calmer.

The thought of her empty home filled her with a sense of doom and Tama's riddle plagued her. Maihi went out of town the weekend before and nobody else provided a ready substitute. "What?" She slammed a hand on the steering wheel at the Wairere Drive roundabout. "Who's your employer, you stupid boy? What could you possibly know that might hurt Logan?"

Hana drove around the roundabout full circle, finding herself on Amy's street. She groaned and pressed her palm against her forehead. "This is stupid," she hissed. Reaching for her phone, she dialled Amy's number. "Are you at home?" she asked, when Amy barked a reply.

Hana shoved her car onto the narrow drive, fighting her way through a large sago palm near the gate. She trotted to the side door and knocked.

"Come in." Amy pulled the door open, alarmed when Hana ran past her. "Oh. What's wrong?"

The unwelcome dose of reality acted like an ice cold shower and Hana shivered in the kitchen, wringing her hands and chewing her lips. "It's started again," she gushed, her voice breaking. "I can't go home. It's not safe."

Amy laid a broad paintbrush on the counter. The smell of waterborne acrylic paint filled the house and a smudge of khaki colour spread across the bridge of her nose. "What's happened?" Her businesslike tone infused Hana with guilt. She bolted towards the door.

"It doesn't matter. You're off duty and busy. I'm sorry. I'll go home."

"No." Amy intercepted her in the doorway. "Don't be silly. Tell me. I'm only painting Jas' bedroom."

Hana took a deep breath and nodded, allowing Amy to take her handbag from her shoulder and place it on the table. She turned sideways and flicked the kettle on to boil. "Would you like to see what I'm doing?"

Hana nodded again without looking up, focusing on her heart and trying to think calming thoughts. Amy took her arm and led her through the house. "I'm so sorry." Hana breathed out through her lips. "I didn't know where else to go."

"It's fine, I needed a break. I started this before dawn. It's a bigger job than I imagined. It always is with old houses; you start something and realise you needed to do something else first. I wanted to paint Jas' bedroom, but then found cracks in the plaster. I spent yesterday filling the cracks and needed to wait for them to dry." She stood back to admire her work. "Do you think he'll like it?"

The afternoon sun streamed through the window and brightened the back bedroom. Jas' furniture stood in the centre of the room and tarpaulins covered the wooden floor. A rolled up rug lay on top of the bed, still in its plastic wrapper. Amy opened one end to show Hana the camouflage scene on it. "He can set up his battlefields. Then he might keep them in one place." Amy rolled her eyes, already hearing her son's angry protests.

One wall bore a coat of khaki paint and the other three displayed a lighter green. The colours contrasted. Amy touched the nearest wall, frowning at the blob of paint on her finger as she drew it away. "I'm doing it for Jas, but wanted a colour that wouldn't put buyers off. I don't want to redo it." A wistfulness echoed in Amy's voice, making Hana feel uneasy.

"Are you planning to leave?" she asked, framing the question with a casual tone. Amy shook her head as they entered the kitchen and picked up the kettle.

"Maybe," she replied, keeping her back to Hana. "This house and all its various problems were my divorce settlement. It's full of memories I don't want anymore. My parents live in Wellington. They keep asking me to transfer there."

"Would you?" Hana asked and Amy shrugged.

"This is an old house with old house structural problems. I don't have the money or inclination to do what it needs. I think it would be easier to cut my losses and start again." She smiled at Hana, a tired grimace which looked more like an attempt at bravery than any semblance of happiness. Amy put a mug of tea on the table for Hana and ran herself cold water from the tap. Then she sat. "Tell me what happened."

Hana licked her lips. "Where's Jas?"

Amy raised an eyebrow. "Didn't you know? Bodie's gone up north for a few days and taken Jas with him. I did six days on shift, so now have three off. I thought I'd get on with it while the house is quiet and I don't have to keep stopping to pull Jas out of paint."

Hana nodded. She sipped her tea and wished things were different with her son. She looked up to find Amy watching her. "Are you going to tell me?" she asked.

Hana put her tea down and rolled her eyes. "I feel stupid now," she admitted. "Logan's nephew got in the car and made this garbled threat. I don't even remember what he said, but he scared me."

"I can call someone," Amy offered, setting her glass on the table.

Hana shook her head. "No, thanks. I feel an idiot. I should have just gone home and told Logan."

"Are you sure?" Amy's brow furrowed. "I wanted to talk to you about Bodie anyway."

Hana groaned. "Please don't." She felt a wave of guilt at the vehemence in her tone and apologised. Amy nodded, suggesting unanimity between the women.

"We share the same sentiment then," she said, her bottom lip wobbling with sadness. "He and I started to get close, but he pulled away for no reason. He makes sure he picks up Jas when I'm not around and doesn't get out of the car when he drops him off. I know he's avoiding me." A tear rolled down Amy's cheek and plopped onto the table. "Now he's taken Jas away and didn't invite me to go. I don't know what he wants."

Hana hauled herself upright and wrapped her arms around Amy's shoulders. "Sweetheart," she whispered. "It's not your fault."

"He's used me again," Amy sobbed. "He slept with me and then left. Why do I always fall for the jerks?"

"I'm so sorry." Hana held her, feeling her pain and silently cursing her son. "I didn't raise him that way, Amy, I promise."

"I know." Amy sniffed and wiped her nose on the back of her hand. "You're a nice person, Hana. It's not your fault."

"It must be." Hana's eyes watered as she sat, her fractured relationship with Bodie seeming to threaten everything. "Please don't leave yet. I'm just getting to know you." She clasped Amy's wrist in her fingers and felt guilty for her plea. She withdrew her hand. "That's not fair. I'm sorry. Do what's best for you and Jas. I'll visit you wherever you go."

Amy swallowed. "So much for the decorating taking my mind off my awful personal life." She sniffed, an ugly, echoing sound. Hana barked out a laugh and Amy covered her mouth. "Sorry."

"For what it's worth, I think he's confused about how he feels." Hana paused and chose her words. "He talks to Izzie. I can ring her if you want."

Amy shrugged and her cheeks coloured. "Is she nice, your daughter?"

Hana nodded and her body relaxed. "Yes. She's gorgeous. I'll see if she knows anything that might help either of us."

A small and squeaky, "Hello," issued from the phone, almost indiscernible from the cacophony of background noise. Squeals, grunts and yells made anything else impossible to hear. Hana held the phone away from her ear, screwing up her face.

"Izzie, are you in labour?" she demanded. "What's that noise?"

"Hang on," her daughter shouted. Hana heard a clang and the background noise dimmed. "Sorry Mum." Izzie giggled. "Marcus organised a family tea night and it's tremendous fun. But I can't hear myself think."

Hana heard the clopping of heels as Izzie walked outside into the cool spring air of an Invercargill teatime. She opened her mouth to chastise her daughter for still wearing stilettos whilst heavily pregnant with twins. Then she peered beneath the table at her own high boots. "I'm actually ringing about Bo," Hana began, wanting to cut her daughter off before she launched into a description of Marcus' latest outreach. She heard the footsteps cease and sensed Izzie's fear. "No, sweetheart, he's fine. Nothing's happened." Hana swallowed. "But he's behaving like an idiot and I wondered if you might know why."

Izzie laughed with relief. "How long have you got?" she chuckled.

The conversation proved short and to the point. Izzie had plonked Elizabeth on somebody's knee and needed to get back. Hana listened, giving nothing away to Amy, who feigned disinterest as though her life didn't depend on the result of the call. She rang off after telling her daughter she loved her when the sound of grizzling became louder and Elizabeth tried to snatch the phone out of her hand. Hana blew noisy kisses to the little girl, hearing giggles in return. She ended the call and took a moment to settle her thoughts. Amy's hungry look met her.

Hana tried not to sound like a village gossip. "She says Bodie told her he's in love with you and wants to settle down." Sadness crossed her face. "He also hates Logan, but I already knew that. He wants to take him down and is looking for any way to do it."

Amy gasped and leaned back, shaking her head in an instant challenge. "He loves me? He's got a funny way of showing it."

Hana nodded. "He told Izzie he wants to get married, but you don't. You're very independent and he doesn't feel there's space for him in your life. He thinks you just want a free childminder." Hana winced. "Sorry. I could have put that nicer."

Amy shrugged. "It's okay. I think I understand. I don't want to get married again and I do like my independence. My last marriage proved such a bloody disaster. Bodie hasn't given me any reason to change my mind so far." She sighed. "So I guess I can stop worrying. My relationship is at an impasse. What will you do about Logan?"

Hana exhaled. "What can I do? He's my husband." She sighed. "At least, he is when I get to see him."

"Problems?" Amy leaned forward, eager to focus on someone else's troubles. Hana waved her hand.

"Nothing that time won't fix." She rose and picked up her handbag. "I should go. I've trespassed on your good nature enough."

"It's impossible to believe Bodie loves me." Amy's face darkened. "He's never said it. I'm not sure he knows how to love anyone except himself."

Hana swallowed and nodded. "He used to, Amy. Before his father died, he was shaping up to be a lovely man." Her eyes dulled. "I don't know what I could have done differently."

"Why has he gone north?" Amy changed the subject, wiping her eyes with a sleeve. "I thought he went camping, but I heard your daughter say something about a case."

Hana cringed, wishing Izzie didn't always shout into the phone. "He's trying to find something out about Laval."

Amy leapt to her feet, mother and police sergeant mingling in a heady mix of responsibility. "He's conducting an unauthorised investigation! With my son?" She pounded the flat of her hand against the table and stalked around the small kitchen like a caged animal, "I'll bloody kill him!"

Hana saw she had made things ten times worse. At the kitchen door she turned to Amy, offering a final parting piece of wisdom. The girl stopped pacing and looked at her, seeming surprised to find Hana on her way out. "Perhaps you need to put more trust in Bodie. He'd do nothing to hurt Jas. Maybe trust is the problem between you. Let him into your life, Amy. If he disappoints you, then that sucks. But what if he doesn't? What if he proves you wrong?"

Hana felt sadness settle on her shoulders as she made her way to the car. Her own philosophy came back to bite her. "Big words off a weak stomach, Hana," she whispered. "Try taking your own advice." Guilt drove her fingers to press in Bodie's number and she sighed when his voicemail clicked in. She didn't leave a message. Ringing Logan elicited the same response. She argued with the sago palm on the way out, tearing a few leaves which her wing mirror scattered on the pavement. Rush hour was almost over, the last stragglers winding their way home before darkness settled over the city.

She left the Flagstaff roundabout and headed into the countryside, aware of the Hakarimata Ranges calling to her. Tama's cryptic threat hung over her like a cudgel and something else gnawed at Hana's sensibility. Grief came like a familiar and unwelcome visitor, running sharp fingers across her fragile peace. Glancing at her watch, she saw the digital date glowing against the darkness and winced. "Please God, no," she whispered, desperation in her voice. "It shouldn't be this way. I'm happy. I don't need to think about it."

But she did think about it. The date gnawed at her like a rabid dog and robbed her of appetite and relaxation. The empty house closed itself around her and Hana rattled aimlessly from one end to the other. Logan's presence might have taken the unrest away, but once again, he wasn't there.

Chapter 22

The heaviness pushed on Hana's chest all night and she slept in fitful bursts which didn't refresh her. Logan arrived home late, falling into bed after midnight. Despite trying to be quiet, he disturbed her and she lay sleepless for hours, turning things over in her mind and listening to him snore next to her. She snuggled up to her husband, putting her leg across him and placing her hands on his body. Craving distraction, she trailed her fingers along his thigh. He sighed in his sleep and didn't wake, compounding her sense of rejection. "Where do you go, Logan?" she whispered into the darkness. "What's happening to us? I can't do this again."

The familiar hard lump grew beneath her rib cage, spreading out from its origins of foreboding the night before. It gripped and pulled and sapped her energy, just like always. The threat of its hold petrified her and by the time the birds roused the dawn, Hana's blood pressure hammered in her ears.

Tired and uncommunicative, Logan readied himself for work. He gave no explanation of where he'd been and Hana felt herself withdrawing from him, the distance growing between them even though she dressed metres away. She could have reached out and touched him, but didn't.

In the car, she opened her mouth to tell Logan about Tama, the fog in her brain muddling her words. "Can we talk?" She swallowed, picking her sentences as gossamer threads from the surrounding air.

"Not if it's about last night," Logan replied, his tone biting. "I'm sick of asking you to trust me and then enduring the third degree."

Hana clenched her jaw. "I don't think wanting to know where my husband went is the third degree. It's normal, Logan. It's called marriage."

"It's called micromanaging," he bit. "I want you to trust me."

Hana held onto her bitter retort, picking at a thread on her mitten. Logan glanced across and she felt his gaze burning into the side of her face as he waited to pull out onto the busy Hakarimata Road. The way became clear but he missed the gap, his attention on her. "Hana?" She looked up at him as though pulling herself back from another world. "You mad at me?" he asked. "I'm sorry, I know this isn't what you signed up for."

Hana looked down at her mitten and went back to worrying the thread. Logan's brow knitted. "Don't lock me out, mate," he said, his voice soft. "It feels like I'm living in the eye of a storm. I didn't mean to shut you down. Let's talk."

Hana turned her face away and ignored him. Everything felt too hard to sum up in a sentence. Even Tama. Especially Tama.

Logan shook his head to clear an unbidden image of Miriam throwing a large saucepan full of water and peeled potatoes at his father's head. The worry ticked in the back of his mind that Hana might be showing signs of depression. Frustration prickled in his chest as he pulled onto the busy road and drove south. "It'll all be over soon. I don't want to keep leaving you like this; you do know that, don't you?" Hana shrugged as though she didn't care and placed a hand against her heart. Logan sighed. "I'm doing this for us, Hana. I don't want to ride around the country in the dark, selling off assets and getting hate mail from board members. The meetings I attend are important."

Hana pursed her lips and looked out of the window, trying to halt the buzz in her head. It told her lies about Logan and placed her at the bottom of his list of importance. Behind business meetings and things she didn't want to dwell on. Thwarted, Logan reacted with stupidity. "Fine! Whatever! I'm not on business at all, Hana. I'm actually whoring my way up and down the country and enjoying every second of it." He slammed his foot on the gas pedal as the traffic lights turned to green and didn't see the look of horror cross Hana's face. Her chest became tight and her breathing laboured. The seat belt cut into her neck.

"You're cheating on me?" Her eyes held a look of frenzy and Logan recoiled.

"No! Of course not. I shouldn't have said it. I just wanted you to answer me." He sighed and rubbed his eyes, her expression haunting him.

Hana didn't speak again on the journey and Logan couldn't break the heavy sense of foreboding. At school, he turned off the ignition and fingered the keys between his fingers while eyeing her sideways. "Is it okay if I keep these?" he asked and Hana shrugged. "I need to nip out at lunchtime." She pressed her lips together, no longer possessing the energy to enquire after yet another clandestine meeting. Logan's reputation took a further nose dive.

"Do whatever you want, Logan," she said with a tired sigh. She pressed her fingers over the top of her stomach as though in pain. The coloured strands of her mitten stretched across Hana's lap like spaghetti. Logan reached over and grabbed her hand, a dismayed expression in his widened eyes. Hana jumped as he pulled the mangled mitten-encased hand towards him.

"I bought those for you," he said. "Why did you do that?"

Hana yanked her hand away, unable to deal with the look of accusation she imagined in his grey eyes. "Leave me alone!" She moved fast for a woman who couldn't get her own socks on earlier, leaving the car before Logan could collect his thoughts. He narrowed his eyes as he watched his wife stalk towards the front of the school. She looked stiff and wooden and he saw her elbow move as she repeatedly clutched at an invisible pain in her chest.

In desperation, he rang Liza. She answered the phone in her usual clipped fashion. "What bro? I'm due in court, be quick."

Logan sighed. The women in his life drained his energy. "The meeting with your lawyer mate last night proved informative." He heard the click of Liza's heels as she walked towards her chambers. "Thanks for recommending him. He issued Reuben with a trespass notice at the weekend and an invoice for full payment of the loan."

"Ah yep," Liza replied. A door closed in the background with a muffled thud. "What do you want, Logan? You don't usually ring me with progress reports. You're big and ugly enough to take care of your own mess."

"I'm worried about Ma," he replied, watching a group of boys pass the car bouncing a rugby ball. It hit the art teacher's ute and set the alarm off. The sound peeled at a high pitched decibel level and they laughed until they noticed Logan's raised eyebrow. Then they moved away at speed. "Kane and his mates paid the hotel a visit last night. I drove up there after I met your lawyer mate. The developers turned up yesterday too and threatened Dad with court action. You know what he's like. No balls. He panics easily and Ma keeps skipping her meds."

"And?" Liza snapped. "What do you want me to do about it? You started this. I warned you what would happen." She sounded haughty.

"Fine! Sorry to bother you. Go hand out some life sentences, Liza. Knock yourself out." Logan disconnected the call and shoved his phone into his inside pocket. When it rang again he answered it, kidding himself she may have regretted her sharpness and called him back. His heart sank. "Oh, hi Dad. What's up?"

Alfred's voice sounded tinny and distant. "You need to come back again. Kane broke the window last night and he might have worse planned. Your ma can't cope with it. It's making her sick."

Logan ground his teeth. "Did she take her meds this morning?"

"It's not the meds!" Alfred shouted. "It's what you're doing to Rueben. She can't cope."

Logan pressed his fingers into his eyes and his vision blurred. Multi-coloured flashes decorated his view of the car park. "You promised to back me. So back me. I can't keep running up there. My life is here. I put you in as managers, so manage."

"But Reuben came back after you left, Logan. He wants to see you."

"What's to see, Dad? He stood in front of me like a stunned mullet!" Logan shook his head at the recollection of his uncle's face as he raced through the front door to confront him. Distaste mingled with fear in the old man's handsome Du Rose features. Logan experienced a peculiar sense of déjà vu in that moment and shuddered at the memory.

"He didn't expect you to be home. He wants to see you alone, just you and him." Alfred's voice wavered, some deeper emotion behind his nervousness. "Come back tonight. I'll ask Toby to ride over and call a hui."

"No." Logan heard the bell ring inside the building and let out a curse. "I'm late for staff briefing. I don't need to see him. He's got instructions on what to do and the lawyer's phone number." He hung up and ran to the meeting, enduring Donald Watson's evil eye as he ran in late and sat at the back. His mind wandered from the discarded chocolate wrappers fluttering from Watson's fingers as the man waxed lyrical about the litter problem. Logan returned to his memory of the previous evening when Reuben stood before him gaping like a fish. Kane sprang back from the damaged window with a cackle of glee and hefted another rock in his fingers, ready to throw again. Toby laid him out flat with one well-timed punch and he squirmed in the gravel. Hotel guests enjoyed the floor show from first floor windows.

"Don't!" Logan saw the stone in Reuben's hand and read his intent. The other man gaped in surprise and shook his head as though trying to clear some inner fog.

"Logan," he said, licking his lips as though tasting the name on his tongue. He moved his hand in a quick motion and Logan covered his head with his forearms, a natural, defensive reaction. A strange expression rode over Reuben's features like a stampede and his voice resonated deep within Logan's soul. The timbre touched a note of familiarity and confused, he lowered his arms.

"Go home!" he snapped. "Leave my family alone."

"You don't understand, tāne," Reuben had protested, taking a step forward. His eyes widened with emotion and tears swam in his grey irises. Logan winced at the unexpected show of weakness and moved aside as other stockmen arrived to remove the unwanted arrivals. Toby hauled Kane from the gravel and gave him a shove towards the dilapidated vehicle he arrived in. Both men stank of alcohol and Logan shook his head and turned away. "Don't turn your back on me!" Reuben shouted and Logan kept walking, moving up the steps of the hotel and in through the heavy wooden doors. Jack slid from the shadows and Logan halted in surprise. He lifted his hand to communicate but Jack shook his head and left, limping along the private corridor and leaving confusion in his wake. Logan heard the outer door click in the bowels of the house and numbed himself against the continuing commotion outside. He understood none of it.

In the meeting, Logan yawned and Pete dug him in the ribs. Masking a grunt of pain and tuning back in to Watson's diatribe about detentions, he forced himself to focus on the day which stretched before him like a murky lake. Pete tried to wipe a bogey on the arm of Logan's chair and he dug his fingers into the tendons either side of the man's bony knee, affecting a nonchalant air as Pete squealed out loud. Dobbs tipped sideways in his seat and glared at Pete. "My office after briefing," he said with authority.

Pete narrowed his eyes at Logan. "Thanks for that!" he hissed.

"Bugger off," Logan replied under his breath. The meeting ended and as the volume increased to a deafening level, Pete leaned across to whisper in Logan's ear. "What?" Logan snapped, recoiling from the man's onion breath. "I told you never to speak to me again, dude. Go away."

"I said you need to watch Hana," Pete whispered. His eyes widened to the size of large blue marbles. Logan's heart hardened in an instant and a defensive barrier crashed down around him.

"Keep out of my marriage," he growled. "I don't care what she thinks. I'm not cheating on her."

"Cheating on her?" Pete's voice rose enough to draw nearby attention. "What's this?"

"Nothing!" Logan felt his energy levels deplete and his shoulders slumped. "Forget it." He slammed from the room and went to meet his tutor group, unnerving them with the dangerous air accompanying him.

Hana met her husband at the car and they travelled home in silence. She appeared even more morose and withdrawn after a day of separation. It was as though she had receded into an untouchable room in her head and Logan couldn't gain admittance. "You know I didn't mean what I said earlier?" he said, pulling her into his arms as she tried to remove her blouse in the bedroom. She shrugged out of his grasp.

"About what?" she asked. Her voice sounded tired and defeatist. "Whoring yourself? Do what you bloody like, Logan. You will anyway."

He jumped back as though shot and felt the power shift. It wrong-footed him. "What do you fancy for dinner?" he asked.

"Nothing." Hana hopped into bed and turned her back on him.

"I'm not going out tonight." He sounded hopeful. "We can talk."

Hana shook her head and snuggled down into the blankets. "I don't want to anymore."

He took a step towards her. "Hana, remember the promise we made to each other?" Her snort of derision forced him to withdraw before he said something he'd regret.

Hana focussed on the hard knot in her gut as Logan's defeated footsteps pattered along the hallway. She pressed a hand over her mouth and a tear trickled onto the pillowcase. Clattering came from the kitchen and the metallic pop of the toaster. Twenty-one steps would take her into his arms but nothing could persuade her to make the distance. "It's too late," she breathed as her chest heaved. "I can't do this again."

Logan's phone chirped on the hall table and Hana heard him pick up. His reply sounded curt. "You what?" he snapped and then cursed. She tried to care about who might have called him at home in the evening, but couldn't summon up the usual feelings of curiosity. The black cloud consumed her, lying heavy on her chest and impairing her breathing. She knew if she kept still and tried not to think too hard about its presence, it would go, washing out with the turn of the calendar like it always did.

Hana felt the lead weight increase as her novel fell to the floor with a thud. The story line geared up for a sad ending and she sensed it coming. It added to her misery and she decided not to read the rest. It had become pointless. All hope and optimism faded from her world and left only the husk of defeat. Praying didn't help. Net curtains obscured the God of Hope from view. Head and heart knowledge failed to line up and lies sprang into her heart, declaring Hana Du Rose unlovable and unworthy. She closed her weeping eyes to sleep and let the inward torture continue.

Logan stayed in the kitchen, making calls to wind up over twenty years work for a woman who had opted out of their marriage. He watched television while marking senior assessments and fell asleep with the cat sprawled on his knee. Waking up cold and stiff, his legs felt dead from the weight of the cat. Tiger dug his claws into Logan's thighs as he shifted beneath him. "Don't!" he complained. "That hurts. I've got enough problems without blood poisoning from you." Tiger hissed and leapt up, retreating behind the sofa to comfort himself with irritated licks of his rough tongue.

Logan stretched and contemplated sleeping in the spare room. He ran a hand over tired eyes and yawned. He couldn't sustain the gruelling pace for much longer and disaster loomed. When his phone vibrated from between the sofa cushions, he dug it out. "Du Rose," he answered.

"Where were you?" the caller demanded. "We made an agreement."

"Yeah, well you can stick it." His body tensed. "I don't want this anymore. It's complicated."

The person on the other end gave an irritated sniff of derision. "You don't make the rules, Du Rose. Same time tomorrow. Be there."

Logan turned his phone off and left it on the sofa, padding through the lobby in his boxer shorts and socks. He heard the agonised sound of a woman crying as he passed the door of the room he shared with Hana. She sobbed and pleaded as though someone else was there. It sounded eerie. Alertness came like a second skin, dulling the pounding of his heart. Logan resisted the urge to bust the door off its hinges, fixing his fingers over the handle. Honing himself into a relentless weapon and tamping down his conscience, he pressed the door open to meet the intruder head on.

A single lamp glowed in the darkness and Hana's shape made a lump on her side of the bed. Logan moved around the room and checked every dark corner, his body rigid and ready to defend. His muscles flexed and veins stood out as ridged lines. Nothing.

Confused, Logan moved to Hana's side of the bed, feeling the fluffy threads of a rug through his socks. She whimpered again and his brow knitted. Sweat beaded on her face and her red hair tumbled across the pillow, suspended against the cream sheets like blood. Her chest hitched as though she'd cried for hours without relenting. Logan took a step back and closed his eyes. He'd spent his whole life knowing what to do in every situation, relying on instinct and avoiding disaster. Yet this woman defeated his ability to control anything. Fear crept into his decision making every time and rendered him useless.

"Oh, Hana," Logan whispered. He crawled into bed next to her and wrapped her in his arms. The pillow felt damp beneath his cheek. She muttered rubbish and put her hand on her upper abdomen, leaning forward into a ball. "Why won't you tell me what's wrong?" he whispered into her hair. "I'm sorry for what I said. I didn't mean you to take me seriously." Logan stroked her back and she moaned. Her nails grazed his ribs as she clung to him. She stirred, her brain moving her through the phases of sleep.

"Stay," she murmured, her voice cracked and desperate. "Stay with me. Why did you want to hurt me?"

Logan released his held breath and pulled Hana closer. "I'm going nowhere," he promised, kissing her hair and holding her tight. "I don't want to hurt you, Hana. Please, trust me. I didn't mean it."

Hana woke at dawn, her eyes puffy and sore. Her lips tasted salty when she licked them and her nose ached from being pressed against Logan's chest. She eased herself from the bed, feeling him tense and clutch at her nightshirt. She slipped it over her head and left him holding the fabric. In the bathroom, she ran hot water over her aching body, letting it race over her head and pound her face. Gentle fingers washed her stomach, caressing the child who kicked and turned against the change in body temperature. Hana pressed her hand against the knot in her chest, the vulnerability overwhelming. "Oh, Vik," she sighed. "Who was the bigger fool? You or me?"

She pressed her forehead against the tiles and let the water pummel her back. Her dead husband had returned in her dream and sat with her at Hamilton Gardens on the wide grassy hill above the lake. Sitting in the sunshine, they talked about their children and Hana felt a familiar safety wrap around her. The light glinted in Vik's black hair and Hana noticed salt and pepper greys around his ears. Age suited him, even though it had been halted within time. He would not alter further. Hana watched him as he lay back on the grassy slope. She forgot how stunning he had been. His long black lashes framed dark brown eyes and when he smiled, she saw Bodie in him. And then she ruined it. "After the accident, a woman came to see me," she said, watching dismay flood his irises. "Please, tell me the truth. You never tell the truth."

Vik turned towards her, his beautiful face ashen and sad. His head shook from side to side in denial. He opened his mouth, but she closed her eyes to avoid the inevitable reply, the nine year secret buried for another year. In her dream, Vik distorted and faded, his head becoming translucent. Hana snatched at his arm and it dissipated beneath her grasp, disappearing and moving like fog. "Stay!" she'd cried. "Why did you want to hurt me?"

Hana crouched beneath the water, making her naked body small and matching the insignificance in her soul. "Fool!" she breathed, bubbles forming against her lips. "You stupid fool."

Logan stumbled into the bathroom as she stepped over the side of the bath. He held his hand out to steady her and she took it with reluctance, snatching up her towel from the rail. "I feel like I've been run over by a truck," he complained, rubbing his eyes with his other hand.

Hana's eyes narrowed into an expression of hatred. "Don't say things like that!" she snapped, remembering Vik's smashed sunglasses returned to her in a police evidence bag. Spots of dried blood remained around the frame where the grill of the truck crashed through the windscreen and smashed his skull.

"Sorry! Again!" Logan bit back oblivious, lifting the toilet seat and knowing she would leave. He spread his legs and shot a look of defiance over his shoulder. The door clicked shut behind her.

Logan showered and rubbed the cricks from his neck, returning to the bedroom in a towel. "We can drive in together if you want," he offered. "But I'll need the car at lunchtime." Hana held her breath and Logan saw her body tense. "I didn't go yesterday." She perched on the edge of the bed in her bra and knickers. Her body contorted as she tried to poke socks onto her feet. "Here, I'll do it." Logan snatched the errant sock from her flapping hand and fitted it over her toes. His eyes crinkled at the edges in amusement. Hana breathed out through pursed lips as he put the other one on for her. She ached to reach out and touch his hair, a mangled fishing net of emotion lodged in her chest. Logan took the leggings from the bed and put the ends over her feet, stepping back as she stood and hauled them over her bump.

"Want me to drive you?" he asked, running his finger along a damp red coil at her shoulder. Hana recognised the need in his grey eyes and almost caved. His face channelled confusion, unease and a sense of self-preservation working overtime. The baby squirmed in Hana's womb as though in silent protest at the neglect of its father's feelings. "Then we can talk," he said.

The cloud of depression settled back over Hana like a hat, shrouding her in self-pity and righteous indignation. She stepped back and shook her head. "Now you want to talk?" she snorted, sarcasm underlying her tone. "Now that it suits you."

"Hana!" Logan's instant irritation strengthened her pique and Hana lifted her chin into the air.

She batted away his hands as he sought to catch her around the shoulders. "You go off and do your super-secret things, Logan. I'd hate to get in your way." She stalked from the bedroom and snatched up the Honda keys, clumping down the back stairs in unlaced boots. Tears fought for release and she swallowed them, letting them add to the hardness in her chest.

Logan heard her reverse up the slope and turn at the top, wincing as she cranked the gears and gunned the gas pedal too hard. He watched the tail lights disappear down the driveway, Hana's face pinched and blank at the wheel. Logan shook himself as a wave of foreboding crept over his soul like an internal shiver, leaving him afraid.

Chapter 23

Hana drove to work on autopilot. She covered half the journey without recognition. When a child wearing a yellow backpack stepped out in front of her, it brought her to her senses. The Honda slid to a stop and her hands shook on the steering wheel. Wide blue eyes stared at her and then the boy ran the rest of the way across the road. It left her trembling. "Snap out of it!" she pleaded with herself, pinching her thigh to break the miserable fog. "Snap out of it, Hana. Before you kill someone!"

Driving along the tree-lined avenue towards school, Hana felt her heart constrict and her blood pressure rise. "It's just work, you'll be fine," she coached herself. "You can do this. It's almost the holidays. It's just another day, an ordinary day. You can't control everything and that's okay. Let it go." Hana bullied and cajoled herself, using the phrases a counsellor taught her after Vik's death. They fitted around her tongue like tasteless food and a wail of hopelessness formed in the base of her chest. "You should have told her the truth!" Hana's breath came in heaves as she relived the never ending nightmare. "How can a counsellor help you if you don't tell the truth?" The wail emerged and Hana bit her knuckles, trying to stop the emotional eruption. Her mind raced in terrible directions, dragging her back through the rabbit hole of history and ramming the bitter memories down her throat like an accusation.

A bus pulled out in front of her as the traffic slowed and irrational thoughts pressed into Hana's brain. Boys poured across the road from the bus like released ants, not waiting for the pedestrian lights in Fairview Downs. The car in front of Hana slammed on its brakes. A teacher on duty waved at the boys in the road. "Get back on the pavement!" he shouted as cars backed up in a metallic stream of impatience. The boys delayed, blocking the road and watching him pull his detention slips from his pocket. He flapped them in the air and the boys retraced their steps to the pavement, heading towards the pedestrian lights in a slow, reluctant shuffle. The teacher recognised Hana waiting in the traffic and shrugged, raising his white bushy eyebrows at her. A member of the elderly physics teaching stock, he resembled a bad caricature of a southern hemisphere Father Christmas in his Bermuda shorts and socks with sandals.

Hana gave a small wave as she battled the emotions raging inside her. "It's just another day. Don't let it get a hold of you. Just think of Logan, think of your husband," she murmured. The man watched her lips move and squinted, thinking she spoke to him.

The car in front of Hana moved away. Thoughts of Logan came with the memory of his foolish, hasty claim and the words slapped her in the face. 'Obviously I'm not on business at all. I'm actually whoring my way up and down the country and enjoying every second of it.' She heard it like an echo in her head. The driver behind Hana honked the horn, an impatient mother wanting to drop her tribe and dash to a high powered job. Hana's body turned to ice in her seat.

The school gate beckoned to her from across the road and she ran through the movements she made every day, in her head. "Indicate-drive-turn. Do it, Hana. Just bloody do it." But a black cloud of depression sat in the entrance waiting for her, blocking her path and daring her to pretend that today might continue as normal. The dark cloud morphed into an animal with bottomless eyes and its mouth opened in a dreadful liquid drool. "It's not normal," she wailed. "Nothing's normal."

She took her foot off the brake and the car rolled forward. The vehicle behind honked again and the teacher on bus duty stared at her, an expression of concern in the set of his square jaw. Something clicked inside Hana's head and the routine and constriction of work moved aside, replaced by the possibility of being somewhere, anywhere else but there.

Cancelling her indicator, Hana floored the gas and drove past the gates. Her wheels made a tiny screech as she took off. The sudden rush of freedom felt exhilarating. Her eyes filled with tears and she laughed, a horrid, maniacal sound. "I'm bunking off," she whispered. "I don't have to stay anywhere I don't want to be." She understood in that moment the desire of truanting boys, needing to duck out of life and wander the streets in an act of avoidance.

Hana drove south with the traffic, trying not to panic as the vehicles in front peeled off left and right onto different routes. She scrambled through her mind for places to go, discounting anywhere involving contact with other people. The prospect of small talk and explanation sent darts of fear shooting through her head. Raglan on the west coast was an hour away, but the cool breeze promised a freezing day at the seaside alone.

Further west Hana drove until forced to negotiate the bottleneck roundabout at the junction with Cobham Drive and Galloway Street. Panicking, she pulled into the left-hand lane and spotted the upright stones and woven rugs marking the entrance to Hamilton Gardens. Making the left turn, she pushed the car towards the town's green oasis. Her knees felt weak and her legs shook in her boots.

Hana managed to park the Honda in the car park without dinging it, despite her crumbling resolve. She rested her face against her forearms over the steering wheel, nausea making her feel heady and out of control. "What have I done?" she groaned. "Watson will fire me." A voice in her head told her she shouldn't care and she obeyed it, realising it wouldn't be the end of the world. She watched a group of Asian tourists clamber aboard their bus and contemplated sneaking into their large baggage compartment and feigning memory loss. The tour company carried them away still clicking their cameras and Hana lost her opportunity. A more urgent need pressed home its advantage and drove her from the safety of her vehicle.

"Please can you tell me where the nearest toilet is?" she asked a park attendant, faking a lousy German accent. He blinked at her in surprise and answered in fluent German. "Thank you," Hana squeaked and took off in the direction of his pointing finger. "Idiot!" she chastised herself. "You make a pathetic runaway!" Her irrational behaviour bemused her. She'd never seen the man before and probably wouldn't again. Stopping half way across the car park, she ruined her sophisticated image by squatting to lace her boots and almost getting run over by a camper van.

She found the new automatic toilets behind a row of neat camellia bushes. The city counsellors opened them earlier that year with a brass band and a party. Hana threw up in the basin without ceremony. She washed her face, wary of the various complicated looking buttons. When the lights gained an eerie blue hue, a clipped voice announced in multiple languages that the facility would be automatically cleaned in five minutes.

Hana shot out like a cork from a bottle, dragging a length of toilet roll on the bottom of her boot. She pondered a story she once read about a woman who had her insides sucked out by an automatic toilet when she didn't get off in time. She reached the fountain before realising she forgot to pee. "Oh for goodness' sake!" she moaned. "Why am I so afraid of everything?" The sound of raucous sluicing filled her ears, preventing any possible return.

Hana dipped her fingers in the cold water of the fountain at the entrance to the gardens. She closed her eyes and sensed the ripples crossing her skin like a sensual massage. When she looked up, a female park attendant in an official green uniform smiled at her. "You should check out the fantasy garden," she said, jerking her head towards the entrance.

Hana started and her gaze strayed to the decorative archway which began the tour. "I suppose I should now I'm here," she mused. She nodded in thanks and walked towards it. In the first themed garden, she struggled with an overwhelming sense of isolation. Modelled on an English rose garden, it reminded her of her childhood home. Memories of her mother enacted a slow painful torture as grief bit. She walked with deliberate slowness, forcing herself to follow the paths through every garden and inspect each of the different themes at length. In her right hand, she carried a fistful of rose petals stolen from the English garden. Red like blood, they held her mother's scent and she closed her eyes and inhaled from her palm. "I miss you," she whispered. "There are so many things I need to tell you." Each garden contained a seating area and she wasted the entire morning sitting on the benches one after another. The sun warmed her back and shoulders as she sat in the shade of the Indian garden, overlooking the treacherous and mighty Waikato River. She contemplated the poor missing woman who Bodie searched its depths for and shivered, wondering if Laval watched her right then.

Lunchtime came and went and Hana ran out of gardens to view. Reality called to her and she resisted, straightening her spine and refusing to obey. She climbed to a familiar patch of grass above the lake, sinking into the damp grass and forcing herself to think of happier times. In her mind's eye, Izzie and Bodie played on the slope, rolling over and over while they waited for the summer performers to entertain them with Shakespearean delights. "Oh, why here?" she groaned, remembering her dream about Vik. Closing her eyes, she ran her palm over the soft grass, feeling the water droplets against her skin.

She sat for a while, reaching for her emotions and letting them escape bit by bit. Overwhelming sadness and loss trumped guilt and fear. Her phone trilled at regular intervals from her handbag and she ignored it as she'd done all day, resisting pressure from the outside world to conform. The damp earth encroached into her clothes until an uncomfortable wetness eked through to her skin and caused her to shiver. She sat cross-legged like a school child before a teacher, her rounded belly balanced on her thighs. Her fingers picked absentmindedly at blades of grass and she threaded daisy stems into a necklace. Concentrating on the greenery halted the clamour of competing voices in her head and Hana relished the momentary rest.

The sun dipped behind a cloud leaving cooler air to nip at her flesh. Hana glanced at her watch and once again, the date taunted her. "Nine years," she murmured. "Nine years to rebuild my life and five minutes to destroy it all over again." She sighed. "Men and their secrets. Now what will I do?"

Hana wondered if her children remembered the date and chided herself for thinking they could ever forget the horror of that day. "Your father's not coming home. He died on the way to work this morning." She mouthed the words engraved on her heart. The memory of their stricken faces crushed her to pieces. Sometimes the date occurred in the holidays and Hana knew she coped better then. She could hide away and wait for it to end. Not this year. The state of her marriage, her ruined relationship with Bodie and her pregnancy all heralded disaster. She'd contemplated taking the day off, but suspected Logan wouldn't understand. He treated every mention of Vik the same way she viewed Caroline. A piece of their respective pasts with no right to trespass on their present.

Hana looked at her watch and saw the hands move towards the hour. Two o'clock in the afternoon. What was she doing at that time nine years ago? Safe and unsuspecting of the horror arriving with a knock on the front door. She tried to look back in time and found herself blocked by some obstacle that wouldn't allow her past. The blackness prevented her accessing the memory. She'd been sick that day and stayed home, but what was she doing at two o'clock? Sleeping? In the bathroom?

"What?" she moaned, pounding her fist into the grass. The child in her womb kicked, upset by the constriction of her position. Hana gasped and snapped her legs apart. She rubbed a hand over her belly and breathed out through half-closed lips, trying to soothe the sharp pains which sliced like a knife through her guts.

The temperature dropped, warning of the cold coming as soon as the sun went down. Hana gave up her wrestle with the past and bringing her knees up, tried to stand. One of her arms and both legs failed to respond, numb and jelly like from her terrible sitting position. The baby kicked her bladder, causing her to give a low moan and clutch her stomach again. The sensation felt like an iron bar wedged sideways inside her, rigid and immovable.

Hana gave in and lay flat on her back, rubbing her numb right arm. She waited through the tingling as the weak tendons came back to life and punished her for the ill treatment. Her foot banged against her handbag as she jerked in pain and Hana heard it fall. The contents clattered out and she watched them slide down the incline. "Damn it!" she exhaled. "Bloody typical!"

"Are you okay?" The question came from near her feet, the questioner silhouetted by the watery sunshine behind him. Hana struggled to sit up, flailing like an upturned tortoise. She admitted defeat and lay there, embarrassment flushing her cheeks as the man stared down at her.

"Dead legs," she said, wishing he would leave.

"Ah yep," he said, holding out his hand. Hana seized it with reluctance, hauling herself back into the uncomfortable sitting position. She didn't know if she trusted her legs enough yet to stand.

"Sorry," she muttered. "I sat for too long. It's painful." She tried to look up, but her eyes watered in the direct sunlight and she shaded them with her hand and turned away.

"Ooh, blinded." The man chuckled and moved uphill, his eyes shielded by the brim of a khaki hat. Mid-twenties, fair-haired and brown skinned, he wore a green park keeper's uniform. He smiled at Hana, rugged and good looking. "Hey Mrs Johal," he said.

Hana's cheeks lit with the flush of mortification. She twisted her lips into a reluctant smile and cursed her rotten luck. "Hey yourself." She tried to sound pleasant, racking her brain for the ex-student's name.

"Don't get many women flailing around on their backs up here," he said, looking at her with expectation. She continued to dig for his name. "We get a few down in the bushes though!" He gave a stilted laugh at his own smutty joke and then had the decency to look sorry. His humour jogged Hana's memory but his name still escaped her. She recalled his very blonde hair against the school jersey. John, Jack, Jason.

"Paul isn't it?" It came to her in a rush and the man's face crinkled into a wide smile.

"I never expected you to remember my name," he lied. "I work here." He waved his arm expansively. "I liked that horticulture course you sent me on so I applied for a job here about six years ago."

Hana winced as the tingle increased to encompass her thighs and the lower half of both legs. "Wonderful," she gasped.

"How's Bodie?" the man asked, changing tack.

"He's good thanks," Hana replied. "He's taken his son for a trip up north for a wee while." She tried not to tell people Bodie's occupation. If he wanted them to know, he would tell them himself.

"Awesome," the young man replied, "He's got a kid? Good on him. Always was a bit of a one with the la…" He left the sentence unfinished, clamping his teeth over his bottom lip. He still had that same habit then.

Paul peered at her bulging stomach, clearly wanting to comment. But somebody wise had drilled into him the danger of that particular subject. A woman might not be pregnant; she might just be fat. He gulped the question away and looked down the hill, pushing his wide-brimmed hat backwards onto his crown. He spotted Hana's paraphernalia spread out over the grass and stepped towards it. To Hana's horror, he dropped to his haunches and started shoving it back into the open bag. "Oh! It's fine, I'll get it later," Hana cried, hearing the alarm in her voice as he scooped up dirty tissues and a forgotten tube of hair remover cream.

"No trouble," he replied, grunting as he leaned over to reach a roll of sticky tape covered in grass.

"I need to clear it out," Hana said, dusting her knees and watching his deft fingers recover the myriad objects. "It's not had a good clear out since, well, a while." Since she whacked Tama with it actually. Hana bit her lip. She heard a lipstick clink on the buckle of her wallet as Paul chucked it into the bag and her keys jingled after it.

Hana pressed her hand over her mouth, not sure whether to laugh or cry as Paul waved her phone at her. He looked bemused by the sanitary towel stuck to the front of the screen. "It's clean," she gasped. "Just a spare. Oh, please just give it here." Dusty from bag-crap, it had escaped its wrapper and dangled from her phone screen like a flapping tongue. Hana looked around her, willing a hole to open up in the ground and swallow her, inflamed cheeks first.

Paul waggled the phone from side to side, making the object perform a little slap-slap dance. Oblivious to Hana's discomfort, he shrugged and dropped it into the bag. He bounced around catching chewing gum wrappers and a few petrol receipts, shoving them into his pocket. "Littering's an offence in the gardens," he said with gravity.

Humiliation settled over Hana, creating the complete crazy-lady picture. She flapped her left arm at him, silently pleading for help to stand. She tensed every muscle in her lower half and prayed she wouldn't add peeing herself to the list of failures. A perfect end to a terrible day.

"Here you go then." Paul helped her up, unaware of her fear of leakage. Hana daren't let out a sigh because it wasn't over until she reached a bathroom.

"Is there another toilet nearby?" she asked, masking the squeak in her voice.

Paul raised an eyebrow. "Nobody likes that automatic one." He jerked his head down the hill. "There are some more at the pavilion. About two minutes' walk that way."

"Thank you so much for your help. All the best," Hana managed in a strangled voice. Paul waved and trotted back to his flowerbeds at the rose gardens on the other side of the hill. Hana maintained a steady pace across the boardwalk and closed the toilet door with a sigh of relief. She groaned at the horrid damp feeling around her bottom from the ground. "These stains won't come out," she muttered, contorting herself to inspect the grassy blur on the back of her coat. She left the bathroom, pulling her leggings from her backside and walking with tentative steps.

Tiredness flanked her and she sank into a seat in the pavilion hallway, dropping her handbag to the floor. A glass cabinet occupied the wall opposite, filled with an enormous carving. From a distance, Hana saw myriad individual characters carved into the huge planes of wood. Delicate fairies peeked from the leaves of trees. Grumpy gnomes sulked in the undergrowth and birds, butterflies and tiny rabbits went about their business in a gentle, fantasy world. Hana rose and pressed her palms to the glass, enthralled by the thing of such beauty. A notice declared that two separate artists worked on sections of the carving, injecting their own techniques and individuality into the piece. "Incredible," Hana breathed. The parts weren't united until the day they arrived at the gardens and were assembled into a complete picture.

Hana squinted to look for the joins and spotted them. A thin line denoted where one section ended and another began. Yet from afar, they resembled a continuous image envisioned and executed by a single craftsman. Thousands of hours of work went into creating a masterpiece. Two minds influenced by experience and with individual autonomy produced a single, perfect design.

Hana sat down again, wondering if the carving offered her the secret to life. She could take all the mixed up, individual parts of herself and unite them with Logan's, trusting when she viewed their marriage with hindsight, the cracks may no longer seem so important. Her phone whined again from her bag, sounding sad and plaintive as the battery waned. She sighed. "I loved you so much, Vik," she breathed. "I gave you everything." Her bottom lip wobbled and she let her head sink to her chest. "It's been so hard lying to everyone. All these years, such a waste." For three hundred and sixty-five days in an average year, Hana allowed Vikram Singh Johal to keep his sainted status, doubting him only on the anniversary of his death. A stranger's posthumous accusation robbed her of a husband, father and friend on the strength of a single, angry conversation. Hana would never know the truth and it tainted every shred of trust she possessed. "Maybe I should ignore the cracks," she whispered. "Perhaps I need to stand back so I can't see them, instead of driving myself insane prying them open and ruining a perfectly good work of art."

"It's amazing, isn't it?" The voice sounded soft and creaked with age. Hana spun in her seat and acknowledged a slender woman walking with splayed sticks. The old lady paused, her head bobbing as she drank in the beauty of the carving.

"Yes," Hana replied. "It's breathtaking."

"Are you a tourist, dear?" the woman asked, smiling at Hana with gentle benevolence. Hana shook her head.

"No, I live above Hamilton. I just came here for my day off." She bit her lip against the lie.

The woman nodded. "My son's visiting from England. His wife didn't like this mural. She stood with her face against the glass and complained about all the joins. I told her to sit where you are and look, but she wasn't interested. You can't see them from there, can you?"

"No," Hana mused. "I was just thinking that exact same thing."

"She's got no class, my daughter-in-law," the woman grumbled, teetering towards the toilets on her sticks. "Doesn't know a good thing when she sees it." She farted and it echoed in the narrow corridor as if rebelling against the notion of class. Hana stifled a snort and pressed a hand over her mouth, praying the old lady made it to the bathroom without further delay.

The baby's activity calmed to a steady rumble of elbows and knees as Hana found her equilibrium. A weight lifted and the dark cloud parted enough for her to see ahead. She resolved to stop punishing Logan for Vik's mistakes. Hana picked mud off the heel of her boot and thought about going home.

Wanting to hear Logan's voice, she pulled her phone from her bag, stripped off the sanitary pad and dialled his number. The small telephone image showed a red arrow and the number twenty-three. Eleven unopened envelopes flashed on the screen. Twenty-three missed calls and eleven texts. Hana bypassed the flashing symbols and waited for Logan's familiar voicemail to ask her to leave a message.

"Hana?" His voice sounded calm and level and she pictured him in a business meeting somewhere, perhaps with the Ches or some other mafia king.

She inhaled. "Vik cheated on me," she blurted. "I found out after the funeral. His mistress came to see me."

Logan sighed and the sound carried as a hiss into Hana's ear. "I'm sorry," he said.

"Logan." Hana held her breath. "I don't want to be alone every night, wondering where you are or who you're meeting. You said you'd sold everything, so why is it worse? Why do you go out more?" She heard him swallow. "You want me to trust you, but I can't Logan. There are too many reasons not to."

Hana listened to the static of a long pause before Logan spoke. "I'm at home, babe. It's you who's not here."

"Oh," Hana whispered, her brow furrowing.

"Come home Hana." His voice sounded soft and soothing. She felt drawn to his presence, wanting to curl up on the sofa next to his powerful body and erase this date from her memory.

To cancel this day's existence from every calendar for the rest of her life.

"Okay," she breathed and disconnected the call.

Chapter 24

At Culver's Cottage, Logan slumped back against the kitchen chair, nausea making him grip his stomach. He dialled a number with shaking fingers. "She's fine," he said to the person on the other end. "She's on her way home. I've no idea where she's been. I'll call you tomorrow." Logan disconnected and called Sheila and Angus separately.

Then he paced as he'd done for the last four hours. When his phone rang, he snatched it up and peered at the caller ID. "Hi, dad, make it quick," he snapped.

"What time will you arrive?" Alfred demanded, a whiny tone to his voice. "Your mother wants to know if you're needing dinner."

"I'm not coming. I'll visit at the weekend sometime, but not tonight."

Alfred upped the anti. "You started this and now we're living with the consequences. Reuben came last night and spent the evening drinking and yelling in the car park. Your mother's giving refunds most mornings. He wants to see you."

Logan sighed. "I told you to call the cops!"

"He will only deal with you. Your mother can't cope. She wants you to retract everything. It's making her ill."

"I've told you. Call the cops, it's easy! I've issued him with a trespass notice and gave the local station the other copy. They'll enforce it and put him under arrest."

"No, he's my brother. I don't want to do that."

"Whatever, Dad! You supported me! You encouraged me to see it through. It's too late to stop it now unless Reuben agrees to settle. He needs to pay me back or abandon the land. I'm hoping he leaves." Logan ended the call, his patience fractured.

He walked onto the front porch and stretched in the cooling air, lifting his arms up above his head and bending his spine backwards. He felt like kicking something. As though on cue, his phone flashed up Pete's number. "What do you want?" he snapped. "I told you to stay away from me."

"Did you find Hana?" Pete sounded fearful and Logan ground his teeth to stop himself feeling sympathy.

"Yes."

"Okay. That's grand. I warned you about the anniversary of her husband's death. She always gets stressed and behaves a bit odd."

"I'm her husband now." Logan spoke through gritted teeth, the words emerging as a growl. He heard Pete give a nervous swallow in recognition of the warning sign.

"I do know that," Pete grumbled. "I've looked out for Hana since long before you arrived on the scene. You can't push me out of her life too."

Logan closed his eyes and put his head back on his shoulders. The huge sigh rocked his whole body. "Is that all?" he demanded.

"No." Pete inhaled and made a chewing sound. Logan cringed and tried not to think about the potential object between his teeth. "Graham from the Physics department said she drove to school and while she waited to turn into the gates, he had a bit of trouble with the bus boys."

"So?" Logan barked. He peered at his watch and tapped an impatient foot on the deck.

"So, he said she looked upset and drove straight past. Said she left tyre rubber on the road and looked in a hurry. Where did she go?"

"Mind your own business." He couldn't admit he didn't know.

"I told Sheila and she told you." Pete paused, waiting for thanks. He didn't get any.

"You want a medal?"

"Logan, how long do you plan to freeze me out? Can you thump me and get it over with? My life sucks without you." Pete sounded tearful. "Just hit me. I don't mind where." He spoke to someone behind him. "Henrietta's asking you not to hurt my face. We're getting engagement photos taken at the weekend."

Logan swallowed and a sense of futility rested on his shoulders. He pushed aside the desire to congratulate his old friend and concentrated on the driveway. If he moved to the left without falling off the deck, he could see the first bend after the gate. The breeze picked up through the trees but the narrow lane remained empty.

"Logan?" Pete persisted. "Can you hit me tomorrow? I want to get it over with."

"No," Logan groaned. "It's the gambling, Pete. That's the problem between us. You made me a promise when I paid off your last debt and you broke it. You're just one in a long line of recent let downs." He disconnected the call and blocked Pete's number.

Logan moved around the house, busying himself making food and tidying. He heard the beep of the gate monitor as he knelt on the living room floor setting the fire. He rubbed his eyes and ran his hands through his dark hair before getting to his feet. "Stay calm, stay calm," he warned himself, aware of the growing desire to shake his errant wife until her teeth rattled.

The need to punish Hana evaporated as soon as he met her on the front porch. She looked so fragile, Logan's breath caught in his chest and he knew he couldn't be angry. Her white face exuded pure exhaustion and she dragged her feet up the steps.

Logan followed her into the house and turned to close the door, noticing mud and grass stains on the back of her coat. "Here, let me help you." He took her coat and fingered the stains. "I'll put it into the washing machine," he offered. Hana held onto his shoulders like a child while he bent down, unlaced her boots and pulled them free. He saw damp patches on her leggings. "Strip those off and I'll take care of them," he said, his tone soothing.

Hana nodded in thanks and covered a yawn with her fingers. "I'm tired," she stated, as though imagining he hadn't noticed. "I think I'm in trouble with Watson."

Logan shook his head. "No. I told him you went home sick." He swallowed, desperate to hear the details of where she'd been, but afraid to ask. "Are you okay, Hana?" he said instead.

She nodded and pulled her feet free of the damp leggings. "I will be."

Logan's heightened awareness searched for signs of his mother's ailment, finding nothing similar in Hana's behaviour. She seemed calm although mascara dotted her cheeks in faded tear tracks. She twisted herself and brushed her fingers across the mud stains on her bottom. "It went through," she mused. Her eyelashes fluttered as she looked up. "I think I'll take a bath."

"Okay. Are you hungry? I made dinner."

Hana shrugged. "I'm not sure. I feel a bit weird." She stroked her lower abdomen. "A drink would be amazing, please."

Logan nodded, relieved to be given a function. He took her hand and led her to the bathroom, reluctant to let her out of his sight. He poured bath crystals into the tub and ran the water, warm but not too hot. Then he helped Hana undress, perplexed at the dampness of her clothes. She seemed passive, letting him peel her free of her clothes and holding his arm as she clambered into the big bath. She closed her eyes and lay back in the bubbles, but the hand on the side of the bath gripped with white knuckled fingers as though seeking a lifeline.

Logan fetched her a mug of green tea, finding her dozing in the hot water. Her hair hung in amber strands and grass dotted the curls. He stripped naked and then touched her hand, regretting the jolt of fear as she opened her eyes. "Everything's fine," he whispered. "Sit up and I'll get in and wash your hair." Hana sat up and shifted forward, giving Logan room to sit behind her. She lay back against his chest and closed her eyes as he scooped water over her hair and massaged conditioner into her clean scalp.

"The water's cooling," she sighed after a long while. Logan moved to turn the tap on with his toe and Hana shrieked as a burst of cold water escaped before the hot.

"Sorry." He got it running hot and she settled, the water covering her stomach but leaving a small mound of baby bump showing. Logan reached for the soap and rubbed his hands over it, caressing the outline of his child and counting his blessings. Hana groaned as the baby responded with a sharp kick. Logan inhaled as the imprint of a foot disappeared from the skin. "Geez!" he gasped. "Is that normal?"

"It happens all the time now," Hana said, sounding sleepy. She pushed Logan's finger away as he pressed the space where he last saw the foot and it appeared again. The skin stretched around the tiny ridge and he laughed.

"It's painful," Hana complained and he put the soap in the dish and rested his palms over her stomach. Conflict vied inside him, wanting to see the baby move but not wishing to cause Hana hurt. He gasped as a quake began in her stomach and something like the Loch Ness Monster emerged as though from the still waters of the Scottish lake. Hana's stomach contorted into an egg-shape and she groaned. Then the form twisted and dove beneath Logan's hand, shape-shifting and moving. The bath water shuddered as a tiny fist poked through Hana's fragile stomach and then all became still. Logan rubbed a hand over the bump as if checking for holes.

"That's just amazing," he breathed.

Hana sat in bed later while he plied her with tea and toast. The nightshirt laid over her shoulders, fastened by one lonely button. Indigestion loomed, stopping her after half a slice of toast and jam. A peculiar tingling sensation in her lower abdomen sent her to the bathroom numerous times, growing more uncomfortable with each visit. "I think I'm getting a bladder infection," she complained. "I drank nothing today. It's my own fault."

Logan fetched her lemon barley cordial laced with cranberry juice and she gulped it, wiping her lips with the back of her hand. "Better?" he asked and she nodded. "About the argument," he began and saw Hana wince. "I said a dumb thing and in the light of what you told me on the phone, it's dumber than I thought. It's thrown up bad memories and it wasn't my intention."

"I know." Hana inhaled and heaved out the breath. "I overreacted. Everything piled up on me and it's always a difficult time because the children don't know Vik cheated. I seem to cope with his sainted image all year round, smiling and nodding when they reminisce. But I get to today and can't do it. There are too many unanswered questions and I feel worthless and stupid." Her brow knitted. "How could I not know, Logan? What kind of wife was I?"

He shrugged and looked down at his hands. "You're my wife, Hana. Not his. Maybe he never deserved you, but I won't let you down. Please don't worry about that issue with me."

She sighed. "I didn't worry about it with him and hindsight taught me I should have. Just don't give me cause, Logan. I refuse to walk through that kind of rejection again. If I get even a hint of infidelity, I will leave and take this baby where you can't reach either of us." Her eyes flashed an ethereal green and burned with vengeance.

"You don't need to threaten me." He swallowed. "It won't happen, Hana." He watched as she ran a hand over her stomach through the nightshirt and gritted his teeth.

When they lay down to sleep, he cuddled against her spine and wrapped his arms around her waist. "Where did you go?" he whispered into her hair.

"Hamilton Gardens. I got scared by a toilet, soaked by wet grass and insulted by an ex-student."

Logan snorted. "It sounds riveting."

"It was." She closed her eyes and savoured Logan's presence like a long, thirst-quenching drink on a hot day. "Do you think everything will turn out okay?" she asked into the silence.

"Yep," he replied with absolute certainty. "I'll make sure it is."

Hana sighed and breathed in his warm scent. He always smelled the same, of hay, sunshine and wood smoke from an outdoor fire. "Did you train with the sports guys at lunchtime today?" she asked, running the backs of her fingers against his flat stomach. She imagined him running around the track, flanked by the other exercise junkies.

He grunted and she heard the rustle of his hair against the pillow. "No. I came home."

"Did you know the old farts watch you from the balcony at lunchtime?" Logan shook his head. "They do," Hana mused. "They clutch their generic pullovers close to their chests and eat their homemade sandwiches, trying to ignore their spreading bellies and multiplying chins."

Logan lifted his head. "And then make fun of us at every opportunity."

"Just jealousy." Hana turned to wrap her arms tighter around Logan and wedged her head beneath his chin. She felt the unevenness of the long scar on his side, knowing every knotted ridge from armpit to hip. Her fingers ran up and over his shoulder, touching the silky smooth skin beneath the tattoo on his bicep. "Whakapapa," she mouthed, her lips brushing the hair on his chest. "Where did your family's waka land in New Zealand?"

"Kawhia," he replied, his speech slurred as his mind battled sleep. "West coast."

"Would you get a moko on your face?" Hana slid her fingers up his neck and over the roughness of his chin.

"No." Logan shook his head a in slow movement. "I'm not kaumatua or chief," he answered.

Hana smiled and pushed her hands beneath the warmth of his armpits. "I think you are," she breathed, hearing the accidental truth behind her words.

Logan exhaled with a tired laugh catching in his breath and gave a satisfied sigh. "Not at the moment. Right now, I'm just your husband and her father." His fingers strayed to Hana's stomach, his eyelids opening as she jerked away from him. Her foot grazed his shin and he hissed. "Ouch!"

"You didn't!" Hana reached sideways and flicked on the overhead lights. "You opened the envelope, didn't you? From the scan."

Logan swallowed and twisted his lips into a grimace. "Sorry."

She sat up, the sheets pooling in a lazy puddle around her belly. "When did you open it?"

Logan sat and leaned against the pillows. He wouldn't look at her. "Didn't you peek already?" he asked innocently.

"No!" Hana sounded scandalised, biting her lip and slapping his chest. "Now you've ruined the surprise!"

"Oh." Guilt laced his voice in the darkness.

"When?"

"This afternoon while I waited for you to call."

Hana tensed and linked her fingers over her knees. "I guess I asked for that."

"No." Logan sighed. "I'm sorry. Please don't be mad at me." He reached out and ran his fingers over her hip.

"I'm trying not to get upset, but we were meant to look together."

"Hana?"

"What?"

"Why was the envelope hidden at the back of the bread bin?"

Hana swallowed. "Is that where it went?"

"You didn't know where it was?" Logan snorted. "That's the only reason you didn't open it!"

"No! I wouldn't." Hana's protest met his raised eyebrow of disbelief. She smirked and looked away.

"Double standards!" He poked his tongue out and moved his fingers over her ribs. Then he tickled. Hana squealed and bent double. "Bloody women!" Logan pulled her into his side, ignoring the sliver of resistance as his lips found hers.

"I want you back," he whispered. "I want you back from that place in your head where you've been the last few weeks." He pushed her fringe away from her forehead and kissed the porcelain skin beneath. "I love you, Hana Du Rose. You're my Circle Line girl." He pressed his lips over hers, relief flooding through him as she responded. Deft fingers parted her from the shirt and her underwear and his tongue touched hers with feather light caresses.

Later, Hana stood on the precipice of sleep, ready to jump off into the black nothingness. She heard Logan's phone chirp from the bedside cabinet. Slumber snatched her away with a renewed sense of exhaustion as he rolled over and killed the call.

Chapter 25

Logan rose before the alarm. He dialled Liza's mobile number from the kitchen, knowing she'd already be awake and glued to her laptop. "Kia ora!" she snapped. "And about bloody time."

Logan sighed. "I couldn't talk last night."

"Your problems won't go away because you ignore them, Logan." Her voice softened. "Your lawyer tells me the sleeping partnerships are almost dissolved, but there's the other issue."

"Uncle Reuben?" Logan's nostrils flared with his impatient inhale. "Yeah. Dad's blowing up my phone over his behaviour. I've seen him and he gaped at me like a moron. What could he possibly have to discuss now? He just needs to pay up by the deadline or abandon the property."

"Just like that?" Liza swallowed and paused. Logan felt she wanted to say more and waited, but she didn't.

"There's something else." Logan walked to the door and closed it, ensuring Hana didn't overhear. "That other thing I mentioned last time we spoke. They're putting me under more pressure and I think it might provide a means to an end."

"You're not considering it!" Liza exploded and Logan heard the murmur of a male voice in the background.

"Is that my lawyer?" he asked. "Can I speak to him?"

"No!" Liza spat. "It isn't."

Logan raised his eyebrows. "Do you have two on the go at the same time or just run through men like wine?"

"Mind your mouth, little brother," she returned. "Don't you dare go near that man or follow through on any of his ridiculous plans. I'm not pulling you out of the shit if you do, Logan! It's on you!"

"Okay. Thanks for the chat."

"It isn't over, Logan. Give the issue with Reuben more thought. He's family. You've gone down this track but think of the implications. I understand how much you hate Kane but you've had your revenge now. They're running scared. Come to an arrangement about the land at the top of the mountain and negotiate the outstanding debt. The developers want to speak to you, not your lawyer. They're offering you a sizeable stake in their project. It's worth considering."

"No." Logan clenched his jaw and disconnected the call. "No." He ran a hand through his hair and spoke to the empty room. "It's my land. She gave it to me. The only house allowed there is mine and I don't want neighbours."

Logan showered and then made Hana a cup of tea. She took a long time to rouse and seemed groggy. It didn't stop the endless stream of slurred complaints which poured from her lips until she disappeared for a shower. "Everything hurts," she grumbled, stumbling from the bedroom.

Logan's phone rang and he snatched it from the bed and pushed the door closed. He recognised the number and rapped out an answer. "What?"

"The developers insist on a meeting." His lawyer sounded jovial, a sickeningly happy early riser. Logan heard the sounds of a coffee shop even though the clock showed just after seven. "They've come up with an offer you can't refuse."

Logan snorted. "Can't I?"

The lawyer laughed too. "Yeah, if you're a crazy man. I wouldn't. They're over committed and you'll put them out of business. We all know it. Let me push them a bit harder and then sign."

"No." Logan balled his right fist and stared at the white knuckles showing through the skin. Scars dotted the flesh from a lifetime of haemophilia.

"Look man, I'm costing you a fortune. Let it go and make a profit."

"No," Logan repeated. "Don't bring me any more of their offers. I want their equipment off the mountain. They can leave the road as compensation. Everything else off."

"I have to bring you the offers. It's my role as your legal counsel. You know that." His voice softened and he took a noisy slurp of his coffee. "My advice is for you to negotiate. Make them squirm and then let them build."

"No. And if you can't do as I instruct you, I'll employ the new guy in my sister's bed. Do as you're told." Logan killed the call and dropped his phone on the bed as though it contaminated his fingers. Hearing Hana clattering in the bathroom, he snatched it up and muted the volume, shoving it into his trouser pocket.

When she didn't reappear, he made the bed and tidied around. "Hana?" His steps took him to the bathroom door and he knocked. "I'll drive today and we can go together. But Donald moved staff briefing forward half an hour because of the athletics exchange. Are you almost ready?"

"No," came a small voice from the bathroom, "I can't get off the toilet. I'm peeing and it hurts."

Logan bit his lip. "That sounds bad. Can I get you more cranberry juice?"

"It's not helping. I need to stay home."

Logan tutted and twisted his lips. "I told Watson to mark you as sick yesterday. He can add another day, but you'll need a doctor's note if you want more."

"I don't care right now," Hana grumbled from behind the door.

Logan walked to the kitchen and filled a pint jug with water. He opened the door enough to set it on the floor inside. "Drink this and refill from the cold tap. I'll wait here until you feel better."

"No, you should go." Hana sighed. "Thanks for the water."

Logan heaved out a breath of exasperation and pushed the door open further. Hana sat like a queen on her throne, a long coat hanging either side of her legs. She sniffed and Logan felt a surge of pity. "Why are you wearing your coat in the bathroom?" he asked, dropping to his haunches next to her.

"I can't get warm." She shivered as though to make her point and Logan's brow knitted. He reached up a hand to feel her forehead and stroked her cheek as he withdrew it.

"You don't feel like you have a temperature," he said. He rose. "I'll call the doctor."

"No, please don't." Hana winced. "I'll stay home, drink gallons of water and rest. It's worked before."

"Ring me if anything changes?" He bent to kiss her forehead. "Promise?"

"I promise." Hana pushed at his thigh. "Now go. This is embarrassing."

Logan nodded. "I don't have time to get my stuff for the bike. I'll leave the Honda and take the truck. In case you need it."

Hana offered a sweet, disarming smile in response. Logan hovered in the doorway, sensing she faked it. "I dunno." He lifted a hand to his hair and mussed up the fringe, confusion showing in the tilt of his head.

"Go! I'm fine!" she persisted. She flapped a hand at waist level. "I need to get off the toilet and you're stopping me."

"Okay." Logan swallowed and retreated to the hall, collecting the keys for his truck and shoving his feet into his boots. Fear lodged in his chest. "Are you sure, Hana? I can stay home with you today."

"No, I'm good," she called, forcing joviality into her voice. "I'll text you every couple of hours."

Logan's phone vibrated in his pocket and he cursed and withdrew it. Distracted, he set off towards the back stairs. "Okay, I'll expect to hear from you, Hana. Don't forget." Pausing to wait for a reply, he heard the flush of the toilet. The sound covered whatever he said and the phone continued to vibrate in his hand. He gritted his teeth and answered, his reply channelling aggression. "Leave me alone!"

The caller gave a low chuckle and his next sentence slowed Logan's steps. "This is the only way," the voice said. "You play the game my way or I'll ruin everything you hold dear, mate. Last warning. I'll call when you've had time to digest my suggestion."

"Suggestion?" Logan spat the word. His feet picked up speed on the steps, pounding the wood with the weight of his frustration. "That's a threat, not a suggestion."

"Too bad." The voice gave a low chuckle. "Time's up." The call ended and Logan's screen paused a moment before retreating to black.

Chapter 26

The gate alarm beeped and Hana heaved a sigh of relief. "I don't feel so good," she sighed, fighting unexpected nausea. "But it's worse with you watching me, Logan Du Rose." Crawling across the floor, she drank the pint of water, followed by two more from the cold tap. She winced in discomfort as she sat on the floor to wait for it to take effect. "Darn kidneys," she cursed. "You always let me down."

A soreness crept into her lower back, along with the nasty suspicion she needed antibiotics. When she stood, the three pints of water which proved difficult enough to get down, threatened to come back up. With a sigh of acceptance, Hana crawled into the lobby and found her mobile phone on the hall cupboard. She searched for the number of her doctor's surgery.

"No appointments today," a sing-song-no-messing-kind-of-voice informed her. "You can come to the surgery and hang around for a drop-in appointment? The wait time is currently four hours."

Hana pictured herself spending four hours in the surgery toilet and declined. She ended the conversation and executed Plan B. None of the midwives picked up so she left a message and leaned back against the cupboard. Her head pounded and she shifted to get comfortable, wishing she'd let Logan stay home with her. The phone rang and she fumbled it, answering the call and then dropping it onto the floor.

"Hello?" a worried voice said. "I'm calling from the midwives' office. You left a message."

"Sorry, I dropped you," Hana replied, feeling like an idiot. "I'm sitting on the hall floor and becoming more certain by the second I need antibiotics."

"Ah. I've checked and your midwife is on leave all this week," continued the female voice. She paused. "Why are you sitting on the hall floor? Have you passed out? I can call an ambulance."

"No, no! I'm fine. I feel a little sick is all. The doctor's receptionist offered me a four hour wait and I didn't want to spend it in the bathroom at the surgery. There must be another way of getting a prescription of antibiotics." Hana sighed. "Is that hot locum still there or did he leave already? I'm sure he'd give me a private script."

The midwife laughed. "That ship sailed sweetheart. I need to see you. Give me half an hour and I'll get to your place. Your doctor might write something up."

"If my midwife is away, he probably is too. They're married." Hana wrinkled her nose. "I'm out of luck today."

"Nothing is insurmountable. I'll bring a test kit and see what I can do. Allergic to anything?"

Hana replied she wasn't and rang off. She stayed on the floor, making herself comfortable and ignoring the peculiar feeling of vertigo. After a few sorties to the bathroom and back, Hana heard the gate buzzer sound and rose onto her knees to press the release button without checking the caller's identity. "Please don't be Laval," she grumbled, crawling to the front door. "I don't have the energy."

The sun shone high in the sky and Hana's body temperature moved from shivering to overheated. She sat on the front steps and waited for the visitor. A silver Nissan laboured to the top of the hill and parked in front of her. A pretty blonde in a blue uniform hopped out and reached into the back seat for a medical bag. "Aren't you hot?" she asked, indicating the coat.

Hana nodded. "I am now, but a minute ago I couldn't stop shivering."

The woman offered Hana her arm. "Let's get you inside. The other doctor wrote you a script but I want to check you out." She waited for Hana to haul herself upright. "I'm Juliet, by the way."

"Thanks." Hana nodded and caught her breath. "I've seen you around the antenatal clinic."

They proceeded inside at a slow pace. Hana let the door slam behind her and walked into the lounge. Juliet looked around, her gaze settling on the rug. "Do you have the energy to walk to the bedroom?" she asked. "Or should I check you here?"

"Here." Hana used the sofa as a midway point and lowered her bottom to the floor. "It's nearer the bathroom."

"Good call." The midwife smiled. "Because you'll need it in a second."

Hana gripped the sofa cushion while the woman examined her belly. She listened to the baby's heartbeat with a funnel and palpated the bump. When she pushed on Hana's sides, she let out a groan. "That hurts, especially on the right."

The woman sat back on her knees. "Definitely kidneys, Hana. The antibiotics I've brought should fix it."

"What do you mean? Brought."

"The doctor had a few days' worth in his bag. You can get the rest of the prescription fulfilled at a pharmacy. He wants you to take them for ten days."

"Wow, thanks." Hana clambered to her feet, using the sofa cushion to haul herself upright. "That's great service." She held her hand out for the container the midwife fished from her bag and waggled her eyebrows. "Is that all you need? I could produce a couple of litres if you need me to."

Juliet laughed. "Nope. Just a few drops is enough. Where's your kitchen so I can wash my hands?"

Hana pointed her in the right direction and then scurried to the bathroom. She kept her eyes on the floor and bent her body to avoid the awful sensation of falling. The midwife found her sitting on the bathroom floor minutes later, clutching a container of yellow liquid. "I'm fine," Hana promised, crawling across to unlock the door. "We've had a rotten few months and it's catching up with me."

"I'm not happy." Juliet leaned against the door frame and pursed her lips. "I think you should go to hospital."

Hana shook her head. "No. I'm safe here."

"Safe?" Juliet's brow knitted. "Isn't the hospital safe?"

"It's fine. Ignore me." Hana closed her eyes and took a moment to pull herself together. She held the sample out to the midwife and resorted to humour to mask the awkwardness. "I can produce a couple more if you need it."

"This is enough." Juliet balanced it on the sink and returned to the lounge for her bag. She tested the urine while Hana leaned against the bath with a blood pressure cuff strapped around her arm and a thermometer in her mouth. "There's blood in it." She washed her hands and knelt down to pump the cuff full of air, peering at the reading with narrowed eyes. "Blood pressure is normal."

Hana chirped her gratitude, but the thermometer garbled her words. Juliet pulled it from her lips with a pop. "I said normal blood pressure is good, isn't it?" Hana repeated.

The midwife raised an eyebrow. "But your doctor's notes state that yours is always low, which means it's raised."

Hana groaned and rested her head back against the bath panel. "Please just give me the antibiotics and I'll take it easy for a few days. I'll behave, I promise."

Juliet helped her up and doubt swam in her irises. "I'll take some blood, but I suspect the results will put you in hospital. You should prepare for that."

"I really can't go to hospital." Hana's chest tightened and she struggled with hysteria. Tama's visit returned to haunt her and panic bridled.

Juliet's face creased in alarm. "Don't get upset, Hana. You'll make it worse. Let's sit in the lounge."

"I'm twenty-three weeks pregnant and only just over half way there. I can't spend another seventeen weeks in hospital."

Juliet remained silent and realising her mistake, distracted Hana with compliments about the lounge decorations. "Where did you buy the curtains?" she asked.

Sensing a trap, Hana baulked. "Nowhere." Her eyes widened. "Somewhere."

Juliet settled next to her on the sofa and smiled. "You made them yourself and climbed a ladder to hang them?"

"I didn't know I was pregnant at first," Hana said, her green irises appearing huge as her pupils shrank. "I'm sorry."

"It's not a crime." Juliet stroked her shaking hand. "And pregnancy isn't an illness. You've hit a speed bump is all."

"I can't go to hospital," Hana whispered. "Please don't make me."

Juliet's face softened. "Look, this might all be caused by a urine infection and if so, the antibiotics will clear it up. I'll schedule your regular midwife to ring you on Monday and in the meantime if you feel no better, go straight to the hospital.

Hana felt the colour drain from her face. "So are you saying even if I'm better, I can't go to work tomorrow?"

Juliet looked at her with sympathy. "I don't think so, Hana. I need you to take things seriously and get some rest."

The gate alarm beeped as Juliet put her bag on the back seat of her car. Hana stiffened and tried to hide her angst as the midwife knitted her eyebrows. "What is it?" she demanded.

Hana swallowed as Bodie's car edged up the driveway and navigated its way onto the slope. He emerged from the driver's door and Jas exploded from his booster seat in the back. "Hanny!" the child squealed.

Juliet read Hana's expression of apprehension and turned to intercept the visitors. Her uniform spoke for her and Bodie darted a glance towards his mother. "Is everything okay?" he asked, trying to catch Jas as he launched himself towards Hana with a fast food wrapper in his fingers.

Juliet nodded and turned to address Hana. "Go into the house," she suggested. "I'll explain."

Jas wriggled free of his father's grip and lurched up the stairs with gargantuan steps. "Look what Daddy bought me," he said, waving the wrapper. "We ate KFC all week and he didn't make me eat nothing green. It's been great."

Hana snorted and soaked up the child's infectious enthusiasm. He wrapped his arms around her neck and a glance at the midwife persuaded her to take his hand instead of hoisting him onto her hip. "Come and tell me all about it," she said and turned her back on the people with the power to lock her in a hospital for another four months. Tama and Laval could visit her any time they liked and nobody would know.

Bodie closed the front door behind him and walked into the kitchen with concern and guilt mingling in his eyes. "She's taken Logan's phone number." He confiscated the teapot and pushed Hana towards a chair. "I'll make tea, Mum. After I've apologised for my behaviour recently. I've been a real arse."

Hana winced and looked at Jas, closing her eyes in mortification as he repeated it. "Dad's a real arrrrse." The child inhaled, his tiny chest puffing to bursting point. Then he let loose with a series of guttural repetitions. "Arse," he growled. "Arse."

Hana exhaled. "It's fine, Bo. Let's forget it." She lurched for Jas as he produced Action Man from inside his tee shirt and ran around the table. Hana missed as he darted past.

"Arse!" he said into the doll's face. "Arse."

"Jas, stop," Hana pleaded. "It's a naughty word. What on earth will Mummy say if she hears you swearing?"

He stopped and cocked his head, considering the scenario. Bodie picked him up and dumped him into a chair. "You know what she'll say," he whispered. "She'll blame me."

Jas shook his head and watched his father like a hawk as Bodie opened the pantry and reached for the biscuit tin. "She won't. Mummy says Dad's a really, really big arse too."

Bodie rolled his eyes and sighed. "Nice. Why am I not surprised?" He dished out two biscuits and closed the lid. Reaching into his trouser pocket, he produced his phone and handed it over. "Play quietly while I talk to Hanny," he said.

Jas' eyes widened with glee and his fingers worked across the keypad, entering the password and finding a game. He alternated between biscuit and game, leaning out of his seat in both directions as he became absorbed in the challenge on the screen. Hana smiled. "Jas you're so cute. I've missed you."

Bodie made tea and sat next to his mother. He put his arm around her and pulled her close. Hana sighed into his neck and closed her eyes. "I phoned you yesterday," he whispered. "You didn't pick up, so I figured you were still mad at me. I can't believe Dad died nine years ago yesterday."

Hana tensed. "I didn't ignore you, Bo. I couldn't speak to anyone."

Bodie nodded. "I hoped you wouldn't hurt so much, not with having Logan and a new baby on the way." He swallowed. "I thought of Dad heaps, but Jas distracted me a fair bit." His lips quirked upwards. "Kid's a nightmare."

Hana sighed. "I'll never forget every moment of that awful day." Her voice sounded strained. "It was one of the worse days of my life."

"One of the worst days?" Bodie's eyes narrowed. "What were the others?"

"Not relevant." Hana pulled away from his embrace. "But it's over now. A new year begins."

Bodie sat forward in his seat. "It felt different this year. Jas kept me busy, so maybe next anniversary will be the start of you letting go. You'll have a new baby and no time to think." He sighed as Jas dropped his biscuit on the floor and leaned sideways to retrieve it. The phone thudded onto the floorboards and the boy followed.

"I'm good," Jas called. A hand appeared on the table top and felt around for the remaining biscuit. When it found the prize, it disappeared. "But your phone's buggered."

Hana pursed her lips and contained both the laugh and the rebuke. Bodie ran a hand through his hair. "What did you do yesterday? I guess Pete kept you entertained."

"I took the day off," Hana replied. "And made some good decisions about looking to the future instead of the past."

Bodie nodded and reached under the table. "Give the phone to me," he demanded, glaring at the pieces which appeared in his hand. He slotted the sim card back in and pressed the battery into position. "Be more careful," he said with a sigh and fitted the back casing into its slots. It disappeared from his hand again as though spirited away by a genie.

Bodie pulled a chair up in front of Hana's feet and told her to put her legs up. "Fit midwife's orders," he told her when she protested.

Hana raised an eyebrow. "I thought you might notice." She reached for her tea. "What did you do up north?" She shifted in her chair and tried to ignore another urge to pee.

"We did in-sti-ga-ting stuff," Jas piped up, whispering behind his hand. "Like proper defectives!" He glanced across at his father and swallowed at the expression he met there. "What? Hanny doesn't count. She's fambly. You said don't tell anyone else."

"No, I said don't tell anyone." Bodie licked his lips. "Sorry. I didn't think you'd be home. Jas wanted to leave a present on your pillow."

"Yeah, but Daddy gave his key back to Poppa Logan when he got cross. So he said I could leave it on the doormat."

Hana twisted her lips and observed her son. He squirmed in his seat and she knew the signs. "What did you do up north, Bodie? Izzie already told me some of it."

Bodie deflated. "Bloody woman!" he snapped. "She promised."

Hana sighed. "I know that shifty look. Out with it, please?"

Bodie bit his lip. "I went looking for answers to your Laval problem."

Hana's jaw dropped. "I thought Izzie got it wrong! And you took your baby!"

"No!" said Jas from under the table, "No babies. Just me and Daddy!"

Bodie gritted his teeth and stood up. "Can't believe I fell for that," he grumbled. He narrowed his eyes at Hana. "She didn't tell you anything, did she?"

"Not as much as she could," Hana replied. "But now you can."

Bodie hauled his son out from beneath the table. "Go and play that game in the lounge, Jas. The beeps are irritating."

"Not again!" said Jas crossly, waiting until Bodie set him on his feet. "You just want rid of me."

Hana fought not to laugh at the child's impertinence. "Tell me!" she demanded once Jas left the room.

Bodie plopped into his seat, his shoulders slumped. "You weren't supposed to be here, let alone interrogating me."

"Just tell me." Hana felt exhaustion crawl up her shins and wanted the story over. "Just say it."

Bodie leaned back in his seat and fidgeted. "Odering is using me. He talks to me, but only about you and Logan. When I ask questions, I find myself frozen out. It's part of what's driven my angst about Logan. Odering is way too interested in your husband for it to be anything other than related to the case." Hana tensed and Bodie waved his hand. "Don't worry. I won't give you a lecture. But I used my week off to see my old diving buddies. We searched lakes and rivers for an old lady at the end of last year and when I asked Odering about her, he talked to my inspector and got me into trouble. I sensed more to it, so spoke to my mates unofficially."

"And?" Hana felt her heart pounding in her chest and rested a palm over it, as though trying to dull the vibration.

"My old boss let me see the case file and I got some information. The missing woman lived at a rural address in

Northland and her will is open to dispute. Odering wanted her body because he suspects foul play. That's why he travelled with us when we searched the Waikato River last year."

"Laval?" Hana breathed the name and it emerged as little more than a whisper. "He killed her?"

"Odering thinks so." Bodie took a sip of his tea. "But there's no evidence."

"So, what now?" Hana used her blouse to dab beads of sweat from her forehead.

"That box you found contained the woman's last will and testament. It was wrapped in an engineer's report."

Hana shrugged. "I didn't see it, Bo. Logan dealt with it."

Bodie made a sound like a snort. "Yeah, and then he let the guy who attacked you live at the hotel his parents own. Did you know that?"

Hana ground her teeth. "Not at the time, but later, yes."

"Do you know why?"

The discussion slipped into the realms of interrogation and Hana shifted in her chair. "No, Bodie. I don't have the energy for this right now. Let's talk about something else."

"Flick is the old lady's stepson." Bodie delivered his punch line and Hana felt the blow.

"What?"

"Logan must know that." He sat back in his seat and tempered his budding sense of victory. "I went to see the family. They're decent people actually."

Hana's eyes widened and she held her breath. "You visited the family?" Her bottom lip hung slack. "Are you kidding me? You took Jas to see the family of a man who tried to kill me, knowing the mother is dead somewhere?" She closed her eyes and pursed her lips to control her breathing.

Bodie raised his hand to halt further interruption. "They're nice people, Mum. I'm not an idiot. Laval's a smooth operator and dated the old lady. He won her over and borrowed money for a mining project in South Africa. By the time her son realised she'd handed over her savings, Laval had already persuaded her to make a new will in his favour. He gave her some rubbish about financial trusts protecting her sons from inheritance taxation if she died. A dodgy lawyer drew it up. But the trust is a farce and he's the only named beneficiary."

Bodie paused at Hana's white complexion. "It's what he did to Ethel Bowman," she breathed and he nodded. Hana ran a shaking hand over her mouth. "She mentioned something about lending capital for a mining project. I wonder how long it would have taken for her to change her will in his favour." She shook her head. "He's a monster."

Bodie eyed Hana sideways but continued, reaching across to take her hand. "The old lady's son found out about the will and went crazy. He made her tell Laval she was reversing her will and going to the cops. Laval dropped under the radar with her savings but instead of letting go of the will, something made him dig in harder. The son called in the cops and made a statement, but not before he got his mother to reassert her original will."

Hana shook her head. "Now you've lost me. If the original will leaves everything to the rightful heirs why did Laval chase after me for his copy? And why hide it on me in the first place?"

"Because you didn't have his copy," Bodie said, leaning forward. "You had a verified copy of the last one. Laval needed to destroy the one you had, so he could assert his."

Hana shook her head. "This makes no sense. Solicitors lodge a copy with some legal body. They'll have digital transcripts. He'll never eradicate them all. He's wasting his time."

"The son got her to reverse her will on a piece of paper, Mum. They didn't get a chance to see a lawyer. He got the neighbours to witness it and took the original and a copy. Two days later, his mother disappeared, before a lawyer even got involved. She drove to the supermarket and hasn't been seen since. Even her vehicle is still missing. The cops used different bits of intelligence and searched watercourses and lakes. They pushed the investigation as far as Hamilton and still found nothing."

"And then Odering transferred to Hamilton." Hana licked her lips. "He's tracking him, isn't he?" Her eyes widened. "Is he using me as bait?"

Bodie sighed. "I'm not sure, Mum. He's shut me out. I followed him to a meeting one night last week, but some new cop pulled me over and said my brake light was out. He didn't care that I had police identification and worked real hard to keep me talking. By the time he let me go, Odering was long gone." He blinked. "And my brake light was fine."

Hana's hand shook and she placed her cup on the table. "So, if I had one copy, what happened to the other? You said the son had an original and a copy. Where is the original?"

Bodie swallowed. "Someone hid that copy under your car for a very good reason. Maybe it was random, but they figured it was safe. Laval has the original."

"How?" Hana's head jerked backwards.

"How do you think, Mum? Heavies turned up at the farm and roughed up the son. After they beat him unconscious in front of his kids, the wife handed it over before they started on her. She told them they'd passed the only copy to a lawyer in town and picked a name at random. The guys left, cops came, usual statements, crime scene investigators at the house, no leads. That night, the lawyer's offices burned down after an arson attack. Again, no evidence."

Hana swallowed. "So then, he thought he had both copies?"

Bodie raised an eyebrow. "Somebody put him straight and nobody knows who. Flick's real name is Robert Dressler and he took possession of the copy but lost it. I've no idea how it ended up under your car, but I've discovered his ex-wife lives in Huntly. She's a drunk and her parents paid for Dressler's boys to board at St Bart's. The younger one could have put the box under your car before the summer holidays and then lost track of it."

Hana exhaled. "Gwynne said the kid who tried to mug me was an ex-student." Her eyes widened. "The woman they never caught might be his mother." Her fingers fluttered to her throat at the memory of female hands choking the life from her.

Bodie reached for her wrist. "Dressler phoned his stepbrother the same night as the careers event at school and told him he was running out of time. Then he met Logan and although I know he's at the hotel, I can't get near him."

"I'll ask Logan." Hana gnawed on her bottom lip. "He'll let you talk to him."

Bodie snorted. "You think I haven't tried?" He held up finger and thumb and showed a tiny distance between them. "I'm this far away from telling Odering that Logan's harbouring a criminal."

"Don't, please?" Hana swallowed. "Logan will have his reasons."

Bodie took a slurp of his tea. "I think someone hid the box on your car before Christmas, because you put your car in the garage all over the summer, remember?"

Hana nodded. "Marcus hates my driving. We went everywhere in his car and then Izzie had Beth. I took off to Invercargill and didn't use my car until the start of term." Her eyes widened. "The first day back, someone followed me into the car park and almost ran me over. They wouldn't know which direction I might come from, so they watched the school and bungled it."

Bodie nodded. "I reckon."

Hana rested her head back on her chair and closed her eyes. Everything seemed too hard. "Why would Flick's sons hide something so precious under my car? If they did it."

Bodie looked worried by her pale countenance and slid his chair closer. "I don't think they knew what they had. It's possible they stole it from their father. Odering tracked the outer casing to a project in the metalwork department. You were right about it being something Year 10s make. Perhaps the ex-wife found out it meant money and went after it. I'm guessing it fell off pretty quickly in the garage at the Flagstaff house."

"Did the missing lady's family know all this? If so, why didn't they tell the cops?"

Bodie shrugged. "Her family don't know any of that. They've no idea where Flick is, or what he's been doing. My information is just bits and pieces, guesswork and speculation." His eyes narrowed. "I reckon Logan knows more than either of us."

"You don't know that." Hana defended her husband, more through misguided loyalty than possession of any concrete evidence. Thinking about it wore her out.

She closed her eyes and Bodie touched her shoulder, making her jump. "Hey, you look terrible, Mum. Why don't you go for a lie down?"

Hana winced. "I'm tired of rattling around an empty house. I like you being here."

"Empty house?" Bodie cocked his head on one side. "But Logan lives here."

Hana nodded and conceded to her son's suggestion, eager not to admit she spent most evenings alone. "I'll lie down for a while. If you need to leave before I wake up, I'll understand." She shuffled to the bedroom after another visit to the toilet. A phone rang as her head hit the pillow and she felt relieved as Bodie answered it. She heard him walking into the kitchen, his voice little more than a low rumble. Hana drifted off to sleep, seeking escape from the steady throb of her right kidney and the urgent need to pee.

Chapter 27

S he woke up two hours later, a rabid thirst drying her throat and lips. The baby constricted her chest where she'd fallen asleep on her back. Her arm stuck out sideways, the muscle numb and painful. A strange wetness coated her armpit.

Jas' dark curly head rested against her and he dribbled through the gap between his lips and thumb. An action figure's legs dug into Hana's side. She shifted, sensing an imminent need for the bathroom. Jas stirred and rolled over onto Logan's pillow, leaving Hana to haul herself into a sitting position.

Slipping from the bedroom and closing the door behind her, she made it to the bathroom and then the kitchen. The wonderful scent of hot stew filled her nostrils and hunger gnawed at her belly. Bodie wore her pink and white apron, standing in front of the stove with his right arm making a stirring motion. Maihi sat at the table slurping strong tea and gave Hana a beaming smile as she stumbled in.

"Logan rang," Bo informed her without turning around. He sounded pleased. "The midwife gave him a serve for leaving you alone. He's coming home after his last English class."

Hana nodded. "She shouldn't have done that. I told him to go."

Maihi patted the table next to her and took Hana's hand in hers as she sat. "Sit by me, sweetie," she whispered. "Youse look like crap."

"Thanks." Hana felt foggy and her words sounded slurred.

Bodie handed her a bottle of pills and a cup of tea. "You need to start these now. You forgot earlier."

Hana tried to swallow a pill with the hot tea. Big mistake. She burned her tongue and the pill stuck to the roof of her mouth. The intercom by the front door buzzed and she squeaked and shot the tablet onto the table. Bodie gave her an odd look. "Is there something you're not telling me?" he demanded, his brow furrowed.

Tama's face rose into Hana's vision and her eyes widened. "No. I need to take this with cold water. I burnt myself."

She reached for the soggy tablet and tried again, holding the tea in her mouth before slotting it between her lips.

Bodie strode out to the intercom and held a conversation in a low voice. Hana heard him release the gate button and the front door slammed. She twisted in her seat as the tablet left a bitter trail along her throat. Maihi patted her hand reassuringly. "It's all fine girly. Nothing to worry about. Youse safe here."

A car grumbled up the driveway and Bodie greeted someone. Footsteps followed muttered thanks and an older man with a black briefcase appeared in the kitchen. "Mrs Du Rose?" He offered his hand to shake and Hana pulled away, alarm growing in her eyes. "Dr Cassidy."

"I'm not going to hospital." She pushed her chair back and tried to stand. "I don't know what they've told you, but I'm fine."

The doctor clutched the handle of his leather bag and surveyed his audience. "Your midwife sent me. I'm making house calls and want to take a look at you." He inclined his hand towards her stomach. "Juliet is concerned."

"I'm not going to hospital," Hana repeated, darting a glance at Bodie. "You can't make me. I won't be safe there."

The doctor's brows met in a dark grey line and he stared at her. "Safe? Of course you're safe in hospital, Mrs Du Rose. Let me take a look at you and then we'll talk."

"Would you like some tea, doctor?" Maihi asked and Hana fought the urge to scream. She didn't want him to stay longer than she could fake wellbeing and joviality. To her relief, the man shook his head.

"Thank you but no. I have other urgent visits to make." He fixed a determined gaze on Hana's face. "I'd like to examine you? It's just a precaution. Juliet noticed some oddities with your heart rate and blood pressure and wanted me to check it out."

Taking the path of least resistance, Hana lay on the lounge rug. Jas watched with a possessive air as the doctor examined her stomach, tapped her chest and back and listened with a stethoscope to something only he could decipher. The man frowned and knitted his brows. He sat back on his haunches and Jas pushed at his shoulder as though sensing Hana's distress and trying to force him away. "You can go now," the child said, kneeling between the doctor and Hana. "Hanny's fine."

The doctor spoke over Jas, his face filled with concern. "You have an irregular heartbeat, Mrs Du Rose. Has anyone picked it up before?"

"No." Hana ground her teeth. "This pregnancy is just hard. I'm half way through, but my age is against me."

He cocked his head on one side. "Juliet found blood and protein in your urine. You definitely have an infection. Your blood pressure is higher than usual and your temperature and heart rate are elevated. Given your age and the stage of your pregnancy, none of those things is good." Hana looked down at her hands, but he wasn't finished. "I should send you to the hospital but doubt you'd go. If you promise to stay home, take it easy and not have any excitement, I'll let you stay here." Hana nodded with enthusiasm and the doctor raised his hand in warning. "Any sign of problems and you must go straight to the hospital. Don't come to the surgery, we'll just send you there." He stood and Hana sensed his unhappiness. "Take care and we'll see what happens."

The doctor packed up his bag despite Jas' well-intended assistance and handed Hana another pill bottle from his bag. "Iron tablets, your blood is deficient. I sent a sample to the lab. I'm confident we've given you the right antibiotics to fight this. Hopefully there should be some improvement by tomorrow. Get the rest of the prescription fulfilled and if there are any other problems, seek help without delay." The doctor left without discussion and Hana heaved a sigh of relief.

Bodie let him through the gate while Hana sat up and leaned against the sofa. Jas plonked himself down beside her. "Sick Hanny?" he asked, his brown eyes wide and concerned. Hana shook her head and swallowed the ready tears.

"No," she whispered. She ran a shaking hand across her stomach. "I've come too far now for my body to let me down. I refuse to give in."

Maihi watched from the doorway. "Aw, none of that my love, none of that." She hurried forward to wipe away Hana's tears with her wizened fingers. "I'm here for you. Everything will turn out okay."

"Thank you." The words stumbled from Hana's lips but she paused too long, feeling guilty as the older woman clicked the front door shut behind her.

Hana clambered up eventually, vertigo making the ground lurch up to meet her. She sat in the kitchen and Jas climbed onto her knee with his doll. She exhaled, fear radiating through her body. Everything piled on top of her like a burden too great to bear and she tried to distract herself.

"Lunch is ready." Bodie donned the apron and dished it into bowls, ladling out a heap for himself and Jas.

"Finally!" Jas exclaimed. "I'm starvin'."

Bodie rolled his eyes and opened his mouth to protest about the fast food wrapper in the child's pocket. Instead, he resisted and Hana hid her face behind Jas so she could smile at the irony. Her most difficult child had spawned one of his own. She picked up her spoon and ate around Jas as he sat on her knee and swung his legs. When she discovered a black flake in the bottom of her bowl, she pulled it out and stared at it. "Bo, did you heat this too fast?" she asked.

"Yeah, sorry. I burned the bottom. The lumps of potato stuck to the pan."

"May I 'ave your burndy bits pees Hanny?" Jas balanced precariously on Hana's knees and wiggled round to speak to her. He pointed his spoon at the crusty black layer at the bottom of her bowl.

Hana shook her head. "I think that's the non-stick layer from the saucepan," she said. Her eyes widened as he dipped in and crunched through a chunk. "No, mate!" She shoved the bowl away and Jas wrinkled his nose.

"Damn it!" he groaned under his breath. "I never get anything good." He snatched up Bodie's phone and chased a worm around the screen with a giant bird.

"What's so great about the piece of land Flick's family own?" Hana asked. "Laval missed his opportunity, so why go to such trouble to get it? A good conman should cut his losses and move on to the next victim."

Bodie spooned beef and vegetables into his mouth. "Well, that's the other thing I found out," he said. "There's a store of some natural resource buried quite far into the property. The son wasn't specific and I couldn't ask without sounding obvious. I made out I knew Flick and blagged my way through. They seemed scared he might be floating face down in the harbour with his mate. I made out I'd heard from him recently and stopped by to catch up with him."

Hana swallowed and her gaze darted to the back of Jas' head. He made no sign he'd heard. She rebuked Bodie through the straightening of her lips and slight shake of her head. Her son shrugged. "He's not listening, Mum. He's engrossed in the game."

"At least speak in code then. He shouldn't hear about murders and thefts at his age."

Bodie snorted. "His parents are both cops. They're bedtime stories for him." Hana gave a long blink and hid her exasperation. Her son hesitated as though considering punishing her for her criticism. Hana waited, knowing he couldn't resist boasting about what he'd learned. He continued, but lowered his voice. The bird on Jas' screen chased the worm, zapping blue light which caused the child to pitch sideways. Hana held onto his waist and concentrated on Bodie's story. "Just over ten years ago, a private company made an exorbitant offer to purchase the family farm, believing they'd found an oil reserve just offshore. Local residents protested and the media got involved. The land runs down to the west coast and the legalities got messy relating to who owned what. The company wanted to set up a subsidiary site to Marsden Point on the other side of the island. An environmental lobby group hired a surveyor to validate the presence of oil and predict the impact of any future drilling. Locals didn't want another operation that extensive on their back doorstep. The surveyor carried out geological mapping and his findings agreed with the oil company about where the drilling could potentially find success. He also researched and documented other attempts to extract oil in similar locations. He recommended it didn't go ahead, but the company railroaded the government. Then the stakes changed. A general election saw more of the Green Party in parliament and the project died a death. The son showed me signed documents left by the surveyor and I recognised one sheet from the metal box. It wasn't in a foreign language, but a geological map of the ocean floor. The family shrugged it off and carried on farming until a few years ago."

"What happened?" Hana held her breath.

"The law regarding foreshore and seabed regulations changed. The private company returned last year and offered more money. And Greg Sefton's mother met Michael Laval at a community centre dance in Kaitaia."

"Oh." Hana swallowed and pressed her fingers over her mouth. "That's awful. Can't the original surveyor reassert his findings? I know a few things have probably changed, but his opinion will stay the same. If it was a bad idea ten years ago, it's a bad idea now."

Bodie stood and made a pretence of searching the pantry for the ketchup. Hana watched Jas dip into his father's bowl and take a big black crust from the bottom. She winced as he popped it into his mouth and crunched. "It's in the fridge, Bo," she said, watching the stiffness of his spine. Her maternal alert system sounded. "What's wrong?" Her voice sounded tired.

Bodie retrieved the ketchup and peered into his bowl. "Oh. I thought I had more than that left." He turned to the stove and dished himself up another portion. When he sat down, his gaze darted everywhere but at her. "The surveyor is dead," he said, his voice little more than a whisper. "He died nine years ago yesterday in a car pile-up in the Kaimai Ranges."

Hana gasped and Jas turned to stare at her. His dark brows knitted and he placed the phone on the table, his game abandoned. In a show of solidarity, he leaned back against her chest and tucked his head under her chin. "Sucks, dunnit?" he sighed.

Hana gulped air and a drowning sensation consumed her. The nightmare seemed to run on forever, biting her each time she got her head above water. "How do you know?" she gasped. "What tied Vik to the survey?"

"His name and signature." Bodie watched her flounder and stopped eating. "Sorry, Mum."

"They killed Vik?" The words emerged as a croak and her vision blurred as tears formed.

"No!" Bodie moved around the table at speed and wrapped his arms around her shoulders. "No. There's no evidence of that."

Hana swallowed and her voice sounded strangled. "But you checked?"

Bodie squatted next to her. "Of course, I checked. Dad died on a known accident black spot on a mountain road in wet weather. It's pure coincidence."

"This is too much." Hana covered her eyes with her palm. Tiny fingers reached backwards and snaked up the side of her face, patting her cheek and offering comfort. Bodie pulled a chair alongside and sat down. He snagged Hana's hand and dragged it away from her face.

"I couldn't believe it. I sat there staring at his signature for ages. What are the odds on that happening on the anniversary of his death? Finding out he sat right there ten years earlier. It felt like finding a footprint in the sand belonging to someone you never expected to see again." Bodie's voice cracked. "He missed out on my teenage years and won't meet Jas. Yet he sat in that lounge and signed the paper I held in my hand." Releasing Hana's fingers, he dragged his sleeve across his eyes. "I convinced myself I could sense him there in that room. But it's not like that is it? You don't believe they can still see and watch over us?"

"Catholics do," Hana replied, her tone soft. "Logan does. It gives them comfort sometimes." She remembered her husband's night terrors as he fought ghosts, convinced Barry had returned to hurt him. Upset and incoherent, he frightened her. "I don't want to believe your father's still here. I want to imagine him in Heaven, meeting up with old friends and having a party. Separation from everything he loved is punishment enough, without having to watch it play out without him. But nothing's impossible with God and maybe sometimes they're allowed to glimpse through and see things that encourage them and us."

Bodie gave a shuddering sigh and Hana saw the raw openness in his soul. "Punishment?" he asked, his voice quiet.

Hana rested her fingers over his as he slumped in the chair and stared at something in the distance. "It's an expression, Bo. I meant nothing by it." She licked her lips. "About the feeling you had seeing his signature, if it felt right, then perhaps it was. I don't know, Bo. I used to think I did, but the more I know of God, the less I understand." Hana stroked his fingers in slow, soothing motions to cover her error. "One thing I do know, is that it's best to take things at face value. Embrace the bits which seem right and savour them. Don't over-think it, don't try to work it out and don't go looking for that thing again. You'll drive yourself mad and walk a path which leads nowhere."

"I didn't tell those people anyfink," Jas piped up. He turned to face Hana with a smattering of black particles around his mouth. "They asked me what my daddy did. I got a bit mixed up." He stopped and wiped his mouth on the back of his hand. His tiny front teeth had bits of black in between them like he'd eaten a wax crayon.

Bodie narrowed his eyes. "When did they ask you that, mate? I didn't hear it."

Jas sighed. "You said you needed the bathroom, but you snooped around. The man almost caught you so I tried some terrogations."

Bodie swallowed. "What did you do, Jas?"

Jas made a smacking sound with his lips. "I nearly said you put people in jail, but then I 'membered not to and changed it."

"What did you change it to, sweetheart?" Hana asked. Bodie's eyes started to pop and his complexion paled.

"I said he put people in the, in the, in the hospital!" Jas smiled at his own ingenuity and Hana pressed a hand over her mouth to hide her amusement.

Bodie creaked out a question. "Maybe like an ambulance-man, son?" He looked so hopeful, Hana clamped her teeth over her lower lip.

"No Daddy!" Jas replied, indignation in his tone. "Like a fug!"

"A what?" Bodie looked confused. "A fug?"

"Yes!" said Jas, growing bored with the game. His fingers twitched towards the phone. "A fug, a wobber and a fug."

"Oh crap!" breathed Bodie. "A thug? You told them I beat people up for a living?"

"Yep." Tiny fingers closed around the phone and Jas recommenced his game.

Chapter 28

Hana returned from the bathroom and paused in the lobby listening to her son. Bodie tried to extract from Jas the reason he thought it cool to have a robber and a thug for a father. He wasted his time. Jas made up a song for every word which remotely rhymed with 'fug.' He proved entertaining if exasperating.

The doctor told her to cram the first day's antibiotics in with only a few hours apart. He wanted to hit the infection hard. She took another and realised the ache had lessened in the pit of her stomach.

"Your colour looks better," Bodie noted as she sat at the kitchen table. Hana nodded, wondering if loneliness served to compound her health problems. She pulled Jas onto her knee.

"I like you being here," she admitted. "It's good having company."

"Isn't Logan here much?" Bodie asked. Hana heard the agenda behind his simple question and used a cuddle with Jas to avoid answering.

Logan breezed in mid-afternoon. He ruffled Jas' hair and the child switched allegiance without conscience, demanding instant attention. "How are you?" Logan asked, his voice soft as he squatted on his haunches next to her. His eyes radiated concern and Bodie watched with interest. Hana sensed him studying his stepfather like a bug under a microscope.

"Heaps better, thanks." Hana stroked his forehead and smelled the fresh aftershave from his shower in the school gym. Strength and safety emanated from him. "I'm taking antibiotics every few hours and then four a day for ten days."

Logan ran a hand over her stomach as Jas scrambled over his back demanding a ride. Bodie cleared his throat and shrouded the moment in awkwardness. "We should be leaving soon, mate," he said, directing his comment at his son. Jas peered from over Logan's shoulder and gave Hana a wink. It involved lots of facial contortion and the use of fingers holding his eye open. Hana laughed and Logan looked round and stood up. Jas dangled from his back like a monkey.

"How tall are you Poppa Logan?" Jas asked. Logan shrugged and raised his arms so he could touch the ceiling with his fingertips. "Six feet, four inches."

"Wow," Jas replied, with no comprehension of what the measurement meant. He slithered to the floor and stared at Logan's legs. "I see two. Where do you keep the rest?"

"Not those kinds of feet." Hana laughed. "It's a measurement."

Logan's mobile phone rang from his pocket and he walked into the lobby to answer it. Hana heard his footsteps move into the lounge and he closed the door behind him. Her gaze strayed to Bodie and she felt his condemnation from across the room. Eyes narrowed and brows dark, he gave a slow shake of his head.

"Stop judging," Hana hissed. "You don't know who that is."

Bodie wrinkled his nose. "I don't, but I could hazard an educated guess."

When Logan returned to the kitchen, his brow knitted in response to the tension. "What's up?" he demanded.

Hana inhaled through her nose, the sound like a snort. "Bodie thinks Mr Che just rang you with the low down on his latest drug deal." Her lips quirked upwards in amusement at the horror on Bodie's face. Logan laughed.

"Che hates drugs. He's more into property and protection." He raised one eyebrow. "His wife is a different matter though."

Bodie's face twisted as he acknowledged defeat and Logan fetched himself a glass of cold water and sat at the table. Bodie spun the milk jug in slow, deliberate arcs. "Who called you?" he asked.

Hana held her breath and closed her eyes. She'd spent enough time questioning Logan to know he gave away nothing unless it suited him. To her surprise, he sipped his water and viewed Bodie over the glass. "My lawyer," he replied. His grey eyes narrowed. "I've liquidated all my assets and apart from shares in a restaurant in Rangiriri, I'm cash rich and stress free." He hooked a nearby chair with his foot and rested his ankle on the seat. "Now I can concentrate on my family without distractions."

Bodie nodded and visibly relaxed. He leaned back and lost the haunted look from his eyes. Hana exhaled and rested her head against the chair, listening to the hum of voices as the men talked about trivia. Jas flopped on his belly on the kitchen floor and ticked his head as the bird chased the poor worm on the phone screen.

She dozed, rousing towards the end of a conversation which had grown heated and disturbed her. "You should tell her!" Bodie hissed. "She has a right to know."

Hana kept her eyelids closed and forced her limbs not to tense. Logan shifted in his seat and lowered his voice to a growl. "You say a word and I'll make you sorry." Hana heard his teeth grind and Bodie gave a sharp exhale.

"You're playing with fire."

Logan snorted. "Shut up, Supercop! I'm trying to trust you here. My mistake!" He spat the last two words with something like regret and Hana cringed. "She doesn't need anything else to worry about right now. Just let me take care of things."

Bodie made a sound as though starting to speak and then halted. Hana decided to feign waking before her son gave her away. If Tama had contacted Logan himself, he could arrive uninvited at any moment and attempt to ingratiate himself back into her home. The thought made her feel sick. She tried to move and her back twinged, sending a shooting pain down her legs. A groan of pain escaped along with the start of her protest. "Tama!"

"What about him?" Logan's brows knitted and he dropped to his knees.

The thought of the baby and the doctor's warning made Hana's breath catch in her throat and fear danced on her heart. The teenager's message resounded in her head, garbled and wrong. "Did you see him? Is that what you're talking about?"

"No." Bodie rose to his feet and darted a glance at Logan. His eyes narrowed in suspicion. "Why would we?"

"Oh, I don't know." Hana rested her forehead on her arms. "I don't know anything anymore." A meltdown threatened. Ugly, out of control and filled with angst. She felt her chest tighten. "I can't do this," she breathed. "You can't let him come here again."

Logan stroked her cheek and his grey eyes channelled sincerity. "I haven't seen Tama, Hana. Do you want me to get the doctor?"

"No!" She squirmed in her seat, hospitalisation the last thing she needed. With a tiny grunt of exertion, Logan scooped her from the chair and lifted her into his arms.

"You need rest," he said, his tone authoritative. He shot Bodie a pointed look and knowledge passed between them. Hana regretted messing up her chance to gain entry into their conspiracy, but the moment had passed and exhaustion nipped at her heels.

"Oh my!" Jas exclaimed, watching Logan's biceps bulge with Hana's pregnant weight. "You're like Mr Incredible!" he breathed. He followed as far as the bedroom door and saw Logan's tenderness as he settled Hana on the bed. Turning the soaking doll to face the scene, he whispered in its damp ear. "You're crap at swimming," he muttered. "Reckon you can lift girls instead?"

Bodie appeared behind him and ruffled his hair. The affectionate smile faded as he noticed a trail of water into the bathroom. "No! No!" he groaned. "Mate! Is this why you went quiet? What are you doing?"

"Swimming lessons, Daddy," he said, his cute lips forming a pout. "But he's wubbish."

"You've soaked the bathroom floor!" Bodie exclaimed and Jas shrugged. He pointed a skinny finger at Logan.

"Yeah, but Daddy, can you lift girls like that?" Jas flexed tiny muscles and peered at Bodie's arms. He didn't look impressed. "I bet you can't," he said with disgust. He turned back to look at Hana and his lips twitched. "But I seen you putting Mummy to bed."

Bodie's eyes bugged and he swallowed. His large palm clapped over the child's mouth before Jas could betray any more secrets. Logan's expression remained impassive, but Hana turned her face away to hide her smile. "What?" he mouthed and she shook her head.

"Nothing." Hana pushed her fingers through his and clasped them, holding him in place. His other hand strayed to her belly, smoothing her jumper over her bump.

"It'll turn out okay," he promised and she nodded, praying God agreed with Logan's verdict.

Jas karate chopped his way into the room, making Hana jump. He let rip with an almighty chop which sent him onto the rug. His doll took flight, missing Hana's head by inches and whacking Logan in the middle of his back. Bodie sighed in defeat and called time on the visit. "I'll get our gear together," he said, disappearing into the kitchen.

Logan picked up the doll and peered at it, noting the interesting pen marks on the plastic arm. "What's this?" he asked as Jas picked himself up. "Why did you draw on him?"

"It's you." Jas pouted and held his hand out for the doll. "He's got tats like you."

Logan nodded and held the doll above his head. Jas jumped for it and missed. Liking the game, he jumped again. "White boys shouldn't copy whakapapa," Logan said, his voice serious but his eyes mischievous. "Seeing as you're whānau, I'll let you use it."

"Fambly?" Jas stopped jumping and stood on one leg. He considered the proposition with great seriousness. "Me an' you?"

"Yeah." Logan narrowed his eyes. "What of it, dude? Wanna fight it out?"

Jas' eyes widened and Hana held her breath. Her lips parted to halt a coming storm, dreading Bodie returning to find Logan threatening his son. But the child beat her to it. "Yeah!" he shouted, taking a step forward and balling his fists. In a split second, Logan turned him upside down and clasped him around the stomach.

"Right then," he said. "Let's do this." Logan flipped the boy on the bed and tickled him. Jas squealed so loud, Hana stuffed her fingers in her ears. When Logan stopped, the boy squawked for him to continue.

Bodie appeared in the bedroom door, his expression anxious. He swallowed at the antics taking place on the bed and Hana saw jealousy creep across his face. Logan shoved Jas onto the floor and the child popped up like a Jack-in-the-box, lurching at him again. He pushed tiny fingers behind Logan's knees and revelled in finding a weak spot. As Hana winced at the noise, Logan tossed Jas over his shoulder and carried him into the lobby. Bodie moved aside to let them exit and listened to them chasing each other around the furniture. He approached the bed and Hana saw a sense of failure in his eyes. "He doesn't do that with me," he said, his voice sad.

Hana swallowed. "Logan?" she replied. "I'm sure he will if you ask."

A moment of annoyance evaporated as Bodie licked his lips. "Yeah, whatever," he breathed.

"Just meet him where he is," Hana said, softening her voice. "Jas wants love and attention. He needs a father, Bodie. You've a heap of catching up to do and I know it's not your fault."

"It's not." Bodie slumped onto the bed and defeat shrouded him. "I didn't know he existed until a few months ago. I'm doing my best, Mum."

"I know." Hana reached for his fingers and gave them a squeeze. "The best things take time."

Bodie jerked his head towards the doorway. "Not so. He just met Logan and they're running around like old friends." Screams of glee issued from the lounge. Logan swore as an ornament crashed to the ground and then Hana heard laughter. Bodie sighed. "Best take him back to his mother." He licked his lips and poked at a hangnail. "You know, I thought we'd maybe put things back together once I moved to Hamilton." He shook his head. "It's not working out."

Hana raised an eyebrow. "You two need to talk."

"She won't." His lips quirked upwards at the thought of the other things they did which didn't involve speech. "I want to."

"Try keeping your pants on," Hana suggested and watched her son's cheeks flush. She raised a hand in warning as he tried to deny it. "Your son misses nothing, Bo. Don't forget that."

"Yeah." He nodded.

"I hope it works out for you." Hana gave his fingers one more stroke and then released them. "But honesty is important."

Bodie snorted. "Yeah, Mum." He said nothing else, leaning down to kiss her cheek before leaving the room. It left Hana with a knot in her chest and a burgeoning concern. The men's whispered conversation echoed in her mind. More secrets. It couldn't relate to something illegal, otherwise Logan wouldn't have confided in a cop. It also didn't involve Tama.

"Tama," Hana groaned, struggling to sit up as the front door slammed and she heard gravel crunch beneath footsteps. She stepped to the window and watched her husband chase Jas into the car. The teenager's ultimatum swam in her brain, changing shape and order the more she focussed on it. Perhaps Logan would sort out the point of Tama's visit. Laying on the bed and pressing herself against the pillows, she waited for her husband's reappearance.

Jas little voice piped over the birdsong on the drive. "I'm gonna do that carrying-thing with my girlfriend. How do you do it Poppa Logan?"

"Oh crap! Don't Jas," Bodie pleaded. "You'll drop her on her head and your mum will get a phone call!"

Hana heard Logan's roar of laughter. Then the car engine started and they left. She dozed, waiting for Logan to come to her. An hour passed and she awoke with a start, hearing the sound of his bike engine fire outside. Her heart pounded as she ran to the window, seeing him readying the machine for a trip out. His helmet lay on the gravel in the rays from the dying sun and his bike jacket rested over the seat.

"Logan!" Hana's shout made him jump and he spun around in alarm. Seeing her there, he turned the bike off. She ran to the porch with one hand clutching her stomach and Logan met her there. His furrowed brow conveyed anxiety.

"What's wrong?" His irises disappeared behind the black of his pupils as he seized her upper arms. "Are you okay?"

"You're going out again." Hurt accompanied the statement and Hana shook her arms free. "You promised."

"I have a meeting." Logan's expression shuttered and all emotion disappeared behind the familiar portcullis. "It won't take long." His jaw flexed and Hana's chest tightened as temper took hold.

"Don't leave." She gritted her teeth. "Please." The added nicety masked a wail of desperation.

"I won't be long," he repeated, taking a step backwards and severing the connection between them.

"Do not go," Hana shouted. "Don't, Logan!"

"I don't want to." Desperation flared in his eyes and a dark emotion crept beneath the mask before Logan slammed it back inside.

"Tama," Hana said, wringing her hands. "He came to see me."

"What?" Logan's head shot up, his eyes lighting in rage. "Where?"

Hana inhaled, realising her error of keeping it from him. She blamed circumstance but suspected she wanted a secret too. "He got into my car at work," she said, colour flushing her cheeks.

"Did he touch you?" Logan said the words through gritted teeth and Hana opened her mouth and closed it again. The possession in his face frightened her.

"No. But he confused me." She swallowed, disliking Logan's abject attention now she had it. "What does he know that can hurt you?"

"Is that what he said?" Logan reached for her wrist and Hana put both hands behind her back. "Hana!" he bit. "Is that what he said?"

"I don't remember." The pain in her eyes felt real as her sense of pathetic uselessness overrode anger. "He scared me and it wiped the message."

Logan's teeth ground in his jaw. "Tell me what he said."

Hana inhaled. The cooling air nipped her legs and ankles and she shivered. "He wants you to call someone off his family or he'll tell you something you don't want to hear." Her brows knitted and she sighed, knowing she'd repeated it wrong. "What can he tell?"

Logan leaned forward, his voice low and menacing. "Our address, Hana. He knows where we live and he works for Laval."

Hana gave a sharp intake of breath. "I'm sorry, I'm sorry," she whispered. "It happened so fast and I had other things on my mind. I should have told you sooner."

"Yeah, you should." Logan ran a hand through his hair and his body stiffened as he considered his options. "Pack up. I'm moving you to the hotel."

"No!" She took a step back. "I don't want to."

"This has gone too far!" He spoke through gritted teeth and his fingers fluttered towards her belly. "This isn't just about you, Hana."

"Then call the lawyers off!" Hana shouted, stepping backwards and tripping over the doorstep. Logan caught her arm and hauled her upright before she hit the ground. "Do what he wants." She shoved at his hands, wanting to dodge the fury which darkened his features and reduced his irises to gun metal grey disks. "This is on you, not me."

"Thanks!" Logan spat. "Blame everything on me."

"My nephew doesn't work for Laval." Her words cut Logan and she swallowed as his rage hiked. His fingers around her forearm dug in and hampered the circulation. He pulled her towards him and Hana saw white puffs of condensated breath drift from his lips as he spoke.

"Pack and be ready to leave when I get home. Do as you're told for once."

"You're still leaving?" Hana's eyes widened and disbelief flooded her psyche. "It's this important and you're going out?" She wrenched free of his grip, sensing he could have held on if he wanted. The sneer pursed her lips into an ugly line. "Great." She gave his chest a shove and retreated. "Wonderful."

As Logan fumed on the door mat, Hana turned and slammed the door in his face. "Say hello to Caroline for me!" she shouted. She shot the dead bolt home to prevent him using his key and stamped to the bedroom. Not hearing the immediate roar of his bike, she peered through the window and cracked it open enough to eavesdrop.

Logan held his phone to his ear and his voice carried up to her. "Michael, don't be a dick!" he snapped. "Tell me what I need to know."

He turned the key on his bike and drowned out further conversation, speaking into his phone and hoisting his helmet into his hand. The phone went into his inside jacket pocket and the helmet onto his head. Hana slammed the window as he straddled his bike and set off down the steep driveway towards the main road.

The self-deprecation began immediately. "You bloody left me, you pig!" she raged and kicked Logan's bedside table, stubbing her toe and making herself angrier. "I'm not going to your boring hotel with your crazy family either!"

Despite the stupidity of the idea which formed in her tired brain, it grew and took shape as a concrete plan. Logan left her for another mysterious liaison, so she would do likewise. She packed in minutes, stuffing a change of clothes into a small case and slamming the lid. Taking another antibiotic, she convinced herself she felt much better. Decisiveness proved a fantastic antidote to fear and failure. "Screw you, Logan Du Rose!" she spat, turning off her mobile phone and loading the suitcase into the back of the Honda.

The empty roads glinted with a light sheen of rain on the fifty minute journey. Darkness disguised her progress and Hana reached the sign for Hamilton Airport without incident. She shivered with cold and anticipation as she pulled her case inside and half an hour later, owned a boarding pass for a departing flight. Her credit card sported a four hundred dollar dent and growing fog delayed all flights in or out.

"Hopefully it won't settle for too long, madam," the flight desk operator said, regret in her voice. "We'll call for boarding as soon as it lifts enough to take off."

"Am I able to check my hand luggage?" Hana asked, staring down at her small case.

The operator shook her head. "Sorry, that will cost extra."

Hana sighed and turned away, wheeling the suitcase behind her to the book stall. She killed time by flicking through the bestsellers and moved from fiction to books offering advice about life. As she became engrossed in a study on how to live with psychopaths, the attendant made her jump. "Would you like to buy that?" the girl asked her. Hana flushed and pursed her lips, figuring she'd lingered too long.

"No thanks," she said, placing it back on the shelf. "I'm sure I'll work it out." She snatched up a chick lit type novel with a muffin on the cover and raised an eyebrow at the bloodied knife sticking from the cake's icing. "I'll take this," she said and handed over the credit card.

Reading helped her detach from her current situation and Hana managed to forget her husband ran out on her even when she begged him not to. It proved more difficult to forget the fact she was in her forties, pregnant and abandoned, but she tried. Wide awake at midnight, she took her antibiotic on time and used the toilet as often as required. The fog increased and she waited, half expecting Logan to appear any moment. He would check the credit card online and hunt her down. Then he'd embarrass her, cancel her ticket and drag her to the hotel. Hana shivered at the thought, alternately watching the main door and then swivelling to stare at the group of irritated flight staff, grounded in Hamilton against their will.

The night passed with painful slowness. Hana devoured the novel and bought another. At six o'clock the next morning, she wheeled her suitcase from the toilet and heard the magical sound of a boarding call. "Passengers for Invercargill please go to Gate One. Your plane is ready for boarding."

Hana ran, her boot soles slapping against the tiled floor and her suitcase wheeling after her. She joined the queue of tired, frustrated passengers with a skip in her heart. In two hours, she would have all the sympathy and compassion she needed to shake off Logan's neglect and mistreatment. A sigh of relief escaped her and she wedged herself into the small seat and fastened her belt. As the plane taxied towards the runway and lifted into the air, it occurred to her that she should have warned Isobel she was coming.

Chapter 29

Hana emerged into the sunshine with exhaustion dragging her heels to painful slowness. Dark shadows ringed her green eyes and the flattened curls on one side of her head gave her a lopsided appearance. She paused at the nearest taxi and her voice croaked from lack of use. The driver jumped out and put his hand over the suitcase handle. "Last leg of a long international flight?" he asked with a smile.

Hana shook her head. "Hamilton."

"Oh." He lifted the case and pushed it into the boot of his car. "Sorry. You look like you've walked here."

Hana's lips parted but sapped of energy, she left the biting retort where it lay. She suspected a peek in a mirror might prove the man right. He opened the door for her and she sank into the back seat, muttering Izzie's address in a lifeless monotone.

Izzie lived in an older part of town, on Drury Lane. Hana loved the flatness of Invercargill and the neat perpendicular streets. There was an openness about it which made her instantly relax. After a short drive, the taxi pulled up outside the small weatherboard vicarage. Nerves struck Hana as she paid the driver with cash snatched from Logan's bedside table. She loitered on the curb as the taxi faded to a small white blob in the distance. The winter sun warmed her face and she put off the moment of truth. She'd left her husband.

Her case bumped over the uneven driveway and made her arm ache. An old sedan straddled the cracks in the concrete and a bright pink car seat occupied the rear. Hana took a deep breath and encouraged her feet to move forward, dragging her heels like a naughty schoolgirl about to meet the headmaster.

Her fingers trembled as she knocked on the faded blue front door and Hana took a fortifying breath.

"I'll get it!" a male voice shouted from inside. The door whipped open fast enough to make Hana blink and her son-in-law stood in front of her, a slice of toast half way to his mouth. The toast stopped midway through its trajectory and a gob of butter slid from the crust onto the door mat. He gaped in shock and turned to shout into the narrow hallway behind him. "Izzie. Come here quick!"

Hana swallowed and remained silent, her face a blank mask. Escaping to the home of a priest wasn't her finest idea and she wondered if he might put her back on the plane and send her home. The sound of grunting and shuffling ensued and Izzie appeared behind him. Or what used to be Izzie before a giant marshmallow took over her swollen body. "Mum!" she shrieked, clapping a hand over her mouth. "Mum!!!"

She almost fell over the doorstep in her eagerness to embrace Hana. Their pregnant bellies bumped together and Izzie's huge stomach seemed to suck the air from around them.

Marcus took a last bite of his cooling toast and stepped back so Izzie could enfold her mother in pudgy, waterlogged arms. "Izz, you clown!" he complained with his mouth full. "Let her go. You look like you're trying to eat her."

Izzie stepped back, wiping tears from her cheeks with an arm streaked with pink stuff. "Sorry," she sniffed. "I needed you so much this last week." She made a sound like a cough and glared at Hana. "How did you know?"

Marcus raised an eyebrow and Hana swallowed. "Marcus didn't call me, I promise. Call it mother's instinct," she said.

Her fingers crossed behind her back as she prayed Izzie didn't pry about her abandoned marriage. She almost wished Marcus had called and provided an excuse for escape. Marcus twisted his lips upwards and backed himself between them, offering an arm to each. He heaved the women up the steps where they became wedged in the doorway.

He laughed and extracted himself, watching the tussle as two pregnant women fought their way through the small hall. Annoyed, Izzie tried to lift one of her legs to boot him in the butt, but her stomach prevented her. "Get Mum's case," she ordered, narrowing her eyes as though warning him to say nothing. Hana heard the sound of her suitcase bumping up the steps and followed Izzie into the sunlit kitchen. Her daughter listed from side to side like a trawler caught in a swell.

"Bethie!" Emotion overwhelmed Hana at the sight of the little girl in the highchair and she felt her chest give an embarrassing hitch. Her distress of the day before caught her up and the sight of such pure innocence released the valve. "I've missed you so much." Hana's voice broke and Izzie's lips parted in alarm. Beth waved her arms and burbled unintelligible words. Her little bald head had sprouted a prolific ball of blonde fluff since Hana saw her last and two white pearly teeth shone from a smiley, dribbly mouth. Her almond shaped eyes looked wide and curious and she poked her tongue down to touch her chin. Hana inhaled the scent of baby and reached out to stroke the beautiful face. "Hi lovely," she breathed. "How's my angel?"

Elizabeth squeaked and waved the piece of toast in her hand. Jam streaks showed on the underside and at the end of her nose. As Hana bent to kiss the fluffy head, she noticed the absent jam splatted on the tiled floor. More coated Izzie's arm and the side of her dress. Marcus breezed into the kitchen and shot a glance at his wife. "I'll change Beth's nappy," he announced, unhooking his daughter from her restraints and lifting her onto his hip. He pursed his lips in mock irritation. "Now the mother-in-law's here, I should pretend I'm a good father. How long are you staying, Hana?"

"Marcus, stop," Izzie coached with a sigh.

"I just want to know how long to keep the pretence up." Marcus pouted and Hana allowed herself a smile.

"Sorry to descend on you," she murmured, the rashness of her decision exposed in all its foolishness. "I should have phoned first."

"It's fine." Marcus leaned forward to kiss her forehead and Beth snagged a handful of Hana's curls. "I've put your suitcase in the front bedroom." His eyes radiated a kindness which almost unpicked Hana from the inside out. He covered her obvious distress with humour. "I'll ask my mistress to find somewhere else to sleep for a few nights." With expert fingers, he freed Hana's hair from Beth's grasp and whirled on the spot, his heels clicking along the bare floorboards. Hana glanced back at his dark shirt and white dog collar, finding herself wondering if Logan had enough shirts to last the week. She stopped herself and faced her daughter's enquiring eyes.

"Please don't ask," she begged, her eyes filling with tears. "I can't talk about it."

"I'm glad you're here," Izzie whispered and Hana heard the sob exit her own lips as though she listened to someone else. The sadness and disappointment refused to stay hidden and her wrestling proved futile. She cried, soaking her daughter's shoulder and hair as Izzie held her tight. Her chest heaved with the pain of the emotional purge and when the shuddering breaths stopped, exhaustion attacked Hana's body.

Marcus stayed away long enough to give the women space. He gave Elizabeth a wash and change of clothes and lay her down in her cot for her morning nap. She held out fat little arms and he leaned over so she could feel the contours of his face. Her long lashes fluttered around stunning blue irises which compensated poorly for her lack of vision. Marcus let her sense his features with her fingers like he always did and kissed her button nose. "Nap time little one," he whispered. "Daddy needs to plan his great escape." He stroked her fluffy topknot and heaved out a sigh.

Comfortable in her routine, Beth squeezed her blue eyes tight shut and pushed her thumb between her lips. Marcus covered her with blankets and left the room. His steps took him to just outside the kitchen where Hana sniffed as she struggled for control. His feet slowed. Lifting the car keys from his pocket without letting them jangle, he pushed his head around the doorframe. Hana jumped as he spoke and Izzie narrowed her eyes. "I've put Beth down for her nap." He avoided eye contact with Hana, sensing her embarrassment across the room. "I've got some things to do at church." His hand gave a pathetic wave in Hana's direction. "See you both later."

"Coward!" Izzie sighed as the front door slammed. "He's great with the congregation and awful at home."

Hana ran a shaking hand over her eyes and resorted to wiping her nose on her sleeve. "I'm so sorry for turning up like this. I didn't want to force him out of his own home."

Izzie laid a possessive arm across Hana's shoulder. "Don't be ridiculous. You're an answer to prayer. Poor guy's glad to escape, to be honest. I cried for you so hard last night, I'm surprised you didn't hear me. I'm sick and tired of this pregnancy and I think Marcus is sick of hearing me complain about it. We're both tense. We argued last night about toilet paper usage, for goodness' sake."

Hana wiped her eyes again and gave a disgusting sniff. "I'll contribute to costs if I can stay here."

Izzie laughed. "You don't need to, Mum. It got heated over nothing. I can't see the holder and I also can't see my you-know-what, so I use too much. He keeps unblocking the toilet. Stay as long as you like." Izzie lurched at the chair and heaved herself into it. "I'm turning into a whale. Everything's swollen. If I put shoes on, I can't get them off again an hour later. Nothing fits and the midwife says it's water retention. I'm glad you're here. You might keep me out of hospital."

Hana swallowed and chewed the inside of her lip. "Perhaps we can keep each other out," she agreed.

Despite Hana's protests, Izzie rose to make a pot of tea and they sipped in silence. The tick of the clock seemed to calm everything.

"What's your actual due date," Hana asked, letting the hot drink warm her insides. "You weren't sure."

"It keeps changing." Izzie sounded fed up. "I don't know when I fell pregnant and sustaining two babies complicates everything. They might be small for date or huge for date. The obstetrician is guessing and changes his mind every time I see him."

"Could you have conceived so soon after Beth?" Hana's brow furrowed. "Sorry, that's a bit personal."

Izzie shrugged. "No such thing anymore, Mum. Personal left when the first wave of medical students peered at my naked stomach. It ran out with Dignity and Embarrassment followed not long after. There are midwives, student doctors on practicum and a few nurses begging to be called when I'm admitted. If I manage a natural birth, there won't be room for Marcus in there."

"I need to get you a television for your bedroom." Hana smirked. "Stop the vicar being so randy."

Izzie laughed out loud. "Says you! Yours must have been a honeymoon baby."

Hana smiled and ran a hand over her bump. "I think so."

"And how's the expectant daddy?" Izzie lowered her voice and Hana cringed.

"I don't know and right now I don't care. He ran out on me last night on some stupid pretext and I couldn't take anymore. I'm tired of all the secrets."

Izzie's eyes grew wide, her irises like huge chocolate buttons. "But he knows you're here?"

Hana shrugged and tossed her hair. "I don't think he knows me well enough to hazard a decent guess. I'm happy with that. I need time out."

"Mum! You should ring him. He'll panic."

Hana snorted. "Logan? Panic?" The notion amused her more than she cared to admit. "Isobel, Logan Du Rose never panics."

Izzie used Elizabeth's nap time to lie on her bed and take the weight off her swollen feet. Hana found her suitcase in the room she used once before. Light and airy, the bedroom gave her a view of the street and she opened the window to breathe in the sharp sea air. Wind rustled the new growth on trees which stood like sentries along the roadside. It reminded her of Culver's Cottage and she sighed and closed her eyes against the glass. "What am I going to do?" she whispered.

With its lid flung wide, her suitcase displayed woeful contents thrown together in haste.

Make-up, a spare bra and two remaining pairs of knickers sat in the cavernous space. She'd grabbed the wrong leggings, Logan's shirt to use as a nightdress and one of his pullovers. Hana sat on the bed to rue her packing skills and woke up five hours later.

Her back ached, she'd laid on her left arm until it was numb and soaked her shoulder with dribble. Stumbling along to the kitchen felt like scaling Kilimanjaro.

Izzie and Marcus sat at the table and Elizabeth sang to herself in her high chair. Her fingers clasped a hunk of bread smeared in something brown and gooey. "Ugh, Marmite!" Hana exclaimed, putting her hand up to her mouth and considering the likelihood of vomiting. "Izzie, how could you?"

Izzie laughed and held her hands out in front of her in a gesture of innocence. "Not me Mama, her daddy is the Marmite freak."

Hana looked at Marcus with distaste. "I knew there was a reason I never liked you."

He grinned back at her. Hana plonked herself down on the nearest chair and rested her head in her hands. Marcus gave her an affectionate wink and carried on with his activity. He took a small red object and laid it over the knuckle of his index finger near to the nail and clicked. Collecting the resulting drop of blood on what looked like litmus paper, he peered at it before pushing it into a black device. When it beeped, he took a reading and messed around with syringes. Hana noticed dark rings around his eyes and his skin looked unusually pasty. "Still struggling?" she asked and he shrugged and wrinkled his nose.

"They want to fit a pump," he said. "I don't like the idea of all the pipes and it's invasive."

Izzie gave a snort and pushed more sticky, brown-covered bread at her daughter. Beth seized it with an enthusiastic, "Ooh."

"Yeah, it's really invasive Marc. And I'd miss your hypos like a hole in the head. I mean, it's such fun when you collapse in the bathroom and have to knock your head on the wall to get my attention." Marcus opened his mouth to speak, but Izzie robbed him of the chance. "How could I cope without getting phone calls in the early hours from the church warden who sees lights on in the vestry? How many times has he discovered you collapsed on the floor? Four? Five? I've lost count, Marc."

Marcus raised his hand to stop her and his false smile contained pain. "My wife thinks it's a good idea," he said. "I can't be trusted to take care of myself."

"It's not just you though, is it?" Izzie moved into full attack mode. "It's me and the children. If we can't rely on you because you forgot to eat or worse still, thought you could sneak in a visit to a drive through and overdosed on glucose, where does that leave us?"

"Quite," he said under his breath. The down-turned set of his mouth showed how often they'd had the same conversation. He strived to change the subject. "That's an interesting vocabulary your husband possesses, isn't it?"

Hana sat up straight and her gaze darted to Izzie. "What?" Her complexion paled to the colour of candle wax.

Isobel huffed and slapped her husband's arm. "That's right, change the focus onto someone else. Thanks a lot for that!" She reached over towards Hana in an attempt to take her hand, but Hana backed away from the sticky brown stuff on her fingers. "I'm sorry, Mum, I needed to know what happened. You neglected to mention they're all worried sick!"

Hana narrowed her eyes and shook her head. "I don't care. They don't understand."

"So tell us." Marcus studied her with the practiced air of one who read people for a living. "Explain."

"No." Hana scraped her chair back. "I don't want to. Please don't make me." She raised a hand to squeeze the bridge of her nose and saw the agitated tremble in her fingers.

"Logan swore heaps." Izzie licked her lips, conflict in her expression. "That's what Marcus meant."

"I don't care." Hana's body tightened and her shoulders flexed up to meet her neck.

"You didn't ask who we meant by 'they', Hana," Marcus persisted. "You frightened more than just Logan. Bodie spent the night at your place too."

Hana felt the familiar urgency for the toilet and left the room without excusing herself. She walked to the bedroom to retrieve her antibiotics and rattled around in the suitcase looking for them. Needing to take them with water sent her back to the kitchen for a glass. Izzie's brown eyes looked glossy with unshed tears and guilt sparked in Hana's breast. She stroked her daughter's dark hair. "It's not your problem," she said. "I made a huge mistake and need to face up to it."

Marcus gave her a knowing look and stabbed the insulin needle into his stomach wall. Hana glanced away, the sight making her queasy. She filled her glass and leaned back against the counter to take the tablet. Marcus put the sharp into a container with a clunk and raised an eyebrow. "Did you know eight expletives could make a completely intelligible sentence, as long as the expression in the voice betrays the meaning?"

"Shut up, Marcus!" Izzie warned.

Hana sighed. "No, Marcus. I didn't know that."

"It's true." He snapped his diabetes paraphernalia box closed. "It's all about what people don't say."

"I don't care," Hana repeated, swallowing the chunky tablet with difficulty. It still slid down far easier than the hidden meaning of Marcus' words, which seemed to stick in her gullet.

Elizabeth squealed in her high chair and sat her bread on top of her head. Then she looked everywhere for it. Hana laughed. "Marmite hat. Lovely." The little girl grinned, showing two beautiful white pearls covered in sticky brown yuk. Hana chased the feeling of vomit back down her throat. "Please may I take a shower?" she asked Izzie.

Her daughter smiled and nodded. "Yep. The hot water runs out after twenty minutes, so watch out," she warned.

Hana washed her hair and lathered up her body, using only five of the allotted twenty minutes. As she clambered over the side of the bath and reached for her towel, someone knocked on the bathroom door. "Hana, you missed a call!" Marcus shouted, followed by whispering and shuffling around.

"My phone's off!" she replied, sounding surprised.

"Not anymore." Izzie paused and her voice held a note of pleading. "I turned it back on and you've got loads of texts and missed calls. It started ringing and when I answered, Logan insisted he needs to speak to you. If he rings again, can I answer it?"

"No!" shouted Hana, dragging the towel around her soaked shoulders. Her hair sent uncomfortable trickles of cold water down her back. "I won't talk to him. I don't want to talk to anyone!"

More whispering came from outside the door and Hana lost patience. She wrenched the door open and stormed into the hallway, the towel clasped in a precarious knot at her breast. Marcus and Izzie scattered before her, but followed her into the bedroom. Elizabeth dangled from her father's arms and tipped her head from side to side as though her ears contained water. Hana waved her hands in anger, but stopped when the action compromised the safety of the towel. Izzie clouted Marcus around the back of the head and he obediently turned to face the wall. "Mum, we need to talk about this!" She put her hands on her hips and her twin bump occupied most of the available space next to the bed. "You got married five minutes ago and you've already left him! If I did that, you'd send me straight back home and tell me to get on with it!"

Marcus turned his head to look at his wife, his expression filled with hurt. "Steady on!" he complained. "I'm awesome. You wouldn't need to leave me."

Izzie slapped his shoulder and he turned back to face the wall, grumbling to Beth. She wagged a finger at Hana, but her mother stemmed the promised tirade. "It's more complicated than me just leaving him," she retorted, ashamed of the whine in her voice. "It's perspective. He says he loves me and would do anything for me, but when I need him to stay he sneaks off like a..."

"Gigolo?" Marcus offered helpfully.

Hana let out a groan of exasperation and Izzie slapped him on the back of the head again. He turned back to the wall. "Mum, he loves you. You need to go home."

Hana's mouth dropped open in amazement. "You're throwing me out?"

"No!" Izzie stamped her foot. "No, not throwing you out. Just promise that in a few days, you'll talk to your husband."

"I can't!" Hana put her hands over her eyes. "I'm scared."

"Of what? Of Logan?"

"No!" Hana squirmed and the towel threatened to reveal more than she wanted. She grappled with the knot and narrowed her eyes at the sight of Marcus' shoulders heaving. "He's laughing at me!" she shrieked and pointed at her son-in-law.

"Marcus, stop being an egg!" Izzie demanded and he snorted, diving from the room before a pillow hit his head. It slapped against the door frame and slid down. Hana slammed the door behind him and pulled the towel free.

"What's so funny about my chaotic life?" she whined. "How does that man get paid to be privy to other people's problems?"

"He doesn't laugh at them," Izzie qualified and Hana huffed in outrage.

"Thanks. It's nice to know I'm special." She dragged clean underwear and leggings from the suitcase. "Izzie, I'm naked. You should leave."

Her daughter shrugged and threw herself down on Hana's double bed. It made a sickening twang as she loaded the springs with the weight of herself and her babies. "At least I can see where I get my childbearing hips," she remarked.

"Oh, shut up!" Hana bit, dangling her knickers in front of her foot and trying to hook them enough to shove one leg in.

Izzie lay on her back staring up at the ceiling. "What's the best thing about Logan, Mum?" she asked.

"He's great in bed," Hana quipped, attempting to shock Izzie into quitting.

She giggled. "I bet he is," she said and shot her mother a lascivious look.

Hana pursed her lips and tried not to think about a naked Logan. "Lots of things are good about him. Too many to mention. But he's also infuriating and has this overwhelming need to solve the world's problems." Hana shimmied into her leggings. "And he walked away when I asked him not to."

She ratched around in the case and pulled out Logan's sweater. Despite herself, she enjoyed her husband's scent during the moments she was sequestered beneath its voluptuous folds. Then she yanked her head through with determination and pulled it down over her bump.

"Is that the only clothing you brought?" Izzie narrowed her eyes.

Hana nodded. "I just grabbed things off the bedroom chair," she admitted. "I couldn't think straight." She patted the jumper over her tummy, wincing at how it rose at the front.

Izzie shook her head. "I've got loads of clothes you can borrow. People at church are really kind. I bring a plastic bag home most Sundays. I won't need them in a while." She tapped her stomach with fondness. "Huey and Luey should come out soon."

Hana plonked onto the bed next to her. "I suppose they will, won't they? Such fun going in and such a bugger coming out." She lay back on the bed. It groaned beneath their combined weight and Hana giggled at the thought of them disappearing through the floorboards.

"Remember that time Mrs Bowman broke the chair at the drama production." Izzie shrieked with laughter at the memory. "I can still see her legs wiggling in the air."

Hana felt a wave of guilt for laughing. "Poor Ethel," she sighed. Izzie's infectious laugh got to her and she giggled behind her hand. She groaned. "Laughing makes me need the toilet."

"Me too." Izzie snorted and they laughed again. "Is Logan really good in bed?" she asked, mischief in her chocolate brown eyes.

Hana rolled onto her side and shoved her daughter in the arm. But her eyes sparkled and Izzie cackled. "Oh my gosh, at your age, that's terrible."

She giggled and Hana shoved her again to make her stop, feigning upset. "How do you think I got pregnant so fast?" she demanded. "He's a stud."

"Mum?" Izzie said, turning towards her with a serious expression marring her prettiness. "Logan's gorgeous and would walk across broken glass for you. And I know you love him." She wagged her finger at Hana, a throwback from her childhood and a moment of role reversal. The mood sobered. Izzie stroked her mother's wet hair back from her face. It was such a tender movement, Hana felt tears prickle behind her eyelids. She reached out a hand and rested it on Izzie's babies, rewarded by a firm kick. "Luey said hi," Izzie whispered. "Huey's further down."

"How can you tell?" Hana asked, "That's so amazing."

Izzie nodded. "I'm very blessed."

Hana nodded in agreement. Sensing her daughter wishing to return to the subject of her fated marriage, she sat up and issued a gentle warning. "I don't want to talk about Logan at the moment, Izz. I'm sorry, but I can't."

Izzie reached for her hand again and gave her a smile of reassurance. Hana searched her daughter's kind face and found only compassion without judgement. "What can I do to help you while I'm here?" she asked. "I'd like to prove useful."

Izzie shook her head. "Got it covered, Mum. Just enjoy being with me?"

Hana smiled and leaned over to kiss Izzie's olive forehead. "That, my darling, will be the easiest thing I've done all year."

Chapter 30

A knock on the front door heralded a lady from Marcus' church. She let herself in and Hana started in surprise. The octogenarian bustled into the kitchen and flicked the oven switch on at the wall. White haired and stooped, she surveyed the washed crockery stacked on the draining board and her mouth turned down in a pout. "I came to do the washing up," she said, turning to face Marcus. "But somebody already did it."

Marcus held his arm out wide to indicate Hana. "Meet the mother-in-law," he said.

The woman gave a curt nod and retreated to the hallway. Hana watched as she hefted a covered basket onto the table. Marcus rose to help her, receiving a slap on the hand as he tried to peek beneath the floral covering. "You know that's my absolute favourite, don't you Mrs McLaughlin?" he said, his eyes lighting up. She winked in reply, her features softening and losing their harsh edges.

"Mrs McLaughlin's great grandfather founded our church, Mum." Izzie leaned across from feeding Beth and smiled at Hana. "I struggled so much at the start of my pregnancy, she organised a dinner rota. That's why I'm much happier, but Marcus is so fat."

Her husband's jaw dropped open in shock and he peered down at his burgeoning waist. His brows knitted but the sight caused him to offer no challenging retort. Hana baulked at the horrible thread of resentment which seeped through her veins and made her dislike the other woman. The sense of having lost her place in Izzie's world invoked guilt and anger. "I should be grateful someone else takes care of you, I suppose." She bit her lip and Izzie narrowed her eyes.

"You can't be there for everyone, Mum," she rebuked. "Right now you need to take care of yourself."

Hana gave herself an attitude check in the bathroom mirror and emerged wearing a fake smile. If Marcus and Izzie saw through the charade, they allowed her to keep her dignity. Shepherd's pie smells wafted from the oven, peas boiled on the hob and Beth regarded the old lady as a favourite aunty.

"Stay and eat with us," Marcus urged Mrs McLaughlin. "You made it. Doesn't seem fair you don't get to eat it. Here, bring up a chair."

The woman glanced across at Hana as though seeking silent permission. Hana played the role of benevolence with practiced ease. "Yes, please stay. I'd love to hear more about the history of your church."

Relief chased a spectre of loneliness from the woman's eyes and Hana felt chastened by the raw emotion she recognised from her own life. Her feigned acceptance gained a note of genuine compassion. "Call me Peg," the elderly lady insisted, smiling as she struggled into a chair. "You must tell me about life in the north."

Hana ate well, savouring every mouthful of the home cooked dinner. On time with her antibiotics, she felt the infection loosen its hold on her kidneys and her good nature restored a little. Peg pushed a tiny spoon laden with mashed potatoes between Beth's lips, gasping in horror as an ill-timed sneeze sent it right back out.

"Sorry. She did that to me earlier." Izzie leaped to her feet and retrieved a dampened dish cloth, smothering a grimace as Peg wiped her face with it. Pain shot through her expression and she glanced across at Hana's look of instant alert. "It's nothing," she said, dismissing the moment of pure agony as a twinge.

As the meal resumed, Hana answered Peg's questions but raised her eyebrows at Izzie when it seemed the woman already knew her most intimate details. Izzie smiled without guile and Hana wondered if the women had discussed the state of her underwear yet. Her appetite abandoned her as Peg asked, "Will your husband join you soon? Izzie showed me a picture. He's quite something." She pushed a gnarled hand through her fluffy hair for effect and winced at the feel of crusted mince in her coiffed perm.

"Not this time, no. He's busy." Hana's wooden reply drew Marcus' interest and he chewed whilst staring at her. Hana glared at him across the table and received a mischievous grin in wordless reply.

Elizabeth squished mashed potato sludge through her tiny teeth and Hana laughed at her, grateful for the distraction. The baby cackled and waved her own spoon, letting fly with a globule of mince. It landed in Marcus's plate and he hoovered it up with his next mouthful.

"Is your husband excited about the baby?" Peg asked, a natural enough question. Hana thought of Logan with sadness in the pit of her stomach.

"I think he'll hate the mess a child brings," she admitted. "He's a clean freak. I'm not sure how he'll cope." She glanced at her plate and stopped trying to force herself. Her cutlery clanked against each other as she lay the pieces down. The reality struck fear into her heart.

"Mum?" Izzie's voice brought Hana back to the table. "Are you okay?"

"Sorry, excuse me," Hana scraped back her chair and stood. "I need to get an antibiotic. I just remembered."

In the bedroom, she covered her face with her hands and sank onto the bed. A spirit of disgrace swirled around her and she felt wanting in front of the nice, Christian people. Forty-something, pregnant and alone, she considered having the word, 'harlot' tattooed on her forehead. Self-loathing created a knot inside her chest.

"Stop judging yourself." Marcus' voice came from the doorway and Hana jumped. He leaned against the frame with a casual air, a mince stain leaving a line of grease along the front of his clerical shirt. "Nobody else is."

Hana sighed. "They will, once I file for divorce after less than six months of marriage."

Marcus snorted. "On what grounds?"

Hana gritted her jaw and felt her muscles tense. "I haven't decided yet. There are too many choices."

"Really?" His lips curved upwards into a disbelieving smile. "You say that whilst wearing his jumper?"

Hana tugged at the cuff and Logan's scent drifted over her. Love and regret mingled in her breast. "He isn't reliable and I don't trust him. There. Now you know."

She cast her mind back to her trip to Logan's rental like a line seeking fish. She found the memory with ease. Her feelings for him had blossomed in her stomach, making her awkward and breathless as he handed the jumper to her for warmth. Even their legs touching through their jeans had set her on fire. She knew then she loved him. Hana pressed the sleeve to her forehead and sighed. "You don't understand."

"Maybe I understand more than you think." He offered her a lifeline, but Hana shied away.

"Don't play the vicar role with me, Marcus," she bit. "I remember you in short pants."

She glanced up to see him biting his lower lip and concealing a grin. "I didn't realise my hairy knees left such trauma in their wake." He raised an eyebrow. "I married you both in the sight of God." He crossed his arms and channelled determination. "I didn't do that lightly and I can't let you walk away from a commitment so serious."

Hana drew in a giant breath. "It's complicated."

Marcus snorted and looked wiser than his years. "It always is Hana and always will be. It's not Facebook. You can't just change your relationship status and walk away."

"He left!" Hana spat, the anger in her voice surprising herself. "He promised! I mustn't drive him away and he wouldn't leave. And he left! I begged him not to and he did it anyway." She spoke through gritted teeth and her hands balled into fists. Anger shook her body from head to toe.

"Is that it?" Marcus demanded. "You asked him not to go out and he still did?"

Hana's head whipped up, frustration turning her green irises to flashing emerald gems. Marcus leaned against the door frame with a casual air, dismissing her catastrophe in just a few words. Pent up anger filled her cheeks with a pink hue.

"Fine!" she exploded, a nasty edge to her voice. "I'll pack my things and leave."

"Why would you do that?" Marcus asked, his expression quizzical.

"Because you just trivialised my whole marriage!"

"No, Hana. You trivialised it."

"I did not!" She stood, stamping on the floorboards like a child.

"Yeah, you did." Marcus licked food from behind his teeth, his casual body language jarring against his combative words. "You asked Logan not to go somewhere and he went. I've never seen it listed as a reason for divorce. Where'd he go? To see a prostitute? Rob a bank? Izzie asks me not to go to fast food joints all the time because of my diabetes, but I do. She yells a bit, but doesn't leave me."

"I don't know where he went!" Hana took short, angry breaths and resembled a bull about to charge.

Marcus shrugged, surprisingly unfazed by Hana's temper. She seemed to strobe with anger, her body pulsing in waves of rage. He held his ground, refusing to concede anything until he'd sunk his point home. "So he's behaving to type, Hana? He's done something which fits a category in your head and you're calling time on your marriage already." Marcus shook his head. "I'm surprised at you. It wouldn't matter what Logan did, he'd never reach your exacting standards. He was doomed the minute he put the ring on your finger."

"How dare you!" Hana seethed through lips barely open. "You know nothing!"

Marcus shrugged. "I know enough, Hana."

Her chest hitched in fear and she heard the warning behind his words. It caused her brain to stall. "No," she gasped shaking her head. "Shut up, Marcus. You know nothing so just shut up."

"You're making a big mistake." He lowered his voice to a whisper, aware their conversation had hiked in volume. He studied her, looking more perceptive than she wanted him to be and Hana closed her eyes to avoid seeing his judgement.

"I know you loved Vik," she conceded. "This is different. It's more complicated." Hana felt the familiar void beneath her feet threatening to crack wide open. She struggled to keep it closed. The burden of her first husband's infidelity clung to her like a badge of office, 'victim' blazed across the front. She'd kept the secret for almost a decade, preserving the image of the fine, Christian husband. The veneer lifted under pressure and she sought to tamp down the panic in her heart. A shaking hand strayed to her stomach and caressed the child within. "Please, leave it," she begged, her voice breaking. "I'm tired, Marcus. I'm tired of everything."

"I know." His words offered reassurance. "I won't let you make any drastic decisions right now, Hana. You're under my roof and I'm telling you to rest up, do nothing and prepare to give your husband a fair hearing."

Hana swallowed and gave a jerky nod of acceptance. Marcus left her to her private agonies. She calmed her shakes and collected herself enough to go back to the kitchen, sit at the table and finish her dinner.

"It's Mrs McKiernan's turn to cook for you tomorrow night," Peg announced to Hana over her shoulder as she and

Marcus stacked dishes in the dishwasher. She wrinkled her nose. "She's English. It'll be something fried."

Izzie battled a fit of the giggles as Hana floundered. "Right. That's wonderful." She sighed. "I'm rather jealous that a community feeds my daughter. Perhaps you should all move in with me."

"Does no one take care of you, Hana?" Peg's expression softened and Hana remembered Maihi's tender loving care.

"Yes, actually. My neighbour pops over with food regularly. She walks quite a way in bad weather sometimes just to bring us a casserole or some meat. She's very kind."

"Was she at the wedding?" Izzie demanded. "Did I meet her?"

Hana tensed at the mention of her nuptials as images of Logan flooded back. His shaking hands as he read his vows and the way his gaze sought her across the crowded room. She shivered. "No."

"Is she a Believer, dear?" Peg asked.

"I think so," Hana replied. "Her husband prays to God before dinner. I realise that doesn't mean anything of itself, but she's a beautiful person." Her chest prickled with guilt. "I should text her and let her know I've arrived safe and sound."

"Great idea, Hana," Marcus intoned. His narrowed eyes held a wealth of undertone. "You could do with sending a few of those."

Hana skulked into the small lounge to activate her phone. The missed calls and texts took ages to load and then flashed on the screen like a rebuke. The delete button wiped them from view without her reading them and she flicked a text to Maihi. *'I'm fine,'* she typed. *'I'm just thinking of you and needed you to know how much I value your friendship and appreciate your care.'*

Losing her nerve, she pressed the off button after sending. The battery light showed only one bar and she realised she'd forgotten her charger.

"Everything okay, Mum?" Izzie asked from the doorway and Hana gave a shallow nod.

"Yes thanks. I didn't bother reading all the messages. I told her I'm fine."

"Well done." Her daughter smiled. "What did she say?"

Hana waved the device in an action of futility. "I don't know. I turned it off."

"Mum!" Frustration lurked behind Izzie's use of her name and Hana cringed. She allowed her daughter to take the phone from her fingers and reactivate it. Her lips curved upwards into a smile as the phone bleeped in her hand. "She called you kōtiro," she said, her gaze boring into Hana's face as she pushed the phone back into her fingers. "Daughter. How lovely."

Hana swallowed and looked away. Again, she deactivated the phone and sat it on the mantelpiece. "What else did she say?"

"Just that." Izzie cocked her head and her black fringe strayed into her eyes. "Perhaps she knew what you needed to hear."

Hana nodded and felt her throat lock up. Determined not to cry, she squeezed her daughter's shoulder as she passed and walked into the kitchen to heft Beth onto her hip while the others finished clearing up after their dinner.

Peg showed no sign of leaving. It occurred to Hana that perhaps her daughter's home was usually filled with lonely strangers. She sighed and kissed the baby's downy head, adding herself to the stereotype of heartsore, middle aged woman.

"Have you seen Beth's impression of an aeroplane?" Marcus clapped and held his arms out. Beth pitched forward into them.

"No." Hana dragged herself into the present and tried to push tiredness aside. "Show me."

"Don't!" Izzie shouted from the bathroom. "It's too soon after her dinner."

Marcus crinkled his nose and his eyes flashed with rebellion. He lifted Beth onto his head and she balanced on her stomach, her legs pointed straight out behind her like a ballerina. He gripped her tiny hands and she squealed with delight. Her toes twitched back and forth with anticipation. Hana cringed. "It looks dangerous, Marcus. She pulled the front of Beth's dress out of his eyes and tucked it beneath her writhing body. "Give her here. I've seen now."

"She hasn't flown yet," Marcus insisted. His eyes glinted with mischief. "We need to take off on the runway."

"She loves it," Peg chipped in, waving at the child on her vicar's head as though it represented usual behaviour. Hana rolled her eyes and shook her head.

Take off involved Marcus running up and down the narrow hallway, wearing Beth like a hat. The child shrieked and giggled, her chest hitching with hiccups and mirth in equal measure. Izzie narrowly avoided a collision as she emerged from the bathroom, huffing out of the way with difficulty as Marcus thundered past.

"Marcus, stop now," she warned. "Stop winding her up before bed. You can deal with her when she's overexcited."

"Yep," came Marcus' muffled reply. He hurtled along the hallway, Beth heaving with laughter from her lofty perch. "Last one." He performed yet another lap of honour and bowed to fake applause. Instinct made Peg, Izzie and Hana take a step back.

Beth projectile vomited.

"Marcus!" Izzie shouted as a stream of puke landed on the floorboards with a splat and sprayed out to the sides. "I asked you to stop."

"I did," he replied, sounding piqued. "Good shot!" he complimented his daughter. "Well done for missing Daddy!"

Izzie grumbled about the mess as she fetched wet wipes and kitchen towels. The adults stared at the disgusting addition to the floorboards.

"My arthritis won't let me kneel down," Peg said, sounding thankful for her condition.

"I'll get Beth ready for bed." Marcus at least sounded a little chastened.

Izzie sighed and shook her head at Hana. "Looks like the two fat ladies get the job then." She handed over a wad of wipes and paper.

The women crawled around on the floorboards, their bellies hanging low as they cleared up streaks of vomit. Hana tried not to focus on the nature of the mess for fear of adding to it. Peg hopped around with a plastic bag, collecting soiled tissue and wipes.

Marcus returned with Beth on his hip. Her hair stood on end and her cheeks shone with a healthy blush. She wore a clean vest and her arms and legs pumped the air with excitement as her poor eyesight saw the women as indistinct shapes swirling around on the floor. "Smile ladies." Hana heard a click and turned to see Marcus taking a photograph.

"Stop that!" she ordered. "It's not funny. I don't think I can get up again."

He chuckled and clicked again. "I might put these on social media," he teased. "Your butts look like four little boys fighting under a tent."

"Oh, Vicar!" Peg stifled a snort and Hana glared at her.

Beth squealed and her laugh sounded fake. A guttural burp shot the rest of her dinner down her father's shirt. Marcus lost his sense of humour with immediate effect. "Beth!" he groaned. "Not funny!"

Hana laughed. "That serves you right!" Keeling up, she used her last wipe to clean her hands. She hauled herself into a standing position using the wall and a doorframe. "I'm done now, Izzie. I need a lie down." She sighed and closed her eyes against a wave of dizziness.

"Isobel?" The tone of Marcus' voice caught her attention and Hana's eyes snapped open. Her daughter remained on the floorboards on all fours, head down and spine rigid. Dread snaked its black fingers through Hana's heart. "Izzie!" Marcus sounded sharp and she followed his gaze to the floor beneath her daughter. "Did you just pee yourself?" he demanded. "Izzie, what's wrong?"

"Oh, no!" Hana breathed. "It's too early."

Marcus handed Beth to Peg as Izzie let out a gargled groan which seemed wrenched from her toes. Peg caught the baby with skill and her face brightened. "Mrs McKiernan will be so jealous," she whispered.

Marcus seemed to morph before Hana's eyes, becoming a man imbued with instant calm and authority. She saw the man his parishioners knew and the panic in her breast subsided. Snatching towels from the hall cupboard, he pushed them beneath Izzie and knelt beside her. "Is this it, sweetheart? Are they coming?"

Izzie answered with a series of pants and a horrible, prolonged groan. Marcus pulled his phone from his shirt pocket and dialled a number, rubbing Izzie's with gentle circular movements. Peg rocked Beth who writhed in her arms and Hana remained frozen in position, her spine pressed against the doorframe.

"Can we get to the car?" Marcus leaned down and spoke into Izzie's ear. She replied with a louder groan and her rigid body bore down into the floor. Marcus spoke into the phone, his voice an octave higher, "Isobel's gone into labour in the middle of the hall floor." He paused as Izzie gave a gargantuan wail. "She's pushing!" Panic seeped through his voice. "She's pushing. No, there's been no labour." He tilted to see into Izzie's eyes and his groan matched hers. "Oh, Izzie! When? How long ago did this start?"

Izzie failed to reply, balling her fists and panting. Marcus' gentle strokes on her back turned to pats which looked a little hard. He dropped his phone to the floor and the screen remained alight, a disembodied voice speaking to him and receiving no reply. Hana ordered her limbs to respond, but they refused. She remained glued to the doorframe as Elizabeth squirmed and let out pitiful wails of frustration.

"Milk, Hana!" She jumped as Marcus shouted and his expression softened at the horror on her face. He jabbed a finger towards the kitchen. "Beth's bottle is in the fridge. Heat it in the microwave for forty seconds. She's tired."

Given a purpose, Hana forced her body to move and jerky, wooden footsteps took her to the kitchen. She found the bottle and heated it, giving it to Peg with a trembling hand. Tipped onto her back, Beth took the bottle, instantly soothed by routine and familiarity.

"It's happening too fast," Hana breathed. Peg swayed from side to side, feeding the baby and bumping shoulders with her in solidarity.

"I'm praying," she whispered. "The Lord's delivered babies before. He knows what he's doing."

Hana swallowed. "Good, because I've had two children and never seen one born. I have no clue what to do." Glancing back at Marcus, she saw his command of the situation slipping.

"Not here, Izz," he hissed. "Not on the floor, sweetheart." The puddle spread out beneath them, soaking the knees of his trousers. Hana's chest hitched as terror gripped her soul. Too early, too fast, too risky.

"What can we do?" Her voice held an edge of hysteria.

Marcus glanced up and she saw her fear mirrored in his eyes. "Help me take her into the bathroom. She can kneel in the bath. I can contain the mess and the light's better in there. I need to see what I'm doing." All colour had faded from his complexion and his skin looked waxy and ashen in the dim light of the hallway bulb.

"No!" Izzie slapped at his hands and panted through the next contraction. "Not the bath again!"

Peg slipped away with a sleeping Beth, pushing the pram ahead of her. A night's supplies bulged in the bag dangling from the handle. "Will she manage?" Hana hissed, taking the weight of Izzie's legs as Marcus hauled his writhing wife into the bathroom.

"Yeah." The veins in his neck bulged as he lifted Izzie over the side of the bath and laid her in the nest of towels Hana made in the bottom. "It's part of the birth plan. She's practiced and I can't worry about Beth now." His hand shook as he rubbed his face, watching as Izzie struggled back onto her knees. "Wouldn't it feel easier lying down?" he asked, watching his wife flounder.

A mask of pain shuttered her dark eyes and Izzie gritted her teeth. "You do it then!" she hissed.

Marcus swallowed at the rebuke and Hana released a nervous laugh. The smile disappeared from her lips as Izzie screwed herself into a ball of agony and her groan echoed off the bath tiles.

A wave of faintness attacked Hana as she mopped Izzie's brow with a wet flannel. She sat on the side of the bath and tried to sooth her daughter. Marcus sweated in his black clerical shirt, dark stains showing beneath his armpits and Beth's vomit still staining the front. Izzie's maternity dress lay in a corner of the room, hauled over her head and discarded. A maternity bra barely contained engorged breasts. "Oh, God!" she groaned at intervals. "God help me."

"I need to cut your knickers off." Marcus produced a pair of nail scissors from the bathroom cabinet and Izzie screamed and flapped her hand at him.

"No! Let Mum do it. I don't trust you."

Marcus gritted his teeth. "Fine!" he snapped. The scissors clattered onto the side of the bath and a tearing sound solved the issue. "You don't get to call the shots. Not when you kept this from me. How long, Izzie?"

"Not long." She paused to give a series of gut wrenching moans interspersed with panting. "I felt uncomfortable last night and the contractions started earlier. They didn't feel real until I went to the toilet just then."

Hana clung to the doorframe, her eyes wide with terror. Izzie's face poked over the top of the bath and she tried to smile, the action halted by another contraction. "I'm pushing!" she yelled. Two deep groans truncated her announcement.

Hana held her breath, giving herself an unwelcome headiness. Memories of Elizabeth's birth flooded back, her home filled with ambulance staff and awkwardness. Marcus however, reacted with incredible calm, possibly the result of Peg hitting the prayer chain. "Concentrate, Izz," he ordered, his voice steady and confident. "Help's coming but concentrate. Breathe like we practiced."

"Sod off!" Izzie groaned as another contraction tightened the skin over her stomach. "I bloody hate you. I'm gonna kick you in the balls if you don't get the snip."

Marcus smirked and glanced at Hana with a look of apology. His eyes narrowed. "I dare you," he replied. "But I can't remember the last time you got your leg up that high."

"Just you wait!" Izzie snapped. "Just you bloody wait!"

A screech of brakes, running feet and the slam of the front door heralded the arrival of Izzie's midwife. She appeared in the bathroom with an air of competence. "Where are we up to?" she asked, kneeling next to the bath.

Hana backed into the hall feeling grateful. She leaned against the wall outside the door, unsure where to go. Emptiness leached its way into her soul and left her shaking. The sounds from inside the bathroom filled her with terror as the precariousness of Izzie's circumstances bit home. She jumped as the front door slammed again. A paramedic appeared around the corner and she pointed wordlessly at the bathroom. "Thanks, love," he said. His gaze strayed to her protruding stomach and up to her face. "Are you okay?"

"Yes." Hana spoke the affirmation, although her head shook in betrayal of her inner misgivings. An angry roar split the airwaves and made them both jump. Hana's eyes widened and the paramedic put his hand over hers.

"I'd love a cup of coffee," he said, raising an eyebrow. "Can you flick the jug on to boil?"

Hana stifled a sob as Izzie made noises as though being rent in two. "It's my daughter," she whispered. "The babies are supposed to be born in the hospital, not an old iron bathtub."

"Hey, I've seen worse," he replied, patting Hana's hand. "You concentrate on making me that drink. Milk and three sugars."

Hana nodded and moved along the hallway. She didn't go to the kitchen, hiding in her bedroom. She sat on the edge of her bed and leaned forward, sending up arrow prayers and wishing she'd escaped with Peg. The noise from the bathroom intensified as poor Izzie dealt with the contents of her distended womb. "Oh God," Hana pleaded. "Please help Izzie, please help her babies."

Chapter 31

U nable to sit still, Hana emerged from her room to the sound of more footsteps and new voices, finding two St John's ambulance-men outside her door. One turned towards her. "Hi, love. Has our advanced paramedic arrived?"

She nodded, unable to persuade her voice to croak over the sound of Izzie's noises. He took a step towards her and took her arm. "Please can I check you out?" he asked, his voice gentle. "You don't look so good."

Hana went with him to the kitchen and sat in a chair while he measured her blood pressure. His colleague filled the kettle and flicked the switch on so it would boil. She answered questions with robotic monotony and worried about her daughter. She wrangled with the dilemma of which seemed worse, being inside the cramped bathroom with Izzie's groans, or outside not knowing. "I can't stand this," she breathed and the man squeezed her fingers.

"Not long now," his colleague said, putting a mug of hot tea on the table next to her. "Nearly over."

"Three sugars." Hana remembered the advanced paramedic's request and tried to rise. "Coffee with three sugars."

The men glanced across at each other with an unspoken communication. Hana sensed she'd been sent on a false errand to distract her. She squeezed her fingers hard on either side of the bridge of her nose to stop the threatening tears.

A scream pierced the night, but it wasn't Izzie's. One of the men set off towards the bathroom and Hana rose. Her head swam and faintness threatened as she listened for anything which might offer a clue. The other ambulance-man patted her shoulder. "Here he comes," he soothed as footsteps echoed along the hall. His colleague clutched a tiny pink bundle wrapped in an old, faded green bath towel. It gave the baby's screwed up face an odd hue in the kitchen's murky light.

"One down," he said, waggling his eyebrows at the man next to Hana. "I need to go back in. You okay here?"

"Yep." The ambulance-man hefted Hana's grandson into his arms and peered down at the waxy skin. "A little early but he's got a good pair of lungs."

Hana held out her arms, needing to hold the child as a proxy for reconnecting with Izzie. Her hands shook as she collected the tiny bundle and sat resumed her vigil at the table.

"Drink your tea," the man said as his colleague left the room. He pushed it towards her and she shook her head, unable to trust her shaking hands with a hot drink over the newborn. "Are you her sister?" he asked, making conversation as more awful noises issued from the bathroom. Other circumstances may have raised a smile on Hana's lips as she swallowed the compliment. Instead, she shook her head and stared at the tiny boy in her arms. Marcus' gene pool struck lucky in its influence over him and he mirrored Beth's pale skin and tufty blonde hair. Enormous blue eyes blinked as he struggled to focus on her face. His mouth gulped and his lips puckered as though he might cry. Hana stroked his cheek and tried to soothe him. "Your brother isn't far behind you," she whispered. "And then Mummy will feed you." Yellow flecks around his irises made her wonder if his eyes may turn green eventually in acknowledgement of her Irish

McKay heritage. The baby blinked again and Hana fancied she saw a look of her older brother.

Her lips released a tiny sound and the ambulance-man appeared at her elbow. "Okay?" he asked, tweaking the blanket to examine the baby's complexion.

"Yes." Hana nodded. "He reminds me of my brother, Mark." Saying his name out loud after so long gave her a pain in her chest. The strange ethereal cord, which binds siblings whether they like it or not, snaked around her heart and reminded her of the loss.

"That's nice." The ambulance-man checked his watch and Hana saw traces of anxiety in his expression. He frowned. "Five more minutes and the second baby must be out. Otherwise we're in trouble."

Hana swallowed. "What kind of trouble."

The man shook himself and settled a blank mask over his face. "Nothing for you to worry about. I need to just check the radio in the ambulance. Back in a second." He whirled around and she listened to his footsteps take him through the front door.

"Room for another?" The first paramedic took Hana by surprise as she gazed at her new grandson and worried about Izzie. She looked up to see another tiny bundle in his arms. This time, a newer towel shrouded the infant.

"He's here?" Hana's voice caught and she felt tears prick behind her eyelids. "I didn't hear him."

"He's fine." The paramedic smiled at her and she sensed his pleasure at a job well done. "He's three minutes old exactly."

Hana stood and peered at the swaddled baby, seeing darker blue eyes peering at something beyond her face. Olive skinned and black haired, Isobel had accidentally produced a carbon copy of her father. Hana breathed out through pursed lips and felt glad for her daughter. She had worshipped the ground Vikram Singh Johal once walked upon.

Unfurling a tiny hand from the towel, Hana stretched the little arm towards the other bundle. The child in the paramedic's arms grew fractious and made a series of spluttering cries. He stilled at the feeling of his twin's fist against his cheek and turned his head towards the sensation. Again, Hana sensed the keen loss of her relationship with Mark and silenced the gnawing ache in the pit of her stomach. "How's my daughter?" Hana asked, her eyes searching the man's face for truth.

"She's done well," he said, his blue eyes sincere. "Midwife is cleaning her up and we'll get to the hospital as soon as she's able to travel."

Hana nodded and her heart filled with gratitude which locked up her throat and rendered her speechless. The paramedic squeezed her shoulder. "I know," he said. "We take childbirth for granted, don't we? Yet it's still one of the calls which makes me tense for a second, even after thirty years in this game." He smiled. "There's so much to lose, but this time it's turned out great." The inference behind his words spoke of times when it didn't turn out well at all. Hana pushed those thoughts away.

The child in the paramedic's arms began to snuffle and make little popping noises as though about to cry. He forced his tiny fist into his mouth and sucked. "I'll take this chap to the ambo," the man said. "Then come back for his brother."

"What about Izzie?" Hana asked. "She'll want to go with them." The thought of separation set up a pounding in her brain.

He smiled back at her, offering reassurance. "We won't keep them apart on purpose, I promise. If she's ready we'll go together. If not, we'll reunite them in the hospital. It'll turn out fine."

The man from the ambulance reappeared. He held his arms out for the child which Hana clutched. A moment of instinct made her turn away. The paramedic stopped in the doorway, still holding Luey. "If you give the baby to Mike here and then fetch some things for their mum, we can probably take them all together."

Hana nodded and reluctantly parted with Huey. In Izzie's room she spied a suitcase leaning up against the wardrobe door.

A tiny, knitted matinee jacket peeked from beneath the zipper. Hana wheeled it along the hallway and bumped it down the front steps. The ambulance-man jumped down to meet her and she held the handle out towards him. "Promise you'll wait?" she asked him, chewing her lower lip.

"As long as we can," he agreed. "But these babies need to go to the neonatal ward and get fed as soon as possible. I won't risk their health."

"Thank you." Hana backed away, shivering against the cool night air. Darkness shrouded the street and she wondered when the day disappeared from under her.

Back inside the house, she knocked on the closed bathroom door. Marcus snapped it open one handed and the second ambulance-man nodded to her. "Has Bob left yet?" he asked, pushing a blood pressure cuff back into a medical bag.

"Bob?" Hana asked. "From the ambulance?"

"No." He shook his head and rose. "The advanced paramedic. I heard the controller call him to a road traffic accident near the beach.

Hana watched her daughter reel as Marcus propped her upright. The midwife fitted a tatty bathrobe around her shoulders and drew it closed at the waist. She looked back at the ambulance-man, robbed of speech. "Don't worry," he said with understanding. "Did someone check you out?"

Hana shook her head and then nodded. "Bob," she repeated, without knowing why. Izzie looked sick, her skin glossy with sweat and a greyness beneath her eyes. The rush of love and complete inadequacy overcame Hana. She felt utterly lost. Like the helpless voyeur of a train crash, she watched, unable to move as paralysis spread through her body. Marcus heard the little sob as it escaped from between her lips and responded. He propped Izzie against his body and reached out to drag Hana into the small space. "Look," he said, pulling her into him. "She's fine. Hold her arm while I fetch some knickers."

Hana held her daughter close and cried into her hair, supporting her in arms which turned to jelly and made their combined bodies shake. The screech of a siren split the night air and Hana tensed in terror. The ambulance-man shook his head. "Just Bob," he said. "Gone to that other call. We've got this one."

The midwife struggled with a giant, bloody dinner plate. Hana widened her eyes in curiosity before realising what it was. The placenta tumbled into a white dustbin liner and the midwife handed it to the ambulance-man. "It's intact," she said. "Thank God."

The small bathroom resembled the scene of an axe murder. Izzie's dress lay trampled in a corner and towels filled the sink, streaked with blood and gore. Hana swallowed back nausea and focussed on the cleaning products she might use to restore the room, distracting herself as Izzie listed against her shoulder. Marcus returned, shoving Izzie's feet into panties and fixing a huge sanitary towel in the gusset. He pulled them up around her waist and kissed her on the forehead. "Never accuse me of not embracing the modern male stereotype," he joked and Hana felt eternally grateful for this man. If she left this world prematurely, at least Izzie would know a life with love in it. Izzie began to sag and Hana grunted against her weight. "I'm dropping her," she hissed.

Marcus took his wife in his strong arms, lifting her like a child.

"Where are the boys?" Izzie pleaded, exhaustion lacing her voice.

"In the ambulance waiting for you, sweetheart," the midwife replied. "Are you ready to go?"

Hana stepped back as the ambulance-man passed her, carrying his medical bag in one hand and the afterbirth in the other. "I'll bring a trolley," he said over his shoulder.

"No need." Marcus followed him along the narrow hallway and disappeared around the corner. Izzie's head lolled against his shoulder and a sense of powerlessness consumed Hana. She hurried to the front door in time to see the doors of the ambulance close the second Marcus sat down. The vehicle roared away into the night, carrying off three blood ties she couldn't live without. She stood in the cold doorway and watched the lights disappear, not sure what to do when she could no longer see them in the distance.

"I'll help you clean up and then I should follow them." The midwife spoke from the hallway and then disappeared. Hana followed her to the bathroom and the slaughterhouse scene.

"Where do we start?" she asked, her voice small and without enthusiasm.

The midwife stopped putting her instruments back into her case and turned to smile. "When are you due?"

"January," Hana replied, bending to pick up Izzie's stained dress. She clutched it to her chest like a trophy. "It looks like a massacre took place in here."

The midwife looked around her. "I must just be used to it by now. Find some plastic bags, cloths and strong cleaner. Then we can make a start. I need to follow Izzie."

"I actually don't know where things are yet," said Hana replied, looking lost. She felt the silky material of the dress and imagined Izzie's dark silky hair beneath her fingers. "I only arrived today. You go, I'll sort this out myself."

Hana rounded up the filthy towels and put them straight into the washing machine with Izzie's dress. She set it all on a long wash cycle with extra detergent. The midwife packed away the paraphernalia of her trade and loaded it into her car. She returned long enough to reassure Hana. "The babies looked much better than I expected when I arrived," she admitted. "Izzie won't want to be away from Elizabeth for too long, so I imagine she'll break out of hospital as soon as she can." She smiled at Hana's ashen face. "Everything will be fine," she promised and squeezed her writhing fingers. "Relax, clear up what you can and then get some rest. You look beat."

Hana spent the next two hours cleaning the bathroom. She mopped the stain from the hall floorboards and scrubbed every surface twice. The peal of the house telephone cut into the silence and she almost slipped on the wet floor in her haste to answer it.

"Hey, Hana. How are you?" Marcus asked. She studied every cadence of his voice for bad news but detected nothing.

"I'm okay," she replied. "How's Izzie and the boys?"

"That's why I'm ringing. They're all fine. Izzie says you need to go to bed."

"But what happened?" Hana leaned against the wall and closed her eyes. "When you got to the hospital."

"Nothing." Marcus sounded casual. "The midwives checked Izzie and the boys over and said they're fine. I'm staying the night to help with feeding and all that baby stuff. I'll come home tomorrow because I've got something on early in the morning. Peg will keep Beth because that's the plan. So, go to bed, Hana."

She sighed. "But Izzie looked terrible when she left. You carried her."

"Just knackered," Marcus replied. "I promise you she's fine. She needed a couple of stitches because of the speed, but she's fine. Do you want me to wake her up so you can speak to her?"

"No." Hana shook her head. "Don't do that. I'll finish cleaning up and then sleep."

"Don't forget your antibiotics." Hana nodded at the prompt but didn't reply. Marcus sounded concerned, his sentence lifting at the end. "Hana? Antibiotics. Don't forget to take them."

"Okay," she conceded. "What about you? Your insulin must still be here."

"Yeah, but I'm in a hospital," he said, laughter behind his words. "I've got everything I need. Go to bed, Hana."

Hana hung up the phone and stumbled towards her bedroom. Flicking the light on revealed her open suitcase on the bed and her antibiotics next to her washbag. At the sight of the comfortable pillow, her energy levels autocorrected and extreme fatigue hit her like a speeding train. She forced herself to clean up the kitchen before taking her tablet and crawling into the cold, empty bed.

Images of her father, Mark and Logan swirled around her exhausted mind, torturing her with aloneness. "What's wrong with me?" she sniffed into her pillow. "I always end up by myself, no matter where I go."

Chapter 32

Logan Du Rose travelled to the lake in the darkness, worrying more about dealing with his volatile wife than meeting with a man who made an art form out of hounding him. A sense of exposure crawled across his flesh and his brain wrangled with the unusual deal he'd struck. He'd broken his own rules of never going alone and always keeping his opposition at arm's length. His breathing sounded loud in his helmet and he held it for a few beats, wanting the moment over without sounding like a pussy. Indicating a right, Logan made the turn into Lake Crescent and the prearranged rendezvous with trouble.

He parked his bike with meticulous care and considered keeping his helmet on. "No sense fighting doom," he muttered and pulled it off, before locking it to the back wheel. Thrusting his hands into the pockets of his leather jacket, he moved through the shadows and skirted a lone white van parked near the cafe. A bakery sign on the side panel tied it to the cafe owner and a faint light glinted from the kitchens out back.

The weight of the world pressed down on Logan's shoulders as he walked. He passed the barriers preventing late night traffic around the lake and wondered if his opponent would honour the deal. No weapons, no vehicles. Somehow he doubted it. He whistled beneath his breath as he walked, masking the drumming of his heart. Better to sound nonchalant than terrified. A figure waited for him at the edge of the lake, his hunched shape leaning on a walking stick. A nikau palm soared above him like a crazy, mop-headed silhouette.

"Logan Du Rose," Laval said, savouring his name almost as much as a fine Marlborough wine. Logan knitted his brows and narrowed his grey eyes, nothing about the man even vaguely familiar.

"I don't know you," he replied, removing his hands from his pockets and bracing himself on legs planted solidly and ready for a fight. Logan jerked his head behind him. "We agreed no heavies and yet I've counted six. You're not a man of your word." He sneered. "You have no mana."

Laval laughed, the left side of his face drooping from a mild stroke. "I heard you saw off the Triads back in the day. I got your message."

Logan snorted. "And yet you ignored it."

The stick ground against the grass with a hiss as Laval turned. The scrape of his feet echoed off the water as he shuffled closer. "We are both too old for this, Mr Du Rose," he sighed, a picture of exhaustion as age bowed his body almost in half. "Just give me the box and we'll call it quits."

"Quits?" Logan took a step forward and his fingers curled into fists. "You're not serious."

"I am old and sick and have no time for this. Give me the box." Laval held out his hand, the fingers shaking with a tremor generated from an inner source. Logan glanced at the outstretched hand and then back at the wizened face.

"Why do you need it?" he demanded. "Just let it go."

"I can't." Laval's lips glinted with spittle in the dull overhead light and sweat beaded on his forehead. "I must end this."

"Why?" Logan pushed for the truth, wanting to hear the words from the old man's lips. "What did my wife ever do to you?"

Laval sighed and his knees gave, forcing him to lean harder on his stick. He shuffled away from the edge of the lake and Logan saw a medical tube swing in an arc beneath the pale trench coat. "Nothing," he replied. "She got in the way."

"You're dying." Logan stated the fact without compassion. He took another step forward. "You had a massive stroke a month ago and almost didn't wake up. Just let it go."

Laval turned rheumy eyes in Logan's direction and they widened in surprise. "Che is surprisingly well informed," he concluded. "But I still want that box."

"No." Logan chewed the inside of his lower lip and contemplated the sorry old man before him. "It's over. You're giving no more orders in this life."

"Your reputation precedes you." The old man's slippery voice complimented him, the words sliding like pond scum across Logan's heart. "You have friends in high places, but I have no interest in your affairs. You will give me the box now, or you will lose. This battle will extend beyond my death, Du Rose. It will continue. Best you end it now."

Logan ground his teeth as Laval's men emerged from their hiding places. His eyes darted left and right as he assessed them. "What is this really about?" he asked, his senses on overdrive. He raised his right hand in a universal stop sign and heard the men halt, sensing their unease.

Laval nodded to his heavies and his eyelashes fluttered. "You needn't search him. Wires aren't his style." He inclined his head in a regal acknowledgement of Logan's physique. "He'll have no weapons because he rarely needs them, or so I've heard."

Logan ground his teeth, aware of the proximity of Laval's men. "What is this about?" he repeated, enunciating every word.

Laval smiled, his lips turning down in a peculiar, lopsided grimace. "It started as a con and will end with revenge, Logan. Can't you see it?" His eyes darkened with gimlet hardness and he spoke to the man at Logan's right shoulder. "Get the box and then do as you wish." The stick clattered against gravel as he staggered off the grass and onto the path. Two of the six men moved across to help him, leaving Logan with four. He cursed inwardly. He knew nothing more than when he'd arrived. "Where is she?" he demanded, clutching at straws as they seized his arms from behind. "What did you do with the old lady's body?"

Laval stopped and pushed away the man supporting his right arm. He turned his sickly features back towards Logan and a wicked smile creased his face. "Swimming with the fishes," he replied. Jerking his head towards the far side of the lake, his eyes glinted. "In plain sight."

Logan's gaze raked the darkness, seeing only shadows and the scattering of residential lights. "Where?"

Laval snorted, a high sound containing exasperation. "Storm drain," he bit, the sentence permeated by coughing.

The men spun Logan around and two held him while a third searched his jacket. The man withdrew the box from his inside pocket with a whoop of victory. Logan lifted his knee, contacting the man's groin with painful accuracy and he dropped like a stone at his feet. The box rolled into the grass and rested at the bottom of the palm tree.

Logan squirmed backwards, but the two men held him firm. The fourth came into view, a nasty grin splitting his face as he stepped from the shadows. Lithe and fit, with delicate features and a dark hat pulled over his hair, he showed enjoyment at Logan's gape of surprise. "Hey, Du Rose," the man said. "It's been too long." The sharp uppercut to the face made Logan's head rattle and white spots danced in front of his vision. Tasting blood, he waited for another blow, but the man took a step back. "He's all yours," he said to the other two. "Sink him in the lake and make sure he doesn't come back up." His eyes glinted. "Ever."

Shock struck Logan dumb and robbed him of his usual fight instincts. The two men dragged him backwards and cable tied his wrists before he could wrestle his head back into the game. As they pulled him upright, he managed to smash the back of his skull into the nose of the man to his left and he let go with a curse. Logan's eyes searched the ground for the box but saw nothing. It had gone, along with the unexpected opponent who knew both his name and history. His heart quailed with the realisation this would never be over and distracted from the fight, took a punch to the stomach without tensing first.

The taste of acid filled his mouth as his guts objected. Shock and surprise took Laval's side and left Logan unguarded. His eyes watered from the blow to his nose and blood seeped down the back of his throat. He shoulder barged the man to his right, but met no resistance as his captor dodged clear. Rough hands shoved him in the centre of his spine and the lake water rose to swallow him whole.

Instinct dictated he splay his arms and legs to buoy himself, but the plastic cable ties around his wrists nullified the task. The freezing cold lake closed around him, sucking at his heavy biker gear and eating him in a single bite. As he struggled, his temple hit the metal siding and his eyes rolled back in his head. Many forms of death had played across his mind over the years, but never drowning.

The water filled his mouth and nose with frightening speed, probing and infiltrating his airways. A dead weight, he sank like a brick, leaving only air bubbles in his wake. Blood from his nose and the cut to his temple swirled around him in the dark water and a copper taste infused his open, gasping mouth. The pain in his lungs became unbearable and he sent a silent apology to his wife. Being widowed twice in a lifetime would damage her beyond repair. He hated Vikram Singh Johal in that moment, for the time he'd stolen with Hana and squandered at the end.

Unconsciousness came, but death stayed its hand. It wasn't his turn to meet his maker and give an account of his life. Bodie, the police diver saved him, yanking his heavy body from the lake bottom and hauling him to the side. "Help me somebody! I can't hold him up!" he shouted as he surfaced. Another splash sent someone else to his side and flashlights bounced across the grass as police officers poured from the innocuous catering van.

Logan found emerging from the water more painful than suffocating in it. His lungs burned, the inside of his nose felt raw and his eyes smarted. Bloody water trickled from his nose and mouth and he couldn't breathe. His eyes flickered as Bodie rolled him onto his back, his stepson's dark hair dripping water into Logan's eyes. His irises looked black in the flashlights and he gave a nonchalant shrug as Logan coughed up blood and lake water. "I couldn't let you die when it came to it," Bodie admitted, his chest still heaving from the effects of the freezing water. "For some stupid reason, my mother seems to love you."

Chapter 33

Hana woke with a start and lay awake, watching the street lights play on the ceiling from a chink in the curtains. The room felt different to home and it took a moment for her to remember. She'd run away again, after making Logan promise he wouldn't do likewise. Darkness penetrated the room and her heart in equal measure. She lay in the inky gloom and strained her ears for the familiar bird sounds she was used to, hearing nothing from their suburban cousins. "Please bless Izzie and her babies," Hana whispered to God, at least guaranteeing his wakefulness in the silent world around her.

She shuddered at the memory of Izzie's labour and powerlessness flooded her soul. Elizabeth's birth returned to haunt her, a painful, induced labour protracted by complications. The hospital released a distraught Izzie on Christmas Day as the pains stopped and staff shortages made them empty the ward. Marcus delivered their first child in Hana's bath at the Flagstaff house a day later. Frightening and traumatic, it barely held a candle to the previous night's experience. Hana snuggled on her side and feared for her daughter's mental state after such an ordeal. Squeezing her eyes closed against the promised dawn, she fretted about her own.

The sound of a car engine disturbed the night and Hana heard the clunk of an elderly suspension as it clambered over the lip of the driveway. The vehicle stopped beneath her bedroom window and then doors slammed shut. Hana sighed and pushed herself upright, keen for news of Izzie. She recognised Marcus' footsteps as he lumbered through the front door and laid his keys on the hall table. A faint light glowed beneath the bedroom door and then snapped off. Before Hana could call out, his door closed and she felt the thud as he flopped onto his bed, the action shaking the joists in the floor. She retreated beneath the sheets and gave a disappointed sigh, turning to face the wall in defeat.

Silence shrouded the house and Hana forced her eyelids closed in the hope of more sleep. But her mind whirred away, taking her to places not conducive to relaxation. She jumped as an arm snaked over her shoulder and a cold hand clamped over lips parted in a scream. Her heart raced as the bed dipped behind her and the blue-buzz of fear pinned her to the mattress.

A voice whispered in her ear, the lips close enough to caress her cheek. "I'll let go, but don't scream!" As the hand moved away, Hana took a giant inhale and prepared to do exactly that. The hand gripped her cheeks and stopped the sound escaping, returning to cover her mouth. "Please, wahine!" He sounded tired, but rage filled Hana's chest. She forced her body to still and gritted her teeth. A jeans clad leg reached over and trapped her knees while his body pinned her in place. The hand across her mouth relaxed and Hana bit down on the vulnerable flesh of a finger.

"Bloody hell!" Logan hissed. He flipped Hana onto her back and covered her body with his. The child in her womb woke and protested, making her gasp in pain. Logan shifted sideways and Hana raised her knee, hitting him in the groin. Groaning, he pushed her legs flat and buried his face against her shoulder as a vile curse word slipped from his lips.

"I hate you!" she hissed and felt him inhale.

"Liar!" He lifted his head and bit the side of her neck.

"You'll wake Marcus." Hana's body responded to the bite in ways she least expected, sending darts of desire like a lightning flash into her core and muddying her thinking.

"Doing what?" Logan nuzzled beneath her ear and Hana held her breath, refusing to answer. When his lips brushed across hers, she turned her face away and attempted to master her body.

"Go away," she hissed and heard his characteristic snort.

"No!" His reply contained enough familiar stubbornness to harden Hana's resolve a little. She wiggled beneath him and in answer, he raised her arms above her head and held them there one handed. "Sorry, did you say something?" She swore at him and he gave a low rumble of laughter. "I'm a bad influence on you, wahine." His body stilled and Hana felt peppermint breath on her cheek. "I've missed you, Hana," he whispered.

"I haven't missed you!" she replied and Logan sighed.

"That's not what I hear." A cold hand snaked beneath her nightshirt and Hana shivered and tried to wriggle away.

"They're lying!"

"Who's lying, babe? Your daughter or son-in-law?"

"They're both traitors and I haven't missed you at all. I'm having a great time and I'm not coming home. I'm staying here."

"Yeah, right." Logan's summery scents assailed Hana's nose and she sought his brand of peace like fire hunts oxygen. He tipped to one side and she missed the weight of his thigh across her legs. It depleted the sense of safety he exuded and the realisation brought confusion. He released her wrists and gentle fingers stroked her face, tantalising her further. "I love you, Hana Du Rose," Logan whispered. "I've come further south than I've ever been in this country, just to take you home. So start behaving yourself."

Hana snorted with indignation and ordered her thoughts into a barrage of further denial and insults. The effort proved wasted as Logan's lips covered hers. His busy fingers wrested her nightshirt up to expose her knickers and he eased the waistband down with practiced expertise. It knocked the fight from her mind and filled it instead with thoughts of pleasure. By the time she had recovered, Logan was already well into his work and she knew she didn't want him to stop.

Hana administered a few nasty bites on Logan's neck and shoulder to demonstrate her protest. He removed his clothes without leaving the bed, keeping Hana pinned down as though assuming she would run. She wriggled and kicked out, but stilled as his naked body slid over hers. "When will you learn to trust me?" His words jarred in the darkness and no ready jibe presented itself.

"I don't know, Logan." Hana heard him swallow and reached up to meet his lips. "Perhaps never."

He snorted like his Appaloosa stallion and Hana felt his fingers flutter around her face. "That's okay, babe," he whispered. "I love a challenge; you should know that by now."

When Hana woke a few hours later, she felt the cold wall against her bare back. Boxed into the double bed, she couldn't escape. Logan occupied the space nearest the door, his right arm wrapped around her neck so that her face pressed into his chest. He'd left her no room to move and Hana sensed the deliberateness of his position. She wriggled against him, aware of a pressing need for the bathroom. He responded by tightening his grip on the back of her neck and a sense of panic rose in her breast. His sultry grey eyes met her gaze and he smiled.

"Logan!" Hana pushed away in shock and the back of her head hit the wall with a bump. Logan winced.

"Sorry. Should have mentioned the broken nose." He rolled onto his back and touched the medical tape across the bridge. Black bruises gave him a panda bear resemblance and another line of tape clung to his temple. Blood seeped through the white surface. "They almost didn't let me fly."

Hana pushed herself into a sitting position and the sheets puddled over her rounded belly. "You look a mess!" Fear and temper mingled in her chest and robbed her of rational thought. Her hands balled into angry fists, the nails digging into her palm. "You promised no more dodgy dealings." She kicked out and caught him on the shin, a sense of victory budding at his wince of discomfort. "You promised!" Clambering over him as though he didn't exist, Hana exited the bed. She snatched up the leggings and the pullover on her way past the suitcase, snagging clean knickers as she went. Dragging the clothing against her chest, she escaped the bedroom naked and hoped she didn't run into Marcus on the way to the bathroom.

The shower did nothing to salve her mood. Nor did finding another blob of afterbirth on the tiles behind the shower curtain. She dressed, hauling her leggings out of her ass twice before she left the bathroom. "We're done!" she muttered to herself as her temper stoked out of control. "I refuse to stay married to a gangster."

In the kitchen she found a bleary headed Marcus, mechanically shovelling Cornflakes into his face on one of Elizabeth's red, baby spoons. Compassion took the edge off her rage as she remembered his tender actions with Izzie the night before. Hana stroked his blonde hair as she passed him on the way to the sink. "How are you?" she asked.

He nodded and then ruined the moment with an ill-timed smirk. "Knackered. A noisy old couple ruined my beauty sleep with their loud bonking."

Hana's fingers changed the action from a stroke to a slap. "Did you know Logan intended to come here?" she demanded.

Marcus laughed. "Yes. His flight arrived this morning at four. Izzie sent me to get him. Then she made me stay home to play referee."

"Right!" Hana's retort held a nasty edge. "I'll tell her you didn't bother!"

Marcus rose with his cereal bowl clutched in his hand and placed it in the dishwasher. Ruggedly handsome, his blonde hair stuck up at various points around his head and he looked like he'd been pulled through a bush backwards. "You didn't sound like you needed help." He waggled his eyebrows. "I'll walk round to Peg's and take Bethie to see her new brothers at the hospital." He stalked towards the kitchen door and Hana noticed he already had his shoes on.

"Wait!" She raised her hand and her fingers clutched empty air. "Tell me about Izzie. I want to know she's okay."

Marcus paused. "She's good, Hana. I'm surprised at how well she's come through. She's glad you were here."

"When can I see her?" Maternal instinct made her want to grab her shoes and refuse to let him leave without her. It warred with respect for Marcus' role as husband and father.

Marcus' steps carried him across the kitchen and he drew Hana into a gentle hug. "Soon, love. I'll make sure you're the first after Beth. The hospital will keep everyone else away just for today, then it's game on. I imagine a heap of old ladies will take possession of my wife and the children. Their casseroles helped grow my boys so they'll feel entitled." He pressed his lips to Hana's forehead and released her. "I'll keep you updated with texts," he promised.

Hana nodded and accepted his assurances with good grace. Marcus reached the doorway and held onto the frame as he stared back at her. "Spend today working on your marriage, Hana." He raised blonde eyebrows skywards. "There's more to it than just the conjugal bits." The quirk of his lips ruined the effect of wise counselling and Hana's cheeks flushed pink.

"You don't know what you're talking about!" she snapped, instantly riled.

Marcus shrugged. "Logan adores you and I trust him. Don't punish him for another's mistakes, Hana." He whirled around and the front door clicked shut behind him. Hana derived minor satisfaction from hearing him trip down the porch steps, but the victory didn't last. Her temporary bedroom contained a man covered in cuts and bruises and shrouded in half-truths and mystery.

Hana stood at the kitchen window and watched a small mynha bird hop around the garden. It sat above a child's swing set and preened its feathers. The wooden structure leaned to one side and looked on the dangerous verge of precarious. Hana figured Marcus put it up without a spirit level and pictured his misplaced pride in his shoddy workmanship. "And that guy's a priest," she breathed.

"Yep. And a good one." Logan appeared behind her with his usual stealth and Hana jumped. She felt herself bristle with indignation as his strong fingers linked above her breasts. His rough chin grazed the tender skin of her neck and she bit down on her lower lip in an effort at resistance. When she tossed her head in protest, he got the message and gave an exaggerated sigh. But he didn't release her. Hana looked down at the raw skin on his knuckles and her chest tensed in fear. His bare wrists showed oozing welts from a sharp object and the sight caused a clenching in her gut.

Hana forced herself to turn in the small space, the hard edge of the counter digging into her spine. Logan didn't give, keeping his arms clamped around her torso and observing her rotation with a blank expression. The fine chest hairs tickled the end of Hana's nose as she faced him, tilting her head backwards to examine his injuries. Her gaze raked the cuts and bruises as anger re-surged and the grinding of her teeth started a dull ache at the base of her skull.

A deep graze bit into Logan's jawbone. Open and raw, it glistened with clear sticky stuff which had dried into translucent scabs. He'd removed the tape from his temple and the tails of black stitches poked through the skin. He carried his head at an odd angle and every movement raised a wince to his handsome but battered features. Iodine stains showed around the white tape across the bridge of his nose and exhaustion showed in the pale, grey irises.

Hana shut her eyes and tipped her head forward, hearing the groan escape her lips. Logan misinterpreted her distress as physical, bending his knees and catching her beneath her thighs. Before she could protest, he sat her on the counter and wrapped her into his strong arms like a child. "It's over," he whispered, his chin resting on the top of her head and his voice sending a rumble through her body. "I just had that one more thing to do and I'd exhausted all other options. I couldn't tell you."

"Did you kill them?" Hana asked, her voice sounding small and bewildered.

Logan snorted, part annoyance, part amusement. "Why do you always think the worst of me? I've never killed anyone."

Hana remained silent, absentmindedly moving her lips against the hair on Logan's chest. She closed her eyes and turned her head, listening to his strong heartbeat. Relief at his safety vied with the desire to kill him herself.

"When?" she asked eventually, not sure she wanted the answer. "Was it the night you left me?"

"I didn't leave you." Logan's voice hardened. "I went out to meet someone and no, this happened last night."

"Izzie had the babies last night." Hana's tired brain wandered and she shuddered at the memory of her daughter's cries of pain. Shaking fingers strayed to her belly and the realisation struck her that soon, she would endure a similar horror. The years caught up with her and she felt ill-equipped and far too old to face the events looming in her near future. "I can't do this." The sob seemed to come from her toes and rise into her throat, the embodiment of anguish and terror. It gushed from her lips and others accompanied it. Hana cried and Logan crushed her to him, letting her tears roll down his bare chest and soak the waistband of his jeans.

She tried to speak words which conveyed her powerlessness and describe her daughter's agony, but they emerged as unintelligible moans and half sentences snatched away by violent sobs. Logan held her, stroking her back and placing tender kisses across her sweating forehead. When she silenced, her body continued to rock from the spasming of her chest muscles and his arms loosened their grip. "I'll hire a car and take you to see Izzie," Logan promised, jarring the silence.

Hana nodded and pushed herself upright, her cheeks damp and her eyes puffy. "Thanks," she conceded. "Marcus said he'd text me. He's taking Bethie to meet her brothers this morning."

Logan smiled and the dimple in his cheek appeared, the only recognisable feature of his increasingly swollen face. Hana's gaze coasted over the tape and bruises and her eyes narrowed. "Your turn," she said and her irises hardened to a dangerous, emerald hue.

Logan sighed. "Do you really want to know? It might be best you don't."

Hana's jaw tightened and she spoke through gritted teeth. "Don't patronise me, Logan."

"Fine." His arms slackened and his hands settled around her waist in an easy grip. Gentle thumbs made contact with the swell of his child in her womb. Logan swallowed. "But you won't like it."

Hana snorted and jerked her head upwards at his battered face. "You think?" She pushed her face into his chest and wiped it against the soft flesh, leaving an ugly trail of tears as punishment. Her palms rose to shove him backwards so she could study his face for the truth.

Logan's nostrils flared and a wince narrowed his eyes for a split second. "I explored every avenue before agreeing to this, Hana. I need you to understand that."

"Just tell me." She heard her teeth grind in her head. "What did you agree to?"

Logan sighed. "Odering asked me to arrange a meeting with Laval. He used it as leverage to release me on bail when Boris refused to exonerate me. I kept him dangling for a long while but it wore thin. When Boris admitted I didn't assault him, I assumed Odering would back off." He paused and his tongue flicked out to lick his lips. Hana's eyes widened at the sight of blood but Logan raised a hand to stop her. "I cut the inside of my mouth," he said, irritation in his eyes. "It's fine."

Hana swallowed and her voice sounded croaky. "What happened?"

"I knew Tama worked for Laval and when he threatened you, I couldn't leave it any longer. If he told Laval where we lived, he'd come for you and I couldn't risk not being there. I agreed to let Odering use me as bait to lure Laval out."

"That was stupid!" Hana's voice rose and her green eyes widened in fury. "You said nothing!"

"Stupid?" Logan spat the word and took a step back. His body tensed into hard lines and Hana held her breath. He turned away from her and her scrabbling fingers clung to the edge of the counter, aware she couldn't reach the floor without difficulty. "I got desperate, Hana." Logan rested his palms on the edge of the sink and stared through the window, without seeing the haphazard swing set a few metres in front of it. "I turned Odering down because of you, but then I ended up doing it for the same reason." His eyes narrowed. "It's always about you."

He turned and leaned his neat bum against the sink, folding his arms and flexing his muscles as though in defiance against her criticism. Hana clung to the counter, too stubborn to ask for help. "Odering demanded a meeting the night you left. I asked to see his boss because I didn't intend to play his game anymore." Logan's grey eyes sought Hana's for confirmation. "Then you told me about Tama. I promised I wouldn't be long. I arrived home within the hour and you'd gone. Why would you do that to me again?"

"What do you mean, again?" Hana bridled and her words rapped a staccato beat.

Logan shook his head and spoke through gritted teeth. "Oh, so you've forgotten already, have you? You don't remember disappearing for a whole day and telling no one where you were? Odering had a team searching Hamilton for you. Do you know the awful conclusions we came to, Hana? Do you even care we assumed Laval took you?"

Hana swallowed and realisation flickered in her eyes. She shook her head and admitted, "No. I didn't think about it."

Logan snorted. "Did I storm off, Hana? Did I harangue you and demand to know everything? No! I just loved you when you arrived home and trusted you had your reasons. Geez, Hana, why does it feel like you never meet me half way?"

Hana looked down at the kitchen tiles and shame budded in her heart. A flush bloomed on her neck and spread to her cheeks. Anger rose to defend her from inevitable guilt and she looked for someone else to blame. "I asked you not to leave," she countered, putting a stiffness into her voice. "But you still did."

Logan tutted and heaved out a sigh of defeat. "I phoned Odering when I saw you'd taken a suitcase. It seemed obvious you'd left of your own accord. I agreed to flush out Laval and the cops set up surveillance on the lake. They arrested him. It's over, Hana. You can come home."

Logan walked across to the table, pulling out a chair and sitting with a heavy thud of exhaustion. He ran a hand across his face, hissing when his fingers brushed over the myriad bruises. Hana swung her legs and tried to make her precarious perch look intentional. "I might not want to come home." She jutted out her chin and set her face in an expression of defiance. "I might like Invercargill."

Logan ran both hands through his hair, inadvertently catching the bridge of his nose again. He let out a string of expletives and thumped the table in anger. "You're my wife and you're coming home," he snarled. "There's no Plan B, Hana. We're stuck with each other, even if I have to kidnap you." He pushed his finger over the cut, waiting for the pressure to alleviate the pain. When he looked up, his complexion appeared white and sick. "Laval won't last long in jail, anyway. He's dying."

Hana's eyebrows knitted and curiosity obscured all other emotions. "What? How?"

"A stroke a few weeks ago. Che sent guys to look for him because he'd gone off the radar. They found him at the hospital and waited for my word. He's a mess, hanging together with tin and string by the looks of him."

"What happened?" Hana leaned forward, her eyes sparkling and her mind hungry for answers.

Logan's lips quirked upwards, realising she was stuck and leaving her there for good measure. "The cops put a wire on me and told me to get Laval talking. He turned up with some new guys and I asked him the questions which Odering wanted answers to." Logan paused and swallowed, missing out a salient detail. "They slapped me about a little and cable tied my wrists. I didn't imagine I'd end up in the lake though."

"You swam in the lake?" Hana made it sound like a happy occurrence and Logan shook his head.

"More a case of drowning. I hit my head on the metal siding and figured God might laugh in my face sooner than I thought." He licked his lips and paused for thought.

"God won't laugh in your face." Hana sighed. "He's not like that."

"Oh, well." Logan shook off the involuntary shudder. "They found the old lady's body in a storm drain. Residents complained about a smell during the summer, but it drifted through the system so they searched the wrong one." Logan sighed. "Poor old thing. Crap way to end your life."

Hana noticed a smattering of grey hairs in his sideburns in the early morning sunlight. Guilt prickled into sorrow. While she sulked in Invercargill, Logan sacrificed himself for her. She bit her lip and hung her head in shame. Logan spoke again. "As far as you're concerned, it's over. If Laval lives long enough to get to trial, he'll go away for the rest of his life." A deep unease couched his words, but consumed with her own impetuous wrongdoing, Hana missed the cues.

"What was Laval like?" she asked and Logan gave himself a mental shake.

"A spiteful white haired old conman, who thought he was invincible until Nature took him down. I'm glad you never met him, Hana."

"What about Tama? Did the cops get him?" Logan squirmed at her question and she tensed. "What did you do?"

He shifted beneath her scrutiny and the fingers of his left hand fluttered to his painful nose. "I got Che's guys to pick him up and drop him at the hotel. I didn't want him involved anymore."

Hana inhaled in temper and her green eyes flashed. Her body tipped and she almost pitched off the counter. She wanted to think of Tama sitting in a police cell, not getting bed-and-breakfast at the hotel. "Why?" Her lips hardly moved as she snarled the question.

Logan rose with difficulty and placed his hands on his hips. His teacher's stance intimidated Hana, but she refused to back down. "Why?" He repeated her question and Hana flinched as he strode across the room and seized her wrists with bruised fingers. "Why? Because he's known for months where we live. He could have told Laval at any time, but didn't. Tama's whānau and he honoured his family ties!"

"He threatened to tell!" Hana shouted into Logan's face. "He sat in my car and threatened to do it if you didn't call the lawyers off his family!"

Logan looked down, his mind devoid of answers. His grip relaxed. "I don't know what to say to you, Hana. I don't know how to make this right. All I've ever done is what I thought was best and it's never good enough for you."

Tears of anger welled in her eyes. Logan lifted her from the counter, his biceps flexing as he allowed her body to slide down his. He held her upright until the feeling returned to her legs and gave her no option of wriggling free. His arms felt safe around her lower back and Hana blushed at the thought of his expert fingers on her earlier. He took both her shoulders in his hands and stared into her eyes, so close she smelled his toothpaste. "What. Do. You. Want. From. Me?" he demanded.

He shook her with gentleness but spoke as though to a stupid person. Temper surged within Hana's breast as his tone pushed all the wrong buttons. His question troubled some inner chamber in her heart as she realised she didn't know the answer. She no longer knew what she wanted and probably never had. She made a stupid decision, one she knew she would live to regret as the hasty words left her lips. Boxed into an emotional corner, the alternatives evaded her. With the sensation of his butterfly kisses still on her neck, she told him, "I need you to leave and I want a divorce. We can't live like this. I don't know who you are half the time."

Logan jumped back as though she'd slapped him and Hana's heart clenched in anguish. A little voice in her head warned that she'd made a terrible mistake. She ignored it, gnawing on her lower lip as her husband turned and walked away. Hana listened to his feet pad along the hallway and the bathroom door clicked closed.

Her hands shook as she covered her eyes. "Idiot!" she hissed, wishing she possessed the courage to undo her error. Pinching the bridge of her nose, she shook off the regret. "No," she affirmed. "Vik made you a loser. Worse, he made you a loser in secret." Too many people stood to suffer if she revealed her late husband's indiscretion. A congregation revered him and friends admired him. Hana couldn't bring herself to smash the illusion. Vikram Johal's guilt remained ingrained only in her memory, along with the face of the woman who'd visited her the day after his funeral and detonated her life.

Hana straightened her spine and gave herself a shake. She forced her trembling hands to tidy the kitchen while she waited for Logan to walk out of her life for the last time. An hour passed. He made no attempt to speak to her and didn't pass the kitchen on his way to the front door.

Curiosity drove her to the bathroom as anxiety budded in her chest. His extensive injuries promised to fuel Logan's haemophilia and exacerbate any pain he might have already suffered. Hana increased her pace as fear infused her blood and caused her heart to drum in an unhealthy thud between her ears. Her brain warred with her emotions, asserting its right not to care. It failed. The empty bathroom met her and she panicked.

"What's wrong?" Logan responded to her frantic footsteps by placing his bare feet on the floorboards as he rose. His latest textbook tumbled from his fingers and clattered onto the bed. "Is it Izzie?" he demanded, urgency in his voice.

"No." Hana swallowed and took in his casual appearance. He didn't look like a man on the verge of collapse and anger flared at how her heart deceived her. "When are you going?" she asked him, forcing belligerence into her tone. Her hands shook and she pushed them behind her back.

"I'm not." Logan sank back onto the bed and shifted into the comfy nest of pillows he'd stacked behind him. He reached for his book. "I made you a promise. This is what keeping it looks like."

"But I want you leave." The pathos in her voice sickened her.

"No, Hana. You don't ask me to go and I don't leave. That was the deal in case you've forgotten." He sounded calm and smiled, blood lining the edge of his lower lip. He'd shaved and the wounds stood out, even worse against the harsh daylight.

"Don't tell me what to do!" Hana raised her voice and backed away as Logan stood again, his height dwarfing her and his presence filling the room. A single stride brought him level and Hana winced and closed her eyes. Logan's finger stroked her chin and lifted her face.

"And to put the record straight, Hana, I didn't leave the other night. You did." His lips covered hers and Hana jumped and shoved at his chest. Her eyes snapped open. Logan's easy smile infuriated her.

"You left first!" Her eyes widened and injustice pushed her victim's mentality to the forefront. She landed a punch against his wide pectoral muscle and felt the reverberation through her fist. "You left first!" she repeated and took a giant inhale.

"Nope." Logan ran a tantalising finger along Hana's cheek and watched her pupils dilate. His thumb moved along her top lip and she swallowed in a nervous gulp. The tension between them arced like electricity. Something felt ready to snap and Hana suspected it might be her nerve. Logan's finger traced the outline of her chin and his other hand fluttered over the softness of her exposed forearm. Love and hatred trod the same path and confusion vied for prominence.

Inside she smiled a self-satisfied sort of smile; but outside she sulked for effect. He wasn't leaving.

Logan leaned close and kissed her, his lips coasting across hers in a gentle movement. Despite his vast experience around frightened equines, he exhibited a lack of surety around Hana. He'd taught her never to show her fear around the huge beasts and on an impulse, she lifted her left hand and brought it halfway to his face.

Logan caught her wrist before the blow made contact and gripped it tight. He knitted his fingers through hers and his grey eyes twinkled behind their black lashes with amusement and sex appeal. Hana felt the breath escape her and knew as she melted, she would always be a complete pushover when Logan Du Rose touched her.

Chapter 34

They pushed Elizabeth in her pram around Otepuni Gardens in Invercargill. Logan did most of the pushing and Hana retrieved the things Beth threw out. "She likes how your head pops up by her face," Logan said. "Can't you just do the popping up and down and then she might not keep throwing her stuff in the mud?" Hana popped up again with a muddy teddy and grimaced at Beth. The child's face creased into a paroxysm of giggles.

Hana collapsed onto a nearby bench, feeling exhausted. Logan joined her. He fumbled with the brake on the pram and then hooked his foot around the wheel just to be sure. Laying back against the wooden struts, he put his arm around Hana. "Why do they cry so much?" he asked.

Hana shrugged. "Are we talking about the babies, or Izzie and Marcus?"

"Both!" Logan exclaimed, thinking of Izzie's tears that morning when a body part didn't behave as it ought. "I've spent more time skulking through the supermarket with Marcus than at the house."

Hana rolled her eyes. "We know you both ate an ice cream in the car."

"Not me." Logan crossed the fingers of his other hand on the seat next to him and tensed.

"Liar. You dropped chocolate on your tee shirt. Marcus is meant to follow a strict diet."

Logan twisted his lips and wrinkled a nose covered in green bruising. "He's a bad influence. Why was Izzie crying this morning?"

"Breasts," Hana said with a sigh. "Don't ask."

"It's like living in a lunatic asylum," Logan grumbled. "We arrive home and everyone's all smiles again. How did you fix it?"

"I told you not to ask." Hana shot him a sideways glance. "An old wives remedy for sore nipples."

Logan's lips curved upwards and he mouthed the word with clear enjoyment. "I'm thinking of yours, I promise," he added. Then his face fell. "You won't cry all the time after our baby comes, will you?" He sat up in alarm and raked her face for reassurance. "Otherwise I'll have to keep you barefoot and pregnant all the time."

Hana cringed. She ran her teeth over her thumbnail and oozed discomfort. Logan raised an eyebrow in question. "This baby will be the last, Logan." She licked her lips. "I can't do this again."

"Okay." He shrugged. "I never expected to have any children, so one is still awesome."

Hana sighed with relief. "You'll get the operation then." Logan swore and she laughed. "Yeah, I thought not."

Logan shuddered. "You've never lived on a farm. Castrated animals are boring. You wouldn't like boring." Elizabeth squealed and flipped another teddy from the pram and into a layer of wet mud on the path. "Get that." Logan pointed at the toy and channelled mock authority. Hana exhaled and fished it from the ground, her expression shuttered.

"It'll be hard going home," she said wistfully. "I like it down here. I wasn't lying about that."

Logan pulled her into his side and placed a gentle kiss on her forehead. "I know babe," he sighed.

"Can we stay?" Hana asked in a whiny voice.

"No." He nudged her and rose to his feet, disengaging the pram brake. "My ancestors are already reeling in the urupā. Anywhere further south than Tokoroa is forbidden."

"You're such a liar!" Hana exclaimed and slapped his shoulder. Elizabeth squealed and held her fur-clad arms out to him.

They arrived back at the vicarage with Elizabeth riding on Logan's shoulders, hugging his head. "I can't see, Bethie. You need to move those wee hands out of my eyes," Logan said and she squealed at the top of her voice. Hana lumped along behind, pushing the pram and looking thwarted from her pleading.

"Ooh," said Marcus as he opened the front door. "You want to watch that."

"Why?" asked Logan, moving Elizabeth's hands aside so he could pick his way over the threshold. He bent his knees to admit them both without braining the child on the lintel.

Hana shoved the pram up the steps and into the hall. "Because last time Beth played horsey, she puked, narrowly missing Daddy's head. Then mummy went into labour on the hall floor."

"Oh." Logan stood still to let Marcus take his daughter.

"I need to get you two to the airport," Marcus said, turning to look for something. "I've put your stuff in the car. Where's Izzie? She was here a minute ago. The boys are asleep."

"Got names for them yet?" asked Logan. Marcus shook his head. "No. Might run a competition in Sunday School if Izzie doesn't agree on something soon."

Logan pulled a face. "Dangerous! Jedidiah and Zerubbabel. It's a risk."

Marcus nodded in agreement as Hana claimed Elizabeth and walked along the hallway to Izzie's bedroom. The door hung ajar and she pushed her way through with the wiggling baby. Her daughter sat on the edge of the bed, fumbling in a box of tissues. "Oh, Izz," Hana sighed. "No tears, darling. After two weeks, you must be desperate for the space."

Her beautiful half-Indian daughter let out an involuntary sob. "I don't want you to leave," she stammered. "I need you here."

"No, you don't." Hana sat on the bed next to her and balanced Elizabeth on her knee. "You're amazing and you're doing great." Her own voice broke. "I love you, Izz. Nothing will ever change that." Hana kissed her forehead and stood. Beth pitched forward, her arms outstretched for a twin-free cuddle. Hana sighed. Sometimes it felt impossible behaving like the adult. She wanted to hurl herself on the floor and cry in a mimicry of a toddler tantrum fuelled by sadness. "Don't come out to wave us off if you can't face it," she said, her voice breaking, "Logan will understand."

Izzie nodded but couldn't look at her mother. She buried her face in Beth's neck. "Thanks for everything, Mum. It's been so much better with you here to help me." She gave a gargantuan sniff and Hana bent to stroke her dark, glossy hair before striding from the room before she made it worse. Brushing tears from her cheeks, she met Logan in the hallway.

"I'll just say goodbye," he said and smiled, his grey eyes crinkling at the edges. He knocked on the bedroom door and entered before giving Hana a chance to stop him. Marcus intercepted her and wrapped her in a bear hug.

"Thanks for coming, mother-in-law," he said with a smirk. "I forgot you knew about stuff like sore breasts and super-duper haemorrhage sized sanitary towels."

"Good job someone did." Hana dragged a tissue from her pocket and mopped her eyes. "You can stop getting her pregnant now, you've done enough damage."

Marcus threw his head back and laughed. "I'll look forward to an appropriate Christmas gift then. Perhaps a television for the bedroom?"

They turned as Logan emerged from seeing Izzie. His expression appeared blank and Hana frowned. "I'm ready," he said and jerked his head back towards the sound of crying. "We can get a taxi."

Beth's wail joined the melee and Hana's heart clenched. "Marcus, go to them," she pleaded. "We'll be fine."

Marcus shook his head. "I'll drive you to the airport and come straight back," he promised. "The boys are sleeping in the lounge and Beth will distract her." He winked at Hana. "Trust me, I know when I need to stick around and when I don't."

The men made small talk on the way to the airport, but Hana sat in the back of the car with sadness licking at the edges of her heart. Many times she wrestled with the urge to go back. Marcus glanced at her through the rear view mirror. "Hana, stop," he said. "I can see your brain working."

"You don't understand," she grumbled. "But you will one day."

Marcus responded to Logan's raised eyebrow and changed the subject. "Don't you need a certificate to travel on an airline during pregnancy? Izzie did last time we visited you."

Hana shrugged and pulled her coat around her. "I forgot to mention it."

Marcus snorted. "Then don't go into labour. There's no galley on a domestic flight and the aisle will prove way more exposed than a bathroom."

Logan bit his lip and glared at him. "I don't want fifty strangers watching my baby born."

"Shut up!" Hana protested from the back seat. "This baby won't come early. She's like her father and will hang around to the bitter end." The roar of the men's laughter took them through the gates to the terminal.

Marcus pulled over at the drop zone and Hana refused to let him park the car. "No, love. Please go back and take care of Izzie. She needs you more right now."

"If you're sure." Marcus kissed Hana's cheek, but lingered longer over his embrace with Logan. He whispered something and Logan flushed with embarrassment before darting a nervous glance at Hana.

"What's going on with you two?" she demanded as Marcus limped the old car back through the gate and disappeared with a last wave.

Logan waggled his eyebrows. "Jealous, Hana? Haven't you seen male bonding before?"

She narrowed her eyes and pushed the handle of her suitcase at him. "Plenty. I'm also wise enough to recognise two dudes hatching a plan when I see one." She threw her chin out in defiance. "And I bet you paid." Logan swallowed and the blank expression crashed down, freezing her out. Hana smirked in victory. "Yeah, I thought so."

She halted at the departure gate and Logan ran up the back of her. "Damn!" Hana exclaimed. "I forgot to mention the tyres."

"What?" Logan sidestepped her, wheeling the suitcases towards the ticket machine.

"Marcus' car. The front left tyre looks flatter than the others."

Logan shook his head and pressed the button to print their boarding passes. "He knows," he said. "It's not the tyre. The axle isn't sitting right."

Hana inhaled. "Then it's dangerous. He can't carry my daughter and grandchildren in an unsafe car."

"It's all in hand." Logan waved her boarding pass and tugged on her wrist. "Stop worrying about problems you can't fix. He's sorting it."

Hana drew her coat around her bump and pursed her lips. Logan strode off ahead and made for a coffee kiosk in the distance. "Men!" Hana exclaimed. "A good bromance and some number eight wire and the world is fixed."

While she took her second nervous wee before they were called to board, Logan answered his phone. His eyes creased in discomfort at the sound of the person on the other end. Snatches of words rendered the conversation unintelligible, but he got the gist. "It's fine," he said, lowering his voice and turning away from the other patrons in the cafe. "My pleasure." Another voice came on the line and Logan licked his lips. "I swear your wife does more crying than your kids," he remarked.

Marcus chuckled. "Yeah, I reckon. Does Hana know?"

"No." Logan became stern. "Please don't tell her. She'll think I'm buying her favour."

He heard Marcus inhale. "It's not every dad who buys their stepdaughter a seven seater Chrysler as a gift. I don't know how to repay you."

Logan flexed his jaw. "By saying nothing. Please. And don't even think of repaying me financially."

Marcus rang off after thanking him for the people mover, which included a five-year warranty and cost more than a vicar's annual salary. Hana appeared from the bathroom and Logan slipped his phone back into his jacket pocket.

The attendants called their flight and they trooped across the tarmac like ants on a log, sticking to the marked areas and wheeling their small carry on cases. Despite Logan coveting the window seat, the male steward leaned across Hana to hand him a fizzy drink. "Please may I have some?" she asked and the man dragged his eager smile into a line.

"In a minute," he replied. "I just ran out."

She turned to watch his pert buttocks wiggle back along the aisle. "Why does that always happen?" she demanded. "Everyone ignores me when you're around. You're like a demi god they all want to worship."

Logan shrugged. "Don't know and actually don't care." He offered Hana the cup, but she reached into her bag for the bottle of flavoured water she already had. Logan pointed at the bottle. "See, he knew you had your own."

Hana gave a sarcastic smile and bided her time. Logan finished his drink and leaned forward. He stared at the propeller next to his window and dropped his gaze to the expanse of ocean on his right. Certain of his distraction, she squirted him, leaving an unfortunate trail of sickly scented water along his thighs and groin. "Oh, sorry," she said without sincerity.

"Hana!" He brushed at the wet patch with his hand and grimaced. It felt cold and sticky.

Hana grinned, sucking the sippy top like an advert for the stuff. "I wonder how he'll think you did that." Her eyes drifted to Logan's crotch and then back to his face.

He narrowed his eyes. "Just you wait until we get home, wahine!"

Hana's smile disappeared as the landscape changed beneath them. She felt the painful tug of the umbilical cord which linked her to Izzie. Some instincts even age could not erase.

Chapter 35

C ulver's Cottage seemed empty and still after the bustling activity of the vicarage. Hana rattled around, leaving the front door open to let the stagnant air out as she inspected each room. Logan unloaded the car and parked it alongside his bike in the garage. The two-week airport parking fee left a significant dent in his credit card.

He found her in the kitchen, running fresh water into the kettle. "Logan," she began and his eyebrows rose.

"No!" He answered straight away, grabbing her around her waist and kissing her neck. "No. I like the house as it is. No decorating, no loud visitors and no kidnapping Jas until he's twenty-one. It's just you and me until our baby comes. Then it'll be busy enough."

Hana smirked at his mind reading abilities and relaxed into his chest, allowing him to rock her from side to side. "Izzie's house reminded me of my childhood," she mused. "My father's vicarage always had something happening in the kitchen or his study. I didn't know how much I'd missed it."

"I'll send you to the hotel." Logan grinned out of sight and rested his chin on the top of her head. "There's always coming and going there."

Hana sighed. "The operative word in that sentence is send. I don't want to be there alone."

Logan snorted. "I can guarantee you won't have a minute's peace."

"I don't want to go back to work on Monday." Her revelation made him start and he held her shoulders so he could lean back and assess her expression.

"This is new." He narrowed his eyes. "You just had a two week break for the holidays. But you're expected back now, so hard luck for the moment. Anyway, it's a case of not wanting to go to work, but not wanting to stay home alone either. You like company, Hana. You'd go crazy."

"Why are you always the voice of reason?" She huffed with exasperation.

Logan laughed and pulled her tighter. "Somebody needs to be, Mrs Du Rose." He squeezed her and then released his grip. Hana followed him to the bedroom, watching as he tipped the contents of his overnight bag onto the bed. "Do I need a medical certificate for those last few days of term?" She gnawed on her bottom lip.

Logan shook his head. "No. I sorted it out with Alan Dobbs. If you get any trouble from Watson, let me know."

Hana's brow knitted and she wandered to the French doors and fingered the soft fabric of the floor length curtains. Sighing, she lifted it to her cheek.

Logan glanced up and his face broke into a smile. He reached her in two strides and pulled the curtain material from her fingers. "Oh no, you don't. They're fine!"

"I wasn't thinking of changing them!" Hana shrieked as he swept her off her feet and laid her giggling on the bed.

"I'll give you something else to think about," he smirked, wrenching his shirt from his jeans. "I'll keep you too busy to get bored, Hana."

She squealed as Logan straddled her, his bare torso muscular and downy in the light from the window. He bit his lip as he dropped the shirt behind him one handed, keeping eye contact with her as his fingers roved beneath her dress and sought the top of her underwear. "I missed this," he breathed, his eyes the grey of a gathering storm.

"We had two weeks together." Hana pouted.

"Yeah, in a lumpy little bed with Marcus next door."

"I didn't notice it bothering you at the time!" Hana bit her lip and shifted her hips as Logan settled next to her, one of his thighs trapping her legs in place and her stomach rising beneath his palm.

"I found it restrictive." Logan pressed his lips over hers and Hana suppressed her ready retort. Her fingers stroked the soft skin over his ribs and snaked to touch the rough watershed at his side. She followed the scar to his hip and pushed her thumb over the waistband of his jeans. Logan moaned and his tongue caressed the seam of her lips, asking for admittance. Hana sighed and parted them for him.

The gate buzzer sounded in the hall and Logan jumped. The Saint Christopher around his neck bumped against her breasts as he buried his face in her neck and muttered a stream of curse words. "Who is it?" Hana hissed and he popped his head up to look at her, his eyes widening.

"I'm not bloody telepathic." He reached behind him for his shirt. "But I'll give you two guesses!"

Hana stood up and pressed her face to the glass of the French doors, her fingers adjusting her underwear behind her. Bodie's car rumbled up the driveway and her grandson's excited face peeked from a side window. "It's Bodie," she said without guile and heard Logan grunt. She turned in time to see him yank his shirt back over his head and pull his zipper closed. The smouldering look he gave her made no secret of his feelings.

"Hanny!" Jas shrieked and his little feet pounded up the porch steps. "Hanny and Poppa! Let me in!" Logan's socks padded against the floorboards of the lobby and he opened the front door. "Hanny!" Jas yelled. "Hanny, I need both of youse!"

Hana trotted towards the front door, curiosity and a hint of fear burning in her breast. Jas shot through the gap like a thunderbolt, kicking his flip-flops off in different directions in his excitement. Amy followed, snatching at her son's sweater in a futile attempt to restrain him. She failed and sent frantic glances towards Bodie as he brought up the rear. He wore a convincing expression of disapproval, but remained silent.

"What's up, Jas?" Hana gave her grandson an encouraging smile. She couldn't hear his reply through the hand Amy held over his mouth. He kicked and spluttered and fought, but Amy remained resolute.

"Wait for Daddy!"

"I'm here." Bodie closed the front door with frightening precision and Amy waited, still covering her son's mouth. Jas brimmed like a volcano ready to blow. "I've asked Amy to marry me," Bodie said. He looked at his fingers as he spoke and Hana tensed. He glanced up, his expression shuttered. "She's agreed."

Logan shot Hana a look of confusion, masking it as she beamed with enthusiasm. "Maybe he should let his face know he's happy," he muttered and Hana pinched his thigh in warning as she passed. Tamping down any latent misgiving, she celebrated with Jas, hugging him and wishing him congratulations. Logan offered Bodie his hand to shake and forced a smile onto his lips. "Time for a celebration then," he concluded with a smile. He disappeared into the kitchen and the sound of a cork popping echoed around the lobby.

"Oh, oh! Campaign. I'll help!" Jas charged in behind him and Amy tensed at the ensuing noises involving the chink of delicate glass.

"Campaign!" Hana snorted. "What is he like?"

Bodie bit his lip and fought to hide his obvious stress as she hugged him and asked for details of the proposal. "Tell you later," he whispered.

Jas' portion of champagne matched the one Logan allowed Hana. She wrinkled her nose in disdain before clinking glasses with everyone in the circle.

"To the Johal family," Logan said.

Hana's face clouded almost imperceptibly and she knew Logan noticed. She experienced mixed emotions at being distanced from the Johal name as though cast out over time without having noticed. A sadness bit deep in her gut that seemed about more than just a change of title. The Johals had released her and let her go. Hana smiled and showed an interest in Jas' antics. She did all the things expected of her, but Logan saw her pain and it caused his jaw to tighten.

Jas fell asleep on the lounge rug and snored amidst jokes about lightweights and his inability to hold his drink. Hana slapped her son's arm. "Don't be mean," she chided. "He had two sips." Her lip curled. "The same as me."

"So tell us about the proposal then," Logan demanded, raising an eyebrow which revealed his curiosity.

"Tell us about yours," Bodie bit back. "You never quite got around to it."

Hana opened her mouth to oblige but Logan got there first. "Hana was naked," he said, his lips quirking in a lopsided smile. She kicked him under the table but too late. Bodie recoiled.

"On second thoughts, don't bother," he snapped.

"I was getting in the bath," Hana protested, looking to Amy for solidarity. "And I wasn't naked!"

Bodie shuddered. "I don't want to hear it."

"He proposed at the station." Amy interrupted, tapping the table for attention. "He took Jas out of kindy early so he could be there and it felt special." Her cheeks flushed pink. "I loved it."

"Did he get on one knee?" Hana asked and Amy nodded.

"Yes. In the charge room in front of my team and a few guys arrested for burglary."

Bodie rolled his eyes, the memory giving him discomfort. Logan pursed his lips to stop himself laughing and Bodie jabbed a finger in his direction. "At least she had clothes on!"

"Oh, stop you two!" Hana groaned. Her smile took on the strain of tiredness. "Thanks for pulling Logan from Hamilton

Lake, Bo," she said, leaning across to pat the dark fingers picking at a knot in the table top. "He told me."

"Shouldn't have bothered," Bodie grumbled and through the corner of her eye, Hana saw Logan grin. She sensed nothing would suppress their rivalry over her affection, not even life threatening danger.

"Is there a ring?" Hana asked, having already spotted the rock on Amy's finger. She held out her hand palm upwards and Amy rested her fingers against it. "Gorgeous," Hana concluded. To her surprise, Logan inspected it over her shoulder. He nodded in approval.

"Nice. Princess cut diamond. Must have cost you a decent chunk of money."

Bodie's colour intensified and he flushed to the roots of his hair. "Mind your own damn business!"

Logan threw back his head and laughed, the mirth fading from his eyes as Hana glared at him. Amy twinkled her fingers and inspected the stone set into the shiny gold band. "I wasn't expecting it. I thought he didn't like me anymore." Her statement reminded Hana of the night Tama threatened her and she straightened her spine and forced herself to beat down the rising panic in her breast. Tama lay low at the hotel, Logan's hotel, the one he'd invited her to for a family Christmas. "Apparently there's no more sex until the wedding." Amy's comment threw Hana off guard and the champagne Logan spat out dribbled along her forearm. She looked at it and then at him, her lips parting in disgust.

"Sorry." He fetched a roll of kitchen paper and warded it like a weapon. "I'll check on Jas."

Bodie's groan filled the kitchen as Logan retreated. "Do you have to tell everyone?" he demanded. His misery increased, seeming to beat him into the chair. He glanced up at Hana. "I've been speaking to Pastor Allen. I'm trying to right some wrongs."

Hana smiled at her son, willing her face to show her approval as she mopped up splatter from her sleeve. He smiled back with gratitude.

When Logan returned with the news that Jas still hugged the carpet, the conversation moved to the subject of Laval. Hana felt herself diminish, her muscles tightening beneath her and a sweat breaking out on her brow. She glanced at Logan's face, his wounds healing with characteristic slowness but marking him forever with the trace of violence.

"The guys at the station think you're a hero," Amy said, interrupting Bodie's version of events. "Odering might get a promotion out of this. The suits tasked him two years ago with shutting Laval's operation down."

Logan shook his head, pursing his lips and remaining coy. Hana's brow knitted and she rested her fingers on his thigh, sensing the conflict coming from him in waves of alarm.

"Did he tell you that?" Bodie looked annoyed and turned to face Amy. "Even I didn't know that."

"Yeah. He's got a wife and kids in Auckland," Amy said. "He's trying to persuade them to move south to Hamilton."

"Oh." Bodie shrugged. "I quite like the guy. He let me take part in the operation."

Logan ran a hand over his face and squirmed beneath the scrutiny of the conversation. He shifted in his chair and touched the bridge of his nose with tentative movements.

"Laval's on remand at Waitakere Prison," Amy interjected. "His new guys are being held at a different facility. Odering's charged them with attempted murder for dumping Logan into the lake. He's spending long nights at the office, clearing up the different elements of the case."

"I'm sad about the old lady," Hana said, her voice softening. "I prayed she wasn't really dead, but held somewhere by Laval until he got the box back."

Logan shifted in his seat and Bodie sighed. "Yeah, we found her at the lake. There's a record of local residents complaining about an unpleasant smell. The council did remedial work on an area of swamp and assumed that caused it. They did a lot of dredging work in the summer and it stirred up all sorts of crap. Eventually the smell lessened until everyone forgot about it. Odering got the council in and they excavated a drain outlet buried in a raised bank. It wasn't on the plans and caved in years ago. The manhole cover was masked by flax that got out of control and she was so far in, they wouldn't have found her with a cursory investigation. Much of her clothing had dispersed and washed into the lake."

Hana swallowed and her complexion paled. Logan shook his head at Bodie and drew a finger across his throat to shut him up. Hana gulped. "How can they be sure it's her if there's nothing left of her clothing or handbag? It might not be her. She might be hiding somewhere."

Bodie glanced at Logan and spread his hands, looking for guidance. Hana sighed. "Just finish it, please. Otherwise, I'll always wonder if she's sunning herself in Fiji instead."

"Okay, well, they pulled her out, her skeleton mainly intact although the wildlife inhabitants of the lake made the most of her being there. Dental records and DNA positively identified her." One more look at Logan's narrowed grey eyes silenced Bodie. Hana kept her head down and chewed at a snagged nail on her ring finger.

"There were others too," Bodie said, unable to help himself. "This proved the most lucrative is all." Hana shuddered. Bodie continued, the thrill of the tale overriding his mother's discomfort. He looked everywhere but at Logan. "Laval seemed like a plausible old man when I saw him. White-haired, wrinkly, glasses, a limp and a cane. It's amazing how people aren't what they seem, isn't it?"

Everyone around the table except Logan, nodded. Hana remained still and quiet. "Where does he live?" she asked into the silence. Logan's gaze slid sideways in recognition of her strange question.

"One of the units at a residential estate, funnily enough." Bodie gave a small laugh. "He didn't even whoop it up with everything he stole. Bizarre. No idea how he found guys to work for him, not in Alder Dale."

Logan gripped Hana's fingers and gave them a squeeze. They sweated beneath his, sticky and wet. He leaned forward and stared his stepson down. His voice sounded laden with warning. "Guess what everyone? Bodie's gonna shut up now."

Bodie's eyes flashed with anger but to Hana's surprise, he obeyed.

"Yeah, let's talk about something else." Amy joined the consensus with a nervous glance at Logan. Hana looked pale and sick, the healthy glow from her time in the south quickly gone.

"It doesn't work." Hana spoke into the silence. She appealed to Logan with her eyes. "It makes little sense. All those weeks of car-swapping with Angus, yet Laval lived in the same complex the whole time. I was either very fortunate or the alternatives aren't great. Maybe he knew exactly where I was." She turned to her husband. "Could he have been playing with me?" She swallowed at the sight of the cuts and bruises healing on Logan's face. He never complained. She gripped his fingers and when he looked at her, she bit her lip. Instinct told her it wasn't over. His fingers squeezed hers beneath the table and they shared that rare electrical connection which arced between them, offering the only solid base to build anything on.

"Tell me about my new nephews?" Bodie demanded, changing the subject. Logan retrieved the shiny phone Marcus helped him choose and flicked through the photos. They all laughed at Elizabeth sitting on Marcus' head eating an ice cream. Her little mouth opened wide in a giggle, white tongue poking out and her eyes shut tight.

"Marcus had a shower after that," sniggered Hana.

Bodie smiled and stared at the photo of his friend. "I should see more of them," he said wistfully. "The boys look cute, just like Izzie when she was little. Gosh!" He peered with interest at the next photo, the baby boys propped up together against the arm of the sofa. They resembled a set of falling dominoes. "That one's got reddish hair! Mum!" Bodie exclaimed. "Somebody has your genes!"

Hana grinned and nodded with enthusiasm. "I noticed that," she said. Her eyes sparkled. "Under certain lights, one of the boys has a strawberry hint amongst Marcus' mousey tufts. There's hope for this family yet."

"What about this baby?" Amy jerked her head towards Hana's stomach and she wrinkled her nose.

"She's like Logan. I can feel it." Hana ran a hand over her bump and the men observed her like a scientific experiment.

"How do you know?" Bodie demanded.

Hana shrugged. "Just do."

"A girl." Amy zeroed in on the most important fact. "Congratulations."

Bodie returned to the photos, scrolling through Logan's collection with a hunger in his eyes. "The other little boy has black hair like us," he said, ring fencing the Johals without realising it.

"Ah well." Hana sighed. "Who knows how anything will turn out? They have their whole lives ahead of them."

"Izzie texted me about the car," Bodie said, directing his comment at Logan. Logan bit his bottom lip and stared back at him, his grey eyes flashing a warning.

"They need to get rid of it," Hana said, misunderstanding. "It's a heap. I didn't drive it, but you did yesterday, didn't you, Logan?"

Logan looked back at Hana and lifted his hand to brush a strand of curly hair from her eye. "Yeah, I did. You look tired, babe."

She blinked and rested her cheek on his palm as he left it there. "I am."

Amy prodded Bodie beneath the table and for once he silenced. A quick rap on the front door and the turn of a key revealed Maihi. She wore a large anorak and carried a casserole dish. Hemi followed, stamping his boots outside on the porch to shake off the mud. They brought a draught inside with them.

Logan jumped to his feet and welcomed them, pressing his nose to theirs in turn and greeting them as family.

"Kia ora koutou katoa." Hemi's deep voice rumbled a greeting meant to include everyone. "How are you, tamaiti tāne?" He lowered his voice to speak to Logan, gripping his shoulders and staring into the younger man's eyes with incredible perception.

"I'm good," Logan replied. "No worries."

Hemi nodded and his bear like paws clapped Logan on both shoulders. "Tēnā, tēnā, that's good."

Maihi made a beeline for Hana and squashed her from behind after laying the dish on the counter. "How's my girl?" she whispered, hugging Hana and kissing the side of her face.

"Great thanks." Hana waved her into a seat. "Thank you for looking after the house."

Maihi waved her hand in dismissal. "Oh, that's fine. We stole your cat and had a party every night." Hana laughed, her brow narrowing at Maihi's serious expression. "No, for real," Maihi interjected. "Tiger's moved in with us. He don't want to come back no more. He's in love with Ginger."

Hana's mouth formed a little 'o' of surprise and her expression saddened. "But he'll come back now we're home, won't he?"

"Na, I think you've lost him." Maihi grabbed mugs for her and Hemi and filled them with tea. Her words sounded so matter of fact, but left Hana with a burgeoning sense of loss.

Maihi took over the kitchen, heating the casserole and dishing up portions for everyone. She took a peek at Jas and found him still flaked out on the rug. "I'll leave some in the pot for the boy," she said, winking at Amy.

They finished dinner and Maihi waxed lyrical over the photos of Hana's grandbabies. If she noticed the characteristic features of Elizabeth's Down syndrome she made no comment, drawn only to the extra unpaired gene which produced a tiny face filled with joy. Blissful happiness radiated from the small girl like a haze and Hana felt a prick of sadness at the physical distance between them. She sighed. "I've enjoyed reconnecting with Beth. She's like a perfect ray of sunshine."

"Oh!" A tone of disappointment accompanied the small face which appeared at Hemi's elbow. Jas' tousled head nosed its way in to look at the pictures. "You've seen my baby without me!" Hana's eyes shrouded with guilt. She looked to Amy for help, but Logan came to the rescue first.

"I have something for you," he said. "Come with me." He reached out his hand and Jas clasped it, clutching his blanket under his arm. The child followed Logan from the room, but not before he'd eyeballed Hana such a withering look of betrayal that she felt actual physical pain.

He returned in Logan's arms, riding high on his hip and beaming. Still clutching the blanket, his other hand gripped a photo frame. He leaned precariously towards Amy as Logan set him on his mother's knee. "Look," he announced. "Look what Poppa gave me."

The frame contained a picture of Izzie's children. Elizabeth sat in the middle, squinting at the camera and Izzie leaned over the back of the sofa, holding each of her daughter's skinny arms around a tiny boy. They'd printed a physical copy on Marcus' aged printer and stuck it in Hana's suitcase.

She glanced up at her husband, marvelling at the sleight of hand which replaced a cherished photo in a wooden frame with the rugged print. Hana held her breath, realising she needed to practice recognising the great things about Logan and forgiving the negative. "Thanks, babe," she mouthed to him, knowing he'd removed an aerial photo of the hotel from the hand carved frame.

Jas accepted his bowl of casserole from Logan with a sweet little smile and dug into it. The blanket slipped to the ground, but the photo frame remained clamped between the little fingers of his left hand. Jas caught Bodie observing him and pointed his spoon at the frame, smearing tomato on the glass. "Them's my fambly," he said, adding a few more prods for good measure and obscuring Izzie's face. "I'm gonna look after them all forever!"

Bodie smiled at his son and made appreciative noises. But Jas' gaze moved to Logan for approval. Hana heard her husband whisper beneath his breath, "Good boy! Always protect your whānau." Jas nodded, understanding in his eyes. Hana's mind flicked to Tama and she pushed past the memory of his arrogance and cocky aggression. She forced herself to see the desperation in his eyes and the keen sense of fear. Trapped between two factions of the Du Roses, he'd seen no other way. She shuddered and buried the rising compassion. He still threatened a pregnant woman. She still despised him.

Hana enjoyed the gathering and the laughter which filled her kitchen. Maihi and Hemi left on the quad bike around ten and despite the offer of beds for the night, Bodie insisted he take Amy and Jas home. He hugged Hana before he left, clasping her close as though trying to communicate something through his spirit. She pulled back and looked into his eyes, searching for some clue as to his real emotions. Her maternal instinct sounded an alarm but Bodie offered her no help. "Are you okay?" she whispered and he nodded.

"Of course." His tone sounded abrasive and Hana tensed, expecting him to berate her for reading into everything. Logan offered his hand to shake and Bodie clasped his fingers.

"Congratulations," Logan said.

"Thanks." Bodie left, not taking the pervading sense of unease with him.

Hana stood on the cold porch, her left hand stroking her bump. Logan waved as the BMW disappeared around the first bend and the headlights bounced down towards the road. He wrapped his arms around Hana and kissed the top of her head. "Is it just my perception, or was that the weirdest visit?" he asked. "He's proposed to Amy, but doesn't want to get married."

"I'm not sure," Hana mused. "But I know exactly what you mean. He didn't seem happy."

Logan snorted. "I've never seen Bodie happy, babe. I doubt he was born with that setting."

Hana elbowed him in the ribs and he grunted. Turning, he winked at her and leaned his back against the balustrade of the widow's walk. A cool breeze ruffled his hair and he stared up at the overhead stars. The Milky Way soared above them like a wide stripe of glittering light, interspersed with patches of indigo and black. Logan named the constellations for Hana, leaning with his chin on her shoulder to point out the delights of Creation. Like a riotous motorway above their heads, it twinkled and shone for their pleasure.

"It looks amazing from the ridge at the top of the mountain," Logan said. "I'll show you one day."

"Is that the land your grandmother left you?" Hana asked, still staring upwards.

Logan nodded into the darkness and squeezed her hand. "Yeah."

"I'd love to see it," Hana said. "Will you point the same stars out for me?"

"Soon," he replied, his voice wistful. "Soon."

Chapter 36

"I've worked here too long," Hana grumbled, watching Pete slide from the room as soon as Logan appeared in the doorway. The sports teacher shot furtive glances over his shoulder like a dog looking for approval after chewing up the lounge rug.

"Maybe it's time for a change then," Logan soothed, a wistful look in his grey eyes. "For both of us."

Hana shrugged. "Perhaps. I'm not sure what's wrong with me. This was my happy place after Vik died, somewhere I could just be Hana instead of a widow, mother, problem solver and sergeant major." She ran a tired hand over her eyes. "I've worked for three careers advisors and seven counsellors since I took the job. They're all different. I don't like change."

Logan leaned the smooth seat of his pants on the corner of her desk and observed her with narrowed eyes. "What's prompted this? Is Sheila moving on?"

"Dunno." Hana leaned back in her seat and stretched, her stomach protruding forward like a rolling hill. Logan's fingers twitched as though resisting the urge to stroke it. "She's having a long distance relationship with that university rep. Her phone keeps blowing up. Pete reckons she's sexting."

Logan recoiled with obvious distaste. "People are so stupid," he commented. "They put the most ridiculous stuff out there and then complain when it's public knowledge."

Hana grinned and bit her bottom lip. Her eyelashes fluttered and she jabbed a finger in his direction. "Words of wisdom from a man who keeps physical ledgers and hates email. Easier for cooking the books, hey Logan?"

His lips twisted into a sardonic smile and he gave a slow blink. "I do no such thing, Mrs Du Rose. And I love my spreadsheets and data analysis. I just don't make it accessible to the entire world."

Hana waggled her eyebrows and crinkled her nose. "I can't imagine anyone hacking Sheila's randy texts with a chap who needs a nose hair trimmer."

Logan made a fake vomiting noise in his throat and held his hands out in front of him. "Stop," he pleaded. "Not so close to lunchtime, please!" He bent to kiss her, his eyes sparkling with the hint of fire. "See you later, Mrs Du Rose."

Pete shuffled in through the back door as Logan left. Hana sighed. "You shouldn't listen to private conversations."

"I hoped you might talk about me." He flung himself into his chair and pushed papers around on his desk.

"Sorry to disappoint you." Hana rose and peered over his shoulder. Her stomach nudged him against the side of the head as she leaned forward. "Pete! Are these reports from the first term?"

"Get away from my desk!" Pete flattened his upper body across a sheaf of papers bearing coffee stains and pie grease. "Leave me alone."

"You'll miss me," Hana threw over her shoulder as she grabbed a packet of cleaning wipes. The plastic crinkled beneath her fingers and she dragged a wipe free and brushed it across a shelf.

"What?" Pete's complexion drained to an unhealthy ashen. "You're not coming back after your maternity leave, are you?"

He rose and took a tentative step towards her. "Please, don't leave me, Hana. I need you here."

"I don't know what I'm doing, Pete," she answered truthfully. "Because then I have to face the fact that this giant bump needs to come out. Just let me get past that hurdle before I make career decisions."

"Don't leave!" Pete's eyes moistened. "You're my only friend."

Hana's jaw hung slack and she closed her lips with a snap. "That's not true, Pete." She scratched around for names, realising she couldn't dredge up any at short notice.

"It is true." Liquid welled over the red rims of his eyes and cascaded down his cheek. "Logan won't speak to me, so I only have you left. Don't go, please?"

Hana put her hands on her hips. "Pete! Yesterday you slapped my bum because you said it blocked your view everywhere you looked. I thought you'd be glad to get rid of me."

"No, no!" Pete wrung his hands. "I didn't mean it. I love your bum." His face paled. "You didn't tell Logan about that, did you? He'll bloody kill me!"

"I didn't!"

"Don't leave me?" Pete repeated, his voice plaintive and a sniff escaping.

"You're serious?" Hana's eyes widened. She cringed as he took a lengthy stride towards her. "Oh, gosh, no thanks. You don't need to...okay then."

Pete seized her in a bear hug and sniffled into her shoulder. Hana patted him on the back and tried to stop her eyes crossing at the sight of dandruff within inhaling distance. He smelled like an old sofa. "I love you, Hana," he mumbled from underneath her hair.

Hana stiffened. "That's nice. You can let go now." She administered one final pat and dropped her arms. Pete clung on. The scent of greasy hair wafted into her nostrils and she struggled to hold her breath. "Hi, Logan," she said, when he still didn't let go.

Pete gave her a hearty shove to the collarbone which sent her jetting backwards at speed. She lost her footing and a lucky twist of fate sat her in her own office chair. The force swivelled her around to face her desk and left a ringing in her ears. Pete's head whipped from side to side as he spun in a circle, terror emanating from beneath his hooded eyelids. "She started it!" he screeched. "It's all her fault."

Hana shook her head and smirked, settling her fingers over her keyboard and tapping out an email. "So much for friendship, Pete," she mused. "You'd sell your own granny."

Pete shot her a filthy look and slumped into his chair. "I'll still miss you, you bitch!" he griped. Hana turned her chair and gave him a beatific smile of pure, one hundred watt angel. Pete snorted. "I hear Logan's doing well as usual. Angus says his English senior mock exam results were the best the school's ever seen. His younger students also produced a higher cumulative grade than they did last year under Foggy.

"Why did you call her Foggy?" Hana asked. "I never worked it out."

"Because she never knew where she was," Pete frowned. "It's obvious. She walked around in a fog."

Hana shook her head and tapped numbers into a spreadsheet. Pete sighed and continued as though reading from a pamphlet dedicated to Logan's achievements. "The departmental staff enjoy his no-nonsense leadership and Angus is relieved he can re-route the talented teacher to physical education, health, mathematics or French classes, as easily as he can to English, should the need arise. He has even had requests for him in accounting, following a period of relief teaching that proved successful."

Hana whipped round in her chair. "Are you reading from something?"

Pete pursed his lips and slid a piece of paper back under the pile of ratty, coffee stained documents. "No."

"Yes you are!" Hana stood up and eyed him with a nasty glare. "Is that a copy of an official document?"

Pete looked shifty and squirmed in his seat. "Not a copy, no. It's Logan's appraisal. I nicked it off the Rottweiler's desk."

Hana's mouth dropped open. "Pete! You stole it from the desk of Angus' scary assistant? Apart from the high five I want to give you for your audacity that's a sackable offence!"

He made an ugly face and cringed. "I know. She only left her desk for a second and I don't understand what came over me. I just saw his name while I was cutting out a magazine picture of Angelina Jolie in a bikini. The Rottweiler's scissors were on her desk and she must have just printed the document. I wanted to see if Logan was coping without me."

"Pete! You're a shocker!"

"Help me?" His bottom lip wobbled.

"No!" Hana flounced back to her desk and sat down. "You're on your own with that one. And if I find it on my desk, you're dead! Deal with it yourself."

Hana entered more numbers and worked for a while. Pete sniffed and fidgeted, driving her mad with his irritating noises. A memory rose unbidden to the forefront of Hana's mind and she stopped working. She touched her desk with gentle fingers, remembering the day she accidentally ended up with a large silver trophy sitting there, many months ago. Dobbs turned the school inside out looking for it and Hana worried about getting it back to the trophy table without being spotted. She went out on an errand and when she got back, the trophy was gone, returned to its rightful place. Pete got the blame. "Pete," she said with kindness. "That day the trophy ended up in my possession and I left it on the desk, did you put it back for me, to stop me getting into trouble?" She turned so she could see his face and read if he was lying.

"Yeah," he said and nodded.

Hana sighed. "You're a terrible liar."

Pete collapsed forward like a deflated balloon. "Just help me. You can put it back, she likes you."

"No she doesn't. She hates Logan because he's not scared of her, so I'm hated by association. Just for once, Peter North. Tell me the truth!"

"Okay. Logan put the trophy back."

"What? Don't be ridiculous. I didn't even know Logan then!"

"No but he knew you, didn't he? He came to borrow a stapler and saw it there. Before I could stop him, he'd nipped it back downstairs to the trophy table. He said if I told you, he'd staple my head to the noticeboard and if there was any backlash from Dobbs, he'd take the fall."

"Oh," Hana breathed. She felt the hot flush begin in her chest. Logan looked out for her, even back then. The hot new teacher who got female hearts racing in the staffroom and whose grey eyes always seemed turned towards Hana, risked a wrangle with Dobbs for her. "I'm so lucky," she sighed.

"Yeah, you are. So put this paper back for me?" Pete begged. "And don't tell Logan I told you any of that."

"That's two things," Hana said. "I'll do one and you do the other."

Pete looked hopeful. "Yeah?"

"Yeah. I'll put the paper back on the secretary's desk and you confess to Logan you slapped my bum and told me the truth about the trophy."

Pete's eyes widened and he slammed his palms down on the desk. A pile of reports slid onto the floor. "Bloody women!" he shouted. He snatched up Logan's appraisal and marched towards the door. He exited, muttering to himself and Hana held her snort until he stamped out of earshot.

Pete returned without the paper but his ears shone red around the rims. "She shouted at me!" he complained. "I told her it got muddled up with my pages."

"Well, you're still alive, so that's good," Hana replied. "Even though you lied." She peered at a set of numbers which didn't make sense.

"Will you go to the hotel again this weekend?" Pete asked, his irritation replaced by sadness and Hana nodded.

"We go most weekends so Logan can work on the farm. They're short-handed. You should talk to him." Only a few weeks into the new term and exhaustion chased her like a relentless fiend. Hana felt as though she spent most of her life in the car.

Pete put his head down and placed pen marks on the sheets in front of him. "I can't!" he growled. Hana peeked over his shoulder on the way to the bathroom later, expecting to see him marking. Instead she saw his pen scratching noughts and crosses on a boy's assignment. She sighed heavily and shook her head.

Logan's classroom door stood open as he planned for the next lesson. His fringe hung over his eyes and he wiped stanzas of poetry from the board in long strokes. Hana pushed the door, jumping at the agonising creak it made. Logan turned to her with a ready smile. "What's up, babe?" Seeing no urgency in either her expression or body language, he continued cleaning the white surface with a tatty cloth.

"Nothing." Hana slipped through the gap and ran her fingers along the obstacles in her way. A table, a chair, Logan's wide desk. She leaned against a pillar and watched her husband's calculated movements. "Shakespeare," she mused, reading the last of the lines still not smudged.

"Yeah." Logan sighed, the sound filled with tiredness. "The boys mangled it."

"Sorry." Hana ran a hand across her bump. "Must we drive to the hotel this weekend?"

Logan's fingers stilled and he dropped the cloth onto his desk. "Why? Don't you want to?"

Hana shrugged. "I'm just tired, Logan. We both work full time and then drive to the hotel most Fridays. You put in a full weekend's work and then we drive home. I feel like a hamster on a wheel."

His lips tightened and Hana watched his jaw work in his cheek. She sensed his tension. "I don't mind going up on my own."

She swallowed. "You'd go without me?" Hurt laced her voice. "Oh."

Logan's eyes implored her for clemency. "Dad's got really forgetful lately Hana. If I don't go, I get a million texts from the stockmen complaining over how slack he is."

"So what about once the baby arrives? Do you honestly think I'll want to pack up and drive up there every weekend? And don't even consider abandoning me, Logan. It won't fly."

Logan ran a hand over his face and leaned against the wall next to the board. The emotional distance between them stretched to painful levels. "I'll deal with it," he promised, an edge to his voice. "It's just at the moment. The developers are trying everything to keep their project going."

"But you blocked the road. And the district council have rolled over and your lawyer is sorting out compensation."

Logan nodded. "But they keep coming round wanting to negotiate, Hana. My mother can't cope."

"Please get it sorted before the baby comes, Logan." Hana closed the door after her and walked back to the office. Pete barely glanced up as she slouched into her seat and sulked.

The following Friday evening found her in Logan's bedroom at the hotel. The idea of staying at Culver's Cottage alone all weekend meant she accompanied him, although with increasing reluctance. Logan carried their overnight bags upstairs and then left Hana to unpack while he rushed away to meet his head stockman. When a sharp rap came on the bedroom door, she opened it with a faint hope that he'd returned with food and couldn't activate the keypad one handed.

"Is Logan here?" Tama tried to peer past her into the room and Hana recoiled.

"No! Stay away from me."

"But I need him to look over my assignment before I send it off." The teenager's face creased into a goofy grin. "The Correspondence School say I'm on track to graduate."

"Congrats." Hana shut the door in his face and leaned against it, unable to reconcile the eager young man with the home wrecker and woman threatener she remembered. He no longer looked like the spiteful boy who broke her husband's bones with a tyre wrench. "No," she whispered to the empty room. "Don't fall for it, Hana."

Another knock on the door made her bite the inside of her cheek. She flung it open with a barbed comment on her lips, only to find one of the dining room staff standing before her, hand still raised to knock again. "Bad time?" Helena asked, cocking her head on one side.

"No." Hana heaved out a sigh. "It's fine."

Helena's blonde hair flipped from side to side in its ponytail, reminding Hana of Logan's mare. "Leslie asked if you could help with dinner service this evening. We're short-handed."

Hana nodded with relief. The threat of another lonely evening slipped aside. "I'd love to." She patted her work clothes. "When do you need me?"

"Now." Helena gave her an apologetic smile. "Sorry."

"Five minutes." Hana held up her fingers. "I'll change fast and come straight down."

"Cool." Helena hurried away

Hana changed into a plain white blouse and hauled a pair of black maternity pants over her butt. She yanked her hair back into a bun and arrived in the kitchen within the allotted five minutes. Chaos met her. "Where's Miriam?" she demanded, dodging a line of women carrying plates through the open door.

"Don't ask," Helena whispered.

"Took to her bloody bed again," Leslie grumbled. "Last week."

"Last week?" Hana repeated the word, feeling foolish at Logan's lack of sharing. "Should I go to her?"

Leslie snorted. "Only if you want your head severing from your neck. Leave well alone, girly." She jerked her head towards the laden counter. "Grab three and get in line if you don't mind. I wouldn't ask if I wasn't desperate."

"It's okay." Hana balanced a dinner plate on her forearm and tipped her hand, splaying her thumb to take another. Her free hand took up the third and Leslie nodded in approval. She'd mastered the trick Miriam showed her weeks ago when she found herself drafted into the kitchen. Experience made it come easy and Hana proceeded across the corridor and into the back of the ballroom.

"Don't you mind Leslie bossing you around?" Helena asked as the women met back at the counter for the next wave of deliveries. "You're the boss' wife. You should take charge, not her."

Hana laughed, the tinkling sound echoing out into the corridor. "I couldn't run all this. I'm happier delivering plates and collecting dirties. Leslie does a great job." She kept her opinion about Leslie's capabilities to herself. Despite their current short-handed state, the woman ran service like a well-oiled machine, contrary to Miriam's hit and miss approach.

"Hana!" Leslie's voice called from the doorway. The large woman barrelled towards her like a ship in full sail and Helena snatched up three more plates and escaped. "In here." Leslie edged her towards the chiller and Hana went, feeling the bite of the cold air as she stepped inside. The light activated and the door banged the jamb behind them. Without the curiosity of the other women, Leslie softened with instant effect. "Your puku is showing," she said, her voice gentle.

Hana looked down and gasped. Her rounded stomach protruded through the bottom of the blouse which had parted in its eagerness to escape her trousers. "Damn!" she exclaimed. "Sorry."

"No worries." Leslie undid the black apron at her waist and wound it around Hana's. Spinning her, she tied it at the back. Her eyebrows furrowed and she grunted in satisfaction. "That's better kōtiro. Don't want Mr Logan's business on show yet, do we?" She grinned, revealing a missing tooth in the lower set. The openness changed her face and Hana relaxed.

"Thank you."

Leslie reached up and squeezed Hana's left shoulder. "No, thank you." She sighed and ran a tired hand over her nose, dragging it down to her mouth before dropping it to her side. Exhaustion lingered in the action. "The missus does this often. Things don't go her way so she lays in bed and forces poor Alfie to take care of her."

"Logan called it Bi-polar disease once." Hana narrowed her eyes. "You think it's something else?"

Leslie raised her hands in front of her as though in self-defence. Her expression told Hana she regretted the comment. "It's whatever they wanna call it," she said, her eyes reflecting an insincere sentiment. Hana gave a non-committal smile and jerked her head towards the chiller door.

"We should get back," she said and Leslie nodded.

Hana filled her arms with plates and joined the line behind Helena again. "Who are these diners?" she asked as she balanced her load.

Helena nodded towards a whiteboard just visible at the end of the corridor. It stood in the lobby with the name of a company written on it in capital letters. Hana leaned sideways before giving up as gravy from the roast threatened to drip from the plate. "I can't read it."

"It's an engineering company." Helena moved forward and the line of women shifted as one. "They've hired the venue, motel suites and ordered the full menu. There's a Christmas dinner tonight followed by a seminar tomorrow. They'll check out late-afternoon."

"I'll help strip the rooms after they leave," Hana offered.

"Thanks." Helena paused at the ballroom doors and jerked her head towards the far corner of the room. "You can start with the last table on the right. I'll finish up the one before it."

A strange déjà vu came over Hana as she delivered the meals. The group of men barely regarded her as she slipped their meals before them. They continued talking as she backed away. Helena waited for her. "What's wrong, Hana?"

"Nothing." Her brow furrowed. "I feel I should know those men."

Helena shrugged. "You shouldn't be waiting tables, anyway. I'm guessing you'll take over the bookings."

"It's pointless." Hana followed her into the kitchen. "We're not here enough. Logan's got staff issues with the farm. Once that's sorted, I imagine he'll put in managers."

Helena halted and Hana almost ran up her back. Turning sideways at the last moment to avoid clattering her bump, she gasped. "That's not what I heard," Helena said. "Has Mr Logan said that?"

"No." Hana drew out the word as dread filled her heart.

"Come on girls!" Leslie exclaimed. "We're not done yet."

Hana picked up the remaining three plates as Helena set off ahead of her. Her hands shook and she forced herself to shelve her misgivings and concentrate on finishing the dinner service without making a fool of herself. The men at the table nodded their thanks and Hana fetched an extra salt shaker for a man still wearing his suit jacket. His brow furrowed as he looked up to thank her. Their fingers touched and Hana recoiled in shock. The shaker dropped to the tablecloth and white powder sprinkled itself like snow. The man's lips parted but before he could speak, Hana bolted. She strode towards the ballroom doors, her little legs pounding out a hurried tattoo on the floorboards.

The whiteboard in the reception revealed the full horror of Hana's realisation. Her fingers scrabbled at its flimsy frame to hold her upright as she fought to control her heaving breaths. "Oh, God!" she pleaded beneath her breath. "Oh, God." All colour faded from her cheeks as two worlds collided before her eyes and the innocent words, *Key Largo Engineering*, blurred before her.

Running footsteps heralded Leslie. "Is it the baby?" Her gnarled hands ran up and down Hana's back, as though she felt a horse's legs for soundness. "Shall I get Mr Logan?"

Hana shook her head. "No, I'm fine. Just felt a little faint." Sweat beaded on her forehead.

"Sit down here." Leslie led her to a sofa in the wide lobby and Hana gazed towards the bathroom doors with longing. The urge to lock herself into a cubicle for the weekend overrode any sense of dignity. Leslie gave a tug on her arm. "Sit," she ordered and Hana obeyed, sinking into the sumptuous fabric with an awkward plop. "I need to go back to the kitchen." She looked conflicted, her lips turned down and her eyes narrowed. "I'll send someone to help you upstairs."

"I don't need anyone." Hana leaned forward and rested her elbows on her knees. Adrenaline surged through her bloodstream, leaving her heady and sick.

Leslie's footsteps clattered away. "I'll send someone," she promised and Hana ignored her, concentrating on the blood pounding through her brain. A fresh breeze from the open front door smelled of evening in the bush, the sweet scents of kowhai and silver fern drifting into the lobby. Hana took fortifying breaths and forced herself to calm.

Footsteps approached, quick and light and Hana sighed. "I don't need anyone." Reaching behind her, she untied the apron strings and let the material slither loose. The end balled in her sweating fingers and the black fabric trailed to the floor. The breeze coasted over her rounded belly like a caress and Hana leaned forward, sighing as another button popped.

"I thought I recognised you," a woman's voice said.

Hana's head shot up and her gaze ate up the view of the impeccable grey pantsuit, expensive chiffon scarf and trademark blonde hair which cascaded over curvaceous breasts. Oozing elegance, the intervening nine years did nothing to dim her sex appeal. Hana groaned and remained stock still, willing her to disappear in a puff of smoke like a magic trick. She closed her eyes but when she opened them, the woman still stood over her.

"What do you want?" Hana asked, a tired sigh accompanying her words. "I thought you took it all."

A flicker of sadness marred the woman's face, lessening the sheen of her good looks and poise.

"I want nine wasted years back," she replied. "Can you give me that?"

Hana's teeth ground in her head and she snorted in disbelief. "Are you for real?" She struggled to rise to her feet and turned to face the object of her misery. "You think you had nine wasted years? Try being his wife!"

The woman's upper lip curled back in an ugly sneer. "Poor little Hana, just like always. He'd be alive today if you hadn't taken to your bed with some fake illness. We should have been at the airport and instead, he was getting your brats from school because you wouldn't."

Hana swallowed. "I had a kidney infection!" Injustice rose to choke her. She opened her mouth to protest her innocence but a vague inner wisdom warned her not to bother. She shook her head. "He must have told you some grand lies to get you to destroy a family. *My wife doesn't understand me. Our marriage is over.*" Latent fury drove her to mimic the voice of a man who'd been dead almost a decade. He'd separated in her memory. The loving husband. The cheating bastard. They were different men. Vik's mistress' presence forced them together in a painful clash of warring personalities. Loves me. Loves me not.

"You lost." Hana gritted her teeth. "For some reason he stayed with me and neither of us will ever know why. He took the kids to school and drove to work."

"He shouldn't have been at work." Hysteria strangled the woman's words and pity rose into Hana's breast. Her lips tightened and she shook her head.

"He shouldn't. Nobody should die that way." The memories assailed her like a sudden cold shower on a hot day. Emotions she couldn't name slid along her spine and paralysis rendered her legs useless. "Leave me alone." She flapped a hand in front of her face and rising, tried to negotiate the space between the glass coffee table and the edge of the sofa. The patterns on the rug confused her blurred vision as tears sprang behind her eyelids. The apron dropped to the floor and the glass glinted with flashes of red from the late sunset.

Her nemesis gasped. "You're pregnant!" Blue eyes shrouded in perfectly aligned eyeshadow and mascara widened and horror flashed across her face. The fight left the set of her shoulders. "You're over him." Her right index finger jabbed at Hana's stomach and she put her hands up to defend her unborn child. The woman's other hand clasped her own lips, smearing red lipstick over her cheek without care. Hana watched the action and thought of blood. Nausea sent darts of warning into her throat.

"Leave me alone!" she hissed. The distance between the end of the sofa and freedom seemed to shrink as the woman moved to block Hana's escape.

"You bitch!" the woman spat. She moved both hands to the side of her own face as though trying to crush the pain from her skull. "You bloody bitch."

Hana's body shook with fear as her heart rate spiked. The child moved in her womb and maternal instinct drove her backwards, her calves bumping against the sofa placed perpendicular to its matching partner. One hand protected her bump, the other outstretched in a warding off motion.

Vik's mistress advanced and with nowhere to go, Hana tightened every muscle against the imminent blow and closed her eyes. Nothing mattered to her but her baby.

"Hey," a firm voice rapped out. A thud put its owner between Hana and the woman, following a neat leap over the back of the sofa. "Go back to your party please miss, you've no business here." A cushion fell and bounced over Hana's foot, forcing her to open her eyes. She kept her gaze aimed at the floor, seeing the woman's neat stilettos back away in small degrees.

She released a ragged exhale and leaned her forehead against the broad back. A violent tremble rocked her from head to toe and the man in front of her spoke again. "Just go." His muscles moved as he raised a hand and pointed. Michael. Hana's desperate prayers had sent Michael, the rampant sex maniac turned avenging angel. She exhaled against his spine, seeing a familiar hand reach back for hers. She placed the fingers of her right hand between the blunted thumb and his open hand, accepting the contact like a lifeline. A rip across the sleeve of his polo shirt added to the recognition. She remembered him cursing as he noticed it during her fated honeymoon breakfast. Liza had laughed at his irritation. Hana pursed her lips and breathed, trying to establish a pattern less like hyperventilation. Thoughts of Liza didn't help and she forced them away.

The woman's shoes clattered through the lobby and gravel crunched underfoot as she made her escape. The sounds of crying came back to Hana on the breeze and her mind filled with the utter waste of it all. Nine years for each of them. A pointless wasteland. The sob left her lips and Michael turned in the small space. "It's okay," he soothed, his voice gentle. "She's gone." Strong arms enfolded her and Hana pressed her nose into the muscular chest and released the groan she held. It came from a pit deep in her soul, a nine-year-old chasm which had sealed itself beneath countless layers of grief and disappointment.

Chapter 37

"What the hell was that about?" he asked. Her saviour lifted her chin and forced her to look up at him. "Hana. What happened?"

Hana opened her eyes and gasped. Her feet scrabbled against the rug and he snatched hold of her wrists to prevent her falling backwards through the glass coffee table. "Get away from me!" she hissed, yanking one hand free and trying to break his grip on the other. "Leave me alone, Tama!"

He released her. The simple movement of his fingers opening sent Hana sideways instead, the sofa cushion coming up to meet her at speed and jarring her back. Instead of walking away, Tama sat down next to her, trapping her as surely as Vik's mistress had. "Are you okay?" he asked, his tone soft.

"You're wearing Michael's shirt." The sentence confused her as it wasn't the one in her head. Tama's lips quirked upwards in response.

"You're okay then."

Hana sighed. "I don't know, I don't know." She fanned her face with her hands and rose so fast, the blood drained from her head and she listed. "I need to get out of here."

Tama stood to allow her past but when he placed a hand in the small of her back to support her, she reacted with temper. Her elbow dug into his rips and he bent with a grunt. "Geez, Hana. Stop! I just need to make sure you're okay. Logan will kill me if I don't look out for you now."

"Now?" Hana spat, turning. "Why now and not before? You should have thought of that when you climbed into my car and threatened me." She didn't wait for his answer, running towards the corridor where she knew the spiral staircase lay. Hearing Tama's footsteps behind her she kept going past the bottom step, knowing she couldn't mount the awkward staircase without falling with him pursuing her. Lost in the annals of the house, she ran out of floorboards and an outside door met her. The metal bar of a fire exit gave beneath her palms and cool air filled her lungs as she crashed through and almost fell down a set of high steps.

"Wait! Wait!" Tama gripped her shoulders and held her upright. Spinning her, he faced her towards him and took the heat out of her hurried descent. "Careful," he stressed. "Take it slow." Pushing in front of her, he went backwards and held onto her wrists, tugging her after him like a cumbersome trailer.

At the bottom of the stairs, he paused and Hana focused on the gravel of the car park, planning to run as soon as he let go. "Hana," he whispered. "I'm sorry. I'm sorry for everything." He let her go and stepped back, his hands held up in front of him. "I'll fetch Uncle Logan. He'll know what to do." He turned away and then glanced back, angling his body so she could see the weight of fear in his eyes. "Please don't tell him I touched you though. I know you don't owe me anything, but I like my teeth the way they are."

Hana stared down at the gravel. "It's smoke and mirrors," she breathed. In answer to his grunt of confusion, she fixed her gaze on his angular face. A carbon copy of Michael Du Rose, he oozed the same primitive sexuality. "He never killed anyone." She repeated Logan's scoffed assurances and sighed. "He said so."

"Okay." Tama stuck his chin in the air and gave a shallow nod. He turned to face her again, digging his hands into his jeans pockets but leaving his blunted thumbs exposed. His father's shirt hung slack across the stomach and dipped down over his groin.

"I need to sit down." Hana gazed around her, seeing the steep staircase behind. She took a step towards it and Tama moved.

"There's a bench in Miriam's rose garden," he said, glancing across the car park towards an area of trees. "You can sit there."

Hana lifted her head and stared at the mountain rising behind it, a soaring mix of blue and green in the fading light. Tama snorted. "Don't even think it," he said, misunderstanding. "You'd get lost and be out there all night." Hana snatched at the tear which leaked onto her cheek and Tama sighed. "Come. I'll sit with you until you feel better. I won't come too close."

Hana studied his face and let out a sigh of hopelessness, the fight in her heart abandoning her. "Don't come near me," she insisted and he nodded.

He led her to the rose garden as the fading evening light dissipated. The scent of blooms still hung in the air after the day's heat. Tama slumped onto a wooden bench, stretching his arms across the back rail. He faced a small stone angel playing a harp, fixing his attention on it, as though it interested him above all else.

Hana hesitated before sitting, hugging the wooden arm at the farthest end of the bench. She shivered in the dwindling heat, the sweat on her clammy skin drying and leaving her cold. Tama pulled the polo shirt over his head, leaving his dark hair tousled. "Take this," he said, throwing it onto the seat next to her. He straightened the singlet beneath, youthful skin shrouding growing muscles. Hana lifted it with tentative fingers before wrapping it around her neck like a scarf.

"Thank you." The remnant of his warmth soothed the tight muscles in her neck and she dropped her hands, facing forwards like a candidate in a job interview.

"Who's the woman?" Tama kept his voice low. "Leslie said you felt sick. Why did she leave you with a woman screeching at you?"

"She didn't." Hana licked her lips. "I was alone when she left me."

"So, who is she?"

"Just a woman!" Hana snapped. "Nobody!"

Tama shook his head, a small smile gracing the edges of his lips. "I heard her, Hana. She tried to take someone away from you. Nine years puts Logan out of the frame so it must relate to your first husband. Did he cheat on you?"

"Shut up!" Hana's plea emerged as a hiss, tears obscuring her words. She clamped her hands over her ears in a futile act of self-preservation. The mess slithered around before her, a serpent refusing to crawl back into its charmer's basket. It threatened to throttle her and destroy her new life. She rocked forward on her seat and clasped her arms around her belly.

Tama slid across the bench and drew her resistant body into his side, whispering phrases meant to settle and calm a frightened horse. "It's okay," he whispered. "It'll be okay."

"I was a good wife," Hana groaned. "I just don't understand."

Tama wiped her cheek with a tender palm. He stroked her back and held her close as the sun waned and bathed the garden in shadows. His arms felt firm and strong around her and Hana experienced a flash of warning. Tama's affair with Anka caused her abandoned husband to feel everything of Hana's pain. She sat up and put some distance between them, relieved when Tama's fingers rested against the seat of the bench.

Tama dipped forward and rested his elbows on his knees. He shook his head twice and glanced sideways at Hana, his gaze falling on her rounded stomach. His brow knitted and Hana saw regret in the purse of his lips. "You're never gonna like me, are you?" he asked, an ill-timed swallow cutting his sentence in half.

She sniffed and straightened her spine. "I don't know," she replied. "Perhaps there's too much bad stuff between us."

Tama tipped his head sideways to stare at her. "There's years of it between Uncle Logan and me. But he forgave me." His sad smile made her next breath catch in her chest. She sensed he waited for her to reject him, twisting his fingers through each other and just waiting. It felt inevitable for them both.

Hana swallowed and her resolve faltered. "He's a better person than me," she concluded, as though conceding an argument.

Tama shrugged. "That's not what he says."

Hana tipped her head back against the seat and slumped down so she could look at the overhead stars. Logan overestimated her. Always.

Passing her fingers over her face, she felt the stickiness of her tears and scrubbed them away with the sleeve of her blouse. No ready answer presented itself and still Tama waited. Hana cleared her throat. "*Key Largo Engineering* employed my late husband. They sent him on the job that killed him, but he should've left the day before. With that woman. I don't know why he didn't and I wish I could ask him. I didn't know about his affair until the day after his funeral. She came to the house." Her voice faltered. "She blamed me for his death. Obviously still does." Hana sniffed and pushed her chin out in defiance. "It's always haunted me, the sense of unfinished business. I couldn't move on, not until Logan."

Tama nodded. "Your husband chose you."

Hana's head shook from side to side. "Perhaps he chose no one. He cheated on me because I wasn't good enough. I didn't become good enough overnight, Tama." She closed her eyes against the pain. "I'll never be good enough."

Tama's touch made her start and Hana opened her eyes in time to see his tear stained thumb wipe across his jeans. He stared at the wet trail in fascination. "I never saw it like that," he whispered. "It never occurred to me that Ivan might feel he wasn't good enough. He's a better man than I'll ever be." He gnawed on his lower lip and Hana watched him with a fresh perspective. His thumb dug into the bridge of his nose and he squeezed, his fingers forming the other half of the vice. "I loved her so much. I always will. There's something special about your first love and I didn't care who else got burned while I got to wake up next to her." He turned towards her and Hana held her breath. "Forgive me, Hana? I ruined your friendship with Anka and almost smashed the one relationship that meant something to Logan. I'm sorry."

Hana fought down her reluctance, captivated by the grey Du Rose eyes which offered her a view of Tama's damaged soul. She nodded, a shiver snaking its way around her heart. "I do, Tama. I forgive you."

The familiar portcullis crashed down over his relief and Hana saw Logan's genetic code reflected in his expression. "Thanks," he said. He jerked his head towards the hotel on the other side of the rose garden. "You should go inside. Leslie will send out a search party for you."

Hana sniffed and rose. "I won't tell Logan you touched me," she said, offering an olive branch.

Tama grinned, his eyes sparkling with unshed tears. "I'd deny it," he said. He swallowed. "He's foaling, anyway. Sacha went into labour and he wanted to see it through." His boots scuffed at the dry grass beneath his feet. "See ya, Hana."

"See ya, Tama." Hana left the garden and crept in through the wide front doors. She used the spiral staircase to the family wing and buried herself fully dressed in the empty bed. The open ranch slider sent a cool breeze to dry her tears and the voile curtains billowed out like a wedding dress. A weight pressed down between her legs and she ran a gentle palm across her stomach. The pressure seemed loosed from her upper abdomen and her breaths came with less of a hitch. Her child had engaged during the stress, forcing her head into the birth canal and planning her escape. Hana sighed, sensing more than a physical change in her world. She slept with an uncharacteristic peace, not hearing Logan's late night shower as he washed Sacha's blood from his forearms.

Chapter 38

Hana watched Logan sleep. Peace enveloped him in slumber, yet evaded his waking moments. She resisted the urge to stroke his stubbled cheek, not wishing to wake him though bored with her own company. His fingers clasped the material of her blouse and she squirmed beneath the constriction of her clothing. "Nice work, Hana," she whispered to herself. "What kind of idiot goes to bed fully dressed?" Buttons dug into her stomach and she reached for Logan's fingers, eager to release the fabric from his grasp and escape the bed. He grunted in sleep and shifted, transferring his grip from the blouse to Hana's hand.

She sighed in defeat. For a while, she entertained herself counting the scars on his long, olive fingers, trying to remember the story for each separate injury. Finding too many to count, she gave up and examined his thumb instead. Different to Michael's it housed a kink from a soccer injury, but otherwise matched the slender arc of his fingers. Strong and capable, it had been party to horse breaking, steer mustering and wielding a delicate stick of chalk. "You're an enigma, Logan Du Rose," Hana breathed. "You're too many people rolled into one."

Hana sensed his gaze on the side of her face and froze, embarrassment sending a flush to her cheeks. Logan inhaled and stretched, without letting go of her hand. "I'll settle for just husband, right now," he said, his tone teasing.

Hana laughed. "And I bet I know why." She wrestled her hand free, squeaking as Logan snatched it back and held it to his chest.

"What's so interesting about my hand?" he demanded, pulling her body against his.

Hana shrugged and the amusement faded from her eyes. She swallowed and shuttered her misery at the previous night's memories. "Nothing," she lied. "Did Barry have thumbs like you and Michael?"

"Dunno." Logan kissed the end of her nose. "They spent the whole time bunched into a fist, bashing my face in."

Hana's brow knitted and she pursed her lips, knowing better than to venture into those recollections. Logan smirked. "You can caress something else," he whispered and Hana shook her head in mock exasperation.

"I don't feel great today," she said, pushing herself upright. She glanced sideways at him and saw only concern in his expression.

"What's wrong?" His eyes narrowed and he leaned up on one elbow, running a gentle palm across her stomach. "Why are you dressed?"

Hana shrugged and flung the covers back, escaping from the bed before Logan could probe further. "I got tired waiting tables." She paused on the way to the bathroom. "Please may I hang around with you today? I don't feel like waitressing."

"You needn't work when we come home," Logan sighed. His long fingers pulled at a tassel on the pillowcase. "I'd rather you rested."

Hana snorted from the bathroom. "What, in bed with you?"

Logan licked his lips and waited for her to finish washing her hands and return to the bedroom. His pupils dilated as Hana removed her blouse and dragged the black trousers over her underwear. "Yeah," he breathed. "In bed with me."

Hana felt the familiar stirring in her chest as she glimpsed the desire in his eyes. Darts of lust cascaded into her stomach. "Did you know most of the women in this place would love to swap places with me?" She smiled and bit her lip. "They all think you're hot."

Logan screwed his face into a pout. "Well please don't. Waking up opposite Leslie without her teeth in will scar me for life!"

Hana shrieked with laughter and clapped a hand over her mouth. "That's mean!" she chided. "You don't like her, do you?"

Logan shrugged. "No, Hana."

"But she's been lovely to me."

"Good, I'm thrilled for you. And as a special thank you, I won't sack her this year."

Hana opened her mouth to demand explanations and Logan leapt from the bed. Before she could bolt, he seized her in his arms and kissed her to silence her questions. "Leave it, Hana," he whispered. "It's ancient history and needs to stay there. Now wake me up properly, like a good little wife."

"You sexist pig!" Hana squealed and tried to wriggle free.

"Did you say, sex?" Logan laughed. "Wow, great minds think alike. Yes please." He held onto her forearms and pulled her back towards the bed, pressing his lips over hers and teasing them apart with his tongue. His fingers worked her underwear free and Hana became putty in his hands.

The day waned and sunshine glared through a crack in the curtains. Hana sat up in the wide bed and the sheets puddled beneath her breasts. Logan's fingers snaked up her spine and she shivered. "How's Sacha?" she asked. "Did she have her foal?"

Logan blinked. "Yeah. Awesome little colt, full of spirit. He's got great conformation already. I assumed he'd be white, but he's more Appaloosa than Station bred."

"Will you geld him?" Hana asked, trying to display the little knowledge she'd gleaned.

Logan's eyes twinkled. "Not today. That wouldn't be much of a welcome, would it?"

Hana's brow knitted in irritation and Logan pursed his lips. She gathered fresh clothing from the suitcase and closed the bathroom door behind her. As the shower spat cold water into the tray, Logan let himself into the small room.

Hana groaned. "Stop doing that! I locked it for a reason."

"Yeah, because you're mad at me." Logan rested his back against the wall and smirked as Hana's gaze coasted over his muscles. "But you can't resist me."

She huffed out a breath of irritation. "I bet I can!" Testing the water temperature, she clambered into the shower and closed the glass door between them. Satisfaction budded on her lips as she soaped her breasts and heard Logan let out a groan. "Go away!" She snatched at the plastic lip on the door to keep him out as his grey eyes smouldered like storm clouds.

Logan sighed and reached for his toothbrush. "I'm not gelding him at all. Something tells me he could prove good breeding stock. He looks heavier than I expected."

Hana nodded with disinterest. Her fingers coasted over her stomach and she gritted her teeth, remembering the hunger in the woman's eyes the night before. It sickened her and her fingers shook. She jumped as Logan spoke, his tone sharp. "Hana?"

"What?" The shower gel clattered into the tray and she exhaled in frustration. The ground seemed a long way away.

"Would you like to see the foal?" He stared at her with an air of expectation and Hana swallowed.

"Where is he?" She realised the foolishness of her question as she asked it and Logan gave her a look of confusion. Then his shoulders sagged.

"You don't want to. Is it because I upset you?"

"No." Hana stopped the water running and pushed the glass open, reaching for her towel. "I just don't want to hang around here today. I'm bored." The lie tripped off her tongue and Logan's brows gave a momentary jerk.

"He's at the bunkhouse. Do you want to ride up with me?"

She nodded and knotted the towel at her breasts. "I'd love to come, but I don't think I can sit in a saddle."

"We'll go on the quad bike." Logan smiled, an expression of pleasure and relief. He turned back to the sink and scrubbed at his teeth while Hana exited the bathroom.

They dressed in silence, Hana trying to plan her day well enough to keep her away from the hotel and Vik's mistress for the next few hours. She almost didn't hear Logan's question and looked up in surprise. "Sorry, what did you say?"

"I'd like you to name him," he said and his jaw tightened at her lack of understanding. "The foal. He needs something to stand the test of time as a bloodline name. I'll use part of it through any offspring."

Hana's green eyes sparkled with surprise and she swallowed. "What if I can't think of anything good?"

Logan reached for her, placing soft kisses on the nape of her neck. "I married a creative and intelligent woman, Hana. You won't let me down."

"No pressure then," she complained.

Logan reached his arm around her and loosed the knotted towel with a swift movement. He breathed into her ear, gentle, feather light breaths making her skin tingle. "I have this itch I need you to take care of."

Hana shivered and her teeth grazed her lower lip. "You always have that itch." Her voice sounded husky. Logan nipped the soft skin and Hana inhaled before darting free from his grasp. "I'm hungry, Logan. But I'm sure Effie will come straight up and scratch your itch while I eat breakfast."

"Oh, no!" Logan groaned, falling backwards onto the bed. "Not another one with no teeth! What happens if I only want you? Come here woman!"

Hana stopped, her fingers resting over the hem of her tee shirt. She swallowed and pulled it over her head. "Are you sure you only want me?" she asked and old hurts laced her voice. "You might get bored."

"I've only ever wanted you," Logan replied. "Get over here and I'll show you how much."

Chapter 39

Tama sat next to Hana in the kitchen while Logan poked around in the chiller. Leslie's lips pursed with irritation as he emerged carrying a loaf of bread, but she said nothing. "Toast?" he asked, flicking his fringe from his eyes and jabbing his finger towards the industrial toaster.

"I want some," Tama interjected. "Heaps. I'm starving."

Logan halted in the centre of the room and three women carrying plates dodged him. "I'm not your bloody servant!" he exclaimed. "Get your own breakfast." He squared his shoulders and narrowed his eyes. Hana saw an older woman dart a lascivious glance in his direction and smirked. Logan noticed the quirk of her lips and followed Hana's gaze, his grey eyes resting on Effie's broad face.

"I'll get whatever you need, Mr Logan," Effie said. Her lips parted to reveal a toothless mouth and Logan's smile showed kindness without guile.

"You're not a servant either, Effie," he said, patting her shoulder. His gaze tracked to Leslie's glare. "Besides, I don't want to get you into trouble." Antagonism rolled from his angular frame and Hana sensed Tama tense beside her. The teenager rose, shoving his chair back with a screech and striding across the kitchen. Leaning down, he pinched Effie's rounded bum.

"I'll get my own, thanks," he said, giving her a wink filled with sex appeal. "You can help me."

"She's got jobs to do," Leslie growled. "Don't manhandle my staff!"

Logan took a step forward and dumped the bread on the counter. "Whose staff?" he demanded, his voice low and threatening.

Hana watched the colour drain from Leslie's cheeks and sighed. "Your mother's staff," the older woman conceded.

Logan's jaw worked in his cheek and Hana's chair clattered against Tama's abandoned seat. "I'm not hungry," she announced. "I lost my appetite."

"Where are we up to?" The door closed with the hiss of its spring and Miriam stood in the kitchen. "Effie, hurry up, girl. We need to clear up for morning tea." The fire in Logan's eyes met the determination in Leslie's and Hana tasted the bitterness of an old battle. She watched Miriam stride towards them as Effie hurried out of danger with her tower of dirty dishes. Tama busied himself with the toaster and snatched up the loaf.

"I'll make your breakfast, Hana," he said, shooting a nervous glance over his shoulder at Miriam.

"Thanks." Hana plopped into her seat and watched the dangerous confusion flicker across Logan's face. He glanced at Tama and then back at her and she feared the conclusion his mental leap took him to. Oblivious, Miriam negotiated his prone body, jabbing him in the ribs to shift him sideways. Logan's brows narrowed as he glared at Leslie and Hana's appetite abandoned her. Alfred walked into the kitchen in his socks and stared around the milling group. Age crept over him like a cankerous shroud with each passing week. He stared at Miriam's cowed spine as she loaded brownie onto a platter and his fingers writhed behind his back.

Hana stood again, her legs rigid as she took tentative steps around the table. The tension in the room placed choking hands around her throat and her lungs screamed for oxygen. The child pressed its head lower and she winced with pain, fighting the heavy door and making her escape on wobbling legs.

Fleeing through the corridor and across the lobby, Hana kept her head down and supported her stomach with her left hand. "Please don't be here," she whispered to herself as she ran. "Please don't be here." She reached the arch on the other side and skirted the rope barrier into the family's private quarters, waiting for Vik's mistress to accost her. A glance back into the seating area revealed only empty furniture and the quizzical stare of the receptionist. Hana turned into the spiral staircase and paused to catch her breath. Footsteps sounded behind her and she climbed faster, her fingers fluttering at her chest. "Leave me alone!" she shouted, stopping and pressing her spine against the rail. "Please, just leave me alone."

"Hana?" Logan took the stairs three at a time. He towered above her on the same tread, leaning close in the tiny space. "What's going on?" His blank face looked calm, but his threatening stance revealed something else. Hana placed her hands against his chest to keep herself from falling sideways. His body felt taut beneath his sweatshirt, matching the gimlet hard eyes which stared down at her.

"Nothing's wrong. Just let me go." She shoved at his chest and avoided his gaze.

Logan shook his head in warning, a slow calculated movement which accompanied a raised eyebrow. He dared her to take him for a fool. "I'm warning you, Hana, don't lie to me." He smiled but the slight upward hitch of his lips contained no friendliness.

Hana groaned and leaned her head against the wall, feeling the patterned wallpaper against her scalp. "I need to sit down!" she whined.

Logan shrugged, his stubbornness easily outweighing hers. "Any time, babe. Just answer the question."

"Please?" she begged, her knees trembling.

"Fine!" he snapped. He dipped his muscular body and swung her into his arms in the tiny space, refusing to set her down at the top of the stairs. "Behave!" he told her, the veins protruding from his neck. He carried her to the bedroom, ignoring her complaints as he hitched her sideways to activate the keypad.

"You'll drop me!" Hana hissed.

Logan pressed the final digit and narrowed his eyes. "Don't tempt me."

Kicking the door closed with his heel, he dumped her on the bad and collapsed beside her. "Come on, wahine," he coached. "Fess up."

Hana's hands twisted in her lap, her knotting fingers mirroring her internal wrestling. "There's nothing to confess, Logan. I'm not guilty of whatever you think I am."

Logan snorted and raised his voice in a squeaky impression of Tama. "Oh, Hana, I'll make you breakfast. I know you hated me yesterday, but today I'll be your whipping boy."

Hana reached out and slapped his hard stomach, a look of disdain creasing her brow. "That's what's bothering you?"

"Yes!" Logan sat up and his arm rubbed against her shoulder. "I told you to stay away from him."

Hana shook her head and rolled her eyes. "Then why throw us together, Logan? He's everywhere I look. What did you think would happen?"

Logan tensed. "If he made a pass at you, I'll tear his head off."

"No." Hana sighed. "He didn't."

Logan's brow furrowed. "So why did you run away from me?"

Hana snorted. "Really, Logan? You'd call that running?"

His fingers snaked along her spine and he traced the ridges, dwelling on each one for more than a second. Hana turned to face him, running her tongue over her lips and releasing a sigh. "I can't stand the tension right now. The kitchen felt like a powder keg. You dislike Leslie, Miriam dislikes everyone and Alfred resembles a man on the edge of destruction."

"Fair enough." Logan's eyes narrowed. "But why tell me to leave you alone when I came after you?"

"I didn't." Hana gritted her teeth and stretched her hands across her belly until her fingers touched in the middle. "I thought you were someone else."

"I'll kill him." Logan spoke the words with menace and Hana groaned and flopped sideways, pushing her face into the nearest pillow. He nudged her hip and she slapped his hand away.

"Not Tama! Why don't you listen to me, Logan?"

He stood and Hana panicked, wagging her finger at him. "Don't you dare hurt that kid!" she snapped. Sitting up too fast, she held her breath as her vision blurred. She tipped sideways and closed her eyes. "Oh, do what you like, Logan. I'll get a taxi home and you can come here by yourself in future."

"Don't threaten me, Hana." Logan sank his hands into his pockets and ground his teeth. "Talk to me."

"Then shut up and listen!" She drew her feet up onto the mattress and let out a sigh. "Vik's mistress is here with his old engineering firm. She accosted me in the lobby and Tama stopped her."

"Stopped her doing what?" His dark irises flashed and his fists balled by his sides. "Did she hurt you? Did Tama throw her out?"

"No!" Hana sighed. "He came between us and shielded me from whatever she's spent the last nine years saving up. Then she went back to her room and I don't plan on seeing her again if I can help it. If you throw her out, then it feeds the drama and I've had enough for a lifetime."

Logan took an age to blink, the action appearing slowed down and surreal. "So Tama knows?" he asked, his voice deceptively calm. "About Vik's affair."

Hana buried her face in the pillow. "Yes. He mustn't tell my kids, Logan. Not ever."

"He won't. I'll make sure of it." His jaw worked beneath the skin, causing the bristles to stand up.

"Thanks." Hana shifted on the mattress and closed her eyes.

"But he didn't touch you?"

"Oh, Logan!" She resisted the urge to cry. "You have an over-inflated view of my attributes. I resemble an Easter egg!"

Logan's face softened. "Yeah. But you're my Easter egg." He squatted next to the bed and reached for her hand, drawing her fingers into his rough palm.

"How can this marriage ever succeed?" she whispered. "We're both so damaged and suspicious. We'll end up destroying each other."

His brows knitted and he smiled, the expression reaching his eyes enough to crinkle them at the corners. "We'll work it out somehow, Hana." His fringe bounced against his eyelashes as he brought her fingers to his lips. "I love you, Hana Du Rose," he whispered. "Never forget that."

Logan lay on the bed next to her for an hour, his mind whirring. When she fell asleep, he crept from the room and walked to the stables to see Jack. He borrowed the quad bike and parked it next to a side entrance at the rear of the hotel. Then he spoke to Tama and together they went looking for Vik's mistress.

"I brought you lunch," he said, clattering the tray on the bedside table. "Fancy some soup?"

Hana pushed herself up the bed and wiped her mouth on her sleeve. "Sorry. I didn't mean to fall asleep."

"All good." Logan sat down next to her and lifted the spoon. "You didn't get breakfast."

Hana groaned and sat back against the pillows. She ran a hand over her belly. "I think the baby's engaged. I'm more comfortable but I feel so tired."

"Is that meant to happen?" Logan clasped her fingers beneath his, the spoon bumping against her thumb.

"Yeah." Hana soothed away the fear in his eyes with a smile. "It's normal, Logan."

He held the spoon out towards her and she took it in clumsy fingers. "Eat this and I'll take you up to see the foal."

"Really? I'd love that." She bit her lower lip. "Am I still naming him?"

"Yep." Logan settled the bowl on her knee and watched her take a tentative sip. "I'm looking forward to it."

Hana used the bathroom and met Logan by the lift. She watched the indicator light climb to the third floor and her brow furrowed. "Maybe we can do this tomorrow," she whispered.

Logan's lips pursed into a line. "Hana. She left last night."

Her eyes widened. "You don't even know who she is!"

"Not hard to find out, babe. Tama helped me look for her. But she made an excuse and checked out of her motel unit after your fight."

"I'm not sorry." Hana leaned against the wall and rested a hand over her heart. "The thought of running into her again made me ill. I refuse to keep going over the same old ground."

Logan held her hand as they used the lift to the ground floor. She pressed herself against his chest in the privacy of the tiny space and reached up for a kiss. "There's a camera," he whispered and she bit her bottom lip and fluttered her eyelashes.

"Maybe I don't care." She giggled as he kissed her neck and slapped her bum.

The quad bike pitched at savage angles as Logan drove up the mountain. Hana alternated between crashing into his hip on the bench seat and clinging to the other side. "How much further?" she asked, trying to keep her voice level.

"Not far," Logan promised. "Just to the bunkhouse. I kept Sacha away from the other mares. She's vicious at the best of times but I imagine she'll be worse with a foal at heel. The guys will watch her for me after we leave." The quad bike veered off to the right and Hana tensed her thigh muscles to keep her on the seat. She clutched her stomach and hoped the ride would end soon. Native flora whipped past and she closed her eyes to avoid the nauseating blur.

Sacha snorted and shook her head when she saw Logan, showing off for his benefit while giving Hana her blue wall eye.

Glued to her side, the tiny foal's grey flecked legs looked too long for its body and its gait seemed stuttered and clumsy. Hana clambered from the quad and hung back as Logan drew an apple from his jacket pocket. "So cute," she whispered.

Sacha strutted to the fence and nosed at Logan's fingers until he held up the apple. He smoothed the fuzzy fringe from her brow and rubbed at the short tight hair on her forehead. Her eyes rolled back as she took delighted bites from the fruit and caused juice to dribble down his fingers. "Clever girl," Logan murmured. "You did good, Sacha."

The foal stared at the adults with wide-eyed curiosity, hanging behind Sacha's hindquarters and peeking up at them. Hana offered her hand over the rail and it skipped backwards, almost falling over its hooves in haste. "Ooh, sorry." She withdrew her hand, aware of Sacha's ever watchful gaze. "I did it wrong."

"No, you didn't." Logan kissed the side of the mare's cheekbone and rested his hand on the top rail. "Sacha just needs to teach him what's safe and what isn't. He'll spook at everything for a while."

"I've never seen anything born." Hana avoided Sacha's sharp teeth and viewed the scene from a safe distance. The mare's brown eye looked calm as she turned her graceful neck to check on her baby. She made a low sound in her throat and the foal edged nearer. Logan whispered to the mare and Hana felt a stab of exclusion as the horse's ears flicked back and forth in response. Logan spoke often of his kinship with the land and his sense of being tied to the tangata whenua. He fitted into the scene and a sense of hopelessness consumed her as though she didn't belong there with him. She was a city girl making the best of it for his sake and worried she would never fit his mould. Where she failed, many more would step up and attempt to take her place.

"You will if you hang around here long enough." Logan's smile held contentment. "This place is like Nature's maternity wing in the spring." His fingers caressed the velvety skin above Sacha's nostril and he turned to her. "So what's the verdict?"

Hana stared at the small creature in front of her, all legs and twitching, stumpy tail. She tried to imagine him as a fearsome stallion, commanding a herd in the seclusion of the bush. He turned his face towards her and the haughtiness of his expression reminded her of Logan. Sacha moved and the colt stumbled against her, his tiny hooves not responding fast enough. Hana sighed. "I thought of something, but I'm not sure it fits him now. I imagined he'd be pure white, like Sacha. And bigger."

Logan's lips twisted upwards. "You know I won't tell you if I don't like it," he said, his voice soft.

"That's what I'm worried about." Hana chewed the inside of her cheek. "Maybe the truth is best." Her mind drifted to her past, to a husband who devalued her opinion and found fault with her plans.

"I'm not him, Hana." Logan reached out and stroked her cheek and Sacha snuffed, shaking her neck and sending a cloud of dust over them both.

"I know," Hana whispered. "I know."

"Trust me?" he asked. "At least give me a chance to prove myself to you."

Hana felt the intensity of the moment. The foal could mark the beginning of one thing and the end of all else. She hovered in between, lost and frightened. She braced herself for disappointment, waiting for Logan's rejection despite what he promised. "Du Rose le Prochain," she announced, her voice trailing as she lost her nerve.

Logan's expression remained blank for a heartbeat. Then he smiled and Hana relaxed at the sight of approval in his eyes. She released the breath she held and acknowledged the waiting tension in her neck and shoulders. "I like that." Logan held out his hand to the spidery creation. It took a brave step forward but lost its nerve, snuffing and backing into Sacha's legs. "Du Rose Future." Logan translated the French name into English and Hana nodded.

"Whatever that looks like."

"It looks great from where I'm standing." He laid his arm across her shoulders and tucked her into his side. "You need to believe that, Hana. Have a little faith." He stroked back the hair which blew around her face and kissed her forehead.

Hana let him hold her, seeking safety away from her old life and yet fearing the new just as much. "We'll be okay, won't we?" she whispered, seeking reassurance.

"If you behave." Logan winked and his lips felt soft against hers. His fingers caressed the arc of their child and he sighed. "We're doing great, Hana. Our Du Rose future has great potential."

"I hope so." A door banged behind them and Hana tried to turn. Logan blocked her with his arms and kept her facing him.

"We should get back," he said, kissing the end of her nose. "Mum's planning a family roast once the guests leave."

Hana nodded and allowed him to lead her to the quad bike. Sacha's hooves ground in the dirt and her foal skittered after her as she followed them along the fence. Logan helped Hana into the seat and settled her, lingering to press her fingers over the lip on the dashboard. "It's easier going down," he promised, his irises the colour of slate. "I'll use the lower half of the developer's road and it shouldn't feel as steep."

Hana murmured her thanks and watched Logan walk around the front. He started the engine and she rubbed at her forearms, the prickling of her skin eerie and unnerving. When the sensation spread to the back of her neck, she looked around for the source. The darkened windows of a low cedar house gave away nothing and she pointed towards it. "Is that the bunkhouse?"

Logan nodded and negotiated a bend which would take them to the bush and the narrow track downhill. Hana took a final look back at Sacha and her heart stilled.

Flick leaned against the fence, a cowboy hat pushed high on his head. The brim cast his eyes into shadow, but Hana sensed his gaze crawl across her skin. Fear rose into her chest and she gave an involuntary shiver. She'd run from the man for so long, she doubted she would ever feel anything but loathing for him. The bunkhouse disappeared from sight as the quad plunged into the bush, leaving Robert Dressler with his threats and secrets.

Hana remained silent on the trip back, gripping the quad's frame until her fingers smarted. Despite Logan's continued faith in Flick's redemption, Hana doubted and the prickle of unease grew. Her trust in his judgement began to wither on the vine.

Chapter 40

"What would you do if I'd picked a silly name?"

Logan pushed the truck ahead of an idling ute on the highway and glanced across at Hana. "What do you mean?"

"You know, something humiliating, like Flash or Bob?"

He shrugged and contemplated his answer. Hana watched his blank expression, guessing at the thought patterns behind it. He seemed damned whichever answer he gave. When he shrugged, Hana relaxed. "I knew you wouldn't, so it was a safe gamble. You wouldn't disrespect something so incredible with a stupid label. It's not who you are. And I can't ask your opinion if I'm not prepared to accept it." He indicated and made the turn onto the back roads to Huntly. "Whatever you'd decided would be his registered name. He might have ended up with a different stable name, but that's out of my control."

"Who controls that?" Hana lay back against her headrest as contentment washed over her.

"Jack." A smirk lit Logan's lips. "I suspect he just swears and because the stable hands can't understand him, they make stuff up."

Hana closed her eyes and thought of her deaf mother. So many times poor Judith arrived home with the wrong products because shop assistants thought they knew what she wanted. She laughed it off though Hana recalled the look of pain in her eyes at her isolation.

Term four passed in a blur as it gathered pace towards the exams. Summer advanced and less diligent students panicked. Logan held tutorials for his seniors during lunch hours and after school. Sometimes Hana waited for him but mostly she drove herself home. Her stomach bloomed as temperatures rose and her energy levels depleted before home time. With only a few months left to last, the crawl towards the end of term seemed to go backwards for her.

"You've got baby brain," her midwife said as Hana recounted the many things she'd misplaced or couldn't remember. "Slow down. You should go on maternity leave soon."

"I will," Hana promised. "The end of term should give me eight weeks to get ready."

Logan paid Maihi to clean the house and make dinner a couple of times a week. She protested that she'd do it for free, but accepted the cash when he called it a koha, a gift between family.

The student centre filled with panicking boys of all ages. They wore Sheila out with their last minute flapping, despite her failed efforts to coordinate them for the last two years. Year 13s discovered friends had sneakily applied to universities without telling them. Rugby boys watched their final college season end and lost the will to live. Terrified parents arrived, towing young men they foresaw hanging around, eating their food and clogging up their laundry basket as they repeated their final year into their twenties. Then frightened Year 11 and 12s forgot the cut off date for the next year's options and missed out on their chosen classes. Hana fielded each new arrival, funnelling them towards the guidance counsellors or Sheila, depending on their level of angst.

Rory's problems multiplied at the same rate as his Year 13s truanted, fought and suffered meltdowns of a different nature. Real life beckoned and they dealt with it in a variety of odd behaviours. As Sheila closed her door for the fourth time that morning and a boy disintegrated in Rory's visitors' chair, Hana heaved herself through the empty common room, seeking peace.

"The overwintering did our grass no good whatsoever," the gardener complained, peering over the balcony at the rugby pitch. Hana massaged her aching stomach and peered at a swearword etched into the turf using weedkiller. She gulped and peered at the man next to her.

"I don't think the winter caused that," she said, shading her eyes with her other hand.

"What?" He removed his stained spectacles and cleaned them on his shirt. "It's dying, look."

Hana waited for him to replace his glasses and watched the expression of horror pass across his face. When he let out a volley of expletives, she nodded.

"Yes. That's exactly what it says. It looks like a leavers' prank."

The man's face grew ashen and he gaped like a fish. "Little buggers," he breathed.

Hana nodded. "Looks like they did it a few days ago by the way the grass is dying. It should be good and dead by prize-giving."

The gardener stepped back from the rail and his breathing became a series of agonised puffs. Backing away with the heady panic of an asthmatic, he fled from the staffroom and Hana heard him clattering down the stairs.

A sigh from the end of the deck drew her attention and she saw Pete hanging over the rail. An air of hopelessness hung around him and she wound her way through abandoned tables and chairs. Nudging her arm against his, she jerked her head towards his rear. "Do you display your crack on purpose?" Hana asked. "Or does it just enjoy the open air?"

She glanced through the staffroom windows and saw a row of backs. Anyone eating had turned their chair around. Pete snorted and rested his chin on his hands. "I've lost weight," he grumbled. "My pants are falling down."

"Oh. Well done." Hana offered him a smile and to her surprise, saw him wipe a streak of wetness from his cheek. "What's wrong, Pete?" She glanced behind her again, grateful for the unusual lack of an audience, thanks to Pete's backside.

Pete pointed a bony finger towards the running track. Still there after sports' day, it continued in use as the PE teachers drilled the younger boys in sprints and middle distance. A group of black and white striped shirts moved around it at various speeds, resembling humbugs in a food mixer. Hana squinted against the sunshine. "Oh, yeah. Logan said he was covering for Chris Carter this morning. Problems with their newborn, I think."

Pete snorted again, an irritating sound of superiority which made Hana's teeth grind together. "Problems with his marriage!" he bit.

Hana sighed. "Okay, I'll see you back in the office." She turned away from the rail and Pete lurched towards her, pinching her upper arm in grasping fingers.

"Talk to him for me, please Hana!" His saucer eyes blinked against the sunlight and Hana sighed.

"I don't want to get involved in your relationship, Pete. For a start, it's older than mine and I don't have the energy." Hana's gaze strayed back to the track and she watched Logan run with a student. He remained with him, despite the slow pace and Hana saw him bend every few metres as though urging the child on. Numerous boys lapped them, but they kept going at the tortoise pace without stopping.

"Cancer," Pete muttered, releasing Hana's arm. She rubbed at the painful welt from his fingernails.

"What?"

"The boy with Logan. He had Leukaemia. Been back a few weeks and already he's got him running. They'll do anything for Mr Du Rose." Pete's voice dripped resentment and Hana turned away.

"If you tried turning up to classes occasionally, they might like you too," she bit, reaching the open doorway into the staffroom.

Pete lurched for her again, his eyes bright with unshed tears and his cheeks flushed and pink. His wispy hair moved against the breeze, resembling blonde candyfloss. Defeat rose from him like a heat haze. "It's all gone wrong this year," he said, his fingers grabbing air as Hana dodged sideways. "I felt so happy when he turned up here." He jabbed an index finger at Hana's oblivious husband. "This should have been the best year of my life. Me and Logan back together and then meeting Henrietta. It felt amazing." Pete's chest hitched. "It's all ruined."

"What's changed?" Hana asked. She spread her hands and then regretted it as Pete seized one and held on.

"Everything," he whispered. His eyes contained a look of mania. "Everything." Pete blanched, turning paler than usual. He moved so close, Hana smelled the peanut butter sandwich he ate at morning tea. "I stuffed up, Hana. I stuffed up big time. Boris started it, not me."

"Started what?"

"The gambling!" Pete's gaze flicked to the window and back to Hana. "Logan paid the debt last time to stop me getting my legs broken. I promised I'd never do it again. But Boris started and before I knew it, I'd run up a debt I couldn't pay."

"Logan bailed you out again?" Hana recoiled, her brows knitting at the prospect of another secret between them. But Pete shook his head.

"No. Henrietta paid it. Logan won't speak to me. He has this honour code thing and I've broken it. Don't break a promise to him, Hana. He'll walk away from you."

Hana's chest tensed. She yanked her hand free of Pete's grasp. "You caused all that trouble for us?" She backed away. "Did Boris tell Laval's men the address, or you?"

"Boris. Boris did it, I promise." Pete lurched again and Hana backed into a table, the wood pressing against her thighs.

Like a coiled spring, Pete seized her and crushed her to his chest. Hana smelled chip fat and body odour and they tussled as she tried to extract herself. He maintained an admirable headlock, raining tears and snot onto her shoulder. A half full mug plunged to the deck with a thud, emptying its contents through the gaps and onto boys below. Hana heard a confused squeal as warm, brown tea doused them from above.

Dandruff coated the back of Pete's tracksuit jacket and she fought not to breathe it in "Please let go!" she hissed, aware of a prickling sensation working its way up her neck. "Logan's looking!" Using two fingers, she jabbed Pete in the stomach, relieved when he crumpled like an envelope and gave her an opportunity to step away. Hana glanced across the field and met Logan's gaze, seeing the hardness fill his expression. She exhaled and closed her eyes. "Thanks for that!" she snapped at Pete, whirling away from the balcony.

"What's going on 'ere then?" The soft Welsh accent heralded Gwynne and Hana breathed a sigh of relief. She jerked her head backwards as Pete sank to the boards and rocked his body, lunatic style.

"I can't do this," she whispered and he nodded with understanding. Leaning over Pete, he touched his shoulder, gasping as Pete enclosed his legs in a grip of death. Reaching into his pocket, he produced a small packet of tissues, offering it down. Pete snatched it and ripping the plastic wrapper, used all ten to blow his nose at once.

Hana escaped to the office with a glass of water and spent the next half an hour ignoring Rory and the sobbing boy behind her. When Logan didn't visit her during his free period, she felt chastened and a sense of injustice rose into her chest.

They met at the car after the final bell. Logan sat in the driver's seat with the air conditioning belting out cold air. Hana settled herself next to him and waited for him to speak. When he continued fiddling with his phone, she sighed. "Is this how it will be?" she demanded. "I get the silent treatment like Pete for some perceived wrong."

Logan snorted. "Perceived wrong, Hana? You've no idea what he did."

"He told me." She chewed her lower lip. "And it sucks!"

Logan started the engine and refused to engage in the conversation. The traffic lights on Wairere Drive turned red and he stopped the car behind an empty boat trailer. His fingers tapped an irritated beat on the steering wheel.

Hana knew with unexpected clarity she faced The Wall which Logan hid behind and gave a sigh of exasperation. "I don't have the energy for this," she said, staring at a loose wire in the trailer's electrics. She wondered where the boat was. "I don't care what's between you, Logan. You've put me in disgrace for nothing." She pressed the fingers of both hands over her eyes to dull the budding headache, running them down her cheeks and pulling at her jaw. The sudden sense of release washed over her as she let go, acknowledging she should do it more. Closing her eyes and leaning against the headrest, she relaxed.

Hana felt the change in road camber as they turned onto River Road. Then she felt Logan's hand close over hers as she stroked her stomach. "I'll get over it," he said. "But I need him to understand what he did."

Hana nodded. "I don't care, Logan. But what you think you saw was wrong. You demand my trust while giving none in return. It cuts both ways."

"Fair enough." Logan squeezed her fingers and let go. He remained silent for the rest of the journey.

He didn't speak again until they reached Culver's Cottage and he'd switched the engine off in the garage beneath the house. "Twenty grand," he said. Hana paused in the process of clambering down from her seat. Her brows knitted in confusion. "Pete's last gambling debt." Logan ran a hand across his jaw and she heard the dark bristles scratch across his palm. "I earned a black eye and stitches paying it for him, because the kind of guys who lend that amount of money don't like being paid in full. I didn't ask for it back on the understanding he never did it again." Logan sighed. "Guy's an idiot and the debt became repayable once he made that first bet."

"Oh." Hana swallowed. "What will you do?"

"No idea."

Something clicked inside her belly and Hana winced. She exhaled against a slow contraction which started in her lower back.

"What's wrong?" Logan reached her side in seconds and she grimaced against the pain. "Is it the baby?"

"No." She gave him a fake smile of reassurance, knowing he didn't buy it. "Braxton Hicks contractions. They're a practice run but they still bloody hurt."

"Okay." Logan helped her upstairs and settled her with a cup of tea. The pain faded after a few hours but the effort of coping with it wiped out the last of her energy reserves.

"A bit of number eight wire and she'll be right," Hana said, responding to the concern in his eyes as she pushed a hot water bottle against the base of her spine.

Logan threw his head back and laughed. "Now you sound like a Kiwi," he said.

Chapter 41

Hana made it to the last day of term. Alan Dobbs organised a Christmas party at a restaurant in town and the staff gathered to farewell another successful year.

"Well done, one and all," Dobbs said, his voice higher than usual as he slopped his glass of Waikato Draught and raised it in a toast.

"One and all," Angus repeated, beaming around at his exhausted staff. He rose and reached for a sheet of paper, an expensive Scots' malt whisky slurring his voice. "Now, I must farewell a loyal and trusted colleague." He held his hand out to Hana and she cringed. Amidst jeers and wolf whistles, surrounding staff pushed her up and their enthusiasm propelled her forward.

Angus' speech reduced her to tears. The gift of vouchers for a baby wear shop overwhelmed her and exhaustion nipped at her swollen ankles. She escaped back to her seat with a confusing mix of emotions, not knowing whether or not she'd return to her job and alarmed by the general assumption that she would. "I'm so confused," she whispered as Logan pressed a kiss against her forehead. "I don't know what to tell people."

"Tell them nothing," he advised, stroking a curl from her cheek. "We can make decisions after the baby arrives."

Pete grew more trolleyed as the alcohol flowed and his tone became obnoxious. Hana shot a nervous glance in his direction as the female teacher next to him aimed a slap at his head. "Oh, no," she breathed. "Someone else not wanting to compare penis sizes with Pete and their husband."

Logan raised an eyebrow and shook his head. "What do you suggest?"

Hana gave a coy grin. "Nothing, babe. It's none of my business." Logan raised his glass to her and smiled.

"Well played, Mrs Du Rose. I'm guessing Henrietta isn't due home for a few more days." He watched Pete for a moment and then rose to his feet. "I won't be long," he promised.

Hana observed her husband's progress across the room towards where Pete tipped another bottle of beer down his throat and swayed in his seat. Logan pushed his shirt into the back of his pants, a constant losing battle for tall men. Tapping Pete on the shoulder, he jerked his head towards the outside door and the street beyond. Like a dog expecting a kicking, Pete rose and followed him with a drunken, slinking gait.

They returned twenty minutes later, Logan stuffing a napkin and pen into his trouser pocket. Pete clung to his arm, holding himself upright with difficulty. "I love this guy!" he shouted to the whole restaurant and walked into a chair.

"Get off me, you dick," Logan snapped, the old ribaldry returned. Pete's grip switched from Logan's arm to the waistband of his trousers as he sank to his knees and they tussled. "You're pulling my pants down," Logan hissed. Hana felt a frisson of nervousness as Logan leaned into Pete's screwed up face and murmured, "Get off me or I'll break your legs!"

Pete let go in seconds. He slid to the floor tiles and sprawled like a snow angel. A passing waiter stepped over him with a tray of drinks.

"Is that PE teacher gay then?" shouted the physics teacher, his hearing aid making a high pitched whistle. "That explains it." Nearby staff members buried their faces in pint glasses and struggled to contain themselves. He tapped the art teacher on the shoulder. "He asked me to squeeze a spot in his arse crack once. Do you think he fancies me?"

"Would you go for it then, Tom?" Gwynne asked, mirth creasing his face into shadowed lines. The surrounding males guffawed and howled.

"Na." The old man smiled, his top set of false teeth crashing down to meet the bottoms. "But I'd go for that fat chick he's pretending to be straight with."

Hysteria followed and the men roared with laughter. A few of the more sober members of staff helped Pete to his feet. "Good on ya," Gwynne shouted at them. "I'm off duty tonight."

"Are you gay then?" the physics teacher chimed in, silencing Gwynne and sending the others into paroxysms again. "Bloody hell! Nobody tells me anything!" Tom sulked, burying his face in his beer.

Hana watched the exchange with amusement. Drunk teachers proved worse than teenagers.

"This is a great time to admit I am actually gay." The drama teacher made his announcement with a trembling lip and the men dissolved again. "No, I am. Really!" He made numerous protestations, but his confession seemed bound to be lost and then forgotten by the next day.

"My feet are killing me. Can we go yet?" Hana asked as Logan sank into his seat. "You can be the sober driver next year." She offered a sweet smile of consolation as he conceded defeat.

"No! No!" Pete saw them rise and crawled across the floor. "You can't go yet! I wanna spend time with Logan."

Logan swore beneath his breath and Hana grimaced. "Fantastic!" she hissed. "I bet you've missed your best friend."

"Like a hole in the head," Logan hissed.

"Oh, that's bloody disappointing!" Tom slammed his beer glass on the table. He waved his arms towards Logan as Pete clasped his thighs, his face dangerously close to Logan's groin.

"They're all gay! Why am I always the last to know anything in this damn place?" He waved at Hana with enthusiasm, his hearing aid whistling for a new battery. "It doesn't matter, I'm available, Hana!"

"Thanks, Tom." Hana smiled and waved back, growling at Logan through gritted teeth, "I'm leaving before the wife swapping starts."

Logan twisted Pete's finger until he let go and they made a break for it. Hana waddled across to unlock the car. "What's on the napkin?" she demanded, starting the engine and pulling out onto the main road.

Logan took it out and opened it, flapping it in front of him. "A contract."

"What, for a hitman?" Hana laughed at her own joke and Logan wrinkled his nose.

"No, Hana. For repayments. Pete's paying me back from before."

"But you don't need it." Hana's brow furrowed as she turned onto the expressway, navigating the road in the darkness. "Why make him pay up?"

Logan inhaled and thought about his answer. "Because that's the deal I made with him. I'm a man of my word, Hana."

She shrugged. "What will you do with the money?" A thought creased her face into a grin. "Scratch that. He'll pay you five bucks a week for the next three hundred and eighty five years. If at all."

"He had to pay." Logan waved the napkin. "I think he will too. Investing the money will treble it anyway, then when he's finished, I'll give it all back tripled."

"You'd do that?" Hana stole a sideways glance at him.

"Yeah." Logan shrugged. "Wouldn't you?"

Chapter 42

The hotel seemed busier than usual, tourist buses replacing the company conferences. Hana project managed the motel room renovations and Logan gave her full responsibility.

"You look tired." Logan collapsed onto the bed, his cowboy boots dangling over the edge.

"No worse than you." Hana nudged at his side and continued pushing her swollen feet into shoes. "Get off the bed, you're dusty."

Logan's gaze coasted over her rounded stomach. "Have you heard when the kids are visiting?"

"Bodie and Amy arrive after New Year's Day. Are you sure that's okay with your parents?"

"It's fine." Logan inhaled. "What about Izzie and Marcus?"

Hana's nose crinkled. "I might need to fly down to see them after the baby's born. Marcus is booked up for months and they can't leave."

"Bummer." Logan sat up using his stomach muscles and raised his arms above his head. Muscles rippled in his sleeves until the fabric reached breaking point. Hana heard knots crack in his spine and winced.

"The renovations are almost complete." She wiggled her toes in her tight shoes and stood. "Do you want to inspect?"

"I'll come and admire." Logan's quick arms lassoed her around the thighs as she passed and she squeaked. "But I trust you, Mrs Du Rose." He hauled her into his lap and kissed her.

For the next few weeks, their conversations consisted of discussions about stock and values as Logan strived to educate his city girl on the merits of farming and land ownership. He appeared settled and happy, spending his days in the bush and mountains, mustering cattle and mending fences.

Hana watched him painstakingly break in the youngest horses. She sat on the quad bike while he worked with them in a small arena. "I thought you did it like in a rodeo," she said and Logan turned away to hide his smirk.

"Er, na. Bit more to it than that," he replied, his slate grey eyes daring his head stockman to laugh. Toby pulled his hat over his eyes and turned away. "Bugger off and do some work, Toby," Logan snapped and the man left after raising his middle finger. He returned leading a white filly, leaving her in the arena and claiming the feisty colt Logan just finished with.

"Toby's the only one who defies you," Hana noted, watching him saunter away. "He's not scared of you."

Logan pursed his lips. "Never was. What can I say? He's a white guy with a death wish."

Hana raised an eyebrow and joined him at the fence. Logan clambered onto the top rail after unclipping the rope from the filly's head collar. "What are you doing now?" she demanded.

"Just letting her get used to me." Logan forced relaxation into his stance and turned sideways. The filly sniffed the sparse grass in the arena, spooking at every sound in the stable yard. Logan ignored her, but she kept him in her sights as she investigated. The dappled spots on her rump and face resembled the colours of a sylph in the shimmering sunlight. Hana watched as bored, the filly ventured closer, nosing the back pocket of Logan's jeans.

"I'm not sure how I feel about another female sizing up your bum," Hana mused, leaning her face on her forearms on the top rail. Logan laughed and the filly jumped backwards. He kissed the top of Hana's head, winding his fingers through her soft curls.

"Break the bloody horse, man!" Toby's voice startled them both and Hana and the filly let out identical squeals. "If that's how you do it then I might swap jobs."

Logan jumped down into the pen, a hail of hissed threats making Toby laugh harder. Hana watched as Logan picked up a trowel and pulled weeds from around the filly's feet. At first, she skittered away, calming as she grew used to the predictability of his movements.

For an hour each day, Logan repeated the process. He raked the sand, painted the fence and mended the faulty catch on the gate. His endless patience fascinated Hana and she gasped in surprise as the filly cracked by degrees, following him from job to job within the arena by the third day. Then Logan began with the basics, teaching her the principles of personal space and respect. When the filly ran up his heels in her desire to follow, he stamped his foot and splayed his arms. Jumping back in shock, she corrected herself until the trait disappeared altogether.

Hana's interest increased and she watched their relationship grow, jealous of Logan's easy trust in a beast with the potential to break every bone in his body. Whatever task she found herself involved in, she made sure she arrived at the arena when Logan's time with the filly came around. She watched him desensitise the horse until the filly hardly registered the lead rope he stroked across her withers or over her face. He cleaned out her hooves and progressed to the blacksmith's tools he used to shoe the stock horses. His commitment proved relentless and Hana learned more about her husband from observing his work with the filly than she managed in months of marriage. He caught her smiling as he walked the horse around the pen and his eyes narrowed in question.

"Nothing." Hana grinned and watched the filly parade past, her ears flicking back and forth at the unfamiliar saddle resting across her withers. "I'm recognising traits of your courtship, is all."

"Like what?" Logan bit his lower lip and his dark eyelashes gave a seductive flutter.

Hana laughed. "Pressure and release. I can see the pattern now."

"Don't know what you mean." His smile said otherwise.

"Is it a dominance thing?" Hana asked as Logan walked around the arena next to her. She admired his strong physique, his cowboy boots and jeans dusty and his hat tipped back on his head. His whakapapa tattoo snaked from underneath the sleeve of his tee shirt, wrapping itself around a firm brown bicep. "And when do I get my own filly to break?"

Logan's eyes shone with a curious light. He held out the lead rope to her. "It's about trust more. And how about now? You can try this girl."

Hana swallowed in confusion. "I'm asking what I need to do to get my own horse."

Logan pushed his hat back on his head. Sweat beaded his forehead and the sun beat down on them both. He cocked his head and Hana felt her world shift on its axis. "Move up here permanently and choose one," he stated.

Hana accepted the less complicated challenge. Despite her oversized belly, she climbed the fence and accepted the lead rope from Logan's fingers. The filly reacted with a nervous bob of her head, but used to Hana's presence on the other side of the fence made no further protest. Hana grew as dusty as Logan as she held the filly's lead rope and walked the mare, her husband lying on his stomach across the horse's back.

"You'll make a great assistant." Logan held her hand as they walked the horse back to the stable yard. The filly plodded behind, the lead rope hanging like a washing line and her head in a relaxed position.

Logan's other project proved a different matter altogether. Though Hana only watched him with the filly, she heard stories about the black colt which gave Logan a run for his money in the afternoons. A sore wrist, a black eye and a kick to a sensitive part of his anatomy gave the stable yard staff an enormous amount of entertainment, but Logan seemed in no hurry to admit defeat. "That's one way to get yourself sterilised," Toby laughed and slapped Logan on the back as he bent double in the arena, the colt snorting and posturing a safe distance away from him.

"Sod off. You're fired," Logan groaned, hauling himself onto the top rung of the fence but finding it hard to sit down. The war raged as Christmas day advanced, with bets placed in the stable yard and among the stock men. Logan won five days before the deadline of Christmas Eve, riding the colt around the stable yard. Jack collected his small fortune and pocketed it with a toothless grin.

Alfred's behaviour marred Hana's sense of peace, becoming more erratic with each passing day. Instinct warned her that something was wrong, but Logan sidelined her anxieties. "He's fine," he said, shutting the conversation down. "He's worrying about Mum."

"What about her?" Hana demanded. "She seems happier than usual and is back at the helm. It feels like something else."

"It isn't." Logan ground his teeth and Hana heard the danger in his voice. "He just gets like this."

She shook her head. "He's muttering to himself, Logan. He keep saying things like, 'It needs to stop, I can't do this anymore.' What is he talking about?"

"No idea, Hana!" Logan's pronounced irritation at her questions drove her to observe without making further comment.

Michael arrived at the hotel in the week before Christmas. Hana assumed he would ride with Logan on horseback, but he avoided his brother apart from at meals. "What's your favourite bit of the farm?" Hana asked over breakfast.

"None of it!" he scoffed. Bitterness laced his voice.

Hana stopped eating her toast and stared at him in surprise. Butter dribbled onto her plate. Logan snorted and rose from the table, clattering his dishes into the industrial machine near the sink. "He fell off, Hana. Like the pussy he is, he never got back on."

"Maybe I didn't want to get back on." Sarcasm laced Michael's tone and Hana tensed.

Logan rolled his eyes and bent to kiss her. "I'll be back later," he promised. "I won't be far away if you need me."

Michael watched the door close behind him and shrugged. "I've delivered heaps of babies. You can hang with me."

So she did. When Logan didn't return until late that night, Hana spent the day with Michael. She found him easy company and in the absence of a better offer, they settled into an easy rhythm. She realised first hand that the affable doctor was an illusion. Michael possessed deep rooted insecurities and an underlying jealousy of Logan. With the hotel ramping down and little else to do, he attached himself to Hana and followed her everywhere like a puppy dog. "These motel rooms look heaps better," he remarked, winking at the interior designer as she finished up adjusting the swags of a sumptuous curtain.

Hana rolled her eyes. "You're certainly a trier!" she chided him later. "Lily's gay and very much not interested. You're wasting your time."

Michael masked his temporary deflation. At dinner time when one of the waitresses showed him a little too much attention, his ego perked up again and he followed her from the room and didn't return.

Logan's sense of time seemed to fail him in greater degrees. He missed numerous meals despite promising to return, the demands of the farm and hotel sucking every waking minute from his day and leaving nothing for Hana. Michael filled the gap, a gallant and entertaining companion. Hana found him harder to dislike with every passing day. He furnished her with stories from their childhood, overlaying the more disturbing tales with the gloss of time. Hana used the opportunity to press for information which could help her understand Logan better. "Tell me about your brother, Barry," she asked and Michael winced.

"He was a psycho. Less you know about him, the better."

"Can I ask you a question?" she ventured.

"No!" Michael kicked a ball of pumice and sent it skittering into a raised bed. "I know what you're going to ask, so no."

"Oh." Hana sniffed back her offence. She bit her lip and frustration budded. "It was just something Logan said."

"I can imagine what Logan said. Please, just leave it Hana?"

"Okay, sorry." The moment felt awkward and guilt infiltrated Hana's emotions as punishment for trespassing where she didn't belong. Isolation washed over her and she craved the peace and security of Culver's Cottage.

Michael stopped on the path between the rose garden and the imposing hotel facade and faced her. "Some things it's best you don't know."

"Out of respect for Miriam?" Hana asked and Michael looked confused.

"No! Out of respect for your husband."

Hana's cheeks reddened with fear. "What do you mean?"

"See! Right there!" Michael jabbed an angry finger into her chest. "You have too much to learn. Let's just agree to stay away from certain subjects."

Hana nodded, her heart beating fast. Her agreement seemed farcical when she didn't know which subjects to avoid. She remained silent until they reached the house and Michael relented, catching her arm as they went up the wide front steps. "I'm sorry, this must be hard for you."

"No, not hard." Hana shook her head and dragged her arm away. "Just bloody impossible." She waved behind her and made her way towards the main staircase, needing a lie down. The child weighed low in her stomach and her legs ached. She moved without grace, a small elephant creeping along the hallway and thudding onto the bed. Hana closed her eyes.

So, the Du Roses kept secrets. She pushed aside any offence at their lack of sharing, not wishing to reciprocate. But it felt like walking through a mine field; never knowing which footstep would disconnect her head from her body. She napped, the mystery whirling around her dreams, becoming more fantastical with each revolution.

Michael searched for her later, finding her in the library. "Sorry about before," he said, slumping into a wing backed chair. His gaze took in the floor to ceiling shelves and the books crammed into every orifice. The room drew Hana like a magnet to its true north.

"I don't care anymore." Hana stroked the pages of the book in her hand and relaxed back into the cushions.

"Don't be that way," Michael said. "Logan's a secretive bugger but on some things, I can't help you."

"I don't need you to. I said I don't care." Hana closed the Jane Austen classic and blew dust from its cover. The writing on the spine shone gold and the publishing date on the fly leaf marked a day in the late 1800s. "I might borrow this," she mused. "It's a long time since I read Emma."

Michael observed her, cocking his leg over the arm of his chair. "You love books?"

"Yeah. I did an English degree."

"Like Logan?"

Hana nodded and Michael smoothed his hand over his chin, his expression becoming thoughtful. "I didn't bother with all that poetic wrangling. It's more interesting fixing what's wrong, than writing a long soliloquy about it."

"So, you became a doctor? To fix things?"

"Yeah, kind of." Michael bit his lip and looked guarded again and Hana's patience snapped. Her body felt like a beach ball, pumped way beyond its pressure point and her feet ached.

"Please, just leave me alone!" she bit. "You don't want me asking questions and I don't have the energy to play guessing games. I just want some peace. I don't care about your deep, dark secrets." She waved the novel in the air. "To be honest, there's more entertainment value in here. I'm sure there are places you'd rather be than babysitting me, so please, you're released from duty. Just go!"

Michael's face broke into an instant grin. "Sparky! So that's what Logan loves about you? I knew there had to be more than the little English rose you appear to be."

"Sod off!" Hana grew exasperated.

"Anyone ever told you, you're hot when you're angry?" Michael strolled over and without asking, grabbed Hana's wrist and pulled it towards him. He clamped two fingers over her vein. "Why is your heartbeat so irregular?" he asked after a moment's patient observation.

Hana snatched her hand away. "Rubbish! You didn't even time it."

Michael laughed. "I did actually. Look." He twisted his other wrist to show Hana the digital display facing upwards. His smiling eyes made her feel foolish. He smoothed the soft skin of her wrist with his fingers. "But I didn't need to. I've done this for enough years to instinctively know what's normal and what isn't. Did you get it checked after I mentioned it last time?"

"Yes, heaps of times." Hana sounded bored and Michael smirked.

"Don't you trust me? I'm a good doctor."

"So you say," she spat and he sniggered.

"Okay, Hana Du Rose. I'll tell you why I became a doctor, but it wasn't my finest moment."

"Ooh, don't tell me secrets, Michael. I might tell the newspapers and then where would you be?" Hana stood up and reached towards the nearest shelf, pulling out another book which caught her eye. She fingered the dusty, faded copy of Daniel Defoe's Roxana.

"I studied this for my degree." She smiled with a dreamy expression and stroked the spine. "Defoe wrote for money and the inconsistencies in his writing are hilarious." She turned to find Michael's grey eyes observing her with a predatory interest. "Rather like your family and your stories."

Chapter 43

Undeterred by her spirit, Michael stuck close. Two days before Christmas Eve, he offered to drive Hana up the mountain on the quad.

"I'm not sure." She ran a hand over her stomach. "Last time proved quite bumpy, but I'd like to see Sacha's foal again."

"We'll take it slow." Michael offered one of his winning smiles. Hana imagined female colleagues tumbling into his bed at the sight of it. "Logan's mending a fence near the bunkhouse around lunchtime. Why don't we take them a picnic?"

Emboldened with the idea of pleasing her husband, Hana press ganged Leslie into helping her. They made sandwiches and added fruit and muffins, loading it into a cooler which strapped into the bed at the back of the quad. A gallon container of water bounced next to it as Michael pushed the vehicle along a narrow bush track.

Hana didn't make it as far as Sacha's enclosure. Michael's quarrel with Logan destroyed the outing within a few minutes of arriving. It began with Logan giving an upward jerk of his head towards Hana, not stopping his work to greet her properly. She swallowed her disappointment as the other men fell on the food and drink with enthusiasm. "Have I done something to offend you?" she whispered, holding out a bottle of water. Logan shook his head, continuing to hammer the post into the dry earth without answering. Hana sighed. "I must have, Logan. You leave before dawn and you're back after dark. I miss you."

He snorted, a low sound emitted through his nose. "Doesn't look like it," he growled. "You look just fine to me."

Hana glanced back at Michael and scowled. "You leave me no choice," she whispered, trying not to draw attention to herself. "I'm bored and lonely." Logan gave another thwack of the sledgehammer and Hana took a step back. The contact of metal on wood vibrated the ground beneath her and made her stomach feel odd. She put a hand over her bump and frowned. "I don't know what you want from me, Logan," she sighed. "I think I'll drive home for Christmas. Being alone beats being wrong at every turn."

"Don't." Logan put the sledgehammer down and leaned the handle against the fence post. "I'm sorry. Things got busy and I don't want Michael around. Mum won't let me send him away."

"Then learn to live with it." Hana's reply sounded sharp. "And stop leaving me to find my own entertainment. At least at home I'd have Maihi and Jas."

Logan capitulated and removed his gloves. He reached out to stroke Hana's cheek. His fingers smelled like bush fern mixed with dust. "I just don't like it, is all," he said, kissing her forehead and nuzzling her hair. "I don't trust him."

"Does that mean you don't trust me either?" Hana demanded and Logan's face clouded over. Jealousy rose like a green monster between them and she shook her head and took a step back. "And there we have it. One rule for you and another for me." She gritted her teeth and her green eyes flashed. "It's sounding more and more like the Du Rose way the longer I stay, Logan. You can stick it."

Hana whirled away and Logan tossed his gloves to the ground and followed. She heard his feet pounding the earth behind her and cringed. The men stilled their digging into the cooler and stopped to watch, sensing trouble before it began. Embarrassment flushed Hana's cheeks as she contemplated a public argument, but Logan ignored her and made a beeline for Michael. He seized him by the throat and pushed him against the quad. Water sloshed inside the container. "I know your dirty game, man. You touch my wife and I'll bury you!"

Michael's face paled in anger and he balled his fists. "You never forget or forgive, do you Logan?" he replied through gritted teeth. "One mistake in the past and that's it for you, isn't it?"

"Some mistake!" Logan scoffed. "And I heard it was more than once, the last time only hours before she aborted the baby!"

Hana cringed. The stockmen moved wordlessly away and Toby glanced at Hana before subduing his instant swearword to a dull hiss.

"I said sorry!" Michael shouted. "Why do you never let things go? You've got everything you ever wanted and you're still not happy."

"I'll be happy when you get in that fancy car of yours and drive away," Logan hissed. He lowered his voice so only Hana heard. "Mum's little favourite. Stay away from my wife, I'm warning you!"

Hana's face clouded with anger and she moved away, one hand over her stomach. The thought of Caroline and Logan made the bile rise into her throat and she felt prickling heat spread over her body. Caroline's blonde hair and long legs fixed a picture of themselves in Hana's memory, making her feel lumpy and inadequate in her pregnant state. Her confidence drained away and left her shaking. "Don't mind me!" she shouted over her shoulder. "You carry on fighting about an old girlfriend. I'm leaving."

"Hana!" Logan called after her, sorrow in his tone. She ignored him, stalking along the uneven mountain path. Tears of misery streaked her cheeks and she blamed the pregnancy hormones for the rush of emotion. "Bloody men and their bloody egos!" she raged to a wax-eye as it shadowed her down the mountain.

Michael met her a few hundred metres out. "Get on the bike!" he shouted. Hana ignored him and he killed the engine before running on foot to catch her up. She backed away from him and her foot slipped. His grey eyes widened as he caught her wrist and stopped her plunging down an embankment. "Get on the bloody quad bike!" he shouted into her face.

Exhaustion turned Hana's legs to concrete and she allowed him to push her into the seat. She sniffed and cried until the green valley opened out before her, not bothering to wash the tears away. Michael remained furious, opening the last gate and driving the quad through the gap. He slammed it behind them and climbed back in, seizing the wheel and gunning the pedal. Their downward speed increased, bumping Hana into the back of the seat and forcing her to cling on. The ground moved fast in her peripheral vision and merged into a blur of green and yellow. Nausea rose into her chest and she snatched at Michael's sleeve. "Please, stop!" Her clawing nails scratched his bicep and he hauled on the brakes.

"Sorry, sorry!" His voice sounded full of contrition as he glimpsed her ashen face. He accompanied the apology with a swear word. The quad slewed against gravity on its downward run and Hana plunged into the foot well, feet first. Her chin met her knees and she yelped in pain, the metallic taste of blood spilling into her mouth.

"Hana!" Michael got the bike under control and hauled her back into her seat. She panted and clutched her stomach, but when she ran a shaking hand across her lips, it came away bloody.

"Oh, no!" she groaned, peering at her fingers.

"Let me see," Michael demanded, forcing her to open her mouth. Guilt cast his handsome features into shadow. "You bit the inside of your lip. It looks worse than it is."

"It hurts." Hana's tears mingled with the blood and cascaded onto her yellow dress, leaving a slick pink mess.

"I'm sorry," Michael whispered. "I'm really sorry."

"It's fine." Hana pushed his fingers away and dabbed at her lip with the hem of her dress. "Leave me alone."

A dull pain spread out from the base of her spine bringing discomfort and a sense of warning.

Michael berated himself. "He'll never forgive me, will he?" His tone held genuine regret and Hana opened her mouth, ready to offer reassurance.

"We need not tell Logan."

"I meant the Caroline thing," Michael replied. "He'll never forgive me."

Hana closed her eyes. Caroline's absence provided no escape from her pervading influence. She could wreck everything even from a distance. She watched Michael's blunted thumb dig at a rip in the leather of the steering wheel and held her tongue. He only cared about himself and she promised herself she'd stay away from him in the future.

"Are you really leaving?" he asked, pressing the gas pedal and easing the machine forward.

"I don't know," Hana murmured. "That kinda depends on my husband."

Michael drove in silence, sending occasional glances of concern her way. He opened the final gate and drove into the stable yard. "I'm having an affair," he announced, watching as Jack's head bobbed up and down in a distant stable. Hay appeared on a pitchfork and then lowered.

"I don't care." Hana rubbed her lower back and winced. "I don't want to know."

"It's Tama's mother." Michael bit his lower lip. "I love her."

Hana snorted and closed her eyes. "I told you, Michael, I don't care." The baby kicked her in the ribs and she groaned.

"I didn't leave her, Hana. If she'd told me she was pregnant, I'd have married her, but she didn't trust me enough. She got with my deadbeat cousin and tried to pass the baby off as his. Kane bashed the hell out of her and she ran for her own safety.

Her biggest mistake was leaving Tama behind because Reuben never let her take him back."

"Why?" The swelling in her mouth made the word sound strange. Hana glanced up and noticed Jack watching from the stable. He'd stopped working and she sensed his disapproval.

Michael narrowed his eyes. "To hurt Dad. He's Tama's grandfather, not Rueben. He denied him a moko because he already lost a son."

"Your dad lost a son? I know he did. Barry."

"No! Reuben!" Michael's anger startled her and Hana clambered from the bike, fear driving her urgency.

"I'm not interested!" Her chest hitched and the scrape of a stable door alerted her to Jack's steady progress across the yard. He made a beeline for her, pointing to the blood on her dress, his eyes wide with alarm. Hana dodged his outstretched arms and ran, heaving herself towards the hotel with difficulty. She heard a yell of surprise from Michael and glanced behind to see Jack lurch for his throat.

"Get off me, you crazy old man!" Michael shouted. "It's not what you think!"

Hana ignored everyone on the way to Logan's room. She closed the door behind her and leaned against it, relief washing over her. "Logan's room," she whispered to herself. "Not Hana's and Logan's. Just Logan's."

Shaking fingers washed the blood from her dress and laid it over the towel rail to dry. She crawled into bed and feigned sleep when Logan came to see her later. "I'm sorry," she heard him whisper and held her breath. The click of the bedroom door released her from her play act and she sat up. Using her mobile phone, she found the number of a taxi firm and dialled. The operator laughed at her.

"Six hundred bucks from there to Huntly," she said, sniggering as though Hana's call represented the funniest prank she'd ever received. "You're in the ass end of nowhere and the roads are shite. Besides, it's Christmas."

Three other taxi firms delivered the same news and similar prices. Hana daren't risk it, not after her recent great escape to Invercargill. She contemplated sending an SOS to Bodie, but the thought of his enjoyment in her plight deterred her from making the call. Falling asleep in utter misery, Hana missed the last Christmas meal of the year and slept through the exit of all remaining guests. She snoozed on as the hotel quietened to the sounds of the mountain and the last car snaked its way up the drive.

Chapter 44

Logan left before Hana woke, leaving a note stuck to his pillow. The single word of apology seemed to punish her for the call to the taxi firm and she pushed it beneath the covers. "You're all weird," she sighed, rolling onto her back.

When she didn't appear for breakfast, Leslie arrived with tea and toast. She let herself in after knocking and sat on the edge of the bed to watch Hana pick at the food. "What happened yesterday?" she demanded, her tone soothing and confidential. "You can tell me."

Hana shrugged. "I have no idea. It wasn't about me. I got caught in the middle of something old and it made me feel dirty. If I could've got a taxi, I'd be at home by now."

"But this is your home, kōtiro." Leslie reached across and patted her knee through the blankets. "Youse the best thing that's happened to this place in a very long time."

Hana snorted. "So, why doesn't it feel that way?"

"What happened to your lip? Did someone hurt youse, girly?"

"No." Hana realised the veiled question and her fingers flickered over the swelling. "Logan wouldn't do that."

"I didn't mean him."

Hana sighed. "Nobody hurt me, Leslie. The quad slipped on the last hill and I banged my lip on my knee."

Leslie tutted and rose to her feet. "With that great lump in the way? Youse must be more flexible than you look. You take care of that baby. Take a morning off and relax. Nobody will blame you." She gave Hana a toothless smile. "Ring reception if you need anything and I'll come straight up."

Hana nodded her thanks and discarded the unwanted food as soon as Leslie left the room. She lay in bed and sulked for a while, but her painful back drove her to take a long soak in the bath. The effort exhausted her and she dressed in loose clothing and turned on the television. She threw the remote control in disgust. "One hundred and ten channels of utter Christmas crap," she grumbled.

Flinging the ranch slider open to allow air to cool the room, Hana spotted the old cabinet Logan kept near the credenza. With a significant degree of effort, she sank to her knees and opened the door. Her husband's eclectic stash of DVDs tumbled out onto the floorboards and she sifted through them. Wrinkling her lip caused pain and she tried to keep her annoyance in check. "Die Hard meets A Midsummer Night's Dream," she grumbled, sorting them into alphabetical order. "This one." Hana held up a cover displaying zoo animals and Matt Damon, an odd combination, but promising.

Locked in position, her legs tingled and she didn't trust them to carry her to either the bed or the armchair. "Great!" she muttered. Thrusting the corner of the DVD case into the good side of her mouth, she slithered across the floor on her hands and knees. Her forehead hit the footboard of the bed and she dropped the DVD case. It opened with a click and the disc skittered under the bed. Hana groaned and closed her eyes as misery washed over her. The strange position seemed to alleviate the pain in her lower back and she remained there until her knees ached.

"Want a hand up?" The deep voice echoed off the walls and Hana jumped, bumping her nose into the footboard. A stranger stood in front of the closed bedroom door, feet slightly apart and hands behind his back as though on guard duty. Hana's heart rate increased and she heard blood swishing through her eardrums. The heightened throb-throb-pulse made her body shake with the force of it. She stared at him, her lips parting to reveal the cut.

"Did Laval send you to kill me?" she whispered.

The man stared back, his face impassive. His hair curled around his collar, dark and wavy and his irises held Du Rose genetics in their stunning slate grey tones. His olive skin seemed to shine in the sunlight through the window and he shook his head. "No."

He towered over Hana, graced with an elegant natural height which fitted his build. He must have ducked to enter the room. Despite the grey flecks in his hair and the deep crow's feet around his almond eyes, he looked honed and fit, muscle and vein distinguishing themselves through the flesh of his forearms. His resemblance to Alfred seemed to wax and wane, depending on his face expression. At that moment, it held a look of confusion. "Who hurt you?"

"Nobody." Hana shrank onto her haunches at his look of disbelief. "The quad bike."

He stepped towards her and she flinched, still clinging to the footboard. Numbness pervaded her knee joints. "No, kōtiro, please don't fear me." He held his hands out, palms upwards in placation and his face clouded with a bone-deep sadness that reached for Hana's soul. An innate magnetism captured her and drew her in, so that when he offered his hand she took it.

He raised her to her feet with gentleness, a palm cupped beneath each elbow. "You should sit," he said, walking backwards to lead her to the side of the bed. Once she eased onto the mattress, he let go and stepped back. A distant look clothed his dark irises in sadness. "This was my room," he said. "It's where I made my best and worst decisions." He nodded in approval. "The boy made it nice. Ka pai. I hope life will be kinder to you in here than it was to me, Hana Du Rose."

His left hand rubbed at his chin with long, slender fingers. Hana thought they wouldn't look out of place plucking guitar strings or wielding a paintbrush. His curved thumb looked scarred and twisted as though broken and badly set.

Turning, he jumped as a loose board creaked beneath his foot. A look of delight lit his face as the childish memories flooded back. He closed his eyes and when he opened them, misery had replaced them. "They try, but they can't change history, Hana Du Rose. They can't wipe out everything." He offered her a lopsided smile and her heart felt as though it halted in her chest. The shock of realisation drummed through her like an electrical pulse, the paralysis painful and devastating. "May I?" While she still floundered, he placed a palm over her belly, scars criss-crossing the back of his hand. Pinprick grey hairs dotted the black of his sideburns and littered the hair around his chin. His grey eyes pierced her soul and he smiled.

"Reuben," he said, his tone soft and lilting. He kept his left hand over her stomach and stroked her cheek with his right.

Her breath came in short rasps. "Hana," she said, her voice a whisper and he laughed, a sound like distant wind chimes.

"I know who you are." His lips curved upwards and the startling likeness gave Hana the sensation of falling. Reuben stroked his calloused palm across her belly. "And I know who this is."

The baby kicked against his hand and his face creased in pleasure. His lips pursed into a delighted 'o' and his grey eyes glinted. Brought to her senses, Hana pushed his hand away, horrified at the man's forward intimacy. "Why are you here?" she demanded.

The light disappeared from Reuben's eyes and his lips turned down in a sad smile. As if in sympathy, the sun sneaked behind a cloud and bathed the summer day in grey tones. His eyes resembled pools of ice on a dark river, tales of heartache fathoms deep. "I wished to meet my hunaonga," he said. "And I knew you wouldn't come to me."

Hana shook her head, recognising the Māori word but not wanting to hear it spoken. Not by this man. "What do you want?" she pleaded.

Reuben drew himself up to his full height and bowed at the waist, his dark curls falling forward into his eyes. He placed his right hand across his heart and gave the smile which would one day haunt her dreams. "Nothing," he replied, his tone soft. "You've given me more than I deserve. Goodbye, Hana Du Rose."

Reuben left, closing the bedroom door behind him. Hana drew her knees into her chest and cried, dredging tears from a well of misery she believed long since closed.

Chapter 45

"Is this still about my fight with Michael?" Logan closed the bathroom door and leaned against it. "I've said I'm sorry."

"I'm fine!" Hana snapped, running a hand over her stomach. "Just stop, Logan."

"Is it those funny contractions?" His jaw moved from side to side as he chewed the inside of his cheek.

Hana snorted. "Please don't pretend you care, Logan! Otherwise you'd be here with me instead of riding around the mountain all day and night. Just go to work and stop making excuses."

"I'm tidying things up so we can have a proper Christmas break." His voice rose and his brow furrowed. "The grazing on the mountain is tinder dry so we're mustering them nearer home."

Hana spun around, toothbrush in hand. Paste dripped onto the cool white surface surrounding the sink. "Do I look like I care, Logan? Just leave me alone. If I could afford a taxi to take me home, I'd be gone by now."

"Hana!" Logan took a step forward and she repelled him with a look of warning. He heeded it, whirling around and slamming the door behind him.

Logan tried again at lunchtime, making the long ride home despite the sandwiches Leslie packed for him. He found Hana in the library, feeling the uncharacteristic resistance as he pulled her into his side. "Why do I get the feeling you're keeping something from me?" He sounded hurt and Hana reacted with guilty anger.

"Because you imagine stuff," she snapped. "Like imagining your brother would make a pass at a woman who looks like an orange and walks like a penguin." She laced her comment with a smile which didn't reach her eyes.

"I said I'm sorry," Logan replied. "Things between me and Michael are complicated."

"But family's all we have!" Hana implored. "There is nothing else. Without it, we're lost." She wrung her hands and gnawed on her bottom lip. "Logan?" She turned her face upwards and her eyes implored him for clemency. "Logan, please call off the legal action on your uncle?"

"What? No!" Logan removed his arms from around her and slid away. Temper flashed behind his eyes. "Not you as well! I assumed my wife would support me."

"It's important, Logan. Please? Just do it for me?"

"No! And thanks for nothing!" He slammed the door behind him, leaving Hana in agony. She cried to the point of hysteria, a nosy tui bird ruffling his white bow tie and mimicking her tears through the open French doors.

The Du Rose family unit completed itself with the celebrated arrival of the judge. Hana receded more into the fringes as Liza dominated Miriam's attention. Tama allied with her and they hung together, two pieces of driftwood floating loose after a storm.

Logan received a phone call as he mended a fence on the side of the mountain. He walked away from the hammering until the signal grew stronger. "What?" he demanded, sticking a finger into his ear.

"It's done," his lawyer replied. "The settlement is in, your uncle has signed and you can enjoy Christmas." He laughed down the line. "So can I with the overtime I'm billing you for."

"Wow." Logan frowned and saw Toby glance across at him. Someone else picked up the sledgehammer and continued to thump the post into the ground. The lawyer spoke for a while longer and then Logan gave a final reply. "Just email me the bill and I'll get it paid tonight." He returned to the men and shared the news.

"That showed the old bugger." Toby grinned. "Maybe he can call his psycho son off us now."

"Just keep running Kane off with the guns," Logan said with an evil smile. "And if you accidentally trip and shoot him, make the body disappear."

The men laughed and nodded. Toby watched Logan with the understanding of familiarity and he waited for his opportunity as the men broke for lunch. "That's not all, is it?" he asked, lowering his voice. "What's wrong?"

Logan turned away from the group and leaned on the handle of a shovel. "Reuben demands a face-to-face meeting. He's signed on the understanding he'll get one and my lawyer saw no reason not to just appease him."

Toby's brow knitted. "You can't, man. Don't do it."

"I need this finished." Logan ran a dusty hand through his hair. "Even Hana's fighting me over it now. I tried to make a point and failed. If meeting him once gets him off my back, it's worth it."

"But you did meet him, remember? That night last winter when Kane busted the window. Reuben just stared at you."

Logan shrugged. "Yeah, well. Don't mention it to anyone else, please? The lawyer is setting it up for this evening."

Logan shared the news with his family and only Liza celebrated with him. When he slipped away to meet Rueben, Toby stepped from the shadows and offered his support. "I won't come in," he promised. "But I'll wait in the truck. Just in case."

Hana lay in bed later and listened to her husband's snores. He arrived home after midnight stinking of alcohol and weaving across the floor. Tripping over his own feet, he slammed into the bed and Hana struggled to get back to sleep afterwards. She crept down to the library using the light from her phone and read Jane Austen until she fell asleep in an armchair.

Logan woke the next day with a pounding headache, to find Hana already dressed and gone. He rode up the mountain late and the men avoided his quick temper and short patience. Miriam roped Hana into Christmas preparations, chopping and mixing for her homemade marinades. "On Christmas Eve we always have dinner with the workers," she said, slapping a bowl next to Hana. "Those without whānau eat with us and that's the way it's always been."

Hana sighed and poured chopped onion into the bowl. She stuck her tongue out at Miriam's back and rolled her eyes. "I wasn't intending to challenge the way it's always been," she muttered and Miriam whirled around.

"What? Speak up."

"Nothing." Hana swallowed and kept the rest of her comments to herself.

She spent the morning fetching and carrying herbs from the vegetable garden and Leslie stopped her with a basket of rosemary and sage. "You shouldn't be doing that," she grumbled. "Youse look terrible."

Hana sighed through her nose. "I'm fine. I'm glad someone wants me."

Leslie released her with a shake of her head.

"Do you ever keep secrets from Alfred?" Hana asked her mother-in-law as they folded sheets in the laundry. Miriam's hand stilled and her grey eyes fixed on Hana's face as though reading her features.

"Why do you ask that?" Her tone sounded sharp.

"It doesn't matter," Hana responded, unable to reveal the root of her question. "I just wondered how other people deal with things and I've no one to ask."

"Best not doing secret things and then you won't have secrets to keep," Miriam bit and Hana nodded.

"Fair enough," she replied.

Logan's presence forced Hana to think about the enormous lie she carried in her chest and when she saw him naked, the whakapapa tattoo screamed its inaccuracy into her soul. Detailing a heritage he didn't own, it made Hana sick to her stomach.

Miriam's attitude towards Hana changed after her blundered question about secrecy and she treated her like a servant, barking orders as though she was the paid help and not a family member. "That meat won't fully defrost until later. Put those marinades in the chiller in their containers. Then we'll rub them into the steaks and leave them until Christmas Eve. It's Alfie's mother's recipe. I'll give it to you one day, when you've earned it."

They sat at the kitchen table mid-afternoon, Hana peeling potatoes and sipping tea. Miriam swallowed her tablets, but seemed as listless and distracted as Hana. "I'm going out for a while," she snapped, leaving the room without explanation.

Hana sighed and dropped the potato knife onto the table. "Would you like to come, Hana? That would be lovely. It's not like I'm doing anything special right now." Temper budded in Hana's soul and on a whim, she popped her head into the corridor and watched her mother-in-law stride away. The door closed behind her with a click and she held her breath, knowing her brain proposed something ridiculous even as her legs began moving beneath her.

She followed Miriam. "She's probably going to the bathroom," Hana breathed, offering herself reassurances she didn't believe. When Miriam stalked through the lobby, Hana trailed behind, stopping to pull an information brochure from the rack. The reception desk sat empty, the woman gone for the holiday break and Hana heaved a relieved sigh as she scuttled past, shoving the leaflet into her pocket. Miriam's stride took her along the corridor with the rope barrier and Hana slowed, anticipating her using the spiral staircase and then the lift to her attic apartment. She hung back, readying her expression to one of nonchalance in case Miriam turned. She didn't.

Past the spiral staircase, Miriam strode on, using the hidden corridor as a rat run through the house. Hana pressed on after her, aware that if her mother-in-law looked behind, she possessed no ready excuse for following save her own warped curiosity. She kept her steps light and made no sound, her old Converse padding along the wooden floor in silence. Miriam's shoes slapped against the wood, accentuating her uneven, arthritic gait and covering any sound Hana made.

Light spewed into the darkness as Miriam hit the bar on the fire exit at the end of the corridor. It opened beneath her hand and swung outwards as Hana remembered. Miriam's shoes tapped down the stairs outside and the door slammed closed again, condemning Hana to shadow. Picking up speed, Hana stopped worrying about noise and ran to the door, holding one hand beneath her bump for support. She pushed the bar and the door opened beneath her palm. She halted then, scared of coming face to face with Miriam and exercised caution, peeking around it and easing it open with deliberate slowness.

It was as though Miriam reached the bottom of the short staircase and vanished. No sign of her remained. Hana waited, not sure which direction to take in order to continue her futile pursuit. She imagined recounting her adventure to Logan and felt ashamed. Sunshine bathed the stable yard beyond, the loose boxes silent and empty. Jack used a wide broom to brush wisps of hay from the cobbled surface, collecting it into a pile next to a rusty wheelbarrow. He glanced up once and Hana saw him stop, resting his chin on the broom handle. Something caught his eye and he watched it for a while, shaking his head before returning to his task.

Hana held her breath, wondering if he'd seen Miriam. She let the door clang behind her, relieved when Jack didn't even look up. She trotted down the stairs, trying to make her mission look more like a casual walk than a chase in case someone saw her. But she skirted the rear of the stables and set out towards the direction Jack had looked. Crowded around the courtyard, the stable block made up three lengths of single storey buildings and Hana ran around two. She halted with her hand on a low windowsill, seeing Jack's disorganised office beyond the glass. A whisky bottle sat in the centre of a paper pile, a voice of unreason in a demolition site. A rolled cigarette sat next to it. Hana edged to the end of the building and peered around it.

Logan sat on a dark horse at the point where the foothills met the bush. Hana heard the clank of his tack despite the kilometres between them. The day felt still and airless and she held her breath at the sight of his ease in the saddle, wondering why such a demi-god ever allied himself with her. "He could have anyone," she breathed, watching as he lifted his hat and wiped his forehead with the back of his hand. Inadequate fingers sought the security of her bump and Hana let her fingers caress her child's outline. He chose her.

Logan leaned down and pulled open the gate, backing the horse until the metal eased open. His mount pawed the ground beneath them and Hana sensed an air of expectation. A low rumble came to her, crashing through the stillness and trembling the earth beneath her feet. Distracted, she watched as steer streamed down the narrow track like cream emerging from a bottle. The white Charolais poured into the paddock below the bush and spread out in a controlled spill. Hana heard whooping and the crack of a bullwhip as two riders followed the last of the five hundred strong herd. Logan closed the gate and drove his horse into the stragglers, sending them down the mountain and into the back of the herd.

Excitement budded in Hana's heart at the sight of the muster and she longed to join them. Her fingers itched to feel the smooth leather of reins and experience the ground rushing beneath her. She longed to become a seamless part of Logan's other world. Hopelessness washed over her as the thrill dissipated on the wind. Glancing right, her eyes followed the path Logan drove her along when he took her to see Sacha's foal. A ridge below the bush marked the space where she'd plunged into the foot well of the quad under Michael's careless watch. Hana winced and placed a hand in the small of her back. It hurt less, but it still hurt.

"What are you doing?" Hana jumped and banged her hand against the brickwork. It smarted and she hissed and pulled it towards her. A red graze across the knuckles of her left hand blossomed like a marker to her stupidity.

"Nothing!" she snapped, whirling around to glare at Tama. "What are you doing?"

He shrugged and held up a set of keys. "I borrowed Jack's truck to go into town. I'm putting his keys back in the office."

"Through the window?" Hana let sarcasm lace her tone and Tama grinned.

"Nope. I saw you creeping behind here and wanted to see what you were up to."

Hana pointed towards the herd. The cows bunched where the riders drove them, ready to funnel into a lower paddock. "I wanted to see the muster," she lied. "But I didn't want people to think me stupid. I've never seen one before."

"Oh." Tama watched Logan weave his mount behind a stray, cracking his whip and pushing it forward. The horse ducked and dove beneath him and his strong torso moved in tune with it. "It's really something, aye?"

"Do you take part?" Hana turned and looked up at him. Her eyes widened as she spotted her quarry emerge from a low patch of bush and continue climbing. She held her breath as Tama answered.

"Yep. But they didn't need me today. They moved the rest down yesterday, but these came from the top of the mountain so they left them until last." Tama jangled the keys. "Logan sent me on an errand."

Hana watched Miriam pass the ridge and her fingers moved instinctively to her spine in acknowledgement of the pain she endured there. Then her mother-in-law stepped onto the path leading to the bunkhouse and the canopy swallowed her up. Tama turned and followed her gaze. "What are we looking at?"

Hana sighed. "I went in the quad with Michael the other day and we came down too fast." She pointed to a rocky outcrop. "I slipped into the foot well right there and hurt my back."

Tama snorted and his brows knitted into a dark line. "He's a dick. I'm avoiding him."

"I noticed." Hana's green eyes settled on his face. "Miriam just walked up there. Where do you think she's going?"

Tama swallowed. "Best you don't know the answer to that."

Hana snorted. "What a surprise. Another Du Rose secret I'm not part of."

"You and me both!" Tama's face creased in concern and he slipped his hand around the back of her neck. Her face pressed into his chest and she experienced a flush of solidarity. "Guess we're both outcasts."

"Yeah." Gratitude washed over her and she shelved Logan's warnings. It stood to reason under the weight of his neglect she'd seek company elsewhere. Logan Du Rose be damned.

Tama slipped his arm around her shoulders and she let him. They walked around the building and Hana waited while Tama sat the keys next to the whisky bottle on Jack's desk. Then they walked to the rose garden to sit in the shade. Hana inhaled and asked her burning question. "Have you ever known something, something you wish you didn't and not known what to do about it?"

Tama nodded and his eyes widened. "Yes."

"What did you do?" Hana persisted, "Did you tell?"

He shook his head and vehemence crept into his narrowed eyes. His lips turned downwards in a grim line. "Never. It had the potential to detonate someone else's life. Your life and Logan's. I tried to change things, but I never told Laval or Larne where you lived."

Hana fixed him with a searching stare and allowed his answer to sink in. Then she let the matter drop, not liking the implication. She doubted she could live her whole life without telling Logan the truth. Her fingers strayed to her belly and she grimaced. There was more at stake than she'd imagined.

Chapter 46

Hana lingered in the rose garden with Tama. It offered one of the few areas of shade and the intoxicating scent of warmed blooms brought peace. "Do you remember what your Uncle Barry died of?" she asked, keeping her tone casual as she watched a bee collect pollen from a delicate rose head. It emerged as though drunk and seemed to hold in mid-air before weaving across the garden.

"I wasn't born," Tama replied with a smile. "But I heard he died from complications related to a blood disease. Poppa Rueben told me."

"Haemophilia." Hana's teeth ground against the word. "I didn't know Logan had it when we married."

Tama nodded. "We studied it at school. It's genetic. Girls are carriers and don't generally suffer from the disease. They get it from their father and boys get it from a carrier mother. If you've got two parents with it, then you're potentially screwed." He glanced at Hana's stomach. "So, you need your baby to be a boy. Then it stops the line continuing."

Hana sighed and pushed the thought away. She'd done her own research and acknowledged a high chance her daughter would be born a carrier. Tama flicked a fallen leaf off the crest of her belly, his expression thoughtful. "Poppa Reuben has haemophilia. And Uncle Kane." His brow furrowed. "They bleed like stuck pigs. Good job they didn't have daughters, aye?" He grinned. "Koro Alfred doesn't have it, so Barry and Logan got it from Kui Miriam. Poppa Reuben says that's why she gets so depressed. She feels guilty. It's a fifty percent rule, though, so it's a shame Logan got it too. Really unlucky I guess, but statistically correct."

They wandered through the vegetable garden and Hana remembered the half-peeled potatoes on the table. She winced, wondering what Miriam would say when she found them turning brown. "We should dig up more potatoes," she said, chewing her lower lip. "For the dinner tomorrow."

Tama shrugged. "Okay. I'll dig and you pull them off the plant," he agreed. It proved hot work and Tama removed his shirt beneath the hot sun. His olive skin glistened and he winked at Hana and flexed his biceps.

She smirked at his antics. "Logan threatened to bury Michael for driving me round on the quad bike. Are you going for a full execution?"

Tama snorted. "Na, Logan just wants an excuse to start up with his dick brother. He threatens me, but he doesn't follow through."

"You'd better hope not." Hana's voice wavered as she strained to gather the tubers into a bucket. Her belly hung between her legs as she squatted and her lower back began its insistent tugging.

"Logan smacked me hard once though." Tama pressed the fork beneath a wilting plant. "In the face."

Hana gaped and Tama shrugged. "But he used my fist, so maybe it doesn't count."

"Why would he do that?" Hana paused in her work and watched Tama's expression move through a series of emotions from mirth to dread.

"Yeah." He paused with one foot on the fork. "Let's just leave that one hanging."

Hana shook her head as she rolled a potato in her hands to get the loose dust off. "Promise me you'll behave from now on?" she asked. He stopped digging again, his dark eyebrows raised and his grey eyes curious.

"Why do you care?"

"I don't know." Hana looked at Tama with her wide emerald eyes reflecting honesty. "I can stop if you don't want me to."

He bit his lip and looked thoughtful. "I want you to," he replied with certainty. "I'd like it."

Miriam sat at the kitchen table as Tama carried the potatoes through the door. She glanced up and glared at Hana. "I thought you were peeling those," she said, jerking her head towards the stove. The potatoes bubbled in hot water, a brown scum on the surface.

"Sorry." Hana allowed nonchalance to creep into her tone. She bit down on the ready rebuke which would lead to trouble. "We got more potatoes."

Miriam ran cold water into the sink and watched Tama tumble the potatoes into it with a splash. She kissed his bicep and Hana saw her eyes close in pleasure. "You're a good moko," she whispered, her tone confidential and intended to shut Hana out. Hana shook her head as tiredness swamped her body. So much mixed parentage and too many lies. They swirled around her head like irritating gnats, making her want to scream their truths aloud and force them from their dark, destructive corners.

She avoided the family at dinner time, making an excuse and returning to the rose garden. Daylight slid away from the mountain and though Logan sought her, he didn't think to look there. She crawled into bed early, hearing the sound of Du Rose laughter returning as an echo to haunt her. Figuring they enjoyed their dinner more without her, she sank into her pillows with turmoil and confusion for company. Her mobile phone clutched in her fingers, she twice typed a text to her son asking him to fetch her on Boxing Day. Both times she deleted it, not wanting to admit defeat. She knew he'd come, but the thought of his victorious speech put her off. She typed it again and left it on the screen, falling asleep as the back light winked out.

A sense of alarm woke her. Hana lay on the spacious mattress and forced herself to full consciousness, listening to the familiar bush sounds from outside. The room felt stuffy where she'd forgotten to open the ranch slider to the balcony. Her fingers pushed through the covers to Logan's side of the bed, finding it empty and cool.

Liza moved around in the room next door, soft thuds and the sound of a wardrobe door sliding closed. The judge spent the day elsewhere and Hana felt her chest tighten at the thought of Christmas Eve dinner under her accusatorial glare. Sitting up in bed, she felt the sense of unease descend like a band around her head. Urgency accompanied it and she pushed herself from the bed and stumbled to the bathroom. "This is ridiculous." She spoke to her reflection as she washed her hands, the water containing an odd brown tinge. "Find Logan and tell him how you feel. If he doesn't listen, call Bodie."

The power surged and the bathroom light flared and then dimmed as Hana washed her face and cleaned her teeth. Loneliness wrapped familiar arms around her shoulders and she shrugged them loose. Pulling a pair of maternity pants on and tucking in Logan's borrowed shirt, she slipped from the room and into the hallway, steeling herself for the overwhelming mission: How to explain a resolution based on emotion to a man ruled by logic.

A door slammed behind her as she passed along the corridor and she jumped and whirled around. Liza folded her arms and Hana quailed, a guilty expression settling over her features. She opened her mouth to release a barrage of excuses for her pre-dawn wandering, but Liza held up a hand to silence her. "Can you smell it?" she demanded.

"What?" Hana took a step towards her and then halted, proximity to the snake a bad idea. "Smell what?"

Liza puffed out a breath of exasperation and then beckoned her closer. Hana's bare feet padded along the hallway and then stopped again. "Come on!" Liza urged, pushing her door open and flapping her hand. With great reluctance, Hana entered the judge's den.

Liza's ranch slider stood wide open, the net curtains billowing into the room like the skirts from a voluminous wedding dress. Hana smelled it and her eyes widened in fear. Acrid, like the blue smoke from burning tyres, the scent hung on the balmy air and left her throat feeling raw. Listening, she heard faint shouts echo from far away, stilted and distorted noises rolling down the mountainside.

"Fire!" Hana inhaled and winced at the scent which permeated her lungs. She ran from the room and punched numbers into the keypad outside her door, hurry making her fingers error twice before gaining access. She shoved her feet into trainers but didn't stop to tie the laces. Logan's shirt escaped from her maternity pants and she left it loose, the buttons straining over her stomach as she reached for her phone. Turning it over, she pressed keys but the dark screen remained sleeping.

Liza hurried ahead of her along the hallway, halting as Hana called her name. Her voice sounded anguished and high. "Are you going to look?"

Liza swallowed, her grey eyes flashing in the darkness. "If it's a bush fire, they won't be able to stop it. They'll need all the help they can get."

Hana nodded and her fingers fluttered in the air. "Logan didn't come to bed. I think he's up there."

Liza's nostrils flared and she turned away. "We'll see if there's a vehicle left." Hana followed her to the top of the spiral staircase and negotiated her way down. Liza moved with lithe proficiency, not encumbered by an eight month pregnancy or untied shoes. Hana puffed behind her, one hand supporting her rounded belly. She stumbled at the foot of the spiral staircase and Liza glared back at her, irritation overriding concern. "Don't hold me up or I'll leave you!" she bit.

They burst outside into the courtyard and the smell rode over them like a tide. Liza knew it, sniffing the air like a dog. "That's a house fire!" she exclaimed.

In the stable yard, the quad bike sat next to the tack room. The security light flashed on showing the key still in the ignition and Liza cranked it into action with deft, unruffled fingers.

"Jack turned the horses out last night," Hana gushed, remembering him sweeping the empty yard. She clambered into the passenger seat and attempted to sit down on the already moving vehicle. Its dull green paintwork looked eerie in the darkness as they spun away from the hotel and onto the steep paddocks.

Liza forced Hana to get out and open the first few gates, screaming at her when she fumbled the catches or pushed them the wrong way. "You're useless!" she railed. "What does Logan see in you? Get out of the bloody way!" After the third one, she did it herself.

They screeched around the front of the bunkhouse and Hana sighed with relief at Sacha's empty pen. The building looked intact, lights glaring from open doorways and no sign of life. Liza's eyes flashed as she ate up the abandoned scene. "It must be Uncle Reuben's place," she said, her voice a low hush. "Everyone's gone there. That's why the hotel seemed deserted when I got home."

She gunned the accelerator and the quad performed a wide circle, heading back the way they'd come but turning right on the track. The wheels dug into the earth, spitting up dust and making them cough. Higher up the mountain, the smell became overpowering and the fractured noises grew louder and more pronounced. A sinister crackling accompanied male shouts and fear lodged itself in Hana's heart and stayed there. "Oh God!" she whispered, desperate for divine help. "Please, not Logan."

The quad ground to a halt in a clearing where Jack's Jeep blocked the gate. Liza turned it off and abandoned it. She vaulted the gate, leaving Hana to clamber over the rails with her outsized belly getting in the way.

She puffed behind Liza after stopping to tie her flapping laces. Logan's sister seemed confident of the route, despite the eerie blackness surrounding them and the canopy which blocked out the stars overhead. They followed a fence line for ten minutes of hard climbing until Hana's breath came in agonised heaves. Several times she slipped, gripping hold of the boundary to save herself. Her right palm became a pattern of barbed wire cuts and splinters, but she gritted her teeth and forced herself onward. A sickening orange light pulled them towards it and black smoke billowed over their heads as they ascended, making them both cough and stop often to cover their faces. Yet still they climbed, not sure what awaited them but driven on by a primeval desire to know, anyway.

Chapter 47

Hana grabbed for the fence wire as heat rolled over her from the source of the fire. The flickering orange light blinded her and her fingers grasped at nothing. The boundary had gone. Already committed, she felt herself falling forwards. The ground rose to meet her and she put her hands out, jarring her wrists and arms as she made contact. A cliff side swung away beneath her as though a giant took a bite from the hard earth. Hana felt wetness beneath her palms and lifted her hands. The orange glow revealed cuts to her fingers from the barbed wire fence lying beneath her.

Strong hands had hauled out the posts and laid them flat, spreading the wire like a sheet. Liza picked her way across it in her tennis shoes, disappearing from sight as she found a route down. Hana peered over, seeing a rough driveway chipped in lime, weeds poking their faces into the haze. Liza didn't wait for Hana, leaving her to struggle through alone. "Thanks for your help," Hana muttered under her breath. "It's been an absolute pleasure spending time with you."

Moving onto her bottom, she swung her legs over the precipice. Her feet found a narrow ridge and she tested it for reliability before hoisting herself down. Well-worn but narrow, the tiny track zig-zagged down towards the driveway through willowy trees and natural scrub. Hana's painful back twisted and jarred. The descent proved perilous, but she forced herself onward, relying on tufts of grass which yanked free in her hands and banging against trees to break her fall. When her feet found the thin gravel of the driveway, she sat in the mud to cup her stomach in bleeding hands and wait for the pain in her back to pass.

The low wooden house, which Logan once gazed down on during their first trip up the mountain, neared a blackened shell at one end. Hana recognised the silhouettes of several stockmen as they held hosepipes on the burning structure. Her heart clenched as she heard a shout and recognised her husband's commanding tone cutting through the crackle of the hungry fire and other men's voices. "Thank you God!" she clapped her hand to her mouth and stifled a sob.

Liza advanced towards a couple gathered on a tatty, threadbare lawn. Hana saw Miriam's frail outline silhouetted against the orange blaze. Toby held her arms and she struggled against him. The air burned hot with the effects of the super-heated wood and Hana felt the trickle of sweat along her spine. She watched Liza gather her mother into her side as the old lady's shoulders heaved with racking sobs. With a curt nod, Toby released her and ran towards a crowd of men passing buckets of sloshing water from a nearby tap. "Why?" Miriam screeched, her voice cutting over all other sounds. "Why would he do this?" She beat at Liza's arms with fists and Hana's brow knitted in confusion at the implication. Who did what?

She lifted the bottom of her shirt and covered her nose and mouth, attempting to block the acrid fumes billowing from burning plastic and popping electrics. Her bare skin poked through the gap, her baby bump vulnerable and exposed. A knot of people gathered near Miriam without making contact and Hana saw a woman holding a small boy in her arms. She searched for Reuben's imposing outline but didn't see him amongst the line of busy males.

Heaving herself to a standing position, Hana approached Liza, placing her footing with care on the ground strewn with sparks and burning timber. "Is everyone out?" she asked, but the judge ignored her and concentrated her efforts on holding Miriam. At close quarters, Hana realised the embrace showed less comfort and more restraint as the old lady struggled to release herself. Miriam beat against Liza's hands and twisted in her grasp.

"Go away!" Liza snapped, seeing the alarm in Hana's eyes. "You're not wanted here!"

Hana edged away, keeping the shirt raised over her mouth. A hand protected her naked belly. Guilt washed over her like hot water at the sense of voyeurism. She tried to join the line passing water buckets but Toby shook his head at her. "Get back, Mrs Du Rose!" he ordered. Hana retreated, separating herself from the helpers and the observers, belonging in neither camp. The division between her and the Du Roses yawned wider than she ever imagined possible.

Logan unwound another length of hosepipe as the first melted in the heat. His actions appeared jerky against the backdrop of the fire and Hana held her breath. Passing the end of the pipe to other grasping hands, he ran back to the line of buckets and took his place. His strong arms pumped and she watched him wipe his mouth against his forearm as proximity to the fire made him cough.

"I'm sorry," she breathed, fear taking hold in her chest. "Sorry, Logan. Forgive me." The stupidity of the arguments between them seemed dwarfed by the fire and she longed for an opportunity to make peace. As a section of the building behind him collapsed, it sent a shower of orange flecks into the night sky to compete with the watching stars. Smoke billowed out and then it happened. An explosion ripped the building wide, sending the line of men onto their faces. Bowled over by the force of the blast, Hana found herself on her back, gasping for clean air and unable to see through the black smoke surrounding her.

Coughing, she pushed herself to a sitting position. Soreness radiated from the back of her head and a cursory examination beneath her fingers revealed a lump. Bodies moved as others stood and she heard Logan's voice. "The power's gone! The water pump won't work. Get the tanks open and use the buckets!" The line regrouped and Hana heard the grind of a concrete lid being hauled from the water tank.

A hand reached down and she grasped it, feeling strong male fingers grip hers. "What about the fire trucks?" she asked, her voice rasping against the sounds of the fire. Toby hauled her upright, pausing for a moment while she steadied herself.

"Won't get up the mountain," he said, bending double to cough. He vomited and Hana patted his back as he retched.

"What then?" she demanded, heat prickling her cheeks and forehead as the fire ate up a nearby outbuilding.

"Dunno." Toby raised upright and moved away, aiming for the knot of men gathered around two water tanks. Unable to reach the depleted water from above, Logan kicked free a pipe in the side of the one nearest the house and water gushed out. The men resumed their bucket passing, making little difference to the raging inferno. Hana watched it lick at the two storey part of the cedar house, consuming everything in its path with enthusiasm.

Then the water ran out. The final trickle sent a rush of panic through the line and the fire cackled its eerie laughter. The men backed away, a silent respectful death march in reverse.

Miriam screamed and thrashed against Liza's thin arms. "Let me go!" she howled. "Tell them not to stop!" Hana watched with morbid fascination as she lashed out at her daughter, not caring that she hurt Liza. Her final push sent Liza sprawling to the ground. Hana broke into a run, pulling her upright with a grunt of exertion. She clung to the judge's wrist, refusing to let go as Liza tried to follow Miriam.

"No!" she shouted into her face as they wrestled. "It's too dangerous."

For Miriam had run towards the building, braving the inferno of super-heated air just as the two-storey end of the house gave up its battle against gravity and sank into a haze of black dust and victorious flames. The fire celebrated, throwing its orange tendrils high and wide like arms dancing in glee as Miriam disappeared beneath it.

Liza stopped struggling and a hush fell over the gathered group. Disbelief seemed to paralyse them for a fraction of a second before movement restarted, uncoordinated and without focus. Hana screamed as Logan ran forward. She released Liza's wrist and her hands covered her mouth in horror. Like the crack of a whip, several men followed, wrestling Logan to the ground. Hana heard his strangled cries and covered her ears to dull out the sound of her husband's agony.

Michael appeared from nowhere to comfort a writhing Tama. The teenager screamed and cried at the fire with animalistic terror, "Karani!" Grandmother. The gathering breeze snatched up his voice and echoed it across the mountain.

Hot tears coursed over Hana's cheeks, not lasting more than a few seconds in the searing heat. She balled up the bottom of the shirt and stuffed it into her mouth to stop the awful cries which threatened to break her in half. "Why?" she wailed. "Why?" But she suspected she knew the answer and it didn't help at all.

Hana stood alone like a rubber-necker at a road traffic accident as the scene played out before her. Choking breaths heaved in her chest and her green eyes glinted emerald against the myriad of colours the fire produced. Another bang echoed as a second gas tank exploded and shot into the air, showering the scene with molten debris. The fire engulfed the house and powerless, a small knot of cowed silhouettes gathered beneath a stand of trees to watch. Nobody spoke, solidarity forming their only comfort.

Hana watched them, detached and isolated on her lonely patch of brown grass. The other lone woman stood in her nightdress, clutching her tiny boy. A man who resembled Logan in stature wrapped his arms around them and Hana's chest hitched. Nobody offered to enfold her in their arms and she hugged herself as though subconsciously making amends.

Logan lay on the ground, his body prone and spent. Toby sat in the centre of his back and another stockman knelt on his legs. Hana saw them rise as one as though sharing a consensus that he wouldn't attempt to find Miriam in the inferno. She held her breath, knowing her husband but willing sense into his brain. "Don't do it, Logan," she begged. "Please, don't do it."

When he pushed himself upright, Hana knew. Marriage gave her a special insight into the workings of his mind and she screamed as he staggered to his feet. Toby heard her strangled cry over the fire's rabid enjoyment of the upper floor of the two storey and followed the direction of her pointing finger. Logan lurched towards the fire and his mother. She watched Toby's lips move and understood the curse without needing to hear it.

He set off after Logan but another man overtook him. His rugby tackle razed Logan to the dirt fair and square, landing in a patch of charred scrub only metres from the flames. Logan squirmed onto his back and lashed out, but Toby flew into the fight and pinned his legs. Hana held her breath as Flick balled his fist and drove it into Logan's face, the action slowed down by horror and disbelief. Once, twice and then Logan stilled. A heady mix of horror and relief kept Hana pinned in place as Toby seized Logan's boots and dragged him away from the fire's greedy fingers. Flick helped, wiping at his forehead with his sleeve and hauling Logan across the dirt like a rag doll.

Hana took a step towards them and then halted as though finding her trainers glued to the floor. Logan didn't need her. The men crowded around him, hiding him from view as they slapped his face and helped him to sit up. He never needed her. His self-sufficiency left no room for a wife to wrap her arms around him at the moment his world detonated before his eyes. Surplus to requirements, Hana turned away, no longer able to bear the heat of the flames or her isolation amidst the crowd. Her heart hardened in self-defence, focussing her attention on her child and not wasting grief on her displacement from a role she never truly held.

The steep bank loomed ahead of her and she baulked at the thought of the excruciating climb. "You can do this, Hana," she encouraged herself, facing the supplejack covered ridge with determination. The vines glinted in the firelight and conspired to make it harder. She began the climb anyway, hand over hand with tentative toes seeking adequate footholds.

Hana paused on a ledge and forced herself to look at the fire one last time. It swallowed the rest of the house and licked towards more of the dilapidated outbuildings, satiating itself in a feast of wood and sacrificial human flesh. The grass and bushes up to twenty metres around the house glistened with droplets of water in the dancing light, hailing Logan's failed attempt at damping down.

Hana heard her husband's voice in her head, remembered whispered confidences on a shared pillow. "If you can't put a fire out in the bush, you douse as much as you can around it, to prevent it ripping out of control and going for miles," he had said. "But I hope it never happens here, because it'll eat this mountain alive."

In the unreal scene below her, Michael became the family rock, comforting Liza and Tama at the same time. They clung together as everyone else retreated and Hana heard their tears through the roar and hiss of collapsing walls. She sat on her ledge and let her painful fingers coast across her belly, afraid when the child remained still. Her baby's fate was to know none of her grandmothers and the realisation made Hana gulp in a wave of overwhelming sadness. Both of them gone, hers and Logan's.

"Logan, I should have told you," she sobbed, tears making the cuts on her palms sting. Rueben's touch of her abdomen seemed to heighten Miriam's betrayal.

Hana turned back to her task, facing the scarred bank as though it represented the sum of her fears. The supplejack vines did their worst, tying up her legs and tripping her until crawling made the only viable option. Her hands, knees and chin bled from scrapes and scratches in her desperation to protect her stomach.

At the top of the bank, Hana realised the futility of her mission as she faced a rock she couldn't defeat. From her journey down she remembered the jarring slide as she descended on her bottom. On the way up, it proved insurmountable. Lying on her side, she clung to a tree root and sobbed, knowing she needed to let go and face the bone breaking slide to the bottom. Redheaded stubbornness prevented her fingers releasing and she fought for breath and prayed for a solution.

A hand appeared in her eye-line. "Take hold, girl!" a male voice called.

Hana inhaled and grasped the hand with gratitude, allowing herself to be hauled upwards. Her feet scrabbled for purchase and failed. As she swung loose, only the vice-like grip around her fingers dragged her across the rock and released her into the soft earth beyond it. The barbed wire fence bit into her clothing with hungry teeth and she lay on her face and panted for air. "Thank you," she managed through gritted teeth. "Thank you."

"Steady, steady now. Just rest a while," Alfred said. His chest heaved with exertion and his grey eyes looked wild. He folded his body in half and rested his hands against his knees. Dark pain glinted in his eyes, oozing from a damaged soul.

"I'm so sorry!" The words gushed free and a flurry of tears poured over Hana's lower lids and cascaded down her smoke stained cheeks. "They tried to stop her."

Alfred shrugged, his face a blank sheet. "I could never stop her, so how could they?" His voice choked back smoke and emotion. "Now she's got what she always wanted."

Speechless, Hana pushed herself to a sitting position. "You're saying she wanted to die?" The barbed wire snatched at her pants, tearing holes and marking the skin beneath.

Alfred pulled her to her feet but didn't release her hand, the orange glow reflected in his eyes as the fire ate Logan's parents with abandon. "Looks like we're both alone, Hana Du Rose."

He smiled, but the expression didn't reach his eyes, the result ghoulish and sinister.

Hana swallowed and nodded. "I don't think I can make it back," she whispered and Alfred's brow furrowed. He gripped her hand tighter.

"We'll get through this together," he replied. Hana wondered if he referred to the current situation, or the rest of their lives. Nodding, she accepted help for the moment and pushed all thoughts of the future aside.

Together they slipped and slithered down the mountain, following the lights of the hotel as they appeared and disappeared through the trees. Alfred proved surefooted, knowing the ground like the back of his own hand. He took the quad bike, firing it into life and descending with care. They unified, related not by blood or marriage even, but by circumstance. Gratitude filled Hana's heart, replacing the emptiness as she accepted the unexpected hand of friendship and clung to it.

"I want to go home," she whispered as Alfred stopped the quad by the front steps. Hana turned her face towards him and saw her own fears reflected there. "You can come with me," she offered, reaching for his hand. "I don't mind."

He smiled and a tear rolled over his lower eyelid. His irises swam like moonlight on a pond and he nodded. "Everyone will think I did it," he hissed. A sound like a strangled laugh gurgled from his lips. "I've had over forty years of opportunity, kōtiro. It's a bit late now."

Hana nodded and squeezed Alfred's fingers. "I know you didn't," she said. "I believe you."

"Thank you." His chin wobbled and his jaw clenched. The shutter dropped over his emotions. "Let's get inside," he said. "At least I can still help you, Hana."

The hotel's complete desertion with lights on and the doors open to the night, seemed to scream of Miriam's abandonment of her family. Hana let Alfred help her down from the quad and lead her up the front steps. In the mudroom at the back of the house, she watched while he removed his boots, his rough hands shaking as he loosened the zips and pushed the boots aside. When he removed his hat, a black line of soot ringed his head, a clean olive forehead above it and black filthy soot below.

A snort of hysterical laughter bubbled from Hana's lips, her emotions unpredictable and erratic. "I'm sorry," she whispered, clamping her fingers over her mouth.

"For what?" Alfred's eyes searched her face, the shutter dropping long enough for her to see the void within. The ring resembled a black halo trapping his face in darkness.

"For laughing," Hana replied, dragging her fingers away from her mouth. "Sorry for looking like weirdos. But mostly I'm sorry because your wife just died in front of you." She swallowed and sniffed, closing her eyes against the deafening silence which returned to her like whining static. "I'm sorry you might get the blame. Just sorry. Bloody sorry."

Alfred nodded and the void flashed through his eyes again. "Come, kōtiro," he soothed. "Let's take care of you and te pēpe for now. The rest will work itself out." He smoothed his hand across her stomach with longing and heartbreak in his eyes and Hana burst into tears.

Alfred behaved with kindness, soothing her as he knelt to unlace Hana's trainers. It seemed an age since she struggled to tie them. Blackened and ruined, they represented her life. The stink of the acrid fire would never leave her. Like a child, she rested her hands on Alfred's bent shoulders as he knelt on the floor and tugged them from her feet.

"What should we do?" Her fingers writhed and salt water washed pink tracks over her cheeks. "What happens next?"

Alfred shook his head and ran a trembling hand over his face. "I don't know," he whispered. "They'll all think I did it." He released a strange sound as though his heart unlocked with a click. The wail began as a gurgle, erupting from his chest and defying the hand he pressed over his mouth to keep it in. "I loved her!" he howled. "My life is a waste!"

"It isn't!" Hana cried. "It isn't!" She wrapped her arms around the old man's neck and felt his body tremble. Forty years of heartbreak leaked from his soul as Alfred's tears soaked the back of Hana's shirt, drenching her hair and mixing salt and fire soot into a sticky, blackened paste.

Crying seemed almost more exhausting than the descent from the mountain. Every time Hana closed her eyes she saw the orange glow mingling with her tears. Like a vision stuck on replay, it haunted her. Alfred propped her up in the lift, the stains from their clothing leaving black streaks on the walls. At Logan's bedroom door he paused with expectation, holding her up with gargantuan strength. "Press the numbers," he instructed and Hana stared at the keypad in shock.

Her lips parted in a startled gape. "I don't know them anymore," she said. "They're gone." She pressed her fingers to her temple in confusion.

Alfred shook his head, focussing his attention on her to avoid facing his own emotions. "It's fine," he breathed. "Just wait here." He limped towards the spiral staircase and Hana sank to her bottom on the floorboards. The wall felt comfortingly real behind her back. She lost track of time in his absence and when Alfred returned carrying a master list, Hana looked pale and sick, her hair matted to one side of her head.

"I messed up the wall," she said, pointing to the grimy streak above her head.

"Don't worry about that now." Alfred used the keypad and opened the door. His body stiffened and he gave an involuntary shiver. He looked as though a ghost ran ethereal fingers across the raised hairs on his arms. "Take a shower," he ordered, helping Hana to her feet. He swallowed and gave a curt nod. "Wash the fire off."

"What then?" Hana whispered "Can I just go home?"

"No." Alfred shook his head and his brow knitted. "Logan will need you now more than ever."

Hana laughed, the sound cold and bitter. "I don't think so, Alfred."

"Just get into the shower," he bit. "I promise I'll come back."

Hana kept hold of his fingers, afraid to release her grip. The words sounded cruel in her head and she tripped over them in her haste. "You won't do anything stupid?"

"No." Alfred swallowed. "My lifetime's worth of stupid is all used up, Hana." Still she clung to the sleeve of his dirty shirt. "I won't go far," he promised again, more frightened by her physical and emotional fragility than his own. "I just need to get myself clean."

The irony of his words hit Hana like a train. No one who watched Miriam run into the fire would ever feel clean again. He left and Hana stripped off her ruined clothes, dropping them onto the bathroom tiles. Stepping into the hot water, she felt instant guilt. The hotel took its water supply from an uphill stream. Even in drought, the mountains provided with never ending generosity. The fire devoured Rueben's house for lack of electricity or water and she used both to wash its traces from her skin.

It took four attempts to remove the soot and acrid smell from Hana's long hair. She scraped black gel from her arms and face and watched the water run grey down the plughole. Emerging from the shower in a towel, the sight of dark lines in the creases of her elbows sent her back in again.

The day held an essence of unreality as Hana dressed in the only clothes available. The trusty leggings came from the bottom of the suitcase alongside a clean bra and knickers. She pinched a shirt of Logan's, looking for comfort more than consolation.

The leggings slid down beneath her belly, pinching and leaving her round pink stomach exposed. The shirt's lower buttons refused to close. Hana sat on the edge of the bed and massaged her stomach, willing her child to stir and reassure her. When the tiny fist protruded through the fragile skin, she cried with relief.

The scrapes on her knees and palms stung against the fabric and the graze on her chin wept transparent liquid. Reluctant to leave the bedroom, Hana tidied, packing her belongings into her suitcase. The overflowing laundry basket cried out for attention and she forced herself from the room around six in the morning, carrying it to the washroom on the ground floor. Finding powder, she set two loads going and then watched the water slosh through the clothing, mingling hers and Logan's in a peculiar dance of sleeves and legs.

The silence of the hotel shrouded her, robbing her of oxygen as she balled up her sooty clothes and trainers and dropped them into the trash bin. More than anything she longed to take the truck and drive back to Culver's Cottage, sealing herself in until she worked out how to heal. If she ever worked out how to heal.

"Been looking for you." Alfred settled next to her on the bench in the rose garden, the birds strangely silent for the time of day. Ash littered the leaves and delicate petals, blown down from Reuben's ruin.

"I'm going home." Hana accompanied the words with a sigh. "Logan doesn't need me. My life is a disaster."

Alfred laid a gnarled hand over her shoulder. "No more than mine, Hana. The difference is that Logan loves you. Hold onto that. It's important."

"I don't fit in." The petulance in her voice embarrassed her. She ran a hand across her stomach. "I never will. Logan and I aren't getting on and I'm tired of forcing it to work. It's time to cut my losses."

"He needs you," Alfred repeated, his words like a broken record on repeat inducing a tightness in Hana's chest.

The gravel shifted in the carpark behind them, sending up a plume of dust. Car doors slammed. Hana jumped and Alfred spun around, hope flickering in his eyes and then extinguishing. "Cops," he said, squinting through the bushes and then turning back to Hana. "Best get it over with."

She watched as three police officers walked behind the old man into the hotel. After a moment's delay, she rose and followed, feeling she owed him some allegiance. She stepped into the kitchen behind them, half expecting to see Miriam at the sink. Alfred's gaze flicked to her and he afforded her a tight smile.

"Ma'am." The men acknowledged her in turn and she responded with a nod which revealed nothing. Two wore uniform, the third a detective in plain clothes. Hana watched Alfred stare into the cupboard looking for mugs. "I'll make drinks," he whispered. His eyes appeared glazed and his fingers clutched the cupboard door with white knuckles. He reached in and grasped hold of an object and pulled it out, his hand trembling as though he might drop it. Miriam's favourite floral mug shook in his fingers, the pattern flickering with the movement.

"Oh." Hana swallowed, seeing pain bend the old man almost in half. She rushed forward and prized the mug from his hand, struggling when he leant all his weight against her. A silver packet of tablets fell from the mug, making a metal skittering sound on the open blisters. It lay there, curled upwards, some of the small beds occupied while others lay opened and vacant.

"Her pills." Alfred's sob hitched in his throat. "She didn't take her pills."

Hana battled against his weight, relieved when the uniformed officers joined her. "This isn't a good time," she implored, but they ignored her plea, observing through eyes wired to detect unusual behaviour. Hana felt like a freak show.

Alfred's eyes squeezed shut and a tear loosed down his cheek. Hana yanked a chair free and shoved it behind his legs. "What can I do?" she pleaded. "Tell me how to help you."

Alfred collected deep breaths trying to get control, his knuckles white against the seat. The cops stood upright again, watching like automatons. "I don't know," he whispered. "I don't know anything anymore."

Hana replaced Miriam's mug with the others, but left the pills on the tiled floor. She couldn't bend even if she wanted to. She filled the teapot from the wall heater and placed cups before the policemen, indicating the milk jug with a jerk of her head. Then she stood, redundant, her stomach peeking through the bottom of the denim shirt. Covering it with her hand seemed futile as the detective's gaze burned through the wall of her womb.

"You go," Alfred said, his voice wobbling. He waved a hand towards her. "Get some rest."

Hana nodded and obeyed, needing no further excuse to leave the heavy atmosphere. The fire door clicked behind her and she walked towards the family room, not knowing where else to go. The smell of fire seemed to have permeated every corner of the house, a nauseating reminder of death.

"Ma'am?" The voice sounded behind her as she reached the first bend in the hallway. Hana turned and found the detective following her. His notebook flapped in one hand and a small pen poised in the other. She stopped and turned towards him with a question in her eyes. "Sorry to do this now." He sounded guilty but pressed on, anyway. "I need to ask you some questions."

Hana nodded and led the officer to the wooden panelled room. Curtains shrouded the window and the television played to itself. A mug of coffee disgorged crusted liquid in a puddle on the low table and a newspaper strewed its inner pages on the floor. The officer raised an eyebrow. "Looks like someone left in a hurry," he said, peering at the disorder.

Hana nodded and pull back the curtains, sunshine blinding her for a second. "Yes. Looks like it." She searched around for the remote. Unable to find it, she turned the television off at the wall. The old sofa offered some comfort and she eased into it, her legs aching. She hauled the shirt over her stomach, failing as it gaped wide.

The detective sat opposite. "Please can you give me a run through of last evening as you remember it?" His gaze held steady on her face. "You're Logan Du Rose's wife, I believe."

Hana shrugged and gave the information in a flat monotone. She went to bed early. Something woke her and she left the house with Liza. She saw Miriam run into the burning building.

The man wrote everything in a crabbed shorthand, his eyes never leaving her face. "Who do you think set the fire?"

Hana inhaled through her nose and shook her head. "I don't know." She sighed. The image of Miriam disappearing into the flames sent a shudder along her spine. "Where's my husband?"

The man peered at his notebook and flipped a page. "Hospital." As Hana's eyes widened, he raised a hand in apology. "Sorry. Nothing too serious. Smoke inhalation and injuries to the face. Do you know anything about those?"

Hana shrugged. "When the building collapsed he took off after his mother. One of the stockmen tried to stop him and they tussled."

The pages of the notebook fluttered. "Toby Du Rose?"

Hana's lips formed a tight line. Cousins. From some other branch of the family she knew nothing about. "I think so," she lied, protecting Flick despite herself. "It was dark and chaotic. One of them stopped him and I'm grateful." Her fingers strayed to her belly and the cop watched conflict cross her expression. "No child should grow up without a father."

"You were a widow when you met Mr Du Rose?" His eyelashes fluttered and Hana lost patience.

"You're surprisingly well informed for a man investigating a fire." She injected steel into her voice. "I don't think you need anything else from me."

"Where was Alfred Du Rose," he asked, his tone clipped. "Did he attend the family dinner last night?"

Hana's gaze strayed to the upturned newspaper and spilled coffee. The cop's interest followed and he raised an eyebrow. "I don't know. As I told you, I didn't go. I felt unwell and went to bed early. You'll need to ask someone who was there. I'm guessing he and Miriam came in here as usual after dinner and this is where they got the news of the fire." She lifted her eyes to the ceiling and then back to the detective. "Have you accounted for everyone? Did Miriam perhaps survive?" Her voice held such longing and hope, the detective's face softened.

"No, Mrs Du Rose. We found two bodies and they're with the authorities now." He leaned forward in his seat. "I need to ask you about your husband's legal action against Reuben Jacob Du Rose. What do you know about that?"

Instinct told her where he hoped his questions might take him. Hana sighed, seeing the same inquisitive mind which drove Bodie. "Talk to Logan's lawyer. Liza knows his name if you can't ask him. It was over. They settled. Reuben relinquished his hold on the land and they negotiated the loan. Logan wanted the land back. I don't think he cared about the money."

"A hundred grand!" the policeman spluttered. "He didn't care about a hundred grand?"

"They're family. You wouldn't understand." Hana sighed. "It was a matter of principle, not money."

"You're right! I don't understand!" The cop snorted, his shroud of professionalism slipping.

Hana felt exhaustion nipping at the base of her skull. "My husband didn't burn his uncle's house, if that's where you're hoping to go with this," she bit, squaring her jaw and feeling the skin on her chin smart. "Everything was fine. They settled it and everyone got what they wanted. Logan had no reason to burn down a building." The irony of her words returned to bite her. Reuben didn't get what he wanted. He wanted his son's acknowledgement.

The policeman thanked her, expressed his commiserations to her family and stood to leave. Hana rose, seeing his veiled wince as she asked the one question he'd tried to avoid. "You said there were two bodies. Who's the other one?"

The policeman consulted his notebook and fluffed around. "I can't say. We need to notify the family."

"Oh, please?" Hana put her face in her hands. "I saw Miriam run in and you snuffed out any hope of her survival. I just don't want the other person to be Reuben."

"Why?" The cop jumped on her words so fast, it gave her no time to mask her expression.

Hana thought about his salt and pepper sideburns and the gentleness of his speech. She swallowed and her lower lip wobbled. "I like him. I want the chance to get to know him properly."

"I'm sorry," he said, biting his lower lip. His reply told Hana everything she wanted to know.

Her eyes squeezed shut and her head drooped. She thought she had no tears left, but more found their way to the surface and ran unchecked down her cheeks, setting up a steady drip onto the rug. The policeman backed away, the damage done. "Can I get someone to sit with you?" he asked. He gnawed on his lower lip. Hana shook her head and secrecy managed to isolate her once again.

As the heavy door clicked shut, a spirit of desolation shrouded her, pleased for yet another opportunity to drain her lifeblood. She let it. Lying on the sofa, she pressed her face into the cushion and greeted her old friend Grief once again without resistance.

Chapter 48

Hana woke with a start, her cheeks tight from crying and sunlight warming her head. She put out an arm to shield her face and focussed on the cuts and bruises criss-crossing her fingers.

"Hana, wake up babe. I want Michael to check you over."

"No." She pushed Logan's face away, jumping when he hissed in pain. A black eye spread down his cheek and along the bridge of his nose. "Sorry," Hana stammered. "But please go away."

"Hana." Michael squatted next to her, blisters dotted over his nose and forehead. Savage burns left his fingers raw in places and she closed her eyes to avoid the sight. "I need to check you out. We didn't know you were at the fire. Liza only just said."

"Liza." Hana recoiled and shook her head. "Leave me alone. I'm going home." Michael reached for her wrist and she yanked her hand away, the veins standing up in her neck as she whipped herself towards hysteria.

"Leave her," Logan ordered and Michael stood and took a step back. Logan sat on the seat next to Hana and held out his arms. "Can I hold you?" he asked.

Hana reared away and then caught the hidden misery in his eyes. His mother was dead, but he knew only half the grief. She wondered what he would do if he knew the whole truth. In that moment she knew she couldn't share it. The secret pinned her to the sofa and Logan misunderstood. He gathered her into his arms and Hana struggled before giving in. A sense of need rolled off him in waves and it felt new and different. "I'm sorry," she breathed, the list of her sorrows both deep and wide.

"It's okay." Logan's breath shuddered against her. "We'll get through it, Hana. Together." Her gaze flicked upwards to Michael's expression and she saw it all written there. He knew everything. He gave an exaggerated shake of his head behind Logan and Hana swallowed. In that moment she hated him.

A voice inside her head warned her to be careful, but Hana felt irrational and out of control. The nap had done nothing to calm her jangled nerves. The child inside her moved, but with a sluggish, laboured action. A flicker of worry shot through Hana's brain. She offered her hand back to Michael, needing his help. He clasped her wrist and turned his other hand over, measuring her pulse on his watch. He finished with an inhale and released her. "You're cut up pretty bad. Any other injuries?"

"Cuts and scrapes." She wiggled free from Logan's arms. "And back pain."

"Back pain?" Michael cocked his head and narrowed his eyes. "When did that start?"

"When I fell in the quad bike." She watched the realisation dawn alongside the memory and he licked his lips.

"What?" Logan jerked backwards. "When did that happen?"

"I braked too hard." Michael's eyes shuttered his guilt. "I was angry with you. It's my fault."

Rage blossomed in Logan's face and Hana sighed, tired of the fighting, the endless secrets and the damaging lies. She pushed at Logan's thigh. "Stop!" she implored him. "I'm going home, Logan. I can't take anymore and I realise it's a bad time, but I'd already made my decision." His lips moved, but he made no sound. "Bodie will come and fetch me. I'll text him later when I know what's happening."

Logan snorted through his nose, a short sound filled with despair. "Geez, Hana, not him. Don't make me face Supercop now. Please. I'll drive you back myself. Let's just get through Christmas." His irises sparkled as he fought back the weakness of defeat. "And Mum's funeral." He twisted his fingers in his lap and Hana watched the long joints lace together and then divide. Reuben's strong hands.

"Okay," she conceded, not sure what other option remained.

It hadn't felt like Christmas Eve and never would. The family moved around the property, fulfilling roles without commitment, killing time and waiting for answers which wouldn't come. In the chiller Hana found the huge slabs of home-kill, almost defrosted and waiting to be made into steaks for a barbeque which wouldn't happen. The marinades sat on a high shelf anticipating the next part of their process, which Hana didn't know. The family recipe which Miriam promised died with her in the fire.

Fire officials and police appeared and disappeared at intervals. The identity of the second body remained tentative although everyone in the family knew. Nobody spoke and they alternately separated themselves and cannoned together in a desire to unify before drifting apart again.

Hana sat in Logan's bedroom, curled into an armchair reading the same page of the Jane Austen novel over and over. Michael knocked on the door and let himself in. "How are you?" he asked, his tone easy despite the leaden atmosphere which entered with him.

"Fine." Hana rubbed her eyes. Her child moved with more enthusiasm and she realised it was all she cared about. Hope among the ashes.

"You need to take it easy," Michael insisted. "You shouldn't have gone up to the fire." Hana's lips tightened into a thin line and she clamped her teeth over her tongue to stem the ready retort. Michael sat down uninvited on the edge of the bed and faced her. "This next few days needs to be about protecting Logan. Don't mess it up."

"Really?" Hana sniped unkindly at him. "It's a bit bloody late to look out for Logan, isn't it?"

Michael's face hardened and he leaned forward, his manner threatening. "I don't know how you found out, Hana, but you say nothing to him. I'm warning you! And just so you know, you don't get to just walk away from us!"

Hana shook her head. "I'm not doing this again. I refuse to waste another decade of my life protecting a liar." Her thoughts gathered force and the decision surprised her in its cohesion. "You tell him, or I swear, I will."

"No!" Michael lurched forward and gripped Hana's wrist. Her book plunged to the floor with a clunk. She jumped in fright and glared up into Michael's flashing Du Rose eyes. He leaned close, his breath damping her cheeks. "You're not part of this family! You're just grafted on and don't you forget it!" He released her wrist with a painful shove and stormed from the room. He didn't return, withdrawing his medical expertise as punishment.

Hana cried herself to sleep, woken by the excited twitter of birds in the eaves. Life went on. It always did. Tama sought her out, drawing comfort from her presence and she felt grateful. Everyone else avoided her. He created a pillow nest and snuggled on the floor at her side, sometimes watching the television, sometimes exorcising his grief in bouts of tears which he tried to hide. When his pain sounded wretched and his back heaved, she reached out and laid her hand on his shoulder. Tama stilled. His fingers crept upwards until they met hers and he sniffed. "Thanks," he whispered. "It hurts so bad."

"I know." Hana fought her own misery. "Believe me, I know."

Chapter 49

Logan returned to the fire site. He watched as they collected the ruined body of his mother, packing her into a bag and carrying her down the mountain on a stretcher. He bit the inside of his cheek until the blood poured unchecked and his lips were stained with it. Still he watched, his face grim and his heart thudding dull, laboured beats. When he rode back to the house, he looked like a man whose world had collapsed. It had.

Tama broke the news to Hana. After a foray into the kitchen, he returned empty handed, his cheeks soaked and his grey eyes glassy. "I killed her!" he shouted from the doorway. "It's all my fault!"

"What? No!" Hana ran to him, pinning his flailing arms to his sides and wrapping him in her embrace. "Don't say that, Tama. What's happened?"

He sank to the floor, his jacket sliding down the wall and leaving a welt in the wallpaper. Hana crouched in front of him. "Electrical fire," he sobbed. "The bloody Christmas lights. I put them up with Wiri. It's all my fault."

"I'm so sorry, Tama." Hana pulled him into her and held his shaking body. "You're not to blame, sweetheart. It's not your fault."

"Shit, shit, shit!" he cried into her hair, his voice muffled by her shoulder. "I killed Kui Miriam and that cop said my poppa died too." His body grew rigid. "What have I done, Hana? What have I done?"

"It's not your fault!" Hana pleaded, her voice catching in empathy with his distress. "I won't let you carry this! I won't." She held him and rocked his rigid body until her legs numbed and her shirt hung limp with his tears. He cried himself into exhaustion and she remained on her knees, cradling his head in her lap with his face pressed against the outline of Logan's daughter. His body shook with the remnants of hysteria and a mighty weight settled on his young shoulders. Hana recognised its traits from her son's unnamed burden and it frightened her. It settled around the time of Vik's funeral and she wondered if Bodie knew more than he ever revealed. "I won't let you carry this alone," Hana breathed, placing wet kisses on the top of Tama's head. "I won't fail a second time."

He cried himself to sleep in her lap and Hana let him rest, stroking his hair back from his forehead as she'd done with her own babies. When raised voices erupted in the hallway, she jumped. She waited a moment to settle Tama with his head on an abandoned pillow before creeping from the room. Her legs felt like jelly under her and she paused to press a palm against the wall next to Liza's door. Her sister-in-law emerged, sleep tousled and her hair raised in a cockatiel's crest. "What's happening?" she murmured and Hana ignored her, staring beyond her at the knot of people gathered at the head of the spiral staircase. "I said what's happening?" Liza demanded and Hana fixed angry green eyes on her face.

"Screw you!" she hissed. "That's what."

"Electrical fault." Logan's voice sounded calm and his body language betrayed sympathy for the two men facing him. "I'm sorry."

The darker of the strangers lifted a crooked finger and jabbed it into Logan's chest. Hana held her breath as her husband stared down at it and then swallowed. "You did this!" he hissed.

Logan pushed his finger away. "I didn't Kane. We both know that. We all lost someone today."

Kane Du Rose. Reuben's son. Hana swallowed and pursed her lips. She edged forward, alarmed when Liza stuck out her forearm to prevent her moving past. "Leave it!" Liza hissed.

Hana inhaled and gave a retaliatory shove, hitting Liza in the shoulder. "Get off me," she breathed, turning her ire on the other woman. To her surprise, Liza quailed beneath whatever she saw in Hana's eyes. She moved around Liza and crept forward, tasting the tension and danger in the air.

"I lost my mum." Logan's voice cracked and Hana felt a dart of pain cut through her heart at the plea in his voice. "It's time to let this go."

"You lost more than that!" Kane spat, taking an exaggerated step forward. His chest met Logan's and Hana watched her husband take a controlled breath. "You stupid, blind dickhead!"

The other man with Kane intervened. He pressed himself between the men and pulled Kane's chin towards him. "Stop, man!" he urged. "It won't help. Dad's gone. This won't bring him back."

"It's what he wanted, Nev!" Kane shoved his companion's arm and Hana recognised the name. Both olive skinned and muscled, the men resembled Reuben down to the scattering of greys in their sideburns. Logan fit into their mould like a missing piece. Kane jabbed at Nev's chest and his brother took a step backwards as he unbalanced. "It's what he always wanted."

Michael appeared from a doorway leading up to Alfred's loft apartment. He saw the visitors and his expression darkened. As Kane lurched for Logan, Michael advanced and clasped him around the torso. Logan ducked to avoid the fist aimed for his face. "Don't do this!" Michael repeated Nev's command but Kane thrashed in his arms.

"Kane, let's go," Nev pleaded, his tone placatory with the faint hint of a whine. Kane shook himself free of Michael's grip and spun until he faced Logan again.

Hana heard the click of Pandora's Box snapping open and the dark secret leapt out like a ghoulish clown, staining everything it touched. She held her breath, knowing after this moment, they could never go back.

"We hated you. Dad's little favourite!" He spat the words and Logan's narrowed eyes showed a lack of understanding. Kane shoved him in the chest and he reeled backwards. "All he ever wanted was your acknowledgement."

"Kane! He didn't want this. He promised." Nev seized Kane's shoulders, attempting to spin him away with white knuckled fingers. Kane resisted.

"He always wanted this." He lashed out at Nev and caught him in the jaw. "It's what the development was about and you know it." Kane whirled back to face Logan. "He said you were bright, Logan. He wanted you to work it out!" His voice broke and he scrubbed at his eyes with the backs of sharp knuckles. The hallway seemed to empty of oxygen and Hana's fingers scrabbled at her throat.

"Dad?" Tama's sleep fuddled voice sounded behind Hana, the dreadful hitch still torturing his lungs. Michael and Kane looked across at him and both faces softened. Hana saw the irony in that moment, two men, one child, two fathers. Clarity settled over Reuben's spite. He'd already lost a son and sought to deny Alfred a grandchild. Logan. Logan was the son he lost. Truth flowed like a swollen river and nothing would stop it bursting its banks.

"This is all your fault," Kane bit, his teeth gritting in his face. "You won your petty legal game and he gave up. He needed to look you in the eye and see if you knew." Kane's fists balled by his sides. "He cried, man! He broke his heart after you left. You should have seen, Logan. You should have seen the aroha in his face but you didn't." Kane launched again and Michael and Nev used their combined efforts to hold him back.

The muscles of Logan's face twitched and Hana read nothing through the blank wall guarding his emotions. Then he shook his head, a definitive action of denial. "No. Michael's Reuben's son, not me." His gaze flicked right and Hana saw Alfred standing by the door to his apartment. The old man didn't look up or catch Logan's eye. Logan held his hand out, imploring Alfred for validation. "It's Michael. You said it to Mum that night. You have one son and it's me."

"Sorry son." The words acted as a grenade, detonating the last of Logan's foundations with the pulling of a tiny pin. Logan stared around him at the crowd in the hallway as the nature of his family changed shape.

Alfred raised his eyes and fixed his grey irises on Logan's face. A multitude of years seemed to settle into the creases of his weathered cheeks. "Michael's my son," he whispered, his voice soft. "I have one son."

Hana watched Logan's gaze flick towards his arm. The whakapapa tattoo wound itself around his shoulder and bicep, permanent evidence of a colossal lie. He shook his head in disbelief as the knowledge filtered into his psyche. "You bunch of liars!" he roared. Hana heard his pain and took a step forward. "Liars!" Logan spun and his boots carried him down the stairs in a clatter of feet on treads. Nobody else moved.

Except Hana. She lumbered to the top of the stairs and tried to follow, taking an age to descend the spiral staircase and make her way to the front of the hotel. A film of soot and dust covered everything in the carpark but she saw no sign of Logan.

A motor split the air and Hana hurried to the stables, still tasting the acrid burning in her throat as she tried to run. Too late, she saw Logan's dark hair tossed by the wind as he tore from the yard on a motorbike, a bridle looped over his shoulder. The rigidity of his spine told her everything she needed to know. He sped off up the hill, abusing the first of many gates as he went. He didn't close it behind him. And he didn't look back.

"Logan!" Hana cried, hearing her voice return without effect. "Logan, please come back?" She waited until he showed as a tiny dot against the bush line, running away from hurt and betrayal. Running away from Hana, just like he promised not to.

Tama met her on the front steps, his brow furrowing at the sadness in her eyes. She shrugged, but found no acceptable words to describe her misery at watching her husband become more unreachable than she ever believed possible.

Chapter 50

Tama sat with Hana in the kitchen. Dusk set in and with it, an overwhelming sense of foreboding. She paced the room with quick, even footsteps, the twinges in her back and stomach becoming painful. When she bolted for the door, Tama shouted. "Sit the hell down, will you! You're doing my head in."

"I can't!" Hana waddled along the corridor towards reception, letting the door slam behind her. Tama found her in the bedroom, stuffing her feet into boots and yanking her hair back into a ponytail.

"What are you doing?" he demanded, his face settling into a grin as Hana grunted and groaned at the effort of leaning forward to zip up her boots.

"I'm going to find Logan," she wheezed, sitting up pink cheeked and puffed.

"That's ridiculous!" Tama's face curled into a sneer. "It's getting dark and you don't know your way around up there."

"No, but you do." Hana snagged his elbow as she passed and hauled Tama from the room, towing him along the hall to the lift.

"You want to search the bush, but you can't be assed to walk down the stairs?" His sass made her fingers itch to clip him around the ear.

"I don't feel well!" she snapped, rubbing the back of her hand into the small of her back. "Shut up and do as you're told."

Hana paused in the equipment shed and studied the various farm vehicles, dismissing them one at a time. Tama punched a code into a metal box and turned bearing a key like a holy grail. "This one," he said. "You're too fat for any of the others." He walked towards the quad bike and Hana groaned.

"Not that one, please. Anything but that."

Tama fired up the engine with a shrug. "Don't go then. It's this or nothing. The horses are out and you can't ride one, anyway. Jack's Jeep won't go as far as we might need it to and you can't sit behind me on a motorbike. There isn't enough room for your fat ass."

Hana gritted her teeth. "If you call me fat one more time, I'll hurt you!" she growled. She clambered into the passenger seat and held on as the quad blew a cloud of smoke and hayseeds into the air. She sneezed. "You have no idea how much I hate this vehicle."

Tama spun the wheel and headed outside, pointing the battered hood towards the gate at the bottom of the sloping paddock. Hana wrinkled her nose. "Logan left the gate open. Someone's closed it."

Tama shrugged. "Jack. He'll give Logan a slap for leaving it open."

"Don't be daft," Hana sighed, tiredness gripping her in a vice.

"I'm not. Jack's got a nasty right hook. Look." Tama pointed at a scar in his hair line and Hana gasped.

"Your stable manager hits you?"

"Hell yeah!" Tama made it sound normal. He jerked his head towards the gate. "All yours."

Hana fumbled with the catch and took an age to get settled after the first three gates. Tama shook his head. "I thought you wanted to find Logan before next week."

"I can't help it!" Hana complained. "My back is killing me and I have this strange feeling."

Tama narrowed his eyes. "What, like a psychic?"

"No!" Hana pressed her hand between her legs and grimaced. "A strange feeling down here."

"Oh." Tama's lips lifted in a lopsided grin. "I can get rid of that for you."

Hana hit him on the shoulder and he laughed, the joviality of the sound not fitting the seriousness of their mission. "Just drive," she grumbled.

They trailed over the land in the darkness, travelling kilometres into mountainous bush until they discovered Logan's bike abandoned near a paddock gate. The smashed front headlight betrayed the extent of his rage and a dent in the gate marked the point of impact. A discarded halter hung from a nearby fence post and hoof marks left round imprints in the dirt. Tama stared at the horses gathered near a water trough in the centre of the paddock. "He took the mare he rode yesterday."

"Sacha?" Hana sighed with relief, knowing he'd be safe with her. Tama shook his head and pointed to a white mare with a speckled foal at heel.

"No. One of the young ones.

Hana sighed. "Where would he go?"

Tama aimed towards the bush and took a track through the undergrowth. Hana clung to the quad bike with fingers clenched in fear as they lurched around washouts and cannoned through supplejack. Dark trees obliterated the starry sky and a dust haze clouded around them. He stopped on the track, the bike jolting to a standstill. "You don't look good," he said, his brow furrowing. "I should take you back."

"No!" Hana growled. A supernatural urge drove her onward and her green eyes flashed. "I want my husband."

They crested the hill and Hana groaned with relief at the sight of Logan's paddock. Moonlight bathed it in a white glow and the gate hung open. Tama paused the bike and Hana clambered off, picking her way across the delicate roots of the kauri tree and searching in the darkness for her husband. "Logan!" she shouted, her voice echoing off the canopy and returning to her as strangled cries. Tama followed her through the gate and killed the engine, letting out a vile swearword. Hana paused her shouts to glance at him. "What?" She half-turned, seeing his face pale in the darkness.

"Wait!" he snapped. He turned the key and a puff of black smoke issued from the back end. "No, no! Don't do this!" he hissed.

"What now?" Hana demanded. Her swollen belly felt taut beneath her fingers and the shirt flapped in the breeze. "What's happened to it?"

"Do I look like a bloody mechanic?" Tama shouted, jumping down and kicking the nearest tyre. "We're kilometres from the hotel, in the most inaccessible part of the property and this thing's broken down! That's what's happened!"

Tama ranted in the clearing while moonlight poured down in a circle of light amidst palms and punga. After another kick at the tyre, he ran the key again, managing to raise a grating sound and more black smoke. But with a final sputter of choking, the vehicle died. Tama turned the key again, but it remained silent. "This is bad. This is really bad." He clasped his hands behind his head and pointed his elbows out to the sides. "Did you bring a radio?"

Hana's face paled. "No. I don't know how to work one."

"This is unbelievable!" Tama raged. "What the hell are we doing up here?"

"Looking for Logan." Hana's voice lowered as dread snaked its fingers around her heart. "Are we stuck?"

"Yeah, pretty much!" Tama dropped to his knees and examined the soil. "Logan's been here recently." He poked at the fresh hoof prints in the dust. "We're too late, Hana. He's been and gone. It looks like he galloped round the paddock like an idiot and left. He does that when he's pissed off. He rides like a maniac." Tama swore a few times and kicked the quad bike again.

"Swearing at it won't help," Hana said, feeling the bloom of fear grow. It leached through her voice and occupied every thought. Bracing herself, she pushed it away. "Logan said this place is sacred." She waved her arm back towards the faded rahui pole at the gate. "He wants to build his house here." The desolation ebbed away and a strange peace wrapped around her and offered her certainty. "He'll come back for us," she said, her voice light and confident. "We'll wait."

"No, we need to get back to the house." Tama pulled Hana's arm. "Get back on and I'll try the key again. Maybe the engine flooded after the climb." He tugged Hana's wrist, jumping back as a torrent of water hit the baked earth and splashed over his boots. "What are you doing?" His eyes grew round and white in the moonlight.

"No!" Hana wailed. "No!" She cried out, bending double under the familiar back pain. An unseen hand snaked around to encompass her whole stomach in a vicious bite. It gripped like a vice and Hana recognised it. "The baby!" she panted, pinned in place by the pain.

Tama panicked with the skill of a teenager. "Hold it in!" he shouted. "Sit down. You can't have it here!"

"I'm pregnant, not deaf!" Hana yelled back, gripping the side of the quad bike in rigid fingers. "It hurts, it really hurts."

Tama dragged his mobile phone from his jeans pocket and examined the screen. "There's no phone reception here!" His voice sounded high pitched. "That's why we needed the bloody radio!"

"You can still make emergency calls." Hana pressed her face into the warm metal and groaned.

"No. I. Can't!" Tama pressed buttons and lifted the device to his ear. "We're in the middle of bloody nowhere, Hana. It's not working!" With a guttural sound, Hana sank to her knees in the dirt. Tama rushed to her side and tried to haul her upright. "Why can't you hold it in?" he demanded.

Hysterical laughter bubbled from Hana's mouth, mingling with her agonised moans. "I'd like to see you try!" she cried as another contraction drove her into the floor. Tama knelt next to her, patting her back and resting his forehead on her shoulder.

"It'll be okay," he repeated over and over.

"Nothing's okay about this!" Hana's sentence emerged stilted and punctuated by groans of frustration and fear. Tama's hands shook as his futile patting continued. "I need my husband!" Hana wailed, panting interspersed with moans of pure agony. "I want Logan!"

Tama ran down the track, trying to work out how far he could run on foot and if he dared leave Hana to get help. Her cries of pain brought him running back again. "Don't you dare leave me!" she screeched into his face, her eyes wide and glassy.

"I promise I won't," Tama gasped. He gripped her fingers and winced in pain as her nails dug into his palm. "I promise I'll stay."

Chapter 51

Hana knelt in the dirt on her hands and knees, resting her forehead on the grass between contractions. "It hurts," she gasped, panting into the dirt. "I feel like someone's tearing me in half." Tama paced up and down next to her, kicking dust into her face with each turn on his heel.

Hana struggled to regulate her breathing, in through her nose and out through her mouth. She leaned back and down onto her heels, dropping her hand to touch her stomach. The pressure from inside bowed her low again, her spine arched and a groan escaping from between pursed lips.

"How far apart are the thingies?" Panic laced Tama's voice.

Hana panted through a giggle. He was making it up as he went along, cobbled together from science classes and his brief forays into the adult world. "I don't know," Hana puffed. "Not long. Less than a minute." She let out another grunt of pain as the pressure bit again. The truth was she didn't know. The contractions had melded into one giant, never-ending pain, as though an iron bar had been shoved in sideways and two big men crushed her around it. "The baby's coming," she sobbed, snot mingling with the soil.

"But it's too early!" Tama turned again, kicking more dust into her face.

"Tell her that!" Hana spat.

The pressure in her bottom increased and the remaining amniotic fluid soaked her leggings and underwear. Hana experienced an animalistic urge to remove all barriers and she freed up one hand by taking the weight on her other. She grappled behind her, wrenching at her leggings and underwear until they became trapped over her thighs.

Tama squeaked in fear and instead of helping, fought her in an attempt to pull them up. "No!" he protested. "Logan will kill me if you get undressed with me here!"

The bizarre tug of war over Hana's pants ended when the contraction knocked the remaining breath out of her lungs. Agony tore at her chest and the sound of her pain rocked their surroundings. Birds left their nests in alarm and Hana's cries echoed around the mountain. A startled tui sat in the kauri tree and mimicked her, repeating her sounds over and over as though they amused him.

Hana slapped Tama's hands away and yanked her leggings as far as the backs of her knees. He covered his eyes and mouth and turned around, beseeching her for mercy. "Please don't do this," he begged. "I'm too young to die."

Hana's fingers slipped between her legs, withdrawing in shock when she felt the fluffy topknot of her baby's head crowning. She leaned forward and howled in pain and terror.

"What should I do?" Tama's chest hitched. "I don't know what to do."

"Get. Help!" The words became disjointed and Tama stared at Hana on her knees in the deepening darkness.

"I'm so dead," he breathed. He ran to the quad bike and turned the key, hearing only a forlorn click from the engine. His fingers searched the bed of the quad, finding a folded tarpaulin and a first aid box. When he produced them like a special gift, Hana burst into noisy tears.

"I need more than a Band Aid," she sobbed. "I want my husband."

Tama ran back to the quad and used his phone to search the contents of the corrugated bed. Blades of hay slipped beneath his palms and then his fingers closed around a metal shaft. His lips curled back in a grin. "Someone left a shotgun in the quad," he called, hefting the barrel in his hands. "Jack will go crazy."

"So shoot me," Hana wailed. "In the head, please. In the head."

"I'm not gonna shoot you!" Tama felt in his pockets and scraped together enough ammunition for the plan unfolding in his head. "Oh crap." He swallowed a gulping breath. "It was me. I left it there yesterday." He snapped the barrel closed and turned away from Hana. Three rounds fired into the air in quick succession, the sound reverberating off the mountain and echoing back. He checked his pockets for more cartridges and found nothing. The first aid box yielded enough for a repeat and Tama sent the volley of three shots in the opposite direction. The sound drowned out Hana's cries of agony.

"Three quick shots, a hunter in distress." Tama spoke to himself, more than to her. "Someone will come," he promised, kneeling next to Hana. His fingers rubbed her bent spine and he averted his eyes from the sight of her white bottom beneath the moonlight. "I am not horny," he repeated to himself as though surprised. "Uncle Logan will not kill me."

Hana cut a pitiful figure as she paused for breath and smeared tears from her cheeks with dirty palms. "I can't do this," she gasped. "I can't do it."

"You can." Fear laced Tama's voice. "This is my uncle's baby and you can do this. You have to do this, Hana."

"Oh, God!" she wailed. "Oh, God help me!"

"Logan, damn you! I need you now!" Tama shouted and thumped the earth. "If he's still out here, he'll find us," he convinced himself. "It's gonna be fine."

He settled next to her, stroking her hair and soothing her as she strained. Awful noises spilled from her lips but no more conversation. All her effort went into pushing her child into the world. Instinct told him it was taking too long as Hana's grunts reflected more exhaustion and her breathing became laboured. Liquid ran into the dust beneath her, dark and frightening in the moonlight. Tama prayed to a God he'd always scorned and worked hard to disappoint.

A steady rumble began, vibrating through his knees and the palm resting on the earth. Within minutes, it became audible hoof beats and the clank of teeth on a snaffle bit. "Logan!" Tama yelled. "Logan!" Rising, he spun on the spot, willing his uncle to appear from the darkness and relieve him of the overwhelming adult responsibility. Hana let out a piercing scream which began with pain and ended in determination.

Logan's keen sight picked up Tama's shape alongside the quad and he flung his hard body from the horse with ease. "What's wrong?" he demanded, dropping the reins and striding to his nephew's side. Hana crouched on all fours, labouring with more power and energy as she sensed the end coming. Logan gaped, his eyes widening in confusion. Hana's white bottom poked upwards to the night sky and Tama leaned down and patted her back. "What did you do?" Logan's tone sounded dangerous and laden with threat. His fingers flexed at his sides and Tama quailed.

"The baby's coming," he stammered. "Now. She can't hold it in. We came looking for you and she leaked stuff and then this happened." His tone held an accusation. "Do something, Uncle. Help her!"

Logan dropped to his knees and gathered Hana into his side. Her eyes appeared glassy and strange and she offered no acknowledgement of his presence. When his grasp restricted the movement of her shoulders, she gave him a vicious shove and resumed her concentration. Logan glanced back at Tama. "Take the quad. Get help!" he snapped.

Tama flung himself into the seat and turned the key. Nothing. "It's knackered!" he shouted. He shook his head as though surprised at his ability to forget the reason they were there.

Logan jerked his head towards the mare who grazed among the sun-scorched grass where he abandoned her. "Take her!" he insisted. "Take the mare. Go! Tell Toby to bring the old ute up to the bend on the east side of the fortieth and a stretcher. Hurry!"

Tama leapt onto the mare's back, settling into the dip behind her withers. He spun her around, sliding without a saddle and headed her towards the gate. The noise and vibration of her bare hooves returned as a rhythmic echo. Logan swallowed and licked his lips. "He'll make it," he breathed, convincing himself more than Hana.

He jumped as Hana clawed at his forearm. "What, sweetheart, what?" he begged.

She cried out words which garbled and made no sense. Fear radiated from her green eyes and she dragged at his shirt, trying to make him move. Keeping his hand against her spine for comfort, Logan peered at the ground beneath Hana. In the light of a vivid half-moon, he saw his daughter's head emerge into the world.

"Far out!" he gasped, taking the round skull into his palms. She strained again and a shoulder freed itself. Hana faltered, her arms growing numb and weak with leaning on them and her energy almost spent. "Again!" Logan commanded. "Just one more, Hana. One more!"

Hana obeyed and the second shoulder released. The tiny girl slipped into his hands, looking up at the night sky with wide, unfocussed eyes. He laid her twitching body on the baked earth and reached in his jeans pocket for a penknife. Instinct drove him to knot the cord and cut it closest to Hana. Inadequacy plagued him as his inexperienced fingers gathered the child up and held her to his body.

Hana leaned her forehead against her arms and panted. The child gave a tired strangled cry and her eyelids fluttered. "What do I do, Hana?" Logan demanded, gazing down on the tiny pouting lips with awe and terror. "What does she need?" A pathetic wail split the air, gaining traction and volume as the baby fretted with the shock of expulsion. Logan lay her in the sparse grass and her body rigidified in shock, her lips parting wide and emitting a sharp scream which contained dismay and fury. He stripped off his shirt, buttons flicking into the dirt as he ripped them free. Laying it flat, he swaddled his daughter and held her close, rewarded with the snuffle of satisfaction as her horror diminished.

"Hana." Logan spoke to his wife again. "Hana, talk to me."

"I can't," she replied and despite himself, Logan smiled at her sass.

"You just did." He rose still cuddling his child and spotted the tarp which Tama abandoned. One-handed, he managed to shake it loose and lay it beside the quad. "Crawl under this and sit down," he ordered.

"I'm never sitting down again!" Hana groaned.

Logan squatted, shifting his daughter onto his left side. She made snuffing noises and turned her face into his chest. "You need to feed her, Hana. They have to feed straight away." He trotted out the words of life gleaned by watching countless farm animals birth their young. "Get moving." He stroked her hair off her damp forehead. "You're worrying me."

Hana's voice broke and she sniffed into her forearms. "I can't move. I want to go home."

"I'm doing my best here." Logan's voice held an edge of pleading as he nudged her shoulder. Still holding the rooting child, he slipped his other arm around Hana's chest and hauled her upright. "She needs you, Hana. I need you."

With a cry of pain, Hana sank onto her bottom and Logan hauled her back against the quad's wide front wheel. His child began a pitiful mewing and he popped the front of Hana's blouse open one-handed. "I can't do this," she panted, clutching at her stomach. "It hurts so bad."

Logan laid the child in her lap. "Hold her, Hana." He reached behind her and unhooked her bra. To his relief, she pushed the baby into the crook of her right arm as though instinct overrode emotion. But she used the other hand to slap his face.

"Ow!" Logan jumped back in shock and his eyes sought hers in the darkness. "What was that for?"

"Leaving me!" she hissed. "Lying to me about everything! Making me give birth outside."

"The last bit isn't my fault." Logan held his hands out in front of him. The baby's wails grew in intensity and Hana rocked her without looking down. Logan gripped her face in his hand, forcing her to meet his gaze. "Look at her, Hana. She's beautiful. Please, feed her."

Hana glanced down at her daughter, the moonlight casting shadows over her expression. The tiny girl's eyes flickered as they searched for focus and Hana saw the moment she smelled her milk. It seemed to release her from the shock and she inhaled. Natural reflex and maternal memory invaded her mind and dictated her reactions. With confident fingers she guided the child's mouth to her breast and winced as she latched on.

Logan heaved a sigh of relief as the baby stopped fretting and her sucking took on a regular pattern. He squeezed Hana's shoulder and gave her an encouraging smile. "It'll be okay now," he lied, sensing she'd forgotten the next part.

Breastfeeding activated the closing of her womb and it came fast, intense and crippling. The tarpaulin contained the mess she expelled and Logan carried the warm, knotted structure to the bottom of the kauri tree. "Keep feeding her," he instructed. "It makes everything okay."

Hana closed her eyes and leaned her head back against the quad. The child's sucking grew less ordered and her head hung limp against the inside of Hana's elbow. Logan dug a hole with the heel of his boot. As he found softer soil below the parched earth, he dug with his hands until he uncovered a space between the tree roots. He laid the placenta into it, uttering a prayer to his ancestors before covering it over. The tui bird cawed in a trumpet of sound above and Hana jumped and banged her head against the quad. The child stirred and let out a pitiful wail.

Logan rose and wiped his soiled hands on his jeans. He heard her then, the soft tones of his grandmother reaching him on the breeze. "You will begin and end here, my mokopuna," she whispered. "This whenua is home."

Logan froze and a strange sensation crawled from his head to his toes. "Kuia?" he said, a dart of pain driving through his chest. "Āwhina. Help me." He ran his hands over his eyes and the horror returned. Miriam. Reuben. The secrecy and deceit. It bowed his shoulders beneath its weight. Then his gaze settled on Hana, fragile and vulnerable with her leggings and underwear around her ankles. His daughter snuffled and wailed in her arms. Squaring his shoulders and giving himself a shake, he strode back towards his family.

"Let me take her a minute." Logan took the bundle and held her upright over his shoulder. Her head lolled and he supported it with his other hand. The crying ceased, replaced with the sensation of wet lips moving against his neck. "She's still hungry, Hana." He nudged her shoulder. "Wake up, babe. You need to feed her more."

"I can't," Hana groaned. "I'm tired." She closed her eyes and leaned her head back against the quad bike's dark tyre. Her dishevelled hair cascaded over the wheel arch and glittered in the moonlight.

"Tough." Logan shook her awake and knelt beside her. The baby snuffled into his neck and released a tiny, dignified burp. He pushed her against Hana's other breast and she latched on unaided, her zest for life making him smile. "She's so different to the rest of us," he breathed with gratitude. "She's a survivor."

Hana let him curl her arm around the baby to support it and roused more through the discomfort of breastfeeding. Logan kissed her forehead and stroked her cheek to keep her focussed. "How do you feel now?" he asked.

"Hideous!" Hana sighed. "Naked. Dirty. Cold."

Logan looked down at his jeans. "I can give you these," he offered. "I could probably wrap them around your shoulders." Hana smiled and the expression filled Logan with relief. He pressed his forehead to hers and listened to the sound of his baby suckling beneath. "Not lost your sense of humour then," he whispered.

Hana snorted. "I just imagined Tama arriving back and finding you in your boxers and cowboy boots. Do you think he'd say anything or try to pretend you looked normal?"

"I dunno." Logan sat back and narrowed his eyes. "What do you think?"

"He'd fake normal." Hana reached down and stroked the soft cheek at her breast. "He went crazy when I pulled my pants down."

Logan's brow furrowed and Hana rolled her eyes. "Don't be a dick, Logan."

"Sorry." He glanced down at Hana's clothing. "What do you want to do about your leggings? They're soaked."

Hana sighed. "Just help me pull them up. It can't get any worse."

She squirmed as Logan hauled the soaked fabric up her thighs. He held the baby as she finished pulling it over her bottom and shifted herself away from the mess on the ground. The child's head lolled back against his elbow, her cheeks blowing in and out and her lips pursed closed. Moonlight flickered over dark, tufty hair and her skin bore the same olive hue as his. "She's beautiful," he whispered. He touched a hand to his chest. "I didn't know it felt like this."

Hana's teeth chattered as she tried to get comfortable and Logan grew concerned. He checked his watch and licked his lips. "Half an hour there if he gaps it, ten minutes to raise the alarm and fifty minutes back uphill. Then they need to carry the stretcher." Logan tapped his fingers against the baby's back and she snuffled in response. He turned to Hana. "A little longer, babe. They must be on their way by now."

Hana pulled her bra over her breasts and clutched her shirt closer. She found a single remaining button and her fingers fumbled it closed. "It hurts," she whimpered. "My stomach hurts."

"I know, sweetheart. I know." He dropped to his knees still clutching the child and saw Hana's eyes flash in the darkness.

"You don't bloody know!" she bit. "You have no idea. This is all your fault."

Logan raised an eyebrow and his smile gleamed white. "I hope you're not proposing celibacy, Mrs Du Rose. I couldn't go for that. When you fall off a horse, you need to get straight back on."

"In your dreams," she snarled and he laughed.

"You don't want to be in my dreams, babe." Reuben's face mingled in his inner vision, fusing with Miriam's and then separating. Pain rode across Logan's expression and he ran his tongue over dry lips. He knew what his dreams would contain from now on and sleep promised no refreshment.

"I didn't mean it." Hana pressed her fingers over his mouth and Logan kissed her palm.

"I know. It's okay."

"I want to go home though, Logan." Her voice held determination. "I can't stay here."

Logan sighed, the sound wrought with sadness and dread. "I'm not sure I can either."

The tui bird cackled in the tree, awake far later than usual. Its harsh tones contained a rebuke and Logan shook off its warning. Home. He no longer knew where that was.

Hana leaned her head back against the quad and gasped, dragging Logan from his maudlin thoughts. "Look," she whispered. "It's amazing." The Milky Way spread out above them like a motorway lit with headlights. Unadulterated by man-made interference, the sky displayed its full glory.

Logan nodded. "Told you it was." He sighed and reached for her hand. "You did good tonight, sweetheart. I'm so proud of you."

Hana snuggled closer, pulling Logan's free arm around her shoulders. "I'm so cold," she whispered. Her jaw clattered as she spoke, banging her teeth together in an involuntary shiver.

Logan put the sleeping baby against her chest and waited until she felt secure. Pulling the tarp over them, he huddled beneath it, holding Hana's body against his. "Not long now," he promised. "Tama won't let us down."

His daughter woke and grew fractious, giving startled cries as though horrified at her new status in the world. Logan sat her on his knee and leaned her over his big hand, rubbing her back and supporting her wobbling head. She gave a series of burps which rocked her tiny frame and made Logan laugh. "She sounds like Jas," he said.

Hana watched the overhead stars, her eyes glassy and the irises faded from exhaustion. "How much longer?" she asked.

"Soon," he lied, glancing at his watch. "They'll come." He pushed the baby towards her. "Feed her some more. She's still hungry."

Hana sighed and pulled her shirt up, offering the child her darkened nipple. After a performance of head banging, the baby latched on and suckled. Hana groaned. "You never forget that feeling," she said, tiredness in her voice. "I'm sure I'll remember it when I'm an old lady."

They sat in silence and Logan felt Hana's head sag against his shoulder. He lifted the tarp and watched his daughter. Her tiny fists clasped her ears as though raging against something unseen and her head rolled back on her neck. A trail of milk dripped from the side of her mouth. He reached across and felt her chest, checking she still breathed without alarming Hana. The delicate rise and fall of tiny lungs pushed against his fingers. He sighed. "Come on, Tama. Don't let me down, man."

In the silence he thought he heard the sound of male voices. Blaming his imagination on the wind, he pulled the tarp higher over Hana. Her steady breathing reassured him and he replayed conversations in his head, looking for answers where there were none. The child jerked beneath the tarpaulin, letting out a wail against her terrifying dreams as men crashed through the gate and into the clearing.

They gathered in a hush, facing the sight in a ring of disbelief. Logan recognised men from the bunkhouse and workers from the township who had gone home for Christmas. They'd all come, responding to the emergency call. It fetched a lump into his throat. Michael broke the awkward silence, pushing his way to the front of the crowd and squatting before Logan. "Is everything okay?" His gaze strayed to Hana's closed eyes and slumped head and Logan felt the wave of fear drift over them.

"Yeah." He reached beneath the tarp and covered Hana's breast, yanking her blouse down and disturbing her. She inhaled and stirred, opening her eyes to the alarming sight of twenty concerned male faces.

"They came," she whispered and Logan nodded. He folded the plastic sheet back to reveal the tiny bundle wrapped in a tatty farm shirt. The men inhaled as one and then clapping began, a round of applause which shook the clearing and resounded off the nearby mountain ridges.

"Congratulations." Michael spoke to Hana, his eyes crinkling in a smile. "Let's get you home," he said.

"Home," she repeated and Logan cringed, no nearer to understanding its exact location.

Logan staggered to his feet and willing hands helped him. Slaps landed on his back and shoulders as congratulations rang in his ears. Voices clamoured, desperate to be heard amidst the excitement.

"You examining them, Doc?" someone asked and Logan's brows narrowed.

"No," he answered, his tone harsh.

"Not here." Michael replied to the questioner, his voice level. "I can't see much and it's getting cold. Where's the stretcher?"

The scar on Logan's side stood out white beneath the light of the moon. He pulled back the tarp and took his child from Hana's arms. A hand touched his shoulder and he looked at its owner, seeing Jack's eager face next to him. The old man flapped his hands and offered a toothless smile. Without question,

Logan placed his precious daughter into the arms of the only man on the mountain he would ever truly trust.

He bent and hoisted Hana into his arms, whispering an apology into her ear for the indignity and his roughness. He laid her on the stretcher and tightened the straps over her chest and legs. "Try to relax," he said, his voice soft and his eyebrow raised at the irony of his words. "I know it's hard but the next bit will be bumpy and rough going."

Two men rushed forward, eager to make themselves useful. They hefted Hana aloft and Logan experienced the first in many conflicts of interest. He watched his wife's curls bounce against the movement in the stretcher ahead, while his daughter snuffled in Jack's arms behind. He turned to the old man. "What should I do?" he mouthed and Jack's face held sympathy and understanding, though he'd never married or raised a legacy. Jack pushed the baby into his arms and jerked his head towards Hana. The men crowded behind her, blocking her from view. Jack shoved at Logan's shoulder, indicating he should mind both.

The men allowed Logan through and he paced behind the stretcher, watching his footing on the treacherous downward slopes. When he slipped, a strong hand caught him beneath the elbow, ensuring he neither fell nor dropped his daughter. "Thanks, bro." Logan lifted his gaze and met Tama's, seeing sincerity in the grey irises.

Tama swallowed. "I turned your mare loose on the way back up." His earnestness sought approval. "But I didn't groom her or pick out her feet."

Logan smiled, recognising the teenager's need for approval. He nodded. "It won't matter. You did good, boy. I'm grateful."

"Thanks." Tama's eyes glittered with unshed tears and Logan felt the ice in his heart lose some of its bite. The teenager's displacement between two families reflected his own situation and he swallowed the lump rising into his throat. Tama licked his lips and glanced sideways as he trudged next to Logan on the narrow track. His gaze coasted across the tiny pale face peeking from the ugly shirt. "I'm sorry for everything," he whispered. "You didn't deserve any of what I caused."

Logan blew out a breath and halted on the track. The following group bunched behind him and Hana's hair bounced ahead. "It's forgiven, man," he breathed. "Let it go."

"Really?" Tama swallowed and emotion bubbled into his chest. His voice cracked and the shutters disappeared from his expression, leaving a vulnerable, unwanted teenager with no fixed abode. "I don't deserve it."

Logan shook his head and set off down the slope, hauling Tama with him. "None of us get what we deserve, Tama," he breathed. "Haven't you learned that yet?"

The teenager picked up speed and careened alongside his uncle. He knew that to his considerable cost. "If I got what I deserved, I'd be dead," he murmured.

Hana displayed bravery as the men lifted her into the back of the utility vehicle. She clasped her hands over her painful stomach and sought Logan in the surrounding faces. "She's safer in the ute bed," Michael said, turning to find Logan. "And it's quicker than fitting her into the front seat." He indicated the remaining space either side of Hana. "Give her the baby and then you and I can brace either side of her in case she slips.

Logan nodded and leaned over the side, reuniting Hana with her child. Relief relaxed the muscles in her face as she gazed down on the sleeping infant. He leapt into the ute bed and signalled to Tama. "Get up here with me," he said.

Michael's brow narrowed, but he made no protest as he forced himself into the tiny space near Hana's legs. Discarded hay seed fluttered around their faces and made them cough. They gripped the sides of the vehicle as it fired up and started its perilous descent, the men using their bodies to prevent Hana slipping as it lurched along the track.

Hana closed her eyes and clutched her baby to her chest, clinging to the fragile bundle with everything she had left. Michael leaned across and pulled the shirt away from the child's mouth. "She still good?" he asked. Hana nodded and he grunted in satisfaction. "Toby went to the township to get Leslie's daughter. She's a midwife."

Logan nodded and reached for Hana's hair, holding it away from the edge of the ute and the grabbing, snatching branches which clutched at it. The baby's tufty topknot blew against the shirt as they picked up speed, the ute bouncing down through paddocks and across ridges.

Logan smiled across at Tama. "Who's driving?" he mouthed.

"Flick!" he shouted back.

Hana's former enemy handled the ute with the precision of an expert car thief, an even match for the difficult terrain. Behind the ute the men picked up quads, motorbikes and horses, closing gates and restoring order in their wake. Tama nodded to his Uncle Nev as Reuben's son cantered behind the ute on a black and white paint horse and Nev touched the brim of his hat in acknowledgement.

Lights shone from the hotel and the front door stood open. Jack's red Jeep screamed onto the gravel, spinning its wheels as it halted and beat the ute to the front steps. Toby fell from the driver's seat and ran around, yanking the passenger door open. "She's here!" he shouted across the carpark. The passenger descended into his arms and he hauled her without grace, shoving her towards the ute like a captive. "I've got her!" he announced again, his eyes wild and questioning.

The pretty dark-haired woman shoved at his arm and her brows knitted. "Toby! Let go of me," she demanded.

Logan leapt from the ute and landed in the gravel, sending up a cloud of dust to cover her face. She coughed and peered over the side at Hana. "Where are you taking her?" she asked, flapping her hand in front of her face.

"Just inside," Michael said, bouncing next to Logan with less natural elegance. "Then hospital."

"No!" Hana issued her first order, clutching the baby and using her other hand to cling to the side of the ute. "I'm not going to the hospital."

"I'll make that decision," Michael retorted, authority in his tone. The midwife dug him in the ribs.

"No. I will." She narrowed her eyes at Logan. "Put her somewhere comfortable and I'll look her over. I don't care where but let's get on with it. I'm Isla, by the way," she said, smiling at Hana. "I'm a midwife."

Isla held the baby in the lift and Logan cradled his wife. Hana closed her eyes and listened to the thud of his heart through his bare chest wall, the sound drowning out the clamour in her head. Tama and Michael appeared at the top of the spiral staircase as the lift doors slid open. Neither looked pleased to be in the other's company. Logan carried Hana to his bedroom and leaned against the wall as Tama pressed in the code. Once inside, Hana protested, "Put me on the floor, not the bed. I'm disgusting."

Logan tried to lay her gently on the floorboards, dust and leaves falling like a shower around them. He gaffed at the last moment, saving Hana's head by sacrificing his elbow. He winced and chewed the inside of his cheek. Isla's face appeared over his right shoulder. "Mummy first and then baby," she said, handing the sleeping bundle to Tama. The teenager took his cousin with natural ease, staring down into her delicate features with an expression of protectiveness. Isla settled on her knees. "Where do you hurt most, Hana?" she asked.

"My head." Hana pressed her fingers to the back of her skull and winced. "The blast knocked me on my back."

Isla's brow knitted above her. "You just gave birth, Hana." Her voice sounded soft. "The fire was last night. I'm asking about your stomach and other relevant parts."

Hana groaned. "You're not seeing those. Everyone's looking."

Isla glanced around the room. "Everybody out," she demanded.

"Don't be ridiculous. I'm a doctor," Michael retorted and Isla raised an eyebrow.

"If he's staying then so am I!" Logan growled.

"I've got the baby," Tama said and Hana closed her eyes.

A knock at the door heralded Leslie. She bustled into the room with a bundle in her arms. It spewed onto the bed and she listed the items, oblivious to the tension. "Nappies, baby clothes and some other bits I could grab. The women in the township send their best wishes." She looked up and smiled, meeting the combined gaze of the Du Rose men. A sigh escaped her lips. "You boys need to get out," she said. Reaching for the baby, she took her without giving Tama time to protest. "Now you can all wait outside." She jerked her head towards the door and Logan opened his mouth. "Out!" Leslie snapped. "Let my girl do her job!"

The men trooped outside and the door closed behind them. Hana heard them arguing in the hallway. Isla's shoulders slumped and she rolled her eyes. "I forgot what they were like," she breathed. "Testosterone overload."

Leslie unwrapped the baby from her unusual shroud and examined the sleeping pink bundle. "She's beautiful," she sighed. "A little Du Rose treasure."

Isla palpated Hana's stomach and her brow creased in concentration. "I need to take a look at you," she whispered. "Do you mind?"

Hana squirmed. "Please let me take a shower? I feel disgusting." Her eyes widened. "I brought nothing with me. The baby wasn't due until next month."

"It's okay." Leslie waved a packet of sanitary towels in her peripheral vision. "I grabbed whatever you needed."

Isla pushed herself upright and walked to the bedroom door. She pulled it open and spoke through the gap. "Just Logan," she said and stood back for him to enter. Then she closed the door again. "Hana wants to take a shower before I examine her. I've felt her stomach and it seems normal in the time since the birth. If you help her in the shower, I'll check the baby over."

Logan nodded and lurched to help Hana as she flipped herself over and pushed onto her knees. "Hold on," he said, offering his arm as a stronghold.

"I want to see her," Hana grunted, pausing as she crawled into an upright position. "I want to see my baby."

"She's here. She's fine," Leslie promised, picking up the tiny girl and holding her out for Hana to see. Her expression grew thoughtful. "She has a look of old Mrs Du Rose."

Hana recoiled and Logan's brow knitted. "My kuia," he said, his voice filled with reverence. "Not my mother. And she does."

Leslie produced the naked bundle for Hana to see and she placed a gentle kiss on her daughter's forehead. Blue eyes opened, blinking in the light and the tiny lips parted in a snuffling cry. Leslie whipped her away again. "Hurry up in that shower and then you can give her what she needs," she said.

Michael knocked on the bedroom door, his tone sounding urgent with a trace of irritation. "I need to examine Hana!" he called. "If she haemorrhages and it all goes wrong, it's on me when the ambulance gets here!"

Logan's eyes widened in fear and Hana groaned. "I'm fine, please. I just want to be clean," she begged.

"I'll go in with her," Logan promised and Isla nodded her approval.

"Right, well, I'm staying here. Just shout for me if it all goes wrong." Michael sounded grumpy as his voice echoed through the door.

Logan ran the shower until the water felt warm to the touch. Hana leaned against the wall while he helped to peel her filthy clothing from her body. "I'll throw these away," he said, dropping her shirt by the door.

"I've nothing left," she murmured. "My other stuff got ruined in the explosion and the shirt's yours."

"I'll buy you more new stuff," Logan promised. Her stained underwear came apart in his fingers and he sent them to lie with the shirt. He plucked her socks free and smoothed his arms over her shoulders. "I'm so proud of you," he whispered. "Everything will be okay, Hana. Trust me."

She inhaled and looked around as though seeing the bathroom for the first time. Her eyelids hung low and she ran a hand over her naked, empty womb. "I'm scared," she whispered.

"Oh, Hana. Of what?" Logan squatted in front of her, sincerity in the lines of his face.

She swallowed and fought for the right words to express her fears. "Of everything. It's all a big mess and I can't cope with it. Your family hate me."

Logan shook his head and stood. His belt buckle clanked against the shower cubicle as he stripped to his boxer shorts. "You're my family, Hana. You and our baby are all I've got." He pulled off his socks and held out his hands to her. "Don't you abandon me too?"

Hana sighed and accepted his help into the shower. She felt grateful for his strong body as he slipped in behind her and wrapped his arms around her waist. The water pounded the top of her head, robbing her of coherent thought and numbing her senses. Logan washed her hair, soaping her battered body and wincing at the cuts and bruises from her climb up the mountain. He felt the bump on her head caused by the explosion and kissed the nape of her neck in sympathy. "I'm sorry, Hana," he whispered. "I'm sorry I can't change any of this."

Hana nodded, her body aching to the bone. She leaned against the shower cubicle and closed her eyes, filthy water cascading in a waterfall. When the baby cried next door, she started and almost slipped. Logan shut off the water and reached for a towel, draping it around her shoulders. He patted her dry with gentle hands, water running off his shorts and soaking the floor between his legs. He reached for the door handle as Leslie knocked, creating a wide enough gap to peer out. She handed him clean underwear for Hana, sanitary towels and a voluminous night dress.

"Is she okay?" Hana asked, her teeth chattering.

"She's fine, kōtiro." Leslie sounded confident. "You take your time."

Logan helped Hana dress, pulling her hair free from the collar of the nightdress with tenderness. When the baby let out a wail, she grew eager to escape, darting nervous glances towards the door as he pulled a wide comb through her hair. "You're done," he whispered, kissing the back of her head. Hana turned and faced him, exhaustion in the dark shadows beneath her eyes.

"What about you?" she asked. "Are you done?"

Logan swallowed and fingered the soaked fabric of his shorts. His teeth worried at his lower lip and he shuttered his eyes as pain warred behind his lids. "I don't know," he whispered. "Maybe." Hana reached up and stroked his cheek, letting her palm coast over the rough stubble. She sighed as the baby cried again.

She pulled the last towel from the rail and wrapped it around his waist, knotting it over his hip. "Don't be long," she whispered. "We need you."

Logan looked down at the hand towel wrapped around his waist. His lips quirked upwards in a smirk. "Very funny," he chided her. Water droplets littered his shoulders and back and Hana placed a kiss on his chest.

"It is." She flicked her hair over her shoulder and left the bathroom, closing the door behind her. She relented enough to snatch clean underwear and jeans from Logan's suitcase and push them through the gap between the door and frame.

Leslie clucked her tongue. She balanced the baby over her shoulder and the child bounced her head up and down against the rolls of flesh near her face. "Let Isla check you out and then this little girl needs her mummy," she said, rocking her large hips back and forth in a motion which made Hana feel seasick.

"Thanks, Mum!" Isla said, narrowing her eyes in a grimace of embarrassment. "I actually do this as a job." She rolled her eyes at Hana and indicated the bed.

Hana climbed onto the bed and settled her head into the pillows. "I'm so tired." She let out a yawn and apologised, covering her mouth with a shaking hand.

"Can I come in now?" Michael's voice sounded hollow.

"And me." Tama's plea followed.

"In a minute! Just wait!" Isla ordered. She smiled at Hana. "Let's see what the damage is."

Logan took that moment to leave the bathroom, his hair wet and his torso still glistening with droplets of water. He stalked across the bedroom bare foot, his jeans hanging low on his hips. He shoved his hands deep in his pockets and his biceps tensed, the strong muscles across his chest rippling. Isla raised her eyebrows and winked at Hana. "I can see how you got into this mess."

Hana gave a tired smile. "It won't happen again."

"Yeah, whatever," Isla snorted.

Leslie gave a low whistle and Logan scowled. "Stop it, old woman!" he bit. "You can try my older brother, if you like." He held his arms out for the baby and Leslie's face crumpled into a mask of disappointment.

"I might just do that," she snapped and Isla bit her lower lip.

"Mother! Stop it! You're embarrassing me!"

Logan cradled his daughter, a look of awe in his eyes. Her soft downy body encased in its white sleep suit contrasted with the ugly welts and scars on her father's body. Logan turned towards the window, shielding his emotions from view. Hana watched as his shoulders flexed, catching sight of the child's gaze stuttering across his face.

"You feeling okay?" Isla pulled Hana's nightdress down and squeezed her shoulder. She jerked her head towards Leslie. "Stop ogling your boss and tell Michael he can come in."

The door opened before Leslie got to it and the men burst in. Hana scrabbled to cover her legs with the sheet. "She's fine." Isla raised a hand to Michael and hauled the sheet higher.

"I need to check her out," he replied, pausing at the end of the bed. "Did you check her pulse?"

Isla sighed. "It's a little fast, but that's understandable. She's had a harrowing couple of days and is still in pain."

"She should go to the hospital." Michael pushed his thumbnail into his mouth and glanced across at Logan. "You should take her to hospital," he repeated.

Logan turned, his child nestled into the crook of his elbow. He looked a picture of satisfaction as though the last few days hadn't touched him. Hana knew differently. He got eye contact with his wife and raised an eyebrow. "What do you want, Hana?" he asked.

She yawned again, her eyelids drooping. "I want to go to sleep," she mumbled and Michael's brow knitted. He shook his head and glared at Isla.

"A word outside?" he asked, his tone not allowing for disobedience.

Isla followed him out and the door clicked shut behind them. Logan's gaze tracked to Leslie and she shrugged. "My girl won't let him push her around," she stated. Her eyes devoured the baby as though desperate to snatch her from Logan's arms.

When they returned, Michael ground his teeth in temper. Isla squeezed Hana's hand. "Stay here for now. But if anything changes, Michael will call an ambulance and you'll go straight to Auckland Hospital." She wrinkled her pretty nose. "They'll be understaffed because of the Christmas break and it'll be horrible if you go tonight. I won't make you. Your baby's a good weight and she looks absolutely fine." She avoided Michael's gaze with a determined smirk on her lips.

Leslie kissed Hana's forehead and bore her daughter away with great reluctance. Logan heaved a sigh of relief as they left. Tama had remained silent, sitting on the end of the bed and observing the discussion. He gave Hana a wry smile as she yawned again. "Busy day?" he asked and laughed at his own joke.

Hana nodded. "Yeah. Thanks for being my birth partner."

He snorted. "I missed the good bit. Too busy picking my sorry ass out of the dirt four times on the way down the mountain."

Hana wrinkled her nose. "Sorry. Maybe Isla will check you over."

"I should be so lucky." Tama's left eyebrow jerked upwards and he looked away. Standing, he waved to Hana and nodded to Logan. "Night," he said. His exit from the room left them alone, a newly formed band of three.

Hana dozed on her back, the child tucked into her side. The baby murmured often, little sounds of distress as though life outside the womb wasn't preferable to safety and seclusion. A table lamp cast a yellow glow into the room and offered comfort after the nightmare. Hana pulled the sheet back and examined her daughter. Already stunning, her olive skin held a healthy glow and when her eyes flickered open, they displayed a peculiar blue as they searched without focus.

Hana heard the movement of fabric and turned her head, seeing Logan's rigid spine in her peripheral vision. She shifted to see him better, raising the child onto her chest and pushing herself upright. The ranch slider stood open and the net curtains moved in the breeze. Smoke still lingered in the air and Logan leaned against the doorframe. One hand dug deep into his jeans pocket and the muscles around his spine looked bunched and tight. His left hand moved over his face and Hana heard the scratch of bristles. His body language oozed pain and she saw his head move back and forth as he bumped a balled fist against his forehead. "Logan?" She watched him jump and turn in a sharp movement, too fast to shutter the misery in his eyes.

"You okay?" His brow furrowed and he left his sentry duty, standing by the bed and looking down on her.

Hana nodded. "I'm glad you were there. You knew what to do." She swallowed and glanced at her sleeping daughter's face. "It could have gone so wrong."

"About that," Logan began and his voice sounded husky. He squatted next to the bed and Hana placed a finger over his lips.

"You handled yourself with dignity today. Walking away from Kane took courage, Logan. I know you wanted to hurt him." Her gaze grazed the scar beneath his armpit and he pressed his arm closer to his body to hide it from view.

"But I left you." Pain twinkled in his irises. "After everything we agreed, I ran. I can't seem to break the habit of a lifetime, can I?"

Hana shook her head. "You planned to come back, didn't you?"

Logan nodded. "Yeah. I thought riding would straighten out my head, but it didn't."

Hana smiled. "Maybe I'll let you have this one. But if you do it again, I'll break your legs." Her lips tweaked upwards and Logan smirked.

"I think you would too." His mirth didn't last. "You still want me to drive you home?"

Hana swallowed and looked down at her daughter. Her tiny lips moved and her bottom lip poked out as her face twitched in slumber. Hana sighed. "I don't think that would be very grown up, would it?"

Logan's eyelashes fluttered and he clenched his jaw, the lahar of emotions in his chest moving beyond his ability to cope. "Thanks," he whispered and his lips pursed into a thin line.

"Could you hold her so I can use the bathroom?" Hana asked and Logan nodded. He gathered the delicate bundle from her arms and looked into his daughter's face. His calloused hands dwarfed the baby, his Adam's apple rising and falling as he gazed on her innocence.

Hana excused herself, returning with little sound so she could observe her husband. He stood with his back to her, rocking the child as she fretted and facing the darkness beyond the windows. Hana sensed the mountain hold its breath as a gentle cadence reached her ears. Logan spoke in Māori to his daughter, infusing her with his knowledge of the tangata whenua. When she heard him sniff and his voice crack, she realised he was crying.

Chapter 52

On New Year's Eve, they made the return journey up the mountain. Bright sunshine warmed their heads, yet Hana still shivered in anticipation of her memories. Logan urged Jack's old Jeep up the developer's new road and she sat in the back next to the car seat.

"Sure you can manage?" Logan asked, opening Hana's door and helping her out. She nodded, descending into an empty cul-de-sac where an architect's grand designs would never spring from the dry earth. She remained silent on the upward climb, watching her husband keep one hand beneath his daughter's body which curled in the baby sling against his chest. Though the sudden rains had sluiced away the scent of burnt foliage, she sensed the blackened driveway running parallel to their ascent. Logan reached for her hand and squeezed her fingers, his turmoil mirroring hers.

The gate to Logan's paddock stood open as though in deference to the changed status of the mountain. Hana sighed as the tui greeted them with raucous cackles and a trill which echoed around the bush canopy. She turned to face the kauri tree, its high branches sweeping overhead and its leaves lush and plentiful. Logan walked ahead, pausing at the patch of ground where his daughter entered the world. Nourished by summer rains, it nurtured fresh green shoots of a healthy lime, the arid dust and traces of gore long gone. He glanced back at Hana and waited to take her hand.

"It makes you look softer," she said, jerking her head towards the sling. "You'll drive the women even crazier with a baby strapped to your chest."

"I don't care about other women." He smiled, his face growing lighter despite the increased flecks of grey along his hairline. "Just you, Hana Du Rose."

They stood at the edge of the cliff and watched the Tasman Sea lick the coastline with gentle flicks of its white tongue. The breeze attacked their summer clothing, pulling at loose ends as though desperate to rid them of their cares and worries. Logan's jaw flexed and he gnawed on his lower lip. "I'm glad she's with him now," he said, his voice low. His lips pursed and his eyelashes fluttered.

Hana nodded and squeezed his fingers. "A joint tangihanga seemed appropriate," she agreed. "Keeping them apart in death made no sense."

Logan smiled, an upward lift of one side of his mouth. "Thanks. Not everyone liked them farewelled together."

"Alfred?" Hana remembered his ashen face as he refused to attend.

Logan shook his head. "No. He suggested it. But he stayed away for his own reasons."

Hana nodded but didn't probe. She no longer wished to know everything, finally understanding the cost. She shivered. "I needed to come back here while the sun shone and the world seemed back in order."

Logan shrugged. "It feels impossible. What order should it be in?"

"Yours." Hana pressed his fingers against her lips. "It just takes time."

The green countryside stretched before them, tumbling over the ragged cliff edge to greet the aqua sea. Its rhythm bowed to a higher power, continuing regardless of the whims and errors of fragile, temporary men. Hana tasted salt on the breeze and licked her lips. Despite everything, this place still radiated peace and brought healing.

"What shall we call her?" Logan asked. His voice broke the silence and the tui barked its irritation.

Hana sighed. "I still don't know. I suggested your mother's name but I'm not sure if that's because I sense it's expected."

Logan nodded. "It is. But my daughter's better than that. I won't label her with it."

Hana kept her relief to herself, the concession costly and fraught with bad reminders of a woman trapped by her own desire.

"What about your mother's name?" he offered. "Judith is nice."

Hana shook her head, declining for reasons she didn't understand. Speaking her mother's name out loud would conjure thoughts of her father's livid face as he expressed his disappointment. "No," she whispered.

Logan looked down at his daughter. "Baby it is then," he said, running his finger over the soft cheek and smiling as her lips puckered.

"What about your grandmother's name?" Hana asked. "Lots of people say the baby looks like her. And you adored her."

Logan stared into the far distance and his expression softened. He saw a woman in her middle years, black haired, brown skinned and delicate. She ran the family with a rod of iron and possessed bones as fragile as a bird's. She represented a powerhouse of energy and competence.

"Rebuild your house, Logan Du Rose," came her whisper down the ages.

"Leslie said she delighted in you." Hana flicked a blade of grass from her pants. "She called you the little rangatira because you reminded her of her father. He was a tribal chief, wasn't he?"

Logan nodded. "Yeah. Tribal royalty with God given leadership." He shook his head and shivered. "I think she carved up the mountain because of me. My birth caused the rift. She must have known about Rueben and my mother." His nose wrinkled and Hana recognised the distress tell. She rested her hand over his.

"Yet she adored you anyway, Logan. And she gave you this piece of land and told you to build a house."

Logan shrugged. The coded message to a small boy through her will was not of wood, bricks and mortar. It was not that kind of house she foresaw. It was about family and a legacy, a house of kin. She saw the flaws in her own and he suspected she saw death, coming like a spectre of doom and sucking the life from everything in its path, killing and stealing. And it had.

"She taught me French and Māori," Logan murmured. "She gave me a love for the land and a desire to preserve it. And she died right here." He pointed to the edge of the cliff, his face creasing in pain. "We rode up to watch the sunset together. I thought she fell asleep but I couldn't wake her when it got dark. I sat with her until Jack came looking. It's the only time I ever saw him cry." Logan swallowed and turned away, facing the green paddock and absorbing the sense of life in its abundance. The tui hopped onto a nearby rock and cocked its dark head. The white bow tie wobbled at its elegant neck. It seemed to wait, holding time in its pointed beak.

"What was her name?" Hana asked.

Logan smiled. "It means renewal. To rise from the ashes." He stared down at his daughter, adoration in the softness of his eyes. "Phoenix," he whispered. "Phoenix Du Rose."

Hana peeked into the sling where the little girl slept. The altitude brought a flush to her tiny cheeks and she seemed dwarfed by the larger mountain peaks which rose above her. Like gathered witnesses to her naming, they appeared to bow their lofty summits in deference. "Hello, Phoenix Du Rose," Hana whispered.

Logan exhaled, sensing his child's heartbeat through his chest wall. A familiar contentment swallowed him. Welcome and safe, it had abandoned him the day his grandmother died and he'd sought it the world over, without success. In a momentary connection with a distraught girl on a train, he'd glimpsed it again, replacing it with an insatiable hunger for trouble to numb the loss. "Phoenix Du Rose," he repeated.

Peace descended on the land like a veil. The tui remained silent, perching on his rock as the tangata whenua rejoiced below his hooked feet. The old lady's mana stirred, passed to her favoured son and then to the child. Reuben's simple touch, an exchange of life force, the passing on of a legacy. The child contained it all.

Logan's dynasty coursed through her veins, bearing the mana given to him by accident. His finger stroked her button nose, his blood brimming with the life force passed on by a foresighted man dying in an English hospital.

The old tui bird warbled and flew to the top of the kauri tree, watching with interest as two ancient forces agreed, the God of Heaven and Māori ancient lore. Tangata whenua - the people of the land rejoiced as an old lady's coded prophecy came to pass.

The New Du Rose Matriarch

Here is a sample of the next book in the series.

Chapter 1

Hana Du Rose pushed the pram across the soccer field without seeing in front of her, willing the baby to stay asleep. A prickling sensation crept up the back of her neck, plaguing her with unease. She turned her head to survey the empty field. Nothing. Yet the sense of someone watching remained.

The child fretted in the pram, raising her tiny hands to her ears and tossing her head in quick movements. "Hush," Hana crooned, placing one foot in front of the other in a haze of misery. "I can't do this," she hissed in desperation. "It's worse than I remember."

Baby Phoenix Du Rose spent the entire night screaming, taxing Hana beyond her ability to stay sane. Reacting to her six-week inoculations, she bumped across the school field as her mother tried the last trick in her repertoire to get her to sleep. Hana shivered beneath the eerie sensation and turned her head again. Still nothing. She sighed and rubbed her eyes. "I'm so tired, I'm creating monsters," she grumbled.

Her feet turned in the direction of the school boarding house and an early dew speckled the cricket pitch. She'd been walking since before dawn and every step seemed more laboured than the one before. "Let's find your father," she murmured. "I bet he enjoyed a lovely night's sleep."

Phoenix groaned in the pram in reply and Hana rubbed at her tired green eyes again. Her eyeballs ached in their sockets. The baby brought her knees up to her chest in pain and opened her mouth, emitting a piercing wail. Hana increased her pace, distress adding itself to the guilt of failed parenting. She'd wanted to vomit as the needle penetrated the spindly little olive-toned leg, feeling a traitor as she held onto her child and allowed the atrocity. This was her punishment for the betrayal. "I'm sorry," she murmured, adding a rocking motion to the handle of the pram. "I'm rubbish at this."

The pram bumped across the crease in the centre of the cricket pitch as Hana registered a momentary stab of anger at her husband. "He promised," she hissed. "He promised it wouldn't be like this." Logan hadn't discussed taking on the extra duty as the boarding house manager as a favour to the principal. He'd announced it days after arriving back in the city. Hana ground her teeth, knowing it impacted on her more than either of them imagined. Four night duties in a row left her coping alone with a new baby. The constant sense of being watched frayed her nerves to breaking point.

"Oi!"

She turned, swinging the pram around to face the shout. A quad bike sped towards her, not slowing until the last moment. The head groundsman hurled his stumpy body from the vehicle and strode the final two metres towards her. His pocked face bulged with fury. "What do you think you're doing?" he shouted into her face, spraying spittle into the air and onto Hana's red curls.

The sleepless night caught Hana up in one overwhelming punch and she gaped, her lips producing no sound. Unsatisfied, the man jabbed a finger into her chest. "Get off the cricket pitch!" he bawled. "Wheeling your effin pram over it. Especially the effin crease!" He waved his arms and backed towards the bike, his expression showing no recognition of Hana's bedraggled state. Jumping onto the quad bike, he whirled it in an arc and drove straight over the hallowed pitch without regard, flicking up dust behind him. Hana's shoulders slumped in defeat. Her gaze strayed to the pram as Phoenix opened her eyes and let out another wail.

Hana abandoned the pram outside the dining hall of the boys' boarding house. Dating from just after the Second World War, St Bartholomew's complimented the illusion of affluence with its gabled roof and mock Tudor facade. As a private institution, The Waikato Presbyterian School for Boys commanded an appropriate price tag for the bespoke education and opportunities it promised. Hana scooped her daughter from the blankets and as Phoenix wailed again, she fought the urge to hand her off to Logan and make a run for it. Guilt coloured her cheeks pink with shame and she kissed the bobbing downy temple. "I'm sorry," she whispered. "Silly thoughts. I'm just exhausted."

The baby's face made a picture of misery as her unfocussed eyes tried to latch on to the shapes and colours whizzing past. Hana walked through the lobby and into the dining room, her eyes downcast and the set of her shoulders oozing defeat. A hundred pairs of eyes turned to watch as she appeared in the entrance. Phoenix gave a pitiful wail and Hana cringed.

"Hey Miss." A tall, dark haired boy greeted her. Dressed in a prefect's white shirt with black-and-white striped blazer, he cut an imposing figure as he separated himself from a group of younger boys.

"Hi, Acton." Hana dropped her gaze, aware of her red hair escaping from its ponytail accompanied by shapeless tracksuit bottoms and sick-stained hoodie.

"You looking for Mr Du Rose?" He smiled and Hana nodded. Phoenix stopped grizzling and her head nodded comically as she tried to focus on his face.

"She won't stop crying," Hana blurted, surprised by her spontaneous confession of failure.

The teenager reached out an olive finger and slotted it into the baby's little fist. "They do that don't they?" His face held a knowing expression. "My baby brother squalled when he came out and he's still going." His lips curved upwards. "He's fourteen now." Seeing the misery cross Hana's face, his cheeks reddened with guilt and he back pedalled. "This little girl won't be like that, she's a Du Rose."

"What does that mean?" Hana regretted the words as she sensed his confusion. Acton gulped and his gaze coasted across the dining room. He spotted Logan striding towards them and swallowed. "She wouldn't dare do half the stuff my brother has," he hissed. Twisting his lips into a quizzical smile, he retreated back to his knot of adoring fans. The younger boys fell into line behind him like a family of ducklings.

Hana's breath caught in her chest with a familiar sinking sensation as her stomach flip-flopped. Logan Du Rose's Māori heritage exuded from him in the smooth olive skin and dark wavy hair. He moved through the rows of chairs with ease, already lifting his lips in a smile at the sight of his wife and daughter. His immense personality dwarfed Hana, rendering her ragged by comparison. In a split second, she moved from relief to inadequacy.

"How is she?" Logan accompanied his words with a kiss to Hana's forehead and a matching one on his daughter's crown.

Boys turned to stare and he disregarded their smutty interest. His strong arms encased his girls in safety and Hana sighed. She hid her face within the folds of his expensive jacket and heard the murmurings of teenage voices.

Phoenix's head bobbed as she searched for Logan's face, tears still drying on her cheeks. Logan smoothed them away with gentle fingers and responded to the hitch in her chest. "You still unhappy, baby?" he whispered. His grey eyes flicked upwards to regard Hana, irises the colour of slate. "Should we take her to the doctor?"

Hana shook her head. "I took her last night. He thinks it's a reaction to the jabs. I've filled her with pain syrup, but she needs to sleep." She sighed. "I can't get her to drop off, Logan. I'm exhausted." She yawned and Logan winced.

"Sorry." His lower teeth gnawed the inside of his lip. "I need to help you more."

"Mr Du Rose?" A boy spoke his name and waited to the side, twisting his fingers in expectation. When Logan turned to face him, the boy gushed out his problem. "Darren's puked up in his bed. He asked me to fetch you."

Hana sensed the wave of uncontrolled emotion rise from her chest into her throat. She tamped down the urge to shout and scream, to wrestle her husband's attention back from the seething mass of fragile male egos in his care. Her eyelashes fluttered with the effort of controlling her tears and she stared at the parquet floor while Logan dealt with the child.

"I should go," she muttered, turning away to release him. "I'm in the way."

Logan's fingers clamped around her forearm, holding her in place. "Ask Matron to take a look at him," he said, his tone impassive as he spoke to the edgy boy. "I'll go up to see him in a minute."

The child nodded with relief and Hana ached to dump her problems on someone else and run. She backed away, her daughter's cheek bumping against her chest. "Will I see you later?" she asked, the question holding more rebuke than she intended.

"I'll walk outside with you." Logan made a hand action to one of the prefects and the boy nodded. Like a well-oiled machine, the teenager assumed command of the dining room without question. A hundred pairs of eyes watched Hana leave and she sifted the sensation in her tired brain. It felt different. Curious, not hostile eyes followed her progress and instinct told her whoever watched from the shadows didn't possess teenage acne and raging hormones. She sighed and in the corridor, Logan rested an arm around her shoulders. "You're doing great," he whispered. "I promise."

"No, I'm not!" Hana raised her voice and then swallowed. An embarrassed flush coursed up her throat and added colour to her cheeks. "I didn't agree to be a single parent, Logan. This isn't fair."

"I know, I know." Logan looked around him before drawing her through the front doors. He pulled her to the side and waited until a group of boys passed out of earshot. "It's not what we agreed, but I'm getting there, I promise. A few more weeks and we can go home once the new manager arrives."

Hana groaned and turned her face towards the brightening sky. "But it's too hard, Logan! The staff unit is uninhabitable and you're never home. The last time I had a tiny baby to care for I was twenty-five years younger."

Logan's eyelashes fluttered and Hana saw conflict flicker behind his eyes. Sighing, he reached for Phoenix, hoisting her over his shoulder in strong, tender hands which belied his physical strength. Hana felt naked without the child in her arms, not sure what to do with her hands. Her fingers twisted and writhed in front of her. Logan edged her away from the entrance. "The boys will stampede in a second. Let's get out of the way." He pressed a kiss against Hana's forehead, his brows knitting when she didn't respond.

Hana straightened her spine as the bell sounded from the main building, a raucous peal ripping through the airwaves. She held her hands out to collect the baby. "Go back to work, Logan. I'm fine." Forcing a fake smile onto her lips, she ignored his narrowing eyes and the suspicion in the line of his lips. She lay Phoenix in the pram and the child fussed before closing her eyes and pushing a tiny thumb into her mouth. Hana felt the tension ease in her shoulders at the promise of peace.

"Hana." Logan waited for her to finish releasing the pram brake and then spoke her name again, putting more force into it. "Hana?"

She rubbed her eyes and turned to face his perceptive scrutiny. "I'll see you later." With a dismissive wave, she walked away. The oppressive staff units appeared in her peripheral vision and she bit her lip against the scream bubbling into her chest.

"Hana!" Logan raised his voice and forced her to turn, his authority tugging at their tenuous connection.

"What?" After a cautious look at her sleeping daughter, Hana turned.

"I know something's going on." He kept his tone even and Hana fought the instant desire to swallow.

She clenched her jaw and shook her head with a little too much emphasis. The lie tripped off her tongue. "I'm just tired," she insisted. Forcing a smile onto her lips, she gave a final wave and left.

Shouts and jeers betrayed a fight breaking out on the first floor and Hana capitalised on Logan's distraction to push the pram away with as much confidence as she could manage. The prickling sensation returned, raising the hairs on the back of her neck. She resisted the urge to look for its source. Experience told her she wouldn't find it. Boys milled around her in obedience to the bell's summons, their presence holding no fear. Hana's knuckles showed white as she gripped the handle of the pram and she put her head down and stalked across the field.

She didn't see the shake of Logan's head before he let the front doors swing behind him. Nor did she notice the figure watching her from the boundary of the school grounds. Hana didn't see. But she felt the burn of the intense interest as she bumped the pram up the front steps and into the dilapidated staff unit.

Author's Note

DEAR READER

If you have enjoyed my novels, please consider leaving a short review at the site where you purchased them and at Goodreads. I have learned many things on my publishing journey, one of which is that I cannot succeed without reviews, no matter how good my work might be. It doesn't have to be an essay, a few short words about what you liked will be good enough for me.
Thank you,
K T Bowes

About the Author

K T Bowes is a bestselling teen and women's author. Her novel A Trail of Lies was the winner of the genre award for Author's Cave in 2014.

She is an Englishwoman in exile in New Zealand, swapping rugged cosmopolitan for mountain ranges and terrifying rivers. The culture around her is infused into most of her novels.

You can find her hanging out on social media in the following places.

Check in and say hello. Maybe suggest she gets back to writing and stops watching cat videos.

FACEBOOK

https://www.facebook.com/NZauthorKTBowes/

TWITTER

https://twitter.com/ktboweswrites

INSTAGRAM

https://www.instagram.com/k_t_bowes

Other books by this author:

The Hana Du Rose Mysteries:
Logan Du Rose
About Hana
Hana Du Rose
Du Rose Legacy
The New Du Rose Matriarch
One Heartbeat
The Du Rose Prophecy
Du Rose Sons
Du Rose Family Ties
Du Rose Vendetta
Phoenix Du Rose
Wiremu Du Rose

The Calculated Risk Series:
The Actuary
The Actuary's Wife
The Actuary in Trouble
The Heart of The Actuary

Troubled series for teens/young adults:
Free from the Tracks
Sophia's Dilemma
A Trail of Lies
Gone Phishing

Escaping the Back Country NZ Series:
Pirongia's Secret
Deleilah

A Keeper's War Fantasy Trilogy:
Perpetual Winter
The Bee Queen
Hive

Standalone novels:
Artifact
Demons on Her Shoulder
Her Quiet Legacy
All Saints

The Curly Fan Club
Dead Straight
Bad Hair Day
Side Parting

www.ingramcontent.com/pod-product-compliance
Lightning Source LLC
Chambersburg PA
CBHW051202120726
47905CB00004B/948